KT-574-200

MY STRUGGLE: BOOK 2

A MAN IN LOVE

Karl Ove Knausgaard's My Struggle cycle has been heralded as a masterpiece all over the world. From *A Death in the Family* to *The End*, the novels move through childhood into adulthood and, together, form an enthralling portrait of human life. Knausgaard has been awarded the Norwegian Critics Prize for Literature, the Brage Prize and the Jerusalem Prize. His work, which also includes *Out of the World*, *A Time for Everything* and the Seasons Quartet, is published in thirty-five languages.

Don Bartlett lives in Norfolk and works as a freelance translator of Scandinavian literature. He has translated, or co-translated, a wide variety of Danish and Norwegian books by such writers as Karl Ove Knausgaard, Per Petterson, Roy Jacobsen, Jo Nesbo and Ida Jessen.

Also by Karl Ove Knausgaard

A Time for Everything
A Death in the Family: My Struggle Book 1
Boyhood Island: My Struggle Book 3
Dancing in the Dark: My Struggle Book 4
Some Rain Must Fall: My Struggle Book 5
The End: My Struggle Book 6
Home and Away: Writing the Beautiful Game (with Fredrik Ekelund)
Autumn (with illustrations by Vanessa Baird)
Winter (with illustrations by Lars Lerin)
Spring (with illustrations by Anna Bjerger)
Summer (with illustrations by Anselm Kiefer)
So Much Longing in So Little Space: The Art of Edvard Munch

A MAN IN LOVE

MY STRUGGLE: BOOK 2

KARL OVE KNAUSGAARD

Translated from the Norwegian by Don Bartlett

VINTAGE

12

Vintage
20 Vauxhall Bridge Road,
London SW1V 2SA

Vintage is part of the Penguin Random House group of companies whose addresses can be found at global.penguinrandomhouse.com

Penguin
Random House
UK

Copyright © Forlaget Oktober 2009
English translation copyright © Don Bartlett 2013

Karl Ove Knausgaard has asserted his right to be identified as the author of this Work in accordance with the Copyright, Designs and Patents Act 1988

This edition published in Vintage in 2019
First published in Vintage in 2014
First published in hardback by Harvill Secker in 2013
First published with the title *Min Kamp Andre Bok* in 2009 by Forlaget Oktober, Oslo

penguin.co.uk/vintage

A CIP catalogue record for this book is available from the British Library

ISBN 9780099555179

Printed and bound in Great Britain by Clays Ltd, Elcograf S.p.A.

Penguin Random House is committed to a sustainable future for our business, our readers and our planet. This book is made from Forest Stewardship Council® certified paper.

MIX
Paper from
responsible sources
FSC
www.fsc.org   FSC® C018179

A Man in Love

29 July 2008

The summer has been long, and it still isn't over. I finished the first part of the novel on 26 June, and since then, for more than a month, the nursery school has been closed, and we have had Vanja and Heidi at home with all the extra work that involves. I have never understood the point of holidays, have never felt the need for them and have always just wanted to do more work. But if I must, I must. We had planned to spend the first week at the cabin Linda got us to buy last autumn, intended partly as a place to write, partly as a weekend retreat, but after three days we gave up and returned to town. Putting three infants and two adults on a small allotment, surrounded by people on all sides, with nothing else to do but weed the garden and mow the grass, is not necessarily a good idea, especially if the prevailing atmosphere is disharmonious even before you set out. We had several flaming rows there, presumably to the amuse-ment of the neighbours, and the presence of hundreds of metic-ulously cultivated gardens populated by all these old semi-naked people made me feel claustrophobic and irritable. Children are quick to detect these moods and play on them, particularly Vanja, who reacts almost instantly to shifts in vocal pitch and intensity, and if they are obvious she starts to do what she knows we like least, eventually causing us to lose our tempers if she persists. Already brimming with frustration, it is practically impossible for us to defend ourselves, and then we have the full woes: screaming and shouting and misery. The following week we hired a car and drove up to Tjörn, outside Gothenburg, where Linda's friend Mikaela, who is Vanja's godmother, had invited us to stay in her partner's summer house. We asked if she knew what it was like living with three children, and whether she was really sure she wanted us there, but she said she was sure; she had planned to do some baking with the children and take them swimming and go crabbing so that we could have some time to ourselves. We took her up on the offer. We drove to Tjörn, parked outside the summer house, on the fringes of the beautiful Sørland countryside, and in we piled with all the kids, plus bags and baggage. The intention had been to stay there all week, but three days later we packed all our stuff into the car and headed south again, to Mikaela and Erik's obvious relief.

People who don't have children seldom understand what it involves, no matter how mature and intelligent they might otherwise be, at least that was how it was with me before I had children myself. Mikaela and Erik are careerists: all the time I have known Mikaela she has had nothing but top jobs in the cultural sector, while Erik is the director of some multinational foundation based in Sweden. After Tjörn he had a meeting in Panama, before the two of them were due to leave for a holiday in Provence, that's the way their life is: places I have only ever read about are their stamping grounds. So into that came our family, along with baby wipes and nappies, John crawling all over the place, Heidi and Vanja fighting and screaming, laughing and crying, children who never eat at the table, never do what they are told, at least not when we are visiting other people and really *want* them to behave, because they know what is going on. The more there is at stake for us, the more unruly they become, and even though the summer house was large and spacious it was not large or spacious enough for them to be overlooked. Erik pretended to be unconcerned, he wanted to appear generous and child-friendly, but this was continually contradicted by his body language, his arms pinned to his sides, the way he went round putting things back in their places and that faraway look in his eyes. He was close to the things and the place he had known all his life, but distant from those populating it just now, regarding them more or less in the same way one would regard moles or hedgehogs. I knew how he felt, and I liked him. But I had brought all this along with me, and a real meeting of minds was impossible. He had been educated at Oxford and Cambridge, and had worked for several years as a broker in the City, but on a walk he and Vanja took up a mountainside near the sea one day he let her climb on her own several metres ahead of him while he stood stock-still admiring the view, without taking into account that she was only four and incapable of assessing the risk, so with Heidi in my arms I had to jog up and take over. When we were sitting in a café half an hour later – me with stiff legs after the sudden sprint – and I asked him to give John bits of a bread roll I placed beside him, as I had to keep an eye on Heidi and Vanja while finding them something to eat, he nodded, said he would, but he didn't put down the newspaper he was reading, did not even look up, and failed to notice that John, who was half a metre away from him, was becoming more and more agitated and at length screamed until his face went scarlet with frustration, since the bread he wanted was right in front of him but out of his reach. The situation infuriated Linda, sitting at the other end of the table – I could see it in her eyes – but she bit her tongue, made no comment, waited until we were outside and on our own, then

she said we should go home. Now. Accustomed to her moods, I
said she should keep her mouth shut and refrain from making
decisions like that when she was in such a foul temper. That
riled her even more of course, and that was how things stayed
until we got into the car next morning to leave.

The blue cloudless sky and the patchwork, windswept yet
wonderful countryside, together with the children's happiness
and the fact that we were in a car, and not a train compartment
or on board a plane, which had been the usual mode of travel
for the last few years, lightened the atmosphere, but it was not
long before we were at it again because we had to eat, and the
restaurant we found and stopped at turned out to belong to a
yacht club, but, the waiter informed me, if we just crossed the
bridge, walked into town, perhaps 500 metres, there was another
restaurant, so twenty minutes later we found ourselves on a
high, narrow and very busy bridge, grappling with two buggies,
hungry, and with only an industrial area in sight. Linda was
furious, her eyes were black, we were always getting into situations like this, she hissed, no one else did, we were useless, now
we should be eating, the whole family, we could have been really
enjoying ourselves, instead we were out here in a gale-force wind
with cars whizzing by, suffocating from exhaust fumes on this
bloody bridge. Had I ever seen any other families with three
children outside in situations like this? The road we followed
ended at a metal gate emblazoned with the logo of a security
firm. To reach the town, which looked run-down and cheerless,
we had to take a detour through the industrial zone for at least
fifteen minutes. I would have left her because she was always
moaning, she always wanted something else, never did anything
to improve things, just moaned, moaned, moaned, could never
face up to difficult situations, and if reality did not live up to
her expectations, she blamed me in matters large and small.

Well, under normal circumstances we would have gone our separate ways, but as always the practicalities brought us together again: we had one car and two buggies, so you just had to act as if what had been said had not been said after all, push the stained rickety buggies over the bridge and back to the posh yacht club, pack them into the car, strap in the children and drive to the nearest McDonald's, which turned out to be at a petrol station outside Gothenburg city centre, where I sat on a bench eating a sausage while Vanja and Linda ate theirs in the car. John and Heidi were asleep. We scrapped the planned trip to Liseberg Amusement Park, it would only make things worse given the atmosphere between us now; instead, a few hours later, we stopped on impulse at a shoddy so-called 'Fairytale Land', where everything was of the poorest quality, and took the children first to a small 'circus' consisting of a dog jumping through hoops held at knee height, a stout manly-looking lady, probably from somewhere in eastern Europe, who, clad in a bikini, tossed the same hoops in the air and swung them around her hips, tricks which every single girl in my first school mastered, and a fair-haired man of my age with curly-toed shoes, a turban and several spare tyres rolling over his harem trousers, who filled his mouth with petrol and breathed fire four times in the direction of the low ceiling. John and Heidi were staring so hard their eyes were popping out. Vanja had her mind on the lottery stall we had passed, where you could win cuddly toys, and kept pinching me and asking when the performance would finish. Now and then I looked across at Linda. She was sitting with Heidi on her lap and had tears in her eyes. As we came out and started walking down towards the tiny fairground, each pushing a buggy, past a large swimming pool with a long slide, behind whose top towered an enormous troll, perhaps thirty metres high, I asked her why.

'I don't know,' she said. 'But circuses have always moved me.'

'Why?'

'Well, it's so sad, so small and so cheap. And at the same time so beautiful.'

'Even this one?'

'Yes. Didn't you see Heidi and John? They were absolutely hypnotised.'

'But not Vanja,' I said with a smile. Linda returned the smile.

'What?' Vanja said, turning. 'What did you say, dad?'

'I just said that all you were thinking about at the circus was that cuddly toy you saw.'

Vanja smiled in the way she often did when we talked about something she had done. Happy, but also keen, ready for more.

'What did I do?' she asked.

'You pinched my arm,' I answered. 'And said you wanted to go on the lottery.'

'Why?' she asked.

'How should I know?' I said. 'I suppose you wanted that cuddly toy.'

'Shall we do it now then?' she asked.

'Yes,' I said. 'It's down there.'

I pointed down the tarmac path to the fairground amusements we could make out through the trees.

'Can Heidi have one as well?' she asked.

'If she wants,' Linda said.

'She does,' Vanja said, bending down to Heidi, who was in the buggy. 'Do you want one, Heidi?'

'Yes,' Heidi said.

We had to spend ninety kroner on tickets before each of them held a little cloth mouse in their hands. The sun burned down from the sky; the air beneath the trees was still, all sorts of shrill, plinging sounds from the amusements mixed with 80s disco music from the stalls around us. Vanja wanted candyfloss, so ten minutes later we were sitting at a table outside a kiosk with angry persistent wasps buzzing around us in the boiling-hot sun, which ensured that the sugar stuck to everything it came into contact with – the tabletop, the back of the buggy, arms and hands – to the children's loud disgruntlement; this was not what they envisaged when they saw the container with the swirling sugar in the kiosk. My coffee tasted bitter and was almost undrinkable. A small dirty boy pedalled towards us on his tricycle, straight into Heidi's buggy, then looked at us expectantly. He was dark-haired and dark-eyed, possibly Romanian or Albanian or perhaps Greek. After pushing his tricycle into the buggy a few more times, he positioned himself in such a way that we couldn't get out and he stood there with eyes downcast.

'Shall we go?' I asked.

'Heidi wanted a ride,' Linda said. 'Can't we do that first?'

A powerfully built man with protruding ears, also dark-skinned, came and lifted the boy and bike and carried him to the open space in front of the kiosk, patted him on the head a couple of times and went over to the mechanical octopus he was operating. The arms were fitted with small baskets you could sit in, which rose and fell as they slowly rotated. The boy began to cycle across the entrance area where summer-clad visitors were constantly arriving and leaving.

'Of course,' I said, and got up, took Vanja's and Heidi's candyflosses and threw them in the waste bin, and pushed John, who was tossing his head from side to side to catch all the interesting things going on, across the square to the path leading up to 'Cowboy Town'. But Cowboy Town, which was a pile of sand with three newly built sheds labelled, respectively, MINE, SHERIFF and PRISON, the latter two covered with WANTED DEAD OR ALIVE posters, surrounded on one side by birch trees and a ramp where some youngsters were skateboarding and on the other by a horse-riding area, was closed. Inside the fence, just opposite the mine, the eastern European woman sat on a rock, smoking.

'Ride!' Heidi said, looking around.

'We'll have to go to the donkey ride near the entrance,' Linda said.

John threw his bottle of water to the ground. Vanja crawled under the fence and ran over to the mine. When Heidi saw that she scrambled out of her buggy and followed. I spotted a red and white Coke machine at the rear of the sheriff's office, dredged up the contents of my shorts pocket and studied them: two hairslides, one hairpin with a ladybird motif, a lighter, three stones and two small white shells Vanja had found in Tjörn, a twenty-krone note, two five-krone coins and nine krone coins.

'I'll have a smoke in the meantime,' I said. 'I'll be down there.'

I motioned towards a tree trunk at the far end of the area. John raised both arms.

'Go on, then,' Linda said, lifting him up. 'Are you hungry, John?' she asked. 'Oh, it's so hot. Is there no shade anywhere so that I can sit down with him?'

'Up there,' I said, pointing to the restaurant at the top of the hill. It resembled a train, with the counter in the locomotive and the tables in the carriage. Not a soul was to be seen up there. Chairs were propped against the tables.

'That's what I'll do,' Linda said. 'And feed him. Will you keep an eye on the girls?'

I nodded, went to the Coke machine and bought a can, sat down on the tree trunk, lit a cigarette, looked up at the hastily constructed shed where Vanja and Heidi were running in and out of the doorway.

'It's pitch black in here!' Vanja shouted. 'Come and look!'

I raised my hand and waved, which fortunately appeared to satisfy her. She was still clutching the mouse to her chest with one hand.

Where was Heidi's mouse, by the way?

I allowed my gaze to drift up the hill. And there it lay, right outside the sheriff's office, with its head in the sand. At the restaurant Linda dragged a chair to the wall, sat down and began to breastfeed John, who at first kicked out, then lay quite still. The circus lady was making her way up the hill. A horsefly stung me on the calf. I smacked it with such force that it splattered all over my skin. The cigarette tasted terrible in the heat, but I resolutely inhaled the smoke into my lungs, stared up at the tops of the spruce trees, such an intense green where the sun caught them. Another horsefly landed on my calf. I lashed out at it, got up, threw the cigarette to the ground and walked towards the girls with the half-full still cold can of Coke in my hand.

'Daddy, you go round the back while we're inside and see if you can see us through the cracks, OK?' Vanja said, squinting up at me.

'All right, then,' I said, and walked round the shed. Heard them banging around and giggling inside. Bent my head to one of the cracks and peered in. But the difference between the light outside and the darkness inside was too great for me to see anything.

'Daddy, are you outside?' Vanja shouted.

'Yes,' I said.

'Can you see us?'

'No. Have you become invisible?'

'Yes!'

When they came out I pretended I couldn't see them. Focused my eyes on Vanja and called her name.

'I'm *here*,' she said, waving her arms.

'Vanja?' I shouted. 'Where are you? Come out now. It's not funny any more.'

'I'm here! Here!'

'Vanja?'

'Can't you see me, really? Am I really invisible?'

She sounded boundlessly happy although I sensed a touch of unease in her voice. At that moment John started screaming. I looked up. Linda got up clutching him to her breast. It was unlike John to cry like that.

'Oh, there you are!' I said. 'Have you been there the whole time?'

'Ye-es,' she said.

'Can you hear John crying?'

She nodded and looked up.

'We'll have to go then,' I said. 'Come on.'

I reached out for Heidi's hand.

'Don't want to,' she said. 'Don't want to hold hands.'

'OK,' I said. 'Hop into the buggy then.'

'Don't want buggy,' she said.

'Shall I carry you then?'

'Don't want carry.'

I went down and fetched the buggy. When I returned she had clambered onto the fence. Vanja was sitting on the ground. At the top of the hill Linda had left the restaurant; she was standing in the road now looking down, waving to us with one hand. John was still screaming.

'I don't want to walk,' Vanja said. 'My legs are tired.'

'You've hardly walked a step all day,' I said. 'How can your legs be tired?'

'Haven't got any legs. You'll have to carry me.'

'No, Vanja, that's rubbish. I can't carry you.'

'Yes, you can.'

'Get in the buggy, Heidi,' I said. 'Then we'll go for a ride.'

'Don't want buggy,' she said.

'I haven't got any leeegs!' Vanja said. She screamed the last word.

I felt the fury rising within me. My impulse was to lift them up and carry them, one pinned under each arm. This would not be the first time I had gone off with them kicking and screaming in my arms, oblivious of passers-by, who always stared with such interest when we had our little scenes, as though I was wearing a monkey mask or something.

But this time I managed to regain my composure.

'Could you get into the buggy, Vanja?' I asked.

'If you lift me,' she said.

'No, you'll have to do it yourself.'

'No,' she said. 'I haven't got any legs.'

If I didn't give way we would be standing here until the next day, for though Vanja lacked patience and gave up as soon as she met any resistance, she was infinitely stubborn when it was a question of getting her own way.

'OK,' I said, lifting her up into the buggy. 'You win again.'

'Win what?' she asked.

'Nothing,' I said. 'Come on, Heidi. We're going.'

I lifted her off the fence, and after a couple of half-hearted 'No, don't want's we were on our way up the hill, Heidi on my arm, Vanja in the buggy. As we passed, I picked up Heidi's cloth mouse, brushed off the dirt and popped it into the net shopping bag.

'I don't know what's up with him,' Linda said as we arrived at the top. 'He suddenly started crying. Perhaps he's been stung by a wasp or something. Look . . .'

She pulled up his jumper and showed me a small red mark.

He squirmed in her grip, his face red and his hair wet from all
the screaming.

'Poor little lad,' she said.

'I've been bitten by a horsefly,' I said. 'Perhaps that's what
happened. Put him in the buggy though and we can get going.
We can't do anything about it now anyway.'

When he was strapped in, he wriggled about and bored his
head down, still screaming.

'Let's get into the car,' I said.

'Yes,' Linda replied. 'But I'll have to change him first. There's
a nappy changing room down there.'

I nodded, and we began to walk down. Several hours had
passed since we arrived, the sun was lower in the sky and
something about the light it cast over the trees reminded me
of summer afternoons at home when we either drove to the
far side of the island with mum and dad to swim in the sea
or walked down to the knoll in the sound beyond the estate.
The memories filled my mind for a few seconds, not in the
form of specific events, more as atmospheres, smells, sensations.
The way the light, which in the middle of the day was whiter
and more neutral, became fuller later in the afternoon and
began to make the colours darker. Oh, running on the path
through the shady forest on a summer day in the 70s! Diving
into the salt water and swimming across to Gjerstadholmen
on the other side! The sun shining on the sea-smoothed rocks,
turning them almost golden. The stiff dry grass growing in the
hollows between them. The sense of the depths beneath the
surface of the water, so dark as it lay in the shadow beneath
the mountainside. The fish gliding by. And then the treetops
above us, their slender branches trembling in the sea breeze!
The thin bark and the smooth leg-like tree beneath. The green
foliage . . .

'There it is,' Linda said, nodding towards a small octagonal wooden construction. 'Will you wait?'

'We'll amble down,' I said.

In the copse inside the fence there were two gnomes carved in wood. That was how the place justified its status as Fairytale Land.

'Look, *tompen!*' Heidi shouted. *Tompen*, or in correct Swedish *tomten*, was a gnome.

She had been fixated on gnomes for quite a time. Well into spring she had pointed to the veranda where the gnome had appeared on Christmas Eve and said '*Tompen*'s coming,' and when she played with one of the presents he had given her she always stated first of all where it had come from. What sort of status he had for her, however, was not easy to say, because when she spotted the gnome outfit in my wardrobe after Christmas she wasn't in the least bit surprised or upset. We hadn't said a word; she just pointed and shouted '*Tompen*' as if that was where he changed his clothes, and when we met the old tramp with the white beard who hung around in the square outside our house she would stand up in the buggy and shout '*Tompen*' at the top of her lungs.

I leaned forward and kissed her chubby cheek.

'No kisses!' she said.

I laughed.

'Can I kiss you then, Vanja?'

'No!' Vanja said.

A meagre though regular stream of people flowed past us, most wearing summery clothes – shorts, T-shirts and sandals – some in jogging pants and trainers, a striking number of them fat, almost none well dressed.

'My daddy in prison!' Heidi shouted with glee.

Vanja turned in the buggy.

'No, daddy's not in prison!' she said.

I laughed again and stopped.

'We'll have to wait for mummy here,' I said.

Your daddy's in prison: that was what kids in the nursery used to say to one another. Heidi had understood it as a great compliment, and often said it when she wanted to boast about me. Last time we were returning from the cabin, according to Linda, she had said it to an elderly lady sitting behind them on the bus. My daddy's in prison. As I hadn't been there, but was standing at the bus stop with John, the comment had been left hanging in the air, unchallenged.

I leaned forward and wiped the sweat off my forehead with my T-shirt sleeve.

'Can I have another ticket, daddy?' Vanja said.

'Nope,' I said. 'You've already won a cuddly toy!'

'Nice daddy, another one?' she said.

I turned and saw Linda walking over. John was sitting upright in the buggy and seemed content under his sun hat.

'Everything OK?' I said.

'Mm. I bathed the sting in cold water. He's tired, though.'

'He'll sleep in the car then,' I said.

'What time do you think it is?'

'Half past three maybe?'

'Home by eight then?'

'Or thereabouts.'

Once again we crossed the tiny fairground, passed the pirate ship, a pathetic wooden façade with gangways behind, where one-legged or one-armed men with headscarves brandished swords, the llama and ostrich enclosures, the small paved area where some kids rode four-wheelers and finally arrived at the entrance, where there was a kind of obstacle course, a few logs, that is, and some plank walls with netting in between, a stand with a bungee trampoline and a donkey-riding ring, where we stopped. Linda took Heidi, carried her to the queue and put a helmet on her head, while Vanja and I stood watching by the fence with John.

There were four donkeys in the ring at a time, led by parents. The circuit was no more than thirty metres in length, but most of the animals took a long time to complete it because these were donkeys, not ponies, and donkeys stop when the whim takes them. Desperate parents tugged at the reins with all their strength, but the creatures would not budge. In vain they patted them on their flanks; the accursed donkeys were as motionless as ever. One of the children was crying. The woman taking the tickets kept shouting advice to the parents. Pull as hard as you can! Harder! Just pull, they don't mind! Hard! That's the way, that's it!

'Can you see, Vanja?' I said. 'The donkeys are refusing to move!'

She laughed. I was happy because she was happy. At the same time I was a little concerned about how Linda would cope; she wasn't much more patient than Vanja. But when it was her turn, she managed with aplomb. Whenever the donkey stopped she turned round and stood with her back to its flank while making smacking noises with her lips. In her youth she had ridden horses, they had formed a large part of her life, so that must have been how she knew what to do.

Heidi was beaming astride the donkey's back. When the donkey no longer responded to her trick Linda pulled so hard on the bridle it was as if there was no room left for any obstinacy.

'You're such a good rider!' I called to Heidi. Looked down at Vanja. 'Do you want a go?'

Vanja firmly shook her head. Straightened her glasses. She had ridden ponies from the age of eighteen months, and the autumn we moved to Malmö, when she was two and a half, she had started at a riding school. It was in the middle of Folkets Park, a sad down-at-heel riding hall with sawdust on the ground, which was a wonderful experience for her, she absorbed everything and wanted to talk about it when the lesson was over. She sat erect on her straggly pony and was led round and round by Linda, or on those occasions I went with her on my own, by one of the eleven- or twelve-year-old girls who seemed to spend their lives there, while an instructor walked about in the middle telling them what to do. It didn't matter that Vanja wouldn't always understand the instructions; the main thing was the experience of the horses and the environment around them. The stable, the cat that had kittens in the hay, the list of who was going to ride which horse that afternoon, the helmet she chose, the moment the horse was led into the hall, the riding itself, the cinnamon bun and the apple juice she had in the café afterwards. That was the high point of the week. But things changed during the course of the following autumn. They had a new instructor, and Vanja, who looked older than her four years, came face to face with demands she couldn't meet. Even though Linda told the instructor, things didn't get any better and Vanja began to protest when she had to go – she didn't want to go, not at all – and in the end we stopped. Even when she saw Heidi riding the little donkey in the park free of any demands, she didn't want a ride.

Another thing we had signed her up for was a playgroup where the children sometimes sang together, but also did drawings and various other creative activities. The second time she went they were supposed to draw a house, and Vanja had coloured the grass blue. The playgroup leader had gone over to her and said grass wasn't blue but green. Could she do another one? Vanja had torn up her drawing and then shown her annoyance in a way which made the children's parents raise their eyebrows and consider themselves lucky to have the well-brought-up children they had. Vanja is a great many things, but above all she is sensitive, and the fact that this attitude is already hardening – and it is – causes me concern. Seeing her grow up also changes my view of my own upbringing, not so much because of the quality but the quantity, the sheer amount of time you spend with your children, which is immense. So many hours, so many days, such an infinite number of situations that crop up and are lived through. From my own childhood I remember only a handful of incidents, all of which I regarded as momentous but which I now understand were a few events among many, which completely expunges their meaning, for how can I know that those particular episodes that lodged themselves in my mind were decisive, and not all the others of which I remember nothing?

When I discuss such topics with Geir, with whom I talk on the telephone for an hour every day, he is wont to quote Sven Stolpe, who has written somewhere about Bergman that he would have been Bergman irrespective of where he had grown up, implying, in other words, that you are who you are whatever your surroundings. What shapes you is the way you are towards your family rather than the family itself. When I was growing up I was taught to look for the explanation of all human qualities, actions and phenomena in the environment in which they originated. Biological or genetic determiners, the givens, that is, barely existed as an option, and when they did they were viewed with suspicion. Such an attitude can at first sight appear humanistic, inasmuch as it is intimately bound up with the notion that all people are equal, but upon closer examination it could just as well be an expression of a mechanistic attitude to man, who, born empty, allows his life to be shaped by his surroundings. For a long time I took a purely theoretical standpoint on the issue, which is actually so fundamental that it can be used as a springboard for any debate – if environment is the operative factor, for example, if man at the outset is both equal and malleable and the good man can be shaped by engineering his surroundings, hence my parents' generation's belief in the state, the education system and politics, hence their desire to reject everything that had been and hence their new truth, which is not found within man's inner being, in his detached uniqueness, but on the contrary in areas external to his intrinsic self, in the universal and collective, perhaps expressed in its clearest form by Dag Solstad, who has always been the chronicler of his age, in a text from 1969 containing his famous statement 'We won't give the coffee pot wings': out with spirituality, out with feeling, in with a new materialism, but it never struck them that the same attitude could lie behind the demolition of old parts of town to make way for roads and car parks, which naturally the intellectual left opposed, and perhaps it has not been possible to be aware of this until now, when the link between the idea of equality and capitalism, the welfare state and liberalism, Marxist materialism and the consumer society is obvious because the biggest equality creator of all is money, it levels all differences, and if your character and your fate are entities that can be shaped, money is the most natural shaper, and this gives rise to the fascinating phenomenon whereby crowds of people assert their individuality and originality by shopping in an identical way, while those who once ushered all this in with their affirmation of equality, their emphasis on material values and belief in change, are now inveighing against their own handiwork, which they believe the enemy created, but like all simple reasoning this is not wholly true either: life is not a mathematical quantity, it has no theory, only practice, and though it is tempting to understand a generation's radical rethink of society as being based on its view of the relationship between heredity and environment, this temptation is literary and consists more in the pleasure of speculating, that is of weaving one's thoughts through the most disparate areas of human activity, than in the pleasure of proclaiming the truth. The sky is low in Solstad's books, they show an incredible awareness of the currents in modern times, from the feeling of alienation in the 60s, the celebration of political initiatives at the beginning of the 70s, and then, just as the winds of change were starting to blow, to the distance-taking at the end. These weathervane-like conditions need be neither a strength nor a weakness for a writer, but simply a part of his material, a part of his orientation, and in Solstad's case the most significant feature has always been located elsewhere, namely in his language, which sparkles with its new old-fashioned elegance, and radiates a unique lustre, inimitable and full of elan. This language cannot be learned, this language cannot be bought for money and therein lies its value. It is not the case that we are born equal and that the conditions of life make our lives unequal, it is the opposite, we are born unequal, and the conditions of life make our lives more equal.

When I think of my three children it is not only their distinctive faces that appear before me, but also the quite distinct feeling they radiate. This feeling, which is constant, is what they 'are' for me. And what they 'are' has been present in them ever since the first day I saw them. At that time they could barely do anything, and the little bit they could do, like sucking on a breast, raising their arms as reflex actions, looking at their surroundings, imitating, they could all do that, thus what they 'are' has nothing to do with qualities, has nothing to do with what they can or can't do but is more a kind of light that shines within them.

Their character traits, which slowly began to reveal themselves after only a few weeks, have never changed either, and so different are they inside each of them that it is difficult to imagine the conditions we provide for them, through our behaviour and ways of being, have any decisive significance. John has a mild, friendly temperament, loves his sisters, planes, trains and buses. Heidi is extrovert and talks to everyone she meets; she's obsessed with shoes and clothes, wants to wear only dresses, and is at ease with her little body, such as when she stood naked in front of the swimming pool mirror and said to Linda, Mummy, look what a nice bottom I've got! She hates being reprimanded; if you raise your voice to her she turns away and starts crying. Vanja, on the other hand, gives as good as she gets, has quite a temper, a strong will, is sensitive and gets on easily with people. She has a good memory, knows by heart most of the books we read to her as well as lines in the films we see. She has a sense of humour and is always making us laugh when we are at home, but when she is outside she is easily affected by what goes on around her, and if the situation is too new or unaccustomed she goes into her shell. Shyness made its appearance when she was around seven months, and manifested itself through her shutting her eyes as if asleep whenever a stranger approached; she simply shut her eyes, as if she were asleep. She still does that on rare occasions; if she is sitting in the car and we bump into a parent from the nursery, for example, her eyes suddenly close. At the nursery in Stockholm, which was directly opposite our flat, after a tentative, fumbling start, she attached herself to a boy of her age called Alexander, and together they ran riot on the playground equipment, so much so that the staff said they sometimes had to protect Alexander from her – he couldn't always handle her intensity. But by and large he brightened up when she came, and was sorry when she left, and since then she has always preferred to play with boys; there is something about their physical and unrestrained side she obviously needs, perhaps because it is uncomplicated and easily gives her a feeling of control.

When we moved to Malmö she went to a new nursery, near the Western Harbour, in the newly built part of town where the most affluent lived, and as Heidi was so small I was the one who had to be responsible for settling her in. Every morning we cycled through the town, past the old shipbuilding yards and out towards the sea, Vanja with her little helmet on her head and her arms around me, me with my knees at stomach height on the undersized ladies' bike, light-hearted and happy, for everything in the town was still new to me, and the shifts of light in the morning and afternoon sky had still not been dulled by the debilitating gaze of routine. I thought it would be no more than a transitional phase, Vanja telling me first thing every morning, with an occasional tear, that she didn't want to go to the nursery; she would like it after a while, of course she would. But when we arrived she would not budge from my lap, no matter what the three young women who comprised the staff enticed her with. I thought it would be best to throw her in at the deep end, just walk away and leave her to fend for herself, but neither they nor Linda would hear of such brutality, so I sat there on a chair in a corner of the room with Vanja on my lap, surrounded by children at play, with the sun blazing outside, but the weather became gradually more autumnal as the days passed. In the break, for a snack consisting of apple and pear slices served by the staff in the yard, she would only take part if we sat ten metres away from the others, and when I agreed to that, me with an apologetic smile on my face, it was no surprise to me, for this was my way of relating to other people: how had she, only two and a half years old, managed to pick it up? Of course the staff eventually succeeded in coaxing her away from me, and I was able to cycle back to do some writing while she shed heart-rending tears, and after a month had passed I dropped her off and picked her up as normal. But sometimes in the mornings she still said she didn't want to go, still cried now and then, and when another nursery close to our flat rang to tell us they had a place free we didn't hesitate. It was called Lodjuret and was a parents' cooperative. That meant that all the parents had to put in two weeks' work a year on the staff, as well as filling one of the many administrative or practical posts. How far this nursery was to eat into our lives we had no idea; we talked only of the advantages it would bring: we would get to know Vanja's playmates and, through the duties and meetings, their parents. It was normal, we were told, for the children to go home together, so soon we would have some relief when we needed it. Furthermore, and this was perhaps the weightiest argument, we didn't know anyone in Malmö, not a soul, and this was an easy way to make contacts. And it was true: after a couple of weeks we were invited to one child's birthday party. Vanja was really looking forward to it, not least because she had just got a pair of gold-coloured party shoes she was going to wear, while at the same time not wanting to go, understandably enough, since she still didn't know the others very well. The invitation lay on the shelf in the nursery one Friday afternoon, the party was a week later on the Saturday, and every morning that week Vanja asked if it was Stella's party that day. When we said no, she asked if it was the day after tomorrow; that was about the furthest extent of the future horizon for her. The morning we were at last able to nod and say yes, we were going to Stella's today, she jumped out of bed and headed straight for the

cupboard to put on her golden shoes. A couple of times every
hour she asked whether it would soon be time to go, and it
could have been an unbearable morning of nagging and scenes,
but fortunately there were activities to fill it with. Linda took
her to a bookshop to buy a present, afterwards they sat at the
kitchen table and made a birthday card. We bathed the girls,
combed their hair and put on their white stockings and party
dresses. Then Vanja's mood suddenly changed – she didn't want
to wear stockings or a dress, there was no question of her going
to any party, and she threw the golden shoes at the wall – but
after patiently sitting through the few minutes the outburst
lasted we managed to get her into everything, including even
the white knitted shawl she had been given for Heidi's christening, and when at last the girls were sitting in the buggy in
front of us they were again filled with expectation. Vanja was
serious and quiet, her golden shoes in one hand and the present
in the other, but when she turned to say something to us it was
with a smile on her lips. Beside her sat Heidi, excited and happy,
for although she didn't understand where we were going, the
clothes and preparations must have given her an indication that
something unusual was in the offing. The apartment where the
party was to take place was a few hundred metres up the street
where we lived. It was full of the bustle that marks late Saturday
afternoons, the last heavily laden shoppers mingling with kids
who have come to the town centre to hang around outside Burger
King and McDonald's, and the stream of traffic passing is no
longer purely with a purpose in mind, families on their way to
and from multi-storey car parks. Now there are more and more
of the low shiny black cars with the bass throbbing through the
bodywork driven by immigrant men in their twenties. Outside
the supermarket there were so many people that we had to stop
for a moment, and when the skinny wizened old lady who usually

sat there in her wheelchair at this time of day caught sight of Vanja and Heidi she leaned towards them, rang the bell she had hanging from a stick and beamed a smile that was clearly meant to be engaging but to the girls must have been terrifying. But they said nothing, just looked at her. On the other side of the entrance sat a drug addict of my age, with a cap in his outstretched hand. He had a cat inside a cage next to him, and when Vanja saw it she turned to us.

'When we move to the country I want a cat,' she said.

'Cat!' Heidi said, pointing.

I steered the buggy over the kerb onto the road to pass three people walking so damned slowly, probably thought they owned the pavement, walked a few metres as fast as I could and steered back onto the pavement after we had passed them.

'That could be a long way off, you know, Vanja,' I said.

'You can't keep a cat in an apartment,' she said.

'Exactly,' Linda said.

Vanja looked ahead again. She was squeezing the bag containing the present with both hands.

I looked at Linda.

'What was his name again, Stella's father?'

'My mind's gone blank . . .' she said. 'Oh, it was Erik, wasn't it?'

'That's right,' I said. 'What was his job again?'

'I'm not sure,' she said. 'Something to do with design.'

We went past Gottgruvan and both Vanja and Heidi leaned forward to look through the window. Next door was a pawnbroker's. The shop beside that sold a variety of small statues and jewellery, angels and Buddhas, as well as joss sticks, tea, soap and other New Age knick-knacks. Posters hung in the windows giving information about when yoga gurus and well known clairvoyants were coming to town. On the other side of the street was a clothes shop with cheap brands, Ricco Jeans and Clothing, FASHION FOR THE WHOLE FAMILY, beside it was Taboo, a kind of 'erotic' boutique luring passers-by with dildos and dolls in various negligees and corsets in the window by the door, hidden from the street. Next to it was Bergman Bags and Hats, which must have remained unchanged in terms of interior and range from the day it was founded in the 40s, and Radio City, which had just gone bankrupt but where you could still see a window full of illuminated TV screens, surrounded by a wide selection of electrical goods, with prices written on large almost luminous orange and green bits of cardboard. The rule was that the further you advanced up the street, the cheaper and more dubious the shops became. The same applied to the people frequenting the area. Unlike in Stockholm, where we had also lived in the centre, the poverty and misery which existed here were visible in the street. I liked that.

'Here it is,' Linda said, stopping by a door. Outside a bingo hall a little further on three pale-skinned women in their fifties stood smoking. Linda's gaze glided down the list of names beside the intercom; she pressed a number. Two buses thundered past one after the other. Then the door buzzed, and we went into the dark hallway, parked the buggy by the wall and went up the two flights of stairs to the flat, me with Heidi in my arms, Linda holding Vanja's hand. The door was open when we arrived. The inside of the flat was dark too. I felt a certain unease walking straight in, I would have preferred to ring, that would have made our arrival more obvious, because now we were standing in the hall without anyone paying us the slightest attention.

I set Heidi down and took off her jacket. Linda was about to do the same with Vanja, but she protested: her boots were to come off first, then she could put on her golden shoes.

There was a room on either side of the hall. In one, children were playing excitedly; in the other some adults were standing around talking. In the hall, which continued deeper into the flat, I saw Erik standing with his back to us chatting to a mother and father from the nursery.

'Hello!' I said.

He didn't turn. I laid Heidi's jacket on top of a coat on a chair and met Linda's eye. She was looking for somewhere to hang Vanja's jacket.

'Shall we go in then?' she said.

Heidi wrapped her arms round my leg. I lifted her up and took a few steps forward. Erik turned.

'Hi,' he said.

'Hi,' I replied.

'Hi, Vanja!' he said.

Vanja turned away.

'Aren't you going to give Stella her present?' I asked.

'Stella, Vanja's here!' Erik said.

'You do it,' Vanja said.

Stella got up from the group of children on the floor. She smiled.

'Happy birthday, Stella!' I said. 'Vanja's got a present for you.' I looked down at Vanja. 'Do you want to give it to her?'

'You do it,' she said in a low voice.

I took the present and passed it to Stella.

'It's from Vanja and Heidi,' I said.

'Thank you,' she said, and tore off the paper. When she saw it was a book she put it on the table next to the other presents and went back to the other children.

'Well?' said Erik. 'Everything OK?'

'Yes, fine,' I said. I could feel my shirt sticking to my chest. Was it noticeable? I wondered.

'What a nice apartment,' Linda said. 'Are there three bedrooms?'
'Yes,' Erik said.

He always looked so wily, always looked as though he had got something on the people he spoke to, it was hard to know where you stood with him; that half-smile of his could equally well have been sarcastic or congenial or tentative. If he'd had a pronounced or strong character, that might well have bothered me, but he was dithery in a weak-minded, irresolute kind of way, so whatever he might be thinking didn't worry me in the slightest. My attention was focused on Vanja. She was standing close to Linda and looking down at the floor.

'The others are in the kitchen,' Erik said. 'There's some wine there, if you fancy a glass.'

Heidi had already entered the room, she was standing in front of a shelf with a wooden snail in her hand. It had wheels and a string you could pull.

I nodded to the two parents down the hall.

'Hi,' they said.

What was his name, now? Johan? Or Jacob? And hers? Was it Mia? Oh hell. Of course. Robin, that was it.

'Hi,' I said.

'You all right?' he said.

'Yes,' I said. 'What about you two?'

'Everything's fine, thank you.'

I smiled at them. They smiled back. Vanja let go of Linda and hesitantly entered the room where the children were playing. For a while she stood observing them. Then it was as if she had decided to take the plunge.

'I've got golden shoes!' she said.

She bent forward and took off one shoe, held it up in the air in case anyone wanted to see. But no one did. When she realised that she put it back on.

'Wouldn't you like to play with the children over there?' I suggested. 'Can you see? They've got a big doll's house.'

She went over, sat down beside them but did nothing, just sat watching.

Linda lifted Heidi and carried her to the kitchen. I followed. Everyone said hello, we returned the greeting, sat down at the long table, I was by the window. They were talking about cheap air tickets, how they started out dirt cheap, slowly became more expensive as you had to pay one surcharge after another, until you were left with a ticket that cost as much as those from more expensive airlines. Then the topic moved to buying CO_2 quotas and after that to the newly introduced chartered train journeys. I could definitely have offered an opinion about that, but I didn't – small talk is one of the infinite number of talents I haven't mastered – so I sat nodding at what was said, as usual, smiling when others smiled, while ardently wishing myself miles away. In front of the worktop was Stella's mother, Frida, making some kind of salad dressing. She was no longer with Erik, and even though they were good at working together where Stella was concerned, you could still occasionally notice the tension and irritation between them at committee meetings in the nursery. She was blonde, had high cheekbones and narrow eyes, a long, slim body, and she knew how to dress, but she was much too pleased with herself, too self-centred for me to find her attractive. I have no problem with uninteresting or unoriginal people – they may have other, more important attributes, such as warmth, consideration, friendliness, a sense of humour or talents such as being able to make a conversation flow to generate an atmosphere of ease around them, the ability to make a family function – but I feel almost physically ill in the presence of boring people who consider themselves especially interesting and who blow their own trumpets.

She placed the dish of what I thought was a dressing but which turned out to be a 'dip' on a board beside a dish of carrot sticks and one of cucumber sticks. At that moment Vanja came into the room. When she had located us she came over and stood close.

'I want to go home,' she said softly.

'We've only just got here!' I said.

'We're going to stay a bit longer,' Linda said. 'And look, now you're all getting some goodies!' Was she referring to the vegetables on the board?

She had to be.

They were crazy in this country.

'I'll go with you,' I said to Vanja. 'Come on.'

'Will you take Heidi as well?' Linda asked.

I nodded, and with Vanja at my heels I carried her into the room where the children were. Frida followed holding the board. She placed it on a little table in the middle of the floor.

'Here's something to eat,' she said. 'Before the cake arrives.'

The children, three girls and a boy, went on playing with the doll's house. In the other room two boys were running around. Erik was in there, by the stereo system with a CD in his hand.

'I've got a bit of Norwegian jazz here,' he said. 'Are you a jazz fan?'

'We-ell . . .' I said.

'Norway has a great jazz scene,' he said.

'Who's that you have there?' I asked.

He showed me the cover. It was a band I had never heard of.

'Great,' I said.

Vanja was standing behind Heidi trying to lift her. Heidi was protesting.

'She says no, Vanja,' I said. 'Put her down.'

As she carried on I went over to them.

'Don't you want a carrot?' I asked.

'No,' Vanja said.

'But there's a dip,' I said. Went over to the table, took a carrot stick and dunked it in the white, presumably cream-based, dip and put it in my mouth.

'Mm,' I said. 'It's good!'

Why couldn't they have given them sausages, ice cream and pop? Lollipops? Jelly? Chocolate pudding?

What a stupid, bloody idiotic country this was. All the young women drank water in such vast quantities it was coming out of their ears, they thought it was 'beneficial' and 'healthy', but all it did was send the graph of incontinent young people soaring. Children ate wholemeal pasta and wholemeal bread and all sorts of weird coarse-grained rice which their stomachs could not digest properly, but that didn't matter because it was 'beneficial', it was 'healthy', it was 'wholesome'. Oh, they were confusing food with the mind, they thought they could eat their way to being better human beings without understanding that food is one thing and the notions food evokes another. And if you said that, if you said anything of that kind, you were either reactionary or just a Norwegian, in other words ten years behind.

'I don't want any,' Vanja said. 'I'm not hungry.'

'OK, OK,' I said. 'But look here. Have you seen this? It's a train set. Shall we build it?'

She nodded, and we sat down behind the other children. I began to lay railway track in an arc while helping Vanja to fit her pieces. Heidi had moved into the other room, where she walked alongside the bookcase studying everything in it. Whenever the two boys' capers became too boisterous she swivelled round and glared at them.

Erik finally put on a CD and turned up the volume. Piano, bass and a myriad of percussion instruments that a certain type of jazz drummer adores – the kind that bangs stones against each other or uses whatever materials happen to be at hand. For me it sometimes meant nothing, and sometimes I found it ridiculous. I hated it when the audience applauded at jazz concerts.

Erik was nodding to the music, then turned, sent me a wink and went into the kitchen. At that moment the doorbell rang. It was Linus and his son Achilles. Linus had a pinch of *snus* under his top lip, was wearing black trousers, a dark coat and beneath it a white shirt. His fair hair was a touch unkempt, the eyes peering into the flat were honest and naïve.

'Hello!' he said. 'How are you doing?'

'Fine,' I said. 'And you?'

'Yep, jogging along.'

Achilles, who was small with large dark eyes, took off his jacket and shoes while staring at the children behind me. Children are like dogs, they always find their own in crowds. Vanja eyed him as well. He was her favourite, he was the one she had chosen to take over the role of Alexander. But after he had removed his outer clothing he went straight over to the other children, and there was nothing Vanja could do to stop him. Linus slipped into the kitchen, and the glint I thought I detected in his eye could only have been his anticipation of a chance to have a chat.

I got up and looked at Heidi. She was sitting beside the yucca plant under the window, taking earth from the pot and making small piles on the floor. I went over to her, lifted her, scraped what I could back with my hands, and went into the kitchen to find a rag. Vanja followed me. Once there, she climbed onto Linda's lap. In the living room Heidi started to cry. Linda sent me a quizzical look.

'I'll see to her,' I said. 'Just need something to wipe with.'

People were crowded round the worktop, it looked as if a meal was being prepared, and instead of squeezing through, I went to the toilet, unfurled a hefty handful of toilet paper, moistened it under the tap and went back to the living room to clean up. I lifted Heidi, who was still crying, and carried her to the bathroom to wash her hands. She wriggled and squirmed in my grip.

'There, there, sweetheart,' I said. 'Soon be done. Just a bit more, now, OK. There we are!'

As we came out the crying subsided, but she wasn't entirely happy, didn't want to be put down, just wanted to be in my arms. Robin stood in the living room with his arms crossed following the movements of his daughter Theresa, who was only a few months older than Heidi, although she could already speak in long sentences.

'Hi,' he said. 'Writing at the moment, are you?'

'Yes, a bit,' I said.

'Do you write at home?'

'Yes, I've got my own room.'

'Isn't that difficult? I mean, don't you ever feel like watching TV or washing some clothes or something, instead of writing?'

'It's fine. I get less time than if I had an office, but . . .'

'Yes, of course,' he said.

He had quite long blond hair that curled at the nape of his neck, clear blue eyes, a flat nose, broad jawbones. He wasn't strong, nor was he weak. He dressed as if he were in his mid-twenties, even though he was in his late thirties. What went through his mind I had no idea, I didn't have a clue about what he was thinking, yet there was nothing secretive about him. On the contrary, his face and aura gave the impression of openness. But there was something else nevertheless, I sensed, a shadow of something else. His job was to integrate refugees into the community, he had told me once, and after a few follow-up questions about how many refugees were allowed into the country and so on, I let the matter drop because the opinions and sympathies I had were so far from the norm I assumed he represented that sooner or later they would shine through, whereupon I would come across as the baddie or the idiot, which I saw no reason to encourage.

Vanja, who was sitting on the floor slightly apart from the other children, looked towards us. I put Heidi down, and it was as though Vanja had been waiting for that: she got up at once and came over, took Heidi by the hand and led her to the games shelf, from which she passed her the wooden snail with feelers that whirred when you pulled it along the floor.

'Look, Heidi!' she said, taking it out of her hands and putting it on the floor. 'You pull the string like this. Then it whirrs. See?'

Heidi grabbed the string and pulled. The snail toppled over.

'No, not like that,' Vanja said. 'I'll show you.'

She placed the snail upright and slowly dragged it a few metres.

'I've got a little sister!' she said aloud. Robin had gone to the window, where he stood staring out into the backyard. Stella, who was energetic and presumably extra lively since it was her party, excitedly shouted something which I didn't understand, pointed to one of the two smaller girls, who handed her the doll she was clutching, took out a little buggy, placed the doll in it and began to push it down the hall. Achilles had found his way to Benjamin, a boy eighteen months older than Vanja who usually sat deeply absorbed in something, a drawing or a pile of Lego or a pirate ship with plastic pirates. He was imaginative, independent and well behaved, and was sitting with Achilles now, building the railway track Vanja and I had started. The two smaller girls ran after Stella. Heidi was whimpering. She was probably hungry. I went into the kitchen and sat down beside Linda.

'Will you go and see to them for a bit?' I said. 'I think Heidi's hungry.'

She nodded, patted my shoulder and got up. It took me a few seconds to figure out the subject of the two conversations going on round the table. One was about the car pool, the other about cars, and I inferred that the conversations must have gone off in opposite directions. The darkness outside the windows was dense, the light in the kitchen was frugal, the creases in the Swedish faces around the table were in shadow, and eyes gleamed in the glow from the candles. Erik and Frida and a woman whose name I didn't remember were standing at the worktop with their backs to us, preparing food. The tenderness I felt for Vanja filled me to the brim, but there was nothing I could do. I glanced at the person speaking, gave a faint smile whenever there was a witticism and sipped at the glass of red wine someone had put in front of me.

Directly facing me was the only person who stood out. His face was large, his cheeks were scarred, features coarse, eyes intense. The hands on the table were large. He was wearing a 50s-style shirt and blue jeans rolled up to the calf. His hair was also typical of the 50s, and he sported side burns. But that was not what made him different; it was his personality, you could sense him sitting there, even though he didn't say much.

Once I had been to a party in Stockholm at which a boxer had been present. He was sitting in the kitchen, his physical presence was tangible, and he filled me with a distinct but unpleasant sensation of inferiority. A sensation that I was inferior to him. Strangely enough, the evening was to prove me right. The party was hosted by one of Linda's friends, Cora, her flat was small, so people were standing around chatting everywhere. Music was blaring from a system in the living room. Outside, the streets were white with snow. Linda was heavily pregnant, this was perhaps the last party we would be able to go to before the child was born and changed everything, so even though she was tired, she wanted to try and stay there for a while. I had a drop of wine and chatted to Thomas, who was a photographer and friend of Geir's; he knew Cora through his partner, Marie, who was a poet and had been one of Cora's instructors at Biskops-Arnö Folk High School. Linda was sitting on a chair pulled back from the table because of her stomach, she was laughing and happy, and I was probably the only person aware of the slight introversion and faint glow that had come over her during these last few months. After a while she got up and went out, I smiled at her and turned my attention back to Thomas, who was saying something about the genes of redheads, so prevalent here this evening.

Someone was knocking.

'Cora!' I heard. 'Cora!'

Was it Linda?

I got up and went into the hallway.

The knocking was coming from inside the bathroom.

'Is that you, Linda?' I asked.

'Yes,' she said. 'I think the door lock has jammed. Can you get Cora? There must be some sort of knack to it.'

I went into the living room and tapped Cora on the shoulder. She was holding a plate of food in one hand and a glass of red wine in the other.

'Linda's locked in the bathroom,' I said.

'Oh no!' she said, set the glass and the plate down and dashed out.

They conferred for a while through the locked door. Linda tried to follow the instructions she was given, but nothing helped, the door was and remained jammed. Everyone in the flat was aware of the situation now, the mood was both amused and excited, a whole flock of people were in the hall giving advice to Linda while Cora, flummoxed and anxious, kept saying that Linda was heavily pregnant, we had to do something now. In the end the decision was taken to ring for a locksmith. While we waited for him I stood by the door talking to Linda inside, unpleasantly conscious of the fact that everyone could hear what I said and of my own helplessness. Couldn't I just kick the door in and get her out? Simple and effective?

I had never kicked a door in before. I didn't know how solid it was. Imagine if it didn't budge. How stupid would that look?

The locksmith arrived half an hour later. He laid out a canvas bag of tools on the floor and began to fiddle with the lock. He was small, wore glasses and had the beginnings of a bald patch, said nothing to the circle of people around him, tried one tool after another in vain, the damned lock wouldn't budge. In the end, he gave up, told Cora it was no good, he couldn't get the door open.

'What shall we do then?' Cora asked. 'She's due soon!'

He shrugged.

'You'll have to kick it in,' he said, starting to pack his tools.

Who was going to kick it in?

It had to be me. I was Linda's husband. It was my responsibility.

My heart was pounding.

Should I do it? Take a step back in full view of everyone and kick it with all my might?

What if the door didn't give? What if it swung open and hit Linda?

She would have to take shelter in the corner.

Calmly, I breathed in and out several times. But it didn't help, I was still shaking inside. Attracting attention like this was anathema to me. If there was a risk of failure it was even worse.

Cora looked around.

'We have to kick the door in,' she said. 'Who can do that?'

The locksmith disappeared through the door. If it was going to be me, now was the time to step forward.

But I couldn't bring myself to do it.

'Micke,' Cora said. 'He's a boxer.'

She swivelled to fetch him from the living room.

'I can ask him,' I said. In that way I wouldn't be hiding my humiliation at any rate, I would tell him straight out that I, as Linda's husband, didn't dare to kick in the door, I was asking you, as a boxer and a giant, to do it for me.

He was standing by the window with a beer in his hand chatting to two girls.

'Hello, Micke,' I said.

He looked at me.

'She's still locked in the bathroom. The locksmith couldn't open the door. Could you kick it in, do you think?'

'Of course,' he said, eyeing me for a moment before putting down his beer and going into the hallway. I followed. People moved to the side as he made his way to the door.

'Are you in there?' he asked.

'Yes,' said Linda.

'Stand as far back from the door as you can. I'm going to kick it in.'

'Right,' Linda said.

He waited for a moment. Then he raised his foot and kicked the door with such force that the lock was knocked inwards. Splinters flew.

When Linda came out, some people clapped.

'Poor you,' Cora said. 'I'm so sorry. Subjecting you to that, and then . . .'

Micke turned and went.

'How are you?' I asked.

'Fine,' Linda said. 'But I think maybe we should go home soon.'

'Of course,' I said.

In the living room the music was turned down as two women in their early thirties were about to read their gushing poems. I passed Linda her jacket, put on mine, said goodbye to Cora and Thomas, my shame seared inside me, but the last duty remained, I had to thank Micke for what he had done. I made my way through the poetry audience and stopped by the window in front of him.

'Thank you very much,' I said. 'You rescued her.'

He blew out his cheeks and shrugged his shoulders. 'It was nothing.'

In the taxi on the way home I hardly looked at Linda. I hadn't risen to the task. I had been so cowardly as to let someone else do the job, and all of that was visible in my eyes. I was a miserable wretch.

When we were in bed she asked what was wrong with me. I said I was ashamed that I hadn't kicked in the door. She looked at me in astonishment. The thought had not even occurred to her. Why should I have done it? I wasn't the type, was I.

The man sitting on the opposite side of the table radiated some of the same vibes the boxer in Stockholm had. It didn't have anything to do with the size of his body or muscle mass, for even though several of the men here had well-trained powerful upper bodies they still made a lightweight impression, their presence in the room was fleeting and insignificant like a casual thought. No, there was something else, and whenever I met it I came off worse, I saw myself as the weak trammelled man I was, who lived his life in the world of words. I sat musing on this while taking occasional peeps at him and listening to the ongoing conversation with half an ear. Now it had turned to various teaching styles, and which schools each of them was considering for their children. After a short intermezzo in which

Linus talked about a sports day he had attended, the conversation moved to house prices. There was agreement that house
prices had soared over recent years, but more in Stockholm than
here, and that presumably it was just a question of time before
the tide would turn, maybe they would even fall as steeply as
they had risen. Then Linus turned to face me.

'What are house prices like in Norway, then?' he asked.

'About the same as here,' I said. 'Oslo's as expensive as
Stockholm. It's a bit cheaper in the provinces.'

He kept his eyes fixed on me for a while, in case I might exploit
the opening he had given me, but when this proved not to be
the case, he turned back and continued chatting. He had done
the very same thing at the first general meeting we had attended,
though at that time with a kind of critical undertone, because,
as he had put it, the meeting was drawing to a close and Linda
and I still hadn't said anything, the point was that everyone
should have their say, that was the whole idea of a parents'
cooperative. I had no idea what to think about the matter under
discussion, and it was Linda who, with a faint blush, weighed
up the pros and cons on behalf of the family, with the whole
assembly staring at her. First on the agenda was whether the
nursery should get rid of the cook who was employed there, and
instead go for a catering firm, which would be cheaper, and
second, if they did that, what kind of food they should opt for:
vegetarian or the standard? Lodjuret was actually a vegetarian
nursery, that was the principle on which it had been founded
in its day, but now only four of the parents were vegetarians,
and since the children didn't eat much of the numerous varie-
ties of vegetables that were served up, many parents thought
they might as well dispense with the principle. The discussion
lasted for several hours and scoured the subject like a trawl net
on the seabed. The meat percentage in various types of sausage

was brought up; it was one thing that the sausages bought in shops had the meat percentage printed on the label, but quite another what catering companies did with their sausages, because how could you know how much meat they contained? To me sausages were sausages. I didn't have the slightest idea about the world that was opening before my eyes that evening, least of all that there were people who could delve so deeply into it. Wasn't it nice for the children to have a cook who made food for them in their kitchen? I thought but didn't say, and I was beginning to hope that the whole discussion would pass without our having to say anything, before, that is, Linus fixed his astute and naïve eyes on us.

From the living room came the sound of Heidi crying. Again I thought of Vanja. Usually she solved situations like these by doing exactly the same as the others. If they pulled out a chair, she pulled out a chair, if they sat down, she sat down, if they laughed, she laughed, even if she didn't understand what they were laughing at. If they ran around calling a name, she ran around calling a name. That was her method. But Stella had seen through it. Once I happened to be there and heard her say, You just copy us! You're a parrot! A parrot! That hadn't deterred her from continuing, so far the method had proved too successful for that, but now when Stella herself was holding court it probably did inhibit her. I knew she understood what this was all about. Several times she had said the same to Heidi, that she copied her, she was a parrot.

Stella was eighteen months older than Vanja, who admired her above all else. When she was allowed to tag along, it was at Stella's grace, and she had this hold on all the children in the nursery. She was a beautiful child, she had blonde hair and big eyes, was always nicely, sensibly dressed, and the streak of cruelty she possessed was no worse and no better than that displayed by other children at the top of the hierarchy. That was not why I had problems with her. The problems for me were that she was so aware of the impression she made on adults, and the way in which she exploited this charming innocence. During my compulsory duties at the nursery I had never fallen for it. No matter how sparkling the eyes she clapped on me when she asked for something, my reaction remained one of indifference, which of course confused her, and she redoubled her endeavours to charm me. Once she had stayed with us after nursery to go to the park and sat beside Vanja in the double buggy while I carried Heidi on one arm and pushed them with the other. She jumped out a few hundred metres before the park to run the last stretch, which I reacted sharply to. I called her back and said that she was to sit nicely in the buggy until we arrived, there were cars around, couldn't she see them? She looked at me in surprise, she wasn't used to that tone, and even though I was not satisfied with the way I had resolved the situation, I also thought that a *No!* was not the worst thing that could befall this creature. But she had taken note of it, because when, half an hour later, I swung them round by their feet to their immense glee, and then knelt down to fight with them, which Vanja loved, especially when she took a run-up and knocked me over onto the grass, Stella, when it was her turn, kicked me on the calf instead, and that was all right once, all right twice, but when she did it a third time I told her, That hurts, that does, just stop it now, Stella, which of course she ignored, now it had become exciting, and she kicked me again, with a loud laugh, and Vanja, who always aped her, also laughed, whereupon I got up, grabbed Stella around the waist and stood her up. 'Listen to me, you little brat,' I felt like saying, and would have done had her mother not been coming to collect her in half an hour. 'Listen, Stella,' I said instead, harshly, with annoyance, looking her in the eye.

'When I say no, I mean no. Do you understand?' She looked down, refusing to answer. I raised her chin. 'Do you understand?' I asked again. She nodded, and I let her go. 'I'm going to sit on that bench over there. You can play on your own until your mother comes.' Vanja sent me a bemused look. But then she laughed and tugged at Stella. For her, scenes like this were everyday occurrences. Fortunately, Stella dropped the matter at once, for I was really skating on thin ice – what on earth would I do if she began to cry or scream? But she went with Vanja over to the big 'train' which was teeming with kids. When her mother came she had two paper cups of latte in her hand. Usually I would have gone as soon as she arrived, but when she passed me a cup of coffee I had no option but to sit down and listen to her chatter on about her job, while squinting into the low November sun and keeping half an eye on the children.

The week when I'd had nursery duty and in principle had been like any employee ran more or less like clockwork; I had worked a lot in institutions before and soon had all the routines off pat, which the staff were not accustomed to seeing with parents, nor was I a stranger to dressing and undressing children, changing their nappies and even playing if it was required. The children reacted to my presence in different ways, of course. For example, one of them who hung around without any friends, a gangling white-haired boy, wanted to crawl up onto my lap all the time, either to have a story read or just to sit there. I played with another one for half an hour after the others had gone, his mother was late, but he forgot all about that when we played pirate ships. To his great delight, I kept adding new features like sharks and marauding boats and fires. A third boy, on the other hand, the oldest there, immediately discovered one of my weak spots by taking a bunch of keys from my pocket while we were at the table eating. The mere fact that I didn't stop him, even though I was angry, allowed him to follow the scent. First of all, he asked if there was a car key. When I shook my head he asked me why not. I haven't got a car, I said. Why not? he asked. I haven't got a licence, I said. Can't you drive a car? he said. Aren't you an adult, then? he asked. All adults can drive cars, can't they? Then he jingled the keys under my nose. I let him do it, thinking he would soon tire of it, but he didn't; on the contrary he persisted. I've got your keys, he said. And you can't get them. He kept jingling them under my nose. The other children watched us, the three members of staff as well. I made the mistake of lunging for the keys, He managed to pull them away in time, and laughed and jeered. Ha, ha, you didn't get them! he crowed. Again I tried not to show my annoyance. He started banging the keys on the table. Don't do that, I said. He just smiled cheekily and persisted. One of the nursery staff told him to stop. And he did. But continued to dangle them from his hand. You'll never get them, he said. Then Vanja broke in.

'Give the keys to daddy!' she said.

What kind of situation was this?

I acted as if nothing was happening, leaned over the food again and went on eating. But the little devil continued to tease me. Jingle, jingle. I decided to let him keep them until we had finished eating. Drank some water, feeling my face strangely flushed over such a tiny matter. Was that what Olaf, the head of the nursery, saw? At any rate, he ordered Jocke to hand back the keys. And Jocke did, without any fuss.

All my adult life I have kept a distance from other people, it has been my way of coping because I come so incredibly close to others in my thoughts and feelings they only have to look away dismissively for a storm to break inside me. That closeness naturally informs my relationship with children too, that is what allows me to sit down and play with them, but as they lack any veneer of courtesy and decency that adults have, this also means they can freely penetrate the outer bulwarks of my personality and then wreak as much havoc as they wish. My only defence, when it all started, was either sheer physical strength, which I was not able to use, or else simply to pretend I wasn't bothered, possibly the best approach, but something I wasn't so adept at, since the children, at least the most forward of them, immediately discovered how uncomfortable I was in their presence.

Oh, how undignified this was!

Everything was suddenly turned on its head. I, who wasn't fond of the nursery Vanja attended, who just wanted it to look after Vanja for me so that I could work in peace for some hours every day without knowing what she was doing or how she was, I who didn't want any closeness in my life, who could not get enough of distance, could not be alone enough, who all of a sudden had to spend a week there as an employee and get involved in everything that happened, but it did not stop there, for when you dropped off your children or picked them up it was normal to sit for a few minutes in the playroom or dining room or wherever they were, and chat to the other parents, perhaps play a little with the children, and every day of the week . . . I usually kept this to the bare minimum, took Vanja and put on her coat before anyone discovered what was going on, but now and then I was trapped in the corridor, a conversation was initiated, and, hey presto, there I was sitting on one of those low deep sofas making agreement noises about something or other that was of no interest to me whatsoever while the brashest of the children yanked and tugged at me, wanting me to throw them, carry them, swing them round or, in the case of Jocke, who incidentally was the son of the kind book-loving banker Gustav, was content merely to stab me with sharp objects.

Spending Saturday afternoon and evening squeezed between

others at a table and eating vegetables with a strained but courteous smile on your face was part of the same obligation.

Erik lifted down a stack of plates from a cupboard above the worktop while Frida counted knives and forks. I took a sip of wine and could feel how hungry I was. Stella stopped in the doorway, her face red and a little sweaty.

'Is it time for the cake now?' she called.

Frida swivelled round.

'Soon, sweetheart. But first we have to eat some proper food.'

Her attention wandered from the child to those sitting around the table.

'The food's ready,' she said. 'Help yourselves. There are the plates and cutlery. And you can take some food for your children too.'

'Ah, that sounds good,' Linus said, getting up. 'What is there?'

I had planned to stay seated until the queue had died down. When I saw what Linus had returned with – beans, salad, the ever-present couscous and a hot dish I assumed was chickpea casserole – I got up and went into the kitchen.

'Food's in there,' I said to Linda, who was standing with Vanja wrapped around her legs and Heidi in her arms chatting to Mia. 'Shall we swap?'

'Yes, that's good,' Linda said. 'I'm ravenous.'

'Can we go home now, daddy?' Vanja said.

'But we're eating,' I said. 'And afterwards there's cake. Shall I get you some food?'

'Don't want anything,' she said.

'I'll get you something anyway,' I said, and took Heidi by the arm. 'And you come with me.'

'Heidi's had a banana, by the way,' Linda said. 'But she'll probably want some food as well.'

'Come on, Theresa, let's go and get something for you,' Mia said.

I followed them in, lifted Heidi into my arms and stood in the queue. She rested her head against my shoulder, which she only did when she was tired. My shirt stuck to my chest. Every face I saw, every glance I met, every voice I heard, hung like a lead weight on me. When I was asked a question, or asked a question myself, it was as if the words had to be dynamited out. Heidi made it easier, having her there was a kind of protection, both because I had something to occupy myself with and because her presence diverted others' attention. They smiled at her, asked if she was tired and stroked her cheek. A large part of my relationship with Heidi was based on me carrying her. It was the basis of our relationship. She always wanted to be carried, never wanted to walk, stretched up her arms as soon as she saw me, and smiled with pleasure whenever she was allowed to hang from my arms. And I liked having her close, the little chubby creature with the greedy mouth.

I put some beans, a couple of spoonfuls of chickpea casserole and a dollop of couscous on a plate and carried it into the living room, where all the children were sitting around the low table in the middle, with a helpful parent behind.

'Don't want anything,' Vanja said as soon as I set the plate in front of her.

'That's OK,' I said. 'You don't have to eat if you don't want to. But do you think Heidi wants some?'

I speared some beans on the fork and raised it to her mouth. She pinched her lips together and twisted her head away.

'Come on now,' I said. 'I know you're both hungry.'

'Can we play with the train?' Vanja asked.

I looked at her. Normally she would have stared either at the train set or up at me, begging as often as not, but now she was staring straight ahead.

'Of course we can,' I said. I put Heidi down and went to the corner of the room where I had to press my knees against my body, almost into my chest, to make room between the tiny children's furniture and the toy boxes. I took the railway track apart and passed it piece by piece to Vanja, who tried to reassemble it. When the pieces didn't fit she forced them together with all her strength. I waited until she was on the point of throwing them down in fury before intervening. Heidi constantly wanted to tear the track up, and my eyes searched for something to give her as a diversion. A puzzle? A cuddly toy? A little plastic pony with large eyelashes and a long pink synthetic mane? She hurled all of them away.

'Daddy, can you help me?' Vanja said.

'Course I can,' I said. 'Look. Let's put a bridge here, so the train can go over and under it. That'll be good, won't it.'

Heidi grabbed one of the bridge pieces.

'Heidi!' Vanja said.

I took it from her, and she began to scream. I took her in my arms and stood up.

'I can't do it!' Vanja said.

'I'll be there in a sec. I'm just going to take Heidi to mummy,' I said, and went to the kitchen carrying Heidi on my hip like an experienced housewife. Linda was chatting with Gustav, the only one of the Lodjuret parents with a good old-fashioned profession, and with whom for some reason she got on well. He was jovial, his face shone, his short always neatly dressed body was robust and stocky, his neck strong, his chin broad, his face chubby but open and cheerful. He liked talking about books he had enjoyed, the latest of which were by Richard Ford.

'They're fantastic,' he would say. 'Have you read them? They're about an estate agent, an ordinary man, yes, and his life, so recognisable and normal. Ford captures the whole spirit of America! The American mood, the very pulse of the country!'

I liked Gustav, especially his decency, which was thanks to nothing more complicated than his having a basic, honest job, which incidentally none of my friends had, least of all myself. We were the same age, but I thought of him as ten years older from his appearance. He was adult in the way our parents had been when I was growing up.

'I think perhaps Heidi ought to go to sleep soon,' I said. 'She seems tired. And probably hungry too. Will you take her home?'

'Yes, just have to finish eating first, OK?'

'Of course.'

'Now I've held your book in my hand!' Gustav said. 'I was in the bookshop, and there it was. It looked interesting. Was it published by Norstedts?'

'Yes,' I said with a strained smile. 'It was.'

'You didn't buy it then?' Linda asked, not without a teasing tone to her voice.

'No, not this time,' he said, wiping his mouth with a serviette. 'It's about angels, isn't it?'

I nodded. Heidi had slipped from my grasp, and when I lifted her up again I noticed how heavy her nappy was.

'I'll change her before you go,' I said. 'You brought the changing bag, didn't you?'

'Yes, it's in the hall.'

'OK,' I said, and went out to fetch a nappy. In the living room Vanja and Achilles were running around, jumping from the sofa onto the floor, laughing, getting up and jumping off again. I felt a surge of warmth in my breast. Leaned over and picked up a nappy and a packet of wipes while Heidi clung to me like a little koala bear. There was no changing table in the bathroom, so I laid her on the floor tiles, took off her stockings, tore off the two adhesive tabs on the nappy and threw it in the bin under the sink while Heidi watched me with a serious expression.

'Just wee-wee!' she said. Then she turned her head to the side and stared at the wall, apparently unmoved by my putting on a clean nappy, the way she had done ever since she was a baby.

'There we are,' I said. 'That's you done.'

I grabbed her hands and pulled her up. Then folded her tights, which were slightly damp, and took them to the bag on the buggy, whereupon I dressed her in some jogging pants I found, and then the brown bubble-lined corduroy jacket she had been given for her first birthday by Yngve. Linda came in while I was putting on Heidi's shoes.

'I'll be coming soon too,' I said. We kissed, Linda took the bag in one hand, Heidi in the other, and they left.

Vanja ran at top speed down the hallway, with Achilles in tow, into what must have been the bedroom, from where her over-excited voice could be heard soon afterwards. The thought of going in and sitting at the kitchen table again was not exactly appealing, so I opened the bathroom door, locked it behind me and stood there motionless for a few minutes. Then washed my face in cold water, dried it carefully on a white towel and met my eyes in the mirror, so dark and in a face so rigid with frustration I almost started with alarm at the sight.

No one in the kitchen noticed that I was back. Except for a stern-looking little woman with short hair and ordinary angular features, who stared for a brief moment at me from behind her glasses. What did she want now?

Gustav and Linus were discussing pension arrangements, the taciturn man with the 50s shirt had his child, a wild boy with blond, almost white hair, on his lap, and was discussing FC Malmö with him, while Frida chatted with Mia about club evenings she and some friends were going to start. Meanwhile, Erik and Mathias compared TV screens, a discussion which Linus wanted to join, I could see that from his long glances and the shorter ones to Gustav so as not to appear impolite. The only person not deep in conversation was the woman with cropped hair, and even though I looked in every direction apart from hers she still leaned across the table and asked if I was satisfied with the nursery. I said I was. There was perhaps a bit too much to do there, I added, but it was definitely worth the investment of time; you got to know your children's playmates, and that could only be good, I opined.

She smiled at what I said without any great fervour. There was something sad about her, some unhappiness.

'What the hell?' Linus said suddenly, thrusting his chair back. 'What are they *doing* in there?'

He got up and went to the bathroom. The next moment he came out with Vanja and Achilles in front of him. Vanja had put on her broadest smile, Achilles looked rather more guilt-ridden. The sleeves of his small suit jacket were soaked. Vanja's bare arms glistened with moisture.

'They had their hands as far down the toilet as they could get them when I went in,' Linus said. I met Vanja's eyes and couldn't help smiling.

'We'll have to take this off now, young man,' Linus said, leading Achilles into the hall. 'And you make sure you wash your hands properly.'

'The same applies to you, Vanja,' I said, getting up. 'Into the bathroom with you.'

She stretched out her arms over the basin and looked up at me.

'I'm playing with Achilles!' she said.

'I can see that,' I said. 'But you don't have to stick your hands down the loo to do that, do you?'

'No,' she said, and laughed.

I wetted my hands under the tap, soaped them, and washed

her arms from the tips of her fingers to her shoulders. Then I
dried them before kissing her on the forehead and sending her
out again. The apologetic smile I wore when I sat down was
unnecessary, no one was interested in pursuing this little
episode, not even Linus, who as soon as he returned continued
the story about a man he had seen attacked by monkeys in
Thailand. His face didn't even break into a smile when the others
laughed, but he seemed to inhale their laughter, as if to give
the story renewed vigour, which it did, and only when the next
wave of laughter broke did he smile, not much, and not at his
own wit, it struck me; it was more like an expression of the
satisfaction he felt when his face could bask in the merriment
he had evoked. 'Yeah, yeah, yeah,' he said, jabbing his hand in
the air. The stern woman, who thus far had been looking out
of the window, pulled her chair up and leaned across the table
again.

'Isn't it tough to have two children so close in age?' she asked.

'Yes and no,' I answered. 'It is a bit wearing. But it's still better
with two than one. The single-child scenario seems a bit sad, if
you ask me . . . I've always thought I wanted to have three children. Then there are lots of permutations when they play. And
the children are in the majority vis-à-vis the parents . . .'

I smiled. She said nothing. All of a sudden I realised she had
an only child.

'But just one can be brilliant too,' I said.

She rested her head on her hand.

'But I wish Gustav had a brother or a sister,' she said. 'It's too
much with just us two.'

'Not at all,' I said. 'He'll have loads of pals in the nursery, and
that's great.'

'The problem is I haven't got a husband,' she said. 'And so it's
not possible.'

What the *fuck* had that got to do with me?

I sent her a look of sympathy and concentrated on preventing my eyes from wandering, which can easily happen in such situations.

'And I can't imagine the men I meet as fathers to my children,' she continued.

'Nonsense,' I said. 'These things sort themselves out.'

'I don't believe they do,' she said. 'But thank you anyway.'

From the corner of my eye I detected a movement. I turned and looked towards the door. Vanja was coming my way. She stopped right next to me.

'I want to go home,' she said. 'Can't we go now?'

'We have to stay for a just a little longer,' I said. 'Soon there'll be cake too. You want some of that, don't you?'

She didn't answer.

'Do you want to sit on my lap?' I asked.

She nodded, and I moved my wine glass and lifted her up.

'You sit with me for a bit, and then we'll go back in. I can stay with you. OK?'

'OK.'

She sat watching the others round the table. I wondered what she was thinking. How did it seem to her?

I observed her. Her blonde hair was already over her shoulders. A small nose, a little mouth, two tiny ears, both with pointed elfin tips. Her blue eyes, which always betrayed her mood, had a slight squint, hence the glasses. At first she had been proud of them. Now they were the first thing she took off when she was angry. Perhaps because she knew it was important for us that she should wear them?

With us her eyes were lively and cheerful, that is if they didn't lock and become unapproachable when she was having one of her grand bouts of fury. She was hugely dramatic and could rule the whole family with her temperament; she performed large-scale and complicated relational dramas with her toys, loved having stories read to her but watching films even more, and then preferably ones with characters and high drama which she puzzled over and discussed with us, bursting with questions but also the joy of retelling. For a period it was Astrid Lindgren's character Madicken she was mad about, and this caused her to jump off the chairs and lie on the floor with her eyes closed; we had to lift her and think at first that she was dead, then realise she had fainted and had concussion, before carrying her, with eyes closed and arms hanging down, to her bed, where she was to lie for three days, preferably while we hummed the sad theme from this scene in the film. Then she leaped to her feet, ran to the chair and started all over again. At the nursery's Christmas party she was the only one who bowed in response to the applause and who obviously enjoyed the attention. Often the idea of something meant more to her than the thing itself, such as with sweets; she could talk about them for an entire day and look forward to them, but when the sweets were in the bowl in front of her she barely tasted one before spitting it out. However, she didn't learn from the experience: the next Saturday her expectations of the fantastic sweets were as high again. She wanted so much to go skating, but when we were there, at the rink, with the small skates Linda's mother had bought for her on her feet and the little ice hockey helmet on her head, she shrieked with anger at the realisation that she couldn't keep her balance and probably wouldn't learn to do so any time soon. All the greater therefore was her joy at seeing that she could in fact ski, which happened once when we were on the small patch of snow in my mother's garden trying out equipment she had come by. But then too the idea of skiing and the joy at being able to do it were greater than actually skiing; she could function quite happily without that. She loved to travel with us, loved to see new places and talked about all the things that had happened for several months afterwards. But most of all she loved to play with other children, of course. It was a great experience for her when other children at the nursery came back home with her. The first time Benjamin was due to come she went around the evening before, inspecting her toys, worried stiff that they were not good enough for him. She had just turned three. But when he arrived they got on like a house on fire and all prior concerns went up in a whirl of excitement and euphoria. Benjamin told his parents that Vanja was the nicest girl in the nursery, and when I told her that – she was sitting in bed playing with her Barbies – she reacted with a display of emotion she had never manifested before.

'Do you know what Benjamin said?' I said from the doorway.

'No,' she said, looking up at me with sudden interest.

'He said you were the nicest girl in the nursery.'

I had never seen her filled with such light. She was glowing with happiness. I knew that neither Linda nor I would be able to say anything to make her react like that, and I understood with the immediate clarity of an insight that she was not ours. Her life was utterly her own.

'What did he say?' she answered, she wanted to hear it again.

'He said you were the nicest in the nursery.'

Her smile was shy but happy, and that made me glad too, yet a shadow hung over my happiness, for was it not alarmingly early for others' thoughts and opinions to mean so much to her? Wasn't it best for everything to come from her, for it to be rooted in herself? Another time she surprised me like this was when I was in the nursery. I had gone to pick her up and she ran towards me in the corridor and asked if Stella could go with her to the stables afterwards. I said that things didn't work like that, it had to be planned in advance, we had to speak to her parents

first, and Vanja stood watching me say this, obviously disappointed, but when she went to pass on the news to Stella, she
didn't use my reasons. I heard her as I was rummaging in the
hall for her rain gear.

'It'll be a bit boring for you at the stables,' she said. 'Just
watching isn't cool.'

This way of thinking, putting others' reactions before your
own, I recognised from myself, and as we walked towards Folkets
Park in the rain I wondered about how she had picked that up.
Was it just there, around her, invisible but present, like the air
she breathed? Or was it genetic?

I never expressed any of these thoughts I had about the children, except to Linda of course, because these complex questions
belonged only where they were, in me and between us. In reality,
in the world Vanja inhabited everything was simple and found
simple expression, and the complexity arose only in the sum
of all the parts, of which naturally she knew nothing. And the
fact that we talked a lot about them did not help at all in our
daily lives, where everything was a mess and constantly on the
verge of chaos. In the first of the Swedish 'progress conversations' we had with the nursery staff there was a lot of talk about
her not making contact with the teachers, not wanting to sit
on their laps or be patted, as well as her shyness. We should
work on toughening her up, teaching her to play a more dominant role in games, taking the initiative and talking more, they
said. Linda replied that she was tough enough at home, took
the lead in all the games, always showed initiative and could
talk the hind leg off a donkey. They told us the little she said
in the nursery was unclear, her Swedish wasn't correct, her
vocabulary was not that large, so they were wondering if we
had considered speech therapy. At this juncture in the conversation we were handed a brochure from one of the town's speech

therapists. They are crazy in this country, I thought. A speech therapist? Did everything have to be institutionalised? She's only three!

'No, speech therapy's out of the question,' I said. Until that point Linda had been the one to do all the talking. 'It will sort itself out. I only *started* talking when I was three. Before that I said nothing, apart from single words which were incomprehensible to anyone except my brother.'

They smiled.

'And when I started speaking it came in long, fluent sentences. It all depends on the individual. We are not sending her to a speech therapist.'

'Well, that's up to you,' said Olaf, the head of the nursery. 'But you're welcome to hang on to the brochures and give it some thought.'

'OK then,' I said.

I collected her hair in one hand and stroked her neck and the top of her back with one finger. Usually she loved this, especially before going to sleep, until she settled for the night, but this time she squirmed away.

On the other side of the table the stern woman had struck up a conversation with Mia, who gave her her undivided attention while Frida and Erik had begun to clear away the plates and cutlery. The white layer cake, which was the next item on the agenda, stood proudly on the worktop, decorated with raspberries and five small candles, beside a column of square cartons containing Bravo, a sugar-free apple drink.

Gustav, who until now had been sitting beside me with his back half-turned, swivelled round to face us.

'Hi, Vanja,' he said. 'Are you having fun?'

As he didn't get a response, nor any eye contact, he looked at me.

'You'll have to come and play with Jocke one day,' he said, winking at me. 'Fancy doing that?'

'Yes,' Vanja said, regarding him with eyes that suddenly dilated. Jocke was the biggest boy in the nursery. Going to his house was more than she dared hope for.

'We'll fix something up,' Gustav said. Raised his glass, took a swig of red wine and wiped his mouth with the back of his hand.

'Are you writing anything new then?' he asked.

I shrugged.

'Yes, I'm keeping busy,' I said.

'Do you work at home?'

'Yes.'

'How do you go about it? Do you sit waiting for inspiration?'

'No, that's no good. I have to work every day like you.'

'Interesting. Interesting. There are not many distractions at home then?'

'I manage fine.'

'Ah, you do, do you? Well . . .'

'Let's all go into the living room then,' Frida said. 'And we can sing for Stella.'

She took a lighter from her pocket and lit the five candles.

'What a wonderful cake,' Mia said.

'Yes, isn't it?' Frida said. 'And it's healthy too. There's hardly any sugar in the cream.'

She lifted it up.

'Will you go in and switch off the light, Erik?' she said as people began to move from their seats and leave the room. I followed holding Vanja's hand, and just managed to find a position against the wall furthest away when Frida entered the darkened hall with the illuminated cake in her hands. As she came into view from the table she began to sing *Ja må hon leva,* whereupon the other adults immediately joined in, and the birthday song rang around the small room as she placed the cake on the table in front of Stella, who was watching with gleaming eyes.

'Shall I blow now?' she asked.

Frida nodded as she sang.

Everyone clapped afterwards, me too. Then the lights came back on, and for a few minutes slices of the cake were distributed among the children. Vanja didn't want to sit at the table, but on the floor by the wall, where we settled down, her with a plate of cake on her lap. It was only then I noticed she wasn't wearing her shoes.

'Where are your golden shoes?' I asked.

'They're stupid,' she said.

'No, they're not, they're lovely,' I said. 'They're a proper princess's shoes!'

'They're stupid,' she repeated.

'But where are they?'

She didn't answer.

'Vanja,' I said.

She looked up at me. Her mouth was white with cream.

'Over there,' she said, motioning towards the other room. I got up and went in, looked around, no shoes. I went back.

'Where did you put them? I can't see them anywhere.'

'By the flower,' she said.

Flower? I went back, peered between the flower pots on the windowsill, no, not there.

Could she have meant the yucca?

Yes, indeed. They were in the pot. I grabbed them, brushed the earth off over the pot, took them to the bathroom and wiped off the rest, then put them under the chair where her jacket was.

The interruption for cake, which had occupied all the children's attention, might give her a chance for a new beginning, I thought, perhaps it would be easier to be there after that.

'I'm going to have a piece of cake too,' I said to her. 'I'll be in the kitchen. Just come and find me if there is anything you want, OK?'

'OK, daddy.'

It was only half past six according to the clock above the kitchen door. No one had left yet, so we would have to wait for a while. I cut myself a thin sliver of the cake on the worktop, put it on a plate and sat at the other side of the table as my seat was occupied.

'There's coffee as well if you'd like some,' Erik said, looking at me with a kind of pregnant smile, as if there lay more in the question and what he said than met the eye. For all I knew, it was a technique he had learned so as to appear important, more or less like the tricks the average writer resorts to when trying to lend his stories the semblance of immense profundity.

Or had he really seen something?

'Yes, please,' I said and got up, took a cup from the pile and filled it with coffee from the grey Stelton pot nearby. By the time I got back to my seat he was on his way out of the room. Frida was talking about a coffee machine she had bought, it was expensive and she had been torn, but she had no regrets, it was definitely worth the money, the coffee was fantastic, and it was important to spoil yourself with such things, perhaps more important than was generally thought. Linus talked about a Smith and Jones sketch he had seen once, two guys sitting at a table with a cafetière in front of them, one presses the plunger, but everything is pushed down, not just the coffee grains, until the jug is empty. No one laughed, and Linus hunched his shoulders and raised his palms.

'A simple coffee anecdote,' he said. 'Anyone got a better one?'

Vanja stood in the doorway. Her gaze took in the table, and when she had found me, she came over.

'Do you want to go home?' I said.

She nodded.

'Right, do you know what?' I said. 'I do too. I'll just eat this cake first. And drink my coffee. Do you want to sit on my lap in the meantime?'

She nodded again. I lifted her up.

'Nice you could come, Vanja,' Frida said to her with a smile from the other side of the table. 'Soon it'll be fishing time. You want to join in, don't you?'

Vanja nodded and Frida turned back to Linus. There was a TV series on Home Box Office she had seen, but he had missed it, and she couldn't praise it enough.

'Do you want to?' I asked. 'Shall we wait for the fishing game before going?'

Vanja shook her head.

In the game each child was given a little fishing rod which they would cast over a sheet behind which an adult sat waiting to attach a bag containing a prize, some sweets or small toy or the like. In this family they would probably fill it with peas or artichokes, I thought, manoeuvring my fork down past Vanja to my plate, where I cut off a piece with the edge – brown crust under the white cream, yellow inside, with red streaks of jam – twisted my wrist so that the piece of cake remained on the fork, raised it past Vanja, and inserted it in my mouth. The base was too dry, and there was far too little sugar in the cream, but with a mouthful of coffee it wasn't too bad.

'Would you like a bit?' I asked. Vanja nodded. I forked a piece into her open mouth. She looked up and smiled.

'I can go into the living room with you,' I said. 'Then we can see what the others are doing. And maybe join in the fishing game as well?'

'You said we were going home,' she said.

'I did. Let's be off.'

I placed the fork on the plate, finished off the coffee, put her on the floor and stood up. Looked around. No eyes met mine.

'We'll be on our way now,' I said.

Right then Erik came in with a small bamboo pole in one hand and a plastic Hemköp bag in the other.

'We're going to do the fishing now,' he said.

Some got up to join in, others remained where they were. No one had noticed that I had said goodbye. And since people's attention around the table had been drawn in different directions now, I saw no need to say it again. Instead I laid my hand on Vanja's shoulder and led her out. In the living room Erik shouted 'Fishing!' and all the children hurried past us to the end of the hall where the cover, a white sheet, hung from wall to wall. Erik, who followed them like a shepherd, told them to sit down. Standing in the hall with Vanja and putting on her jacket, we could see right into the room.

I pulled up the zip on her red bubble jacket, which was already a little tight, set the red Polarn O. Pyret woolly hat on her head and buttoned up the chinstrap, placed her boots in front of her so that she could stick her feet in them herself, and zipped them from the back when she was ready.

'There we are,' I said. 'Now all we have to do is say thank you and we can go. Come on.'

She raised her arms towards me.

'Can't you walk?' I said.

She shook her head, keeping her arms outstretched.

'OK,' I said. 'But first I'll have to put on my things.'

In the hall Benjamin was the first to 'fish'. He cast his line, and someone, I suppose Erik, caught it on the other side.

'I've got a bite!' Benjamin shouted.

The parents standing along the wall smiled, the children on the floor shouted and laughed. The next second Benjamin yanked at his rod, and a red and white Hemköp goodie bag came flying over the sheet, attached by a clothes peg. He removed it and took a few steps away to open the bag in peace and quiet while the next child, Theresa, grabbed the fishing rod, helped by her mother. I wound my scarf round my neck and buttoned up the reefer jacket I had bought on sale last spring at Paul Smith in Stockholm, put on the hat I had bought at the same place, bent down over the pile of shoes by the wall, found mine, a pair of black Wrangler shoes with yellow laces I had bought in Copenhagen when I was at the book fair, and which I had never liked, not even when I bought them, and which furthermore were now tainted by the thought of the catastrophe that had befallen me there, as I had been incapable of answering sensibly a single question the enthusiastic and insightful interviewer had asked me on the stage. The reason I hadn't thrown them out long ago rested exclusively on the fact that we were hard up. And the laces were so yellow!

I tied them and stood up.

'I'm ready,' I said. Vanja stretched out her arms again. I lifted her, walked along the hall and stuck my head into the kitchen where four or five parents were chatting.

'We're off now,' I said. 'All the best, and thanks for a nice evening.'

'Thank *you*,' Linus said. Gustav half-raised his hand to his forehead.

Then we went into the hall. I patted Frida's shoulder to catch her attention. She was standing by the wall, smiling, fully absorbed in the scene on the floor.

'We're off now,' I said. 'Thank you for inviting us. It was a lovely party. Very nice company.'

'But doesn't Vanja want to catch a fish?' she said.

I made a very expressive kind of grimace, intended to mean something on the lines of 'You know how illogical children can be.'

'Right, right,' she said. 'Well, thanks for coming. Take care, Vanja!'

Mia, who was standing alongside, with Theresa in front of her, said, 'Just a moment.'

She leaned over the sheet and asked Erik, who was on his haunches, if he could give her a goodie bag. He certainly could, and she passed it to Vanja.

'Here, Vanja. You can take this home with you. And perhaps share it with Heidi if you want.'

'I don't want,' Vanja said, holding the bag to her chest.

'Thank you very much.' I said. 'Bye, everyone!'

Stella turned and looked at us.

'Are you going, Vanja? Why?'

'Bye, Stella,' I said. 'Thanks for inviting us to your party.'

I turned and went. Down the dark stairs, through the hall and onto the pavement. Voices, shouting, footsteps and the noise of engines rose and fell continuously in the street. Vanja wrapped her arms around me and leaned her head against my shoulder. Which she never did usually. This was Heidi's way.

A taxi swept past with its roof light on. A couple with a buggy passed us; she had a scarf round her head and was young, twenty maybe. A rough complexion I saw as they walked past, her face was thick with powder. He was older, my age, and kept looking around nervously. The buggy was the ridiculous type with a thin stalk-like rod going from the wheels which the basket-seat with the child rested on. Coming towards us from the other side of the road was a gang of youngsters aged fifteen or sixteen. Black combed-back hair, black leather jackets, black trousers, and at least two of them wore Puma trainers with the logo on the toe, which I had always thought looked idiotic. Gold chains around their necks, slightly unsteady, clumsy arm movements.

The shoes.

Shit, they were still up in the flat.

I stopped.

Should I just leave them there?

No, that was too pathetic. We were right outside the door.

'We have to go back up,' I said. 'We've forgotten your golden shoes.'

She stiffened.

'I don't want them,' she said.

'I know,' I said. 'But we can't leave them there. We'll have to take them home with us, and they don't have to be yours any more.'

I dashed up the stairs again, put Vanja down, opened the door, stepped inside and grabbed the shoes without looking any further into the flat, but could not avoid doing so as I straightened up and met Benjamin's eyes. He was sitting on the floor in his white shirt with a car in one hand.

'Hi!' he said, and waved with the other.

I smiled.

'Hi, Benjamin,' I said, closed the door behind me, lifted Vanja and went back downstairs. It was cold and clear outside, but all the light in the town, from street lamps, shop windows and car lights, seeped upwards and lay like a shimmering dome above the rooftops, through which no starry lustre could penetrate. Of all the heavenly bodies only the moon, hanging, almost full, above the Hilton hotel, was visible.

Vanja clung to me as I hurried down the street, our breath like white smoke around our heads.

'Maybe Heidi wants my shoes?' she said.

'When she's as big as you she can have them,' I said.

'Heidi loves shoes,' she said.

'Yes, she does,' I said.

We continued for a while in silence. By Subway, the big sandwich bar beside the supermarket, I saw the white-haired crazy woman staring through the window. Aggressive and unpredictable, she walked back and forth around our district, more often than not talking to herself, always with her white hair tied in a tight knot, and in the same beige coat, summer and winter alike.

'Will I have a party when it's my birthday, daddy?' Vanja asked.

'If you want,' I said.

'I do,' she said. 'I want Heidi and you and mummy to come.'

'That sounds like a nice little party,' I said, shifting her from my right to my left arm.

'Do you know what I want?'

'No.'

'A goldfish,' she said. 'Can I have one?'

'We-ell . . .' I said. 'To have a goldfish you have to be able to take care of it properly. Feed it, clean the water and so on. And you have to be a bit bigger than four, I think.'

'But I can feed it! And Jiro's got one. He's smaller than me.'

'That's true,' I said. 'We'll have to see. Birthday presents are supposed to be secret, you know, that's the whole point about them.'

'Secret? Like a secret?'

I nodded.

Oh bugger! Oh bugger! said the crazy woman, who was now only a few metres ahead. Warned by the movement, she turned and looked at me. Oh, her eyes were evil.

'What are those shoes you're carrying?' she said behind us. 'Hey, *pappa*! What are those shoes you're carrying? Let me have a word with you right now!'

And then louder: 'Bugger! Oh BUGGer!'

'What did the old lady say?' Vanja asked.

'Nothing,' I answered, squeezing her tighter to me. 'You're the best thing I've got, Vanja, do you know that? The very, very best.'

'Better than Heidi?' she asked.

I smiled.

'You're both the best, you and Heidi. *Exactly* the same.'

'Heidi's better,' she said. Her tone of voice was completely neutral, as if she were stating an incontrovertible fact.

'What nonsense,' I said. 'You little monkey.'

She smiled. I looked past her and into the large almost deserted supermarket, where the goods lay gleaming on each side of the narrow avenues of shelves and counters. Two women sat at their cash desks staring into the middle distance waiting for customers. At the traffic lights across from us a car was revving, and when I turned my head I saw the sound was coming from one of those enormous jeep-like vehicles that had begun to fill our streets in recent years. The tenderness I felt for Vanja was so great it was almost tearing me to pieces. To counteract it, I broke into a jog. Past Ankara, the Turkish restaurant with belly dancing and karaoke on the menu, and its door, where well dressed men from the east often stood in the evenings, smelling of aftershave and cigar smoke, but which was empty now, on past Burger King, where an incredibly fat girl, wearing a hat and fingerless gloves, sat alone on the bench outside devouring a hamburger, then over the crossing, past the Systembolaget and the Handelsbanken, where I stopped as the lights were on red, even though there were no cars in any of the lanes. All this while holding Vanja tight to my chest.

'Can you see the moon?' I asked, pointing to the sky as we stood waiting for the lights to change.

'Mm,' she said. And then, after a short pause, 'Have any people been there?'

She knew very well there had, but she also knew that I liked talking about such things.

'Yes, there have,' I said. 'Just after I was born three men flew there. It's a long way and it took several days. And then they flew around it.'

'They didn't fly; they had a spaceship,' she said.

'You're right,' I said. 'They went in a rocket.'

The lights changed to green, and we crossed to the other side, where the square began and we had our flat. A slim man in a leather jacket with hair down his back was standing by a cash-point. He put out one hand to receive his card; with the other he stroked the hair from his face. It was a feminine gesture, and amusing, as everything else about him, the entire heavy-metal look, was designed to be dark and hard and masculine.

The tiny pile of bank receipts on the ground by his feet blew up in a gust of wind.

I shoved my hand in my pocket and took out a bunch of keys.

'What's that?' Vanja asked, pointing to the two slush machines outside the little Thai takeaway next to our front entrance.

'Slush ice,' I said. 'But you knew that.'

'I want some!' she said.

I looked at her.

'No, you're not having that. But *are* you hungry?'

'Yes.'

'We can buy some chicken satay if you like. Would you like that?'

'Yes.'

'OK,' I said, put her down on the ground and opened the

door to the restaurant, which was not much more than a hole in the wall and filled our veranda, seven floors up, with the smell of noodles and fried chicken every day. They sold two dishes in a box for forty-five kroner, so it was not exactly the first time I was standing at the glass counter and ordering from the young skinny expressionless hard-working Asian girl. Her mouth was always open, her gums visible above her teeth, her eyes always neutral as if they couldn't make any distinctions. In the kitchen were two equally young men – I had caught only brief glimpses of them – and between them flitted a man in his fifties, his face expressionless as well, though a touch more friendly, at least whenever we bumped into each other in the long labyrinthine corridors beneath the house: he was fetching something from or taking something to a storeroom, I was washing clothes, throwing out rubbish or pushing my bike in or out.

'Can you carry it?' I asked Vanja and passed her the hot box which appeared on the counter twenty seconds after the order had been placed. Vanja nodded, I paid, and then we went into the next front hall entrance, where Vanja put down the box on the floor so as to press the button for the lift.

She counted all the floors aloud on the way up. When we were standing outside our flat she handed me the box, opened the door and called for her mother even before she was inside.

'Shoes first,' I said, holding her back. At that moment Linda came from the living room. The TV was on, I could hear.

A faint odour of putrescence and something worse rose from the large bag of rubbish and the two small nappy bags in the corner by the folded double buggy. Heidi's shoes and jacket were on the floor next to it.

Why the HELL hadn't she put them in the wardrobe?

The hall was awash with clothes, toys, old advertising leaflets, buggies, bags, bottles of water. Hadn't she been here all after-noon?

But she had plenty of time to lie on the sofa and watch TV.

'I got a goodie bag even though I didn't do any fishing!' Vanja said.

So that was what she considered important, I mused, bending forward to remove her shoes. Her body was twitching with impatience.

'And I played with Achilles!'

'Nice,' Linda said, crouching down in front of her.

'Let me see what's in the goodie bag, then,' she said.

Vanja showed her.

As I thought. Ecological goodies. Must have come from the shop that had just opened in the mall opposite. A selection of chocolate-covered nuts in various colours. Candied sugar. Some raisin-like sweets.

'Can I eat them now?'

'Chicken first,' I said. 'In the kitchen.'

I hung her jacket on a hook, put her shoes in the wardrobe and went into the kitchen, where I served the chicken, spring rolls and noodles on a plate. Took out a knife and fork, filled a glass with water, put everything in front of her on the table, which was still littered with felt-tips, watercolour paint boxes, glasses of water, brushes and sheets of paper.

'Everything go all right there?' Linda asked, and sat down beside her.

I nodded. Leaned back against the worktop, with arms folded.

'Did Heidi go to sleep easily?' I asked.

'No, she's got a temperature. That must be why she was so crotchety.'

'Again?' I said.

'Mm, but not so high.'

I sighed. Turned and looked at the piles of washing-up on the side and in the sink.

'Looks a hell of a mess here,' I said.

'I want to watch a film,' Vanja said.

'Not now,' I said. 'It was bedtime ages ago.'

'I want to!'

'What were you watching on TV?' I asked, meeting Linda's eyes.

'What do you mean?'

'Nothing special. You were watching TV when we came. I was wondering what you were watching.'

Now it was her turn to sigh.

'I don't want to go to bed!' Vanja said, lifting the chicken skewer as if about to throw it. I grabbed her arm.

'Put it down,' I said.

'You can watch for ten minutes and have a bowl of sweets,' Linda said.

'I just said she couldn't,' I said.

'Ten minutes, that's all,' she said and got up. 'Then I'll put her to bed.'

'Oh yes?' I said. 'So I'm supposed to do the washing-up, am I?'

'What are you talking about? Do what you like. I've had Heidi here the whole time, if you really want to know. She was ill and grumbly and –'

'I'll go out for a smoke.'

'– quite impossible.'

I put on my jacket and shoes and went onto the east-facing balcony where I usually smoked, because it had a roof and because it was rare you saw anyone from there. The balcony on the other side, which ran alongside the whole flat and was more than twenty metres long, didn't have a roof, but it had a view of the square below, where there were always people, and the hotel and the mall on the other side of the street as well as the house fronts all the way to Magistrat Park. What I wanted, however, was peace and quiet, I didn't want to see people, so I closed the door of the smaller balcony behind me and sat on the chair in the corner, lit a cigarette, put my feet on the railing and stared across the backyards and roof ridges, the harsh shapes against the vast canopy of the sky. The view changed constantly. One moment immense accumulations of cloud resembling mountains, with precipices and slopes, valleys and caves, hovered mysteriously in the middle of the blue sky, the next moment a wet weather front might drift in from the far distance, visible as a huge greyish-black duvet on the horizon, and if this occurred in the summer a few hours later the most spectacular flashes of lightning could rip through the darkness at intervals of only a few seconds, with thunder rolling in across the rooftops. But I liked the most ordinary of the sky's manifestations, even the very smooth grey rain-filled ones, against whose heavy background the colours in the backyards beneath me stood out clearly, almost shone. The verdigris roofs! The orangey red of the bricks! And the yellow metal of the cranes, how bright it was against all the greyish white! Or one of the normal summer days when the sky was clear and blue and the sun was burning down, and the few clouds drifting by were light, almost contourless, then the glittering, gleaming expanse of buildings stretched into the distance. And when evening fell there was an initial flare of red on the horizon, as though the land below was aflame, then a light gentle darkness, under whose kind hand the town settled down for the night, as though happily fatigued after a whole day in the sun. Stars lit the sky, satellites hovered, planes twinkled, flying into and out of Kastrup and Sturup.

If it was people I wanted to see I had to lean forward and look down to the yard on the other side, where faceless figures occasionally appeared in the windows, in the eternal merry-go-round between rooms and doors: a fridge door is opened, a man wearing only boxers takes out something, closes the door and sits at a kitchen table, somewhere else a front door is slammed, and a woman in a coat with a bag over her shoulder hurries down the stairs, round and round it goes, and over there what must be an elderly man, judging by the silhouette and the paucity of movement, is ironing; when he finishes he switches off the light and the room dies. So where should you look? Above, where a man sometimes jumps up and down on the floor waving his arms in front of something you can't see but is no doubt a little baby? Or at the woman in her fifties who so often stands by the window looking out?

No, those lives were spared my gaze. It searched upwards and outwards, and not to scrutinise what it found there, nor to be struck by the beauty, but to rest. To be utterly alone.

I grabbed the half-full two-litre bottle of Coke Light that stood on the floor beside the chair and filled one of the glasses on the table. The screw top was off and the Coke was flat, so the taste of the somewhat bitter sweetener, which was generally lost in the effervescence of the carbonic acid, was all too evident. But it didn't matter, I had never been bothered much by how things tasted.

I returned the glass to the table and stubbed out my cigarette. There was nothing left of my feelings for those I had just spent several hours with. The whole crowd of them could have burned in hell for all I cared. This was a rule in my life. When I was with other people I was bound to them, the nearness I felt was immense, the empathy great. Indeed, so great that their well-being was always more important than my own. I subordinated myself, almost to the verge of self-effacement; some uncontrollable internal mechanism caused me to put their thoughts and

opinions before my own. But the moment I was alone others
meant nothing to me. It wasn't that I disliked them, or nurtured
feelings of loathing for them; on the contrary, I liked most of
them, and the ones I didn't actually like I could always see some
worth in, some attribute I could identify with, or at least find
interesting, something which could occupy my mind for the
moment. But liking them was not the same as caring about
them. It was the social situation that bound me, the people
within it did not. Between these two perspectives there was no
halfway house. There was just the small self-effacing one and
the large distance-creating one. And in between them was where
my daily life lay. Perhaps that was why I had such a hard time
living it. Everyday life, with its duties and routines, was something I endured, not a thing I enjoyed, nor something that was
meaningful or made me happy. This had nothing to do with a
lack of desire to wash floors or change nappies but rather with
something more fundamental: the life around me was not meaningful. I always longed to be away from it, and always had done.
So the life I led was not my own. I tried to make it mine, this
was my struggle, because of course I wanted it, but I failed, the
longing for something else undermined all my efforts.

What was the problem?

Was it the shrill sickly tone I heard everywhere, which I
couldn't stand, the one that arose from all the pseudo people
and pseudo places, pseudo events and pseudo conflicts our lives
passed through, that which we saw but did not participate in,
and the distance that modern life in this way had opened up to
our own, actually inalienable, here and now? If so, if it was more
reality, more involvement I longed for, surely I should be
embracing that which I was surrounded by? And not, as was the
case, longing to get away from it? Or perhaps it was the prefab-
ricated nature of the days in this world I was reacting to, the

rails of routine we followed, which made everything so predict-
able that we had to invest in entertainment to feel any hint of
intensity? Every time I went out of the door I knew what was
going to happen, what I was going to do. This was how it was
on the micro level, I go to the supermarket and do the shopping,
I go and sit down at a café with a newspaper, I fetch my children
from the nursery, and this is how it was on the macro level,
from the initial entry into society, the nursery, to the final exit,
the old folks' home. Or was the revulsion I felt based on the
sameness that was spreading through the world and making
everything smaller? If you travelled through Norway now you
saw the same everywhere. The same roads, the same houses, the
same petrol stations, the same shops. As late as in the 60s you
could see how local culture changed as you drove through
Gudbrandsdalen, for example, the strange black timber buildings, so pure and sombre, which were now encapsulated as small
museums in a culture which was no different from the one you
had left or the one you were going to. And Europe, which was
merging more and more into one large, homogeneous country.
The same, the same, everything was the same. Or was it perhaps
that the light which illuminated the world and made everything
comprehensible also drained it of meaning? Was it perhaps the
forests that had vanished, the animal species that had become
extinct, the ways of life that would never return?

Yes, all of this I thought about, all of this filled me with sorrow
and a sense of helplessness, and if there was a world I turned
to in my mind, it was that of the sixteenth and seventeenth
centuries, with its enormous forests, its sailing ships and horse-
drawn carts, its windmills and castles, its monasteries and small
towns, its painters and thinkers, explorers and inventors, priests
and alchemists. What would it have been like to live in a world
where everything was made from the power of your hands, the

wind or the water? What would it have been like to live in a
world where the American Indians still lived their lives in peace?
Where that life was an actual possibility? Where Africa was
unconquered? Where darkness came with the sunset and light
with the sunrise? Where there were too few humans and their
tools were too rudimentary to have any effect on animal stocks,
let alone wipe them out? Where you could not travel from one
place to another without exerting yourself, and a comfortable
life was something only the rich could afford, where the sea
was full of whales, the forests full of bears and wolves, and there
were still countries that were so alien no adventure story could
do them justice, such as China, to which a voyage not only took
several months and was the prerogative of only a tiny minority
of sailors and traders, but was also fraught with danger.
Admittedly, that world was rough and wretched, filthy and
ravaged with sickness, drunken and ignorant, full of pain, low
life expectancy and rampant superstition, but it produced the
greatest writer, Shakespeare, the greatest painter, Rembrandt,
the greatest scientist, Newton, all still unsurpassed in their fields,
and how can it be that this period achieved this wealth? Was it
because death was closer and life was starker as a result?

Who knows?

Be that as it may, we can't go back in time, everything we
undertake is irrevocable, and if we look back what we see is not
life but death. And whoever believes that the conditions and
character of the times are responsible for our maladjustment is
either suffering from delusions of grandeur or is simply stupid,
and lacks self-knowledge on both accounts. I loathed so much
about the age I lived in, but it was not that that was the cause
of the loss of meaning, because it was not something that had
been constant . . . The spring I moved to Stockholm and met
Linda, for example, the world had suddenly opened, the intensity

in it increased at breakneck speed. I was head over heels in love and everything was possible, my happiness was at bursting point all the time and embraced everything. If someone had spoken to me then about a lack of meaning I would have laughed out loud, for I was free and the world lay at my feet, open, packed with meaning, from the gleaming futuristic trains that streaked across Slussen beneath my flat, to the sun colouring the nineteenth-century-style church spires in Ridderholmen red, sinisterly beautiful sunsets I witnessed every evening for all those months, from the aroma of freshly picked basil and the taste of ripe tomatoes to the sound of clacking heels on the cobbled slope down to the Hilton hotel late one night when we sat on a bench holding hands and knowing that it would be us two now and for ever. This state lasted for six months, for six months I was truly happy, truly at home in this world and in myself before slowly it began to lose its lustre, and once more the world moved out of my reach. One year later it happened again, if in quite a different way. That was when Vanja was born. Then it was not the world which opened – we had shut it out, in a kind of total concentration on the miracle taking place in our midst – no, something opened in me. While falling in love had been wild and abandoned, brimming with life and exuberance, this was cautious and muted, filled with endless attention to what was happening. Four weeks, maybe five, it lasted. Whenever I had to do some shopping in town I *ran* down the streets, grabbed whatever we needed, shook with impatience at the counter, and *ran* back with the bags hanging from my hands. I didn't want to miss a minute! The days and nights merged into one, everything was tenderness, everything was gentleness, and if she opened her eyes we rushed towards her. Oh, there you are! But that passed too, we got used to that too, and I began to work, sat in my new office in Dalagatan writing every day while Linda was at home with Vanja and came to see me for lunch, often worried about something but also happy, she was closer to the child and what was happening than me, for I was writing, what had started out as a long essay slowly but surely was growing into a novel, it soon reached a point where it was everything, and writing was all I did, I moved into the office, wrote day and night, sleeping an hour here and there. I was filled with an absolutely fantastic feeling, a kind of light burned within me, not hot and consuming but cold and clear and shining. At night I took a cup of coffee with me and sat down on the bench outside the hospital to smoke, the streets around me were quiet, and I could hardly sit still, so great was my happiness. Everything was possible, everything made sense. At two places in the novel I soared higher than I had thought possible, and those two places alone, which I could not believe I had written, and no one else has noticed or said anything about, made the preceding five years of failed writing worth all the effort. They are two of the best moments in my life. By which I mean my whole life. The happiness that filled me and the feeling of invincibility they gave me I have searched for ever since, in vain.

A few weeks after the novel was finished life began as a house husband, and the plan was it would last until next spring while Linda did the last year of her training at the Dramatiska Institut. The novel writing had taken its toll on our relationship. I slept in the office for six weeks, barely seeing Linda and our five-month-old daughter, and when at last it was over she was relieved and happy, and I owed it to her to be there, not just in the same room, physically, but also with all my attention and participation. I couldn't do it. For several months I felt a sorrow at not being where I had been, in the cold clear environment, and my yearning to return was stronger than my pleasure at the life we lived. The fact that the novel was doing well didn't matter. After every good review I put a cross in the book and waited for the next, after every conversation with the agent at the publisher's, when a foreign company had shown some interest or made an offer, I put a cross in my book and waited for the next, and I wasn't very interested when it was eventually nominated for the Nordic Council Literature Prize, for if there was one thing I had learned over the last six months it was that all writing was about *writing*. Therein lay all its value. Yet I wanted to have more of what came in its wake because public attention is a drug, the need it satisfies is artificial, but once you have had a taste of it you want more. So there I was, pushing the buggy on my endless walks on the island of Djurgården in Stockholm waiting for the telephone to ring and a journalist to ask me about something, an event organiser to invite me somewhere, a magazine to ask for an article, a publisher to make an offer, until at last I took the consequences of the disagreeable taste it left in my mouth and began to say no to everything at the same time as the interest ebbed away and I was back to the everyday grind. But no matter how hard I tried, I couldn't get into it, there was always something else that was more important. Vanja sat there in the buggy looking around while I trudged through the town, first here, then there, or sat in the sandpit digging with a spade in the play area in Humlegården, where the tall lean Stockholm mothers who surrounded us were constantly on their phones, looking as if they were part of some bloody fashion show, or she was in her high chair in the kitchen at home swallowing the food I fed her. All of this bored me out of my mind. I felt stupid walking round indoors chatting to her, because she didn't say anything; there was just my inane voice and her silence, happy babbling or displeased tears, then it was on with her clothes and tramping into town again, to the Moderna Museet in Skeppsholmen, for example, where at least I could see some good art while keeping an eye on her, or to one of the big book-shops in the centre, or to Djurgården or Brunnsviken Lake, which was the closest the town came to nature, unless I took the road out to see Geir, who had his office in the university at that time. Little by little, I mastered everything with regard to small children, there wasn't a single thing I couldn't do with her, we were everywhere, but no matter how well it went, and irrespective of the great tenderness I felt for her, my boredom and apathy were greater. A lot of effort was spent getting her to sleep so that I could read and to making the days pass so that I could cross them off in the calendar. I got to know the most out-of-the-way cafés in town, and there was hardly a park bench I had not sat on at some time or other, with a book in one hand and the buggy in the other. I took Dostoevsky with me, first *Demons*, then *The Brothers Karamazov*. In them I found the light again. But it wasn't the lofty, clear and pure light, as with Hölderlin; with Dostoevsky there were no heights, no mountains, there was no divine perspective, everything was in the human domain, wreathed in this characteristically Dostoevskian wretched, dirty, sick, almost contaminated mood that was never too far from hysteria. That was where the light was. That was where the divine stirred. But was this the place to go? Was it necessary to go down on bended knee? As usual I didn't think as I read, just engrossed myself in it, and after a few hundred pages, which took several days to read, something suddenly happened: all the details that had been painstakingly built up slowly began to interact, and the intensity was so great that I was carried along, totally enthralled, until Vanja opened her eyes from the depths of the buggy, almost suspicious, it seemed: where have you taken me now?

There was no option but to close the book, lift her up, get out the spoon, the jar of food and the bib if we were indoors, set a

course for the nearest café if we were outside, fetch a high chair,
put her in it and go over to the counter and ask the staff to
warm the food, which they did grudgingly because Stockholm
was inundated with babies at that time, there was a baby boom,
and since there were so many women in their thirties among
the mothers who had worked and led their own lives until then,
glamorous magazines for mothers began to appear, with children
as a sort of accessory, and one celebrity after another allowed
herself to be photographed with and interviewed about her
family. What had previously taken place in private was now
pumped into the public arena. Everywhere you could read about
labour pains, Caesareans and breastfeeding, baby clothes, buggies
and holiday tips for parents of small children, published in books
written by house husbands or bitter mothers who felt cheated
as they collapsed with exhaustion from working and having
children. What had once been normal topics you didn't talk
about much were now placed at the forefront of existence and
cultivated with a frenzy that ought to make everyone raise their
eyebrows, for what could be the meaning of this? In the midst
of this lunacy there was me trundling my child around like one
of the many fathers who had evidently put fatherhood before
all else. When I was in the café feeding Vanja there was always
at least one other father there, usually of my age, that is, in his
mid-thirties, almost all of whom had shaved heads to hide hair
loss. You hardly ever saw a bald patch or a high forehead any
longer, and the sight of these fathers always made me feel a
little uncomfortable. I found it hard to take the feminised aspect
of their actions, even though I did exactly the same and was as
feminised as they were. The slight disdain I felt for men pushing
buggies was, to put it mildly, a two-edged sword as for the most
part I had one in front of me when I saw them. I doubted I was
alone in these feelings, I thought I could occasionally discern

an uneasy look on some men's faces in the play area, and the restlessness in the bodies, which were prone to snatching a couple of pull-ups on the bars while the children played around them. However, spending a few hours every day in a play area with your child was one thing. There were things that were much worse. Linda had just started to take Vanja to Rhythm Time classes for tiny tots at the Stadsbiblioteket library, and when I took over responsibility she wanted Vanja to continue. I had an inkling something dreadful was awaiting me, so I said no, it was out of the question, Vanja was with me now, so there would be no Rhythm Time. But Linda continued to mention it off and on, and after a few months my resistance to what the role of the soft man involved was so radically subverted, in addition to which Vanja had grown so much that her day needed a modicum of variety, that one day I said, yes, today we were thinking of going to the Rhythm Time course at the Stadsbiblioteket. Remember to get there in good time, Linda said, it fills up quickly. And so it was that early one afternoon I was pushing Vanja up Sveavägen to Odenplan, where I crossed the road and went through the library doors. For some reason I had never been there before, even though it was one of Stockholm's most beautiful buildings, designed by Asplund some time in the 1920s, the period I liked best of all in the previous century. Vanja was fed, rested and wearing clean clothes, carefully chosen for the occasion. I pushed the buggy into the large completely circular interior, asked a woman behind a counter where the children's section was, followed her instructions into a side room lined with shelves of children's books, where on a door at the back there was a poster about this Rhythm Time class starting here at 2 p.m. Three buggies were already present. On some chairs a little further away sat the owners, three women in heavy jackets and worn faces, all around thirty-five, while what must have been their snot-nosed children were crawling around on the floor between them.

I parked the buggy by theirs, lifted Vanja out, sat down on a little ledge with her on my lap, removed her jacket and shoes and lowered her gently to the floor. Reckoned she could crawl around a bit as well. But she didn't want to, she couldn't remember being here before, so she wanted to stick with me and stretched her arms out. I lifted her back onto my lap. She sat watching the other children with interest.

An attractive young woman holding a guitar walked across the floor. She must have been about twenty-five; she had long blonde hair, a coat reaching down to her knees, high black boots and she stopped in front of me.

'Hi!' she said. 'Haven't seen you here before. Are you coming to the Rhythm Time class?'

'Yes,' I said, looking up at her. She really was attractive.

'Have you signed up?'

'No,' I said. 'Do you have to?'

'Yes, you do. And I'm afraid it's full today.'

Good news.

'What a shame,' I said, getting up.

'As you didn't know,' she said. 'I suppose we can squeeze you in. Just this once. You can sign up afterwards for the next time.'

'Thank you,' I said.

Her smile was so attractive. Then she opened the door and went in. I leaned forward and watched her putting her guitar case on the floor, removing her coat and scarf and hanging them over a chair at the back of the room. She had a light fresh spring-like presence.

I had a hunch where this was going, and I should have got up and left. But I wasn't there for my sake, I was there for Vanja and Linda. So I stayed put. Vanja was eight months old and absolutely bewitched by anything that resembled a performance. And now she was attending one.

More women with buggies came, in dribs and drabs, and soon the room was filled with the sounds of chatting, coughing, laughing, clothes rustling and rummaging through bags. Most seemed to come in twos or threes. For a long time I seemed to be the only person on my own. But just before two a couple more men arrived. From their body language I could see they didn't know each other. One of them, a small guy with a big head, wearing glasses, nodded to me. I could have kicked him. What did he think: that we belonged to the same club? Then it was off with the overalls, the hat and the shoes, out with the feeding bottle and rattle, down on the floor with the child.

The mothers had long since gone into the room where Rhythm Time was due to take place. I waited until last, but at a minute to, I got up and went in with Vanja on my arm. Cushions had been strewn across the floor for us to sit on, while the young woman leading the session sat on a chair in front of us. With the guitar on her lap she scanned the audience smiling. She was wearing a beige cashmere jumper. Her breasts were well formed, her waist was narrow, her legs, one crossed over the other and swinging, were long and still clad in black boots.

I sat down on my cushion. I put Vanja on my lap. She stared with big eyes at the woman with the guitar, who was now saying a few words of welcome.

'We've got some new faces here today,' she said. 'Perhaps you'd like to introduce yourselves?'

'Monica,' said one.

'Kristina,' said another.

'Lul,' said a third.

Lul? What sort of bloody name was that?

The room went quiet. The attractive young woman looked at me and sent me a smile of encouragement.

'Karl Ove,' I said sombrely.

'Then let's start with our welcome song,' she said, and struck the first chord, which resounded as she was explaining that parents should say the name of their child when she nodded to them, and then everyone should sing the child's name.

She strummed the same chord, and everyone began to sing. The idea behind the song was that everyone should say 'Hi' to their friend and wave a hand. Parents of the children too small to understand took their wrists and waved their hands, which I did too, but when the second verse started I no longer had any excuse for sitting there in silence and had to start singing. My own deep voice sounded like an affliction in the choir of high-pitched women's voices. Twelve times we sang 'Hi' to our friend before all the children had been named and we could move on. The next song was about parts of the body, which, of course, the children should touch when they were mentioned. Forehead, eyes, ears, nose, mouth, stomach, knee, foot. Forehead, eyes, ears, nose, mouth, stomach, knee, foot. Then we were handed some rattle-like instruments which we were supposed to shake as we sang a new song. I wasn't embarrassed, it wasn't embarrassing sitting there, it was humiliating and degrading. Everything was gentle and friendly and nice, all the movements were tiny, and I sat huddled on a cushion droning along with the mothers and children, a song, to cap it all, led by a woman I would have liked to bed. But sitting there I was rendered completely harmless, without dignity, impotent, there was no difference between me and her, except that she was more attractive, and the levelling, whereby I had forfeited everything that was me, even my size, and that voluntarily, filled me with rage.

'Now it's time for the children to do a bit of dancing!' she said, laying her guitar on the floor. Then she got up and went to a CD player on a chair.

'Everyone stand in a ring, and first we go one way, stamp with our feet, like so,' she said, stamping her attractive foot, 'turn round once and go back the other way.'

I got up, lifted Vanja and stood in the circle that was forming. I looked for the other two men. Both were completely focused on their children.

'OK, OK, Vanja,' I whispered. '"Each to his own," as your great-grandfather used to say.'

She looked up at me. So far she hadn't shown any interest in any of the things the children had to do. She didn't even want to shake the maracas.

'Away we go, then,' said the attractive woman, pressing the CD player. A folk tune poured into the room, and I began to follow the others, each step in time to the music. I held Vanja with a hand under each arm, so that she was dangling, close to my chest. Then what I had to do was stamp my foot, swing her round, after which it was back the other way. Lots of the others enjoyed this, there was laughter and even some squeals of delight. When this was over we had to dance alone with our child. I swayed from side to side with Vanja in my arms thinking that this must be what hell was like, gentle and nice and full of mothers you didn't know from Eve with their babies. When this was finished there was a session with a large blue sail which at first was supposed to be the sea, and we sang a song about waves and everyone swung the sail up and down, making waves, and then it was something the children had to crawl under until we suddenly raised it, this too to the accompaniment of our singing.

When at last she thanked us and said goodbye, I hurried out, dressed Vanja without meeting anyone's eye, just staring down at the floor, while the voices, happier now than before they went in, buzzed around me. I put Vanja in the buggy, strapped her in and pushed her out as fast as I could without drawing attention to myself. Outside on the street I felt like shouting till my lungs burst and smashing something. But I had to make do with putting as many metres between me and this hall of shame in the shortest possible time.

'Vanja, O Vanja,' I said, scurrying down Sveavägen. 'Did you have fun then? It didn't really look like it.'

'Tha tha thaa,' Vanja said.

She didn't smile, but her eyes were happy.

She pointed.

'Ah, a motorbike,' I said. 'What is it with you and motorbikes, eh?'

When we reached the Konsum shop at the corner of Tegnérgatan I went in to buy something for supper. The feeling of claustrophobia was still there, but the aggression had diminished, it wasn't anger I felt as I pushed the buggy down the aisle between the shelves. The shop evoked memories, it was the one I had used when I had moved to Stockholm three years earlier, when I was staying at the flat Norstedts, the publishers, had put at my disposal a stone's throw further up the street. I had weighed over a hundred kilos at the time and moved in a semi-catatonic darkness, escaping from my former life. It hadn't been much fun. But I had decided to pick myself up, so every evening I went to the Lill-Jansskogen forest to run. I couldn't even manage a hundred metres before my heart was pounding so fast and my lungs were gasping so much that I had to stop. Another hundred metres and my legs were trembling. Then it was back to the hotel-like flat at walking pace for crispbread and soup. One day I had seen a woman in the shop, suddenly she was standing next to me, by the meat counter of all places, and there was something about her, the sheer physicality of her appearance, which from one

moment to the next filled me with almost explosive lust. She
was holding her basket in front of her with both hands, her hair
was auburn, her pale complexion freckled. I caught a whiff of
her body, a faint smell of sweat and soap, and stood staring
straight ahead with a thumping heart and constricted throat for
maybe fifteen seconds, for that was the time it took her to come
alongside me, take a pack of salami from the counter and go on
her way. I saw her again when I was about to pay, she was at the
other cash desk, and the desire, which had not gone away, welled
up in me again. She put her items in her bag, turned and went
out of the door. I never saw her again.

From her low position in the buggy Vanja had spotted a dog,
which she was pointing a finger at. I never stopped pondering
about what she saw when she watched the world around her.
What did this endless stream of people, faces, cars, shops and
signs mean to her? She did not see it in an undiscriminating way,
that at least was certain, for not only did she regularly point at
motorbikes, cats, dogs and other babies, she had also constructed
a very clear hierarchy with respect to the people around her: first
Linda, then me, then grandma and then everyone else, depending
on how long they had been near her over the last few days.

'Yes, look, a dog,' I said. I picked up a carton of milk, which
I put on the buggy, and a packet of fresh pasta from the adjacent
counter. Then I took two packets of serrano ham, a jar of olives,
mozzarella cheese, a pot of basil and some tomatoes. This was
food I would never have dreamed of buying in my former life
because I had no idea it existed. But now I was here, in the midst
of Stockholm's cultural middle classes, and even though this
pandering to all things Italian, Spanish, French and the repu-
diation of all things Swedish appeared stupid to me, and gradually, as the bigger picture emerged, also repugnant, it wasn't
worth wasting my energy on. When I missed pork chops and

cabbage, beef stew, vegetable soup, dumplings, meatballs, lung mash, fishcakes, mutton and vegetables, smoked sausage ring, whale steaks, sago pudding, semolina, rice pudding and Norwegian porridge, it was as much the 70s I missed as the actual tastes. And since food was not important to me, I might as well make something Linda liked.

I stopped for a few seconds by the newspaper stand wondering whether to buy the two evening papers, the two biggest publications. Reading them was like emptying a bag of rubbish over your head. Now and then I did buy them, when it felt as though a bit more rubbish up there wouldn't make any difference. But not today.

I paid and went into the street again, with the tarmac vaguely reflecting the light from the mild winter sky, and the cars queueing on all sides of the crossing resembling a huge pile-up of logs in a river. To avoid the traffic I went along Tegnérgatan. In the window of the second-hand bookshop, which was one of the ones I kept an eye on, I saw a book by Malaparte that Geir had spoken about with warmth and one by Galileo Galilei in the Atlantis series. I turned the buggy, nudged the door open with my heel and entered backwards with the buggy following.

'I'd like two of the books in the window,' I said. 'The Galileo Galilei and the Malaparte.'

'Pardon me?' said the shirt-clad man in his fifties who ran the place, as he peered at me over the square-rimmed glasses perched on the tip of his nose.

'In the window,' I said in Swedish. 'Two books. Galilei, Malaparte.'

'The sky and the war, eh?' he said, and turned to pick them out for me.

Vanja had gone to sleep.

Had it been so exhausting at Rhythm Time?

I pulled the little lever under the headrest towards me and lowered her gently into the buggy. She waved a hand in her sleep, and clenched it exactly as she had done just after she had been born. One of the movements that nature had supplied her with but which she had slowly replaced with something of her own. But when she slept it reawakened.

I pushed the buggy to the side so that people could pass, and turned to the shelf of art books as the bookshop owner rang up the prices of the two books on his antiquated cash till. Now that Vanja was asleep I had a few more minutes to myself, and the first book I caught sight of was a photographic book by Per Maning. What luck! I had always liked his photos, especially these ones, the animal series. Cows, pigs, dogs, seals. Somehow he had succeeded in capturing their souls. There was no other way to understand the looks of these animals in the pictures. Complete presence, at times anguished, at others vacant, and sometimes penetrating. But also enigmatic, like portraits by painters in the seventeenth century.

I put it on the counter.

'That one's just come in,' the owner said. 'Fine book. Are you Norwegian?'

'Yes, I am,' I said. 'I'd like to browse a bit more if that's OK.'

There was an edition of Delacroix's diary, I took it, and then a book about Turner, even though no paintings lost as much by being photographed as his, and Poul Vad's book about Hammershøi, and a magnificent work about orientalism in art.

As I placed them on the counter my mobile rang. Almost no one had my number, so the ringtone, which found its way out of the depths of the side pocket in my parka a touch muffled, aroused no disquiet in me. Quite the contrary. Apart from the brief exchange with the Rhythm Time woman I hadn't spoken to anyone since Linda cycled to school that morning.

'Hello?' Geir said. 'What are you up to?'

'Working on my self-esteem,' I said, turning to the wall. 'And you?'

'Not that, at any rate. I'm just sitting here in the office watching everyone scurry past. So what's been happening?'

'I've just met an attractive woman.'

'And?'

'Chatted to her.'

'Mm?'

'She invited me to hers.'

'Did you say yes?'

'Of course. She even asked what my name was.'

'But?'

'She was the teacher in charge of a Rhythm Time class for babies. So I had to sit there clapping my hands and singing children's songs in front of her, with Vanja on my lap. On a little cushion. With a load of mothers and children.'

Geir burst into laughter.

'I was also given a rattle to shake.'

'Ha ha ha!'

'I was so furious when I left I didn't know what to do with myself,' I said. 'I also had a chance to try out my new waistline. And no one was bothered about the rolls of fat on my stomach.'

'No, they're nice and soft, they are,' Geir said, laughing again. 'Karl Ove, aren't we going out tonight?'

'Are you winding me up?'

'No, I'm serious. I was planning to work here till seven, more or less. So we could meet in town any time after.'

'Impossible.'

'What the hell's the point of you living in Stockholm if we can never meet?'

'You realise you just used a Swedish word, don't you,' I said.

'Can you remember when you first came to Stockholm?' Geir said. 'When you were in the taxi lecturing me about the expression "hen-pecked" when I didn't want to go to the nightclub with you?'

'There you go. And another. Your Norwegian's gone to pot,' I said.

'For Christ's sake, man. What we're talking about is the expression you used. Hen-pecked. Do you remember?'

'Yes, I'm afraid I do.'

'And?' he said. 'What do you deduce from that?'

'That there are differences,' I said. 'I'm not hen-pecked. I'm a hen-pecker. And you're a woodpecker.'

'Ha ha ha. Tomorrow then?'

'We're eating out with Fredrik and Karin tomorrow night.'

'Fredrik? Is he that idiot of a film producer?'

'I wouldn't express it in that way, but, yes, he is.'

'Oh my God. All right. Sunday? No, that's your day of rest. Monday?'

'OK.'

'There are lots of people in town then, too.'

'Monday at Pelikanen then,' I said. 'By the way, I'm holding a Malaparte book in my hand here.'

'Oh yes? Are you in a second-hand bookshop then? It's good, that one.'

'And Delacroix's diary.'

'That's supposed to be good as well. Thomas has talked about it, I know. Anything else?'

'*Aftenposten* rang yesterday. They wanted to do an interview.'

'You didn't say yes, did you?'

'Yes.'

'You idiot. You said you were going to stop doing them.'

'I know. But the publishers said the journalist was particularly good. And so I thought I would give it one last chance. It *could* turn out all right after all.'

'No, it can't,' Geir said.

'Yes, I know,' I said. 'But never mind. Now I've said yes anyway. Anything new with you?'

'Nothing. Had some bread rolls with the social anthropologists. Then the old institute head popped by with crumbs in his beard and his flies open, wanting to talk. I'm the only one who doesn't give him the heave-ho. So he comes here.'

'The one who was so tough?'

'Yes. And who's now terrified of losing his office. That's all he's got left of course. And so now he's as nice as pie. It's a question of adapting. Tough when he can be, nice when he has to be.'

'I might pop round tomorrow,' I said. 'Have you got any time?'

'Dead right I have. So long as you don't bring Vanja along, that is.'

'Ha ha. Right, but I've got to pay now. See you tomorrow.'

'OK. All the best to Linda and Vanja.'

'And to Christina.'

'See you.'

'Yes, see you.'

I rang off and stuffed the mobile back in my pocket. Vanja was still asleep. The bookshop owner was studying a catalogue. He looked up as I approached the counter.

'That'll be 1,530 kroner,' he said.

I passed him my card. I put the receipt in my back pocket – the only way I could justify these purchases of mine was that they could be written off against tax – I put the two bags of books underneath the buggy, and then I pushed it out of the shop to the sound of the doorbell ringing in my ears.

It was already twenty minutes to four. I had been up since

half past four in the morning going through a problematic
translation for Damm until half past six, and even though it
was tedious work in which all I did was weigh one sentence
against the other in the original, it was still a hundred times
more interesting and rewarding than what I did during the
morning in terms of nappy changing and children's activities,
which for me were no longer any more than a means of occupying my time. I wasn't exhausted by this lifestyle, it had nothing
to do with expending energy, but as there wasn't even the
slightest spark of inspiration in it, it deflated me nonetheless,
rather as if I'd had a puncture.

By the crossing at Döbelnsgatan I took a left turn, walked
up the hill below Johanneskyrk, which with its red brick walls
and green tin roof was similar to Johanneskirk in Bergen and
Trefoldighetskirk in Arendal, followed Malmskillnadsgatan for
a while, then turned down David Bagares gata and through
the gate to our backyard. Two torches were burning on the
pavement outside the café opposite. There was a stench of piss,
because people stopped here on their way home from Stureplan
at night and pissed through the railings, and a stink of rubbish
from the line of dustbins along the wall. In the corner was
the pigeon that had taken up residence here when we moved
in two years before. At the time it lived in a hole in the wall.
When it was bricked up and sharp spikes were cemented into
all the flat surfaces higher up, she moved down to ground
level. There were rats here too. I saw them occasionally when
I went out for a smoke at night, black backs sliding through
the bushes and suddenly scuttling across the open illuminated
square towards the security of the flower beds on the other
side. Now one of the women hairdressers was standing there,
talking on her mobile while smoking. She must have been
about forty, and I guessed she had grown up as a small-town

beauty, at any rate she reminded me of the type you can see in restaurants in Arendal in the summer, women in their forties with hair dyed much too blonde or much too black, skin that was much too brown, eyes much too flirtatious, laughter much too loud. Her voice was raucous, she spoke broad Skåne dialect, and today she was dressed all in white. She nodded on seeing me, and I nodded back. Even though I had barely spoken to her I liked her, she was so different from all the other people I met in Stockholm, who were either on their way up, or were up, or thought they were. She had no truck, to put it mildly, with their homogeneous style, which not only applied to clothes and objects but also their thoughts and attitudes.

I paused in front of the door and pulled out my key. The smell of detergent and clean clothes streamed out from the vent above the cellar window. I unlocked the door and walked as quietly as I could into the hall. Vanja knew these sounds and the order in which they occurred so well that she almost always woke when we came in here. She did so this time too. With a scream. I let her scream, opened the lift door, pressed the button and regarded myself in the mirror as we went up the two floors. Linda, who must have heard the screams, was waiting for us at the door when we arrived.

'Hi,' she said. 'Have you had a good time? Have you just woken up, sweetheart? Come here then and I'll . . .'

She undid the belt and lifted Vanja up.

'We've been fine,' I said, pushing the empty buggy in while Linda unbuttoned her cardigan and went into the living room to feed her.

'But I'll never set foot in the Rhythm Time session for as long as I draw breath.'

'Was it that bad?' she asked, glancing at me with a fleeting smile before looking down at Vanja and nestling her against her bared breast.

'Bad? It's the worst experience I've ever had. I was furious when I left.'

'I see,' she said, no longer interested.

Her care for Vanja was so different. It was all-embracing. And completely genuine.

I went into the kitchen with the shopping, put the perishables in the fridge, placed the pot of basil on a dish on the windowsill and watered it, fetched the books from under the buggy and put them in the bookcase, sat down in front of the computer and checked my emails. I hadn't looked since the morning. There was an email from Carl-Johan Vallgren, he congratulated me on the nomination, said he was afraid he hadn't read my book yet, and that I just had to ring if I felt like a beer one day. Carl-Johan was someone I really liked, I valued his extravagance – which some found disagreeable, snobbish or stupid – especially after two years in Sweden. But it was impossible for me to have a beer with him. I would just sit there in silence, I knew I would; I had already done it twice. Then there was one from Marta Norheim about an interview in connection with NRK 2's Novel Award, which I had won. And one from my uncle Gunnar, who thanked me for the book and said he was building up his strength to read it, wished me luck with the Nordic championship in liter-ature and concluded with a PS that it was a shame Yngve and Kari Anne were going to divorce. I closed the window without answering.

'Anything interesting?' Linda asked.

'Well. Carl-Johan congratulated me. And then NRK wanted to do an interview in two weeks. Gunnar wrote as well, of all people. He just thanked me for the book. But that's not bad, considering how angry he was about *Out of the World*.'

'No, it isn't,' Linda said. 'Aren't you going to call Carl-Johan and get him to come over?'

'Are you in such a good mood?' I said.

She pouted at me.

'I'm just trying to be nice,' she said.

'I know that,' I said. 'Sorry. Didn't mean it. OK?'

'That's all right.'

I walked past her and picked up the second volume of *The Brothers Karamazov*, which was lying on the sofa.

'I'm off then,' I said. 'Bye.'

'Enjoy,' she said.

Now I had an hour to myself. It was the sole condition I had made before taking over responsibility for Vanja during the daytime, that I would have an hour on my own in the afternoon, and even though Linda considered it unfair since she'd never had an hour to herself like that, she agreed. The reason she'd never had an hour, I assumed, was that she hadn't thought of it. And the reason she hadn't thought of it was, I also assumed, that she would rather be with us than alone. But that wasn't how I felt. So for an hour every afternoon I sat in a nearby café reading and smoking. I never went to the same café more than four or five times at a stretch because then they started to treat me like a *stammis*, that is, they greeted me when I arrived and wanted to impress me with their knowledge of my predilections, often with a friendly comment about some topic on everyone's lips. But the whole point for me of living in a big city was that I could be completely alone in it while still surrounded by people on all sides. All with faces I had *never* seen before! The unceasing stream of new faces. For me the very attraction of a big city was immersing myself in that. The Metro swarming with different types and characters. The squares. The pedestrian zones. The cafés. The big malls. Distance, distance, I could never have enough distance. So when a barista began to say hello and smile on catching sight of me and not only brought me a cup of coffee before I asked but also offered me a free croissant, it was time to leave. And it wasn't very hard to find alternatives, we were living in the city centre, and there were hundreds of cafés within a ten-minute radius.

This time I followed Regeringsgatan down towards the centre. It was packed with people. I thought about the attractive woman in the Rhythm Time class as I walked. What had that been all about? I wanted to sleep with her but didn't believe I would get an opportunity, and if I'd had an opportunity I wouldn't have taken it. So why should it be of any importance if I behaved like a woman in front of her?

You can say a lot about my self-image, but it was definitely not shaped in the cool chambers of reason. My intellect may be able to understand it, but it did not have the power to control it. One's self-image not only encompasses the person you are but also the person you want to be, could be or once had been. For the self-image there was no difference between the actual and the hypothetical. It incorporated all ages, all feelings, all drives. When I pushed the buggy all over town and spent my days taking care of my child it was not the case that I was adding something to my life, that it became richer as a result; on the contrary, something was removed from it, part of myself, the bit relating to masculinity. It was not my intellect which made this clear to me, because my intellect knew I was doing this for a good reason, namely that Linda and I would be on an equal footing with regard to our child, but rather my emotions, which filled me with desperation whenever I squeezed myself into a mould that was so small and so constricted that I could no longer move. The question was which parameter should be operative. If equality and fairness were to be the parameters, well, there was nothing to be said about men sinking everywhere into the thralls of softness and intimacy. Nor about the rounds of applause this was met with, for if equality and fairness were the dominant parameters, change was an undoubted improvement and a measure of progress. But these were not the only parameters. Happiness was one; an intense sense of being alive was another. And it may be that women who followed their careers until they were almost in their forties and then at the last moment had a child, which after a few months the father took care of until a place was found in a nursery so that they could both continue their careers, may have been happier than women in previous generations. It was possible that men who stayed at home and looked after their infants for six months may have increased their sense of being alive as a result. And women may actually have desired these men with thin arms, large waistlines, shaven heads and black designer glasses who were just as happy discussing the pros and cons of Babybjørn carriers and baby slings as whether it was better to cook one's own baby food or buy ready-made ecological purées. They may have desired them with all their hearts and souls. But even if they didn't, it didn't really matter because equality and fairness were the parameters, they trumped everything else a life and a relationship consisted of. It was a choice, and the choice had been made. For me as well. If I had wanted it otherwise I would have had to back out and tell Linda before she became pregnant: listen, I want children, but I don't want to stay at home looking after them, is that fine with you? Which means, of course, that you're the one who will have to do it. Then she could have said, no, it's not fine with me, or, yes, that's fine and our future could have been planned on that basis. But I didn't, I didn't have sufficient foresight, and consequently I had to go by the rules of the game. In the class and culture we belonged to, that meant adopting the same role, previously called the woman's role. I was bound to it like Odysseus to the mast: if I wanted to free myself I could do that, but not without losing everything. As a result I walked around Stockholm's streets, modern and feminised, with a furious nineteenth-century man inside me. The way I was seen changed, as if at the stroke of a magic wand the instant I laid my hands on the buggy. I had always eyed the women I walked past, the way men always have, actually a mysterious act because it couldn't lead to anything except a returned gaze, and if I did see a really beautiful woman I might even turn round to watch her, discreetly of course, but nevertheless: why, oh why? What function did all these eyes, all these mouths, all these breasts and waists, legs and bottoms serve? Why was it so important to look at them? When a few seconds, or occasionally minutes, later I had forgotten everything about them? Sometimes I had eye contact, and a rush could go through me if the gaze was held a tiny second longer, because it came from a person in a crowd, I knew nothing about her, where she was from, how she lived, nothing, yet we looked at each other, that was what it was about, and then it was over, she was gone and it was erased from memory for ever. When I came along with a buggy no women looked at me, it was as if I didn't exist. One might think it was because I gave such a clear signal that I was taken, but this was just as evident when I was walking hand in hand with Linda, and that had never prevented anyone from looking my way. My God, wasn't I only getting my just deserts, wasn't I being put in my place for walking around ogling women when there was one at home who had given birth to my child?

No, this was not good.

It certainly was not.

Tonje told me once about a man she had met at a restaurant, it was late, he came over to their table, drunk but harmless, or

so they had thought, since he had told them he had come straight
from the maternity ward, his partner had given birth to their
first baby that day, and now he was on the town celebrating.
But then he had started to make advances, he became more and
more insistent and in the end suggested they should go back to
his . . . Tonje was shaken deep into her soul, full of disgust,
though also fascination, I suspected, because how was it possible,
what was he thinking of?

I couldn't imagine a greater act of betrayal. But wasn't it what
I was doing when I sought the eyes of all these women?

My thoughts inevitably went back to Linda sitting at home
and washing and dressing Vanja, their eyes, Vanja's inquisitive
or happy or sleepy eyes, Linda's beautiful eyes. I had never ever
wanted anyone more than her, and now I had not only her but
also her child. Why couldn't I be content with that? Why couldn't
I stop writing for a year and be a father to Vanja while Linda
completed her training? I loved them; they loved me. So why
didn't all the rest stop plaguing and harrying me?

I had to apply myself harder. Forget everything around me
and just concentrate on Vanja during the day. Give Linda all she
needed. Be a good person. For Christ's sake, being a good person,
was that beyond me?

I had reached the new Sony shop and was considering going
into the Akademi bookshop on the corner, buying a few books
and settling down in the café there when I spotted Lars Norén
across the street. He had a Nike carrier bag in his hand and was
walking in the direction I had just come from. The first time I
saw him was a few weeks after we had moved into our flat here,
it was in Humlegården, the mist was hanging over the trees,
and towards us walked a hobbit-like man dressed all in black. I
met his gaze, it was as black as the night, and my spine ran
cold, what kind of person was this? A troll?

'Did you see *him*?' I said to Linda.

'That was Lars Norén,' she said.

'Was *that* Lars Norén?' I said.

Linda's mother, who was an actress, had worked with him in a play at the Royal Dramatic Theatre a long time ago, and Linda's best friend, Helena, also an actress, had done as well. Linda told me he had chatted to Helena, in a friendly way, and described how her precise words had appeared later in the play, put into the mouth of the character she was playing. Linda was always pestering me to read *Chaos Is the Neighbour of God* and *Night Is the Mother of Day*, which she said was quite fantastic, but I never did, my list of books to read was as long as my arm, and for the time being I had to make do with an occasional sighting, for he appeared on the street at regular intervals, and when we went to our favourite café, Saturnus, he was not infrequently there being interviewed or just talking to someone. He wasn't the only writer I bumped into; in the bakery close to ours I once saw Kristian Petri, whom I was on the point of saying hello to, unaccustomed as I was to meeting faces I had seen before, and on another occasion Peter Englund was in the same place, while Lars Jakobson, who wrote the fantastic *In the Red Queen's Castle*, once came into Café Dello Sport while we were there, and Stig Larsson, whom I had been addicted to when I was in my twenties and whose book *Watch Over Mine* had hit me like a clenched fist, I saw on the terrace at Sturehof. He was reading a book, and my heart beat so fast it was as if I had seen a corpse. Another time I saw him at Pelikanen, where I was with some people who knew the crowd he was with, and I shook his hand, dry as a bundle of withered straw as he gave me an apathetic smile. I saw Aris Fioteros at Forum Culture House one night, Katarina Frostenson was also there, and I met Ann Jäderlund at a party in Södermalm. I had read all these authors when I was in Bergen, back then they were no more than foreign names living in a foreign country, and seeing them now in the flesh they were shrouded in the aura of that time, which gave me a strong historical sense of the present, they wrote in our era and filled it with moods on which generations to come would base their understanding of us. Stockholm at the beginning of the millennium, that was the feeling I had when I saw them, and it was a good uplifting feeling. I didn't care that many of these writers had had their heyday in the 80s and 90s and had long been pushed aside, it wasn't reality I wanted but enchantment. Of the young writers I had read there was only Jerker Virdborg I liked; his novel *Black Crab* had something that raised it above the mist of morals and politics others were cloaked in. Not that it was a fantastic novel, but he was searching for something different. That was the sole obligation literature had, in all other respects it was free, but not in this, and when writers disregarded this they did not deserve to be met with anything but contempt.

How I hated their journals. Their articles. Gassilewski, Raattamaa, Halberg. What terrible writers they were.

No, not the Akademi bookshop.

I stopped by the zebra crossing. On the other side, in the passage leading to the old, traditional NK department store, there was a little café, and I decided to head for it. Even though I often went there the flow of customers was so great and the surroundings so anonymous that you were invisible nevertheless.

There was one free table by the railings of the staircase leading down to the DIY shop in the cellar. I hung my jacket on the back of the chair, put the book on the table, front cover down, spine facing away, so that no one could see what I was reading, and joined the queue by the counter. The three people working there, two women and a man, looked like sisters and a brother. The oldest of them, now standing by the hissing coffee machine, had the appearance and radiance of someone you normally only ever saw in magazines, and her photo-like appearance almost cancelled out any lust I felt as I watched her flit about behind the counter, as though the world I moved in was incommensurable with hers, and I suppose it was. We didn't have a thing in common, apart from the gaze.

Hell. There I go again.

Wasn't I supposed to be stopping all this?

I took out a crumpled hundred-krone note from my pocket and smoothed it in my hand. Scanned the other customers, who were almost all sitting on a chair with their gleaming carrier bags on another. Shiny boots and shoes, elegant suits and coats, the odd fur collar, the odd gold necklace, old skin and old eyes in their old mascaraed sockets. Coffee was drunk, Danish pastries consumed. I would have given a fortune to know what the people sitting there were thinking. What the world looked like to them. Imagine if it was radically different from what I saw. If it was full of pleasure at the dark leather of the sofa, the black surface of the coffee and its bitter taste, not to mention the yellow eye of custard in the centre of the puff pastry's winding and cracked terrain. What if the whole of this world sang inside them? What if they were full to bursting with the many delights the day had bestowed on them? Their carrier bags, for example, the ingenious and extravagant handles of string some of them were fitted with instead of the small cardboard handles stuck on the bags in the supermarkets. And the logos which someone with all their specialist knowledge and expertise had spent days and weeks designing, the meetings with feedback from other departments, more work refining the design, perhaps they had shown samples to friends and family, lain awake at night, for there was always someone who would not have liked it, despite all the meticulous care and ingenuity that had gone into it, until the day it became a reality, and now lay, for example, in the lap of that woman in her fifties with the stiff hair dyed a golden tint.

Maybe she didn't seem that elated. More like mildly contemplative. Filled with a great inner peace after a long and happy life? In which the perfect contrast between the coffee cup's cold, hard, white stoneware and the coffee's hot, fluid, black liquid was only a temporary stopping point on a journey through the world's noumena and phenomena? For had she not seen foxgloves growing in rocky scree once? Had she not seen a dog pissing against a lamp post in the park on one of those misty November nights that fill the town with such mystique and beauty? Ah, ah, for isn't the air full of tiny rain particles then that not only lie like a film over skin and wool, metal and wood, but also reflect the light around such that everything glistens and glimmers in the greyness? Had she not seen a man first smash the basement window on the other side of the backyard, and then lift the hasp and crawl in to steal whatever might be inside? The ways of man are indeed weird and wonderful! Did she not have in her possession a little metal stand with salt and pepper cellars, both made of fluted glass, the top made of the same metal as the stand and perforated with lots of small holes so that the salt and pepper, respectively, could *sprinkle* out? And what had she seen them sprinkle on? Roast pork, a leg of mutton, wonderful yellow omelettes with chopped green chives in, pea soups and joints of beef. Filled to the brim with all these impressions, each and every one, with all their tastes, smells, colours and shapes, in themselves an experience of a lifetime, was it perhaps not surprising that she sought peace and quiet where she sat, and did not appear to want to absorb *any* more of the world?

At last the man in front of me in the queue had his order placed on the counter, three latte coffees, evidently an extremely demanding task, and the woman serving, with the shoulder-length black hair, the gentle lips and the black eyes which brightened in an instant if there was a customer she knew, they were watching, but now they were neutral, now she was looking at me.

'A black coffee?' she said before I had time to ask.

I nodded, and sighed as she turned to get it. So she too had noticed the tall drab man with the jumper stained by baby food who never washed his hair any more.

In the few seconds it took her to find a cup and fill it with coffee I ran my eyes over her. She too had knee-high black boots. It was this winter's fashion, and I wished it would last for ever.

'Here you are,' she said.

I handed her a hundred-krone note, she took it with her well-manicured fingers, I noticed the nail varnish was transparent, she counted up the change at the till and placed it in my hand as the smile she gave me transmuted into a smile for three friends behind me in the queue.

The sight of the Dostoevsky book on the table was not exactly tempting. The threshold for reading became higher the less I read; it was a typical vicious circle. In addition, I didn't like being in the world Dostoevsky described. However rapt I could be and however much admiration I had for what he did, I couldn't rid myself of the distaste I felt when reading his books. No, not distaste. Discomfort was the word. I was uncomfortable in Dostoevsky's world. But I opened the book anyway and settled down on the chair to read, after glancing round the room to make sure no one saw me doing it.

Before Dostoevsky, the ideal, even the Christian ideal, was always pure and strong, it was part of heaven, unattainable for almost everyone. The flesh was weak, the mind frail, but the ideal was unbending. The ideal was about aspiring, enduring, fighting the fight. In Dostoevsky's books everything is human, or rather, the human world is everything, including the ideals, which are turned on their heads: now they can be achieved if you give up, lose your grip, fill yourself with non-will rather than will. Humility and self-effacement, those are the ideals in Dostoevsky's foremost novels, and inasmuch as they are never realised within the framework of the storyline, therein lies his greatness, because this is precisely a result of his own humility and self-effacement as a writer. Unlike most other great writers, Dostoevsky himself is not discernible in his novels. There are no brilliant turns of phrase that can point to him, there is no definitive moral that can be elicited; he uses all his ingenuity and diligence to individualise people, and since there is so much in man that will not allow itself to be humbled or effaced, the struggle and active striving are always stronger than the passives of mercy and forgiveness, which is how they end up. From here one might go on and examine, for example, the concept of nihilism in his work, which never seems real, always seems like a mere *idée fixe*, a piece of his era's intellectual history heaven, for the very reason that humanness bursts forth everywhere, in all its forms, from the most grotesque and brutish to the aristocratically refined and the besmirched, impoverished and worldly splendour-repudiating Jesus ideal, and it quite simply packs everything, including a discussion about nihilism, to the brim with meaning. With a writer like Tolstoy, who also worked and wrote during the period of great upheavals that was the latter half of the nineteenth century and which furthermore was riddled with all manner of religious and moral qualms, everything looks different. There are long descriptions of landscapes and space, customs and costumes, a rifle barrel smoking after a shot has been fired, the report reverberating with a faint echo, a wounded

animal rearing up before falling down dead, and the blood
steaming as it flows to the ground. Hunting is discussed in
lengthy analyses which do not pretend to be anything other
than that, an informed account of an objective phenomenon,
inserted in an otherwise eventful narrative. This preponderance
of deeds and events for their own sake does not exist in
Dostoevsky, there is always something lying hidden behind them,
a drama of the soul, and this means there is always an aspect
of humanness he doesn't include, the one that binds us to the
world outside us. There are many kinds of wind that blow
through man, and there are other entities inside him apart from
depth of soul. The authors of the books in the Old Testament
knew that better than anyone. The richest conceivable portrayal
of the possible manifestations of humanness is to be found there,
where all possible forms of life are represented, apart from one,
for us the only relevant one, namely our inner life. The division
of humanness into the subconscious and the conscious, the
rational and the irrational, whereby one always explains or
clarifies the other, and the perception of God as something you
can sink your soul in, such that the struggle ends and peace
prevails, are new concepts, inextricably linked to us and our
time, which not without reason has also let things slip out of
our hands by allowing them to merge with our knowledge of
them or with our image of them, while at the same time turning
the relationship between man and the world on its head: where
before man wandered through the world, now it is the world
that wanders through man. And when meaning shifts, meaninglessness follows. It is no longer the abandonment of God
which opens us to the night, as it did in the nineteenth century,
when the humanness that was left took over everything, as we
can see in Dostoevsky and Munch and Freud, when man, perhaps
out of need, perhaps out of desire, became his own heaven.

However, a single step backwards from that heaven was all that
was necessary for all meaning to be lost. Then it was evident
that there was a heaven over and above humanness, and that it
was not only empty, black and cold, but also endless. How much
was humanness worth in the context of the universe? What was
man on this earth other than an insect among other insects, a
life form among other life forms, which might just as well take
the form of algae in a lake or fungi on the forest floor, roe in a
fish's stomach, rats in a nest or a cluster of mussels on a reef?
Why should we do one thing rather than another when there
was no goal anyway, nor any direction in life, apart from to
huddle together, live and then die? Who enquired about the
value of this life when it was gone for ever, turned into a fistful
of damp earth and a few yellowing brittle bones? The skull,
wasn't it grinning with derision down there in the grave? What
difference did a few extra dead bodies make from that perspective? Oh yes, there were other perspectives on this same world;
couldn't it be seen as a miracle of cool rivers and vast forests,
whorled snail shells and deep potholes, veins and grey matter,
deserted planets and expanding galaxies? Yes, it could, because
meaning is not something we are given but which we give. Death
makes life meaningless because everything we have ever striven
for ceases when life does, and it makes life meaningful too,
because its presence makes the little we have of it indispensable,
every moment precious. But in my lifetime death was removed
from our lives, it no longer existed, except as a constant item
in all the newspapers, on the TV news and in films, where it
didn't mark the end of a process, discontinuity, but, on account
of daily repetition, represented, on the contrary, an extension
of the process, continuity, and in this way, oddly enough, had
become a source of our security and our anchor. A plane crash
was a ritual, it happened every so often, the same chain of events,

and we were never part of it ourselves. A sense of security, but also excitement and intensity, for imagine how terrible the last seconds were for the passengers . . . everything we saw and did contained the intensity that was triggered in us, but had nothing to do with us. What was this? Were we living other people's lives? Yes, everything we didn't have and were not experiencing we had and were experiencing even so, because we saw it and we took part in it without being there ourselves. Not only once in a while but every day . . . And not just me and everyone I knew but all major cultures, indeed almost everyone in existence, all bloody humanity. It had explored everything and made it its own, as the ocean does with rain and snow, there were no longer any things or places we had not made our own, and thereby loaded with humanness: our mind had been there. In the context of the divine, humanness was always small and insignificant, and it must have been because of this perspective's enormous import – which perhaps can only be compared with the significance contained in the recognition that knowledge was always a fall – that the notion of the divine arose in the first place, and had now come to an end. For who brooded over the meaninglessness of life any more? Teenagers. They were the only ones who were preoccupied with existential issues, and as a result there was something puerile and immature about them, and hence it was doubly impossible for adults with their sense of propriety intact to deal with them. However, this is not so strange, for we never feel more strongly and passionately about life than in our teenage years, when we step into the world for the first time, as it were, and all our feelings are new feelings. So there they are, with their big ideas on small orbits, looking this way and that for an opportunity to launch them, as the pressure builds. And who is it they light upon sooner or later but Uncle Dostoevsky? Dostoevsky has become a teenager's writer, the issue of nihilism a teenage issue. How this has come about is hard to say, but the result is at any rate that the whole of this vast question has been disregarded while at the same time all critical energy is directed to the left, where it is swallowed up in ideas of justice and equality, which of course are the very ones that legitimise and steer the development of our society and the abyss-less life we live within it. The difference between nineteenth-century nihilism and ours is the difference between emptiness and equality. In 1949 the German writer Ernst Jünger wrote that in the future we would have something approaching a world state. Now, when liberal democracy reigns supreme in modern societies, it looks as though he was right. We are all democrats, we are all liberal, and the differences between states, cultures and people are being broken down everywhere. And this movement, what else is it at heart, if not nihilistic? 'The nihilistic world is in essence a world that is being increasingly reduced, which naturally of necessity coincides with the movement towards a zero point,' Jünger wrote. A case in point of such a reduction is God being perceived of as 'good', or the inclination to find a common denominator for all the complicated tendencies in the world, or the propensity for specialisation, which is another form of reduction, or the determination to convert everything into numerical figures, beauty as well as forests as well as art as well as bodies. For what is money if not an entity that commodifies the most dissimilar things? Or as Jünger writes, 'Little by little all areas are brought under this single common denominator, even one with its residence as far from causality as the dream.' In our century even our dreams are alike, even dreams are things we sell. Undifferentiated, which is just another way of saying indifferent.

That is where our night is.

*

I had a sense the crowds around me were thinning and that the streets outside were dark, but not until I put the book down to go and get a refill of coffee did it strike me that this was a sign that time was passing.

It was ten minutes to six.

Bloody hell.

I should have been home at five. And it was Friday today, when we always went to a bit of extra trouble with the dinner and the evening that followed. At least that was the idea.

Shit. Fuck and bollocks.

I put on my jacket, stuffed the book in my pocket and hurried out.

'Bye!' the girl behind the counter said as I left.

'Bye!' I replied, without turning. I had to do some shopping before going home too. First of all, I went into the Systembolaget opposite, blindly grabbed a bottle of red wine from the most expensive shelf, after first checking there was a bull's head on the label, then followed the passage into the mall, which was so big and luxurious it always made me feel shabby, like a hobo, to the staircase and down into the supermarket in the basement, where the selection of goods on offer was the most exclusive in Stockholm, and where a large slice of our income ended up, not that we were gourmets by any stretch of the imagination, but because we were too lazy to walk to the cheap supermarket in the subway in Birger Jarlsgatan, and because I didn't care two hoots about the value of money, in the sense that I had no hesitation about spending it like water when I had it and hardly missed it when I didn't. Of course it was stupid; it made life harder for us than it needed to be. Our finances, though limited, could easily have been regular and healthy, instead of me splashing money around as soon as I had it and then living for the next three years on the basic minimum. But who could be bothered to think like that? Not me at any rate. So it was off to the meat counter, where they had wonderful well-hung and matured but by our standards staggeringly expensive entrecote steak from a farm in Gotland, meat which even I could tell tasted especially good, and where there were also some plastic pots of home-made sauces, which I grabbed hurriedly, along with a bag of potatoes, some tomatoes, broccoli and mushrooms. I saw they had fresh raspberries and grabbed a punnet, dashed to the freezer counter and selected the vanilla ice cream with the little label they had just started stocking, and lastly, at the other end of the shop, picked up some of the French waffles that were so good with it, where, fortunately, there was also a till.

Dear oh dear oh dear, now it was a quarter past.

It wasn't only that I had been away for an hour and a half longer than I should have been, and that she was waiting, but also that the evening would be so short now, as we went to bed very early. For my part, it didn't matter, I was just as happy eating sandwiches in front of the TV and could go to bed at half past seven if necessary, it was her I was worried about.

Furthermore, I had recently been on a three-day mini-tour doing readings and was going to Oslo to give a talk next week, so the leash was even tighter than usual.

I put the goods on the metal disc that slowly rotated towards the checkout assistant. She lifted them one by one and twisted them in the air until the bar code was over the laser reader, placed them on the small black conveyor belt after the beep, all with somnambulistic movements as if she were moving in a dream. The light above us was sharp and not a pore in her skin was left unexposed. Her mouth drooped at the corners, not because she was old, but because her cheeks were so big and fleshy. Her whole head was bloated with flesh. She might have spent a lot of time on her hairdo but it did nothing to improve the overall impression; it was like titivating the green top on a carrot.

'Five hundred and twenty kroner,' she said, looking at her nails, which she splayed for a brief moment. I swiped my card and tapped in my PIN. While staring at the display as I waited for the transaction to be accepted it struck me I had forgotten to buy a carrier bag. When this happened I was always careful to pay, so they didn't think I had forgotten it on purpose, hoping they would say I could have one free, as they often did. But this time I had no change on me, and it was ridiculous to use my card for such a small sum. On the other hand, did it matter what she thought about me? She was so fat.

'I forgot to take a bag,' I said.

'That'll be two kroner,' she said.

I took a bag from the box underneath the cash till and produced my card again.

'Haven't you got any cash?' she said.

'I'm afraid not,' I said.

She waved her hand.

'But I'd like to pay,' I said. 'It's not that.'

She smiled wearily.

'Go on, take it,' she said.

'Thank you,' I said, stuffing the goods inside and walking towards the stairs which, on this side, led up to a hall with some auction firm's display cases along the walls. I left by the door there, and NK was on the other side of the street, glittering in the underground shopping street which, on the left, was connected to another mall, Gallerian, and further up on the same side to the Kulturhus, while straight ahead it came out at Plattan and thus the Metro, from which tunnels led to the main station. On rainy days I always walked this way, on others too, for I found everything subterranean fascinating, it was like an adventure. I suppose this must have originated in my childhood when a cave was absolutely the most exciting find we could have made. One winter, I remembered, more than two metres of snow had fallen, it must have been in 1976 or 1977, and one weekend we dug small dens connected by tunnels stretching right across the garden to the neighbour's. We were like creatures possessed and totally enchanted by the result when evening fell and we could sit chatting deep beneath the snow.

I walked past the crowded American bar. It was Friday, and people went there after work for a beer or before their night out started in earnest, sat with their thick jackets over the backs of the chairs smiling and drinking, their faces flushed, most of them in their forties, while young, slim men and women with black aprons walked round taking orders, placing trays of beer on the tables and collecting empty glasses. The sound of all these happy people, this warm good-natured buzz, spiced as it were with the occasional roar of laughter, met me as the door was opened and a group of five people stopped outside, all busy doing something, whether searching a bag for cigarettes or lipstick, or keying in a number on a mobile and raising it expectantly to one ear, scanning the street while waiting, or searching out one of the others in order to send a smile, nothing more than that, just a friendly smile.

'Taxi to Regeringsgatan . . .' I heard behind me. Along the road a line of cars slipped past, slowly and sombrely, the faces in them illuminated by the gleam from the street lamps, which lent them a mysterious glow, or in the case of the drivers, by the bluish light from the dashboards. Some throbbed with the sound of bass and drums. Across the street people were streaming out of NK, where soon there would be a loudspeaker announcement that the store was closing in fifteen minutes. Thick furs, small whimpering dogs, dark woollen coats, leather gloves, clusters of carrier bags. The occasional youthful Puffa jacket, the occasional drop-crotch trousers, the occasional woollen beanie. Then there was a woman running past, holding on to her hat with one hand, the tails of her coat flapping around her legs. Why was she in such a hurry? It seemed to be urgent and I turned my head to watch. But nothing happened, she disappeared round the corner towards Kungsträgården. Three tramps were sitting by the wall on some grating. One had a sheet of cardboard in front of him on which he had written in felt-tip that he needed money for a place to stay the night. A hat containing a few coins lay beside him. The other two were drinking. I looked away as I passed them, crossed the road by the Akademi bookshop, hurried along past the stern somehow faceless façades, thinking about Linda, who perhaps was cross, who perhaps was thinking the evening was ruined, thinking how I was not looking forward much to meeting her. Over another crossing, past the expensive Italian restaurant, a quick glance up at the Glen Miller Café, where two people were getting out of a taxi, and then over to Nalen, the jazz club. An enormous band bus with a trailer was parked there, a white Swedish Broadcasting Corporation bus right behind it. A thick bundle of cables ran from it across the pavement, and in vain I struggled to recall who was playing there tonight, before striding up the three steps in front of our door, tapping in the code and entering. As I started on the stairs I heard a door being opened and shut again on the floor above. From the slam I knew it was the Russian woman. But it was too late to take the lift, so I went on up, and sure enough, a moment later, there she was, on her way down. She pretended she hadn't seen me. I greeted her anyway.

'Hi!' I said.

She mumbled something or other, but not until she had passed. The Russian woman was our neighbour from hell. For the first seven months we lived in the block her apartment was empty. But then one night at half past one we were awakened by a racket in the corridor – it was her front door being slammed shut – and straight afterwards music was played so loud we could not hear each other speak. Euro disco, with a bass and bass drum that made the floor vibrate and the windowpanes rattle. It was as though we had our stereo on at full blast. Linda, who was eight months' pregnant, had problems sleeping anyway, but even I who was usually able to remain comatose through any sort of noise could forget all about sleeping. Between the songs we heard her shouting and yelling beneath us. We got up and went into the living room. Should we ring the hotline that had been set up for situations like this? I didn't want to. That was too Swedish for me. Shouldn't we just go downstairs and ring the bell and complain? Fine, but then I would have to do it. And I did, I rang, and when that didn't help I knocked, but no one came. Another half an hour in the living room. Perhaps it would stop of its own accord? But in the end Linda was so furious that she went down herself, and then all of a sudden the woman opened the door. And was full of understanding! She stepped forward and laid a hand on Linda's stomach, and there's you expecting a baby, she said in her Russian-sounding Swedish, I'm so sorry, apologies, but my husband has left me and I don't know what to do, do you understand? Music and a bit of wine, it helps me in cold, cold Sweden. But you're going to have a baby and you need your sleep, don't you, my dear.

Happy to have made progress, Linda came back up and told me what was said before we went into the bedroom and got into bed. Ten minutes later, just after I had fallen asleep, the infernal racket started again. The same music at the same crazy volume, with the same hollering between the songs.

We got up and went into the living room. It was getting on

for half past three. What should we do? Linda wanted to ring the hotline, but I didn't, because even if in principle this was supposed to be anonymous, in the sense that the house-disturbance patrol was not allowed to say who had rung to complain, it was obvious the Russian woman would know, and with her as unstable as she evidently was, it would be asking for trouble later. So Linda suggested we should wait until it was all over this once and then write a friendly letter the day after in which it would emerge that we were understanding and tolerant, but this kind of volume late at night was in fact unacceptable. Linda lay down on the sofa, breathing heavily with her huge belly in the air, I went to bed, and an hour later, at almost five o'clock, the music finally stopped. The next day Linda wrote the letter, popped it through her letter box before going out in the morning, and everything was quiet until about six in the evening, when there was a terrible hammering and banging on our door. I went to open. It was the Russian woman. Her gritted alcohol-ravaged face was white with fury. In her hand she was clasping Linda's letter.

'What the hell is this!' she shouted. 'How *dare* you! In my own home! You're not bloody telling me what to do in my own home!'

'It's a friendly letter—' I said.

'I don't want to speak to you!' she said. 'I want to speak to the person in charge here!'

'What do you mean?'

'You're not the man in your own home. You're chased out when you want to smoke. You stand in the yard, you're a laughing stock. Do you think I haven't seen you? It's her I want to talk to.'

She took a few steps forward and tried to pass me. She stank of alcohol.

My heart was pounding. Fury was the one emotion I was really afraid of. I never managed to ward off the feeling of weakness that flooded through my body in these circumstances. My legs went weak, my arms went weak and my voice trembled. But she didn't need to notice.

'You'll have to speak to me,' I said, advancing towards her.

'No!' she said. 'She's the one who wrote this letter. It's her I want to talk to.'

'Listen,' I said. 'You were playing unbelievably loud music late last night. It was impossible for us to sleep. You can't do that. And you've got to understand.'

'Don't *you* tell me what to do!'

'Well, it's not me,' I said. 'We've got something called house rules. Everyone who lives in this place has to abide by them.'

'Do you know how much rent I pay?' she said. 'Fifteen thousand kroner! And I've lived here for eight years. No one has ever complained before. Then you come along. You snobby little snobs. "Actually, I'm preeegnant."'

As she said the latter she mimicked a snob, pursed her lips and stuck her nose in the air. Her hair was unkempt, her skin pale, cheeks plump, eyes staring.

She regarded me with that fiery gaze of hers. I looked down. She turned and went downstairs.

I closed the door and turned to face Linda, who was leaning against the hall wall.

'Well, that was a clever move,' I said.

'You mean the letter?' she asked.

'Yes,' I said. 'Now we're really in for it.'

'You mean it's my fault? It's her, not me who's gone completely off her rocker. That's nothing to do with me.'

'Relax,' I said. 'You and I are not at daggers drawn.'

In the flat below the music blared out, as loud as the previous night. Linda looked at me.

'Shall we go out?' she said.

'I don't really like the idea that we're being driven out,' I said.

'But it's impossible to stay here.'

'True.'

As we were putting on our coats the music stopped. Perhaps it was too loud even for her. But we went out nevertheless, down to the harbour by Nybroplan, where the lights glittered on black water and great layers of brash ice collected in front of the bows of the Djurgården ferry as it slowly approached. The Royal Dramatic Theatre stood like a castle on the other side of the road. It was one of my favourite buildings in Stockholm. Not because it was beautiful, for it was not, but because it exuded its own special atmosphere, as did the area around it. Perhaps it was simply that the colour of the stone was so light, almost white, and the surface area so vast that the entire building shone, even on the darkest of rainy days. With the constant wind coming off the sea and the flags fluttering outside the entrance there was an openness about the space it stood in, and the oppressive monument-like status that buildings often have about them was not present. Was it not like a small mountain by the sea?

We walked hand in hand down Strandgatan. The surface of the water out to the island of Skeppsholmen was wreathed in darkness. Moreover, when only a few lights were on in the houses it created a singular rhythm in the town, it was as if it came to an end, merged into the periphery and nature, only to pick up again on the other side of the water where the Old Town, Slussen and all the sheer cliffs towards Södermalm lay glittering and twinkling in the murmuring wind and sea.

Linda told me some anecdotes about the Royal Dramatic Theatre, where she had practically grown up. While her mother had worked there she had sole responsibility for Linda and her brother, so they had often been with her to rehearsals and performances. For me this was mythological, for Linda trivial, something she preferred not to talk about and quite definitely would not have done now had I not asked her directly. She knew everything about actors, their vanity and their tendency to burn themselves out, their angst and their intrigues, she laughed and said that the best of them were often the most stupid, the ones who understood least, that an intellectual actor was a contradiction in terms, but even though she despised the play-acting, despised their gesticulations and pomposity, their cheap, hollow, volatile lives and feelings, there was little to which she gave higher priority than their stage performances when they were at their best. She spoke, for example, with passion about Bergman's production of Ibsen's *Peer Gynt*, which she had seen countless times as she was working in the theatre wardrobe at that time, the fantastical and fairytale-like elements in it, and also the baroque and burlesque aspects. Or Wilson's production of Strindberg's *A Dream Play* at Stockholm City Theatre, where she worked on the dramaturgy, which of course was purer and more stylised but equally magical. She had wanted to be an actress herself once, reached the final round of auditions for the Theatre School two years in a row, but when they didn't take her the last time, that was fine, they would never take her, so she turned her attentions in a different direction, applied for the writer's course at Biskops-Arnö, and made her debut there with the poems she had written the year after.

Now she told me about a tour she had been on. The Royal Dramatic Theatre, Bergman's travelling company, they were stars wherever they went, and this time it was to Tokyo. Tall, noisy and drunk, the Swedish actors piled into one of the city's finer restaurants. There was no question of removing shoes or adapting to their surroundings in any other way, they swung their arms about, stubbed out their cigarettes in the sake cups and called loudly for the waiter. Linda, in short skirt, with red lipstick, black hair in a page cut, cigarette in hand, a little in love with Peter Stormare, was only fifteen years old and must have seemed grotesque to Japanese eyes, as she put it. But of course they didn't bat an eyelid, they just tripped quietly around them, not even when one of them burst through a paper partition and fell flat on his face.

She was laughing as she told me.

'When we were about to leave,' she said, glancing towards Djurgårdsbrunn, 'a waiter came over to me with a bag. It was a present from the chef, he said. I looked down into it. Do you know what it was?'

'No,' I said.

'It was full of small live crabs.'

'Crabs? What was that supposed to mean?'

She shrugged.

'I don't know.'

'What did you do with them?'

'I took them to the hotel. Mum was so drunk she had to be helped home. I caught a taxi on my own, with the bag of crabs by my feet. Back in my room I ran cold water into the bath tub and put the crabs in. They crawled around all night while I was asleep in the adjacent room. In the middle of Tokyo.'

'What happened then? What did you do with them?'

'The story ends there,' she said, squeezing my hand while looking up at me with a smile.

There was something about Japan and her. For her poetry collection she had been awarded a Japanese prize, of all things, a picture with Japanese characters, which until recently had hung above her desk. And wasn't there also something faintly Japanese about her wonderful small facial features?

We went up towards Karlaplan, with its circular pool, in the middle of which there was an enormous fountain during the summer months, but which was dry now, the bottom covered with withered leaves from the tall surrounding trees.

'Do you remember the time we went to see *Ghosts*?' I asked.

'Of course!' she said. 'I'll never forget that.'

I knew that – she had stuck the theatre ticket in the album she had started making when she became pregnant. *Ghosts* was Bergman's final production at the theatre, and we went to see it before we really got together, it was one of the first things we did, one of the first things we had shared. That was only eighteen months ago, but it felt like a whole lifetime.

She gazed at me with that look of affection that could make my heart melt. It was cold outside: a raw biting wind was blowing. It made me think how far east Stockholm actually was, a hint of something foreign, quite unlike where I came from, although I was unable to put my finger on what it was. We were in the richest district in Stockholm, and it was absolutely dead. No one went out here, the streets were never busy, yet they were broader than in any other part of the centre.

A man and a woman with a dog came towards us, him with his hands behind his back and a large leather hat on his head, her in a fur coat with the little terrier snuffling ahead.

'Shall we go for a beer somewhere?' I asked.

'Let's,' she answered. 'I'm hungry too. What about the bar in Zita?'

'Good idea.'

A shiver ran through me, and I drew the coat lapels tighter around my neck.

'Brass monkeys tonight,' I said. 'Are you cold?'

She shook her head. She was wearing the enormous Puffa jacket she had borrowed from her best friend, Helena, who last

winter had been as pregnant as Linda was now, and the fur hat
I had bought for her when we were in Paris, with two furry
pompoms dangling from it.

'Is it kicking?'

Linda placed both hands on her stomach.

'No, the baby's sleeping,' she said. 'It invariably does when I
go for a walk.'

'The baby,' I said. 'A tingle goes through me when you say
that. Most of the time it's as if I haven't quite clicked that there's
a human being inside you.'

'But there is,' Linda said. 'I already know the baby, or so it
seems. Do you remember how angry it got when they did that
diabetes test?'

I nodded. Linda was at risk as her father had diabetes, so she
had been given a kind of sugary mixture, the most nauseating
and foulest medicine she'd ever had, she said, and the baby in
her belly had kicked like crazy for more than an hour.

'That must have given him or her a jolt,' I said with a smile,
glancing towards Humlegården, which started on the other
side of the street. There was something bewitching about the
atmosphere here at night, with domes of light illuminating in
some places the trees with their heavy trunks and spread
branches, and in others the wet yellowing grass carpet, in
between which it was pitch black. But it was not bewitching
as in a forest, more like the bewitching atmosphere of a theatre.
We followed one of the paths. In some places there were still
small piles of leaves, otherwise the lawns and paths through
them were bare, much like the wooden floor in a sitting room.
A jogger shuffled around the statue of Linné, another came
sprinting down the gentle slope. Beneath us, I knew, lay the
enormous storehouses belonging to the Royal Library, which
towered up before us. A block further on was Stureplan with

the most exclusive nightclubs in the city. We lived a stone's
throw from Stureplan, but it might just as well have been in
another part of the world. People were shot in the streets down
there without us knowing anything about it until it was in the
newspapers the day after; international stars dropped by when
they were in town; the whole of Sweden's business and celebrity
elite put in an appearance there, which the whole country read
about in the evening papers. People didn't queue up to get in,
they stood in a line, and then the security guards walked round
and pointed at those who were allowed to enter. I hadn't seen
this cold hard side of the town anywhere before, and I had
never experienced such a clear cultural divide. In Norway
almost all distance is geographical, and since the population
is so small, the way to the top, or to the centre, is short everywhere. In every class at school there is always someone who
reaches the top within some field, or at least in every school.
Everyone knows someone who knows someone. In Sweden the
social distance is much greater, and since the countryside has
been depopulated and almost everyone lives in towns, and
anyone who wants to be someone goes to Stockholm where
everything of any significance happens, this is extremely conspicuous: so near, yet so far.

'Do you sometimes think about where I come from?' I asked,
looking at her.

She shook her head.

'No, not really. You're Karl Ove. My handsome husband. That's
what you are for me.'

'A housing estate on the island of Tromøya. Nothing has less
in common with your world than that. I know nothing about
life here. Everything is *deeply* alien. Do you remember what my
mother said when she came into our flat for the first time? No?
"Grandad should have seen this, Karl Ove," she said.'

'That's great, isn't it,' Linda said.

'But do you understand? For you this apartment is nothing special. For my mother it was like a little ballroom, wasn't it?'

'And for you?'

'Yes, for me too. But *that*'s not what I mean. Whether it's nice or not. But the fact that I come from something quite different. Something incredibly unsophisticated, right? I don't give a shit, and I don't give a shit about this either, the point is that it isn't mine, and it can never be mine however long I live here.'

We crossed the road and went down the narrow street in the residential quarter close to where Linda had grown up, past Saturnus Café and down Birger Jarlsgatan, where Zita cinema was. My face was stiff with cold. My thighs were frozen.

'You're lucky to be in this situation,' she said. 'Just think how much good it has done you. To have a place to go to. To have an outside where you've come from and an inside where you are going.'

'I know what you're getting at,' I said.

'Everything was here for me. I grew up in it. And I can barely separate it from myself. And there are also expectations. No one expected anything from you, did they? Except of course that you would study and get a job?'

I shrugged.

'I've never thought about it in that way.'

'No,' she said.

There was a pause.

'I've always lived in the middle of it. Perhaps *mummy* didn't wish anything else of me than that I should be all right . . .' She looked at me. 'That's why she loves you.'

'Does she?'

'Haven't you noticed? You must have noticed!'

'Yes, I suppose I have.'

I recalled the first time I had met her mother. A little house on an old smallholding in the forest. Autumn outside. We sat down to eat the moment we arrived. Hot meat broth, freshly baked bread, candles on the table. I could occasionally feel her eyes on me. They were curious and warm.

'But there were other people than mummy where I grew up,' Linda continued. 'Johan Nordenfalk the Twelfth, do you think he became a schoolteacher? So much money and culture. Everyone had to be a success. I had three friends who took their own lives. I daren't even think about how many of them have, or have had, anorexia.'

'Yes, what a bloody mess that is,' I said. 'Why can't people just take it easy?'

'I don't want our children to grow up here,' Linda said.

'Children now, is it?'

She smiled.

'And?'

'It'll have to be Tromøya then,' I said. 'I only know of one person who committed suicide there.'

'Don't joke about it.'

'OK.'

A woman in high heels and a long red dress click-clacked past. She was holding a black bag in one hand and clutching a black net shawl around her chest with the other. Behind her were two bearded young men in parkas and climbing boots, one with a cigarette in his hand. After them three women, friends by the look of them, also dressed up, with pretty little bags in their hands, but at least with windbreakers covering their dresses. Compared with the streets in Östermalm this was nothing less than a carnival. On both sides of the street, lights shone from restaurants, all packed with people. Outside Zita, which was one of two alternative cinemas in the district, a small shivering crowd was assembled.

'Honestly though,' Linda said. 'Perhaps not Tromøya, but Norway by all means. People are friendlier there.'

'That's true.'

I pulled at the heavy door and held it open for her. Took off my gloves and hat, unbuttoned my coat, loosened my scarf.

'But I don't want to go to Norway,' I said. 'That's the whole point.'

She didn't say anything, she was on her way to the posters in the showcases. She turned to me.

'*Modern Times* is on!' she said.

'Shall we see it?'

'Yes, let's! But I have to get a bite to eat first. What's the time?'

I searched for a clock. And found a small chunky one on the wall behind the box office.

'Twenty to nine.'

'It starts at nine. So we can make it. If you buy the tickets, I'll go and see if I can get something in the bar.'

'OK,' I said. Dug out a dog-eared hundred-krone note from my pocket and went to the ticket window.

'Have you got any tickets for *Modern Times*?' I asked in Norwegian.

A woman who could not have been any older than twenty, with plaits and glasses, looked down her nose at me.

'*Ursäkta?*' she said. Excuse me.

'Have – you – got – tickets – for – *Modern – Times*?' I asked in Swedish.

'Yes.'

'Two please. At the back, in the middle. *Två.*'

To be on the safe side, I held two fingers in the air.

She printed the tickets, placed them without a word on the counter in front of me, straightened the hundred-krone note and put it in the till. I went into the bar, which was jam-packed, spotted Linda and squeezed in beside her.

'I love you,' I said.

I hardly ever said that, and her eyes beamed as she looked up at me.

'Do you?' she said.

We kissed. The bartender set down a small basket of taco chips in front of us and what looked like a guacamole dip.

'Do you want a beer?' she asked.

I shook my head.

'Maybe afterwards. But by then you'll probably be too tired.'

'Probably. Did you get the tickets?'

'Yes.'

I saw *Modern Times* for the first time at the film club in Bergen when I was twenty. There was one scene where I couldn't stop laughing. Most people can't remember when they last laughed, but I remember when I laughed twenty years ago, because of course it doesn't happen that often. I remember both the shame of losing control and the pleasure of letting myself go. What started me off is still crystal clear in my memory. Chaplin has to perform in a kind of variety show. It's an important performance, there's a lot at stake, he is nervous and jots down the lyrics as an aide-memoire and slips them up his jacket sleeves before he goes on. As he steps onto the dance floor he welcomes the audience with a broad, sweeping flourish and the scraps of paper are sent flying. Then he is left standing there without the lyrics while the orchestra strikes up behind him. What should he do? Yes, he chases after them, improvising a dance to cover the fact that something has gone wrong, while the band plays the intro again and again. I laughed until I cried. But the scene moves into a different phase because he can't retrieve the pieces of paper, however much he dances around, and in the end he *has* to start singing. He stands there in total silence, and when he does begin it is with words that do not exist, but they are similar because although the meaning has gone, the notes and the melody remain, and I was filled with joy, I remember, not only for me but for the whole of humanity, as there was such warmth there and it was one of our own who had produced it.

When I took my seat in the auditorium beside Linda this evening I was unsure what was awaiting us. *Chaplin,* well, yes. Something someone like Fosnes Hansen writes an essay about when the topic is humour. And would I still find what I had laughed at fifteen years ago funny?

I would. And in exactly the same place. He comes on, greets the audience, his crib sheets fly out of his sleeves, he dances round the floor, with his feet somehow *behind* him, in tow, he doesn't lose contact with the audience for one second; the whole time he's dancing and searching he nods politely to them. A tear ran down my cheek at the ensuing pantomime. Everything was so wonderful that evening, I thought. We were giggling as we left the cinema, Linda was happy that I was so happy, I imagined, but also for her own part. We walked hand in hand up the stone steps beside the Finnish Cultural Institute, laughing as we regaled each other with scenes from the film. Then it was along Regeringsgatan, past the bakery, the furniture shop and US Video, unlock the door and up the stairs to our flat. It was a few minutes after half past ten, and Linda could barely keep her eyes open, so we went straight to bed.

Ten minutes later the music blared out beneath us again. I had completely forgotten about the Russian, and sat up in bed with a start.

'For Christ's sake,' Linda said. 'This can't be true.'

I could hardly hear what she was saying.

'It's not even eleven o'clock yet,' I said. 'And it's Friday evening. So we won't get anywhere.'

'I don't care,' Linda said. 'I'm going to ring. This is damn well not on.'

She had barely got up and left the room when the music stopped. We went back to bed. This time I was asleep when it started. At the same unbelievable volume. I looked at the clock. Half past eleven.

'Will you ring?' Linda asked. 'I haven't had a wink of sleep.'

But the same thing happened. After a few minutes she switched it off and there was silence below.

'I'll sleep in the living room,' Linda said

That night she turned on the music full blast twice more. The last time she had the audacity to play it for a full half-hour before switching off. It was ridiculous but also unpleasant. She was out of her mind, and had apparently developed a hatred for us. Anything could happen, we felt. But more than a week passed before the next incident occurred. We were putting some potted plants on the windowsill in the stairwell outside our door, this was a communal area and strictly speaking not any concern of ours, but on the floor above they had done the same, and surely no one could object to the cold staircase being brightened up a bit? Two days later the plants were gone. That didn't matter so much, but the pots had once belonged to my great-grandmother, some of the few items I had brought with me from the house in Kristiansand when my father's mother died – they were from the early 1900s, and so it was quite irritating that *they* had gone. Or had someone stolen them? But who would steal flower pots? Or had someone removed them because they took exception to our initiative? We decided to put a notice on the board asking if anyone had seen them. That same evening the notice was adorned with expletives and accusations written in blue ink and bad Swedish. Were we accusing the residents of stealing? If so, we could move out this minute. Who the hell did we think we were? A few days later I was assembling a nappy-changing table we had bought at Ikea, a bit of hammering was required, but as it was only seven in the evening I didn't think this would be a problem. But it was: after the first bangs with the hammer there was a wild pounding on the pipes below, it was our Russian neighbour's way of protesting about what she clearly regarded as a violation of house rules. But I couldn't let her stop me finishing, so I continued. A minute later the door below slammed and she was outside ours. I opened up. How could we complain about her when we made such a racket ourselves? I tried to explain to her the difference between playing loud music in the middle of the night and assembling a table at seven in the evening, but this fell on deaf ears. With the same wild eyes and indignant gestures she stuck to her guns. She had been asleep; we had woken her up. We thought we were better than her, but we were not . . .

From that day on she had a set strategy. Whenever a sound carried down to her, even if it was only me walking heavily across the floor, she banged on the pipes. The reverberation was penetrating, and since the sender was not visible, like a kind of bad conscience in the room. I hated it; it was as though I wasn't allowed to have any peace anywhere, not even in my own home.

Then, in the days before Christmas, all went quiet downstairs. We bought a Christmas tree from a stall in Humlegården; it had been dark, the air was laden with snow, and the typical pre-Christmas chaos reigned in the streets, with people racing past, oblivious to one another and the world. We chose one, the overalls-clad salesman pulled a net over it for ease of transport, I paid and lugged it over my shoulder. Only then did it strike me it might have been a trifle on the large side. Half an hour later, after innumerable stops on the way, I dragged it into our flat. We laughed when we saw it upright in the living room. It was enormous. We had bought a gigantic Christmas tree. But perhaps that was not so stupid, as this was the last Christmas we would be celebrating on our own. On Christmas Eve we ate the Swedish festive fare Linda's mother had brought us, unwrapped presents and watched Chaplin's *Circus* because we had bought ourselves a box set of all his films. We worked our way through the lot over the Christmas period, went for long walks in the holiday-empty streets, waited and waited. We forgot about the Russian, the outside world didn't exist for the whole of the Christmas weekend. We went to see Linda's mother, stayed there a few days, and on our return we started to prepare for a New Year's Eve dinner with Geir and Christina and Anders and Helena.

I cleaned the whole flat that morning, went shopping for dinner, ironed the big white tablecloth, inserted the extra leaf in the dining room table and laid it, polished the silverware and candlesticks, folded the serviettes and placed bowls of fruit on the table, such that by the time the guests arrived at seven the place was sparkling and glittering with bourgeois respectability. The first to arrive were Anders and Helena and their daughter. Helena and Linda had got to know each other when Helena took lessons with Linda's mother, and even though Helena was seven years older than Linda they had become the best of friends. Anders had been with her for the last three years. She was an actress; he was . . . well, a kind of criminal.

Faces flushed with the cold, they stood in the stairwell smiling when I opened the door.

'Hi there, old boy!' Anders said. He was wearing a brown leather cap with ear flaps, a large blue Puffa jacket and smart black shoes. Elegant he was not, but in some bizarre way he still blended in with Helena, who with her white coat, black boots and white fur hat most definitely was.

Beside them sat their daughter in her buggy, examining me with a serious gaze.

'Hi,' I said, looking her in the eye.

Not a muscle moved in her face.

'Come in!' I said, retreating a few steps.

'Can we bring the buggy in?' Helena asked.

'Of course,' I answered. 'Will it fit, do you think? Or should I open the second door?'

While Helena pushed the buggy forward and coaxed it into position between the door frames, Anders removed his outdoor clothing in the hall.

'Where's the señorita?' he asked.

'She's having a lie-down,' I said.

'Everything OK?'

'Yes, fine.'

'Good!' he said, rubbing his hands. 'So bloody cold outside!'

Helena came through the door, her hands gripping the buggy handle tightly. She activated the brake and lifted her daughter out, took off her hat and unzipped the red romper suit while her daughter stood stock still on the floor. Underneath, the little girl wore a dark blue dress, white tights and white shoes.

Linda came in from the bedroom. Her face was beaming. First of all, she hugged Helena, they held the embrace for a long time and looked each other in the eye.

'How pretty you look!' Helena said. 'How do you do it? I remember when I was in the ninth month . . .'

'It's just an old maternity dress,' Linda said.

'Yes, but all of *you* looks so nice!'

Linda smiled with pleasure, then leaned forward and gave Anders a hug.

'What a spread!' Helena exclaimed as she entered the living room. 'Wow!'

I didn't quite know what to do with myself so I went into the kitchen as if to check something or other while waiting for them to come down to earth. The next moment there was another ring at the door.

'So?' Geir said as I opened the door. 'Have you finished cleaning the place up?'

'Didn't know you two were coming,' I said. 'Thought we said Monday, didn't we? We're having a New Year's party here, so I'm afraid it's not very convenient right now. But, well, perhaps we can squeeze you in . . .'

'Hi, Karl Ove,' Christina said, giving me a hug. 'Everything all right with you?'

'Yes,' I said, stepping back to give them more room as Linda came through to welcome them. More hugs, more coats and shoes removed, everyone went into the living room, where Anders and Helena's daughter, who had begun to crawl around, was a welcome focus of attention for the first few minutes until the situation settled.

'You keep up the Christmas traditions, I see,' Anders said, nodding towards the enormous tree in the corner.

'It cost eight hundred kroner,' I said. 'It's going to stand there for as long as there is any life in it. We don't chuck money around in this house.'

Anders laughed.

'The boss has started to crack jokes!'

'I crack jokes all the time,' I said. 'It's just you Swedes who don't understand what I say.'

'Well,' he said. 'At the beginning at any rate I understood nothing of what you said.'

'So you bought yourselves a nouveau riche Christmas tree, did you?' Geir said while Anders started speaking pidgin Norwegian in the way that is so common in Sweden and which consists of a high-pitched *kjempe*, meaning huge, an occasional *gutt*, boy, which to Swedish ears sounds so comical, all pronounced in an enthusiastic tone that rises at the end of every sentence. It had nothing to do with my dialect, which they therefore assumed was *nynorsk*.

'It wasn't planned,' I said with a smile. 'It's a bit embarrassing to have such a big Christmas tree, I have to confess. But it seemed small when we bought it. It was only when we got it here that it became clear how enormous it was. But then I've always had problems with my sense of proportion.'

'Do you know what *kjempe* means, Anders?' Linda asked.

He shook his head.

'I know *avis*, newspaper. And *gutt*. And *vindu*, window.'

'It's the same as *jätte* in Swedish, big, huge.'

Did Linda think I was offended, or what?

'It took me six months to understand that,' she continued. 'It's used in exactly the same way. There must be loads of words I think I understand, but I don't. It hardly bears thinking about that I translated Sæterbakken's book two years ago. At that time I couldn't understand Norwegian at all.'

'Could Gilda?' Helena asked.

'Her? No. She knew even less than me. But I had a look at it not so long ago, the first pages, and it seemed fine. Apart from one word that is. I blush whenever I think about it. I translated *stue*, living room, with *stuga* . . . so he was sitting in a *stuga* when the text said he was in a living room.'

'What's *stuga* in Norwegian then?' Anders asked.

'*Hytte*,' I said.

'Oh, it's a *hytte*, a cabin! Yes, there's certainly a difference then . . .' he said.

'But no one has remarked on it,' Linda said. She laughed.

'Anyone fancy some champagne?' I asked.

'I'll fetch it,' Linda said.

On her return she gathered the five glasses together and started to loosen the wire holding the cork in place. Her face was slightly averted and her eyes were narrowed, as though anticipating a huge explosion. In the end the cork came off into her hand with a wet plop, and then she held the bottle, with the champagne pouring out, over the glasses.

'You managed that well,' Anders said.

'I worked in a restaurant a long time ago,' Linda said. 'But this was the one thing I could never do. I have no sense of depth anyway, so when I had to fill customers' glasses, it was hit and miss.'

She straightened up and passed the sparkling, bubbly champagne to us one by one. For herself she poured a non-alcoholic variant.

'*Skål*, then, and nice to see you!'

We toasted. When the champagne was finished I went into the kitchen to get the lobsters ready. Geir followed me and sat down at the table.

'Lobster,' he said. 'It's unbelievable how quickly you've adapted to Swedish society. I come to your place on New Year's Eve two years after you moved here and you serve traditional Swedish New Year fare.'

'I'm not exactly on my own,' I said.

'No, I know,' he said with a smile. 'We had a Mexican Christmas at home once, Christina and I did. Have I told you about it?'

'Yes,' I said and split the first lobster into two, placed it on a dish and started on the next. Geir began to talk about his manuscript. I listened with half an ear. Oh yes? I said now and then to signal that I was following even though my attention was elsewhere. He was unable to talk about his manuscript with everyone so it was only here he had the chance, and when I went out for a smoke, he saw his opportunity. He had written a rough draft, spent eighteen months on it, which I had read and commented on. The comments were comprehensive and detailed, they extended over ninety pages, and sadly the tone of the criticism was often sarcastic. I had imagined that Geir could take anything, but I should have known better, no one can take anything, and few things are as difficult to swallow as sarcasm when your own work is the target. But I couldn't stop myself, it was the same when I wrote reader reports, irony was never far away. The problem with Geir's manuscript, as he knew and admitted, was that the narrative was often too far removed from events, and a lot was often left unsaid. Only a fresh pair of eyes could remedy it. And that was what he got. But I was always ironic, much too ironic . . . was it perhaps caused by a subconscious desire on my part to get one over on him, the man who otherwise always reigned supreme.

No.

No?

'I'm terribly sorry about that,' I said now, placing the third lobster on its back and cutting through the shell on the stomach. It was softer than crab shell, and something about the consistency made me think it was artificial, like plastic. The red colour, wasn't there something unnatural about that too? And all the attractive, intricate details, like the grooves in the claws or the armour-like tail shell: didn't they look as if they had been forged in the workshop of a Renaissance craftsman?

'And so you should be,' Geir said. 'Ten Hail Marys for your evil, sinful soul. Can you imagine what it is like to pore over your comments and voluntarily allow yourself to be mocked by

them every single day? "Are you an absolute idiot or what?" Ye-es,
I suppose I am . . .'

'It's just a technical point,' I said, glancing at him while I
sawed through the shell with the knife

'Technical? Technical? Easy for you to say, that is. You can
spend twenty pages describing a trip to the loo and hold your
readers spellbound. How many people do you think can do that?
How many writers would not have done that if only they could?
Why do you think people spend their time touching up their
modernist poems, with three words on each page? It's because
they have no other option. After all these years surely you must
understand that, for Christ's sake. If they could have done, they
would have done. You can, and you don't appreciate it. It means
nothing to you, and you would rather be clever and write in
essayistic style. But everyone can write essays! It's the easiest
thing in the world.'

I looked at the white flesh with the red fibres which appeared
as soon as the shell was pierced. Recognised the faint tang of
seawater.

'You say you don't see the letters when you write, don't you?'
he continued. 'I don't see anything but bloody letters. They
intertwine like damn spiders' webs in front of my eyes. Nothing
can force its way out through that, you understand, everything
is turned inwards like some ingrowing toenail.'

'How long have you been working on it?' I asked. 'A year?
That's nothing. I've been writing for six years now, and all I have
to show for it is a stupid essay of a hundred and thirty pages
about angels. Come back in 2009 and I'll be more likely to feel
sorry for you then. Besides, it was good, the bit I read. Fantastic
story, great interviews. All it needs is to be checked over.'

'Ha!' Geir said.

I put two halves of lobster on the dish, shell up.

'You know that this is in fact the only hold I have over you?' I said, grabbing the last lobster.

'Not sure about that,' he said. 'There are at least a couple of other things you know about me that are best kept quiet.'

'Oh that,' I said. 'That's a completely different matter.'

He laughed loud hearty laughter.

Then a few seconds passed without a word being said.

Was he sulking?

I started to part the lobster with the knife.

It was impossible to say. If I hurt his feelings, he had once said, I would never know. He was as proud as he was haughty, as arrogant as he was loyal. He lost friends one after the other, perhaps because he so seldom backed down and was never afraid to say what he thought. And there was no one, or virtually no one, who liked what he thought. Last winter, a year ago, a very bad atmosphere had developed between us: whenever we went out we generally sat in silence on our bar stools, and if anything was said at all it was usually him making some acid remark about me or mine, with me trying to give as good as I got. Then I heard nothing from him. Two weeks later Christina rang to say he had gone to Turkey to do some fieldwork and would be away for several months. I was surprised, it was an unexpected development, and a little offended too, as he hadn't said anything about this to me. A few weeks later I heard from a friend in Norway that Geir had been interviewed by *Dagsrevyen* in Baghdad, where he had volunteered as a human shield. I smiled to myself, this was typical of him, although I was unable to understand why he had kept this a secret from me. Later it transpired that I had in fact upset him in some way. I never found out what had caused him to take umbrage. But when he came back to Stockholm four months later, loaded down with micro-cassettes of interviews, after having been under attack by bombs for several weeks, he seemed to be reinvigorated. All of the autumn and winter's crisis-like despondency had gone, and when we resumed our friendship it was where it had been when it started.

Geir and I were born in the same year, we had grown up a few kilometres from each other, on our separate islands outside Arendal – Hisøya and Tromøya – but without knowing each other as the initial natural point of contact would have come with *gymnas*, by which time I had long left for Kristiansand. The first time I met him was at a party in Bergen, where we both studied. He was on the periphery of the Arendal set, with whom I was also loosely connected through Yngve, and when I spoke to him I felt he might be the friend I was missing, for at that time, my first year in Bergen, I didn't have one and clung to Yngve. We went out some nights, he laughed all the time and had a devil-may-care attitude I liked, and he was genuinely interested in people around him and had something to say about them. He was the kind to cut through to the essence, and thus someone who made a difference. I had found a new friend; that was the good feeling I went around with during the spring of 1989. But then it transpired he was going to move on. Bergen was no place to set roots for him, he packed up as soon as the exams were over and went to Uppsala in Sweden. I wrote a letter to him that summer, never posted it however, and then he disappeared from my life and my thoughts.

Eleven years later he sent me a book in the post. It was about boxing and entitled *The Aesthetics of a Broken Nose*. After reading a few pages I was able to confirm that both his devil-may-care attitude and ability to cut through to the essence were intact, and also that a lot had been added since our student days. He had boxed at a club in Stockholm for three years in order to gain first-hand experience of the milieu he described. There the values that the welfare state had otherwise subverted, such as masculinity, honour, violence and pain, were upheld, and the interest for me lay in how different society looked when viewed from that angle, with the set of values they had retained. The art was to confront this world without everything you had from the other world – to try and see it as it was, on its own terms, that is – and then, with that as a platform, look outwards again. Then everything looked different. In his book Geir linked what he saw and described with the great classical anti-liberal cultures, in a line extending from Nietzsche and Jünger to Mishima and Cioran. There nothing was for sale, nothing could be measured in terms of monetary value, and therein, or seen from this perspective, I discovered to what great extent things I had always assumed were nature-given were in fact the opposite, namely relative and random. In this sense, Geir's book became as important to me as *Statues* by Michel Serres had been, where the archaic past in which we are and always have been steeped is thrown into relief with alarming clarity, and as *The Order of Things* by Michel Foucault had once been, where the grip that present time and contemporary language have on our notions and concepts of reality is made patently clear, and we see how one conceptual world, in which we are all completely immersed, is succeeded by another. What all these books had in common was that they established a reference point outside the present, either on its periphery, such as in the boxing club, which was a kind of enclave where some of the most important values from the recent past lived on, or in the depths of history, from where what we were, or imagined we were, became totally transformed. Presumably I had moved towards this point by small degrees, groping my way almost imperceptibly and more or less invisibly to my thinking, and then these books came into my life, they were virtually banged down on the table in front of me, and something new became clear to me. As is always the case with books that seem to be ground-breaking, they put into words what for me had been suspicions, feelings, hunches. A vague discomfort, a vague displeasure, a vague, untargeted anger. But no direction, no clarity, no exactitude. The reason Geir's book was so important to me also had to do with the fact that our backgrounds were so similar – we were exactly the same age, we knew the same people from the same places, we had both spent our adult lives reading and writing and studying – so how could it be that he had ended up in such a radically different place? Ever since I went to my first school I, and everyone around me, had been urged to think critically and independently. It had not occurred to me until I was well over thirty that this critical thinking was only of benefit up to a certain point and that beyond this it was transformed into its own opposite and became an evil, or evil itself. Why so late in life? one might wonder. Partly it was a result of my loyal-follower naïvety, which in its country-cousin gullibility might well cast doubt on opinions but never on the premises of those opinions, and hence never asked whether 'the critical' really was critical, whether 'the radical' really was radical, whether 'the good' really was good, things which all intelligent people do as soon as they escape the clutches of the self-intoxicated and emotion-laden views of youth; and partly it was because I had been trained, like so many of my generation, to think abstractly, in other words to acquire knowledge of various schools of thought in various fields, to reproduce them in a more or less critical manner, preferably contrasted with other schools of thought, and then to be judged on that, but sometimes it was for the sake of my own insight, my own intellectual curiosity, not that this gave my mind cause to abandon abstractions, such that thinking was in the end wholly an activity played out among secondary phenomena, the world as it appeared in philosophy, literature, social science, politics, whereas the world in which I lived, slept, ate, spoke, made love and ran, the one that had a smell, a taste, a sound, where it rained and the wind blew, the world that you could feel on your skin, was excluded, was not deemed a topic for thought. Actually, I did think there too, but in a different way, a more practical, phenomenon-by-phenomenon-orientated way, and for other reasons: while I thought in abstract reality in order to understand it, I thought in concrete reality in order to deal with it. In abstract reality I could create an identity, an identity made from opinions; in concrete reality I was who I was, a body, a gaze, a voice. That is where all independence is rooted. Including independent thought. Geir's book was not only about independence, it was also enacted within its terms of reference. He described only what he saw with his own eyes, what he heard with his own ears, and when he tried to describe what he saw and heard, it was by becoming a part of it. It was also the form of reflection that came closest to the life he was describing. A boxer was never judged by what he said or thought but by what he did.

Misology, the distrust of words, as was the case with Phyrros, Phyrromania; was that a way to go for a writer? Everything that can be said with words can be contradicted with words, so what's the point of dissertations, novels, literature? Or put another way: whatever we say is true we can also always say is untrue. It is a zero point and the place from which the zero value begins to spread. However, it is not a dead point, not for literature either, for literature is not just words, literature is what words evoke in the reader. It is this transcendence that validates literature, not the formal transcendence in itself, as many believe. Paul Celan's mysterious cypher-like language has nothing to do with inaccessibility or closed-ness, quite the contrary, it is about opening up what language normally does not have access to but which we still, somewhere deep inside us, know or recognise, or if we don't, allows us to discover. Paul Celan's words cannot be contradicted with words. What they possess cannot be transformed either, the word only exists there, and in each and every single person who absorbs it.

The fact that paintings and, to some extent, photographs were so important for me had something to do with this. They contained no words, no concepts, and when I looked at them what I experienced, what made them so important was also non-conceptual. There was something stupid in this, an area that was completely devoid of intelligence, which I had difficulty acknowledging or accepting, yet which perhaps was the most important single element of what I wanted to do.

Six months after I had read Geir's book, I emailed him and asked if he would like to write an essay for *Vagant*, where I was on the editorial staff. He said he would, we emailed back and forth, all in formal and factual terms. A year later, when from one day to the next I left Tonje and my life with her in Bergen, I emailed to ask if he knew of anywhere to live in Stockholm; he didn't, but I could stay at his place while I was looking for something. Sounds good, I wrote. Fine, he wrote, when are you coming? Tomorrow, I wrote. Tomorrow? he wrote.

Some hours later, after a night on the train from Bergen to Oslo, and a morning on the train from Oslo to Stockholm, I schlepped my bags from the platform down to the corridors beneath Stockholm Central in search of a left-luggage locker big enough to take them both. I had spent the whole journey reading to avoid thinking about what had happened in the preceding days, all of which was the reason for my departure, but now in the midst of the thronging crowds of people heading to or from commuter trains it was impossible to suppress my unease any

longer. Feeling cold to the depths of my soul, I walked down the
corridor. After stowing the two bags in separate lockers and
putting the two keys in the pocket where I normally kept my
house keys, I entered the toilet and washed my face with cold
water to make myself feel more alive. I studied myself in the
mirror for a few seconds. My face was pale and slightly bloated,
hair unkempt and eyes ... yes, my eyes ... staring, but not in
an active outward-facing fashion, as though they were looking
for something, more as if what they saw was drawn into them,
as if they sucked everything in.

Since when had I had such eyes?

I turned on the hot-water tap and held my hands underneath
it for a while, until the heat began to spread through them, tore
off a sheet of paper from the dispenser and dried them, threw
it in the bin beside the sink. I weighed 101 kilos and had no
hopes for the future, but now I was here, that was something,
I thought, and then went out, up the steps and into the
concourse, where I stood in the middle, surrounded by people
on all sides while I tried to devise some kind of plan. It was just
past two o'clock. I was due to meet Geir here at five. So I had
three hours to kill. I had to eat. I needed a scarf. And I ought to
have a haircut.

I walked out of the station and stopped at the taxi stand. The
sky was grey and cold, the air damp. To the right was a jumble
of roads and concrete bridges, behind them a lake, behind that
a line of monument-like buildings. To the left, a broad street
full of traffic; directly in front of me a street which some way
off swung left alongside a filthy wall, beyond that a church.

Which way to go?

I placed one foot on a bench, rolled a cigarette, lit it and
started walking down to the left. After a hundred metres or so
I stopped. It didn't look promising, everything here had been

built with the cars which whizzed past in mind, and I turned
and went back, tried the road ahead instead, which led into a
wide avenue with an enormous brick department store on the
other side. Beyond that was a kind of square, sunk into the
ground as it were, from which rose a large glass construction
on the right. KULTURHUSET it said in red letters, and I went in,
took the escalator up to the first floor on which there happened
to be a café, bought a baguette with meatballs and red cabbage
salad and sat down by a window from where I had a view of the
square and the street in front of the department store.

Was I going to live here? Was this where I lived now?

Yesterday morning I had been at home in Bergen.

Yesterday, that was yesterday.

Tonje had accompanied me to the train. The artificial light
above the platforms, the passengers outside the carriages, who
were already prepared for the night and talking in hushed voices,
the rolling of suitcase wheels over the tarmac. She cried. I didn't,
just hugged her, brushed the tears from her cheeks, she smiled
through the tears and I boarded the train, thinking I didn't want
to see her walk away, didn't want to see her back, but I couldn't
stop myself, peered out of the window and watched her walk
down the platform and disappear through the exit.

Would she stay there?

In our house?

I took a bite of the baguette and looked down at the black
and white checked square to divert my thoughts. The line of
shops on the other side was black with people. In and out of
the doors to the Metro they went, in and out of the tunnel to
the gallery, up and down the escalators. Umbrellas, coats, jackets,
bags, plastic carrier bags, rucksacks, hats, buggies. Above them
cars and buses.

The clock on the department store wall said ten minutes to

three. Perhaps it would be best to have a haircut now to avoid
having to rush it at the end, I thought. Going down the escalator,
I took out my mobile phone and perused the names saved under
contacts, but I didn't feel I could ring any of them, there was
too much that would have to be explained, too much that would
have to be said, too little in return, so emerging into the dreary
March afternoon again with a few heavy snowflakes falling, I
switched it off and put it back in my pocket before heading
down Drottninggatan on the lookout for a hairdresser's. Outside
the department store a man was playing the harmonica. Or
rather, he wasn't playing, he was just blowing into the instru-
ment with all his might while jerking his body backwards and
forwards. His hair was long, his face ravaged. The immense
aggression he radiated flowed straight into me. As I passed him
fear pounded in my veins. Behind him, by the entrance to a shoe
shop, a young woman was bending down over a buggy and lifting
up a child. It was swathed in a kind of fur-lined bag, with its
head wreathed by a fur-lined hat, and staring straight ahead,
seemingly unaffected by what was happening to it. She squeezed
it to her chest with one hand and opened the shoe-shop door
with the other. The snow that was falling melted as it hit the
ground. A man was sitting on a folding chair holding a large
sign proclaiming that fifty metres to the left there was a restaurant where you could buy a planked steak for the sum of 109
kroner. Planked steak? I wondered. Many of the women passing
by looked alike: they were in their fifties, wore glasses, coats,
were plump and carrying bags inscribed with Åhléns, Lindex,
NK, Coop or Hemköp. There were fewer men of the same age,
but many of them looked alike too, albeit in different ways.
Glasses, sandy hair, pallid eyes, greenish or greyish jackets with
a touch of casualness about them, more often thin than fat. I
longed to be alone, but there was no chance of that, and I

wandered up the street. All the faces I saw were of strangers, and would continue to be so for weeks and months as I didn't know a soul here, but that didn't prevent me from feeling that I was being watched. Even when I lived on a tiny island far out into the sea with only three inhabitants I felt I was being watched. Was there something wrong with my coat? My collar, shouldn't it be turned up like that? My shoes, did they look the way shoes should? Was I walking a bit oddly? Leaning too far forward maybe? Oh, I was an idiot, what an idiot. The flame of stupidity burned bright inside me. Oh, such an idiot I was. What a stupid, idiotic bloody idiot. My shoes. My coat. Stupid, stupid, stupid. My mouth, shapeless, my thoughts, shapeless, my feelings, shapeless. Everything was spongy. There was nothing firm anywhere. Nothing solid, nothing vital. Soft, spongy and stupid. Oh fuck. Oh fuck, fuck, fuck, how stupid I was. I couldn't find any peace in a café, within a second I had taken in everyone there, and I continued to do so, and every glance that came my way penetrated into my innermost self, jangled about inside me, and every movement I made, even if only flicking through a book, was likewise transmitted outwards to them, as a sign of my stupidity, every movement I made said, 'This is an idiot sitting here.' So it was better to walk, for then the looks disappeared one by one, admittedly they were replaced by others, but they never had time to establish themselves, they just glided past, there goes an idiot, there goes an idiot, there goes an idiot. That was the chorus as I walked. And I knew it didn't make sense, this was of my own making, inside myself, but it didn't help, because they still got inside, into my inner self, they rumbled around inside me, and even the most maladjusted of these people, even the ugliest, the fattest and the shabbiest of them, even that woman with the drooping jaw and the vacant idiot-eyes, even she could look at me and then say there was something

wrong with me. Even her. That was how things were. There I
was, walking through the crowds beneath the darkening sky,
through falling snowflakes, past shop after shop with illuminated interiors, alone in my new town, without a thought as to
how things would be here, because that made no difference, it
really didn't make any difference, all I was thinking about was
that I had to get through this. 'This' was life. Getting through
it, that was what I was doing.

I found a hairdresser's I hadn't seen when I passed by the first
time, in a passage beside the big department store. I just had to
take a seat. No wash, my hair was moistened with water from
a spray. The hairdresser, an immigrant, a Kurd I guessed, asked
how I wanted it, I said short, indicated with my thumb and first
finger how short I had in mind, he asked what I did, I said I was
a student, he asked where I came from, I said Norway, he asked
if I was here on holiday, I said yes, and that was it. My locks fell
on the floor around the chair. They were almost completely
black. That was strange because when I looked in the mirror I
had fair hair. It had always been like that. Even though I knew
my hair was dark I couldn't see it. I saw fair hair, as it had been
in my boyhood and teens. Even in photos I saw fair hair. Only
when it had been cut and I saw it separately, against white floor
tiles for example, as here, could I see it was dark, almost black.

In the street half an hour later, the cold air gathered around
my shorn head like a helmet. It was almost four o'clock, the sky
almost pitch black. I went into an H&M shop I had spotted earlier
to buy a scarf. The men's department was in the basement. As
I was unable to find the scarves after searching around for a
while I went to the counter and asked the young girl standing
there where they were.

'*Ursäkta*?' she said in Swedish.

'Where do you keep the scarves?' I repeated in Norwegian.

'*Jag fattar tyvärr inte vad du säger,*' she answered, before saying, in English: 'I'm sorry. What did you say?'

'The scarves,' I said in Norwegian, holding my neck. 'Where are they?'

'Do you speak English?' she said. 'I don't understand.'

'Scarves,' I said in English. 'Do you have any scarves?'

'Oh, scarves,' she said. 'We call them *halsduk*. No, I'm sorry. It's not the season for them any more.'

Back in the street, I wondered for a second whether to go into Åhléns, as the large department store was called, to look for a scarf there, but rejected the idea, I had been through enough idiocy for one day, and instead started to walk up the street again, towards the boarding house where I had stayed two years previously, for no other reason than that it was better to walk with a goal than without. On the way I passed a second-hand bookshop. The shelves inside were tall and so close to each other that there was barely room to turn around. After casting an indifferent glance at the spines of the books I was about to leave when I caught sight of a Hölderlin on the top of a pile at the corner of the counter.

'Is this for sale?' I asked the assistant, a man of my own age who had already been eyeing me for a while.

'Of course,' he said blankly.

Sånger it was called. Was that perhaps a translation of *Die vaterländischen Gesänge*?

I flicked through to the colophon page. The year of publication was 2002. So it was quite new. But there was nothing about the title there, so I skimmed through the afterword, stopping at every word in italics. And yes. There it was: *Die vaterländischen Gesänge. Hymns of the Fatherland.* But why on earth had they translated the title as *Sånger*?

It didn't matter.

'I'll take it,' I said, again in Norwegian. 'How much do you want for it?'

'Excuse me?'

'How much does it cost?'

'Let me have a look and I'll check . . . A hundred and fifty kroner, please.'

I paid, he put the book in a little bag and handed it to me with the receipt, which I shoved into my back pocket before opening the door and leaving with the bag dangling from my hand. Outside it was raining. I stopped, took off the rucksack, stuffed the bag in it, put the rucksack back on and continued along the brightly illuminated shopping street, where the snow which had been falling for several hours had left no trace other than a grey slushy layer on all surfaces above ground level: roof projections, window-sills, the heads on the statues, floors of verandas, awnings, which sagged making the canvas bulge close to the outer frame, tops of walls, dustbin lids, hydrants. But not the street. It lay black and wet, glistening in the lights from windows and street lamps.

The rain caused some of the gel the hairdresser had rubbed into my hair to run down my forehead. I wiped it away with my hand, wiped it on the thighs of my trousers, spotted a small gateway on the right-hand side of the street and went there to light up. Inside, there was a long garden with at least two different restaurant terraces. With a small pool in the middle. On the wall beside the entrance was the name of the Swedish Writers' Association. That boded well. The association was one of the places I had intended to ring to enquire about somewhere to live.

I lit the cigarette, took out the book I had bought, leaned back against the wall and somewhat half-heartedly started to flick through it.

*

Hölderlin had long been a familiar name to me. Not that I had read him systematically, not at all, a couple of sporadic poems in Olav Hauge's collection of translations was the sum total, apart from knowing, in the most superficial of ways, about the fate that befell him, the years of madness in the tower in Tübingen; nevertheless his name had been with me for a long time, roughly since the age of sixteen, when my uncle Kjartan, my mother's ten-year-younger brother, first started talking about him. He was the only sibling to live in his childhood home, a modest smallholding in Sørbøvåg in Ytre Sogn, with his parents: grandad, my mother's father, who at that time was approaching eighty but was still active and full of vitality, and grandma, who was in the latter stages of Parkinson's disease and therefore needed help to do virtually everything. As well as running the smallholding, which, though it was no bigger than five acres, demanded considerable time and energy, and caring for his mother, which, in effect, was a twenty-four-hour job, he also worked as a ship's plumber at a yard over twenty kilometres away. He was an unusually sensitive man, as delicate as the most delicate of plants, with absolutely no interest in or talent for the practical sides of life, so everything he did, what consti- tuted the basis of his everyday life, he must have had to force himself to do. Day in, day out, month in, month out, year in, year out. Sheer unmitigated willpower. That he had come to this was not necessarily due to the fact that he had never succeeded in breaking out of the conditions he was born into, as one might perhaps imagine, just staying in his familiar environment because it was familiar, it was more likely a conse- quence of his sensitive nature. For where could a young man with a proclivity for ideals and perfection turn in the mid-1970s? Had he been young in the 1920s, like his father, maybe he would have sought out and felt at home in the vital nature-loving late

romantic current that swept through our culture, at least in
the *nynorsk*-writing section of it, the one within which Olav
Nygard, Olav Duun, Kristoffer Uppdal and Olav Aukrust wrote
and which Olav Hauge was later to carry over into our own age;
had he been young in the 1950s it might perhaps have been
the notions and theories of cultural radicalism he would have
absorbed, unless, that is, its opposite, the slowly dying forces
of cultural conservativism had caught hold of him first. His
youth, however, had been spent neither in the 1920s nor the
1950s, but in the early 1970s, so he became a member of the
(Marxist–Leninist) Communist Workers' Party and proletari-
anised himself, as the expression went in those days. Started
working as a pipe fitter on ships because he believed in a better
world than this. Not only for a few months or years, as was the
case for most of his party colleagues, but for nigh on two decades.
He was one of the very few who didn't give up his ideals when
times changed, but clung to them even though the cost, both
social and private, increased as time passed. Being a communist
in a rural community was a different matter from being a
communist in an urban setting. In a town you were not alone,
there were other, like-minded people, there was a community
spirit, in addition to which your convictions were not visible
in all contexts. In the country you were 'the communist'. That
was his identity, his life. Being communist at the beginning of
the 70s, being borne on the wave, was also quite a different
matter from being a communist in the 1980s, when all the rats
had long since left the ship. A lonely communist sounds like a
paradox, but that was how it was for Kjartan. I remember my
father having discussions with him those summers when we
visited my grandparents, their loud voices coming from the
living room below when we were trying to sleep, and even
though I couldn't articulate it, nor think it, I could sense there

was a difference between them, and that the difference was fundamental. For my father the discussions had limited scope, their sole function was to point out to Kjartan how he was deluding himself, for Kjartan they were a question of life and death, all or nothing. Hence the irritation in my father's voice, the fervour in Kjartan's. It was also apparent, or so it seemed to me at any rate, that my father's words were grounded in the real world, that what he said and thought belonged here, was related to us, to our schooldays and football matches, our comics and fishing trips, our snow-shovelling and Saturday porridge, while Kjartan spoke of something else, something related to another place. Of course he could not accept that what he believed in, and in a way had dedicated his life to, had nothing to do with reality, as my father, along with everyone else, asserted on every occasion. That reality was not as Kjartan described it and never would be. That would have implied he was a dreamer. And a dreamer was precisely what he was not! Concrete, material, physical, down-to-earth reality was precisely what he was talking about! The situation was highly ironic. There he was defending theories about sticking together and solidarity, yet he was the one who had been ostracised and stood alone. He was the one who observed the world through idealistic abstract eyes, who had a more refined soul than any of the others, he was the one who lifted and carried, hammered and pounded, welded and screwed, scrabbled and crawled round ship after ship, who milked the cows and fed them, who shovelled muck into the muck cellar and in the spring spread it over the fields, who mowed the grass and dried the hay, maintained buildings and looked after his mother, who needed more and more help as the years passed. That became his life. The fact that communism began to wane at the beginning of the 1980s, and that the intense discussions he'd had on all sides imperceptibly abated until one day they were completely gone might have changed the meaning of it, but not the content. It continued as before, along the same course: up at the crack of dawn to milk and feed the cows, catch the bus to the shipyard, work all day, come home and see to his parents, walk his mother around the living room, if she was capable of it, or sit bending and massaging her legs, help her to the toilet, maybe get her clothes ready for the following day, do whatever had to be done outdoors, whether it be bringing in the cows and milking them or something else, then back to his place, have supper and sleep until the next morning – unless grandma was taken so ill that grandad had to fetch him in the course of the night. This was Kjartan's life, as it appeared from the outside. When his communist phase started I was only a couple of years old, and when it ended, at least the active, rhetorical part, I had just finished first school, so all of it was no more than a vague backdrop to the image I had of him when I turned sixteen and started taking an interest in who people 'were'. More significant by far for my image of him was the fact that he wrote poetry. Not because I was fond of poetry, but because it 'said' more about him. You didn't write poems if you didn't have to, that is, unless you were a poet. He didn't talk to us about it, but made no secret of it either. At any rate, we knew about it. One year some poems were published by *Dag og Tid*, another year in *Klassekampen*, small simple pictures of an industrial worker's reality which despite their modest proportions had gained a certain prestige in the Hatløy family, where books enjoyed great popularity. When he had a poem published on the back page of the literary journal *Vinduet* beside a small photograph of himself, and then a few years later his poems covered two whole pages of the same publication he was, in our eyes, a fully blown poet. It was at this time he started reading philosophy. Of an evening he sat in the house high above the fjord fighting his way through Heidegger's incredibly intricate German in *Sein und Zeit* – presumably word by word, because to my knowledge he had not read or spoken German since his schooldays – and the poets Heidegger wrote about, especially Hölderlin and the pre-Socratic writers he referred to, and Nietzsche. Nietzsche. He later described reading Heidegger as like a homecoming. It is no exaggeration to say that it filled him to the brim. And that it was a kind of religious experience. An awakening, a conversion, an old world was filled with new meaning. At that time my father had left the family, so Yngve, my mother and I had begun to celebrate Christmas at our grandparents' where Kjartan, now in his mid-thirties, still lived and worked. The four or five Christmas Eves we were there are without doubt the most memorable I have experienced. Grandma was ill and sat huddled at the table, shivering. Her hands shook, her arms shook, her head, her feet. Now and then she had bouts of cramp and had to be taken to a chair where her legs had to be practically forced into a bent position and then massaged. But her mind was clear, her eyes were clear; she saw us and she was happy to see us. Grandad, small and rotund and lively, told us stories whenever he could, and when he laughed, as he always did at his own stories, the tears rolled down his cheeks. But this didn't happen as often as it could have done because Kjartan was there, and Kjartan had sat for a whole year reading Heidegger, had been filled with Heidegger amid the grinding pointless working life of his without a soul to share it with, because no one within a radius of several kilometres had even heard of Heidegger, and no one wanted to either, although I had an inkling he had tried various people, he must have done, so taken with him was he, but it led nowhere, no one understood, no one wanted to understand, he was on his own with this, and then in we walked, his sister Sissel, who was a nursing teacher, interested in politics, literature and philosophy, her son Yngve, who went to university, something Kjartan had always dreamed of doing, more and more so in recent years, and her son Karl Ove. I was seventeen years old, at *gymnas*, and even though I didn't understand a word of his poems he knew I read books. That was enough for him. We came in the door and his sluice gates opened. All the thoughts that had accumulated over the last year came flooding out. It didn't matter that we didn't understand, it didn't matter that it was Christmas Eve, that the mutton ribs, potatoes, mashed swede, Christmas ale and aquavit were on the table; he talked about Heidegger from within, without a single communicative link to the outside world, it was *Dasein* and *Das Man*, it was Trakl and Hölderlin, the great poet Hölderlin, it was Heraclitus and Socrates, Nietzsche and Plato, it was the birds in the trees and the waves in the fjord, it was man's *Dasein* and the advent of existence, it was the sun in the sky and the rain in the air, the cat's eyes and the plummeting waterfall. With his hair sticking out in all directions, his suit askew and his tie full of stains he sat there talking, his eyes aglow, they were really glowing, and I will always remember it, for it was pitch dark outside, the rain was beating against the windows, it was Christmas Eve in Norway 1986, our Christmas Eve, the presents were under the tree, everyone was dressed up, and the sole topic of conversation was Heidegger. Grandma was shivering, grandad gnawing at a bone, mum listening attentively, Yngve had stopped listening. As for me, I was indifferent to everything, and above all happy it was Christmas. But even though I didn't understand a word of what Kjartan said, and nothing of what he wrote, nor anything of the poems he praised with such passion, I did understand intuitively that he was right, that there was such a thing as a supreme philosophy and a supreme poetry, and that if you didn't understand it, were unable to partake in it, you only had yourself to blame. Since then, whenever I have thought about the supreme, I have thought about Hölderlin, and when I've thought about Hölderlin it has always been associated with mountains and fjords, night and rain, the sky and the earth and my uncle's glowing eyes.

Although much had changed in my life since then my attitude to poetry was basically the same. I could read it, but poems never opened themselves to me, and that was because I had no 'right' to them: they were not for me. When I approached them I felt like a fraud, and I was indeed always unmasked, because what they always said as well, these poems, was, Who do you think you are, coming in here? That was what Osip Mandelstam's poems said, that was what Ezra Pound's poems said, that was what Gottfried Benn's poems said, that was what Johannes Bobrowski's poems said. You had to earn the right to read them.

How?

It was simple. You opened a book, read, and if the poems opened themselves to you, you had the right, if not, you didn't. In my early twenties and still full of notions of what I could be, it bothered me a lot that I was one of those for whom the poems did not open. For the consequences of this were serious, much more so than merely being excluded from a literary genre. It also passed judgment on me. The poems looked into another reality, or saw reality in a different way, one which was truer than the way I knew, and the fact that it was not possible to acquire the ability to see and that it was something you either had or you didn't condemned me to a life on a lower plane, indeed, it made me one of the lowly. The pain of that insight was immense. And strictly speaking there were only three ways of reacting. The first was to admit it to yourself and accept it for what it was. I was an ordinary man who would live an ordinary life and find meaning where I was, nowhere else. In practice that was the way it looked too. I liked watching football and played too whenever I had the chance, I liked pop music and played drums in a band a couple of times a week, I attended lectures at university, went out a fair amount or lay on the sofa at home watching TV in the evenings with the woman I was with at the time. The second way was to deny everything, by telling yourself that it existed inside you but it had not yet come to fruition, and then live a life in the world of literature, perhaps as a critic, perhaps as a university lecturer, perhaps as an author, because it was entirely possible to stay afloat in that world without literature ever opening up to you. You could write a whole dissertation about Hölderlin, for example, by describing the poems, discussing what they dealt with and in what ways the themes found expression, through the syntax, the choice of words, the use of imagery; you could write about the relationship between Hellenic and Christian modes, about the role of the countryside in his poems, about the role of the weather, or how the poems relate to the actual politico-historical reality in which they had arisen, independent of whether the main emphasis was on the biographical, for example his German Protestant background, or on the enormous influence of the French Revolution. You could write about his relationship to other German idealists, Goethe, Schiller, Hegel, Novalis, or the relationship to Pindar in the late poems. You could write about his unorthodox translations of Sophocles, or read the poems in the light of what he says about writing in his letters. You could also read Hölderlin's poetry with reference to Heidegger's understanding of it, or go one step further and write about the clash between Heidegger and Adorno over Hölderlin. You could also write about the whole history of his work's reception, or of his works in translation. It was possible to do all of this without Hölderlin's poems ever opening themselves. The same could be done with all poets, and of course it has been. You could also, if you were willing to put in the hard work, write poems yourself if you were one of those for whom poems did not open themselves; after all, only a poet would see the difference between poetry and poetry that resembles poetry. Of these two methods the first, accepting the fact, was the better, but also the more difficult option. The second method, denying it, was easier but also more unpleasant because you were constantly on the verge of the insight that what you were doing actually had no value. And if you lived in the world of literature it was precisely value you were seeking. The third method, which was based on rejecting the whole issue, was therefore the best. There is nothing higher. There is no such thing as privileged insight. Nothing is better or truer than anything else. The poems did not open themselves for me, but that did not necessarily mean I was inferior to them, or that what I wrote necessarily had less value. Both of them, the poems that did not open themselves and what I wrote, were basically the same, namely text. If mine proved to be worse, which of course it was, this was not the result of an irremediable condition – I didn't have it in me – but was something that could be changed through hard work and increasing experience. Up to a certain limit, of course, concepts such as talent and quality were still indispensable; not everyone was able to write well. The crux was that there was no barrier, nothing insuperable, between those who had it and those who did not; those who saw and those who did not. Rather, it was a question of degrees within the same scale. This was a gratifying thought, and not hard to justify, after all this way of thinking had been dominant in all spheres of art and criticism, as well as at universities from the middle of the 1960s until now. The ideas I had nurtured, and which had been such a natural part of me that I didn't even realise they were ideas, and accordingly had never articulated, only felt, but which nonetheless had had a controlling influence over me, were Romanticism in its purest form, in other words antiquated. The few who engaged seriously with Romanticism were preoccupied with those aspects that fitted into the contemporary world of ideas, such as the fragmentary or the ironic. But for me Romanticism was not the point – if I felt an affinity to any era, it was the Baroque period. I was attracted to its sense of space, its dizzying heights and depths, its notions about life and theatre, mirrors and bodies, light and dark, art and science – it was more my sense of standing outside the essence, standing outside what was most meaningful, outside what constituted existence. Whether this sense was Romantic or not was beside the point. To dull the pain it caused I had over the years defended myself using all three of the above-mentioned methods, and for long periods believed in them, especially the last. My notion that art was the place where the flames of truth and beauty burned, the last remaining place where life could show its true face, was crazy. But now and then this notion broke through, not as a thought, for it could be argued out of existence, but as a feeling. I knew with my whole being that the notion was a lie, that I was deceiving myself. This was what was in my mind as I stood there in the gateway outside the Swedish Writers' Association in Stockholm one afternoon in March 2002 flicking through Fioreto's translation of Hölderlin's last great hymns.

Oh, wretched me.

A constant stream of new people walked past the gateway. The light from the lamps hanging from cables above the street glinted on padded jackets and carrier bags, tarmac and metal. A faint hum of footsteps and voices traversed the space between the lines of houses. Two pigeons stood motionless on a first-floor window ledge. Water collected in heavy drops at the end of the rail on the awning projecting from the wall and every so often detached themselves and fell to the ground. I had put the book into my rucksack, and now I took out my mobile phone from my jacket pocket to see what the time was. The display was dark, so I turned it on as I began to walk. A message came in. It was from Tonje.

Have you arrived? Thinking about you.

Those two sentences made her feel close. The image of her, the woman she was for me, completely overcame me for a moment. Not just her face and manner, the way it is when you think about someone you know, but everything her face could be, all the indefinable features, incredibly clear nonetheless, which a person radiates to those who love them. But I wasn't going to answer. The whole point of leaving was to get away from her, so as a wave of sorrow at everything washed through me I deleted the message and clicked back to the clock screen.

16.21.

I had just over half an hour before I was to meet Geir.

Unless we had said half past four?

Had we?

Shit, we had! We were meeting at half past four, not five.

I turned and set off at a run. After a couple of blocks I stopped to regain my breath. The man sitting with the arrow-shaped board in his hands looked at me with listless eyes. I took that as a sign, and turned into the street where the arrow was pointing. When I reached the crossroads at the other end, sure enough the railway station was right in front of me, and on a wall down a short side street I spotted a yellow sign saying Arlanda Express. The train to the airport. It was 16.26. If I was going to be punctual I would have to run the last stretch as well.

Across the street, into the airport train terminal, along the platform, into the entrance hall, past the kiosks and cafés, benches and left luggage lockers and into the main concourse, where I stopped so out of breath that I had to lean forward and support myself with my hands on my knees.

We had agreed to meet by the circular railings in the middle of the concourse, where you could look down at the lower floor. When I straightened up to look for the railings, I saw the clock on the wall stood at exactly half past.

There.

I chose a somewhat circuitous route, right over by the line of kiosks, and waited by the wall some distance away so that I could see Geir before he saw me. It was twelve years since I had seen him, and even then maybe only four or five times over two months, so from the moment he had answered my email and said I could stay with him, I had feared I wouldn't be able to recognise him. 'Recognise' is perhaps an inappropriate term in that I didn't have a single picture of him. When I thought about Geir it was not his face I visualised but the letters in his name – Geir that is – and a vague memory of someone laughing. The only scene I remember with him was in the bar at Fekterloftet in Bergen. Him laughing and saying, 'You're an existentialist!' Why I should remember that of all things I had no idea. Perhaps because I didn't know what an existentialist was? And was flattered because my opinions fitted into a well-known philosophical category?

I still didn't know what an existentialist was. I knew the concept, could cite a few names and a time, but was unable to recall the precise definition.

The king of approximation, that was me.

I took off my rucksack and placed it on the floor between my feet, rolled my shoulders as I watched the people at the railing.

None of them could be Geir. If anyone appeared answering to the vague description I had remembered I would go over to him and hope he recognised me. At worst I could ask, 'Are you Geir?'

I looked up at the clock at the end of the concourse. Five minutes late.

Had we said five after all?

For some reason I was sure he was the punctual type. In that case it must have been five we had arranged. I had seen an Internet café in the entrance hall, and after waiting a bit longer I went there to confirm my suspicions. I also felt a need to read his email again, gauge the tone, then perhaps the impending situation would seem slightly less unfamiliar.

The language problems I'd encountered so far resulted in my confining what I said to the girl behind the counter to: *Internet?* She nodded and pointed to one of the computers. I sat down, logged into my email site and saw there were five new messages, which I skimmed. All of them from the editorial staff at *Vagant*. Even though it had not been more than twenty-four hours since I was sitting in Bergen, it felt as though the discussion between Preben, Eirik, Finn and Jørgen on screen was taking place in another world where I no longer belonged. As though I had crossed a line, as though in fact *I could not return*.

I was there yesterday, I told myself. And I still haven't decided how long I will be staying here. I can return in a week if I like. Or tomorrow.

But that was not how it felt. It felt as if I would never return.

I turned my head and looked towards the Burger King. On the nearest table a paper cup of Coke had been knocked over. The black liquid had formed a long oval puddle and was still dripping from the table edge onto the floor. At the table behind, a man was sitting with his knees pinched together and eating as if it were a punishment: for a few seconds his hand sped between the carton of chips, the small tub of ketchup and the chewing mouth, then he swallowed, grabbed the hamburger with both hands, put it to his lips and took a large bite. While he munched he held the hamburger as if at the ready, a few centimetres from his mouth, and then took another bite, wiped his lips with the back of one hand and lifted the beaker of Coke with the other, glancing at the three black-haired teenage girls chatting round the adjacent table. One of them looked in my direction, and I glanced first at the entrance, where two uniformed flight attendants came through the door into the concourse, each with a roller bag in tow, and then back at the computer screen, with the sharp, rapidly fading click-clacking sounds of their heels in my ears.

What if I never returned? I had after all been longing for this. To be here, alone, in a foreign town. No lies, no one else, just me, free to do what I wanted.

So why this feeling of heaviness?

I clicked on Geir's emails and began to read.

Dear Karl Ove,

An altogether excellent idea. Uppsala is, as you say, a university town, very much so. The town can be compared with Sørland at the turn of the century, a place to send your children so that they can learn how to roll their 'r's properly. Stockholm is one of the world's most beautiful capital cities, anything but relaxed though. Sweden as such is a fantastic paradox, on the one hand known far and wide for its open borders, on the other Europe's most segregated country. If you don't fancy Uppsala, I would recommend you live in Stockholm. (Whatever you choose they're only 40–50 minutes apart by train and one goes every half an hour.)

As for flats, bedsits and rooms for rent, they are by no means easy to get hold of. It's worse if anything in Uppsala because of all the new students. Difficult, though not impossible. Off the top of my head I can't think of anyone with a room to rent, but I'll ask around. Since you, if I've understood correctly, are not moving for good, but to begin with only until the end of the year it should be possible to get hold of what is known here as a 'second-hand flat'. There are agencies that specialise in them. Have you contacted SFF, the Swedish Writers' Union, by the way? It is not inconceivable that they have flats for foreign writers or at least that they know someone who does. If you want I can ring round to agencies, associations, etc.

Today is Saturday 16 March. Would you like to come over one weekend, or perhaps better midweek when everything's open, just to see whether you like it here? Or have you already decided? In which case, next week I'll start to enquire about available flats at the beginning of next week. At all events, you're welcome to stay here whether you're on holiday or flat hunting.

Looking forward to seeing you,

Geir

Karl Ove,

Unless you're already on the train, give me a ring as soon as you're in Oslo or Stockholm! Don't waste your money on a hotel, and don't be shy. I have selfish reasons for this – you speak fluent Norwegian. My vocabulary is shrinking. Incidentally, Uppsala University was founded in 1477.

My number in Stockholm is 708 96 93.

Geir

So you don't like phones, eh? Let's say the main railway station then (where your train arrives) at five this afternoon. There's a circular railing (in local parlance, the poof ring) in the middle of the concourse. I'll meet you there. But call me if you get held up! (You can't object to phones that much.)

Geir

That was the correspondence. I didn't doubt the sincerity of his offer to let me stay with them, but still I found it hard to accept. Meeting somewhere for a cup of coffee would have been more appropriate for the circumstances. On the other hand, I didn't have anything to lose. And he did come from the island of Hisøya.

I closed the email and cast a glance at the table where the three girls were, before grabbing my rucksack and getting to my feet. The one doing the talking spoke with a kind of aggrieved passion, immensely self-assertive, and was applauded with the same passion. If they hadn't been speaking I would have thought they were around nineteen. Now I knew they were closer to fifteen.

The nearest of them turned her head and met my stare again. Not to offer me anything – it was not an open look – but to confirm that I was looking at her. Nevertheless it opened up something. A flash of something like happiness. Then, as I went to the cash desk to pay, the thunder of consciousness followed. I was thirty-three years old. A grown man. Why was I thinking as if I was still twenty? When would these youthful fancies leave me? When my father was thirty-three he had a son of thirteen and one of nine, he had a house and a car and a job, and in photos of him from that time he looked like a man, and from what I could remember he also behaved like a man, I thought as I stepped up to the counter. Placed a warm hand on the cool marble surface. The assistant rose from a chair and came over to take payment.

'How much is it?' I asked in Norwegian.

'*Ursäkta?*'

I sighed.

'What does it cost?'

She glanced at the screen in front of her.

'Ten,' she said.

I handed her a creased twenty-krone note.

'That's fine,' I said, walking away before she had a chance to answer with another *Ursäkta?*, which this country seemed to be awash with. The clock on the wall in the main concourse said six minutes to five. I took up my old position and watched the people hanging around the rail. As none of them fitted the little I had to go on I allowed my gaze to wander among those walking through the station. From the kiosk on the other side came a short man with a large head and an appearance so unusual I couldn't take my eyes off him. He was in his fifties, his hair was a yellowish colour, his face broad, nose large, mouth slightly askew and his eyes were small. He looked like a gnome. But he was dressed in a suit and coat, in one hand he held an elegant leather briefcase, tucked under his arm he had a newspaper, and perhaps another personality was thrusting forth beneath the metropolitan exterior, which meant that my eyes were glued to him until he disappeared down the stairs to the platforms where the commuter trains departed. Suddenly, again, I saw how old everything was. Backs, hands, feet, heads, ears, hair, nails: every single part of the bodies streaming through the concourse was old. The buzz of voices rising from them was old. Even their pleasure was old, even the wishes and expectations of what the future would bring were old. Yet new, for us the future was new, for us it belonged to our time, belonged to the queue of waiting taxis outside, belonged to the coffee machines on the tables in the cafés, belonged to the shelves of magazines in the kiosks, belonged to the mobiles and iPods, the Goretex coats and laptops carried in their bags through the station and into trains, belonged to the trains and automatic doors, to the ticket machines and illuminated boards with changing destinations. Old age had no place here. Yet it completely dominated everything.

What a terrible thought that was.

I stuck a hand in my pocket to check the locker keys were there. They were. Then I patted my chest to feel for my credit card. It was there.

In the thronging masses before me a familiar face appeared. My heart beat faster. But it wasn't Geir, it was someone else. An even more remote acquaintance. A friend of a friend? Someone I had gone to school with?

I grinned as it clicked. It was the man from Burger King. He stopped and looked at the departures board. Between the thumb and first finger of the hand carrying the briefcase he was holding a ticket. As he checked the time on the board with the time on his ticket he raised the whole briefcase towards his face.

I glanced at the clock at the end of the concourse. Two minutes to. If Geir was as punctual as I assumed, he should be somewhere in the station by now, and I systematically scanned all the figures in the approaching crowd. First left, then right.

There.

Surely that had to be Geir?

Yes. It was. I remembered the face when I saw it. And he was not only walking towards me, he also had his eyes fixed on me.

I smiled, wiped my palm over my thigh as discreetly as I could, and reached out as he stopped in front of me.

'Hi, Geir,' I said. 'Long time.'

He smiled too. Let go of my hand almost before he held it.

'You can say that again,' he said. 'And you haven't changed in the slightest.'

'Haven't I?' I said.

'No. It's just like meeting you in Bergen. Tall, serious, wearing a coat.'

He laughed.

'Shall we go?' he suggested. Where are your bags, by the way?'

'In a locker downstairs,' I answered. 'Perhaps we could have a coffee first?'

'Certainly can,' he said. 'Where?'

'Makes no odds,' I said. 'There's a café by the entrance.'

'OK. Let's go there.'

He led the way, stopped at a table, asked without looking at me if I wanted milk or sugar, and went to the counter while I removed my rucksack, sat down and took out my tobacco. Watched him exchange a few words with the waitress, saw him hand her a note. Even though I had recognised him, and the buried image I must have had of him therefore fitted, his aura was different from what I expected. It was much less physical, almost completely lacking the bodily weight I had ascribed to him. Presumably I had done that because I knew he had been a boxer.

I felt a strong desire to sleep, to lie down in an empty room, switch off the light and disappear from the world. That was what I was longing for, while what awaited me, hours of social obligations and small talk, seemed unbearable.

I sighed. The electric light in the ceiling, which spread its lustre over everything in the station concourse, and here and there was reflected in a glass pane, on a piece of metal, a marble tile or a coffee cup, should have been sufficient to make me happy that I was here and able to see it. All the hundreds of people drifting to and fro across the floor of the station hall in such a shadowy fashion should have been sufficient to make me happy. Tonje, who I had been with for eight years, sharing my life with her, as wonderful as she was, should have made me happy. Meeting my brother Yngve with his children should have made me happy. All the music around me, all the literature around me, all the art around me, it should have made me happy, happy, happy. All the beauty in the world, which should have been unbearable to behold, left me cold. My friends left me cold. My life left me cold. That was how it was, and that was how it had been for so long that I could no longer stand it and had decided to do something about it. I wanted to be happy again. It sounded stupid, I couldn't say it to anyone, but that was how it was.

I lifted the half-rolled cigarette to my lips and licked the glue, pressed it down with my thumbs so that it stuck against the paper, pinched off the loose tobacco at each end and dropped it into the gleaming white insides of the pouch, straightened the flap so that it slipped down into the light brown tangled mass of tobacco, closed the pouch, stuffed it in the pocket of the coat hanging over the chair, poked the cigarette in my mouth and lit it with the tall quivering yellow flame from the lighter. Geir had taken two cups and stood pouring coffee while the waitress placed his change on the counter and turned to the next customer, a long-haired man in his fifties wearing a hat and boots and a cape-like poncho-style garment.

No, Geir didn't radiate any aura of physical presence. The aura he gave off, which had been obvious from the moment he no longer had eye contact with me, from when he let go of my hand and his eyes began to roam, was more one of restlessness. He seemed to want constant motion.

He came across the floor with a cup in each hand. I couldn't help but smile.

'So,' he said, putting the cups down on the table, pulling out a chair, 'you're moving to Stockholm?'

'Looks like it,' I said.

'In which case my prayers have been answered,' he said without looking at me. He was studying the table, his hand round the handle of the cup. 'I don't know how many times I've told Christina I wished a Norwegian with literary interests would move here. And then you appear.'

He lifted the cup to his mouth and blew over the surface before drinking.

'I wrote you a letter the summer you went to Uppsala,' I said. 'A long letter. But I never sent it. It's still at my mother's unopened. I haven't a clue what's in it.'

'You're joking!' he said, staring at me.

'Do you want it?'

'Of course I want it! And don't even think about opening it. It has to stay at your mother's. That's a piece of sealed time!'

'Perhaps it is,' I said. 'I don't remember a thing from then. And I've burned all the diaries and manuscripts I wrote in those days.'

'Burned?' Geir asked. 'Not thrown away but burned?'

I nodded.

'Dramatic,' he said. 'But then you were like that when you were in Bergen too.'

'Was I?'

'Oh yes.'

'But you weren't?'

'Me? No. No, I wasn't.'

He laughed. Twisted his head and watched the crowd going past. Twisted it back and surveyed the café's other customers. I tapped the tip of the cigarette against the ashtray. The smoke rising from it billowed gently in the draught from the doors, which kept opening and closing. When I looked at him it was in brief, almost imperceptible, glances. In a way the impression he gave was independent of his face. His eyes were dark and sorrowful, but there was nothing dark or sorrowful about his aura. He seemed happy and diffident.

'Do you know Stockholm?' he asked.

I shook my head.

'Not very well. I've only been here for a few hours.'

'It's a fine town. But as cold as ice. You can live your whole life here without coming into close contact with anyone. Everything is set up in such a way that you don't get close to others. Look at the escalators,' he said, nodding towards the concourse where I presumed the escalators were. 'Those who stand, stand on the right-hand side, those who walk, walk on the left. When I'm in Oslo I'm amazed at all the times I bump into people. There's constant nudging and elbowing. All that business of going left first, then right, then left again when you're in someone's way in the street, you know, that just doesn't happen here. Everyone knows where they're going, everyone does what they are supposed to do. At the airport there's a yellow line by the baggage carousel and you mustn't cross it. And no one does. Baggage distribution is a nice orderly process. And that's the way conversations are organised in this country as well. There's a yellow line you mustn't cross. Everyone's polite, everyone's well mannered, everyone says what they are supposed to say. It's all about avoiding offence. If you're used to this, it comes as a shock to read newspaper debates in Norway. What heated discussions they have! They shout at each other! That's inconceivable here. And if you see a Norwegian professor on TV here – it hardly ever happens, no one cares about Norway, Norway

doesn't exist in Sweden – on the rare occasions they do appear,
they look like wild men with unkempt hair and untidy or unorthodox clothes, and they say things they shouldn't. It's part of
the Norwegian academic tradition, as you know, where education
doesn't have or shouldn't have any outward manifestation . . .
or where the outer manifestation of academia should reflect
idiosyncrasies and individualism. Not the universal and the
collective, as is the case here. But of course no one understands
that. Here they see only wild men. In Sweden they all think the
Swedish way is the only one. Any deviations from the Swedish
way they regard as flaws and deficiencies. The thought of it is
enough to drive you insane.'

Yes, that's right, it was Jon Bing, that's who I had seen just
before I met Geir. He looked all wrong. Long hair and beard, and
I think he was wearing a knitted cardigan.

'A Swedish academic looks neat and tidy, behaves tidily, says
what everyone expects, in a manner everyone expects. *Everyone*
behaves tidily here by the way. That is, everyone in the public
eye. Things look a little different at street level. They released
all the psychiatric patients in this country a few years ago. So
you see them walking around and mumbling and shouting
everywhere. They've arranged it so that the poor live in particular
areas, the affluent in particular areas, those active in cultural
circles in particular areas and immigrants in particular areas.
You'll get to see what I mean.'

He raised his coffee cup to his lips and took a sip. I didn't
know what to say. What he had said was not prompted by the
situation, except that I had just arrived from Norway, and it was
formulated in such a way, came in such a coherent flow, that it
seemed prepared. This was something he *said*, I inferred, this
was one of his favourite topics. My experience of the type of
person who enjoys such topics was that it was important to wait

until the worst pent-up emotion had passed because more often than not a different kind of attention and presence was waiting on the other side. Whether his assertions were right or not I didn't know, my intuition was they were driven by frustration, and he was actually expressing what was causing the frustration. It might have been Sweden. It might have been something in him. It didn't matter to me, he could talk about what he wanted, that wasn't why I was sitting here.

'Sport and academia go together in Norway, and beer drinking and academia,' he said. 'I remember that from Bergen. Sport was big among students. But here they are irreconcilable entities. I'm not talking about scientists but intellectuals. In academic circles here intellectuality is paramount, it's all that exists, everything is subservient to the intellect. The body, for example, is conspicuous by its absence. Whereas in Norway intellectuality is played down. Hence, in Norway the common touch is no problem for an academic. I suppose the idea is that the backdrop should allow the intellect to gleam like a diamond. In Sweden the intellect's surroundings also have to gleam. It's the same for culture with a capital C. In Norway it is downplayed. In fact, it is not allowed to exist. Elitist culture is not allowed to exist unless it's populist at the same time. In Sweden it is emphasised. Popular and elitist cultures are irreconcilable. One should be *here*, the other should be *there*, and there is supposed to be no interchange between the two. There are exceptions, there always are, but this is the rule. Another great difference between Norway and Sweden is to do with roles. The last time I went to Norway I caught the bus from Arendal to Kristiansand, and the bus driver was going on about how he wasn't a bus driver really, really he was something else, he was just doing this to help tide him over to Christmas. And then he said we should look after one another during the festive period. He said that over the loudspeakers!

Unthinkable in Sweden. Here you identify with your work. You simply don't step out of your role. There are no gaps in this role, there is nowhere you can stick your head out and say, This is the real me.'

'So why do you live here?' I asked.

He directed a fleeting glance at me.

'It's a perfect country if you want to be left in peace,' he said, letting his eyes roam again. 'I don't object to coldness. I don't want it in my life, but I can easily live my life within it, if you understand the difference. It's nice to look at. And it's practical. I despise it, but I also benefit from it. So, shall we go?'

'Yes, let's,' I said, stubbing out the cigarette, drinking the last drop of coffee, unhitching my coat from the chair, putting it on, swinging the rucksack over my shoulder and following him into the concourse. When I was alongside him he turned to me.

'Can you walk on the other side? I'm a bit hard of hearing in that ear.'

I did as he asked. Noticed his feet were at ten to two, like duck feet. I had always reacted to this. Ballet dancers walk like this. Once I had a girlfriend who was a ballet dancer. It was one of the few things I didn't like about her, walking with her feet sticking out to the side.

'Where are your bags?' he asked.

'Down below,' I answered. 'Then to the right.'

'Let's go down then,' he said, motioning towards a staircase at the end of the station.

As far as I could see, there was no difference between how people behaved here and in Oslo Central Station. At least nothing obvious. The differences he had been talking about seemed minimal, presumably they had been ratcheted up after many years of exile.

'Looks pretty much like Norway to me,' I said. 'Just as much bumping into one another.'

'Just you wait,' he said with a glance and a smile. It was a wry smile, a superior-knowledge smile. If there was something I couldn't bear it was the profession of superior knowledge, in whatever form it came. It asserted I knew less.

'Look there,' I said, stopping and pointing to the electronic board above us.

'What at?' Geir asked.

'The arrivals board,' I said. 'This is why I came here. For this very reason.'

'What do you mean?' Geir asked.

'Look. Södertälje. Nynäshamn. Gävle. Arboga. Västerås. Örebro. Halmstad. Uppsala. Mora. Göteborg. Malmö. There's something incredibly exotic about it. About Sweden. The language is almost the same, the towns are almost the same. If you look at Swedish rural districts they're similar to the districts in Norway. Apart from minor details. And it's these small divergences, these small differences that are *almost* familiar, *almost* the same, yet aren't, that I find so unbelievably attractive.'

He stared at me in disbelief.

'You're crazy!' he said.

Then he laughed.

We set off again. It was unlike me to say anything like this, out of the blue, but it had felt as if I should make my case, not allow him to dominate.

'I've always felt that attraction,' I continued. 'Not for India or Burma or Africa, the big differences, that has never interested me. But Japan, for example. Not Tokyo or the cities, but the rural areas in Japan, the small coastal towns. Have you seen how similar the landscape is to ours in Norway? But the culture, their houses and their customs, are totally alien, totally incomprehensible. Or

Maine in the USA? Have you seen the coast there? The terrain is
so similar to Sørland, but everything man-made is American. Do
you understand what I mean?'

'No, but I'm listening.'

'That was all,' I said.

We descended into the underground hall, also packed with
people on the move, went to the luggage lockers and I pulled
out two bags. Geir took one and we made our way through the
hall to the Metro platforms a few hundred metres away.

Half an hour later we were walking through the centre of a
1950s satellite town, which in the March street-lamp-illuminated
darkness appeared to be fully intact. It was called Västertorp. All
the buildings were square and made of brick, differing from one
another only in size and surrounded on all sides by high-rise
blocks. The buildings in the town centre were lower with a
variety of shops on the ground floor. Pine trees stood motionless
between the blocks. I could see the occasional hill and glimpse
the occasional lake between the tree trunks in the light from
the many front entrances and windows that seemed to have shot
up from the ground. Geir talked without cease, as he had also
done on the Metro journey here. For the main part he had been
explaining whatever we saw. In between, there had been the
sound of the station names, so wonderful and unfamiliar.
Slussen, Mariatorget, Zinkensdamm, Hornstull, Liljeholmen,
Midsommarkransen, Telefonplan . . .

'There it is,' he said, pointing to one of the houses by the road.

We went in one entrance, up a staircase, through a door. Books
lined the wall, a compact row of jackets on clothes hangers, the
aroma of someone else's life.

'Hi, Christina, aren't you going to say hello to our Norwegian
friend?' he said, peering into the room on the left. I stepped

forward. A woman sitting at a table inside, with a pencil in her hand and paper in front of her, looked up.

'Hello, Karl Ove,' she said. '*Trevligt* to meet you. I've heard so much about you.'

'I haven't heard anything about you, I'm afraid,' I said. 'Well, apart from the little that's in Geir's book.'

She smiled, we shook hands, she began to clear the table and put on some coffee. Geir showed me the flat, it didn't take long. It consisted of two rooms, both covered with floor-to-ceiling bookshelves. In one, the living room, there was a corner where Christina worked; Geir worked in the second, which was a bedroom. He opened some of the glass cabinets and showed me the books. They were so straight you would have thought he had used a spirit level, and they were organised according to series and authors, not alphabetically.

'You're organised, I can see,' I said.

'I'm organised in everything,' he said. 'Absolutely everything. There's nothing in my life that I have not planned or allowed for.'

'That sounds frightening,' I said and looked at him.

He smiled.

'For me it's frightening to meet someone who moves to Stockholm at one day's notice.'

'I had to,' I said.

'To will is to have to will,' he said. 'As the mystic Maximos says in *Emperor and Galilean*. Or to be precise, "What is the value of living? Everything is sport and mockery. To *will* is to *have* to will." That was the play in which Ibsen tried to be wise. Erudite, at any rate. He makes a stab at a huge damn synthesis there. "I defy necessity! I will not serve it. I am free, free, free." It's interesting. "A hell of a good play," as Beckett says about *Waiting for Godot*. I was really taken by it when I read it. He communicates with a time that is past. All the learning, which is a prerequisite, has gone. It's very interesting. Have you read it?'

I shook my head.

'I haven't read any of his historical plays.'

'It was written at a time when everything was being re-evaluated. That's what he does. Catilina, you know, was a symbol of treachery. But Ibsen gives him a makeover. It's as though we should have done the same to Quisling almost. He had balls when he was writing it. But all the values he turns round come from antiquity, and that makes it almost impossible for us to understand. We don't read Cicero, do we . . . We-ell, writing a play in which he attempts to unite emperors and Galileans! He fails, of course, but at least he fails big time. He's too symbolic there. But also bold. You can see how much he wants the big time. I don't think I believe Ibsen when he says he only read the Bible. Schiller gets a look-in here. *Die Räuber.* The Robbers. There's also a kind of rebel figure. Like *Michael Kohlhaas* by Heinrich von Kleist. By the way, there's a parallel with Bjørnson. Is it *Sigurd Slembe*, can you remember?'

'I don't know anything about Bjørnson.'

'I think it's *Sigurd Slembe*. The time to act. To act or not to act. It's classic Hamlet. To be an actor in your own life or a spectator.'

'And you are?'

'Good question.' A silence arose. Then he said, 'I'm probably a spectator, with elements of choreographed action. But I don't really know. I think there's a lot inside me that I can't see. And so it doesn't exist. And you?'

'Spectator.'

'But you're here. And yesterday you were in Bergen.'

'Yes. But this is not the result of any decision. It was forced.'

'That's perhaps another way of making a decision, hm? Letting whatever happens do it for you?'

'Maybe.'

'That's strange, that is,' he said. 'The more unreflective you are, the more active you are. You know, the boxers I wrote about had an incredible presence. But that meant they weren't spectators of themselves, so they didn't remember anything. Not a thing! Share the moment with me here and now. That was their offer. And of course that works for them, they always have to enter the ring again, and if you've been given a pasting in the previous fight it's best if you don't remember it too well, otherwise you've had it. But their presence was absolutely amazing. It filled everything. *Vita contemplativa* or *vita activa*, I suppose they're the two forms, aren't they? It's an old problem of course. Besets all spectators. But not actors. It's a typical spectator problem . . .'

Behind us, Christina stuck her head through the door.

'Would you two like some coffee?'

'Please,' I said.

We went into the kitchen and sat down round the table. From the window there was a view of the road, which lay deserted under the street lighting. I asked Christina what she had been drawing when we arrived and she said she was making models of shoes for a factory in the far north of the country. The absurdity of sitting in a kitchen in the middle of a Swedish satellite town with two people I didn't know suddenly struck me. What was I doing? What was I doing here? Christina started making dinner, I sat in the living room with Geir telling him about Tonje, how it had been, what had happened, how my life in Bergen had been. He summarised in a similar way what had happened in his life since he had left Bergen thirteen years before. What caught my attention most was a debate he'd had in *Svenska Dagbladet* with a Swedish professor who had made him so angry that one morning he had nailed up the last defamatory arguments on the castle door in Uppsala like a second Luther. He had also tried to piss on the door, but Christina had dragged him away.

We had lamb burgers, fried potatoes and Greek salad. I was starving, the plates were empty within seconds and Christina wore a guilty expression. I met her apologies with counter-apologies. She was clearly cut from the same cloth as me. We drank some wine, chatted about the differences between Sweden and Norway, and while I thought to myself, no, Sweden's not like that, and Norway's not like that, I nodded and played along. At around eleven I could barely keep my eyes open, Geir brought some bed linen, I would be sleeping on the living-room sofa, and while we stretched out the sheet his face suddenly changed. *His face was completely different.* Then it changed back, and I had to make an effort to keep it fixed, that was what he looked like, that was him.

It changed again.

I secured the last flap under the mattress and sat down on the sofa. My hands were shaking. What had happened?

He turned to me. His face was once more as it was when I had met him at Central Station.

'I haven't said anything about your novel yet,' he said, taking a seat on the other side of the table. 'But it made an indelible impression on me. I was deeply shaken after reading it.'

'Why's that?' I asked.

'Because you went so far. You went so unbelievably far. I was glad you did, I was sitting here, smiling, because you had brought it off. When we met you wanted to be a writer. No one else had had the idea. Only you. And then you achieved it. But that wasn't why I was shaken. It was because you went so far. Do you really have to go that far, I thought at the time. And it was frightening. Speaking for myself, I can't go that far.'

'What do you mean? How do you mean I went so far? It's just a standard novel.'

'You say things about yourself it's unheard of to say. Not least the story of the thirteen-year-old. I'd never have thought you would dare.'

A cold wind seemed to blow through me.

'I don't quite understand what you're talking about,' I said. 'I made it up. It wasn't so much of an effort, if that's what you think.'

He smiled and looked me straight in the eye.

'You told me about the relationship when we met in Bergen. You'd come from northern Norway the summer before, but you were still full of what had happened up north. That was what you talked about. Your father, and then falling in love when you were sixteen and you had identified with Hamsun's Lieutenant Glahn, and you said you'd had a relationship with a thirteen-year-old when you were a teacher in northern Norway.'

'Ha ha,' I said. 'That's not very funny, in case you think it is.'

He wasn't smiling any more.

'Are you saying you don't remember? She was in your class, you had fallen for her hook, line and sinker, I gathered, but everything was a mess; you said, among other things, you'd spoken to her mother at a party – and the scene is precisely in the novel as you'd described it to me. There's nothing necessarily wrong with that though, if you know the desire is mutual, mind you. But how you know that is quite a different matter. That's the problem. I've got an old school pal who impregnated a thirteen-year-old – he was seventeen I should add, while you were eighteen, but what the fuck, that part is irrelevant here. What's relevant is that you wrote about it.'

He looked at me.

'What is it? You look as if you've seen a ghost.'

'You don't mean it seriously, do you?' I said. 'That I said that?'

'Yes, I do. You did say that. It's etched into my memory.'

'But it didn't happen.'

'You definitely said that it did.'

It felt like a hand was squeezing my heart. How could he say such a thing? Could I have repressed such a major event? Just shrugged it off and forgotten all about it, and then written it all down without thinking for a moment that it was true?'

No.

No, no, no.

It was unthinkable.

Absolutely, totally unthinkable.

So how could he say such a thing?

He got up.

'I'm sorry, Karl Ove,' he said. 'But you did say it.'

'I don't understand,' I said. 'But I don't have the impression you're lying.'

He shook his head and smiled.

'Sleep well then.'

'Sleep well.'

Listening to the faint sounds of a couple settling down for the night in the bedroom on the other side of the door, I lay with my eyes open, staring into the room. It was filled with the weak moon-like light from the street lamps outside. My mind ran wild trying to find a solution to what Geir had said while my feelings had already condemned me: such a firm grip did they have on my innards that my whole body hurt. Now and then there was a low hum, coming, I supposed, from the Metro a few hundred metres away, in which I sought solace. Beneath it there was a kind of distant roar which, if I hadn't known better, sounded like the sea. But I was in Stockholm, there had to be a big motorway nearby.

I rejected all of it, that I might have repressed anything so significant was out of the question. Yet there were large holes in my memory. I had drunk a lot in the days I lived in the north, like the young fishermen I hung around with at weekends, a bottle of spirits vanished in the course of an evening, at least one. Entire evenings and nights had disappeared from my memory, and were left like tunnels inside me, full of darkness and winds and my own skirling emotions. What had I done? What had I done? When I started studying in Bergen it continued, whole evenings and nights disappeared, I was on the loose in the town, that was how it felt, I could arrive home with the front of my jacket covered in blood. What had happened? I could arrive home in clothes that weren't mine. Could wake up on a roof, could wake up under a bush in the park, and once I had woken up in the corridor of an institution. The police had come and taken me away. Questioning followed: someone had broken into a nearby house and stolen money, was it me? I didn't know, but I said no, no, no. All these holes, all this unthinking darkness over so many years in which some mysterious almost ghostly event could be played out on the periphery of my memory had filled me with guilt, large tracts of guilt, and when Geir told me I had said I'd had a relationship with a thirteen-year-old in northern Norway, I could not, with my hand on my heart, say no, I hadn't, for there was some doubt, so much had happened, why not this too?

Part of this burden was also what had happened between Tonje and me, and not least what was going to happen.

Had I left her? Was our life together over? Or was this just a break, a few months of separation for both of us to think things through, each from our own angle?

We had been together for eight years, married for six of them. She was still the person I was closest to, it was barely twenty-four hours since we had shared a bed, and if I didn't turn away now, didn't look in a different direction, it would remain like that because this, I intuited, was up to me.

What did I want?

I didn't know.

I was lying on a sofa just outside Stockholm, knowing not a soul, and everything in me was chaos and unrest. The uncertainty penetrated to my core, through to that which defined who I was.

A face appeared in the glass door to the tiny balcony. It disappeared as I stared at it. My heart beat faster. I closed my eyes, and the same face appeared to me there. I saw it from the side, it turned to me and stared right at me. It changed. It changed again. It changed again. I had never seen any of these faces before, but all of them were profoundly realistic and significant. What kind of parade was this? Then the nose became a beak, the eyes predator eyes and suddenly a hawk was sitting inside me and staring.

I turned on my side.

All I wanted was to be a decent person. A good, honest, upright person who could look people in the eye and everyone knew they could trust.

But such was not the case. I was a deserter, and I had done terrible things. And now I had deserted again.

The next morning I was woken by Geir's high-pitched voice. He sat on the end of the sofa holding a cup of burning hot coffee out for me.

'Good morning!' he said. 'It's seven o'clock! Don't tell me you're a night owl?'

I sat up and scowled at him.

'I usually get up at one in the afternoon,' I said. 'And I can't talk to anyone for the first hour.'

'Worse luck you!' Geir said. 'Anyway, I'm not a spectator of my own life, that's simply wrong. I see others, I'm good at that, but I don't see myself. Not a hope. Besides, spectator is perhaps the wrong word in this context. It's a kind of euphemism. The real question is whether you are capable of action or not. Do you want the coffee or not?'

'I always drink tea in the morning,' I said. 'But I'll take it as a favour to you.'

I took the coffee and sipped.

'*Emperor and Galilean*, to finish the conversation,' he said, 'failed basically for the same reason that *Zarathustra* did. But the point is, and I didn't get round to this yesterday, that what they say can only be said as a result of having failed. That's important.'

He looked at me as if expecting an answer. I nodded a couple of times, took another sip of coffee.

'And as far as your novel is concerned, it wasn't primarily the story about the thirteen-year-old that shook me. It was the fact that you went so far, put so much of yourself into it. That requires courage.'

'Not for me,' I said. 'I don't give a shit about myself.'

'And it's noticeable! But how many are like you?'

I shrugged. I wanted to slump back on the sofa and go on sleeping, but Geir was almost jumping around on the arm.

'How about a trip to town? So that I can show you around. Stockholm has no soul, but it's fantastically beautiful. There's no way of getting away from that.'

'Fine,' I said. 'Though perhaps not right this minute? What is the time actually?'

'Ten past eight,' he said, standing up. 'Get your rags on and we'll have some breakfast. Christina's making bacon and eggs.'

No, I didn't want to get up. And having forced myself to, I didn't want to leave the flat. What I fancied was occupying the sofa for the rest of the day. After breakfast I tried to delay departure, but Geir's energy and willpower were of the inflexible variety.

'Bit of walking'll do you good,' he said. 'In your depressed state staying indoors would be the death of you, surely you understand that. So, up you get! Come on! We're going now!'

On the way to the Metro station, with him striding out and me lagging behind, he turned to me with a grimace which was probably meant to be a smile.

'Have you retrieved the events in northern Norway from your subconscious now, or is it still just as black?' he asked.

'I sussed out what had happened just before I fell asleep,' I said. 'I don't mind admitting it was a relief. For a while I thought you were right and I had in fact repressed the whole business. It was nothing special.'

'And what's the explanation then?'

'You mixed up three different stories and made one, either then or when you read the book. I had a girlfriend up there, but she was sixteen and I was eighteen. No, hang on, she was fifteen. Or sixteen. I'm not sure. Not thirteen anyway.'

'You said you were in love with one of your students.'

'I could not have said that.'

'You bloody well did. I've got the memory of an elephant.'

We stopped by the barriers, I bought a ticket and then we walked down the long concrete tunnel to the platform.

'There was one girl in love with me, I remember. That must be what you can remember. And so you've mixed her up with the girlfriend I had and was actually in love with.'

'It may have been like that,' he said. 'But that's not what you told me.'

'Pack it in now, for Christ's sake. I haven't come to Stockholm to find more problems. The whole point was to get away from them.'

'You've come to the right man then,' he said. 'I won't say another word.'

We caught the Metro to town, emerged from one station after the other all day, each time a new urban landscape revealed itself, all very beautiful. But I couldn't fit it all together: in the four to five days we wandered around from early morning to late afternoon Stockholm was no more than unconnected fragments for me. We walked side by side, he pointed left and we went left, right and we went right, all the while talking in loud enthusiastic tones about what we saw and all his associations. Now and then I got tired of the unequal power distance, with him deciding everything, and then I said no, we won't go right, we're going left, and he smiled and said, OK, if that makes you happy, or fine, if that makes you feel better. We had lunch at a new place every day. In Norway I was used to something on bread, I dined out maybe twice a year; Geir and Christina did it every day, often both lunch and dinner, compared with Norway it cost nothing, and the choice was enormous. My instinct was the student cafés – in other words, those places that most resembled what I knew from Bergen – but Geir refused, he wasn't twenty any more, as he put it, and wanted nothing to do with youth culture. In the afternoons and evenings he forced me to contact all the Swedes I knew, all the Swedes I had dealt with during my time at *Vagant*, all the Swedes my editor knew, because he said it was nigh on impossible to find a place to live in this town, everything worked through contacts. I didn't want to, I wanted to sleep, lounge about, but he kept nudging me, this had to be done, there was no way out. We went to a big poetry slam – Danish, Norwegian, Swedish and Russian writers reading their works, among them Steffen Sørum, who opened by saying 'Hello, Stockholm!' as though he was some sodding rock star, and I blushed on behalf of our country. Inger Christensen read.

A Russian staggered drunkenly around the stage shouting that no one liked poetry – YOU ALL HATE POETRY! he yelled – while his Swedish translator, a bashful man with a little rucksack on his back, tried to calm him down and finally, as the Russian paced the stage in silence, managed to read some poems. It ended with a warm reconciliation when the Russian first poked the translator in the back and then hugged him. Ingmar Lemhagen was in the audience, he knew everyone, and through him I managed to slip backstage and asked all the Swedish writers if they knew of anywhere to stay. Raattamaa had a flat, he said, I could move in next week in fact, no problem. We went out with them, first to Malmen, where the Swedish poet Marie Silkeberg leaned over to me and asked why especially she should read my novel, and the best reply that occurred to me was that perhaps it was the kind of book you were simply drawn into, to which she responded with a fleeting smile and subsequently, not so fast that it was offensive, nor so slowly that it was without significance, glanced round for someone else to talk to. She was a poet; I was a writer of light fiction. Afterwards everyone went back to hers for drinks. Geir was, unlike me, full of contempt for poets and poetry, he viewed them with hatred in his eyes and he ended up at odds with Silkeberg merely by implying that such a large flat in such a central location must have cost quite a packet. As we walked down towards Slussen in the early morning he spoke about the cultural middle class, all the privileges they had, how literature was merely a ticket into society, and he spoke about their manifold ideologies. He talked about their so-called solidarity with the worse off, their flirtations with the working class and their undermining of such entities as quality, and what a catastrophe it was that quality was subordinate to politics and ideology, not only in literature, but also in universities, and its logical conclusion, in the whole of society.

I couldn't relate any of this to the reality I knew, I contradicted him occasionally, saying he was paranoid, that he was making sweeping statements, there was always a person behind an ideology, and sometimes I just let him prattle away. However, he said, as we were going through the station barriers and boarding the escalator, Inger Christensen was unique. She was utterly fantastic. In a league of her own. Although everyone says so, and you know what I think of consensuses, she was.

'Yes,' I said.

Beneath us the draught from the approaching train blew a plastic bag up from the platform. Like an animal with headlamps as eyes, the train appeared at the other end of the darkness.

'She was a different class,' Geir said. 'World class.'

I hadn't experienced anything special when she read. But before the reading I had wondered about her: a small plump elderly woman drinking at the bar with a handbag over her arm.

'*The Butterfly Valley* is a sonnet cycle,' I said, stepping onto the platform as the train came to a halt. 'It must be the most exacting form of all. The first line of all the sonnets has to form the final, concluding sonnet.'

'Yes, Hadle has tried to explain it to me several times,' Geir said. 'But I never remember.'

'Italo Calvino does something similar in *If on a Winter's Night a Traveller*,' I said. 'But it's not quite as strict of course. The title of each narrative in the end forms its own little narrative. Have you read it?'

The doors opened, we went in and sat opposite each other.

'Calvino, Borges, Cortázar, you can keep them,' he said. 'I don't like fantasy and I don't like constructs. For me it's only people that count.'

'But what about Christensen?' I said. 'You'd have to look far and wide for a writer who uses more constructs. What she does sometimes is more like maths.'

'Not from what I heard,' Geir said, and I looked out of the window as the train began to move.

'What you heard was the voice,' I said. 'It overrides all numbers and systems. And it's the same with Borges as well, at least when he's at his best.'

'Makes no difference,' Geir said.

'You don't want to read it?'

'No.'

'OK.'

We sat silent for a while, caught in the silence into which all the other passengers had also sunk. Vacant gazes, motionless bodies, the gently vibrating walls and floor of the train.

'Attending a poetry reading is like being in a hospital,' he said as we left the next station. 'Full of neuroses.'

'Not Christensen though?'

'No, precisely, that's what I was saying. She did something else.'

'Perhaps the tight construct you won't accept balanced it out? Objectivised it?'

'Possible,' he said. 'But for her the evening would have been a total waste of time.'

'And the guy with the flat,' I said. 'Rataajaama, was that his name?'

The next morning I rang the number I had been given by Raattamaa. No one answered. I rang again and again during the day and the next day. No answer. He never picked up the phone, so on the third day we went to another literary event in which he was supposed to be taking part, sat in a bar across the street and waited until it was over, and when he came out I went over to him, he looked down when he recognised me, sorry, it was too late, the flat had gone. Through Geir Gulliksen I managed to fix up a meeting with two editors at Norstedts. I had lunch with them and they gave me a list of writers I should contact – 'They're not necessarily the best, but they're the nicest' – and said I could stay in the company's guest apartment for two weeks. I accepted their offer, and while staying there I received a positive reply from Joar Tiberg, one of whose poems we had published in *Vagant*, a long one, he knew a girl at *Ordfront Magasin* who would be away for a month: I could stay there.

At regular intervals I phoned Tonje, told her how I was and what I was doing, and she told me what was happening where she was. Neither of us asked what we were really doing.

I began to run. And I began to write again. Four years had already passed since the first novel, and I had nothing. Lying on the water bed in the conspicuously feminine room I was renting I decided on one of two options. Either I would begin writing about my life the way it was now, like a diary and open to the future, with everything that had happened over recent years as a dark undercurrent – in my mind I called it the *Stockholm Diary* – or I would continue with the story I had started three days before coming here, about a trip to the skerries one summer's night when I was twelve, when dad caught crabs and I found a dead seagull. The atmosphere, the heat and the darkness, the crabs and the bonfire, all the screaming gulls defending their nests as Yngve, dad and I walked across the island, it had something, but not perhaps enough to carry a novel.

During the day I read in bed, once in a while Geir came down, then we went out for lunch, and in the evenings I wrote or I ran or I caught the train to Geir and Christina's, to whom I had become quite attached in the course of these two weeks. Beside the conversation about literature and beside all the political and ideological topics Geir broached, we also talked continually about subjects that were closer to us. In my case the subject was inexhaustible, everything came up, from events in my childhood to my father's death, from summers in Sørbøvåg to the winter I met Tonje. Geir was shrewd, he was on the outside and saw through everything, time after time. His story, which started to take form later, as though first of all he had to be sure I could be trusted, was the complete antithesis of mine. Whereas he came from a working-class home without any ambitions or as much as a single book on the shelves, I was from a middle-class home, with both my mother and my father having done courses as mature students to get on, and we had the whole of world literature at our fingertips. Whereas he was one of the boys who fought in the playground and was barred and sent to the school psychologist, I was one of the children who always tried to curry favour with the teacher by being as good as possible. Whereas he played with soldiers and dreamed of owning a gun one day, I played football and dreamed of turning professional one day. Whereas I ran for election as a school rep and wrote an essay about the revolution in Nicaragua, he was a member of a Home Guard cadet force and the youth wing of a conservative political party. Whereas I wrote a poem about the amputated hands of children and human cruelty after watching *Apocalypse Now,* he examined the possibility of becoming an American citizen to enlist in the US Army.

Despite all this, we were able to talk to each other. I understood him, he understood me, and for the first time in my adult life I could say what I thought to someone without reservations.

I decided to go for the crab and the seagull story, wrote twenty pages, wrote thirty, my short runs became longer and longer, and soon I ran all the way round Söder, while the kilos flowed off me and conversations with Tonje became fewer and fewer.

Then I met Linda and the sun rose.

I can't find a better way to express it. The sun rose in my life. At first, as dawn breaking on the horizon, almost as if to say, this is where you have to look. Then came the first rays of sunshine, everything became clearer, lighter, more alive, and I became happier and happier, and then it hung in the sky of my life and shone and shone and shone.

The first time I set eyes on Linda was in the summer of 1999 at a seminar for new Nordic writers at Biskops-Arnö Folk High School, outside Stockholm. Standing outside a building with the sun on her face. Wearing sunglasses, a white T-shirt with a stripe across the chest and green military fatigues. She was thin and beautiful. She had an aura which was dark, wild, erotic and destructive. I dropped everything I was holding.

When I saw her for the second time six months had passed. She was sitting at a table in an Oslo café and was wearing a leather jacket, blue jeans, black boots and was so fragile, overwrought and confused that all I wanted to do was hold her in my arms. I didn't.

When I came to Stockholm she was the only person I knew apart from Geir. I had her number, and the second day I was there I rang her from Geir and Christina's flat. What had happened at Biskops-Arnö was dead and buried, there were no longer any feelings for her in me, but I needed contacts in town, she was a writer, she was bound to know many more, perhaps also someone with a place to live.

No one answered. I put the phone down and turned to Geir, who was pretending he hadn't been following.

'No one at home,' I said.

'Try again later then,' he said.

I did. But no one ever answered.

With Christina's help I put an advertisement in the Stockholm newspapers. Norwegian author seeks flat/place to write, it said, we had spoken for ages before arriving at this, they thought there were lots of culture vultures that would jump at the word 'author', and 'Norwegian' was synonymous with easy-going and harmless. They must have had a point because I was inundated with calls. Most of the flats I was offered were in the satellite towns outside Stockholm. I turned them down, there didn't seem to be much point being stuck in a tower block somewhere in a forest, and while I waited for a better offer I moved into the Norstedts flat, then into the very feminine flat. After a week there an offer turned up: someone wanted to rent a flat in Söder, and I went there, waited outside the door, two women so similar they had to be twins, around fifty years old, stepped out of a car, I greeted them, they said they were from Poland and wanted to rent out the flat for at least a year, sounds very interesting, I said, come on up, they said, we can sign the contract straight away if you like it.

The flat was absolutely fine, one and a half rooms, around thirty square metres, kitchen and bathroom, acceptable standard, perfect location. I signed. But something nagged, something was wrong, I couldn't work out what, walked slowly downstairs, stopped by the board with the list of the block's occupants. First of all, I read the address, Brännkyrkgatan 92, there was something familiar about it, I had seen it somewhere, but where? Where? I wondered, scanning the list of names.

Oh, bugger it.

Linda Boström, it said.

A chill ran down my spine.

That was her address! Of course. I had written to her asking for a contribution for *Vagant*, and I had sent it to bloody Brännkyrkgatan 92.

What were the odds of that happening?

One and a half million people lived in this city. I knew one of them. I put an advertisement in the paper, get an interesting response from two complete strangers, Polish twins, and it turns out the flat is in the *same block*!

I sauntered down to the Metro station, squirmed nervously in my seat all the way home to my girly flat. What would Linda think if I moved into the floor above? That I was stalking her?

It was no good. I couldn't. Not after the terrible business at Biskops-Arnö.

The first thing I did when I came in the door was to ring the Poles and say I had changed my mind, I didn't want the flat after all, a better offer had come up, I was really sorry, I really was.

'That's fine,' she said.

Back to square one.

'Are you crazy?' Geir said when I told him. 'You've turned down a flat in the middle of Söder which, on top of everything else, was cheap, because you think someone you don't really know *might* feel she was being stalked? Do you realise how many years I've spent trying to get my hands on a flat in the centre? Do you know how difficult it is? It's *impossible*. Then you come along with a four-leaved clover up your arse and get one, then another, and then you say no!'

'That's how it is now anyway,' I said. 'Is it OK if I drop by occasionally? You feel a bit like my family. And if I come out here for Sunday lunch with you?'

'Apart from the fact that it's Monday, I have the same feeling. But I find it hard to make the father–son relationship fit. So it would have to be Caesar and Brutus.'

'Which of us is Caesar?'

'Don't ask such a silly question. Sooner or later you'll stab me in the back. But just come. We can continue talking out here.'

We ate, I went onto the tiny balcony to smoke and drink coffee, Geir joined me, we discussed the relativist attitude we both had to the world, how the world changed when culture changed, yet everything was always such that you couldn't see what was outside, and therefore it didn't exist, whether this view came from the fact that we had gone to university precisely when post-structuralism and postmodernism were at their zenith and everyone was reading Foucault and Derrida, or whether it actually *was* like that, and whether in that case it was the fixed, unchanging and non-relativist point we were denying. Geir told me about an acquaintance of his who wouldn't talk to him any more after a discussion they'd had about the real and the absolute. I thought it a strange point to invest so much in, but said nothing. For me society is everything, Geir said. Humanity. I'm not interested in anything beyond that. But I am, I said. Oh yes? Geir queried. What then? Trees, I answered. He laughed. Patterns in plants. Patterns in crystals. Patterns in stones. In rock formations. And in galaxies. Are you talking about fractals? Yes, for example. But everything that binds the living and the dead, all the dominant forms that exist. Clouds! Sand dunes! That interests me. Oh God, how boring, Geir said. No, it isn't, I said. Yes, it is, he said. Shall we go in? I said.

I poured myself another cup of coffee and asked Geir if I could use the phone.

'Of course,' he answered. 'Who are you phoning?'

'Linda. You know, the . . .'

'Yeah, yeah, yeah. The woman whose flat you turned down.'

I keyed in the number, probably for the fifteenth time. To my surprise she picked up.

'Linda here,' she said.

'Oh hi, this is Karl Ove Knausgaard speaking,' I said.

'Hi!' she said. 'Is it really you?'

'Yes. I'm in Stockholm.'

'Are you? On holiday?'

'We-ell, I'm not quite sure. I was thinking of living here for a bit.'

'Are you? Cool!'

'Yes. I've already been here a few weeks. I tried to call you, but didn't get an answer.'

'No, I've been away, in Visby.'

'Oh?'

'Yes, I was writing.'

'Sounds good.'

'Yes, it was great. I didn't get a lot done, but . . .'

'Right,' I said.

There was a pause.

'Linda, I was wondering . . . if you fancied a cup of coffee one day?'

'Very much. I'm here for the foreseeable.'

'Tomorrow perhaps? Have you got time?'

'Yes, think so. In the morning anyway.'

'Perfect.'

'Where do you live?'

'By Nytorget.'

'Oh great! Could we meet there then? Do you know where the pizza place is, on the corner? There's a café opposite. There?'

'OK. What time suits you best? Eleven? Twelve?'

'Twelve's fine.'

'Brilliant. See you then.'

'Yes. Bye.'

'Bye.'

I rang off and went in to Geir, who was sitting on the sofa with a cup in his hand and looking at me.

'So?' he said. 'Finally got a bite?'

'Yes. I'm meeting her tomorrow.'

'Good! I'll drop by in the evening and you can tell me all about it.'

I went there an hour before I was supposed to meet her, carrying a manuscript I was doing a report on, the new novel by Kristine Næss, and sat working. Tiny quivers of anticipation ran through me whenever I thought about her. Not that I had any intentions, I had written them off once and for all, it was more the unknown, how things would turn out.

I spotted her as she jumped off her bike outside. She guided the front wheel into the stand and locked her bike, peered through the window, perhaps looking at herself, opened the door and came in. It was pretty full, but she saw me straight away and came over.

'Hi,' she said.

'Hi,' I said.

'I'll just go and order,' she said. 'Anything you want?'

'No, thanks,' I answered.

She was rounder than she had been, that was the first thing I noticed. The boyish leanness was gone.

She placed a hand on the counter, craned her head in the direction of the waiter standing behind the hissing coffee machine. There was a hollow in the pit of my stomach.

I lit a cigarette.

She returned, put a cup of tea on the table and sat down.

'Hi,' she repeated.

'Hi,' I said.

Her eyes were greyish-green and could widen all of a sudden, I recalled, for no apparent reason.

She removed the tea strainer, lifted the cup to her lips and blew on the surface.

'It's been a long time,' I said. 'Is everything going well?'

She took a small sip of the tea and set the cup down on the table.

'Yes,' she said. 'It is. I've just been to Brazil with a girlfriend. And then I went to Visby straight afterwards. I'm still not really here yet.'

'But you're writing?'

She grimaced, looked down.

'I'm trying. And you?'

'Same here. I'm trying.'

She smiled.

'Were you serious when you said you're going to live in Stockholm?'

I shrugged.

'For a while at any rate.'

'Nice,' she said. 'We can meet then. I mean do something together.'

'Yes.'

'Do you know anyone else here?'

'Just one person. His name's Geir. Norwegian. Otherwise no one.'

'You know Mirja a little, don't you? From Biskops-Arnö, I mean.'

'Oh, very little. How is she, by the way?'

'Fine, I think.'

We didn't say anything for a few moments.

There was so much we could not talk about. There were so many subjects we could not touch on. But now we were here we had to talk about *something*.

'It was very good, the short story you had in *Vagant*,' I said. 'It was very good, really.'

She smiled, eyes downcast.

'Thank you,' she said.

'The language was so unbelievably explosive. Well, just very beautiful. Like a . . . ah, it's difficult to talk about, but . . . it was hypnotic I think I was trying to say.'

She was still looking down.

'Do you write short stories now?'

'Yes, I suppose I do. Prose anyway.'

'Hm, that's good.'

'And you?'

'Well, nothing. I've been trying to write a novel for four years, but just before I left I binned the lot.'

Another silence. I lit another cigarette.

'It's nice to see you again,' I said.

'And you too,' she said.

'I was reading a manuscript before you came,' I said, nodding towards the pile beside me on the sofa. 'Kristine Næss. Do you know her?'

'Yes, in fact, I do. I haven't read anything by her, but she was at Biskops-Arnö with two male writers when I went there.'

'Is that right?' I said. 'That's odd. You see she writes about Biskops-Arnö. About a Norwegian girl who goes there.'

What the hell was I doing? What was I blathering about?

Linda smiled.

'I don't read much,' she said. 'I don't even know if I'm a real writer.'

'Of course you are!'

'But I can remember the writers from Norway. I thought they were so incredibly ambitious, especially the two men. And they knew so much about literature.'

'What were their names?'

She took a deep breath.

'One was called Tore, I'm sure of that. They were from *Vagant*.'

'Oh, *that*'s who they were,' I said. 'Tore Renberg and Espen Stueland. I can remember they went there.'

'Yes, that's them.'

'They're two of my best friends.'

'Are they?'

'Yes, but they fight like cat and dog. You can't have them in the same room any more.'

'So you know them separately?'

'Yes, you could put it like that.'

'I was impressed by you as well,' she said.

'By me?'

'Yes. Ingmar Lemhagen was talking about your book a long time before you came. And that was all he wanted to talk about when we were there.'

Another silence.

She got up and headed for the toilet.

It was hopeless, I thought. What idiotic things was I coming up with? But what else could you say?

What the hell did people talk about, actually?

The coffee machine hissed and sputtered. A long queue of people with impatient body language stood at the bar. It was grey outside. The grass in the park below was yellow and wet.

She returned and sat down.

'What do you do during the day? Have you started to get to know the town?'

I shook my head.

'Only a bit. No, I write. And then I swim in the pool at Medborgarplatsen every day.'

'Do you? I swim there too. Not every day, but almost.'

We smiled at each other.

I took out my mobile and checked the time.

'I'm afraid I'll have to go soon,' I said.

She nodded. 'But we can meet again, can't we?'

'Yes, we can. When?'

She shrugged. 'You can just ring me, can't you?'

'Yep.'

I put the manuscript and the mobile phone in my bag, and got up.

'I'll phone you then. Nice to see you again!'

'*Hej då*,' she said. Bye.

Bag in hand, I strode down the street, alongside the park and into the broad avenue where the flat was. Nothing had changed, we hadn't changed anything; when we took our leave it was all as it was before we met.

But what had I been expecting?

We weren't going anywhere after all.

I hadn't asked about flats, either. Or contacts. Nothing.

I was fat as well.

After arriving home I lay back on the water bed and studied the ceiling. She had been completely different. She was almost like a different person.

At Biskops-Arnö perhaps the most striking feature of her personality had been her determination to go as far as she had to, which I had sensed at once and was deeply attracted by. It had disappeared. The hardness, bordering on ruthlessness, yet as fragile as glass, was gone too. There was still something fragile about her, but in a different way, this time I hadn't thought that she could be crushed or go to pieces, as I had then. Now her fragility was joined by a softness, and her indifferent side, which said you'll never get close to me, had changed. She was shy but somehow also open. Hadn't there been something open about her?

*

The autumn after we had been to Biskops-Arnö she had got together with Arve, and through him I had heard what happened to her in the winter and spring. She had gone through a manic-depressive phase, was eventually admitted to a psychiatric hospital, that was all I knew. During the manic periods she had rung me twice to ask if I could get hold of Arve. I did both times, asked his friends to tell him to call me, and when he did I could hear he was disappointed it was actually Linda trying to contact him. And once she rang just to talk to me, it was six o'clock in the morning, she told me she was about to begin a creative writing course, and was leaving for Gothenburg in an hour. Tonje was awake in the bedroom, wondering who would ring at this crazy hour, I said, Linda, you know, the Swede I met, who's with Arne. Why would she ring you? Tonje asked, no idea, I said, think she's going through a manic-depressive phase.

We couldn't talk about any of this.

And if we couldn't talk about this, we couldn't talk about anything.

What was the point of sitting there and saying hi, hi, erm, erm, how are you?

I closed my eyes and tried to picture her.

Had I felt anything for her?

No.

Or yes, I liked her and perhaps I felt some tenderness for her, after all that had happened, but there was no more to it than that. The rest I had put behind me, quite definitely.

Best like that.

I got up, stuffed my trunks, a towel and some shampoo in a bag, put on my jacket and walked to Medborgarplatsen, into Forsgrénska Badet, which was almost empty at this time of day, changed, entered the swimming hall, onto the block and dived in. I swam a thousand metres beneath the pale March light that fell in through the large window at the end, to and fro, up and down, under the water, over the water, without thinking about anything but the number of metres, the number of minutes, all while trying to perform the strokes as perfectly as possible.

Afterwards I went to the sauna, thought about the time I tried to write short stories based on small ideas, like a man with a prosthetic limb in the swimming pool changing room, without knowing what, why or how.

What had been the big idea?

A man tied to a chair in a room, in a flat, somewhere in Bergen, in the end shot through the head, dead, but still alive in the text, an ego that lasted well into its funeral and the grave.

Gesticulating, that was what I had been doing.

And for so long.

I wiped the sweat from my brow with the towel, looked down at the rolls of fat sagging from my stomach. Pale and fat and stupid.

But in Stockholm!

I got up, went to the showers and stood under one.

I knew no one here. I was utterly free.

If I left Tonje, if this was the path I was to take, I could stay here for a month or two, perhaps all summer, and then go to . . . well, wherever I felt like going. Buenos Aires. Tokyo. New York. Go down to South Africa and take the train to Lake Victoria. Or Moscow, why not? That would be fantastic.

I closed my eyes and soaped my hair. Rinsed it, went in and opened my locker, dressed.

I was free if I wanted to be.

I didn't *need* to write any more.

I put the towel and my wet shorts in the bag, went out into the grey chilly day, to Saluhallen, the food hall, where I had a ciabatta roll leaning against a counter. Went home, tried to

write a little while hoping that Geir would come earlier than
he had said. Went to bed and watched TV, an American soap,
fell asleep.

When I woke it was dark outside. Someone was knocking at
the door.

I opened up, it was Geir, we shook hands.

'Well?' he said. 'How was it?'

'Good,' I said. 'Where shall we go?'

Geir shrugged while walking round and inspecting all the
ornaments inside, stopping in front of the bookshelves and
turning.

'Isn't it strange that you find the same books everywhere you
go? I mean, she's around twenty-five, isn't she? Works at *Ordfront*,
lives in Söder? But these are the books she's got and no others.'

'Yes, very strange,' I said. 'Where shall we go? Guldapan?
Kvarnen? Pelikanen?'

'Not Kvarnen at any rate. Guldapan maybe? Are you hungry?'

I nodded.

'Let's go there. The food's not bad. Good chicken.'

Outside, it felt as if it could start snowing at any moment.
Cold and raw and damp.

'Come on then,' Geir said as we strode along. 'Good in what
way?'

'We met, chatted and left. That's pretty much how it was.'

'Was she how you remembered her?'

'We-ell, bit different maybe.'

'In what way?'

'How many times are you going to ask that?'

'I really mean it. What did you feel when you saw her?'

'Less than I thought I would.'

'Why's that?'

'Why? What sort of sodding question is that? How can I know?

I feel what I feel. It's not possible to identify every tiny fluctuation of the soul, if that's what you believe.'

'Isn't that what you make your living from?'

'No. I make my living from all the embarrassing situations I have been put in. That's different.'

'So there are fluctuations then?' he said.

'Here we are,' I said. 'We're eating, isn't that what you said?'

I opened the door and went in. The bar was in the first room, the dining room in the second.

'Why not?' Geir said, and walked through the café. I followed. We sat down, read the menus and ordered chicken and a beer when the waiter came.

'Did I tell you I've been here with Arve?' I said.

'No.'

'When we came to Stockholm we ended up here. Well, first of all we were up at what I gather now must have been Stureplan. Arve went in and asked if they knew where writers drank in Stockholm. They just laughed at him and answered in English. So we wandered round for a while, it was terrible actually, for I held Arve in great esteem, he was an intellectual, was at *Vagant* from the very start, and then we met at the airport and I couldn't say a word. Next to nothing. Landed at Arlanda, couldn't speak. Came into Stockholm, found the accommodation, said nothing. Went out to eat, *nada*. Not a word. My only chance, I knew, was to drink my way through the sound barrier. So I did. A beer in Drottninggatan, where we asked someone where it was good to go out, they said Söder, Guldapan, and so we took a taxi here. I drank spirits and started to open up. A few words here and there. Arve leaned over to me and said, that girl's looking at you. Do you want me to go so that you can be alone with her? Which girl? I asked, that one, Arve said, and I looked at her, and shit, she was so good-looking! But it was Arve's offer that had the most impact. Wasn't it a bit odd?'

'Yes, indeed.'

'We got rat-arsed. So there was no longer any need to talk. We wandered round the streets here, it was getting light, I had barely a thought in my head, then we found a beer hall and went in, there was a great atmosphere, and I was out of my head, chucking beer down while Arve talked about his child. Suddenly he was in tears. I hadn't even been listening. And then, there he was, with his hands in front of his face and his shoulders shaking. He was sobbing his heart out, I thought from somewhere deep inside me. Then they closed, we took a taxi to somewhere further up, they didn't let us in and we found a large open area with a kiosk at the end, it might have been Kungsträdgården, could well have been. There were some chairs which had chains attached to them. We lifted them above our heads and hurled them at the wall, ran wild, completely out of our heads. Strange that the police didn't come. But they didn't. So we took a taxi to our lodgings. The following morning we woke up two hours after the train had departed. But we didn't give a shit anyway, so it didn't matter. We made our way to the station, caught the next train and I talked all the way back. I was unstoppable. It was as if everything that had been inside me for the last year came out. Something about Arve made it possible. I don't know quite what it was, or is. A kind of enormous tolerance in him. Nevertheless, he got the whole story. Dad dying, the hell it had been, the debut and everything that came with it, and after I had told him that, I just went on. I remember us waiting for a taxi at the station, not a soul around, just Arve and me, him looking at me, me talking and talking. Childhood, teenage years, I didn't leave a stone unturned. Just me, nothing else. Me, me, me. I ladled it all over him. Something about him made that possible, he understood everything I said and thought, I had never experienced that with anyone else before. There were always limitations, attitudes, assertion needs that halted what was being said at a certain point, or led it in a certain direction, so that what you said was always reshaped into something else, it could never exist in its own right. But Arve, it seemed to me on that day, was a truly open person, as well as being curious and constantly striving to understand what he saw. But there was no ulterior motive about his openness, it was not a damned psychologist's openness, nor was there any ulterior motive about the curiosity. He had a shrewd eye for the world, so it appeared, and like all those who have accumulated experience, by and large what remained was laughter. Laughter was really the only appropriate way to confront human behaviour and notions.

'I understood that, and while taking advantage of it, for I was not strong enough to resist all that his openness gave me, it also frightened me.

'He knew something I didn't know, he understood something I didn't understand, he could see something I couldn't see.

'I told him.

'He smiled.

'"I'm forty years old, Karl Ove. You're thirty. That's a big difference. That's what you've noticed."

'"I don't think so," I said. "There's something else. You have some sort of insight into things, which I lack."

'"Tell me more! Tell me more!"

'He laughed.

'His aura was centred around his dark intense eyes, but he was not himself dark, he laughed a lot, the smile barely left his slightly twisted lips. His aura was strong, he was the kind of person whose presence you noticed, but it wasn't a physical

presence because you simply didn't notice his light slim body.
At least I didn't. Arve, he was a shaven head, dark eyes, a perma-
nent smile and a hearty laugh. His reasoning always led, for me,
to unexpected conclusions. The fact that he had opened up for
me was more than I could have hoped for. All of a sudden I
could say everything that I had kept inside me so far, and more,
for it was as if it had rubbed off on me. Now my reasoning set
off on expected paths, and the feeling it gave me was one of
hope. Perhaps I was a writer after all? Arve was. But me? With
all my ordinariness? With my life of football and films?

'How I prattled on.

'The taxi arrived, I opened the boot lid and babbled away,
hungover and the worse for wear. We put our two bags in, got
in the car, I babbled the whole way through the Swedish countryside to Biskops-Arnö, where the seminar had long started.
They'd just had lunch when we rolled out of the taxi.'

'And that was how it continued?' Geir asked.

'And that was how it continued,' I said.

A man stepped forward and introduced himself as Ingmar
Lemhagen. He was the course director. He told me he had enjoyed
my book and that it had reminded him of another Norwegian
author. 'Who?' I asked, he smiled wryly, said it would have to
wait until we went through my texts in the plenary.

I pondered. Had to be Finn Alnæs or Agnar Mykle.

I deposited my bags outside, went into the hall, shovelled some
food onto a plate and devoured it. Everything swayed, I was still
drunk, but not so much that I didn't feel my chest bursting with
the excitement and pleasure of being there.

I was shown to a room, dropped off my luggage, went over to
the building where the course was being held. That was when
I saw her. She was leaning against the wall, I didn't say anything

to her, there were lots of people around, but I looked at her, and there was something about her I wanted, the second I saw her, it was there.

A kind of explosion.

We were put in the same group. The group leader, a Finnish woman, said nothing as we took our places, it was some sort of teaching trick she was employing, but no one was taken in, everyone was silent for the first five minutes, until it became too unpleasant and someone took the initiative.

I was aware of her the whole time.

What she said, how she spoke, but most of all her presence, her body in the room.

Why I don't know. Perhaps the state I was in made me more receptive to what she had or the person she was.

She introduced herself. Linda Boström. Her debut had been a collection of poems called *Gör mig behaglig för såret*, she lived in Stockholm and was twenty-five years old.

The course lasted five days. I circled round her the whole time. In the evenings I got drunk, as drunk as I could, I hardly slept. One night I followed Arve into a crypt-like cellar, down there he danced round and round, it was impossible to communicate with him, and when we left and I realised he was beyond reach I cried. He saw. You're crying, he said. Yes, I said. But you'll have forgotten by tomorrow. One night I didn't sleep a wink. When the last ones left for bed at five, I went out for a long walk in the forest, the sun was up, I saw deer leaping between the old deciduous trees and was happy in a mysterious way I didn't recognise. The writing I did during the course was unusually good, it was as if I was in touch with a spring, something all of my own and yet foreign to me gushed up, clear and fresh. Or perhaps it was just the euphoria that caused me to misinterpret. We had classes together, I sat beside Linda,

she asked me if I remembered the scene in *Blade Runner* where
the light through the window fades. I said I did, and that the
moment when the owl turns is the most beautiful in the whole
film. She looked at me. A questioning look, not acknowledge-
ment. The course directors went through the texts we had
written. They came to mine. Lemhagen started to talk about
it, and it was as though what he said elevated itself higher
and higher, I had never heard anyone talk about a text in that
way, elevate what was actually the bare essence, and he didn't
deal with characters or themes or what lay on the surface, he
dealt with the metaphors and the unseen function they
performed, bringing everything together, uniting them in an
almost organic fashion. I had never known that was what I
did, but now he said it I knew, and for me it was trees and
leaves, grass and clouds and a glowing sun, that was all, I
understood everything in the light of this, also Lemhagen's
interpretation.

He looked at me.

'What this reminds me of, above all else, is Tor Ulven's prose.
Are you familiar with his work, Karl Ove?'

I nodded and looked down.

No one was allowed to see the blood foaming in my veins,
trumpets blaring and knights galloping in my insides. Tor Ulven,
that was the summit.

Oh, but I knew he was mistaken, he was exaggerating, he was
Swedish and probably didn't understand the finer points of the
Norwegian language very well. But the mere mention of Ulven's
name . . . *Wasn't* I a pulp fiction writer? *Was* there anything in
my writing that had *resonances* of Tor Ulven?

My blood roared, my elation rushed screaming along my nerve
channels.

I looked down, wishing intensely that he would stop and go

on to the next person, and when he did I slumped back with relief.

That night all the drinking continued in my room, Linda said we could smoke if we took down the fire alarm, I did, we drank, I played Wilco's *Summerteeth*, she didn't seem to be interested in it, from what I could see, I showed her a Roman cookery book I had bought on an excursion to Uppsala the day before, so wonderful to cook the way the Romans did, I thought, but she didn't agree, quite the contrary, she turned abruptly away from me and her eyes sought something else. People began to drift off to their rooms, I hoped Linda would not follow suit, but then she was gone too, and I went into the forest again, roamed around until seven, and when I returned an angry man came running after me. 'Knausgaard, are you Knausgaard?' he shouted. 'Yes, I am,' I said. He stopped in front of me and began to tear me off a strip. Fire alarm, dangerous, irresponsible, he yelled. I said yes, I'm sorry, wasn't thinking, apologies. He stood glowering at me with fury in his eyes, I swayed to and fro, I couldn't care less, went to my room, slept for two hours. When I appeared for breakfast Lemhagen came over to me, he apologised profusely for what had happened, the caretaker had gone too far, it wouldn't happen again.

I understood nothing. Was *he* apologising to me?

What had happened fitted all too well, in my view, with the person I had become in the course of these days: a sixteen-year-old. My feelings were the feelings of a sixteen-year-old, my actions the actions of a sixteen-year-old. All of a sudden I was as unsure of myself as I had ever been. Everyone assembled in one room, we were going to read our texts, one after the other, the idea being that all of us together would form a choir with individual voices chiming in. Lemhagen pointed to someone;

he started reading. Then he pointed to me. I looked at him, disconcerted.

'Shall I read now? While he's reading?' I asked.

Everyone laughed. I blushed scarlet. But as we got going I could hear how good my text was, so much better than the others, rooted in something quite different and more vital.

When we were outside on the gravel talking, I said that to Arve.

He just smiled, said nothing.

Every evening two or three people read to the others. I looked forward to my turn, Linda would be there, I would show her who I was. I read well, I usually got applause. But not this time, from the very first sentence I began to doubt the text, it was ridiculous and I felt myself becoming smaller and smaller, until, flushed with shame, I sat down. Then it was Arve's turn.

Something happened when he read. He had us all spellbound. He was a magician.

'That was incredible!' Linda said to me after he had finished.

I nodded and smiled.

'Yes, he really is good.'

Furious and desperate, I left, got a beer and sat down on the staircase outside the room. I thought, Linda, now leave the room and come here. Do you hear me! Leave and come here. Follow me. If you do that, if you come here now, we belong together. And that's it.

I stared at the door.

It opened.

It was Linda!

My heart pounded.

It was Linda! It was Linda!

She walked across the square, and I trembled with happiness.

Then she turned off and walked towards the other building, raising her hand in greeting to me.

The next day everyone went for a walk in the forest, and I was beside Linda, first in the line, and those behind us fell away and I was alone with her in the forest. She twisted a blade of grass and occasionally glanced at me with a smile. I was unable to say anything. Nothing. I looked down, I looked through the forest, I looked at her.

Her eyes sparkled. There was nothing of the dark deep-set, alluring eyes now, she was all lightness and coquettishness, twisting and twirling the grass, smiling, looking at me, looking down.

What was this?

What did it mean?

I asked if we should exchange books, she said, yes, of course. She came over while I lay on the grass peering up at the clouds, passed me her book. *Biskops-Arnö, 01.07.99, To Karl Ove*, it said on the title page. I ran in and fetched a copy of mine, already dedicated, and passed it to her. After she had gone I went to my room and settled down to read. I ached with desire for her as I was reading, every word came from her, was her.

In the midst of all this, my unbridled yearning for her and my descent into teenager-hood, I saw everything differently. All the greenery that grew, I saw how wild and chaotic it was, yet how plain and clear the shapes were, and it evoked a sense of ecstasy in me, the old oak trees, the wind blowing through the foliage, the sun, the endless blue sky.

I didn't sleep, barely ate, and I drank every night, nonetheless I was not tired or hungry and had no difficulty participating in the course. The conversation with Arve continued unabated, that is I continued to talk about myself to him, and as time progressed, more and more about Linda. He saw me, and he saw the others on the course, and then we talked about literature. My way of talking changed, I became freer and freer in my thoughts the more I was with him, and I considered it a gift. Between the lessons we lay on the lawn outside the buildings and chatted, then the others were there, and I became jealous of him, I saw the impact his words had on others, and I longed to have the same impact myself.

One evening, sitting on the grass drinking and chatting with everyone, he told us about an interview he'd had with Svein Jarvoll for *Vagant*, how everything had opened the evening they spoke, how precise everything that was said had been and how in some way it had opened the way for something extraordinary.

I talked about an interview I'd done with Rune Christiansen for *Vagant* in which the same thing had happened, I had been nervous before I met him, I knew nothing about poetry, but then there had been great openness, what it hadn't been possible to talk about, we were suddenly talking about. It was a really good interview, I concluded.

Arve laughed.

He could disqualify everything I said simply by laughing. Everyone present knew Arve had right on his side, all the authority was gathered there, in the hypnotic focal point formed by his face on that evening. Linda was with us, she saw that too.

Arve touched on boxing, Mike Tyson, his last fight when he bit off Holyfield's ear.

I said it wasn't so hard to understand, Tyson needed a way out, he knew he was going to lose, so he bit off an ear, it brought the fight to an end without him losing face. Arve laughed again and said he doubted that. That would have been a rational act. But there wasn't a single ounce of rationality in Tyson. And then he discussed the scene in a way that made me think about *Apocalypse Now*, where they cut off the bull's head. The darkness and the blood and the trance. Perhaps my thoughts were led in this direction because earlier in the day Arve had been talking about the determination the Vietnamese showed when they chopped off the arms of children who had been vaccinated, how this was impossible to confront or could only be confronted with a determination that was willing to go to the same lengths.

The next day I gathered a few of us together to play football, Ingmar Lemhagen found us a ball, we played for an hour, afterwards I sat down on the grass beside Linda with a Coke in my hand, and she said I had a footballer's gait. She had a brother who played football and hockey, and we had more or less the same way of standing and walking. But Arve, she said, have you seen how he walks? No, I said. He walks like a ballet dancer, she said. Light and ethereal. Haven't you noticed? No, I said, and smiled at her. She responded with a fleeting smile and got up. I lay full-length and stared up at the white clouds drifting slowly past, far into the blue expanse of sky.

After dinner I went for another long walk in the forest. Stopped in front of an oak and stared up into the foliage for a long time. Pulled off an acorn and walked on, turning it round and round in my hands, studying it from all angles. All the small, regular patterns in the tiny, gnarled basket-like section in which the nut rested. Along the smooth surface, the lighter stripes in the dark green. The perfect form. Could be an airship, could be an egg. It's oval, I mused with a smile. All the leaves were identical, they were spat out every spring, in grotesque quantities, the trees were factories, producing beautiful and intricately patterned leaves from sunlight and water. Once the thought was there the monotony was almost unbearable to think about. All this came from some texts I had read by Francis Ponge early in the summer – they had been recommended to me by Rune Christiansen – and his view had changed trees and leaves for me for ever. They surged forth from a well, the well of life, which was inexhaustible.

Oh, the instinctiveness of it.

It was frightening to walk there, surrounded by the blind potency of everything that grew, under the light of the sun which shone and shone, also blindly.

It was a strident tone that resonated in me. At the same time there was another tone in me, one of yearning, and this yearning no longer had an abstract goal, as had been the case over recent years, no, this was palpable and specific, she was moving around below, only a few kilometres away, at this very moment.

What sort of madness was this? I thought as I walked. I was married, we were fine, soon we would be buying a flat together. Then I came here and wanted to wreck everything?

I did.

I wandered beneath the sun-dappled shade from the trees, surrounded by the warm fragrances of the forest, thinking that I was in the middle of my life. Not life as an age, not halfway along life's path, but *in the middle of my existence*.

My heart trembled.

The last night came. We were assembled in the largest room, wine and beer had been set out, it was a kind of end-of-course party. I suddenly found myself beside Linda, she was opening a bottle of wine and placed her hand over mine, gently stroking it while looking into my eyes. It was obvious, it was decided, she wanted me. I thought about that for the rest of the evening as I slowly drank myself more and more senseless. I was getting together with Linda. Didn't need to return to Bergen, could just leave everything there and stay here with her.

At three in the morning, when I was as drunk as I had seldom been, I left with her. I said there was something I had to tell her. And then I told her. Exactly what I felt and what I had planned.

She said, 'I like you well enough. You're a great guy. But I'm not interested in you. I'm sorry. But your friend, he's really fantastic. I'm interested in him. Do you understand?'

'Yes,' I said.

I turned and crossed the square, aware that behind me she was walking in the opposite direction, back to the party. A crowd of people had gathered around the front door beneath the trees. Arve wasn't there, so I went back, found him, told him what Linda had said to me, that she was interested in him, now they could be together. But I'm not interested in her, you see, he said. I've *got* a wonderful girlfriend. Shame for you, though, he said, I said it wasn't a shame for me, and crossed the square again, as though in a tunnel where nothing existed except myself, passed the crowd standing outside the house, through the hallway and into my room where the screen of my computer was lit. I pulled out the plug, switched it off, went into the bathroom, grabbed the glass on the sink and hurled it at the wall with all the strength I could muster. I waited to hear if there was any reaction. Then I took the biggest shard I could find and started cutting my face. I did it methodically, making the cuts as deep as I could, and covered my whole face. The chin, cheeks, forehead, nose, underneath the chin. At regular intervals I wiped away the blood with a towel. Kept cutting. Wiped the blood away. By the time I was satisfied with my handiwork there was hardly room for one more cut, and I went to bed.

Long before I woke I knew something terrible had taken place. My face stung and ached. The second I woke I remembered what had happened.

I won't survive this, I thought.

I had to go home, meet Tonje at the Quartfestival, we had

booked a room six months before, with Yngve and Kari Anne. This was our holiday. She loved me. And now I had done this.

I smacked my fist against the mattress.

And then there were all the people here.

They would see the ignominy.

I couldn't hide it. Everyone would see. I was marked, I had marked myself.

I looked at the pillow. It was covered in blood. I felt my face. It was ridged all over.

And I was still drunk, I could barely stand up.

I pulled the heavy curtain aside. Light flooded into the room. There was a group of people sitting outside, surrounded by rucksacks and suitcases, it would soon be time for farewells.

I smashed my fist against the bedhead.

I had to face the music. There was no way out. I had to face the music.

I packed my things in my case, with my face smarting, and inside I was smarting as well, I had never experienced such shame before.

I was marked.

I grabbed the case and walked out. At first no one looked at me. Then someone cried out. Then everyone looked at me. I stopped.

'I apologise for this,' I said. 'Sorry.'

Linda sat there. She looked at me with wide-open eyes. Then she started to cry. Others cried as well. Someone came over and placed a hand on my shoulder.

'It'll be all right,' I said. 'I was just very drunk yesterday. I'm sorry.'

Complete silence. I showed myself as I was, and there was silence.

How would I survive this?

I sat down and smoked a cigarette.

Arve looked at me. I essayed a smile.

He came over.

'What the hell have you been up to?' he asked.

'I just had a skinful. I can tell you about it later. But not right now.'

A bus arrived, it took us to the station and we boarded the train. The plane didn't depart until next day. I didn't know how I would cope until then. On the streets of Stockholm everyone stared at me, and they gave me a wide berth. The shame burned inside me, it burned and burned and there was no way out, I had to endure it, hold on, hold on, and then one day it would be over.

We walked down to Söder. The others had arranged to meet Linda, we thought in the square I now know is called Medborgarplatsen, whereas at that time it was just a square, and there we stood, she cycled up, surprised to see us, we had arranged to meet at Nytorget, hadn't we, that's over there, she said, and didn't look at me, she didn't look at me, and that was fine, her stare in particular would have been more than I could have stood. We had pizzas, the atmosphere was strange, afterwards we sat on the grass with flocks of birds hopping around us, and Arve said he didn't believe in the theory of evolution, in the sense that it wasn't survival of the fittest, just look at the birds, they don't do what they have to do, they do what they feel like doing, what gives them pleasure. Pleasure is undervalued, Arve said, and I knew he was talking to Linda because I had told him what she said, I had done what she asked me to do, they would get together the two of them, I knew that.

I went back to the lodgings, the others stayed to drink. I watched TV, it was unbearable, but I got through the evening, and fell asleep at last, with the bed beside me empty, Arve didn't come back that night, in the morning I found him asleep in the stairwell. I asked if he had been to Linda's, he said no, she had gone home early.

'She sat crying and only wanted to talk about you,' he said. 'I drank with Thøger. That's what I did.'

'I don't believe you,' I said. 'You can tell me, it doesn't matter. It's you two now.'

'No,' he said. 'You're wrong.'

When we landed in Oslo the following morning, people continued to stare at me although I wore sunglasses and kept my face lowered as far as possible. A long time ago I had agreed to do an interview for the Norwegian Broadcasting Company with Alf van der Hagen, I was to go to his house, it would be a long interview and we would spend a bit of time on it. So, I had to go there. On the way I decided I wouldn't give a damn and would say exactly what I thought to all his questions.

'My God,' he said when he opened the door. 'What happened to you?'

'It's not as bad as it looks,' I said. 'I just got very drunk. It's the sort of thing that can happen.'

'Are you still up for an interview?' he asked.

'Yes, yes. I'm fine. I just don't look so good.'

'No, you certainly don't.'

When Tonje saw me she burst into tears. I said I had got terribly drunk and that was all that happened. Which was true. People stopped and stared at the festival as well, and Tonje cried a lot, but it improved, whatever had been holding me tight, not letting go of me, started to slacken its grip. We saw Garbage, it was a fantastic concert, Tonje said she loved me, I said I loved her and decided I would put all the past events behind me. I wouldn't look back, wouldn't think about it, wouldn't let it have a place in my life.

Early that autumn Arve rang to say he had got together with Linda. I told you it would be the two of you, didn't I, I said.

'But it didn't happen there. It happened later. She wrote me a letter and then she came here. I hope we can still be friends. I know it's difficult, but I hope we can.'

'Of course we can be friends,' I said.

And it was true, I didn't bear any grudges, why should I?

I met him in Oslo a month later, I was back to square one, couldn't bring myself to say a word to him. Barely a word passed my lips, not even if I drank. He said Linda talked a lot about me, and she often said I was so good-looking. With regard to that, I thought 'good-looking' was not a parameter that was relevant to us, it was more like a curious fact, approximately the same as if she had said I was lame or a hunchback. Besides, it was Arve who told me, why would he pass on this comment? Once I met him at Kunsternes Hus and he was so drunk it was hardly possible to talk to him, he took my hand and led me to a table and said, look, everyone, isn't he good-looking? I fled, bumped into him an hour later, we sat down, I said I had told him so much about myself while he had never told me anything about himself, I mean, intimate details, and he said, now you disappoint me, you sound like a psychologist in *Dagbladet*'s Saturday supplement or something, I said, OK. He was right, of course, he was always right, or always situated somewhere above arguments about right and wrong. He had given me a lot, but I had to put this behind me as well, I couldn't live with it and at the same time live the life I had in Bergen. That didn't work.

In the winter I met him again, when Linda was there, she wanted to meet me, and Arve led her to where I was sitting, left us in peace for half an hour, then came to collect her.

She sat huddled in a large leather jacket, weak and trembling, there was almost nothing left of her, and I thought, it's gone, it no longer exists.

While I told the story to Geir he looked down at the table in front of him. After I had finished he met my gaze.

'Interesting!' he said. 'You turn *everything* inwards. All the pain, all the aggression, all the emotions, all the shame, everything. Inwards. You hurt yourself, not anyone else out there.'

'That's what any teenage girl would do,' I said.

'No, they don't!' he said. 'You cut your face to ribbons. No girl would ever cut her face. I've never heard of *anyone* doing it in fact.'

'They weren't deep cuts,' I said. 'They looked bad. But it wasn't so bad.'

'Who would do that kind of thing to themselves?'

I shrugged.

'It was everything together building up into one climax. Dad's death, all the media attention around the book, life with Tonje. And of course Linda.'

'But you didn't feel anything for her today?'

'Nothing strong at any rate.'

'Are you going to see her again?'

'Maybe. Probably. Just to have a friend here, if so.'

'*Another* friend.'

'Yes, exactly,' I said, raising my finger in the air to attract the waiter's attention.

The next day the woman I was renting from rang. She had a girlfriend who needed to sublet her flat to reduce the rent.

'What do you mean *sublet*?'

'You get your room and then you share the rest of the flat with her.'

'Doesn't sound like anything for me,' I said.

'But it's a fantastic flat, you know,' she said. 'It's in Bastugatan. It's one of the best addresses in the whole of Stockholm.'

'OK,' I said. 'I can go and talk to her anyway.'

'She's very interested in Norwegian literature.'

I took her name and telephone number, rang, she picked up at once, just pop round, she said.

The flat really was fantastic. She was young, younger than me, and the walls were plastered with photographs of one man. It was her husband, she said, he was dead.

'I'm sorry to hear that,' I said.

She turned and walked through the flat.

'This is your room,' she said. 'If you want it, that is. You've got your own bathroom, own kitchen, and then there's a room with a bed, as you can see.'

'Looks great,' I said.

'You've got your own entrance as well. And if you want to write, you just have to close the door here.'

'I'll take it,' I said. 'When can I move in?'

'Now, if you like.'

'So quickly? Right, I'll bring my things over this afternoon then.'

Geir just laughed when I told him.

'It's impossible to come here without knowing a soul and get a flat in Bastugatan,' he said. 'It's impossible! Do you understand? The gods like you, Karl Ove, that's for sure.'

'But Caesar doesn't,' I said.

'Oh yes, Caesar does too. He's just a little envious, that's all.'

Three days later I rang Linda, told her I had moved, did she fancy a coffee? Yes, she did, and within an hour we were sitting in a café on the 'hump' overlooking Hornsgatan. She seemed happier, that was my first thought as she sat down. She asked if I had been swimming today, I smiled and said no, but *she* had, at the crack of dawn, it had been fantastic.

So we sat there stirring our cappuccinos. I lit a cigarette, couldn't think of anything to say, thinking this would have to be the last time.

'Do you like the theatre?' she asked.

I shook my head and told her the only plays I had seen were traditional performances at the National in Bergen, which had been about as captivating as watching fish in the aquarium, and a couple at Bergen International Theatre Festival, among them a production of *Faust* in which actors wandered across the stage mumbling and sporting big black noses. When I said that, she said we would have to go and see Bergman's production of *Ghosts*, and I said OK, I'll give it a go.

'Have we got a date then?' she asked.

'Yes,' I said. 'Sounds amusing.'

'Do bring your Norwegian friend along,' she said. 'And I can meet him as well.'

'Right, I'm sure he'd love to come,' I said.

We stayed for another quarter of an hour, but the silences were long, and she was probably dying to leave as much as I was. In the end, I put my cigarettes in my pocket and got up.

'Shall we buy the tickets together?' she asked.

'Can do,' I answered.

'Tomorrow?'

'Yes.'

'Half past eleven here?'

'Yes, that's fine.'

For the twenty minutes it took to go from the hump to the Royal Dramatic Theatre we barely exchanged a word. It felt as though

I could say everything to her or nothing. Now it was nothing, and presumably that was the way it would stay.

I let her order the tickets, and once it was done we started on the way back. The sun flooded the town in light, the first buds had appeared on the trees, there were people everywhere, most of them happy, as you are on the first decent days of spring.

As we crossed Kungsträdgården she squinted into the bright low rays of the sun at me.

'I saw something odd on TV a few weeks ago,' she said. 'They were showing CCTV footage from inside a large newspaper kiosk. Suddenly one of the shelves started smoking. At first there were a few small flames. The assistant was unsighted where he stood. But the customer by the counter could see. He must have known something was going on because while he was waiting for his purchases to be rung up he turned to the shelf. He couldn't help but see the flames. Then he turned back, took his change and left. While there was a fire burning behind him!'

She looked at me again and smiled.

'Another customer came in and stood by the counter. By now the fire was well alight. He turned and looked straight at the flames. Then he turned back, finished what he had to do and went out. But he looked straight at the flames! Do you understand?'

'Yes,' I said. 'Do you think he didn't want to be involved?'

'No, no, not at all. That wasn't the point. It was that he saw the flames but couldn't believe what he was seeing, flames in a shop, and so he trusted his brain more than his vision.'

'What happened after that?'

'The third person, who came in straight afterwards, shouted, "Fire!" as soon as he saw it. By then the whole stand was ablaze. By then it was impossible not to see it. Odd, eh?'

'Yes,' I said.

We had reached the bridge leading to the island where the Royal Palace was and zigzagged through the tourists and immigrants standing and fishing off it. Now and then over the following days I thought about the story she had told, gradually it detached itself from her and became a phenomenon in itself. I didn't know her, knew as good as nothing about her and the fact that she was Swedish meant that I couldn't interpret anything from the way she spoke or the clothes she wore. An image from her poetry collection, which I hadn't read since that time at Biskop-Arnö and had taken out only once, when showing her photo to Yngve, was still imprinted on my brain, the one of the first-person narrator clinging to a man like a *baby chimpanzee* and seeing this in the mirror. Why that of all images had made an impression I didn't know. When I arrived home I took out the collection again. Whales and land and huge animals thundering around a sharp-witted and vulnerable narrator.

Was that her?

Some days later we went to the theatre. Linda, Geir and I. The first act was terrible, truly wretched, and in the interval, sitting at a terrace table with a view of the harbour, Geir and Linda chatted away about quite how terrible it had been, and why. I was more sympathetic, for despite the small, cramped feel of the act, which coloured the play and the visions it was supposed to be depicting, there was an anticipation of something else, as if it was lying in wait. Perhaps not in the play, perhaps more in the combination of Bergman and Ibsen, which ultimately *had* to produce something? Or else it was the splendour of the auditorium that fooled me into believing there had to be something else. And there was. Everything was raised, higher and higher, the intensity increased, and within the tightly set framework, which in the end comprised only mother and son, a kind of

boundlessness arose, something wild and reckless. Into it disappeared plot and space, what was left was emotion, and it was
stark, you were looking straight into the essence of human
existence, the very nucleus of life, and thus you found yourself
in a place where it no longer mattered what was actually
happening. Everything known as aesthetics and taste was eliminated. Wasn't there an enormous red sun shining at the back
of the stage? Wasn't that Osvald rolling naked across the stage?
I'm not sure any more what I saw, the details disappeared into
the state they evoked, which was one of total presence, burning
hot and ice-cold at once. However, if you hadn't allowed yourself
to be transported, everything that happened would have
appeared exaggerated, perhaps even banal or kitsch. The master
stroke was the first act, everything was done there, and only
someone who had spent a whole lifetime creating, with an
enormous list – more than fifty years' worth – of productions
behind them, could have had the skill, the coolness, the courage,
the intuition and the insight to fashion something like this.
Bright ideas alone could not have brought this off, it was impossible. Hardly anything I had seen or read had even been close
to approaching the essence in this way. As we followed the audience streaming out into the foyer and onto the street, not one
of us said a word, but from their distant expressions I could see
they had also been carried away into the terrible but real and
therefore beautiful place Bergman had seen in Ibsen and then
succeeded in shaping. We decided we would have a beer at KB,
and as we made our way there the trance-like state wore off to
be replaced by an elated, euphoric mood. The shyness I would
normally have felt at being so near such an attractive woman,
which was further complicated by the events of three years ago,
was suddenly gone. She talked about the time she had acciden-
tally nudged a floodlight stand during one of Bergman's tests

and got to feel the sharp edge of his tongue. We discussed the difference between *Ghosts* and *Peer Gynt*, which were at opposite ends of a spectrum, one mere surface, the other mere depth, both equally true. She parodied the dialogue between Max von Sydow and Death and talked about individual Bergman films with Geir, who had gone on his own to see the Cinemathek performances, all of them, and had consequently seen the classic films that were worth seeing, while I sat and listened, happy about everything. Happy to have seen the play, happy to have moved to Stockholm, happy to be with Linda and Geir.

After we parted company and I was trudging up the hills to my bedsit in Mariaberget I realised two things.

The first was that I wanted to see her again as soon as possible.

The second was that was where I had to go, to what I had seen that evening. Nothing else was good enough, nothing else did it. That was where I had to go, to the essence, to the inner core of human existence. If it took forty years, so be it, it took forty years. But I should never lose sight of it, never forget it, that was where I was going.

There, there, there.

Two days later Linda rang and invited me to a Walpurgis night party she was going to throw with two girlfriends. It was fine if I brought along my friend Geir. Which I did. One Friday in May 2002 we walked across Söder to the flat where the party was to take place, and soon found ourselves ensconced on a sofa, each with a glass of punch in our hands, surrounded by young Stockholmers who all had some connection with cultural life: jazz musicians, theatre people, literary critics, authors, actors. Linda, Mikaela and Öllegård, who were the party organisers, had met when they were working at Stockholm City Theatre. At the time the Royal Dramatic Theatre was performing *Romeo and Juliet* together with Circus Cirkör, so apart from actors the room was full of jugglers, fire-eaters and trapeze artists. I couldn't get through the evening without speaking, even if I wanted to, so I heaved my body round from one group to another, exchanging civilities and, after I'd had a few gin and tonics, the odd sentence beyond what was strictly necessary. I particularly wanted to talk to the theatre people. I would never have expected to feel that, and it made my enthusiasm for theatre soar on this evening. I stood with two actors and said how fantastic Bergman was. They just snorted and said, *That old sod! He's so bloody traditional it makes you want to puke.*

How stupid could you be! Of course they loathed Bergman. Firstly, he had been the master all their lives and the whole of their parents' lives as well. Secondly, they were for the new, the great, Shakespeare as circus, the play everyone should see, which, with its torches and trapezes, stilts and clowns, was so refreshing. They had gone as far from Bergman as it was possible to go. Then a podgy clearly depressed Norwegian stands there hailing Bergman as the new man.

Meanwhile I confirmed that Linda and Geir were *still* chatting on the sofa, both with excited smiles, the stab in the heart that gave me, was she going to fall for another of my friends? I mingled, bumped into some jazz fans, who asked me if I knew anything about Norwegian jazz, to which I responded with a half-nod, which of course meant they wanted some names. Norwegian jazz musicians? Was there anyone apart from Jan Garbarek? Fortunately I realised that wasn't exactly what they meant and remembered Bugge Wesseltoft, whom Espen had talked about once, and had also invited to play at a *Vagant* party where I had given a reading. They nodded, he was good, I breathed out with relief and went off to sit on my own. Then a dark-haired woman with a broad face, large mouth, intense

brown eyes, wearing a flowery dress, came over to me and asked
if I was the writer from Norway. Yes, I was. What did I think
about Jan Kjærstad, John Erik Riley and Ole Robert Sunde?

I gave my opinions.

'Do you mean that?' she queried.

'Yes,' I said.

'Stay where you are,' she said. 'I'll just get my husband. He
writes about literature. Very interested in Riley. Wait a moment.
I'll be back.'

I watched her push past people towards the kitchen. What
did she say her name was? Hilda? No. Wilda? Shit. No, Gilda.
Shouldn't be impossible to remember.

Then she reappeared through the throng, this time with a
man in tow. Oh, as soon as I saw him I knew the type. He had
university written all over his face from a long distance.

'Now you can say what you told me!' Gilda said.

I did. But her passion was wasted on both him and me, so
when the conversation tailed off, and it didn't take long, I made
my apologies and went to the kitchen to get some food, now
that the queues were shorter. Geir stood chatting with someone
by the window and Linda was with a small group by the bookshelves. I sat down on the sofa and began to gnaw at a chicken
thigh when I met the eyes of a dark-haired woman, who took
this as an invitation, because the very next moment she was
standing in front of me.

'Who are you?' she asked.

I swallowed and put the chicken down on the paper plate as
I looked up at her. Tried to sit up straight on the deep soft sofa,
unsuccessfully, I felt as though I was falling to one side. And my
cheeks, they must have glistened with chicken fat.

'Karl Ove,' I said. 'I'm from Norway. I've just moved here. A
few weeks ago. And you?'

'Melinda.'

'And what do you do?'

'I'm an actor.'

'Oh yes!' I said with what was left of the Bergman euphoria in my voice. 'Are you in *Romeo and Juliet* then?'

She nodded.

'Who do you play?'

'Juliet.'

'Ah!'

'That's Romeo over there,' she said.

A good-looking muscular man came over to join her. He kissed her on the cheeks and looked at me.

Damn the bloody sofa. I felt like a dwarf from where I was sitting.

I nodded and smiled. He nodded back.

'Have you had some food?' he asked.

'No,' she said, and then they were gone. I lifted the chicken back to my mouth. There was nothing for it but to drink.

The last thing I did before I left that evening was to look at a photo album belonging to an equine homeopath with a plunging neckline. The alcohol had not made me soar, as it was wont to do, into a mood where everything was great and there were no obstacles; it made me sink into a spiritual well, from which nothing I had inside could raise me. All that happened was that everything became foggier and more unclear. The day after, I was profoundly grateful I'd had the presence of mind to go home, and not sit there until everyone had gone in the hope that something interesting might happen of its own accord. I assumed Linda was a lost cause – we had hardly exchanged a word all evening, which for the most part I had spent slumped in the chair I had begun to consider as 'mine' – and the little I said, which could have been written on a postcard, no woman

in the world would have found interesting. Nonetheless, I rang
her the following evening, politeness demanded I thank her.
And then, while I was standing with my mobile to my ear
surveying Stockholm spread out beneath me, illuminated by the
broad red light from the setting sun, a pregnant moment arose.
I had said hi, thanked her, said it had been a nice party, she had
thanked me, said she thought it had been nice too, and she
added she hoped I'd had a *trevlig* time. I had, I said. And then
there was a silence. She didn't say anything; I didn't say anything.
Should I wrap up the conversation? That was my natural instinct.
I had taught myself in such situations to say as little as possible.
In that way I wouldn't say anything foolish. Or should I go on?
The seconds ticked. If I had said, yes, well, I just wanted to thank
you and had rung off, that would have probably been that. Such
a mess I'd made of everything the night before. But what the
hell, what did I have to lose?

'What are you doing?' I asked after this long silence, by any
criteria.

'Watching ice hockey on TV,' she said.

'Ice hockey?' I said. And then we chatted for a quarter of an
hour. And decided we would meet again.

We did, but nothing happened, there was no excitement, or
rather the excitement was so great it didn't allow us to move,
it was as if we were caught in it, all the things we wanted to
say to each other, but couldn't.

Polite phrases. Little openings, leading elsewhere, her everyday
life, she had a mother in Stockholm, and a brother, and all her
friends. Apart from six months in Florence she had lived in
Stockholm all her life. Where had I lived?

Arendal, Kristiansand, Bergen. Six months in Iceland, four
months in Norwich.

Did I have any brothers or sisters?

A brother, a half-sister.

You were married, weren't you?

Yes. In a way I still am.

Oh.

Early one evening, in the middle of April, she rang. Did I feel like meeting her? Of course. I was out with Geir and Christina, I said, we were in Guldapan, you could join us if you like.

Half an hour later she was there.

She was beaming.

'I've been accepted by the Dramatiska Institut today,' she said. 'I'm so happy, it's just wonderful. And then I suddenly felt like meeting you,' she said, looking at me.

I smiled at her.

We were out all evening, got drunk, walked back to my place together, I gave her a hug outside the gate and went up to the flat.

The next day Geir rang.

'She's in love with you, man,' he said. 'You can see it miles off. That was the first thing Christina said when we left. She's almost luminous with it. Unbelievably in love with Karl Ove.'

'I don't think so,' I said. 'She was happy she's got into the Dramatiska Institut.'

'Why would she ring you if that was all it was?'

'How should I know? Why don't you ring her and ask?'

'And what's the situation with your feelings?'

'Fine.'

Linda and I went to the cinema. For some idiotic reason we saw the new Star Wars film, it was for children, and having confirmed that, we went to Folkoperan and sat without saying much.

I was depressed as I left, I was so incredibly sick of having everything inside me, being unable to say the simplest thing to anyone.

It passed. I was fine on my own, Stockholm was still new to me, spring had arrived, every second day at twelve I put on my trainers and ran around Söder, it was ten kilometres, on the days between I swam a thousand metres. I had lost ten kilos, and I had started to write again. I got up at five, had a cigarette and a couple of coffees on the roof terrace, from which there was a view of the whole of Stockholm, then I worked until twelve, ran or swam, and afterwards went into town and sat in a café reading, or just drifted around, unless I met Geir. At half past eight, as the sun was setting and colouring the wall blood-red above the bed, I lay down to read. I started *The Karinhall Hunters* by Carl Henning Wijkmark, Geir had recommended it, I read in the glow of the sinking sun, and suddenly, out of nowhere, I was imbued with a wild, dizzy feeling of happiness. I was free, completely free, and life was fantastic. I could on occasion be seized by this feeling, perhaps once every six months, it was strong, it lasted for a few minutes, and then it passed. The oddity this time was that it didn't pass. I woke up and was happy, buggered if I could remember that happening since I was a little boy. I sat on the terrace and sang in the pale sunlight, and when I wrote I didn't care if it was bad, there were other, better things in the world than writing novels, and when I ran my body was as light as a feather, while my brain, which was usually focused on surviving and not much else on my runs, looked around and enjoyed the dense leafy greenery, the blue water of the many canals, the crowds of people everywhere, the beautiful and less beautiful buildings. After returning home and taking a shower I had some soup and crispbread, and then I went to the park to read some more of Wijkmark's

debut novel, about the Norwegian marathon runner who slips
into Goering's hunting castle during the Berlin Olympics in
1936, rang Espen or Tore or Eirik or mum or Yngve or Tonje,
whom I was still with, nothing else had been said, went to bed
early, got up in the middle of the night and ate plums or apples
without knowing until I woke and found the remains on the
floor beside the bed. At the beginning of May I went to Biskops-
Arnö, six months ago I had agreed to give a talk there, phoned
Lemhagen when I came to Stockholm and said I would have to
cancel, I had nothing to talk about, he had said I could go
anyway, listen to the other talks, perhaps participate in the
discussions and do a reading or two in the evening, if I had
anything new.

He met me outside the main building, told me without delay
that he had never experienced anything like the time I had been
at the seminar for debut writers, nothing even remotely near it.
I understood what he meant, the atmosphere had been so special
then, not only for me.

The lectures were boring and the discussions tedious, or else
it was just that I was too happy to show any interest. A couple
of older Icelandic men were the only ones with anything original to say, so they were also the ones who had to face the
strongest arguments. At night we drank, Henrik Hovland was
there and entertained us with stories of life under canvas, one
he told us was about how after a certain number of days the
smell of your shit became so strong and individual that you
could smell your way to each other in the dark, like animals,
which no one believed, but everyone laughed, while I described
the fantastic scene from one of Arild Rein's books where the
protagonist shits such a large turd that it can't be flushed, so
he takes it, puts it into the pocket of his suit jacket and goes
out wearing it.

The next day two Danes arrived, Jeppe and Lars; Jeppe's talk was good, and they were great drinking company. They travelled back with me to Stockholm, we went on the booze, I texted Linda, she met us at Kvarnen, embraced me when she arrived, we laughed and chatted, but suddenly my spirits sank, for Jeppe was charismatic, more than usually intelligent and had a strong masculine presence, by which Linda was not unaffected, I sensed. Perhaps that was why I started a discussion with her. Of all the subjects to choose I chose abortion. It didn't seem to bother her, but she went home afterwards, while we continued, ending up going to a nightclub where Jeppe was refused admittance, it must have been something to do with the plastic bag he was carrying, his worn appearance and the fact that he was very drunk. We went back to my place instead, Lars fell asleep, Jeppe and I sat up, the sun rose, he told me about his father, a good person in all ways, and when he said he was dead, a tear ran down his cheek. It was one of those moments that will live long in the memory, perhaps because the confidence came without warning. There was just his head resting against the wall, illuminated by the first soft light of morning, the tear running down his cheek.

The following day we had breakfast in a café, they left for Arlanda Airport, I went back to sleep, left the window open, it rained, the computer, without any form of back-up, was soaked.

I switched it on the next day and it worked fine. Nothing could go wrong any more. Geir called, it was 17 May, Norwegian Independence Day, should we go out for a meal? Him, Christina, Linda and me? I told him about our discussion, he said there were very few topics you should never discuss with women, abortion was one of them. Bloody hell, Karl Ove, almost all of them have had an abortion at some point. How can you wade

out into such deep waters? Call her and ask her out, it may not
mean anything. She probably hasn't given it a thought.

'I can't ring her after that.'

'What's the worst that can happen? If she's angry with you,
she'll just say no. If she isn't she'll say yes. You'll have to suss it
out. You can't stop meeting her because you *suspect* she doesn't
want to know about you.'

I rang.

Yes, she would like to go out.

We went to Creperiet, talked mostly about the relationship
between Norway and Sweden, Geir's showpiece. Linda kept
looking at me, she didn't seem to be offended, but I couldn't be
sure until we were on our own and I could apologise. Well,
there's nothing to apologise for, she said, you have the opinions
you have. No big deal. What about Jeppe then? I thought, but
said nothing of course.

We went to Folkoperan. It was Linda's favourite place. Every
night when they closed they played the Russian national anthem,
and she loved all things Russian, especially Chekhov.

'Have you read Chekhov?' she asked.

'No,' I said.

'Haven't you? You *must*.'

Her lips parted over her teeth when she became enthusiastic,
before she was on the point of saying something, and I sat
watching her talking. She had such beautiful lips. And her eyes,
greyish-green and sparkly, they were so stunning it hurt to look
into them.

'My favourite film's Russian as well. *Burned by the Sun*. Have
you seen it?'

'Afraid not, no.'

'We'll have to see it one day. There's a fantastic girl in it. She's
in the Pioneers, a fantastic political movement for children.'

She laughed.

'It's like I've got a lot to show you,' she said. 'By the way, there's a book reading at Kvarnen in . . . five days. I'm going to read. Do you fancy going?'

'Of course. What are you going to read?'

'Stig Sæterbakken.'

'Why's that?'

'I've translated him into Swedish.'

'Have you now? Why didn't you say?'

'You didn't ask,' she said with a smile. 'He's coming too. I'm a bit nervous about that. My Norwegian's not quite as good as I thought. But he's read the book anyway and didn't have any comments about the language. Do you like him?'

'I like *Siamese* very much.'

'That's the one I translated. With Gilda. Do you remember her?'

I nodded.

'But we can meet before. Are you busy tomorrow?'

'No. It'll be fine.'

Over the tannoys came the first notes of the Russian national anthem. Linda got up, put on her jacket and looked at me.

'Here then? Eight?'

'OK,' I said.

We stopped outside. The shortest route to hers was along Hornsgatan while my place lay in the opposite direction.

'I'll walk you home,' she said. 'May I?'

'Of course,' I said.

We walked in silence.

'It's strange,' I said as we turned into one of the diagonal streets towards Mariaberget. 'I'm so happy to be with you, yet I'm unable to say anything. It's as if you rob me of the power of speech.'

'I've noticed that,' she said, taking a swift glance at me. 'It doesn't matter. Not for me at any rate.'

Why not? I thought. What can you do with a man who says nothing?

We fell into silence again. Our footsteps on the cobbled stones were amplified by the brick houses on either side.

'It was a nice evening,' she said.

'Bit strange,' I said. 'It's 17 May, a date that is evidently in my blood, and I've felt there has been something missing all the time. Why is no one celebrating?'

She stroked my upper arm softly.

As if to tell me it didn't matter if I came out with stupidities?

We stopped in the street beneath my flat. We looked at each other. I stepped forward and gave her a hug.

'See you tomorrow then,' I said.

'Yes,' she said. 'Goodnight.'

I stopped inside the door and went back out a moment later. I wanted to see her for a last time.

She was walking down the hill alone.

I was in love with her.

So what the hell was it that was so painful?

The next day I wrote as usual, ran as usual, sat outdoors reading as usual, this time at Lasse in the Park, across from Långholmen Island. But I couldn't concentrate, I couldn't stop thinking about Linda. I was looking forward to seeing her, there was nothing I wanted more, but a shadow hung over these thoughts unlike all the others I'd had that day.

Why?

Because of what had happened that time?

Of course. But I didn't know what, it was just a feeling I had, and I couldn't hold it to shape it into a clear thought.

The conversation this evening was as tough going as before, and now it was dragging her down too, the enthusiasm and cheeriness of the previous day was almost totally gone.

After an hour we got up and left. In the street she asked me if I wanted a cup of tea at her place.

'Very much,' I said.

Ascending the stairs, I suddenly remembered the incident with the Polish twins. It was a good story, but I couldn't tell it. Too much of the complexity of my feelings for her would be revealed.

'This is where I live,' she said. 'Grab a chair and I'll make us some tea.'

It was a one-room flat: at the far end there was a bed, at the other a dining table. I removed my shoes but kept my jacket on and perched on the edge of the chair.

She was humming in the kitchen.

As she placed a cup of tea in front of me, she said, 'I think I'm becoming fond of you, Karl Ove.'

'Fond'? Was that all? And she said that to my face?

'I like you a lot as well,' I said.

'Do you?' she asked.

There was a pause.

'Do you think we could become anything other than friends?' she asked after a while.

'I want us to be friends,' I said.

She looked at me. Then she looked down, seemed to discover her cup and raised it to her lips.

I got up.

'Have you got any female friends?' she asked. 'I mean ones who are only friends.'

I shook my head.

'Or rather yes. When I went to *gymnas* I had some. But that's a long time ago of course.'

She looked at me again.

'I think I should go,' I said. 'Thanks for the tea.'

She got up and accompanied me to the door. I stepped into the corridor before turning, so that she would not be able to give me a hug.

'Bye,' I said.

'Bye,' she said.

The next morning I went to Lasse in the Park. Laid a pad on the table and started writing her a letter. I wrote down what she meant to me. I wrote what she had been for me when I saw her for the first time, and what she was now. I wrote about her lips sliding over her teeth when she got excited, I wrote about her eyes, when they sparkled and when they opened their darkness and seemed to absorb light. I wrote about the way she walked, the little, almost mannequin-like, waggle of her backside. I wrote about her tiny Japanese features. I wrote about her laughter, which could sometimes wash over everything, how I loved her then. I wrote about the words she used most often, how I loved the way she said 'stars' and the way she flung around the word 'fantastic'. I wrote that all this was what I had seen, and that I didn't know her at all, had no idea what ran through her mind and very little about how she saw the world and the people in it, but that what I could see was enough, I knew I loved her and always would.

'Karl Ove?' someone said. I looked up.

There she was.

I turned the pad over.

How was that possible?

'Hi, Linda,' I said. 'Thanks for the tea yesterday.'

'It was nice to see you. I'm here with a friend. Would you prefer to be on your own?'

'Yes, if you don't mind. I'm working, you see.'

'Of course, I understand.'

We looked at each other. I nodded.

A woman of her age came out holding two cups. Linda turned to her, they went off to the other end and sat down.

I wrote that she had just sat down at the back.

If only I could bridge this distance, I wrote. I would give everything in the world for that. But I can't. I love you, and perhaps you think you love me, but you don't. I believe you like me, I'm fairly sure of that, but I'm not enough for you, and you know that deepest down. Perhaps you need someone now, and then along I came, and you thought, well he might do. But I don't want to be someone who might do, that's not good enough for me, it has to be all or nothing, you have to be ablaze, the way I am ablaze. To want the way I want. Do you understand? Oh, I know you do. I have seen how strong you can be, I have seen how weak you can be and I have seen you open up to the world. I love you, but that isn't enough. Being friends is meaningless. I can't even talk to you! What kind of friendship would that be? I hope you don't take this amiss. I'm just trying to say it as it is. I love you. That is how it is. And somewhere I always will, regardless of what happens to us.

I signed my name, got up, glanced at them, only the girlfriend was in a position to see me, and she didn't know who I was, so I escaped unnoticed, hastened home, tucked the letter into an envelope, changed into running gear and did my route round Söder.

Over the next days it was as though the speed I had within me increased. I ran, I swam, I did everything I could to keep my unease, which consisted of as much happiness as sorrow, at bay, but I failed, I was shaking with an agitation that never seemed to abate, I went on endless walks around the town, ran, swam, lay awake at night, couldn't eat. I had said no, it was over, it would ease.

The reading was on a Saturday, and by the time it arrived I had decided not to go. I rang Geir to see if he wanted to meet me in town, he did, four o'clock at KB, we agreed, I ran to Eriksdal Baths, swam for more than an hour, to and fro in the outdoor pool, it was wonderful, the air was cold, the water warm, the sky grey with light rain, and not a soul around. Up and down I swam. When I got out I was hot with exhaustion. I changed, stood outside for a while smoking, then made a move towards the centre with my bag over my shoulder.

Geir wasn't there when I arrived. I sat down at a window table and ordered a beer. A few minutes later he was in front of me and holding out his hand.

'Anything new?' he asked, sitting down.

'Yes and no,' I said, and told him what had happened over recent days.

'You always have to be so dramatic,' he said. 'Can't you calm down a bit? It doesn't have to be all or nothing.'

'No,' I said. 'In this particular case it's exactly that.'

'Have you sent the letter?'

'No. Not yet.'

At that moment I received a text message. It was from Linda. *'Didn't see you at the reading. Were you there?'*

I started to answer.

'Can't you do that afterwards?' Geir said.

'No,' I said.

'Couldn't make it. Did it go well?'

I sent the message and raised my glass to Geir.

'*Skål*,' I said.

'*Skål*,' he said.

Another message.

'*Missed you. Where are you now?*'

Missed me?

My heart pounded in my chest. I started a new answer.

'Pack it in,' Geir said. 'If you don't, I'm off.'

'I'll be quick,' I said. 'Hang on.'

'*I miss you too. I'm at KB.*'

'It's Linda, isn't it,' Geir said.

'It is,' I answered.

'You're all over the place,' he said. 'Do you realise? I almost felt like turning round in the door when I saw you.'

New message.

'*You come to me, Karl Ove. At Folkoperan. Waiting.*'

I got up.

'Sorry, Geir, but I've got to go.'

'Now?'

'Yes.'

'Come on, man. Surely she can bloody well wait half an hour? I caught the Metro all the way here, and I didn't do that to sit and have a drink on my own. I can do that at home.'

'Sorry,' I said. 'I'll call you.'

I ran into the street, flagged down a taxi, could have screamed with impatience at the lights, but then it pulled over by Folkoperan, I paid and went in.

She was sitting on the ground floor. As soon as I saw her I knew there was no hurry.

She smiled.

'How quick you were!' she said.

'I had the impression it was urgent.'

'No, no, no, not at all.'

I gave her a hug and sat down.

'Do you want a drink?' I asked.

'What are you going to have?'

'I don't know. Red wine?'

'That sounds good.'

We shared a bottle of red, chatted about this and that, nothing of any significance, it was all between us, every time our eyes met a quiver ran through me, and then there was a heavy thud, that was my heart.

'There's a party at Vertigo now,' she said. 'Feel like coming along?'

'OK, sounds good.'

'Stig Sæterbakken's there.'

'That's perhaps not so good. I panned him once. And then I read an interview in which he said he had kept all the reviews which had panned him. The one I wrote must be one of the worst. A whole page in *Morgenbladet*. And then he went after me and Tore in a debate once. Called us Faldbakken and Faldbakken. But I don't suppose that means much to you.'

She shook her head.

'We can go somewhere else?'

'No, no, God, no. Let's go to the party.'

As we left Folkoperan it had started to grow dark. The cloud cover that had been there all day was thickening.

We caught a taxi. Vertigo was situated in a cellar, it was jam-packed, the air was hot and dense with smoke, I turned to Linda and said perhaps we didn't need to stay so long.

'Isn't that Knausgaard?' a voice said. I turned. It was Sæterbakken. He smiled. 'Knausgaard and I are foes,' he said, and added, 'aren't we?' with a look up at me.

'I'm not,' I said.

'Don't chicken out now,' he said. 'But you're right. We've put it behind us. I'm writing a new novel, and I'm trying to do as you've done. Write a bit more in your style.'

Jesus, I thought. That was quite a compliment!

'You don't say,' I said. 'Sounds interesting.'

'Yes, it is very interesting. You wait and see!'

'Talk to you later,' I said.

'Right.'

We went to the bar, ordered gin and tonics, found two unoc-cupied chairs and sat down. Linda knew lots of people here, mingled and kept coming back to me. I became more and more drunk, but the congenial, relaxed mood I had when I saw Linda at Folkoperan continued. We looked at each other. We were a couple. She placed her hand on my shoulder. We were a couple. She met my gaze through the room in the middle of a conversation with someone and smiled. We were a couple.

After we had been there for a few hours and had settled down in two armchairs in a little room at the back of the club Sæterbakken joined us and asked if he could give us a foot massage. He was good at it, he claimed. I said no, not for me. Linda removed her shoes and put her feet in his lap. He started to knead and stroke while looking into her eyes.

'I am good at it, aren't I?' he said.

'Yes, that's wonderful,' Linda said.

'But now it's your turn, Knausgaard.'

'Not for me.'

'Don't be a coward. Come on, take off your shoes.'

In the end I did as he asked, took off my shoes and rested my feet in his lap. In itself it was pleasant, but the fact that it was Stig Sæterbakken sitting there and squeezing my feet with a fixed smile on his face it was difficult to interpret as anything other than devilish, gave the situation a certain ambivalence, to put it mildly.

After he had finished I asked him about his last collection of essays, dealing with evil, then went for a little wander, drank one glass after another, and caught a glimpse of Linda, she was leaning against a wall with a girl I had seen at Valborg, Hilda, Wilda? Shit. No, Gilda.

Linda was so beautiful.

And so unbelievably alive.

Could she really be mine?

Hardly had I articulated the thought when her gaze brushed mine.

She smiled and waved to me.

I walked over.

The time was ripe.

It was now or never.

I swallowed, put my hand on her shoulder.

'This is Gilda,' she said.

'We've met before,' Gilda said with a smile.

'Come here,' I said.

She sent me a quizzical look.

Her eyes were dark.

'Now?' she said.

I didn't answer, just took her hand.

Without a word, we walked through the room. Opened the door, went up the steps. The rain was pelting down.

'I've taken you aside once before,' I said. 'That time it didn't go very well. And maybe this will go belly up too. In which case, so be it. But there is something I want to say. About you.'

'About me?' she said, standing in front of me and looking up, her hair already wet, her face shiny with raindrops.

'Yes,' I said.

And then I began to tell her what she was to me. Everything I had written in the letter I told her. I described her lips, her eyes, the way she walked, the words she used. I said I loved her even though I didn't know her. I said I wanted to be with her. It was all I wanted.

She stretched up onto the tips of her toes, raised her face to me, I bent forward and kissed her.

Then everything went black.

I woke up with two men dragging me by the feet across the tarmac into a gate entrance. One was talking on his mobile, he said, might be drugs, we don't know. They stopped, leaned towards me.

'Are you conscious?'

'Yes,' I said. 'Where am I?'

'Outside Vertigo. Have you been taking drugs?'

'No.'

'What's your name?'

'Karl Ove Knausgaard. I think I fainted. There's no problem. I'm absolutely fine.'

I saw Linda coming towards me.

'Is he conscious?' she asked.

'Hi, Linda,' I said. 'What happened?'

'You don't need to come,' the man said on the phone. 'It's fine here. He's conscious and appears to be coping all right.'

'You fainted, I think,' Linda said. 'You suddenly collapsed.'

'Oh Christ,' I said. 'I'm sorry about that.'

'Nothing to be sorry about,' she said. 'What you said. No one has ever said anything as nice to me.'

'Are you OK?' one of the men asked.

I nodded and they left.

'It was when you kissed me,' I said. 'It was like I felt something black come *shooting* up. And then I woke up over here.'

I got up, staggered a few steps.

'It's probably best to go home,' I said. 'But you can stay if you want.'

She laughed.

'We'll go to my place. I'll take care of you.'

'I love the idea of you taking care of me,' I said.

She smiled and took a mobile phone from her jacket pocket. Her hair was plastered to her forehead. I surveyed my clothes. My trousers were dark with rain. I ran a hand through my hair.

'Strangely enough, I'm not drunk any more,' I said. 'But I am hellishly hungry.'

'When did you last eat?'

'Yesterday some time, I think. In the morning.'

At that moment she got through to the taxi rank, rolled her eyes at me, gave the address and ten minutes later we were in a taxi on our way through the night and the rain.

When I first woke up I didn't know where I was. But then I saw Linda and remembered everything. I snuggled up to her, she opened her eyes, we made love again, and it was so right, was so good I knew with the whole of my being it was her and me, and I told her.

'We must have children together,' I said. 'Anything else would be a crime against nature.'

She laughed.

'It's meant to be,' I said. 'I'm absolutely sure. I've never felt like this ever.'

She stopped laughing and looked at me.

'Do you really mean that?' she asked.

'Yes, I do,' I replied. 'If you don't feel the same then that's something else. But you don't, do you. I can feel that too.'

'Is this real?' she said. 'Are you lying here in my bed? And saying you want children with me?'

'Yes, you do feel the same, don't you?'

She nodded.

'But I would never have said so.'

For the first time in my life I was completely happy. For the first
time there was nothing in my life that could overshadow the
happiness I felt. We were together constantly, suddenly reaching
for each other at traffic lights, across a restaurant table, on buses,
in parks, there were no demands or desires except for each other.
I felt utterly free, but only with her, the moment we were apart
I began to have yearnings. It was strange, the forces were so
strange, and they were good. Geir and Christina said we were
impossible to be with, we had eyes only for each other, and it
was true, there was no world beyond the one we had built. On
Midsummer's night we went to the island of Runmarö, where
Mikaela had rented a cabin, I found myself laughing and singing
through a Swedish night, a happy chuntering idiot, for everything gave meaning, everything was laden with meaning, it was
as if a new light had been cast over the world. In Stockholm we
went swimming, we lay in parks reading, we ate in restaurants,
it didn't matter what we did, it was the fact that we did it that
was important. I read Hölderlin, and his poems flowed into me
like water, there was nothing I didn't understand, the ecstasy
in the poems and the ecstasy in me were the same, and above
all this, every single day throughout June, July and August, the
sun shone. We told each other everything about ourselves, the
way lovers do, and even though we knew it couldn't last, and
the thought that in fact it might was frightening because there
was also something unbearable about it, all this happiness, so
we lived in it as if we didn't know. The fall had to come, but we
didn't bother ourselves about it – how could we when everything
was so great?

One morning when I was in the shower, she called me, I went

into the bedroom, she was lying naked on the bed, it was by the window now, so that we could see the sky.

'Look,' she said. 'Can you see the cloud?'

I lay down beside her. The sky was perfectly blue, there were no clouds apart from the one which was drifting slowly closer. It was shaped like a heart.

'Yes,' I said, squeezing her hand.

She laughed.

'Everything's perfect,' she said. 'I've never ever been like this. I'm so happy with you. I'm so happy!'

'Me too,' I said.

We took a boat to the skerries. Rented a cabin in the forest outside a youth hostel. We walked round the island for hours, delved deep into the forest, everything smelt of pine and heather, suddenly we encountered a steep rock face: beneath us was the sea. We went on, came to a meadow, stopped and watched the cows, they watched us, we laughed, took pictures of each other, climbed up a tree, sat in it chattering like two children.

'Once,' I said, 'I had to buy cigarettes for my father at a petrol station. It was a couple of kilometres from home. I must have been about seven or eight years old. The path there went through a forest. I knew it like the palm of my hand. I still know it like the palm of my hand. Suddenly I heard a rustling in the bushes. I stopped and looked over. There I saw an absolutely fantastic bird, you know, big and multicoloured. I had never seen anything like it before, it was more like a visitor from some distant exotic continent. Africa or Asia. It scampered off and then flew away and disappeared. I've never seen that kind of bird since and I've never found out what it might have been.'

'Is that true?' Linda asked. 'I had exactly the same experience once. At a girlfriend's summer house. I was sitting in a tree, yes, like now, waiting for my friends to return. I got impatient and jumped down. Strolled around aimlessly and suddenly saw a fantastic multicoloured bird. I've never seen it since either.'

'Is that true?'

'Yes.'

That was how it was, everything gave meaning and our lives were interwoven. On the way home from the island we discussed the name of our first child.

'If it's a boy,' I said, 'I would prefer a simple name. Ola, I've always liked that. What do you think?'

'It's good,' she said. 'Very Norwegian. I like that.'

'Yes,' I said, looking out of the window.

A little boat bobbed up and down on its way across. The registration plate on the side said OLA.

'Look there,' I said

Linda leaned forward.

'Then it's decided,' she said. 'Ola it is!'

Late one evening we had been walking up the hill towards my flat, still in the first, feverish phase of the relationship and, after quite a silence, she had said, 'Karl Ove, there's something I have to tell you.'

'Oh yes?' I said.

'I tried to take my life once.'

'What did you say?' I said.

She didn't answer and looked down at the ground in front of her.

'Was that a long time ago?' I asked.

'Two years ago maybe. It was when I was in the clinic.'

I looked at her, she didn't want to meet my eyes, I went up to her and hugged her. We stood like that for a long time. Then we went up the stairs and into the lift, I unlocked the flat, she sat down on the bed, I opened the window and the sounds of a late summer night rose to meet us.

'Would you like some tea?' I asked.

'Please,' she said.

I went to the kitchenette, switched on the kettle, took out two cups and put a teabag in each. After I had passed her one and stationed myself by the open window, sipping at the other cup, she began to tell me what had happened. Her mother had collected her from the hospital, they were on their way to her flat to pick something up. As they got closer Linda set off at a run. Her mother ran after her. Linda ran as fast as she could, through the door, up the stairs, into the flat, to the window. By the time her mother arrived, a few seconds later, Linda had opened the window and clambered up onto the ledge. Her mother sprinted to the window as Linda was about to jump, grabbed her and pulled her back in.

'I went ballistic,' she said. 'I think I wanted to kill her. I pummelled away at her. We fought for maybe ten minutes. I tipped the fridge over her. But she was stronger. Of course she was stronger. In the end she sat astride my chest and I gave up. She rang the police and they came to take me back to hospital.'

There was a pause. I looked at her, she met my gaze, quickly, like a bird.

'I'm ashamed about this,' she said. 'But I thought you should know at some point.'

I didn't know what to say. There was an abyss between the place she had been then and where we were now. At least that was how it felt. Perhaps not for her though?

'Why did you do it?' I asked.

'I don't know. I don't think it was clear in my mind then, either. But I remember the process. I had been manic for several weeks at the end of the summer. One evening Mikaela came to my place, I was crouching on the worktop reciting numbers. She and Öllegård took me to the acute psychiatry clinic. They gave me some sleeping tablets and asked me if Mikaela would have me at home for a few days. Afterwards, over the autumn, one phase alternated with another. And then I hit the buffers in a depression that was so vast I didn't know if there was a way out. I avoided everyone I knew because I didn't want anyone to be the last person to see me alive. The therapist who attended me asked if I had suicidal thoughts, I just burst into tears and she said she couldn't be responsible for me between therapy sessions and so I was admitted to the clinic. I've seen the papers of the admission meeting. Several minutes pass between my being asked a question and my answering, it says, and I can remember that. It was almost impossible for me to speak, impossible to say anything, the words were so far away. Everything was so far away. My face was a stiff mask. There was no expression in it.'

She looked up at me. I sat down on the bed. She put the cup down on the table and lay back. I lay beside her. There was a heaviness in the darkness outside, a kind of body to it that was alien to a midsummer night. A train rattled across the bridge by Ridderfjärden.

'I was dead,' she said. 'It wasn't that I wanted to leave my life. I had already left it. When the therapist said I was going to be admitted to the clinic I felt relief that someone wanted to take care of me. But when I got there it was all totally impossible. I couldn't stay. And that was when I began to hatch a plan. My sole chance of getting out was a day permit to fetch clothes and so on from my flat. Someone had to be with me, the only person I could think of was my mother.'

She fell silent.

'But if I'd *really* wanted it I would have succeeded. That's what

I think now. I wouldn't have needed to open the window; I could have thrown myself through it. It wouldn't exactly have made much of a difference. But the care I took . . . Yes, if I had really wanted to, with all my heart, it would have worked.'

'I'm happy it didn't,' I said, running my hand through her hair. 'But are you afraid it will happen again?'

'Yes.'

There was a silence.

The woman I rented the bedsit from was making a noise on the other side of the door. Someone coughed on the roof terrace above us.

'I'm not,' I said.

She turned her face to me.

'Aren't you?'

'No. I know you.'

'Not all of me.'

'Of course not,' I said, and kissed her. 'But it will never happen again, I'm sure of that.'

'Then I'm sure too,' she said with a smile, and put her arms around me.

The endless summer nights, so light and open, with us drifting between a selection of bars and cafés in various parts of town in black taxis, alone or with others, the drinking not menacing, not destructive, but a wave raising us higher and higher, it started slowly and darkened imperceptibly, it was as though the sky was attached to the earth, and the light airiness had less and less room, something filled it and held it firm, until at last the night was still, a wall of darkness descended in the evening and rose in the morning, and the light eddying summer night was no longer imaginable, like a dream you try in vain to recapture on waking.

Linda started at the Dramatiska Institut. The introductory
course was hard, they were thrown into all kinds of difficult
situations. I suppose the idea was that it was best to learn
from their experience under pressure as they went along.
When she cycled up to the school in the morning I went to
the flat to write. I had woven the story of the angels into a
story about a woman in a maternity ward in 1944, she had
just given birth, her mind drifted hither and thither, but it
didn't work, the text was too remote, the distance too great.
Nevertheless I continued, slogged through page after page, it
didn't matter, the most important, no, the only focus in my
life was Linda.

One Sunday we were having lunch at an Östermalm café called
Oscar near Karlaplan, we were sitting outside, Linda with a
blanket over her legs, me eating a club sandwich, Linda a chicken
salad, the street was Sunday-still, the bells below us had just
pealed for the church service. Three girls sat at a table behind
us, two men a little way behind them. Some sparrows were
hopping on the tables closest to the road. They seemed quite
tame, approached the plates left behind with small hops,
nodding their whole heads as they poked their beaks into the
food.

Suddenly a shadow plummets through the air, I look up, it is
an enormous bird, it screams towards us, brushes the table of
small birds, grabs one of them in its claws and soars upward
again.

I turned to Linda. She was staring into the air with her mouth
agape.

'Did a bird of prey just take one of the sparrows or was I
dreaming?' I asked.

'I've never seen anything like that before. It was horrible,'

Linda said. 'In the middle of town? What was it? An eagle? A hawk? Poor little bird!'

'It must have been a hawk,' I said, laughing. The sight had excited me. Linda looked at me with smiling eyes.

'My grandfather on my mum's side was bald,' I said. 'He had only a corona of white hair left. When I was small he used to say the chicken hawk had taken it. Then he demonstrated how the hawk had set its claws in his hair and flown off with it. The proof was the corona that was left. And for a while I believed him. I squinted into the sky looking for it. But I never saw it.'

'Not until now,' Linda said.

'I'm not sure it was the same one,' I said.

'No,' she said with a smile. 'When I was five I kept a little hamster in a cage. In the summer we went to our summer house, where I used to let it free. I put the cage on the lawn and let it potter around in the grass. One morning while I was on the terrace watching it, a bird of prey dived down, and whoosh, my hamster was on its way up through the air.'

'Is that true?'

'Yes.'

'How terrible!' I laughed, pushed my plate away, lit a cigarette and leaned back. 'Grandad had a gun, I remember. Sometimes he used to shoot crows. He injured one of them – that is, he shot off a leg. It survived and it's still at the farm now. At least, according to Kjartan, it is. A one-legged crow with staring eyes.'

'Fantastic,' Linda said.

'A kind of avian Captain Ahab,' I said. 'And grandad patrolling the ground like the great white whale.'

I looked at her.

'What a shame it is you never met him. You would have liked him.'

'And you would have liked mine.'

'You were there when he died, weren't you?'

She nodded.

'He had a stroke, and I went up to Norrland. But he died before I arrived.'

She grabbed my cigarette pack, looked at me, I nodded and she took one.

'But it was my grandma I was close to,' she said. 'She used to come down to Stockholm to see us and took charge of everything. The first thing she did was to clean the whole house. She baked and cooked and was with us. She was really strong.'

'Your mother is too.'

'Yes. In fact, she is becoming more and more like her. I mean, after she stopped at the Royal Dramatic Theatre and moved into the country it's as if she's resumed her life from those days. She grows her own vegetables, makes all her own food, has *four* freezers full of food and produce she's bought on offer. And now she doesn't care what she looks like, at least not compared with how she was before.'

She looked at me.

'Have I told you about the time my grandma saw red northern lights?'

I shook my head.

'She saw them when she was out walking. The whole sky was red, the light billowed backwards and forwards, it must have been beautiful, but also a bit doomsday-like. When she came back and told us no one believed her. She barely believed it herself, red northern lights, who's ever heard of that? Have you?'

'No.'

'But then, many, many years later, I was out with my mother in Humlegården late one night. And we saw the same thing! We have the northern lights here now and then, it's rare, but it does happen. That night they were red! Mummy rang grandma as soon as she was home. Grandma cried. Later I read about it and discovered it was a rare meteorological phenomenon.'

I leaned across the table and kissed her.

'Would you like a coffee?'

She nodded and I went in and ordered two coffees. When I returned and put her cup in front of her she was looking up at me.

'I remembered another strange story,' she said. 'Or perhaps it isn't so strange. But it seemed like it was. I was on one of the islands outside Stockholm. Walking in the forest on my own. Above me – and it wasn't far above either, directly above the trees – I saw an airship gliding through the air. It was quite magical. It came from nowhere and floated above the forest and was gone. An airship!'

'I've always been fascinated by airships,' I said. 'Ever since I was little. For me, it's as close to fantasy as I can imagine. A world of airships! Oh, it does something to me, that does, but I'm damned if I know what. What do you think it is?'

'If I've understood you correctly you used to be fascinated by divers, sailing boats, space travel and airships when you were a boy. You said once that you made drawings of divers, astronauts and sailing boats, didn't you? Was that all?'

'Yes, more or less.'

'Well, what can one say about that? An insatiable travel bug? Divers, that's as far down as you can go. Astronauts, that's as high as you can go. Sailing boats, that's a long way back in our history. And airships, that's the world that never materialised.'

'I suppose that's right. Not as a big, dominant mode of transport anyway. It was more on the periphery, if you know what I mean. When you're small you're full of the world, that's what life's all about. It's impossible to resist. And you don't have to, either. At least not always.'

'Well then?' she said.

'Well what?'

'Do you long to get away now?'

'Are you crazy? This summer must be the first since I was sixteen that I haven't.'

We got up and headed towards Djurgården Bridge.

'Did you know that the first airships couldn't be steered, and so to solve the problem they tried to train birds of prey, falcons I suppose, but perhaps eagles as well, to fly with long cables in their beaks?'

'No,' I said. 'All I know is that I love you.'

Even during these new days, which in quite a different way from previously were filled with routines, there was a great feeling of freedom for me. We got up early, Linda cycled off to school, I sat writing all day, unless I popped up to Filmhuset and had lunch with her, and then we met again early in the evening and were together until we went to bed. At the weekends we ate out and got drunk at night, in the bar at Folkoperan, which was our local, or at Guldapan, another favourite haunt, at Folkhemmet or the big bar in Odenplan.

Everything was as it had been, yet it wasn't, for imperceptibly, so imperceptibly that it seemed as if it wasn't happening, something in our lives lost its lustre. The fire that drove us towards each other and into the world no longer burned as bright. Atmospheres could spring up. One Saturday I awoke thinking how nice it would be to have some time for myself, visit some second-hand bookshops, go to a café and read the papers . . . We got up, went to the nearest café, ordered breakfast – porridge, yoghurt, toast, eggs, juice and coffee – I read the papers, Linda stared down at the table or into the room, said at length, do you have to read, couldn't we talk? Yes, of course, I said, closing the newspaper, and we chatted, it was fine, the tiny black spot in my heart was barely noticeable, a little hankering to be alone and read in peace without anyone demanding anything of me was forgotten in a flash. But then came the time when it wasn't, when on the contrary it led to ensuing atmospheres and actions. If you really love me, you have to come to me without demands, I thought but didn't say, I wanted her to notice on her own.

One evening Yngve called, he was wondering if I wanted to go with him and Asbjørn to London, I said, yes, of course, perfect. As I rang off Linda was watching me from the other side of the room.

'Who was that?' she asked.

'Yngve. He wanted me to go to London with him.'

'I hope you didn't say yes?'

'I did. Shouldn't I have done?'

'But we were going to travel together. You can't travel with him before you travel with me!'

'What are you talking about? This has nothing to do with you.'

She looked down at the book she was reading. Her eyes were black. I didn't want her to lose her temper. But to have the disagreement hanging in the air was intolerable for me, I needed clarity.

'I haven't spent a moment with Yngve for an incredibly long time. You have to remember I don't know anyone here except your friends. Mine live in Norway.'

'Yngve has just been here, hasn't he.'

'Oh, come on.'

'Just go then,' she said.

'OK,' I said.

Afterwards, when we were in bed, she apologised for having been so uncharitable. It didn't matter, I said. It was nothing.

'We haven't been apart since we got together,' she said.

'No,' I said. 'Perhaps it's time we were.'

'What do you mean?' she said.

'We can't live on top of each other for the rest of our lives,' I said.

'I think we're fine,' she said.

'Yes, we are fine,' I said. 'You know what I mean.'

'Of course I do,' she said. 'But I'm not sure I agree.'

From London I rang her twice every day, and spent almost all my money on a present for her, it was her thirtieth a few weeks later. At the same time I realised, presumably because I saw our Stockholm life from a distance for the first time, that I would have to knuckle down when I got home, start working harder, for not only had the whole of the long summer disappeared in happiness, and inner and outer extravagance, but September had also passed without my having achieved anything. It was four years since I had made my debut, and a second book was nowhere in sight, apart from the 800 pages with a variety of beginnings I had accumulated since then. I had written my debut novel at night, got up at eight in the evening and worked right through until the next morning, and the freedom that lay in it, in the space the night opened, was perhaps what was necessary to find a way into something new. I had been close in recent weeks in Bergen and the first few in Stockholm, with the story that had aroused my interest about a father who went crabbing one summer's night with his two sons, one obviously me, I found a dead seagull I showed dad, he told me seagulls had once been angels, and we left in the boat with live crabs crawling inside a bucket on the deck. Geir Gulliksen had said, 'There's your opening,' and he had been right, but I didn't know where it would lead, and I had been grappling with it for the last few months. I had written about a woman in a maternity ward in the 1940s, the child she gave birth to was Henrik Vankel's father, and the house waiting for her return with the baby was originally an old hovel, full of bottles, which they had demolished to build a new house. But the story wasn't genuine, everything sounded false, I was going nowhere. So I tried another tack, in the same house, where two brothers are asleep at night, their father is dead, one lies looking at the other sleeping. That sounded equally false, and my despair grew, would I ever be able to write another novel?

The first Monday after I had returned from London I told Linda we couldn't meet the next evening because I had to work through the night. Yes, fine, no problem. At nine she texted me, I answered, she sent another message, she was out with Cora, they were at a place nearby having a beer, I texted, have a good time, said I loved her, a couple more texts went to and fro, then all went quiet and I thought she had gone back to her place. But she hadn't, at around twelve she knocked on my door.

'Are you here?' I said. 'I told you I was going to write.'

'Yes, but your texts were so warm and loving. I thought you would want me to come.'

'I have to work,' I said. 'I'm serious.'

'I understand,' she said, already out of her jacket and shoes. 'But can't I sleep here while you're working?'

'You know I won't be able to. I can't even write with a cat in the room.'

'You've never tried with me in the room. I may have a good effect.'

Even though I was angry I couldn't bring myself to say no. I had no right to be because what I was implying was that the miserable manuscript I was writing was more important than her. At that moment it was, but I couldn't say that.

'OK,' I said.

We drank tea and smoked in front of the open window, then she undressed and went to bed. The room was small, the desk was barely a metre away, it was impossible to concentrate with her in the room, and the fact that she had come despite knowing I didn't want her to gave me a feeling of suffocation. But I didn't want to go to bed either, to let her win, so after half an hour I got up and told her I was going out. This was a demonstration, it was my way of saying I couldn't put up with this, and so I went into the misty streets of Söder, bought a grilled sausage at a petrol station, sat in the park below the flat and smoked five cigarettes in quick succession while surveying the glittering town beneath me and wondering what the hell was going on. How the hell had I ended up in this situation?

The next night I worked through till the morning, slept all day, spent a couple of hours at hers, came back and wrote all night, slept and was woken by Linda in the afternoon, she wanted to speak. We went for a walk.

'Don't you want to be with me any more?' she asked.

'Yes, of course I do,' I said.

'But we aren't together. We don't see each other.'

'Yes, but I have to work. Surely you understand that.'

'Well, not that you have to work at night. I love you, so I want to be with you.'

'But I have to work,' I repeated.

'OK,' she said. 'If you keep doing this, it's over.'

'You can't mean that.'

She eyed me.

'I damn well do. Just you try me.'

'You can't control me like that,' I said.

'I'm not controlling you. It's a reasonable request. We're in a relationship, and I don't want to be on my own the whole time.'

'The whole time?'

'Yes. I'll leave you if you don't stop.'

I sighed.

'It's not that bloody important,' I said. 'I'll stop.'

'Fine,' she said.

I mentioned this on the telephone to Geir next day, he said, Shit, man, are you out of your mind? You're a writer, for Christ's sake! You can't let someone tell you what to do! No, I said, but that's not exactly what this is about. It's what it costs. What what costs? he asked. The relationship, I said. I don't understand, he said. This is where you have to be hard. You can compromise on anything else, but not this. But I'm soft, as you know, I said. Tall and soft, he said with a laugh. But it's your life.

September passed, the leaves on the trees turned yellow, turned red and fell off. The blue of the sky deepened, the sun sank, the air was clear and cold. In mid-October Linda gathered all her friends at an Italian restaurant in Söder. She was thirty and filled with an inner light that made her beam and me proud: I was in a relationship with her. Proud and grateful, those were my feelings. The town sparkled around us as we walked home, Linda in the white jacket I had given her as a present that morning, and walking there, hand in hand with her, in the midst of this beautiful and, for me, still foreign town, sent wave after wave of pleasure through me. We were still full of ardour and desire, for our lives had turned, not just on the breath of a passing wind, but fundamentally. We planned to have children. We had no sense of anything awaiting us except happiness. At least I didn't. I never give a thought to issues which are only about life, the way it is lived, inside me and around me and which are not about philosophy, literature, art or politics. I feel, and my feelings determine my actions. The same applies to Linda, perhaps even more so.

At this time I was asked if I would teach at the writers' school

in Bø, this was not my normal fare, but Thure Erik Lund was
going to hold a two-week course and had been asked to choose
a writer he would like to work with. Linda considered two weeks
a long time, she didn't want me to be away from her for so long,
and I thought, yes, it *is* a long time, she *can't* stay here in
Stockholm while I am in Norway. Yet I wanted to accept the
offer. My writing wasn't making progress, I needed to do something different, Thure Erik was one of the writers I admired
most. I mentioned this to my mother on the telephone one night,
and she said we didn't have any children, why couldn't she be
alone for a couple of weeks? It's your job, she said. And she was
right. A little step to the side, and everything would be fine. But
I hardly ever took that step, Linda and I lived so close together
in more ways than one: Linda's flat in Zinkensdamm was dark
and cramped, one and a half rooms was all we had, and it was
as if life was slowly swallowing us up. The previous openness
had closed in, our lives had been as one for so long they were
beginning to stiffen and chafe against each other. There were
little episodes, insignificant in themselves, but together they
formed a pattern, a new system beginning to settle.

Late one evening while I was accompanying her to drama
practice she suddenly turned to me at a petrol station by Slussen,
and gave me an earful over some tiny matter, told me to go to
hell, I asked her what was up, she didn't answer and was already
ten metres ahead of me. I followed.

One afternoon we were at the food hall, Saluhallen, in
Hötorget, to do some shopping for a meal we were going to have
with two of her friends, Gilda and Kettil, and I suggested making
pancakes. She eyed me with obvious scorn. Pancakes are for
children, she said. We're not having a children's party. OK, I
said, let's call them crêpes then. Is that good enough for you?
She turned her back on me.

We walked round this beautiful town at weekends, everything was great, but then all of a sudden it wasn't great any more, a darkness opened inside her, and I didn't know what to do. For the first time since I had come to Stockholm the feeling that I was on my own reappeared.

She fell into a pit that autumn. And she reached out for me. I didn't understand what was happening. But it was so claustrophobic that I turned away from her, tried to maintain a distance, which she tried to close.

I went to Venice, wrote in a flat my publishing house had at its disposal, Linda was supposed to follow and stay for just under a week, then I would work for a few more days and return. She was so black, she was so heavy, kept saying I didn't love her, I didn't really love her, I didn't want her, I didn't really want her, this wasn't working, it would never work, I didn't want it to, I didn't want her.

'But I do!' I said as we walked in the autumn chill in Murano with eyes hidden behind sunglasses. However, when she said I didn't really love her, I didn't really want to be with her, I wanted to be alone all the time, on my own, it became a little truer.

Where did her despair come from?

Had I brought it with me?

Was I cold?

Did I only think of myself?

I no longer knew what it would be like when my working day was over and I went to her place. Would she be happy, would it be a nice evening? Would she be angry about something, if for example we no longer made love every night, and so I didn't love her as much as before? Would we sit in bed watching TV? Go for a walk to Långholmen? And once there, would I be devoured by her demands to have all of me, making me keep her at a distance and have thoughts shooting to and fro in my brain that this had to come to an end, it wasn't working, thus rendering any conversation or attempts to get closer impossible, which of course she noticed and took as proof of her main thesis, that I didn't want her?

Or would we simply have a good time together?

I became more and more closed, and the more closed I became the more she attacked me. And the more she attacked me, the more aware I became of her mood swings. Like a meteorologist of the mind I followed her, not so much consciously as with my emotions, which, almost uncannily fine-tuned, tracked her various moods. If she was angry her presence was all that existed in me. It was like having a bloody great dog in the room growling, and I had to take care of it. Sometimes, when we were sitting and chatting, I could feel her strength, the depth of her experience, and I felt inferior. Sometimes when she approached me and I held her, or when I lay embracing her, or when we chatted and she was all insecurity and unease, I felt so much stronger that everything else became irrelevant. These fluctuations, without anything to hold on to, and the constant threat of some kind of outburst, followed by the unfailing reconciliation and smoothing of feathers, continued unabated, there was no let-up, and the feeling that I was alone, also with her, grew stronger and stronger.

In the short time we had known each other we had never done anything half-heartedly, and this was no exception.

One evening we'd had a row and after we had made up, we began to talk about children. We had decided to have a child while Linda was at the Dramatiska Institut, she could drop out for six months, and then I could take over while she finished her training. For it to work she would have to stop the medication, so she had to set this up; the doctors were reluctant, but the therapist supported her and, when it came to the crunch, the final decision was hers.

We discussed this nearly every day.

Now I said perhaps we should postpone it.

Apart from the light from the television, which was on in the corner, with the sound turned down, the flat was in total darkness. The autumnal darkness was like an ocean outside the windows.

'Perhaps we should put it off for a while,' I said.

'What did you say?' Linda said, staring at me.

'We can wait a bit, see how things go. You can finish your course . . .'

She got up and slapped my face with the palm of her hand as hard as she could.

'Never!' she shouted.

'What are you doing?' I said. 'Have you gone mad? *Hitting me like that!*'

My cheek stung. She had hit me really hard.

'I'm off,' I said. 'And I'm never coming back. So you can forget that.'

I turned and went into the hall, took my coat from the hook. Behind me she was crying, bitter tears.

'Don't go, Karl Ove,' she said. 'Don't leave me now.'

I turned.

'Do you think you can do as you like? Is that what you think?'

'Forgive me,' she said. 'But stay. Just tonight.'

I stood motionless in the darkness by the door and looked at her, vacillating.

'OK,' I said. 'I'll stay here tonight. But then I'm going.'

'Thank you,' she said.

At seven next morning I woke and left the flat without breakfast, went to my earlier flat, which I still had. Took a cup of coffee with me to the roof terrace, sat smoking and looking out over the town wondering what to do next.

I couldn't stay with her. It was impossible.

I rang Geir on my mobile, did he feel like a trip to Djurgården, it was quite important, I had to talk to someone. Yes, he did, just had to finish off a few jobs first, we could meet by the bridge outside the Nordic Museum, and then walk right to the end, where there was a restaurant in which we could have lunch. And that was what we did, we walked under the masonry-grey sky, between the leafless trees, on a path gaily strewn with yellow, red and brown leaves. I said nothing about what had happened, it was too humiliating, I couldn't tell anyone she had slapped me because what would that make me? I said only that we had quarrelled and that I didn't know what to do any more. He said I should listen to my heart. I said I didn't know what I felt. He said he was sure I did.

But I didn't. I had two different sets of feelings for her. One said you have to get out, she wants too much from you, you're going to lose all your freedom, waste all your time on her, and what will happen to all you hold dear, your independence and your writing? The other set said, you love her, she gives you something others can't and she knows who you are. Exactly who you are. Both sets were equally right, but they were incompatible, one excluded the other.

On this day thoughts of leaving were uppermost in my mind.

When Geir and I were in the Metro carriage coming out of Västertorp, she rang. Asked if I wanted to eat with her in the evening, she had bought crabs, my favourite food. I said yes, we would have to talk anyway.

I rang the doorbell even though I had a key, she opened and studied me with a careful smile.

'Hi,' she said.

She was wearing the white blouse I liked so much.

'Hi,' I said.

One hand moved forward as though intending to embrace me, but it stopped and she took a step back instead.

'Come in,' she said.

'Thank you,' I replied. Hung my jacket on the hook, body angled slightly away from her. As I turned she reached up and we gave each other a hug.

'Are you hungry?' she asked.

'Yes, quite,' I said.

'Then let's eat straight away.'

I followed her to the table, which was under the window on the other side of the room from the bed. She had laid a white cloth. Between the two plates and glasses, plus two bottles of beer, there was a candlestick with three candles, and three small flames flickered in the draught. A dish of crabs, a basket of white bread, butter, lemon and mayonnaise as well.

'I'm not so skilled with crabs, it transpired,' she said. 'I didn't know how to open them. Perhaps you do?'

'Sort of,' I said.

I broke off the legs, opened the shells and removed the stomachs while she flipped off the bottle tops.

'What have you been doing today?' I said, passing her a shell which was almost completely full.

'I couldn't even think of going to class, so I rang Mikaela and had lunch with her.'

'Did you tell her what happened?'

She nodded.

'That you slapped me?'

'Yes.'

'What did she say?'

'Not much. She listened.'

She looked at me.

'Can you forgive me?'

'Of course. I just don't understand why you did it. How can you lose control of yourself like that? I assume you hadn't intended to do it? I mean, on reflection?'

'Karl Ove,' she said.

'Yes?' I said.

'I'm very sorry. Terribly sorry. But it was what you said that hit me so hard. Before I met you I hadn't even dared imagine that I might have children one day. I didn't dare. Even when I fell in love with you I didn't. And then you said what you said. It was you who brought up the subject, do you remember? The very first morning. I want to have children with you. And I was so happy. I was so utterly, insanely happy. Just the fact that there was a possibility. It was you who gave me that possibility. And then . . . yesterday . . . well, it was like you were withdrawing the possibility. You said perhaps we should put off having children. That hit me so hard, it was so crushing, and then . . . well . . . I completely lost control.'

Her eyes were moist as she held the crab shell over the slice of bread and tried to lever out the firm flesh along the edge with the knife.

'Do you understand?' she said.

I nodded.

'Of course I do. But you can't do as you please, however strong your emotions are. That's no good. I mean, for Christ's sake. That just won't do. I can't live like that. The feeling that you might turn on me and start slapping me. It won't do, I can't live with that. We're supposed to be together, aren't we. We can't be enemies, I couldn't stand that, I don't have the energy. It's no good, Linda.'

'No, it isn't,' she said. 'I'll pull myself together. I promise you.'

We sat quietly for a while, eating. The moment one of us

changed the topic of conversation to something more usual and humdrum, what had happened would also be over.

I wanted to and didn't want to.

The crab meat on the bread was both smooth and uneven, reddish-brown like the leaves on the field, and the salty, almost bitter taste of sea, softened by the sweetness of the mayonnaise, yet sharpened by the lemon juice, overtook all my senses for a few seconds.

'Is it good?' she asked with a smile.

'Yes, it's really good,' I replied.

What I had said to her on the first morning we had woken up together had not been just something I said but something I felt with all my heart and soul. I wanted to have children with her. I had never felt that before. And this feeling made me certain it was right, that this was right.

But at any price?

My mother came to Stockholm, I introduced her to Linda at a restaurant, it seemed to go well, Linda shone, shy and extrovert at the same time, while I watched mum and her reactions. She was staying in my flat, I said goodnight to her at the gate, she went in and I jogged back to Linda's flat, which was ten minutes away. The next day, when I collected her to have breakfast at a café, mum told me she hadn't been able to put the light on in the hallway and so it had taken her almost an hour to get into the flat.

'The light turned itself off while I was on the stairs,' she said. 'Automatically. I couldn't see a metre in front of me.'

'That's the Swedes saving energy,' I said. 'They never leave a room without switching off the light. And in communal areas there are automatic time switches. But why didn't you turn it back on, if I might ask?'

'It was too dark to see the switches.'

'But the switches are luminous.'

'So *that* was what was shining!' she said. 'I thought they were the fire alarms or something.'

'What about your lighter?' I said.

'Yes, I remembered that eventually. I was so desperate that I fumbled my way downstairs to have a cigarette and that was when I found it. So then I went back up, flicked it on, opened the door and went in.'

'That's so typical of you,' I said.

'Maybe,' she said. 'But this is a different country, that's why. The little details are different.'

'What do you think about Linda?'

'She's a lovely girl,' she said.

'Yes, isn't she,' I said.

She didn't have to say that, of course. Well, I wasn't in any doubt that she would like Linda, it was more that I had just been in such a long, established relationship. Married even. Tonje had been part of the family, it was as simple as that. Even though the relationship was over, the feelings they had for her were not. Yngve was sorry she was no longer around, and perhaps mum was too. At the end of the summer, after Tonje and I had divided all our possessions without any trauma – we were good to each other – the only time a semblance of sorrow came over me was when I was in the cellar fetching something and was suddenly brought up with a sob – we'd had a life together, now it was over. After the days there, which passed without any conflict, I went to mum's place in Jølster with our cat, which she was going to keep. I told her about Linda then. It was obvious she wasn't best pleased, but she didn't say anything. Half an hour later a sentence crossed her lips which caused me to take stock of her. It was so unlike mum to say that sort of thing. She said I couldn't see other people. I was completely blind, I saw only myself everywhere. Your father, she said, he looked straight into people. He saw immediately who they were. You've never done that. No, I said, perhaps I haven't.

I'm sure she was right, but that wasn't so important, the significant issue was partly that she had ranked dad, that terrible human being, above me, and partly that she had done it because she was angry with me. And that was new, mum was never angry with me.

At that time Linda and I were still in the glow zone, and she must have seen that I was glowing with love and *joie de vivre*.

In Stockholm a little more than six months later everything was different. I was full of grudges, the relationship was so claustrophobic and dark that I wanted to leave, but I couldn't, I was too weak, I thought about her, I pitied her, without me she would be lost, I was too weak, I loved her.

Then came the lunches at Filmhuset, where we sat chatting about everything under the sun, gesticulating enthusiastically, or at home in the flat or at cafés, there was so much to say, there was so much to cover, not just my life and hers, as it had been, but also our lives, as they were now, with all the people who populated them. Before, I had always been deep inside myself, observing people from there, like from the back of a garden. Linda brought me out, right to the edge of myself, where everything was near and everything seemed stronger. Then came the films at Cinemateket, the nights out on the town, the weekends with her mother in Gnesta, the stillness of the forest, in which she sometimes looked like a little girl and showed how vulnerable she was. Then there was the trip to Venice, she *shouted* that I didn't love her, she kept shouting it again and again. In the evenings we got drunk and made love with a wildness that was new and alien and also frightening, not at the time, but

the next day, when I reflected on it, it was as though we wanted
to hurt each other. After she had left I could hardly be bothered
to go out, I tried to write in the loft of the flat, I could barely
drag myself the few hundred metres to the grocer's and back.
The walls were cold, the alleyways empty, the canals full of
coffin-like gondolas. What I saw was dead, what I wrote of no
value.

One day, sitting like this, alone in the cold Italian apartment,
I happened to recall what Stig Sæterbakken had said the evening
I got together with Linda. That in his next novel he would try
to write a little more like me.

Suddenly my face burned with shame.

The comment had been sarcastic and I hadn't understood.

I thought he had MEANT it.

Oh, how conceited do you have to be to believe that sort of
comment? How utterly stupid can you be? Were there no limits?

I got up quickly, hurried down the stairs, put on my clothes
and dashed round the alleyways along the canals for an hour
trying to find the beauty in the filthy deep green water, the
ancient stone walls, the splendour in the whole of this crooked
and crumbling world, to stem the enormous bitterness against
myself that the recognition of Sæterbakken's sarcasm caused to
flood over me time and time again.

In a large piazza I entered without warning I sat down and
ordered a coffee, lit a cigarette and considered at length that
perhaps this was not a matter of much import.

I raised the tiny cup to my lips with my index and middle
fingers, which seemed monstrously large by comparison, leaned
back in the chair and peered up at the sky. I never paid any
attention to it inside the labyrinthine network of streets and
canals, it was a bit like wandering through underground
passages. When the narrow streets opened up into piazzas, and

the sky stretched across the rooftops and church spires it always came as a surprise. That was how it was, yes: the sky did exist! The sun did exist! It felt as though I also became more open, lighter in colour and weight.

For all I knew, Sæterbakken might have thought my enthusiastic response was *also* sarcastic.

Later that autumn the temperature plummeted, all the water and the canals in Stockholm froze, one Sunday we walked on the ice from Söder to Stockholm Old Town, I hobbled along like the hunchback of Notre Dame, she laughed and took photos of me, I took photos of her, everything was sharp and clear, including my feelings for her. We clicked on the photos and looked at them in a café, ran home to make love, rented two films, bought a pizza, lay in bed all evening. It was one of the days I will always remember, perhaps precisely because it comprised normal frivolous activities that became overlaid with gold.

The winter came and with it snow whirling in the air above the town. White streets, white roofs, all sounds softened. One evening while we were out wandering aimlessly in all the whiteness and, perhaps from force of habit, approaching the mountain along which Bastugatan ran, she asked me where I was planning to spend Christmas. I said at home, with my mother in Jølster. She wanted to join me. I said that wasn't appropriate, it was too early. Why was it too early? Surely you know. No, I don't. Right.

It developed into a row. We sat in the Bishop's Arms with a beer in front of us without saying a word, incensed. To compensate, my Christmas present to her was a surprise trip; when I returned on the 27th we went to Arlanda Airport and she didn't know our destination until I gave her the ticket: Paris. We were there for a week. But Linda had an attack of nerves, the city stressed her, she lost her temper over nothing and was constantly unreasonable. When we were eating dinner on the first evening and I was flustered with the waiter because I didn't know quite how to behave in fine surroundings, she sent me a glare full of disdain. Oh, it was hopeless. What had I got myself caught up in? Where was my life going? I wanted to do some shopping but could see that was not on, she already disliked Paris and hated it now, and as she hated being alone most, I dropped the idea. The days could begin well, such as when we went to the Eiffel Tower, the building with the most intense nineteenth-century aura I had seen, and then collapse into black, unreasonable moods, or they could start badly and end well, such as when we called on a girlfriend of Linda's who lived in Paris, next to the cemetery where Marcel Proust was buried and which we visited afterwards. And on New Year's Eve, which we spent in an elegant intimate restaurant thanks to a tip from my Francophile friend in Bergen, Johannes, and were spoilt in every conceivable manner, we sat there glowing as in the old days, that is, six months previously, until, an hour into the New Year, we walked hand in hand along the Seine to our hotel. And whatever it was that oppressed her in Paris, it was gone the instant we arrived at the airport heading for home.

The owner of the flat I was renting was going to sell it, so I moved all my possessions, that is all my books, to a warehouse outside town on one of the first days in January, cleaned up, handed over the keys, and Linda enquired around her friends to see if they knew of an office somewhere, and yes, Cora had heard about some sort of collective for freelancers, they had a place at the top of the palace-like construction towering over the peak of the small mountain on one side of Slussen, only a hundred metres from the flat I'd had, I got a room and started working there during the day. It was a new beginning, I added the last hundred pages to the already long file of beginnings, and recommenced. This time I tackled the little angel theme. I bought one of those cheap art books, full of pictures of angels, and one of them attracted my interest: it was of three angels out walking in the Italian countryside, wearing sixteenth-century clothes. I wrote about someone who saw them walking, a boy who was keeping an eye on some sheep, one had gone missing and while looking for it, through some trees, he saw the angels. It was a rare sight, but not so very unusual, angels were to be found in forests and on the margins of human activity and had been for as long as people could remember. That was as far as I got. What was the story?

This had nothing to do with me, nothing of my life was in it, consciously or unconsciously, and that meant I couldn't get involved in it, couldn't drive it forward. I might just as well have been writing about the Phantom and the Skull Cave.

Where was the story?

One meaningless day's work followed another. I had no alternative but to keep going, there was nothing else. The people I shared office space with were nice enough, but so full of radical-left goodness that I was left speechless when – having used the word 'negro' and immediately been corrected in conversation by one of them while waiting for the coffee machine to brew – I discovered that the man who cleaned the offices, the kitchen and the toilet for them was black. They observed solidarity, equality and consideration towards others in their language and spread a kind of net over a reality which continued on its unjust and discriminating path below them. I couldn't say this. Twice there had been break-ins; one morning when I arrived the police were on the premises asking questions. Computer and photography equipment had been stolen. Since the main front door had not been broken, only the one into our offices, they concluded the culprit had to be someone with a key. Afterwards we sat discussing the matter. I said this was not a hard nut to crack. After all, there were several nameless drug addicts on the floor below. One of them must have got hold of the key. Everyone stared at me. You can't say that, one of them declared. I looked at him in surprise. That's prejudice, he said. We don't know who did it. It could have been anyone. Just because they're drug addicts and have a troubled past, it doesn't mean they broke in here! We have to give them a chance! I nodded and said he was right, we couldn't know for certain. But inwardly I was shaken. I had seen the bunch of them hanging around the staircase before and after the meetings they held, they were the types that would do anything for money, it wasn't bloody prejudice, it was bleeding obvious.

This was the Sweden Geir had told me about. And now I missed him. This story was grist to the mill. But he was in Baghdad.

During this period I was still getting visits from Norway, one after the other they made their way over to Stockholm, I showed them around, they met Linda, we ate out, drifted, got drunk. One weekend in late winter Thure Erik was supposed to come over, driving the old banger he had once crossed the Sahara in, according to what he told me, never more to return to Norway. He did though, and had written a novel that meant a lot to me, it was entitled *Zalep*, which I liked so much, the thinking in it was so radical, so different from everything else in Norwegian novels because it was so uncompromising and because the language was so unique, so all of its own. The oddity was how much of the language turned out to be part of his character, or in harmony with it, which I did not pick up the first time I met him, for it was an extremely superficial

evening at Kunsternes Hus, but I did on the second, third and
fourth times, and not least during the weeks we stayed in two
cabins on a wintry and deserted campsite in Telemark with a
rushing river nearby and a starry night sky arched above us.
He was a large man with enormous fists and a gnarled face,
his eyes were alive and always freely revealed his mood. As I
admired the novels he wrote I found it difficult to talk to him,
everything I said was obviously stupid, could not hold a candle
to what he was doing, but there, in Telemark, having breakfast
together, trudging the two kilometres to the school together,
teaching together, having dinner and drinking coffee or beer
together in the evenings, there was nowhere to hide. You had
to speak. He told me that the station before Bø was called
Juksebø, and we laughed long and hard about that. *Bø* was the
word for a settlement and *jukse* meant to cheat. I told him my
jacket wasn't a jacket, it was a *skinn* jacket, punning on the
word for leather and make-believe. He laughed even louder, it
was as easy as that. His brain raced, everything caught his
interest and was refracted in him, which took it further, because
everything in him moved towards a horizon beyond, he had
such a great thirst for the extreme, and this made the world
around him appear in a constantly new light, a thure-erik-lund
light, yet it didn't only apply to him, because the idiosyncratic
nature of this was *also* refracted in him, in a tradition, in his
reading.

Not many people approach the world with the same energy.

He was kind to me, I felt like a kind of younger brother,
someone he took under his wing and showed things while
curious to know what I was getting out of being here, or *herrre*,
as he said. One evening he asked if I wanted to read something
he had written, I said, yes, of course, he passed me two sheets,
I began to read, it was an absolutely fantastic introduction, an

apocalyptic explosion of dynamite in an old rural world, a child running out of school and into the forest, it was magical, but when I happened to glance up at him he was sitting with his head hidden in his great hands like an ashamed child.

'Ooooh, it's so embarrassing,' he said. 'So damned embarrassing.'

What?

Had he gone mad?

This man, with all of his character, as obstinate as he was generous, as movable as he was irrepressible, was going to visit Linda and me in Stockholm.

Two days before, we had to go to a birthday party. Mikaela was thirty. She lived in a one-room flat in Söder, not far from Långholmen, it was jam-packed with people, we found some room in a corner, talked to a woman who was the director of some kind of peace organisation, from what I could glean, and her husband, who was a computer engineer and worked for a telephone company. They were good company, I had a couple of beers, felt like something stronger, found a bottle of aquavit and started drinking from it. I got more and more drunk, night fell, people started going home, we stayed, in the end I was so plastered that I was making paper balls from the serviettes and throwing them at people nearby. There was only the hard core left, Linda's closest friends, and if I wasn't having fun and throwing balls at their heads I was babbling away about whatever occurred to me and laughing a lot. Tried to say something nice about everyone, failed, but at least my intention had been clear. In the end Linda dragged me out, I objected, now that everything was so cosy, but she tugged at me, I put on my coat, and then we were suddenly on our way down the street far below the flat. Linda was furious with me. I didn't understand, what was the matter now? I was so drunk. No one else was drunk, hadn't I noticed? Only me. The other twenty-five guests had been sober. That was how it was in Sweden: one aim of a successful evening was that everyone left the party in the same state as they arrived. I was used to people drinking until the ceiling lifted. Wasn't this a thirtieth-birthday party? No, I had disgraced her, she had never been so embarrassed, these were her best friends, and there I was, her man, about whom she had said such incredibly nice things, there he was talking drivel and tossing paper balls at people and insulting them, completely out of control.

I lost my temper. She had crossed the line. Or else I was so drunk there was no line. I swore at her, shouted that she was terrible, all she ever thought about was making me toe lines, putting obstacles in my way, clinging to me as tightly as possible. It was sick, I yelled, you are sick. Now I'm going to fucking leave you. You'll never see me again.

I walked away as fast as I could. She came running after me.

You're drunk, she said. Calm down. We can talk about this tomorrow. You can't go to town in that state.

Why the hell not? I said, pulling her hand off me. We had reached the tiny patch of grass between her street and mine. I never want to see you again, I shouted, strode across the street and went down towards Zinkensdamm Station. Linda stopped outside her flat and called after me. I didn't turn. Crossed Söder, through the Old Town to Central Station, still fuming the whole way. My plan was simple: I would get on the train to Oslo and leave this shit town and never go back. Never. Never ever. It was snowing, it was cold, but the anger was keeping me warm. Inside the station I could barely distinguish the letters on the departures board, but after some intense concentration, which I also had to apply in order to keep my balance, I saw that there was a train between nine and ten in the morning. It was four o'clock now.

What should I do in the meantime?

I found a bench at the back and settled down to sleep. The last thought I had before falling asleep was that I mustn't waver when I woke up, I had to stick to my decision, Stockholm was the past, irrespective of how sober I was.

A station guard shook my shoulder; I opened my eyes.

'You can't sleep here,' he said.

'I'm waiting for a train,' I said, sitting up slowly.

'Fine. But you can't sleep here.'

'Can I sit?' I asked.

'Hardly,' he said. 'You're drunk, aren't you. Perhaps the best would be to go home.'

'OK,' I said. Got up.

Whoops. Yes, still drunk.

It was just after eight. The station was crowded. All I wanted was to sleep. My head was terribly heavy, it burned in a kind of fever, such that nothing I saw took root, everything glanced off, I trudged down through the Metro corridors, got on a train, got off at Zinkensdamm, up to the flat, no key, so I had to bang on the door.

I had to sleep. Couldn't give a toss about anything else.

Linda came running into the hall on the opposite side of the glass door.

'Oh, there you are,' she said, wrapping her arms around me. 'I've been so afraid. I've rung every hospital in town. Has a tall Norwegian been brought in . . . ? Where have you been?'

'At Central Station,' I said. 'I was going to catch the train to Norway. But now I have to sleep. Leave me be, and don't wake me.'

'OK,' she said. 'Do you want anything when you wake up? Coke, bacon?'

'Couldn't care less,' I said, and stormed into the flat, tore off my clothes, got under the duvet and was asleep in an instant.

When I woke it was dark outside. Linda was sitting on the chair in the kitchen and reading beneath the lamp, which, like a wading bird standing on one leg, long and thin, with its head slightly slanted, was lit above her.

'Hi,' she said. 'How are you?'

I poured myself a glass of water and drank it in one swig.

'Fine,' I said. 'Apart from the angst.'

'I'm very sorry about last night,' she said, putting the book on the armrest and getting up.

'Me too,' I said.

'Is it true that you were going to leave?'

I nodded.

'I was. I'd had enough.'

She put her arms around me.

'I understand,' she said.

'It wasn't just what happened at the party. It's much more.'

'Yes,' she said.

'Come on. Let's go into the sitting room,' I said. Refilled my glass and sat down at the table. Linda followed and switched on the ceiling light.

'Do you remember the first time I came here?' I said. 'To this room, I mean.'

She nodded.

'You said you thought you were becoming *kjær*, fond, of me.'

'It was an understatement.'

'Yes, I know that now. But in fact I was offended. *Kjær* sounds very weak in Norwegian. You can be fond of an aunt. I didn't know that *kjær* in Swedish was the same as *forelsket* in Norwegian. In love. I thought you said you were beginning to like me a little, and it might become something, given time. That was how I interpreted you.'

She gave a faint smile and looked down at the table.

'I plunged in with both feet,' she said. 'Got you up here and told you what I felt for you. And then you were so cold. You said we could be friends, do you remember? I had invested everything and lost everything. I was so desperate after you'd left.'

'But now we're here.'

'Yes.'

'You can't tell me what to do, Linda. That won't wash. I'll leave you. And I don't mean about drinking. I mean about everything. You can't do that.'

'I know.'

There was a silence.

'Didn't we have some meatballs in the fridge?' I asked. 'I'm bloody famished.'

She nodded.

I went into the kitchen, shook the meatballs into a frying pan and put the water on for spaghetti. I heard Linda come in behind me.

'There was nothing wrong this summer,' I said. 'I mean with the drinking. You didn't mind then, did you?'

'No,' she said. 'And it was fantastic. I am frightened of crossing lines, but I wasn't then, not with you, it felt very secure. It never felt as if it was going to tip over and become manic or simply ugly. It felt very safe. And I've never felt that before. But now it's different. We've moved on.'

'Right,' I said, and turned as the butter began to melt among the meatballs in the pan. 'Where are we now then?'

She shrugged.

'I don't know. But it feels as if we've lost something. Something is finished. And I'm frightened the rest will disappear.'

'But you can't force me. That's the best way to make it disappear.'

'Of course. I know that.'

I sprinkled salt into the water for the spaghetti.

'Are you going to have some?' I asked.

She nodded, wiping away tears with her thumbs.

Thure Erik arrived at around two the next day, filled the whole of the tiny flat with his personality the second he stepped inside. We went to some second-hand bookshops, he perused what they had of old natural history, and then we went to Pelikanen, had dinner and drank beer until they closed. I told him about the night on the railway station and my decision to catch the train back to Norway.

'But I was coming!' he said. 'Was I supposed to turn round and go back?'

'That was exactly what I was thinking about when I woke up,' I said. 'Thure Erik Lund is coming. I can't bloody go home now.'

He laughed, and began to tell me about a relationship that was so stormy that mine and Linda's seemed like a midsummer comedy by comparison. I drank twenty beers that night, and all I can remember from the last hours is an old drunk with whom Thure Erik had struck up a conversation, who sat down at our table and kept saying I was so good-looking, such a good-looking lad. Thure Erik laughed and nudged me in the shoulder between his attempts to draw the man out about his life. And then I remember us standing outside the flat and him clambering into the back of his car to sleep as light snowflakes swirled around beneath the cold grey sky.

One room and a kitchen: that was our arena. We cooked there, we ate, slept, made love, chatted, watched TV, read books, quarrelled and received all our visitors there. It was small and cramped, but it was enough, we managed, we kept our heads above water. But if we wanted children, which we talked about non-stop, we would have to find ourselves a bigger flat. Linda's mother had one in the city centre, it had only two rooms, but was more than eighty square metres, a football pitch in comparison with what we had now. She no longer used the flat, but she rented it out and said we could have it. Not quite like that, because it wasn't legal – in Sweden rental contracts are personal and for life – but exchanges are possible: Linda's mother would take Linda's and we would take hers.

One day we went to see it.

It was the most bourgeois apartment I had ever seen. An enormous Russian-style stove from the previous century at one end of the room, with a massive marble front; another one, just as tall, slightly less massive, in the bedroom. White, beautifully carved panels on all the walls, stucco work on the ceilings, which were more than four metres tall. Fantastic herringbone parquet floors from the end of the nineteenth century. Her mother's furniture was in the same style: heavy, artistic, late nineteenth-century.

'Can we live here?' I said as we walked round looking.

'No, of course we can't,' Linda said. 'Shouldn't we swap with a flat in Skärholmen or somewhere like that? It's dead here.'

Skärholmen was one of the immigrant-occupied satellite towns, we had been to a market there one Saturday and been struck by the life and the diversity.

'I agree,' I said. 'It would be almost impossible to make this *ours*.'

At the same time the thought of moving in here had some appeal. Spacious, beautiful, central location. Did it matter that we would be lost in the rooms? Or perhaps we could fight them, control them, make the bourgeois style part of us?

I have always wanted the bourgeois lifestyle. Always wanted the properness. Always wanted the stiff forms and strict rules to be there to keep the inner in place, to regulate it, to mould it into something you can live with, not allow it to tear up your life again and again. But whenever I had been in a middle-class setting, for example with my father's parents or with Tonje's father, the opposite happened, it was as if it made all the otherness in me visible, all that did not fit, that fell outside the forms and structures, all that I hated about myself.

But here? Linda and I and a child? A new life, a new town, a new flat, a new happiness?

This notion overshadowed the sombre, lifeless first impression the flat had made, we warmed to it and became enthusiastic after making love on the bed; as we lay with a pillow beneath our heads afterwards, smoking, we were in no doubt that our new life would begin here.

At the end of April Geir returned from Iraq, we had dinner at an expensive American restaurant in the Old Town, he was so excited and full of life in a way I had never seen before, and it took several weeks for all his experiences, all the people he had met there, whom gradually I became utterly familiar with, to begin to fade so that other matters could occupy his mind and his conversation. At the beginning of May Linda and I moved our possessions across, with help from Anders, and when we had done that we cleaned the flat. We spent the afternoon and all the evening, and when we still hadn't finished at eleven, Linda suddenly slumped back against the wall.

'I've had it!' she called. 'I can't do any more!'

'One more hour,' I said. 'An hour and a half tops. You can manage that.'

She had tears in her eyes.

'Let's ring mummy,' she said. 'We don't have to finish. She'll drop by tomorrow and do it. It's not a problem. I know it isn't.'

'Would you let someone clean your apartment?' I asked. 'Clean up your mess? You can't shout for your mother every time you've got problems. You're thirty years old for Christ's sake!'

She sighed.

'Yes, I know,' she said. 'I'm just worn out. And she *can* do it. It's not a problem for her.'

'But it is for me. And it should be for you too.'

She grabbed a cloth, got up and resumed wiping the bathroom door frame.

'I can do the rest,' I said. 'Off you go, and I'll follow you later.'

'Are you sure?'

'Yes, I am. It's fine.'

'OK.'

She put on her outdoor clothes and went out in the darkness, I finished the cleaning and it was true what I had said: it didn't matter to me. The next day we moved my things, that is to say all my books, which had now grown to number two and a half thousand titles, a fact which Anders and Geir, who were helping me with the move, cursed from the bottom of their hearts as we shifted the boxes from the lift into the flat. Geir compared it of course with unloading ammunition cases alongside the US Marines, an activity which for him was only a few weeks ago but for me was as alien as Wells Fargo stagecoaches or bison hunting. When the removal goods were stacked in two enormous piles in the two rooms I started painting the walls while Linda went to Norway to make a radio programme about 17 May. She was going to stay with my mother, whom she had only met once for a few hours in Stockholm. After she was on the train I rang my mother, something was bothering me, all the signs of Tonje's presence, especially the photograph of the wedding, which was still hanging on the wall when I had been there for Christmas, and the wedding album. I didn't want Linda to be subjected to that, I didn't want her to feel she was on the periphery of my life, a replacement, and after a short preamble, catching up on news since we last met, I began to zero in on the topic. I knew it was stupid, and actually humiliating, for Linda, her and me, but I couldn't stop myself, I couldn't bear the thought that it might hurt Linda, so in the end I said it. Would she mind taking down the wedding photo, or at least putting it in a more discreet position? Not at all, in fact, it was already down. After all we were no longer married. What about the album then? I asked. You know, of the wedding. You couldn't tuck it away somewhere, could you? Oh no, Karl Ove, mum said. That's my photo album. It represents a phase of my life. I don't want to hide it. Linda will be fine with it; she knows you've been married. You're both adults. OK, I said, you're right, it's your photo album. I just don't want to hurt her. You won't, mum said, it'll be fine.

It was a brave decision of Linda's to stay with her, a reaching out of her hand, and it went fine, we spoke on the phone several times a day, she said she was stunned by the Vestland landscape, all the green and the blue and the white, all the high mountains and the deep fjords, almost completely deserted, the sun shining in the sky all the time, she felt transported into a dream-like state. She phoned from a little boarding house in Balestrand, described the view from her window, the lapping of the waves she could hear when she leaned out, and her voice was laden with the future. Whatever she said, it was us she was talking about, that was my interpretation. The world was so beautiful, that was about us, for we were in it together, indeed, it was almost as if we were the world. I told her how nice the large rooms were now that they were no longer grey but white. I was laden with the future as well. I was looking forward to her returning home to see what I had done, and I was looking forward to living here, in the city centre, and to the child we had decided we would have. We rang off, I went on painting, the following day was 17 May, and in the afternoon Espen and Eirik were going to drop by. They had been to a critics' seminar at Biskops-Arnö. We went out to eat, I introduced them to Geir, he got on well with Eirik, in the sense that they talked without inhibition about a variety of topics, but Geir didn't get on so well with Espen. Geir uttered a few truisms, Espen challenged them, and when Geir noticed he froze, and that was that. As usual I tried to mediate – give Espen something with one hand and Geir something with the other – but it was too late, they were never going to be able to talk, like or respect each other. I liked both of them, all three of them in fact, but my life had always been like this, there were heavy bulkheads between the various parts, and I behaved in such different ways with each of them that I felt caught when they came together and I couldn't behave in one way or the other, but had to keep mixing the styles, in other words behave oddly or keep my mouth shut. I liked Espen a lot precisely because he was Espen, and Geir a lot precisely because he was Geir, and this character trait of mine, actually pleasantness, at least in my eyes, always brought with it a sense of hypocrisy.

Linda had been with my family all day, she told me the following morning; she and mum had gone to Dale where mum's sister Kjellaug and her husband Magne lived on their farm high above the village and celebrated 17 May in traditional manner. She had been interviewing people, and from what she told me, she found the whole affair truly exotic. The speeches, the costumes, the band, the children's procession. In the morning they had seen deer on the edge of the forest, and on the way home there were porpoises frolicking in the fjord. Mum had said that was a good omen, they brought luck.

There weren't often porpoises in the fjord, I had seen them only a couple of times, the first time close up, in a boat with grandad, it had been misty and perfectly still, and then they swam up, at first it was only a noise, like the bow of a yacht ploughing through the water, and then there they were, smooth, glistening, dark grey bodies. Up and down, up and down, they swam. Grandma had said, like mum, that they brought good luck. Linda was excited but tired at the same time, which she had been throughout the trip, and going round all the hairpin bends had made her carsick, so she had gone to bed early, she told me. The previous evening she had been up with grandma's youngest sister, Alvdis, ten years older than mum, and her husband Anfinn, a small but powerful man with a cheery disposition and a strong personality, whom Linda loved, and the feeling appeared to be mutual because he had taken out all his souvenirs from the time when he used to go whaling, and talked about his experiences from those days, probably further motivated by the microphone Linda held between them. They made pancakes with penguin eggs, he told her with a laugh, although she was a little concerned about the recording. Anfinn spoke in broad Jølster dialect, which would doubtless be incomprehensible to Swedes.

Espen left in the morning, but Eirik stayed and went to town while I put the final books on shelves and got rid of the last boxes, so that everything would be finished for when Linda came back the next morning. That evening we went out again and afterwards we sat at home drinking duty-free spirits through the night. Linda and I kept texting each other because she had felt sick, she had been tired, surely that could mean only one thing, couldn't it? The texts became more passionate and loving the later it got, but in the end she wrote goodnight, my prince, perhaps tomorrow is going to be a big day!

When I went to bed at seven the clear flame of alcohol was burning in me so strongly that I could no longer see my surroundings, it was as if my inner self was everything, the way it was when I drank myself senseless. Yet I had enough presence of mind to set the clock for nine. I had to collect Linda off the train.

At nine I was still drunk. It was only by mobilising all the willpower I possessed that I managed to stagger to my feet. I dragged myself into the bathroom, showered, put on some clean clothes, shouted to Eirik that I was going, he was lying on the sofa fully dressed, and forced himself up and said he was going out for breakfast, I said we could meet at around twelve in the restaurant where we had been the previous day, he nodded, I swayed down the stairs and made it to the street, where the sun was glaringly bright and the tarmac smelt of spring.

I stopped on the way to buy a Coke, guzzled it down and bought another. Inspected my face in a shop window. It didn't look good. Narrow red eyes. Tired features.

I would have given everything I had to postpone the meeting by three hours. But that was impossible, her train would be arriving at the station in thirteen minutes and I would have to get my skates on.

As she came down the platform she was happy and light of foot, she looked around for me with a smile on her lips, I waved, she waved back and walked towards me trundling her suitcase after her with one hand.

She looked at me.

'Hi,' I said.

'What's up? Are you drunk?' she asked.

I stepped forward and put my arms around her.

'Hi,' I repeated. 'It got a bit late last night, but nothing special. I was at home with Eirik.'

'You reek of alcohol,' she said, wriggling free. 'How could you
do that to me? Today of all days?'

'I'm sorry,' I said. 'But it's no big deal, is it?'

She didn't answer, began to walk. Didn't say a word as we left
the station. On the escalator up to Klarabergsviadukten she
started to swear at me. She shook the door of the chemist at the
top, but it was Sunday and closed. We continued down to the
chemist on the other side of NK. She was furious the whole way.
I walked beside her like a dog. The second chemist was open.
I'm so bloody sick of you, she said. I don't understand why I live
with you. You only think about yourself. Doesn't what we said
yesterday mean anything? she said, and then it was her turn,
she wanted a pregnancy test, was given one, paid for it, we left,
up Regeringsgatan, she continued to hurl abuse at me, it came
in one long stream, passers-by sent us looks, but she didn't care,
her fury, which I had always feared, had her in its grip. I felt
like asking her to stop, asking her to be nice, I had apologised,
and it wasn't as though I had done anything, there was no
connection between our texts and the fact that I had been
drinking with a guest from Norway, nor between the fact that
I had got drunk and the pregnancy test she was holding in her
hand, but she didn't see it like that, for her this was all the
same, she was a romantic, she had a dream about the two of
us, about love and our child, and my behaviour smashed that
dream, or reminded her that it was a dream. I was a bad person,
an irresponsible person, how could I even imagine becoming a
father? How could I subject her to this? I walked beside her,
burning with shame because people were looking at us, burning
with guilt because I had been drinking and burning with terror
because, in her unbridled rage, she went straight for me and
the person I was. This was humiliating, but for as long as she
was in the right, for as long as what she said was true – that

this was the day we might find out if we were going to have a child and I had met her off the train drunk – I couldn't ask her to stop or tell her to go to hell. She was right, or she was within her rights, I would have to bow my head and put up with this.

It struck me that Eirik might be close by and bowed my head even lower, this was almost the worst thought, that someone I knew would see me like this.

We went up the stairs, into the flat. Fresh coat of paint, everything in its place: this was our home.

She didn't even grace it with a glance.

I stopped in the middle of the floor.

She had hit out at me in her anger, the way a boxer hits a punchbag. As though I were an object. As though I had no feelings, yes, as though I had no inner life, as though I were just this empty body that wandered around in her life.

I knew she was pregnant, of that I was absolutely certain, and I had been from the moment we made love. That's it, I had thought, now we are going to have a baby.

And so it was.

Suddenly, while I was standing there everything inside me opened. My defences fell. I had no resistance to muster. I started crying. The type of crying where I lose control of everything and everything is distorted to the point of being grotesque.

Linda stopped, turned and looked at me.

She had never seen me cry before. I hadn't done it since dad died, and that would soon be five years ago.

She looked terrified.

I turned away, I didn't want her to see, that made the humiliation ten times worse, it wasn't just that I wasn't a person, I wasn't a man either.

But turning away didn't help. It didn't help to cover my face with my hands. It didn't help to walk towards the hall. It was so overwhelming, I was sobbing with such abandon, all the sluices were open.

'But Karl Ove,' she said behind me. 'Nice Karl Ove. I don't mean anything. I was just so disappointed. It doesn't matter though. It doesn't matter. Dear Karl Ove. Don't cry. Don't cry.'

Well, I didn't want to either, of course. The last thing I wanted was her to see me crying.

But I couldn't help myself.

She tried to put her arms around me, but I pushed her away. I tried to draw breath. It became a pathetic trembling sob.

'I'm sorry,' I said. 'I'm sorry. I didn't mean to.'

'I'm sorry too,' she said.

'Well, here we are again,' I said, smiling through the tears.

Her eyes were also full of tears, and she was smiling as well.

'Yes,' she said.

'Yes,' I said.

I went to the bathroom, another sob shook me, another tremble as I took a deep breath, but then, after I had washed my face with cold water a few times, it relented.

Linda was still standing in the hall when I came out.

'Is that better?' she asked.

'Yes,' I said. 'That was plain ridiculous. It must be the drinking from last night. Suddenly my defences were gone. Everything seemed so desperate.'

'It doesn't matter that you cried,' she said.

'Not to you it doesn't, no. But I don't like it. I'd rather you hadn't seen. But you did. Now you know. That's the way I am.'

'Yes, you're a good person.'

'Come on,' I said. 'That's enough. Let's move on. What do you think of the flat?'

She smiled.

'Fantastic.'

'Good.'

We hugged each other.

'Linda,' I said. 'Aren't you going to check?'

'Now?'

'Yes.'

'OK. Just hold me a bit longer.'

I did.

'Now?' I asked.

She laughed.

'OK.'

Then she went into the bathroom and came out again with the white test stick in her hand.

'It'll take a few more minutes,' she said.

'What do you reckon?'

'I don't know.'

She went into the kitchen and I followed. She stared at the white stick.

'Anything happening?'

'No, nothing. Oh, perhaps it's nothing. I was so sure there was something.'

'Well, there have been signs. You've been sick. Tired. How many more do you need?'

'One.'

'Look there. That's blue, isn't it?'

She didn't say anything.

Then she looked up at me. Her eyes were dark and serious, like an animal's.

'Yes, it is.'

We couldn't wait the three obligatory months before we told anyone. Three weeks later Linda called her mother, who burst into tears of joy at the other end. My mother's reaction was more reserved, she said it was nice, lovely, but a little later it came out, she also wondered if we were ready for it. Linda had her training, I had my writing. Time will tell, I said, we'll find out in January. I knew mum always was slow to assimilate change, she had to give it some thought first, and then she moved and adapted to the new situation. Yngve, whom I called as soon as mum had rung off, said, Oh, that's good news. Yes, I said, standing and smoking in the backyard. When's it due? Yngve asked. In January, I said. Congratulations, he said. Thanks, I replied. Karl Ove, he said, I'm a bit caught up here actually, I'm at a football match with Ylva. Can we talk later? Course, I said, and we rang off.

I lit another cigarette and noticed I was not completely satis-fied with their reactions. We were going to have a BABY, for Christ's sake! This was an ENORMOUS event!

But something had happened when I moved to Sweden. We had as much contact as before, it wasn't that, yet something was different, and I pondered on whether the change had taken place in me or them. I was further away from them, and my life, so fundamentally changed from one moment to the next, with new places, new people and new emotions, I couldn't communicate this with the same natural ease as before, when we had lived in the same environment, in the continuity that began in Tybakken and continued first with Tveit and then Bergen.

No, I was probably reading too much into it, I thought. Yngve's reaction had not been so different from the one seven years earlier when I had rung to tell him that the novel I was writing had been accepted. Is that right? had been his laconic response. Mm, that's good. For me it had been the greatest thing that had ever happened, I had been stunned by the news and assumed everyone in my circle would be as well.

Naturally enough, it hadn't been like that.

And it is never easy to confront life-changing news, especially when you are deeply embroiled in the everyday and the banal, which we always are. They absorb almost everything, make almost everything small, apart from the few events that are so immense they lay waste to all the everyday trivia around you. Big news is like that and it is not possible to live inside it.

I stubbed out my cigarette and went upstairs to Linda, who looked at me with raised eyebrows as I entered.

'What did they say?' she asked

'They were incredibly happy,' I said. 'Best wishes and congratulations.'

'Thanks,' she said. 'Mummy was out of herself with joy. However, she gets excited about absolutely everything.'

Yngve rang later that evening; we could have all the baby clothes and gear we wanted. Buggy, changing mat, rompers, bodices, bibs, pants, sweaters and shoes, they had kept the lot. Linda was touched when I passed that on, and I laughed at her, her sensitivities had changed over the last few weeks and reacted to the strangest things. She laughed as well. Her mother often dropped by, bringing the most sensational meals, which we put in the freezer, several bin bags of baby clothes she had been given by her partner's children and boxes of toys. She bought us a washing machine; Vidar, her partner, plumbed it in.

Linda continued with her course, I continued in my collective office at the tower, started reading the Bible, found a Catholic bookshop and bought all the angel-related literature I could get my hands on, read Thomas Aquinas and Augustine, Basilius and Hieronymus, Hobbes and Burton. I bought Spengler and a biography of Isaac Newton, reference works about the Enlightenment and Baroque periods, which lay in piles around where I was

writing and trying to get all these different systems and schools
of thought to tie up in some way or other, or to push something,
I didn't know what, in the same direction.

Linda was happy, but there were always these feelings of abyss
inside her which made her afraid of everything. Would she be
able to take care of the baby when it came? And would it come?
She could lose it – that happened – and nothing I said or did
could stem the fear that was roaming loose inside her, out of
her control, but fortunately that too passed.

At the end of June we went on holiday to Norway, first of all
to Tromøya, where we spent a couple of days, then to Espen and
Anne's in Larkollen, who had lent us a cabin to stay in, and
finally to mum's in Jølster. Neither of us had a driving licence,
so I dragged our cases round onto planes, trains, buses and taxis
with Linda, who couldn't carry anything heavier than an apple,
by my side. Arvid met us in Arendal, he was a few years older
than me, from Tromøya, and initially he was one of Yngve's
friends, but we saw quite a bit of one another in Bergen, where
he had also studied, and not so many months ago he had visited
us in Stockholm. Now he wanted to drive us back to his place.
I knew Linda was tired and wanted to go to the cabin we had
rented, and to get the point across I told Arvid straight away
Linda was expecting a baby.

This came as a bolt from the blue in the sunlit Arendal street.

'Oh, congratulations!' Arvid said.

'So it would be best if we went to the cabin first, to have a
rest . . .'

'We can arrange that,' Arvid said. 'I'll drive you there. Then I
can pick you up by boat later.'

It was a log cabin, low quality, I regretted it the moment I
saw it. The idea had been I would show her where I came from.
That was nice for me. This was not.

She slept for a couple of hours, we walked out on the mole, and Arvid arrived, skimming across the water in his boat. We would go to the island of Hisøya, where Arvid lived. Passed small white houses on rocks, reddish in the afternoon sun, surrounded by green trees, in the midst of the blue arch of sea and sky, and I thought to myself, my God, this is wonderful here. And then the wind that came with the sunset every afternoon. It made the landscape alien, I could see that now, and I had seen it when I was growing up here. Alien because what unified all the elements of the landscape fell apart like a rock struck by a sledgehammer when the wind gusted in.

We went ashore, up to the house and sat around a table in the garden. Linda was shut inside herself in a way that appeared unfriendly, and I suffered, we sat there with his family and friends, it was the first time they had met her, of course I wanted to show them what a wonderful partner I had, and then she was so unwilling. I held her arm under the table and squeezed it. She looked at me without a smile. I felt like shouting she should pull herself together. I knew how charming she could be, how talented she was at exactly this, sitting around a table with other people and chatting, telling stories and laughing. On the other hand, I remembered how I used to be when I was with some of Linda's friends I didn't know so well. Silent, stiff and shy, someone who could go through an entire dinner without saying more than what was absolutely necessary.

What was she thinking?

What had put her out?

Arvid? The slightly boastful manner that could occasionally steal over him?

Anna?

Atle?

Or was it me?

Had I said something during the afternoon?

Or was it inside her? Something which had nothing to do with this at all?

After eating we went for a boat ride, around Hisøya and out to Mærdø, and as we came into open water Arvid hit the accelerator. The swift slim boat skimmed across the surface, the waves were crashing into and bouncing off the bows. Linda's face was white, she was three months pregnant, perhaps these violent movements would be enough to cause her to lose the baby, that was what she was thinking, I could see.

'Tell him to slow down!' she hissed. 'This is dangerous for me!'

I looked at Arvid, who sat behind the wheel with a smile on his face, his eyes scrunched up against the fresh salty air streaming towards us. I didn't think this was dangerous and could not bring myself to interfere and tell Arvid to slow down, it was too stupid. At the same time Linda sat there burning with fear and anger. For her sake surely I could step in, even if I made a fool of myself?

'It's fine,' I said to Linda. 'It's not dangerous.'

'Karl Ove!' she hissed. 'Tell him to slow down. This is extremely dangerous. Don't you understand?'

I straightened up and moved closer to Arvid. The island of Mærdø was approaching at a furious pace. He looked at me and smiled.

'She runs well, doesn't she.'

I nodded and smiled back. I was on the point of asking him to slow down, but I held back, sat down beside Linda.

'It's not dangerous,' I said.

She said nothing, sat there with her arms wrapped around her, face tense and white.

We strolled around Mærdø, a rug was spread out on a field,

coffee was drunk, biscuits were eaten and then we went back to the boat. On the way along the quay I sidled up to Arvid.

'Linda was a bit scared when you throttled up. She's pregnant, you know, so the movements . . . well, you understand. Could you take it a bit easier going back?'

'No problem,' he said.

He piloted the boat all the way to Hove at a snail's pace. I wondered if he was trying to tell us something or was being especially considerate. Whatever it was, it was embarrassing. Both the fact that I had spoken to him and that I hadn't been able to intervene on the way there. Surely it should have been the easiest thing in the world to do, shouldn't it, to tell someone to slow down, my girlfriend was pregnant?

Especially because Linda's fears and unease came from a different source than most people's. It was barely three years since she had been discharged after suffering from manic depression for two years. Having a baby after that kind of experience was not without its risks. She had no idea how she would react. Perhaps she would be plunged into a further bout of manic depression? Maybe so serious that she would be readmitted to hospital. And what would happen to the child then? However, she was out of it and anchored in the world in quite a different way from how she had been before the breakdown and, having seen her every day for almost a year, I knew she would be fine. I viewed what had happened as a crisis. It had been lengthy and all-embracing, but it was over. She was healthy; the mood swings that still existed in her life were all within normal behaviour.

We caught the train to Moss, Espen picked us up at the station and we drove to their home in Larkollen. Linda had a slight temperature and went to bed, Espen and I walked to a nearby pitch to kick around a football, in the evening we had a barbecue, I sat up with Espen and Anne, later only Espen. Linda was asleep.

The next day Espen drove us to the cabin on the island of Jeløya, where we stayed for a week while they travelled to Stockholm and occupied our flat. I got up at around five and worked on my novel, for this was what the manuscript had become, until Linda got up at around ten. We had breakfast, now and then I read bits of what I had written aloud, she invariably said it was very good, we went swimming on a beach a few kilometres away, did some shopping and made lunch, I went fishing in the afternoons while she slept, in the evenings we lit the fire and we talked or read or made love. When the week was up we caught the train from Moss to Oslo and took the Bergen line on to Flåm, whence we went by boat to Balestrand and stayed at Kvikne's Hotel and then caught the ferry to Fjærland the next day. Where we met Tomas Espedal – he was on a walking trip with a friend, heading for a place he had in Sunnfjord. I hadn't met him since I lived in Bergen and just the sight of him cheered me up, he was one of the best people I had ever met. Mum was waiting on the quay in Fjærland, and we drove past the glacier, which shone greyish white against the blue sky, through the long tunnel into the long dark narrow valley where so often there were avalanches, and into Skei, where the gentle luxuriant Jølster countryside opened out.

This was the third time Linda and mum had met, and for the rest of the stay I tried, in vain, to bridge the gap I perceived at once. There was always some obstacle, almost nothing seemed to run smoothly. When something did and I saw Linda perk up and react in a way which mum latched on to, I became happy out of all proportion, realised why and longed to move on.

Then Linda started bleeding. She was terrified, truly terrified, wanted to leave at once, rang Stockholm and spoke to the midwife, who couldn't comment without examining her. That made Linda even more frightened, and my saying it'll be fine, it's bound to be fine and it's nothing did not do a lot to help because how could I know? What authority did I have? She wanted to leave, I said we were staying and in the end, when she agreed, everything became my responsibility, so if things went wrong, or if they had already gone wrong, I was the one who had insisted we shouldn't bother with an examination, we should wait and see.

Linda's entire energy was focused on this, I could see it was all she thought about, fear gnawed at her, she no longer spoke when we were eating or were together in the evening, and when she came downstairs after sleeping on the first floor and found mum and me sitting in the garden and chatting she turned and left, her eyes dark with fury, and I understood why: we were talking as though nothing had happened, as though what she felt did not matter. And that was both true and not true. I thought everything would be fine, but I was not sure, and at the same time we were guests there, I hadn't seen my mother for more than six months, we had a lot to talk about, and what purpose was served by saying nothing, by simply wandering around mute, in constant, agonising, all-encompassing fear? I put my arms around her, I comforted her, tried to tell her that everything was bound to be fine, but she wasn't receptive and didn't want to be there. When mum asked her something she barely answered. On our walks through the valley she criticised my mother and everything about her. I defended her, we screamed at each other, she turned and went off on her own, I ran after her, it was a nightmare, but as with all nightmares there was an awakening from this too. But first there was a final scene: mum drove us to Florø, where we would catch the boat. We arrived early, decided to have lunch, found a restaurant on a kind of pontoon, sat down and ordered fish soup. It arrived, and it tasted terrible, of butter and almost nothing else.

'I can't eat this,' Linda said.

'No, it isn't very good,' I said.

'We'd better tell the waiter and ask him to bring something else,' Linda said.

I could not imagine anything more embarrassing than sending food back to the kitchen. And this was only Florø, not Stockholm or Paris. At the same time I couldn't put up with any more moods and so I beckoned to the waitress.

'I'm afraid this isn't very good,' I said. 'Do you think we could have something else instead?'

The robust middle-aged waitress with badly dyed blonde hair gave me a disapproving glare.

'There shouldn't be anything wrong with the food,' she said. 'But if you say there is I'll go and ask the chef.'

We sat around the table, my mother, Linda and I, with three full bowls of soup, saying nothing.

The waitress returned, shaking her head.

'My apologies,' she said. 'The chef says there's nothing wrong with the soup. It tastes the way it is supposed to.'

What should we do?

The only time in my life I send back food to the kitchen and they don't accept what I say. Anywhere else on earth they would have given us an alternative dish, but not on Florø. My face was red with shame and annoyance. If I had been alone I would have eaten the bloody soup, no matter how bad it was. Now I had complained, however embarrassing and unnecessary I thought that was, and they met my complaint with resistance?!

I got to my feet.

'I'll go in and have a few words with the chef,' I said.

'You do that,' said the waitress.

I walked along the pontoon and into the kitchen, which was on land, poked my head over a counter and caught the attention, not of a little fatso, as I had imagined, but a tall well-built man of my own age.

'We ordered fish soup,' I said. 'There's too much butter in it. I'm afraid it's almost impossible to eat. Do you think we could have something else instead?'

'It tastes exactly as it is supposed to,' he said. 'You ordered fish soup and that's what you got. Can't help you there.'

I walked back. Linda and mum looked up at me. I shook my head.

'Wouldn't budge,' I said.

'Perhaps I should have a go,' mum said. 'After all, I'm an elderly lady. That might help a bit.'

If it was against my nature to complain in restaurants it was definitely against hers.

'You don't need to,' I said. 'We'd better just leave.'

'I'll try,' she said.

A few minutes later she came back. She too shook her head.

'Oh well,' I said. 'I'm hungry but after all this we really can't eat the soup.'

We got up, put the money on the table and left.

'We'll have to eat on the boat,' I said to Linda, who just nodded, her eyes black.

It arrived with propellers whirling. I loaded the baggage on board, waved to mum and found a seat at the very front.

We each ate a soft vaguely wet pizza, a potato pancake and a yoghurt. Linda lay back and fell asleep. When she woke up everything that had been in her head was gone. Bright and open, she sat beside me chatting away. I studied her, profoundly astonished. Had all of this been about my mother? Or about being in an unfamiliar place? Or about visiting my life before she became a part of it? And not the fear of losing the baby? Because surely that was just as acute now?

We flew home from Bergen, she was examined the following day and everything was in perfect order. The tiny heart was beating, the tiny body was growing and all the tests that could be done gave the right results.

After the examination, which was carried out at a clinic in the Old Town, we went to a nearby cake shop and talked about what happened during the check-up. We always did that. After an hour I took the Metro the whole way out to Åkeshov, where I had been given a new office. In the end I couldn't stand being in the old one in the tower, and Linda's author friend, the film director Maria Zennström, had offered me a shabby room for next to nothing out there. It was in the basement of a block of flats, no one was around during the day, I sat all alone between concrete walls and wrote, read or stared into the forest where Metro carriages careered through the trees every five minutes or so. I had read Spengler's *The Decline of the West*, and while a lot could be said about his theories on civilisation, what he wrote about the Baroque period and his Faustian concept, about the Age of Enlightenment and his concept of the cyclical nature of civilisation, was original and masterful; some of it I put straight into the novel, so to speak, which I had realised would have to have the seventeenth century as a kind of centre. Everything sprang from there, it was when the world separated: on one side there was the old and useless, the whole magical, irrational, dogmatic and authoritarian tradition; on the other what developed into the world we inhabited.

Autumn passed, the belly grew, Linda fiddled around with all sorts of bits and bobs, she seemed to be like a magnet for everything, there were lit candles and hot baths, piles of baby clothes in the cupboard, photo albums were collated and books about pregnancy and the baby's first year were read. I was so glad to see it, but couldn't go there myself, not even close, I had to write.

I could be together with her, make love to her, talk to her, go for walks with her, but I could not feel or do as she did.

Now and then there were angry outbursts. One morning I spilt water on the kitchen carpet, went off to the Metro without mopping up and when I returned home there was a big yellow stain. I asked what had happened, she looked at me sheepishly, well, she had seen the stain I had left on the carpet when she entered the kitchen and she had been so angry she poured juice over it. But then the water dried out and she realised what she had done.

We had to throw the carpet away.

One evening she gouged the dining-room table she had been given by her mother, part of a small suite she had paid a fortune for, because I had not shown enough interest in the letter Linda was writing to the maternity department. It had been about her wishes and preferences. When she read out a suggestion I nodded, but without the necessary conviction, evidently, for all of a sudden she jabbed her pen into the table and scored the top with as much force as she could apply, again and again. What are you doing? I said. You don't care, she said. Oh, for Christ's sake, of course I care. And now you've ruined the table.

One evening I got so mad at her that I threw a glass at the stove with all my might. Strangely enough, it didn't break. Typical, I thought afterwards, I couldn't even perform the classic act of smashing a glass during a row.

We went to the antenatal classes together, the room was packed and the audience sensitive to every word spoken from the rostrum; if there was anything remotely controversial from a biological point of view, a low sucking of breath ran through the rows, for this was taking place in a country where gender was a social construct, and for the body, outside what everyone agreed was common sense, there was no place. Instinct, came a

voice from the rostrum. No, no, no! the angry women in the
room whispered. How could you say such a thing! I saw a woman
sobbing on a bench – her husband was ten minutes late for the
course – and I thought, I am not alone. When he did finally
arrive she pummelled his stomach with her fists while he, as
carefully as he could, tried to get her out of this state and into
a more controlled and dignified one.

This was how we lived, in abrupt mood swings between being
calm and peaceful, optimistic and affectionate and sudden explo-
sions of fury. Every morning I caught the Metro to Åkeshov, and
the moment I walked down into the underground everything
that had gone on at home was eradicated from my mind. I looked
at the crowd in the subterranean station, inhaled the atmosphere, got on the train and read, looked at the suburban houses
we glided past after we had left the tunnels, read, surveyed the
town as we crossed the big bridge, read, loved, really loved, all
the stops at the small stations, got off at Åkeshov, almost the
only passenger travelling in this direction to work, walked
roughly a kilometre to the office and worked all day. Soon the
manuscript would amount to a hundred pages, and it was
becoming stranger and stranger; after the introduction about
crabbing it shifted into a purely essayistic style, and presented
some theories about the divine that I had never considered
before, but in some peculiar manner, from the premises they
set, in their way, they were right. I had come across a Russian
Orthodox bookshop, it really was a find, all manner of remarkable writings were there, I bought them, took notes and could
barely restrain my glee when yet another element of the pseudo-
theory fell into place, until I went home in the afternoon, when
the life awaiting me there slowly returned as the train approached
the station in Hötorget. Now and then I went to town earlier,
when we had to go for a check-up at the Mother Care Centre,

as it was called in Swedish, where I sat on a chair watching Linda being examined, blood pressure and blood samples, listening for the heartbeat and measuring the belly, which was growing as it should, everything was in order, all the test results were excellent, for if there was one thing Linda had it was physical strength and rude health, which I told her as often as I could. Compared with the body's weight and certainties, worry was nothing, a buzzing fly, a swirling feather, a cloud of dust.

We went to Ikea and bought a baby-changing table, which we loaded with piles of cloths and towels, and on the wall above I stuck a sequence of postcards of seals, whales, fish, turtles, lions, monkeys and the Beatles during their psychedelic period, so that the baby could see what a wonderful world it had been born into, Yngve and Kari Anne sent us their baby cast-offs, but the buggy he had promised was a little time in coming, to Linda's increasing annoyance. One evening she exploded: the buggy was never going to come, we couldn't rely on that brother of mine, we should have bought our own, which she had said from day one. There were still two months to the due date. I called Yngve, dropped a hint about the buggy and mumbled something about the irrationality of pregnant women, he said it was on its way, I said I knew it was, but nevertheless I had to ask. How I hated doing it. How I hated going against my nature to satisfy her. But, I told myself, there was a purpose, there was a goal, and as long as that remained uppermost in my mind I would just have to put up with all the creeping and crawling. The buggy didn't arrive. Another outburst. We bought some contraption to put in the bathtub for when the baby had to be bathed, we bought bodices and tiny shoes, rompers and a sleeping bag for the buggy. We borrowed a cradle from Helena with a little duvet and pillow, which Linda regarded with moist eyes. And we discussed a name.

Almost every night we sat talking about it, batting an enormous variety of names to and fro, always with a shortlist of four or five, always changing it. One night Linda suggested Vanja, and with that we had the name for a girl. We were suddenly decided. We liked the Russianness of it and its associations, something strong and wild, and Vanja was derived from Ivan, which was the same as Johannes in Norwegian, which was Linda's father's name. If it was a boy he would be Bjørn.

One morning, going down the stairs to the Metro platform under Sveavägen, I found my eyes drawn towards two men brawling. Their aggression alongside all the weary passengers was dreadful, they shouted, no, screeched at each other, my heart beat faster and then they pounced on each other with such ferocity as a train drew in to the platform. One of them wrestled himself free to get space to kick the other. I went closer. They were locked in combat again. I thought, I will have to intervene. The boxer incident, when I hadn't dared to kick in the door, and the boat incident, when I hadn't dared to ask Arvid to slow down, as well as Linda's concern about my failure to act, had played on my mind so much that now there was no doubt in my mind. I could not stand by and watch. I had to intervene. The very thought made my knees go weak and my arms tremble. Nonetheless, I put down my bag, this was a test, I thought, shit, now I would have to give a shit, and went straight over to the two brawlers and wrapped my arms around the closest one. I squeezed as hard as I could. As I did, another man stepped forward between them, and a third, and the fight was over. I picked up my bag, got into the train on the other side and sat there until we got to Åskehov, drained, with my heart pounding in my chest. No one could claim I had been slow to act, nor that I had been very smart, they could have had knives, anything, and the fight had absolutely nothing to do with me.

What was odd about these months was the way in which we came closer to each other and grew apart. Linda did not bear grudges, and after something had happened, it had happened, it was over. For me it was different. I held grudges, and every single one of these incidents over the last year lay somehow stored inside me. At the same time I understood what had happened, the sparks of anger that had begun to fly in our lives that first autumn, they were linked with what had been lost in our relationship, Linda was afraid of losing the rest, she was trying to bind me and my shying away from these bonds increased the distance, and that was precisely what she feared. When she became pregnant everything changed, now there was a horizon beyond the one the two of us formed, something greater than us, and it was there the whole time, in my thoughts and hers. Her unease may have been great, but even in its midst there was always a wholeness and security in her. Everything would fall into place, it would be fine, I knew it would.

In mid-December Yngve and the children came to visit. With them they brought the long-awaited buggy. They stayed for a few days. Linda was friendly on the first day and a few hours into the second, but then she turned her back, assumed the hostile air that could drive me insane. Not when it was only me subjected to it because I was used to this and knew how to counter it, but when others were. Then I had to step in, try to mollify Linda, try to mollify Yngve and keep channels open. Six weeks left to the big day, she wanted peace and quiet and considered she was entitled to that, and perhaps she was, what did I know, but surely it didn't mean you no longer needed to be amiable with your guests? Being hospitable, having people over to stay for as long as they liked, was important to me, and I didn't understand how it was possible for Linda to behave as she was doing. Or, yes, I did: she would soon be giving birth and she didn't want crowds of people in the house, also, she and Yngve were light years apart. Yngve had had a good close relationship with Tonje, he didn't have the same with Linda, she noticed that of course, but why the hell did she have to act on it? Why couldn't she hide all her emotions and play the game? Be friendly to my family? Wasn't I friendly to hers? Had I ever said they came round too much and endlessly stuck their noses into matters that did not concern them? Linda's family and friends were with us a thousand times more than mine, the ratio was a thousand to one, and yet, even though the disparity was immense, she could not and would not adapt, she turned her back. Why? Because she was acting on emotions. But emotions are there to be repressed.

I said nothing, held all my reproaches and my anger in check, and when Yngve and the children had left and Linda was happy, light-hearted and excited again, I didn't punish her by keeping my distance and being sullen, which would have been my natural response, no, on the contrary, I dropped the matter, let unreasonable bygones be unreasonable bygones, and the run-up to Christmas and the days afterwards were wonderful.

On the last evening of 2003, with me running to and fro in the kitchen and sorting out the food while Geir sat in a chair chatting away and watching, there was no longer a trace of the life I had left in Bergen. Everything I had around me now was somehow connected with two people I hadn't actually known at all then. Mostly Linda, of course, with whom I now shared all of my life, but also Geir. I had been influenced by him, and not in a small way either, and that could be an unpleasant thought, that I was so easy to influence, that my views could so easily be affected by others. Occasionally I mused that he was like one of those childhood friends you weren't allowed to play with. Keep your distance from him, Karl Ove, he's a bad influence.

I placed the last half-lobster on the dish, put down the knife and wiped the sweat from my forehead.

'There we are,' I said. 'Just the garnish left.'

'If only people knew what you do,' Geir said.

'What do you mean?'

'The general perception of writers' lives is that they are exciting and desirable. But you generally spend most of your time cooking and cleaning.'

'True enough,' I said. 'But now look how well it's turned out!'

I cut the lemons into four and placed them between the lobsters, tore off some sprigs of parsley and laid them alongside.

'People like scandalous writers, you see. You should go to the Theatercafé with a harem of young women running round you. That's what's expected. Not standing here and languishing over your bloody buckets of water . . . The biggest disappointment in Norwegian literature must be Tor Ulven, by the way. He didn't even go out! Ha ha ha!'

His laughter was infectious. I laughed as well.

'And on top of all that he committed suicide!' he added. 'Ha ha ha!'

'Ha ha ha!'

'Ha ha ha! But you have to say Ibsen was also a disappointment. Though not the top hat with the mirror, by the way. That deserves respect. And the live scorpion he kept on his desk. Bjørnson wasn't a disappointment. And definitely not Hamsun. In fact, you can divide up Norwegian literature like this. And I'm afraid you don't come out very well.'

'No,' I said. 'But at least it's clean here. There we are. Now there's just the bread left.'

'Incidentally, you should write that essay on Olav H. Hauge you've been talking about. Soon.'

'The bad man of Hardanger?' I said, taking a loaf of bread out of its brown paper bag.

'Yes, that one.'

'I'll do it one day,' I said, rinsing the knife under a jet of hot water and drying it on the kitchen cloth before cutting. 'In fact, I do think about it now and then. Him lying naked in the coal cellar after smashing all the furniture in the living room. Or the village boys throwing stones at him. Hell, there were some years when he must have been completely off his trolley.'

'Not least the little matter of him writing that Hitler was a great man, and then removing what he had written during the war from his diary,' Geir said.

'Yes, not least,' I said. 'But the most significant part of the whole diary is what he writes when his periods of illness begin. You can read how everything starts going faster and faster as his inhibitions disappear. Suddenly there he is, writing what he *really* thinks about writers and their books. Normally he's *so* punctilious about saying something nice about everyone. Polite and considerate and friendly and nice. And then there's the breakdown. It's strange that no one has written about it, isn't it. I mean the way his judgements of Jan Erik Vold changed so radically.'

'No one dares write about it of course,' Geir said. 'It's crazy. They hardly dare poke a finger in the periods when he lost it.'

'There is a reason for it,' I said, putting the slices of bread in the basket and starting on the next loaf.

'And that would be?'

'Decency. Manners. Consideration.'

'Ah, think I can feel a sleep coming on. It just got so boring in here.'

'I'm serious. I mean it.'

'Of course you do. Listen to me. It *is* in the diary, is it?'

'Yes, it is.'

'And you can't understand Hauge without it?'

'No.'

'And you consider Hauge a great poet?'

'Yes.'

'So what conclusion do you draw from that? That we should ignore an important part of a great poet and diarist's life for the sake of decency? Forget the unpleasantness?'

'What does it matter whether Hauge believed powers from outer space shone lights on him or not? I mean, as far as the poems themselves are concerned. Besides, who knows where his brutish directness stopped and his sensitive politeness started? I mean, where do you *really* draw the line?'

'What? Which bat has taken up residency in your belfry now? You're the one who told me about Hauge's more eccentric side, and in fact you were obsessed by it! You said the image of the wise man of Hardanger cannot go uncontested when you know that he was mad and anything but wise for protracted periods. Or, to be more precise, that the wisdom, whatever *that* might be, cannot be understood without the misery in his life.'

'No bats without fire, as the Chinese say,' I responded. 'Perhaps our laughing at Tor Ulven has had some influence here. My conscience was pricking me.'

'Ha ha ha! Is that so? You can't be that sensitive and cautious. He is dead after all. And I don't think he was much of a party animal, was he? He drove cranes, didn't he? Ha ha ha!'

I cut the last slices and laughed, though not without a tinge of unease.

'Well, that's enough now,' I said, as I put them in the basket. 'If you take the basket of bread, the butter and the mayonnaise we can join the others.'

'Oh, how wonderful!' Helena said as I put the dish on the table.

'You've done us proud, Karl Ove,' Linda said.

'Help yourselves,' I said. Poured what was left of the champagne and opened a bottle of white wine, then sat down and put one of the lobster halves on my plate. Cracked the large claw with the pliers from the seafood set I had been given as a present by Gunnar and Tove some time ago. The meat that grew in such tasty profusion around the tiny flat white cartilage, or whatever it was. The space between the flesh and the outer shell where there was often water: What kind of feeling would *that* have been when the lobster was walking around on the seabed?

'Now we're having a grand time!' I said in Norwegian dialect, and raised my glass. '*Skål!*'

Geir smiled. The others ignored what they didn't understand and raised their glasses.

'*Skål!* And thank you for inviting us!' Anders said.

More often than not it was me who cooked when we had guests. Not so much because I liked doing it but because it gave me something to hide behind. I could stay in the kitchen when they arrived, poke my head in and say hello, carry on cooking in the kitchen, hidden, until the food was ready to serve and I had to appear. But even then I could hide behind something: a glass had to be filled with wine, another with water, I could take care of that and the instant the first course was finished I could clear the table and set it for the next.

That is what I did on this evening as well. As fascinated as I was by Anders, I was unable to talk to him. I liked Helena, but I couldn't talk to her. I could talk to Linda, but now we were responsible for making sure the others were having a good time and therefore we couldn't have a conversation. I could also talk to Geir, but when he was with others another side of his person- ality took over; he was talking to Anders about criminal acquaint- ances, they laughed and carried on, he entertained Helena with his shocking honesty, she reacted with a mixture of gasps and laughter. Beneath this there were also other tensions. Linda and Geir were like two magnets, they repelled each other. Helena was never quite happy with Anders when they were out, it was not uncommon for him to make comments with which she disagreed or which she considered foolish; this tension affected me. Christina could go for long periods without speaking, this too affected me, why was it, wasn't she having a good time, was it us, Geir or herself?

There were almost no similarities between us, there were constant undercurrents of sympathies and antipathies beneath the surface, that is beneath what was said and done, but despite that, or perhaps because of it, it was a memorable evening, most of all because we suddenly reached a point where it felt as if no one had anything to lose and we could tell any story from our lives, even one we usually kept to ourselves.

The conversation stuttered into life, as most do between people who don't know each other but about each other.

I raised the thick smooth flesh from the shell, divided it, forked a mouthful, ran it through the mayonnaise and lifted it to my lips.

Outside there was an enormous bang, like an exploding bomb. The windowpanes rattled.

'That one wasn't legal,' Anders said.

'Ah yes, you're an expert on that, I gather,' Geir said.

'We've brought a sky lantern with us,' Helena said. 'You light it and then the lantern fills with hot air and just climbs into the sky. Higher and higher. And there's no bang. It rises without a sound. It's fantastic.'

'Is it safe to let it off in a town?' Linda asked. 'I mean, what if it lands on a roof and it's alight?'

'Anything goes on New Year's Eve,' Anders said.

There was a silence. I wondered if I should tell them about the time a friend and I collected all the burned-out rockets on the first of January, removed all the powder, tamped it into a cartridge case and lit it. The image was still vivid in my brain: Geir Håkon turning towards me, his face black with soot. The horror that struck me when I realised that dad could have heard the bang and that the soot might not come off completely and that dad would be able to see. But the story didn't have a point, I thought, so I got up and poured more wine, met Helena's smiling gaze, sat down, glanced over at Geir, who had launched into the differences between Sweden and Norway, a theme he resorted to when conversation round the table was flagging. It was one on which everyone had something to say.

'But why compare Sweden and Norway?' Anders asked after a while. 'Nothing happens here. It's cold and horrible as well.'

'Anders wants to go back to Spain,' Helena said.

'What's wrong with that?' Anders retorted. 'We should have moved. All of us. What actually keeps us here? Is there anything?'

'What is it about Spain then?' Linda asked.

He opened his palms.

'You can do what you like. No one bothers. And it's so lovely and hot. There are some wonderful towns down there. Sevilla. Valencia. Barcelona. Madrid.'

He looked at me.

'And there's a slight difference in the level of football. The two of us should go down and see *El Clásico*. Stay overnight. I can fix the tickets. No problem. What do you say?'

'Sounds good to me,' I said.

'Sounds good to me,' he snorted. 'Let's go, man.'

Linda looked at me and smiled. 'You go, I'd be pleased for you,' her look said. But there were other looks and moods, I knew, which would appear sooner or later. You go and enjoy yourself while I sit at home alone, they said. You only think about yourself. If you go anywhere it should be with me. All of this was in her eyes. A boundless love and a boundless anxiety. Fighting for domination all the time. Something new had appeared in recent months, it was tied up with the imminent arrival of the baby, and lay inside her, a mutedness. The anxiety was delicate, ethereal, flickering through her consciousness like the northern lights across a winter's sky or lightning across an August sky, and the darkness that accompanied it was weightless too, in the sense that it was an absence of light, and absence has no weight. What filled her now was something else, I thought it had something to do with earth, it was earthy, a taking root. At the same time I considered it a stupid mythologising thought.

Nevertheless. Earth.

'When is El Clásico then?' I asked, leaning across the table to fill Anders' glass.

'I don't know. But we don't have to go and see that match. Any of them will do. I just want to see Barcelona.'

I filled my glass and poked out the meat from the back of the claw.

'Yes, that would be good,' I said. 'But at any rate we'll have to wait for a week after the birth. After all, we're not men from the 1950s.'

'I am,' Geir said.

'Me too,' Anders said. 'Or at least on the fringes. If I could have done it, I would have paced the corridor during the birth.'

'Why didn't you?' Geir asked.

Anders looked at him, and they laughed.

'Has everyone got something to drink?' I asked. After they had nodded and thanked me, I collected their plates and carried them into the kitchen. Christina followed me with the two serving platters.

'Can I help you with anything?' she asked.

I shook my head and briefly met her eyes before looking down.

'No,' I said. 'But thank you for offering.'

She went back, I filled a pan with water and put it on the stove. Outside, rockets were making fizzing sounds and exploding. The little patch of sky I could see was occasionally illuminated with glittering lights, which showered across it and extinguished themselves as they fell. From the living room came laughter.

I placed two black cast-iron pots on hotplates and turned the temperature setting to maximum. Opened the window, and the voices of passing pedestrians below rose in volume at once. Went into the living room, put on some music, the latest Cardigans' CD, good background ambience.

'I won't even ask if you need help,' Anders said.

'Such nice manners,' Helena said, turning to me. '*Do* you need any help?'

'No, no, everything's fine.'

I stood behind Linda and rested my hands on her shoulders.

'How nice,' she said.

Silence. I thought I should wait until the conversation got going again.

'I had lunch with a few people at Filmhuset just before Christmas,' Linda said after a while. 'One of them had just seen an albino snake. Think it was a python or a boa constrictor, one of the two. Completely white with a yellow pattern. Then someone else said she *used* to have a boa. At home in her flat, as a pet. An *enormous* snake. Then one day she had a shock because it was lying beside her in bed, stretched out to its full length. She had always seen it coiled up, you see, but now it was as straight as a ruler. She was petrified, and so she rang Skansen Zoo to talk to someone who dealt with snakes. Do you know what he said? Well, good job she rang. In the nick of time. Because big snakes stretch out like that when they're measuring up their prey. To see if they can swallow it.'

'Ugh, oh, Christ!' I said. 'Ugh, shit!'

The others laughed.

'Karl Ove's afraid of snakes,' Linda said.

'That's the nastiest story I've ever heard!'

Linda turned to me.

'He dreams about snakes. He can hurl the duvet on the floor and trample on it in the middle of the night. Once he sat up and *leaped* out of bed. Stood absolutely still, as if paralysed, and stared. What is it, Karl Ove? You're dreaming. Come to bed, I said. There's a *slange* there, he said. A snake in Norwegian. There isn't an *orm*, I said. A snake in Swedish. Come to bed. And then he said, full of contempt, "When you say *orm* it doesn't sound quite so dangerous!"'

They laughed. Geir explained to Anders and Helena the difference between *orm* and *slange* in Norwegian – the former was a worm. I said that I knew what was coming, the Freudian interpretation of dreaming about snakes, and I didn't want to hear, and so I went back into the kitchen. The water was boiling, and I added the tagliatelle. The oil in the two pots was spitting in the heat. I sliced some garlic and put it in, took the mussels from the sink, dropped them in and placed the lid on top. Soon it began to rumble and roar. I poured in white wine, chopped some parsley and sprinkled it in, took the mussels off the hotplate after a few minutes, put the tagliatelle in a colander, fetched the pesto and everything was ready.

'Oh, how lovely that looks,' Helena said as I entered with the plates.

'It's not exactly difficult,' I said. 'I found the recipe in Jamie Oliver's cookery book. But it's good.'

'It smells fantastic,' Christina said.

'Is there anything you can't do?' Anders said, staring at me.

I looked down, forked out the soft content of a mussel, it was dark brown with an orange stripe along the top, and when I bit, it crunched like sand between your teeth.

'Has Linda told you about our *pinnekjøtt* meal?' I asked, looking up at him.

'*Pinnekjøtt*? What's that?'

'Traditional Norwegian Christmas food,' Geir said.

'Sheep's ribs,' I said. 'You salt them and hang them up to dry for a few months. My mother posted me some.'

'Mutton in the post?' Anders queried. 'Is that another Norwegian tradition?'

'How else would I get it? Anyway, my mother salts them and hangs them up in our loft at home. It tastes fantastic. She promised to send me some for Christmas. We were going to have them on Christmas Eve, Linda hasn't tried them, and for me it is unthinkable to celebrate Christmas without ribs, but they didn't arrive until the 27th. So I unpacked them, we decided to have another Christmas dinner that evening, and in the afternoon I went to work steaming the meat. We set the table, white cloth and candles and aquavit and everything. But the meat never cooked, we didn't have a pot you could close tightly enough, so all that happened was that the whole flat reeked of sheep. In the end Linda and I went to bed.'

'Then he woke me up at one!' Linda said. 'And we sat here, on our own, in the middle of the night eating Norwegian Christmas food.'

'That was great, wasn't it?' I said.

'Yes, it was,' she said with a smile.

'*Was* it good?' Helena asked.

'Yes. It might not have looked good, but it was.'

'I thought you were going to tell us a story about something you couldn't do,' Anders said. 'But this was nothing short of an idyll.'

'Cut the man a bit of slack,' Geir said. 'He's made a career of telling people what a failure he is. One wretched tragic episode after another. Shame and remorse all down the line. This is a party! Let him talk about how clever he is for a change!'

'I'd like you to talk about a defeat, Anders,' Helena said.

'Remember who you're talking to!' Anders said. 'You're talking to someone who was rich once. I mean really rich. I had two cars, an apartment in Östermalm, an account heaving with money. I could go on holiday anywhere I wanted, when I wanted. I even had some horses! And what am I doing now? Making ends meet with a bacon snacks factory in Dalarne! But I don't sit around bloody moaning like you do!'

'Like who do?' Helena asked.

'Like you and Linda, for example! I come home and you're sitting there with your cups of tea on the sofa whinging about everything under the sun. Every conceivable and inconceivable feeling you have to struggle with all the time. It's not that complicated. Either things go well or they don't. And that's good too, because if they don't then they can only go better.'

'The strange thing about you is that you never want to know where you are,' Helena said. 'But it's not a question of a lack of insight. It's that you don't want to see. Sometimes I envy you. I really do. I struggle so much trying to understand who I am and why what happens to me actually happens.'

'Your story's not so different from Anders', is it?' Geir said.

'What do you mean?'

'Well, you also had everything. You were employed at the Royal Dramatic Theatre, you got the main roles in big productions, great film roles, and then you dropped everything and left. And that was also a pretty optimistic act, if you ask me. To marry an American New Age guru and go to Hawaii.'

'Well, it wasn't a great career move,' Helena said. 'You're right about that. But I followed my heart. And I don't regret anything. Nothing, really!'

She smiled and looked around.

'And Christina has the same story,' Geir said.

'What's your story then?' Anders asked, looking at Christina.

She smiled and raised her head, swallowing the food she had in her mouth.

'I was at the top almost before I had begun. I had my own clothes brand and was chosen as the best designer one year. I was selected to represent Sweden at the London Fashion Fair. I was in Paris with a collection—'

'A TV crew came to our house,' Geir said. 'And Christina's face was on some enormous drapes, no, enormous bloody *sails* at the front of the Culture House. There was a six-page feature article about her in *Dagens Nyheter* . . . We were at receptions where the women serving were dressed as elves. Champagne flowing everywhere. We were so unbelievably happy.'

'What happened then?' Linda asked.

Christina shrugged.

'No money came in. The success had no base. Or not where it should have been. So I went bankrupt.'

'But at least you went with a bang,' Geir said.

'Yes,' Christina agreed.

'The last collection was the nail in the coffin,' Geir said. 'Christina had hired a giant marquee and had it erected in

Gärdet. The tent was a copy of the Sydney Opera House. The models were supposed to arrive on horseback across the open field. She had got them from the Royal Life Guards and the mounted police. Everything was on a grand scale and costly. She hadn't cut any corners. Huge punchbowls of burning ice, you know, drifting smoke, and everyone was there. All the TV channels, all the major newspapers. It looked like the set of a blockbuster movie.

'And then it began to rain. And I mean *rain*. It pelted down, it was insane.'

Christina laughed and put her hand to her mouth.

'You should have seen the models!' Geir went on. 'The men's hair plastered to their skulls. All their clothes drenched and bedraggled. It was a total fiasco. But there was something stylish about it too. Not everyone can fail in *such* a glorious manner.'

Everyone laughed.

'That was why she was designing slippers when you first came to our place,' Geir said, looking at me.

'They weren't slippers,' Christina said.

'Well, whatever,' Geir said. 'One of their old models of a shoe suddenly became a sales hit because Christina wore them at a fashion show in London. She earned nothing. So the design was a small consolation. That was all that was left of the dream.'

'I haven't been at the *top* exactly,' Linda said. 'But the little success I've had follows exactly the same curve.'

'Straight down?' Anders asked.

'Straight down, yes. I made my literary debut, and that was of course a fantastic event in itself, not that it was sensational for others in any way, but it was big, and wonderful for me, and then I was awarded a Japanese prize, of all things. I've always loved Japan. I was supposed to go there to receive it. I'd bought a Japanese phrasebook and so on. Then I fell ill. I was incapable

of coping with anything, and certainly not a trip to Japan . . .
I'd written another series of poems and at first it was accepted.
I went out to celebrate after they told me, but then the accept-
ance was withdrawn. I went to another publisher's with it and
exactly the same happened there. At first the editor rang and
said it was fantastic and they would publish it. It was so embarrassing, I told everyone about it . . . then he rang to say they
wouldn't be publishing it after all. And that was that.'

'That's just so sad,' Anders said.

'Oh, it didn't matter,' Linda said. 'Now I'm pleased it wasn't
published. It's not a big deal.'

'What about you then, Geir?' Helena asked.

'Do you mean, am I a beautiful loser as well?'

'Yes.'

'We-ell, I suppose I could say that. I was an academic
wonderboy.'

'Even though you say so yourself?' I said.

'No one else will. And I *was*. But I wrote a thesis in Norwegian
based on fieldwork in Sweden. That was not a clever move. It
meant that no Swedish publisher was interested, nor were any
Norwegian ones. Nor did it help that I wrote about boxers,
without looking for social explanations or excuses for what they
did, I mean, that they were poor or underprivileged or criminals
or some such thing. On the contrary, I thought that their culture
was relevant and appropriate, much more relevant and appropriate than the feminised middle-class academic culture. That
was not a clever move either. It was still turned down by several
Norwegian and Swedish publishers. I got it published in the
end by paying for it myself. No one read it. The marketing, do
you know what it was? I spoke to a woman at a publishing
house one day and she told me that she read my book every
morning and afternoon on the Nesodden-to-Oslo ferry and she

thought that someone was bound to see the cover and become curious!'

He laughed.

'And now I've stopped teaching, I don't write any academic articles any more, I don't take part in seminars, I sit all on my own writing a book it will take me five years to finish and which I presume no one will want.'

'You should have had a word with me,' Anders said. 'I could have got you on TV at any rate. Where you could have spoken about your book.'

'And how would you have managed that?' Helena enquired. 'An offer you can't refuse?'

'Not even you would've had good enough contacts for that,' Geir said. 'But thanks for the thought.'

'So that's just you left,' Anders said, looking at me.

'Karl Ove?' Geir said. 'He sheds his tears in a limousine. I've said that ever since he came to Stockholm.'

'I don't agree,' I said. 'It'll soon be five years since I made my debut. Journalists still ring now and then, that's true. But what do they ask about? Hey, Knausgaard, I'm writing an article here about authors with writers' block. And I was wondering if I could have a chat with you. Or even worse: Listen up, we're doing a feature on writers who've done only one book. There are quite a few, you know. And you, well, you've written just one book. I was wondering if you had any time to chat to me about that. How it feels. Yeah, you know. Are you writing now? Has the flow dried up a bit?'

'Hear what I said?' Geir said. 'He sheds his tears in a limousine.'

'But I've got nothing! I've been writing for four years and there's nothing! Nothing!'

'*All* my friends are failures,' Geir said. 'Not like the usual mainstream failures, though, these are really beyond the pale.

One of them, when he puts dating ads on the Net, he says he loves forests and fields and grilling sausages over an open fire and so on simply because he can't afford to take someone to a restaurant or a café. He hasn't got a button to his name. Absolutely *nada*. One of my colleagues at university became obsessed with a prostitute, he spent all his money on her, more than 200,000 kroner, he even paid for her to have her breasts enlarged so that they were the way he liked them. Another friend has started up a vineyard. In Uppsala! A third has been writing a doctoral thesis for fourteen years. He'll never finish because there's always a new theory, or a new book appears he hasn't read and he has to include. He never stops writing. He's of normal intelligence, but he's stuck in a dead-end street. And then there was a friend in Arendal who impregnated a thirteen-year-old.'

He looked at me and laughed.

'Relax, it wasn't Karl Ove. Not as far as I know anyway. Then there's my friend, the painter,' Geir went on. 'He's gifted, a talent, but all he paints is Viking longboats and swords and he has gone so far to the right that there's no way back for him now, and certainly no way in. I mean to say, Viking boats are no admission ticket to a life in the arts.'

'Don't drag me into this collection,' Anders said.

'No, no one present belongs there,' Geir said. 'Not yet at any rate. I have a feeling we are all on the slide. We're sitting on a wreck. Well, the situation's fine now, the sky's black and full of stars and the water's warm, but we have started to slip.'

'That was very poetic,' Linda said. 'But it's not how I feel.'

She was sitting with both hands over her belly. I met her gaze. I'm happy, it said. I smiled to her.

My God. In two weeks we would have a baby here.

I was going to be a father.

The table had gone quiet. Everyone had finished. They were

reclining in their chairs, Anders with a glass of wine in his hands. I took the bottle, got up and refilled glasses.

'We've been so open,' Helena said. 'That never happens, I was thinking.'

'It's a competition,' I said, putting down the bottle and catching the drop running down the neck with my thumb. 'Who's worst off? Me!'

'No, me!' Geir said.

'I find it difficult to visualise my parents sitting and talking about this with friends,' Helena said. 'But they really *were* up the creek without a paddle. We aren't.'

'How do you mean?' Christina asked.

'My father's Örebro's wig king. He makes toupees. His first wife, my mother, is an alcoholic. She's so repugnant I can hardly visit her. And if I do, I'm in a state for several weeks afterwards. But when dad remarried he chose another alcoholic.'

She pulled a face and followed up with a few tics, which captured her father's wife to perfection. I had met her once, at the christening of their child; she was both utterly self-controlled and utterly at the end of her tether. Helena often laughed at her.

'When I was small they injected syringes into those small fruit-drink cartons, you know the ones, and filled them with alcohol. So that they would look quite innocent. Ha ha ha! And once when I was alone on holiday with mum she gave me a sleeping tablet, locked the door from the outside and went on the town.'

Everyone laughed.

'But she's much worse now. She's a sort of monster. Devours us if we visit her. Just thinks of herself, there's nothing else. She drinks and is foul all the time.'

She looked at me.

'Your father drank as well, didn't he?'

'Yes, he did,' I said. 'Not when I was a boy. He started when I was sixteen. And died when I was thirty. So he stuck at it for fourteen years. He literally drank himself to death. And I think perhaps that was what he was trying to do.'

'Haven't you got a funny story about him?' Anders asked.

'I'm not sure Karl Ove has the same relish for his own misfortunes as you have for those of others,' Helena said.

'Don't worry. It's fine,' I said. 'I don't have any feelings about this any longer. I don't know if this is funny, but, well, here we go. In the end he was living in his mother's house. Drank nonstop of course. One day he fell down the step into the living room. I think he broke his leg. It may have been only a bad sprain. But at any rate he couldn't move – he just lay on the floor. My grandmother wanted to ring for an ambulance, but he wouldn't have it. So he lay there, on the living-room floor, while she looked after him. Ate and drank where he was. I've no idea for how long. A few days perhaps. My uncle found him. He was still lying there.'

Everyone laughed. I did too.

'What was he like when he didn't drink?' Anders asked. 'The first sixteen years?'

'He was a bastard. I was scared to death of him. Absolutely pissing in my pants. I remember once . . . well, I used to like swimming when I was a boy, going to the baths in the winter, it was the high point of the week. Once I lost a sock there. I couldn't find it. I searched and searched, but it was nowhere to be seen. And then I got so frightened. It was a total nightmare.'

'Why was that?' Helena asked.

'Because my life would have been a living hell if he found out.'

'That you'd lost a sock?'

'Yes, exactly. The chances of him finding out were minimal
of course, I could just sneak into the house and take another
pair of socks as soon as I was home, but I was still terrified
all the way home. Opened the door. No one there. Started
taking off my shoes. And who should come in but my father?
And what does he do? Stand there and watch me take off my
things.'

'What happened?' Helena asked.

'He slapped me and told me I could never go to the swimming
baths again.' I smiled.

'Ha ha ha!' Geir laughed. 'There's a man after my own heart!
Consistent to the last.'

'Did your father hit *you* then?' Helena asked.

Geir hesitated.

'There were some features of a traditional Norwegian
upbringing. You know, over my knees and down with your pants.
But he never hit me in the face and he never hit me on the spur
of the moment, like Karl Ove's father did. It was a punishment,
nothing more, nothing less. I considered it just. But he didn't
like doing it. I think he saw it as a duty he was obliged to fulfil.
He's very kind, my father is. A good person. I don't harbour any
ill will against him at all. Not even for the beatings. It was a
very different culture from what we have today.'

'I can't say the same about my father,' Anders said. 'Well, I
don't want to go into my childhood and all that psychological
crap. But when I was growing up we were rich, as I said, and
when I finished school I joined his company, as a kind of
companion. I lived a wonderful upper-class life. Then he suddenly
went bust. It transpired he had been cooking the books and had
committed fraud. And I had signed everything he gave me. I was
let off prison, but I owe the tax authorities such enormous sums
of money that everything I earn for the rest of my life has to go

towards paying them off. That's why I don't have a proper job any more. There's no point, they take the lot.'

'What happened to your father then?' I asked.

'He legged it. I haven't seen him since. I don't know where he is. Abroad somewhere. I don't want to see him, either.'

'But your mother stayed here,' Linda said.

'You could say that, yes,' Anders said. 'Embittered, abandoned and broke.'

He smiled.

'Yes, I've met her once,' I said. 'No, twice. She's very funny. She sits on a stool in the corner and peppers her conversation with sarcasm for anyone who wants to hear. There's lots of humour.'

'Humour?' Anders queried, and began to imitate her, the cracked old-lady voice calling his name and criticising him for everything under the sun.

'My mother is frightened,' Geir said. 'And one fact sabotages everything else in her life or overshadows it. She wants to have everyone close to her all the time. It was hell when I was growing up, it cost me so much to break free. Her technique for holding me was to make me feel guilty. I refused to accept it. That was how I escaped. The price is that we hardly talk. It's a high price, but it's worth paying.'

'What's she frightened of?' Anders asked.

'You mean how it manifested itself?'

Anders nodded.

'She's not frightened of people. With them she can be very direct, she's fearless. It's space she's afraid of. For example, she always had a cushion with her when we went out in the car. On her lap. Whenever we went into a tunnel she would lean forward and put it over her head.'

'Is that true?' Helena asked.

'Certainly. Every single time. Then we had to say when we were out of the tunnel. From there it developed further: all of a sudden she couldn't be on roads with more than one lane, she couldn't bear to have cars passing us so close. And then she couldn't be alongside water. Our holidays became a virtual impossibility. I remember my father standing over the map like a general before a battle while he tried to figure out a route without motorways, water and tunnels.'

'And my mother's diametrically the opposite,' Linda said. 'She's not afraid of anything. I think she's the most fearless person I know. I remember cycling with her through the town to the theatre. She pedals like a lunatic, onto the pavement, between people, onto the road. Once she was stopped by the police. She didn't nod, listen and apologise, it won't happen again, officer – not her. No, she was indignant. It was up to her where she cycled. That's how she was all my childhood. If any of the teachers complained about me she would reciprocate in kind. There was never anything wrong with me. I was always right. When I was six she let me go on holiday to Greece alone.'

'Alone?' Christine repeated. 'Just you?'

'No, I was with a girlfriend and her family. But I was six years old, and two weeks alone with a family of strangers in a foreign country was probably a bit much, don't you think?'

'It was the 70s,' Geir said again. 'Everything was allowed then.'

'I was so embarrassed by my mother on so many occasions. She is the kind of person who has no sense of shame, she can do the most incredible things, and if it was to protect me, I used to wish the floor would swallow me up.'

'And your father?' Geir asked.

'That's a completely different kettle of fish. He was totally unpredictable. Anything could happen when he fell ill. We were just waiting for him to do something awful so that the police could come and take him away. Often we had to run away, my mother and my brother and I. Flee from him, no less.'

'What did he do then?' I asked, looking at her. She had told me about her father before, but only in broad strokes, with very little detail.

'Oh, anything was possible. He could climb up the drainpipe or throw himself through a window. He could be violent. Blood and smashed glass and violence. But then the police came. And everything was fine again. When he was at home I was constantly expecting a catastrophe. But as soon as it came I was always calm. It's almost a relief for me when the worst happens. I *know* I can handle it. It's the way there that's difficult.'

There was a pause.

'Now I can remember a story!' Linda exclaimed. 'It was when we had to flee from dad and go up to my grandmother's in Norrland. I think I was five and my brother seven. On our return to Stockholm the flat was full of gas. Dad had opened the tap and left it on for several days. It felt like the door was forced open by the pressure when mummy unlocked it. She turned to us and told Mathias to take me down to the street and stay there. She waited until we had gone before going into the flat and turning off the gas. On the street, Mathias said, and I remember it so well, you realise that mummy can die now, don't you? Yes, I answered, I knew. Later that day I overheard mummy talking to him on the phone. "Were you trying to kill us?" she asked. Not as an exaggeration, but as a sober fact. "Do you actually want to kill us?"'

Linda smiled.

'Hard to top that one,' Anders said. And he turned to Christina. 'That leaves you. What are your parents like? They're alive, aren't they?'

'Yes,' Christina said. 'But they're old. They live in Uppsala.

They're Pentecostalists. I grew up there and was riddled with guilt about everything, the tiniest little thing. But they're good people. It's their life's work. When the snow melts and sand is left on the tarmac after the winter do you know what they do?'

'No,' I said, since it was me she was looking at.

'They sweep it up and give it back to the Highways Department.'

'Is that true?' Anders asked. 'Ha ha ha!'

'They don't drink alcohol, that goes without saying. And my father doesn't drink tea or coffee either. If he wants a treat in the morning he drinks hot water.'

'I don't believe that,' Anders said.

'But it's true,' Geir said. 'He drinks hot water and they leave the sand by the gate for the Highways Department. They're so good it's almost impossible to be there. I'm sure having me as a son-in-law must be like the devil testing them.'

'What was it like growing up with them?' Helena asked.

'I thought for ages that their world was the world, that was what it was like. All my friends and all my parents' friends belonged to the movement. There was no life outside it. When I broke with it I also broke with all my friends.'

'How old were you then?'

'Twelve,' Christina said.

'Twelve?' Helena repeated. 'How did you find the strength to do that? Or the maturity?'

'I don't know. I just did. And it was tough. It was. I did lose all my friends.'

'Twelve years old?' Linda said.

Christina nodded and smiled.

'So now you drink coffee in the morning?' Anders asked.

'Yes,' Christina answered. 'But not when I'm there.'

We laughed. I got up and started collecting the plates. Geir got up as well, took his own plate and followed me into the kitchen.

'Have you changed sides, Geir?' Anders shouted after him.

I slid the empty mussel shells into the bin, rinsed the plates and put them in the dishwasher. Geir passed me his, retreated a few steps and leaned against the fridge.

'Fascinating,' he said.

'What is?' I asked.

'What we've been talking about. Or *talking* about it at all. Peter Handke has a word for it. *Erzählnächte* I believe he calls them. Nights when people open up and everyone contributes a story.'

'Yes,' I said, turning round. 'Coming for a walk? I need a smoke.'

'All right,' Geir said.

When we were ready with our coats on, Anders came out.

'Are you going for a smoke? I'll join you.'

Two minutes later we were in the middle of the yard, me with a glowing cigarette between my fingers, the other two with their hands in their pockets. It was cold and the wind was blowing. Everywhere fireworks were going off.

'I had another story on the tip of my tongue upstairs,' Anders said, running one hand through his hair. 'About losing everything you have. But I thought it best to tell it here. It was in Spain. I had a restaurant with a pal. It was a fantastic life. Up all night, high on coke and booze, lying in the sun during the day, starting again at seven or eight in the evening. I think it was the best time in my life. I was absolutely free. Did exactly what I wanted.'

'And?' Geir said.

'Then perhaps I did too much of what I wanted. We had an office on the floor above the bar, I screwed my companion's wife there, I couldn't keep my hands off her. Of course he caught us

red-handed and that was that. No more working together. But
one day I want to go back. It's just a question of getting Helena
on board.'

'It might not be the life she's dreaming of?' I suggested.

Anders shrugged.

'But we can hire a summer house down there at some point.
For a month every six months. Granada or something. What do
you reckon?'

'Sounds good,' I said.

'I don't have any holidays,' Geir said.

'What do you mean?' Anders asked. 'This year?'

'No, ever. I work every day all week, Saturdays and Sundays
included, and all the weeks in the year, apart from Christmas
Eve perhaps.'

'Why?' Anders asked.

Geir laughed.

I threw down my cigarette end and stamped on the ground a
few times.

'Shall we go up?' I said.

The first time I met Anders he picked Linda and me up from
the railway station by Saltsjöbaden, where they were renting a
little flat, and on the way he expressed his contempt for the rat
race there, life was about more than money and status, but even
though I had an inkling he was humouring us and just saying
what he thought we, as 'arty people', wanted to hear, a lot of
months were to pass before I understood that he actually meant
the opposite: his *only* real interest was money and the life money
bought. He was obsessed by the notion of becoming rich again,
everything he did was to that end, and as he could not do this
with the knowledge of the tax authorities, he moved into the
world of illegal earnings. When Helena met him all his affairs

were murky, but she, while fighting her love for him for as long
as she could, although finally she did crumble on a grand scale,
set some demands, because not long afterwards they had a baby
together, and apparently he complied: the money he earned was
still illegal but in a certain light nonetheless 'clean'. What exactly
his work was I didn't know, except that he used his many contacts
from the days when he was in clover to finance a quick succession of projects and these somehow lasted only a few months
at a time. Ringing him was a waste of energy because he was
forever changing mobile phones, the same applied to his cars,
so-called company cars which he exchanged at regular intervals.
When we visited them, one evening there might be an enormous
flat-screen TV along one wall in the living room, or a new laptop
on the desk in the hall, the next they could be gone. The line
between what he owned and what he could lay his hands on
was evidently fluid, and nor was there any clear link between
what he did and the money he had at his disposal. All the money
he made, and frequently it was not trivial amounts, he used to
gamble. He would gamble on anything that moved. Since his
powers of persuasion were impressive he had no problem getting
hold of money, so he was stuck in a real quagmire. As a rule he
kept all this to himself, but now and then his dealings surfaced,
like the time someone rang Helena and said that Anders had
emptied the till of the company where he had gone to renegotiate
contracts, a little matter of 700,000 kroner, and it would be
reported to the police. Anders didn't bat an eyelid when she
confronted him with it; the company's finances were in a mess
and dubious, now they were bent on a cover-up by blaming him.
Even though he was supposed to have run off with the money
and gambled it away, the money was illegal and therefore the
police would be the last people they would contact, so in that
respect he was safe. Presumably he kept a watchful eye on the

people he swindled, but the situation was no less dangerous for that. Once they had been burgled while they were out, Helena told Linda; the burglars probably did it just to show that they could. Then he became the co-owner of a grandiose restaurant scheme, but that became history for him after some months, then there were some building sites he was suddenly running, then he was renting exclusive rooms to a hairdressing salon, then there was a bacon factory he had to save from bankruptcy. The problem, if you can call it a problem, was that it was impossible to dislike him. He could talk to anyone, which is a rare gift, and he was generous, which you noticed as soon as you met him. And he was always happy. He was the person who stood up at parties and thanked the hosts for the spread or congratulated them on whatever occasion it was or did whatever was required, and he had a kind word for everyone, however much or little they had in common with him. More often than not, he knew how to make them feel good. Yet there was nothing of the schemer about him, no subtlety, and perhaps that was the reason – despite his general duplicity, which is one of the few qualities I find hard to accept – I still liked him so much. Naturally enough, he couldn't give a flying fart about me, but whenever we met he didn't pretend to be interested, the way people sometimes do when duty compels and the fracture between thoughts and actions becomes visible in one of those tiny revealing gestures that very few can control, such as the quick glance to another side of the room, meaningless in itself, but when it is followed by a kind of 'jolt' as their attention refocuses on you, the ritual as ritual becomes obvious. The feeling that you have been subjected to a charade will of course be disastrous for someone whose life depends on winning people's trust. Anders did not 'play games'; that was his secret. However, he was not 'genuine' either, in the sense that everything he said necessarily fell in line with what he thought, what he did and what he wanted. But then who is? There is a type of person who consistently says what he means without adapting it to the situation in which he finds himself, but such individuals are few and far between, I have met only two, and what happens to them is that all these social situations become incredibly charged. Not because people disagree and start quarrelling, but because their conversational aim excludes all other aims and their totalitarian attitude automatically rebounds on them and they appear mean and pig-headed, irrespective of their real nature, which in both cases was, as far as I could judge, basically generous and friendly. The social unease I myself could provoke came from the opposite cause. I always let the situation determine events, either by saying nothing at all or playing up to others. Saying what you believe others want to hear is of course a form of lying. Hence the difference between Anders' and my social behaviour was only one of degree. Even though his corroded trust and mine corroded integrity, the result was basically the same: a slow erosion of the soul.

It was of course ironic, though not incomprehensible, that Helena, who was drawn to the spiritual side of life and was continually trying to understand herself, should have ended up with a man who swept all other values apart from money to the side with a smile on his face, for they shared an essential ingredient, a lightness and a *joie de vivre*. And they were an attractive couple. With her dark hair, warm eyes and strong facial features, Helena's appearance was striking, her personality winning and her presence palpable. She was a talented actress. I had seen her in two TV series: in one, a crime programme, she played a widow, and the sombreness she radiated turned her into a stranger for me, it was like watching a different person with Helena's face. In the other, a comedy programme, she played a bitch of a wife, and I had the same impression, a different person with her features.

Anders was also good-looking, in a boyish kind of way, although whether it was his aura, the glint in his eye, the slim body or perhaps the hair – which would have been described as a mane in the 1950s – that did it, was hard to say because Anders was not an easy person to see. Once I had bumped into him in Sergels torg in the city centre, he seemed to be hanging around by a wall, hunched and very, very tired, I had barely recognised him, but when he caught sight of me, he straightened up, he seemed to lift himself and in the twinkling of an eye he transformed himself into the happy energetic man I was familiar with.

When we returned, Helena, Christina and Linda had cleared the table and were now chatting on the sofa. I went into the kitchen and put on the coffee. While waiting for it to brew I went into the adjacent room, which was completely quiet and empty, except for the breathing of Helena and Anders' child, who was asleep on our bed, clothed and with a blanket over her. In the half-light the empty cradle, the empty cot, the changing mat and the dresser with the baby's clothes beside it seemed a bit eerie. Everything was ready for our baby to arrive. There was even a pack of nappies we had bought on the shelf beneath the changing mat, with a pile of towels and clothes, and above it a mobile from which hung tiny planes, quivering in the draught from the window. It was eerie because there was no baby, and the line between what could have been and what was to come was so fluid in these matters.

From the living room came the sounds of laughter. I closed the door behind me, put a bottle of cognac, cognac glasses, coffee cups and dishes on a tray, poured the coffee from the machine into a vacuum flask and carried everything into the living room. Christina had a teddy bear on her lap, she seemed happy, her face was more open and calmer than usual, while Linda, sitting next to her, could scarcely keep her eyes open. At present she was going to bed at about nine. It was getting on for twelve now. Helena searched for some music among the CDs on the shelves while Anders and Geir were at the table continuing their conversation about mutual criminal acquaintances. A whole menagerie of criminals had obviously frequented the boxing club in the years Geir hung out there. I set the table and sat down.

'You met Osman, didn't you, Karl Ove?' Geir asked.

I nodded.

Geir had once taken me up to Mosebacke to meet two of the boxers he knew. One, Paolo Roberto, who had boxed for the world championship title, was now a TV celebrity in Sweden, and was preparing for a new title fight in a kind of comeback. The other, Osman, was at the same level but not as well known. With them was an English trainer whom Geir introduced as a 'doctor in boxing'. 'He's a doctor in boxing!' I shook hands, didn't say much, but carefully followed what went on because this was very different from what I knew. They were very relaxed, there were no tensions in the air, which, it occurred to me, I had always been used to. They ate pancakes, drank coffee, watched the crowds, squinted into the low but still hot sun and talked about the old days with Geir. Even though his body was as calm as theirs, it was filled with a different, lighter and more excited, almost nervous energy, it was apparent in his eyes, always looking for openings, and in the way he spoke – effusive, resourceful but also calculating – because he was adapting to them and their jargon while they just spoke as it came to them. The one called Osman was wearing a T-shirt, and even though his biceps were large, perhaps five times larger than mine, they were not disproportionately large but slim. The same was true for the whole of his upper body. He sat there, supple and relaxed, and every time my eyes rested on him it crossed my mind that he could smash me to pulp in seconds without my being able to do anything about it. The feeling it gave me was one of femininity. It was humiliating, but the humiliation was all my own, it could not be seen, nor could it be sensed. Yet it was still there, damn it.

'Fleetingly,' I said. 'At Mosebacke last year. You introduced them to me as though they were a couple of chimps.'

'We were more like the chimps, I imagine,' Geir said. 'Well, anyway. Osman. He attacked a Securicor van in Farsta with an accomplice. The place they chose was *fifty* metres from the main police HQ. So when they were a bit ham-fisted at the beginning and the crew managed to set off the alarm the police were there in seconds! Then they bundled themselves into their car and drove off without the money or anything. And ran out of petrol! Ha ha ha!'

'Is that possible? It sounds like the Olsen band.'

'Right. Ha ha ha!'

'So how is Osman? Armed robbery is not exactly a minor offence.'

'It wasn't too bad. He was given a couple of years, that was all. But his pal had so much previous that he'll be in for a long stretch.'

'Has this just happened?'

'No, no, no. It was a few years ago. A long time before he started a career as a boxer.'

'I see,' I said. 'Some cognac?'

Both Geir and Anders nodded. I opened the bottle and filled three glasses.

'Any of you like some?' I asked, looking towards the sofa. A shaking of heads.

'I might have a tiny drop, please,' Helena said. As she walked across the floor towards us the music began to pour out of the ridiculously small speakers behind her. It was Damon Albarn's *Mali* CD, which we had played earlier in the evening and she had utterly fallen for.

'There you are,' I said, passing her a glass with the golden-brown liquid just covering the bottom. The light from the lamp hanging above the table made it glow.

'There's one thing I'm happy about anyway,' Christina said from the sofa. 'And that's being an adult. It's sooo much better being thirty-two than twenty-two.'

'You are aware you've got a teddy bear on your lap, Christina, are you?' I said. 'Somehow that undermines what you just said.'

She laughed. It was wonderful to see her laugh. There was something tight-lipped about her, not in a dark way, more as though she was using every ounce of strength to keep every-thing, also herself, together. She was tall and slim, always well dressed, of course, in a self-willed way, and beautiful with her pale skin and freckles, but after the first impressions had passed there was this slight closed-ness that emerged and etched itself in my thoughts about her, at least that was how it had been for me. And yet there was something childlike about her, espe-cially when she laughed or became excited and her self-restraint was overcome. Not childlike as in immature, but childlike as in playful and unrestrained. I saw some of the same in my mother the rare times she let go and did something uninhibited or hasty, for in her too a natural response was indistinguish-able from vulnerability. Once we had been up at Geir and Christina's for a meal. As usual Christina put all her energy and concentration into the cooking. I had been alone in the living room, in the dim light behind the bookshelves, when she came in to get something. She didn't know I was there. With the voices and the noise of the fans behind her in the kitchen, she smiled to herself. Her eyes were sparkling. Oh, I was so happy when I saw that, but sad too, because she had not intended anyone to see how much it meant to her that we were there.

On one of the mornings when I was staying with them Christina had been washing up in the kitchen while I sat at the table drinking coffee, and she suddenly pointed to the pile of plates and dishes in the cupboard.

'When we moved in together I bought eighteen of everything,' she said. 'I envisaged us having big parties here. Loads of friends and wonderful meals. But we've never used them. Not once!'

Geir laughed aloud from the bedroom. Christina smiled.

That was them. That was how they were.

'But I agree,' I said now. 'The twenties were hell. Adolescence was worse. But the thirties are OK.'

'What's changed then?' Helena asked.

'When I was twenty what I had, what made me me, was so little. I didn't know that of course because that was all there was at that time. But now I'm thirty-five there's more. Well, everything that existed in me when I was twenty is still there. But now it's surrounded by so much more. That's sort of how I think about it.'

'That's an incredibly optimistic view,' Helena said. 'That things get better the older you are.'

'Is it?' Geir said. 'Surely the less you have, the simpler it is to live?'

'Not for me at any rate,' I said. 'Now things don't mean as much as they did before. Trivialities could mean everything! They could be all-decisive!'

'That's true,' Geir said. 'But I still wouldn't call it optimistic. Fatalistic, yes.'

'What happens, happens,' I said. 'And now we're here. *Skål* to that, I say.'

'*Skål!*'

'Seven minutes till midnight,' Linda said. 'Shall we put on the TV and watch Jan Malmsjö's countdown?'

'What's that?' I asked, going over and proffering my hand. She grabbed it and I pulled her to her feet.

'He reads poems. The bells chime. It's a Swedish tradition.'

'Put it on then,' I said.

While she was doing that I went over to open the windows. The noise of fireworks was growing steadily, now the bangs, crackles and whizzes were non-stop, a wall of sound above the rooftops. The streets were thick with people. Champagne bottles and sparklers in hand, warm coats and capes over festive outfits. No children, just happy, drunken adults.

Linda fetched the last bottle of champagne, opened it and filled the glasses full with effervescent foam. Holding them, we stood by the windows. I watched the others. They were happy, excited, talking, pointing, *skål*-ing.

Outside, sirens sounded.

'Either war has broken out or 2004 has started,' Geir said. I put out my arms and held Linda to me. We looked into each other's eyes.

'Happy New Year,' I said and kissed her.

'Happy New Year, my darling prince,' she said. 'This is our year.'

'Yes, it is,' I said.

After all the hugs and congratulations were over and people had started to withdraw from the streets, Anders and Helena remembered their sky lantern. We put on our coats and went down to the backyard. Anders lit the wick, the lantern slowly filled with hot air and when, at length, he let go it began to rise alongside the house, glowing and silent. We followed it until it vanished over Östermalm's rooftops. Back upstairs, we sat round the table again. Conversation was more sporadic and less concentrated now, but occasionally it focused on one point, such as when Linda talked about the posh party she had been to when she was a pupil at *gymnas*, in a grand house with a large swimming pool behind which there was an enormous glass partition. During the course of the evening they had swum and as she kicked off from the partition to dive into the water it shattered and smashed into a million tinkling pieces.

'I'll never forget that sound,' she said.

Anders talked about a trip to the Alps – he had been skiing off-piste and suddenly the ground had opened beneath him. Still wearing his skis, he had fallen down a crevasse in a glacier, perhaps six metres, and lost consciousness. He was rescued by a helicopter, he had broken his back, paralysis was feared and he was operated on at once; for weeks he lay in hospital while his father, he told us, sometimes sat in the chair next to him, as if in a dream, reeking of alcohol.

Then he got to his feet, leaned forward and pulled his shirt up so that we could see the long scar on his back from the operation.

When I was seventeen, I told them, we had been doing a hundred kilometres an hour in the frozen wastes of Telemark and a tyre had burst, we had bounced off a telephone pole, flown over a road and landed in a ditch, escaping serious injury by some miracle, but the car was a total write-off. However, the worst had not been the accident but the cold, it was minus twenty, the middle of the night, we were wearing T-shirts, jackets and trainers after an Imperiet gig and stood on the roadside for hours without getting a lift.

I refilled the glasses with cognac for Anders, Geir and myself, Linda yawned, Helena began a story about Los Angeles, then a shrill alarm went off somewhere in the building.

'What the hell's that?' Anders said. 'The fire alarm?'

'Well, it is New Year's Eve,' Geir said.

'Should we go out?' Linda wondered, sitting up on the sofa.

'I'll go and check first,' I said.

'I'll join you,' Geir said.

We stepped into the corridor. There was no smoke anyway. The sound was coming from the ground floor so we hurried down the stairs. The light above the lift was flashing. I leaned forward and looked through the window in the door. Someone was lying on the floor inside. I opened the door. It was the Russian. She was on her back with one foot against the wall. She was in party clothes, a black dress with some sequins on the chest, skin-coloured tights and high heels. She laughed when she saw us. Instinctively, I looked at her thighs and the black panties between them before shifting my gaze to her face.

'I can't stand up!' she said.

'We'll give you a hand,' I said. I grabbed one arm and pulled her into a sitting position. Geir went to the other side and between us we managed to get her upright. She was laughing all the time. The stench of perfume and alcohol in the confined space was overpowering.

'*Tack så mycket*,' she said in Swedish. Then *Tusen, tusen takk*, in Norwegian.

She took my hands in hers, bent forward and kissed them, first one, then the other. Then she peered up at me.

'Oh, what a good-looking man,' she said.

'Come on and we'll help you to your flat,' I said. Pressed the button for her floor and closed the door. Geir was grinning from ear to ear as he glanced from her to me. As the lift started its ascent she slumped against me.

'So,' I said. 'Here we are. Have you got the key?'

She looked into the little bag she wore over her shoulder, swaying to and fro like a tree in the wind as her fingers rummaged through the contents.

'Here it is!' she exclaimed triumphantly, producing a bunch of keys.

Geir held an arm against her shoulder as she toppled forward with the key pointing to the lock.

'Take a step forward,' he said. 'And you'll be fine.'

She obeyed. After some fumbling she succeeded in getting the key into the lock.

'*Tusen takk!*' she thanked us again. 'You're two angels who have come to my aid this evening.'

'Not at all,' Geir said. 'And good luck.'

On our way upstairs to the flat Geir sent me a quizzical look.

'Was that your crazy neighbour?' he asked.

I nodded.

'She's a prostitute, isn't she?'

I shook my head.

'Not as far as I know,' I said.

'She must be, you know. She couldn't afford to live here otherwise. And her appearance . . . She didn't look stupid though.'

'That's enough,' I said, opening the door to the flat. 'She's like any woman. Just very unhappy, an alcoholic and Russian. With an impulse-control disorder.'

'Yes, you can say that again.' Geir laughed.

'What was it?' Helena asked from the living room.

'That was our Russian neighbour,' I said, going in. 'She'd fallen over in the lift and was so drunk she couldn't get up. So we helped her to her flat.'

'She kissed Karl Ove's hands,' Geir said. '"Oh, what a good-looking man," she said!'

Everyone laughed.

'And that's after she's stood here swearing and cursing at me,' I said. 'And driven us mad.'

'It's a nightmare,' Linda said. 'She's totally out of it. When I walk past her on the stairs I'm almost afraid she'll pull out a knife and stab me. She glares at me with hatred in her eyes, doesn't she? Deep hatred.'

'Time's slowly running out for her,' Geir said. 'Then you move in with a bulging belly and impending bliss.'

'Is that it, do you think?' I asked.

'Of course,' Linda said. 'If only we'd kept our distance at the beginning. But we were open with her. Now she's obsessed by us.'

'Yeah, yeah,' I said. 'Anyone up for some dessert? Linda's made her famous tiramisu.'

'Oh!' said Helena.

'If it's famous it's because it's the only dessert I can make,' Linda said.

I fetched it and the coffee, and we sat at the table again. No sooner had we done so than the music blared out from the flat below.

'This is how we live,' I said.

'Can't you get her thrown out?' Anders asked. 'If you want I can fix it for you.'

'And how does that work?' Helena asked.

'I have my methods,' Anders replied.

'Oh yes?' Helena said.

'Report her to the police,' Geir said. 'Then she'll realise it's serious.'

'Do you mean that?' I said.

'Of course. If you don't do something drastic it'll just go on and on.'

The music stopped as abruptly as it had started. The door below slammed. Heels click-clacked on the stairs.

'Is she going to come here?' I said.

Everyone sat still, listening. But the footsteps passed our door and continued up the stairs. Soon after, they returned and faded as they went down. I crossed to the window and looked below. Wearing only the dress and one shoe, she staggered into the white carriageway. She waved, a taxi was approaching. It stopped and she clambered in.

'She's taking a taxi,' I said. 'Wearing one shoe. Can't fault her for effort, anyway.'

I sat down and the conversation drifted into other areas. At around two Anders and Helena made a move to go, wrapped themselves up in their thick winter clothes, hugged us and headed off into the night, Anders with his sleeping daughter in his arms. Geir and Christina left half an hour later, Geir, after returning with a high-heeled shoe in his hand.

'Like a second Cinderella,' he said. 'What shall I do with it?'

'Leave it outside her door,' I said. 'And be off with you now, we need to sleep.'

When I went into the bedroom, after tidying up the living room and putting on the dishwasher, Linda was asleep. But not so soundly that she was unable to open her eyes and send me a drowsy smile as I undressed.

'That was a nice evening, wasn't it,' I said.

'Yes, it was,' she said.

'Did they have a good time, do you think?' I asked, getting into bed next to her.

'Yes, I think so. Don't you?'

'Yes, I really do. I enjoyed it anyway.'

The light from the street lamps cast a faint glimmer across the floor. It was never properly dark in here. And never properly quiet. Fireworks were still exploding outside, voices rose and fell in the street, cars raced by, more now that New Year's Eve was nearing its end.

'But I'm beginning to get seriously worried about our neighbour,' Linda said. 'It doesn't feel good having her there.'

'No,' I said. 'There isn't a lot we can do though.'

'No.'

'Geir reckoned she was a prostitute,' I said.

'She is, no question about it,' Linda said. 'She works for one of those escort companies.'

'How do you know that?'

'It's obvious.'

'Not to me,' I said. 'The thought would never have crossed my mind in a million years.'

'That's because you're so naïve,' Linda said.

'Maybe I am.'

'You are.'

She smiled, leaned over and kissed me.

'Goodnight,' she said.

'Goodnight,' I said.

It was difficult to comprehend that actually there were three of us in bed. But there were. The baby in Linda's belly was fully developed; all that separated us was a centimetre-thin wall of flesh and skin. The baby could be born any day now and this defined Linda's behaviour. She no longer started anything new, barely went out, kept calm, cosseted herself and her body, took long baths and watched films on the sofa, dozed and slept. Her state was like dormancy, but her disquiet had not entirely left her. Now it was particularly my role in the drama that concerned her. On the antenatal course we had been told that the relationship between the pregnant woman and the midwife was important, and if there were any disagreements, if there was a bad atmosphere of any kind, it was important to say so as early as possible in order that another, hopefully better-suited, midwife could take over. Furthermore, we were told that the man's role during the birth was primarily that of a communicator; he knew his wife best of all, he would understand what she wanted and, as she was otherwise engaged, he would have to be the person to pass this on to the midwife. This was where I came in. I spoke Norwegian. Would the midwives and nurses even understand what I said? And, much worse, I avoided conflict and was always considerate to everyone in any situation. Would I be able to say no to a potentially awful midwife and demand a new one, with all the hurt feelings that might entail?

'Relax, relax, it'll be fine,' I responded, 'don't think about it, everything will sort itself out,' but she couldn't settle, I had become the cause of her worry. Would I even be able to ring for a taxi when the moment came?

That she had a point did not make the matter any easier. Any form of pressure knocked me out. I wanted to please everyone, but sometimes there were situations where I had to make a decision and act upon it, and then I suffered dreadful agonies, these were among my most unpleasant experiences. Now I had lived through a series of them over a short period and she had been a witness. The incident with the locked door, the boat incident, the incident with my mother. And the time when I compensated for all this by intervening in a fight one morning on the Metro didn't do me much credit either, because what sort of judgement had I shown? And, more importantly, I knew it would be more difficult for me to show a midwife the door than to be stabbed with a knife in a Metro station.

Then, on my way home late one afternoon, putting down my laptop case and the two shopping bags to press the button on the outside lift up to Malmskillnadsgatan, I happened to glance at my phone and saw that Linda had rung eight times. As I was so close, I didn't ring back. I waited for the lift, which was taking an eternity to come down. I turned round and met the eyes of a tramp dozing against the wall in a sleeping bag. He was thin and his face was discoloured. There was no curiosity in his gaze, but nor was it one of apathy. It just registered my presence. Filled with concern about that and the uncertainty Linda's calls had created, I stood still in the lift as it slowly made its way up the shaft. As soon as it stopped, I tore open the door and ran along the pavement, down David Bagares gata, in the front door and up the stairs.

'Hello?' I called. 'Has something happened?'

No answer.

She must have gone to the hospital under her own steam. Had she?

'Hello?' I called again. 'Linda?'

I took off my boots, went into the kitchen and peeped inside the bedroom door. No one there. I realised the shopping bags were still hanging from my arms and put them on the worktop before going through the bedroom and opening the living-room door.

She was in the middle of the floor staring at me.

'What's up?' I asked. 'Has something happened?'

She didn't answer. I went over to her.

'What's happened, Linda?'

Her eyes were black.

'I haven't felt anything all day,' she said. 'It feels as if there's something wrong. I can't feel anything.'

I put my arm around her. She wriggled away.

'Everything's fine,' I said. 'I'm sure of it.'

'IT BLOODY WELL ISN'T FINE!' she yelled. 'Don't you understand anything? Don't you understand what has happened?'

I tried to hold her again, but she wormed away.

She started to cry.

'Linda, Linda,' I said.

'Don't you understand what's happened?' she repeated.

'Everything's fine,' I said. 'I'm sure of it.'

I waited for another shout. Instead she lowered her hands and looked at me with her eyes full of tears.

'How can you be so sure?'

I didn't reply at first. Her undeviating stare felt like an accusation.

'What do you want us to do?' I asked.

'We have to go to hospital.'

'Hospital?' I said. 'Everything is as it *should* be. Babies move less the closer you are to birth. Come on, everything's great. It's just . . .'

It was only then, as I met her expression of disbelief, that I realised this might be serious.

'Get your coat on,' I said. 'I'll ring for a taxi.'

'Ring and tell them we're coming first,' she said.

I shook my head and went to the telephone on the windowsill.

'We'll just go straight there,' I said, picking up the receiver and dialling the number for the central taxi switchboard. 'They'll help us when we arrive.'

While waiting to get through I watched her. Slowly, as though not present in her movements, putting on her coat, winding the scarf around her neck, putting first one then the other foot on the trunk to tie her shoelaces. In the hall, where she was standing, every detail stood out clearly against the dark living room. Tears were still running down her cheeks.

Beep followed beep as nothing happened.

She was watching me now.

'I haven't got through yet,' I said.

Then the beeps stopped.

'Stockholm Taxis,' said a woman's voice.

'Yes, hello, I need a taxi to come to Regeringsgatan 81.'

'Yes . . . and where are you going?'

'Danderyd Hospital.'

'Right.'

'How long will it be?'

'About fifteen minutes.'

'That's no good,' I said. 'This is for a birth. We need a taxi immediately.'

'What did you say it was for?'

'A birth.'

I realised she didn't understand the Norwegian word for birth, *fødsel*. A few seconds passed while I searched for the correct Swedish word.

'*Förlossning*,' I said at last. 'We need a taxi right away.'

'I'll see what I can do,' she said. 'But I can't promise anything.'

'Thank you,' I replied and rang off, checked I had my credit card in my inside jacket pocket, locked the door and joined Linda in the corridor. She didn't meet my eyes once on the way down.

Outside, it was still snowing.

'Was it supposed to be coming right away?' Linda said on the pavement.

I nodded.

'As fast as they could make it, they said.'

Even though there was a lot of traffic I saw the taxi from far off. It was coming at quite a speed. I waved and it pulled up beside us. I bent forward, opened the door, let Linda in first and got in after her.

The driver turned.

'Are we in a hurry?' he asked.

'It's not quite what you think,' I said. 'But we're going to Danderyd.'

He pulled out and drove towards Birger Jarlsgatan. We sat at the back without speaking. I took her hand in mine. Fortunately, she allowed me to do that. The overhead motorway lights flashed through the car like narrow belts. The radio was playing 'I Won't Let the Sun Go Down on Me'.

'Don't be frightened,' I said. 'Everything's as it should be.'

She didn't answer. We drove up a gentle incline. There were detached houses between the trees on both sides of the road. The roofs were white with snow, the entrances yellow with light. The occasional orange sledge, the occasional dark expensive car. Then we turned off right and drove under the road we had been on into the hospital, which resembled an enormous box with lots of hatches because of all the lit windows. Piles of snow lay scattered around the buildings.

'Do you know where it is?' I asked. 'I mean the *Förlossning* department?'

He nodded ahead, turned left and pointed to a sign saying *BB Stockholm*.

'In there,' he said.

Another taxi with its engine running was by the entrance as we arrived. The driver pulled in behind it, I passed him my Visa card, got out, held Linda's hand and helped her onto her feet as another couple hurried through the door. He was carrying a baby seat and a big bag.

I signed, put the receipt with my card in my inside pocket and followed Linda into the building.

The other couple were waiting by the lift. We stood a few metres behind them. I stroked Linda's back. She was crying.

'This isn't how I imagined it would be,' she said.

'Everything's fine,' I said.

The lift came and we entered after the other couple. The woman suddenly doubled up, tightly squeezing the rail beneath the mirror. The man stood with his hands full looking down at the floor.

They alerted the staff by ringing the bell when we arrived. The nurse who came to meet us exchanged a few words with them first and told us someone would be coming for us, then accompanied them down the corridor.

Linda sat down on a chair. I stood looking down the corridor. The lighting was muted. There was a sign hanging from the ceiling outside every room. Some of them were lit up in red. Whenever a new sign lit up, a signal sounded, also muted, yet with an unmistakably institutional sound. Now and then a nurse appeared, on her way from one room to another. At the end of the corridor a father was rocking a bundle in his hands. He appeared to be singing.

'Why didn't you say this was urgent?' Linda said. 'I can't sit here!'

I didn't answer.

My mind was a blank.

She got up.

'I'm going in,' she said.

'Wait a minute or two,' I said. 'They know we're here.'

It was useless trying to stop her, so when she made a move I followed.

A nurse emerging from the office section came to meet us.

'Are you being looked after?' she asked.

'No,' Linda said. 'Someone was supposed to be coming, but they haven't come yet.'

She peered at Linda over her glasses.

'I haven't felt it stir all day,' Linda said. 'Nothing at all.'

'So you're worried,' said the nurse.

Linda nodded.

The nurse turned and looked up the corridor.

'Go into that room,' she said. 'It's free. Then someone will come and see to you at once.'

The room was so alien that all I saw was us two. Every single movement Linda made went right through me.

She took off her coat, hung it over the back of a chair and sat down on the sofa. I walked over to the window and stood there, looking down at the road, at the stream of cars passing. The snow fell as tiny vague shadows outside the window, seeming to be visible only when the snowflakes drifted into the circles of light from the lamps in the car park.

There was a gynaecological chair by one wall. Beside it, several instruments were organised on shelves on top of one other, like in a hi-fi rack. There was a CD player on a shelf on the other side.

'Did you hear that?' Linda said.

A low muffled howl came from the other side of the wall.

I turned and looked at her.

'Don't cry, Karl Ove,' she said.

'I don't know what else to do,' I said.

'It'll be fine,' she said.

'Are *you* comforting *me* now?' I said. 'How's *that* supposed to work?'

She smiled.

Then all went quiet again.

After some minutes there was a knock at the door, a nurse came in, she asked Linda to lie down on the bed and uncover her belly, she listened to it with a stethoscope and smiled.

'No problems there,' she said. 'But we'll do an ultrasound to make absolutely sure.'

When we left half an hour later Linda was relieved and happy. I was completely drained, and also a little embarrassed that we had bothered them unnecessarily. Judging by all the people going through the doors they had more than enough to deal with already.

Why is it we always believe the worst?

On the other hand, I thought as I lay alongside Linda in bed, with my hand on her belly, in which the baby was now so big it hardly had space to move, the worst could have happened, life could have ceased inside, for that does happen, and as long as the possibility existed, small though it might be, the only correct action was surely to take it seriously and not to allow yourself to be put off by feelings of *embarrassment*? Or fear of bothering other people?

The next day I went back to my office and continued to write the history of Ezekiel, which I had started in order to rework the angel material into a story, as Thure Erik had quite rightly suggested, and not just an essayistic account of them as a phenomenon. Ezekiel's visions were so grandiose and mysterious, and the Lord's command that he should eat the scroll so as to turn the words into flesh and blood were absolutely irresistible. At the same time Ezekiel himself became visible in the writing, the insane prophet with the doomsday images, surrounded by everyday lives of misery, with all that entailed of doubt and scepticism and sudden shifts between the interior of the visions, where angels are burned and humans slaughtered, and the exterior, where Ezekiel stands with a brick that is meant to represent Jerusalem and draws shapes that are meant to be armies, bulwarks and ramparts, all at the Lord's instructions, outside his house, before the eyes of the town's menfolk. The specific details of the resurrection: 'You dry bones, hear the words of the Lord!' Then the Lord God says to these bones, 'See, I shall put my spirit in you and you shall live again. I shall cover you with sinew and flesh and skin.' And then when it was done: 'They arose and stood. It was a vast army.'

The army of the dead.

This is what I was doing, I was trying to create a gestalt, although without much success – there were so few props, sandals, camels and sand, not much more, perhaps the odd sparse bush as well – and my knowledge of the culture was close to zero, while Linda waited at home, occupied in a very different way with what was going to happen. The due date passed, nothing happened, I rang her about once an hour, but no, nothing new. We talked of nothing else. Then, a week afterwards, at the end of January while we were watching TV her waters broke. I had always imagined this as a dramatic event, a dam bursting, but it wasn't like that, quite the contrary, there was so little water Linda was not entirely sure that that was what had happened. She rang the hospital, they were sceptical, there was not usually any doubt about whether waters had broken or not, but in the end they said we should go in, we grabbed the bag, got into a taxi and went to the hospital, which was surrounded by the same high piles of snow and as brightly lit as before. Linda was examined in the gynaecological chair; I looked out of the window, at the motorway, the rushing cars and the orange sky above. A little cry from Linda made me turn my head. It was the rest of her waters.

*

Since nothing else had happened and contractions had not started for the moment, we were sent home. If the situation stayed the same, they would induce labour with a drip two days later. So at least we had a deadline. Linda was too tense to sleep much when we came home; I slept like a log. The next day we watched a couple of films, went for a long walk in Humlegården, took photos of ourselves with the camera on my outstretched arm, our glowing faces close to each other, the park in the background white with snow. We warmed up one of the many meals Linda's mother had put in the freezer to be used during the first weeks, and after we had eaten, as I was putting on the coffee, I heard a protracted groan from the living room. I hurried out and found Linda doubled up with both hands on her belly. Ooohh, she said. But the face she lifted to me was smiling.

Slowly she straightened up.

'Now it's started,' she said. 'Can you write down the time so that we know how long it is between contractions?'

'Did it hurt?' I asked.

'Bit,' she said. 'But nothing much.'

I went to collect a pen and a pad. The time was a few minutes past five. The next contractions came exactly twenty-three minutes later. Then half an hour was to pass before the next came. And so it continued all evening, the gap between the contractions varied, while the pain evidently increased. When we went to bed at eleven she screamed when they came. I lay beside her and tried to help, but didn't know how. She had been given a piece of apparatus known as a TENS by the midwife, which was supposed to ease the pain and consisted of some electrodes you could put on the skin where it hurt. They were connected to a machine which regulated the strength, and we tried this for a while. There was a mass of wires and some buttons I fiddled with, but the sum total of my efforts was to

give her a few electric shocks and cause her to scream out in
pain and anger, Turn that crap off! No, no, I said, I'll have
another go, there we are, now I think it's working. Ow, for
Christ's sake! she shouted. Don't you understand? It's giving
me shocks. Get rid of it! I put it away, tried massaging her
instead, covered my hands with the oil I had bought for this
purpose, but it was never right for her, either too high or too
low or too soft or too hard. One of the things she had been
looking forward to was the big bath they had in the ward,
which, when it was full of hot water, was supposed to ease the
pain before the birth started in earnest, but now the waters
had broken she could no longer do that, nor use the bathtub
at home. Instead she sat up in it and showered herself with
boiling hot water as she groaned and whimpered whenever a
new wave of pain washed through her. I stood there, grey with
tiredness in the bright light, watching her, with no chance of
reaching the place where she was, let alone helping her. We
only managed to fall asleep at daybreak, and a couple of hours
later we decided to go to hospital, even though there were still
six hours to the appointment we had been given, and they had
explained in no uncertain terms that the gap between contractions had to be down to three or four minutes if we were planning to go in before. Linda's contractions came at around every
quarter of an hour, but she was in such pain there was no
question of reminding her of that. Another taxi, this time in
the grey morning light, another trip on the motorway to
Danderyd. When Linda was examined they said the cervix was
open only three centimetres, that wasn't much, I gathered, and
was surprised after all Linda had been through, I thought it
had to be over soon. But no, quite the opposite, actually we
ought to go home again, they said; however, they happened to
have a room free and we must have looked so tired and bedrag-

gled they let us stay. Get some sleep, they said as they closed the door behind them.

'Well, at least we're here finally,' I said, putting the bag down on the floor. 'Are you hungry?'

She shook her head.

'I fancy a shower. Do you want to join me?'

I nodded.

When we stood under the shower, holding each other, there were new contractions, she leaned forward and hung onto a rail on the wall as the sound I had heard for the first time the night before was emitted again. I stroked her back, but it felt more like an insult than a comfort. She stood up and I met her eyes in the mirror. Our faces looked drained, completely vacant, and I thought, we're in this all on our own.

We went into the room, Linda put on the garments she had been given, I lay down on the sofa. The next minute I was fast asleep.

A few hours later a little delegation came into our room and labour was induced. Linda didn't want any chemical painkillers and instead was given something they called sterile water injections, that is water injected under the skin, on a pain-to-combat-pain principle. She stood in the middle of the floor, holding my hand, as the two nurses injected the water. She screamed and shouted SHIIIT! from the very bottom of her lungs while instinctively trying to wriggle away, and the two nurses held her tight with experienced hands. I had tears in my eyes from seeing her in such pain. Yet I had an inkling that this was nothing, and that worse was to come. And what would it be like now it was clear that Linda had such a low pain threshold?

Dressed in a white hospital smock, she sat in bed while they inserted a cannula into her arm, which from then on was connected to a transparent bag on a metal stand via a thin plastic pipe. Because of the drip they wanted to keep a close eye on the foetus, they said, and attached a small sonar device to its head, from which a wire ran out of Linda, across the bed to a machine next to her, where soon afterwards a number began to flash. It was the foetus's pulse. As if that wasn't enough, Linda had a strap tied around her, on which there were some sensors connected via a further wire to another monitor. A number flashed on it as well, and above it there was a wavy electronic line that rose sharply as the contractions started. In addition, a sheet of paper issued from this machine, showing the same graph.

It was as though they had decided to launch her to the moon.

When the probe was attached to the head of the foetus Linda screamed again and the midwife patted her on the cheek. Why do they treat her like a child? I wondered in my inactivity, standing and staring at all that was suddenly going on around me. Was it because of the letter she had sent them, which was probably somewhere in the nurses' office now, where she had written that she needed a lot of support and encouragement despite being strong and looking forward to what was about to occur?

Linda's eyes met mine through the confusion of hands and she smiled. I smiled back. A dark-haired stern-looking midwife showed me how to read the monitors, the baby's heartbeat was especially important, if there was a dramatic rise or fall I was to call them by pressing a button. If the reading sank to zero I shouldn't worry, contact had probably been lost. Are we really going to be left on our own in here? I wanted to ask, but I didn't, nor how long this would take. Instead I nodded. She would come and see us every so often, she said, and then they were gone.

Not long afterwards the time between contractions shrank.

And, judging by Linda's reactions, they were a lot stronger. She screamed and began to move differently, as though she was searching for something. Again and again she shifted her position, she was restless, she screamed, and I realised she was looking for a way out of the pain. There was something animal about this.

The contractions passed, and she settled down.

'I don't think I can do this, Karl Ove,' she said.

'Yes, you can,' I said. 'It's not a problem. It's painful, but it's not a problem.'

'It hurts so much! So bloody much!'

'I know.'

'Can you massage me?'

'Yes, of course.'

She sat up, holding on to the upright side-rails of the bed.

'There?' I asked.

'Bit lower down,' she said.

On the screen a curve began to rise.

'Looks like one's coming,' I said.

'Oh no,' she said.

It rose like a tidal wave. Linda shouted, lower down! shifted position, groaned, shifted position again, wrapped her fingers around the side-rail as tightly as she could. As the curve began to fall and this pain retreated I saw the baby's pulse had increased dramatically.

Linda slumped back.

'Did the massage help?' I asked.

'No,' she answered.

I decided to ring them if the pulse hadn't gone down after the next contraction.

'I can't do this,' she said.

'Yes, you can,' I said. 'You're managing just fine.'

'Hold my forehead.'

I laid my hand on her forehead.

'Here comes another,' I said. She straightened up, whimpered, groaned, shouted, slumped back again. I pressed the button and a red sign began to flash above the door.

'The pulse went very high,' I said when the midwife was in front of me.

'Hm,' she said. 'We'll have to slow the drip a bit. Perhaps it was too high.'

She went over to Linda.

'How are you doing?' she asked.

'It's terribly painful,' Linda said. 'Is there a long way to go yet?'

She nodded.

'Yes, there is.'

'I've got to have something. I'm not coping. It's no good. Can I have laughing gas, do you think?'

'It's too early for that,' the midwife said. 'The effect wears off after a while. It's better to have it later.'

'But that's no good,' Linda said. 'I need it now! That's no good!'

'We'll wait for a bit,' she said. 'OK?'

Linda nodded and the midwife went out again.

The next hour passed in much the same way. Linda searched for a way to deal with the pain, couldn't, it was as though she were trying to escape it as the waves beat against and pounded her. It was awful to see. All I could do was wipe away her sweat, hold my hand on her forehead and make occasional half-hearted attempts at massage on her back. Outside, in the darkness which had fallen unobserved, it was snowing. It was four o'clock, one and a half hours since labour had been induced. It was nothing, I knew that. Hadn't Kari Anne been in labour for twenty hours or something like that when Ylva was born?

There was a knock at the door. The cool dark-haired midwife came in.

'How are you both doing?' she asked.

Linda turned from her hunched position.

'I want laughing gas!' she shouted.

The midwife mulled this over. Then she nodded and went out, returning with a stand holding two bottles, which she positioned in front of the bed. After fiddling around for some minutes she had it ready and a mask was put in Linda's hand.

'I'd like to do something,' I said. 'Massage. Can you show me where it's most effective?'

At that moment the contractions started, Linda pressed the mask over her face and greedily breathed in the gas as her lower body writhed. The midwife placed my hands at the bottom of her lumbar region.

'There, I reckon,' she said. 'OK?'

'OK,' I said.

I rubbed in the oil, the midwife closed the door behind her, I put one hand on top of the other and pushed the heel of my hand against her spine.

'Yes!' she shouted! Her voice was muffled by the mask. 'There! Yes, yes, yes!'

As the contractions subsided, she turned to me.

'The laughing gas is fantastic,' she said.

'Good,' I said.

The next times the contractions came something happened to her. She was no longer trying to escape, she wasn't searching vainly for refuge from the pain, in the way that had been so heart-rending to watch, something new came over her, she seemed to be confronting the pain instead, acknowledging its presence and meeting it face to face, in an initially inquisitive manner, thereafter with more and more force, like an animal,

I thought once again, but not in a light, frightened, nervous
manner, for when the pain came now she stood up with both
hands clenched round the bed rail, moving her hips to and fro
as she howled into the gas mask, exactly the same procedure
every time, it repeated itself and repeated itself and repeated
itself. Pause, mask in hand, body on the mattress. Then came
the wave, I always saw it slightly before her on the monitor,
massaged as hard as I could, she got up, swayed to and fro,
shouted until the wave retreated and she slumped back again.
It was no longer possible to have any contact with her, she had
totally disappeared into herself, she was oblivious to everything
around her, it was all about meeting the pain, resting, meeting
it, resting. When the midwife came in she spoke to me as though
Linda wasn't present, and in a strange way that was right, it did
seem as if we were a long, long way from her. But not completely
removed, suddenly she could shout in an incommensurately
loud voice, WATER! or CLOTH! and when she was handed it,
THANKS!

Oh, what a strange afternoon and evening it was. The darkness
outside was dense and heavy with falling snowflakes. The room
was filled with Linda's wheezing as she breathed in the gas, the
great roars when the contractions were at their peak, the electronic beeping of the monitors. I wasn't thinking about the baby,
I was hardly thinking about Linda, everything inside me was
concentrated on massaging, lightly when Linda was lying down,
harder and harder when the electronic waves began to rise,
which was the signal for Linda to get up, and then I massaged
as hard as I could until the wave sank again, while keeping a
constant eye on the pulse. Numbers and graphs, massage oil and
lumbar region, wheezing and howling, this was everything.
Second after second, minute after minute, hour after hour, this
was everything. The moment swallowed me up, it was as though

time was not passing, but it was, whenever something outside the routine happened, I was dragged out of it. A nurse entered, asked if everything was going all right, and suddenly it was twenty past five. Another nurse came in, asked if I wanted any food and suddenly it was twenty-five to seven.

'Food?' I queried, as though I had never heard the word before.

'Yes, you can choose between vegetarian lasagne and normal lasagne,' she said.

'Oh, that's nice,' I said. 'Normal lasagne,' I said.

Linda didn't seem to notice that someone was there at all. A new wave came, the nurse closed the door behind her, I pressed my hands against Linda's back as hard as I could, watched the curve subside and when Linda did not release the mask I carefully took it from her. She didn't react, just stood there staring inside herself, her brow dripping with sweat. When the next contractions started, the cry she emitted continued dully inside the mask she held tight to her face. Then the door opened, the nurse put a plate on the table and it was seven o'clock. I asked Linda if it was OK with her if I ate, she nodded, but the second I took my hand away she shouted, no, don't do that, and I continued, I pressed the button, the same nurse came in, could she take over the massaging? Of course, she said and carried on where I had left off. Linda shouted. No, it has to be Karl Ove! It has to be Karl Ove! That's too light! Meanwhile I gorged down the food as fast as possible, so that, two minutes later, I could resume the massaging, and Linda settled back into her rhythm.

Contractions, gas, massage, pause, contractions, massage, gas, pause. There was nothing else. Then the midwife came in, rolled Linda authoritatively onto her side, examined her to see how far she had dilated, Linda screamed and it was a different kind of scream, one she let out, she didn't meet halfway.

She got up again, fell into the rhythm, was gone from this world and the hours passed.

A sudden shout: 'Are we alone?'

'Yes,' I said.

'I LOVE YOU, KARL OVE!'

It seemed to come from deep inside her, from a place she never went, or for that matter had ever been. I had tears in my eyes.

'I love *you*,' I said, but she didn't hear, another wave was on its way.

Time ticked by: eight o'clock, nine o'clock, ten o'clock. I didn't have a thought in my head, I massaged her and kept my eye on the monitors until I had a sudden flash of insight: a child is being born. Our child is being born. Just a few hours more. Then we'll have a child.

The insight was gone, now it was all graphs and numbers, hands and back, rhythm and howls.

The door opened. Another midwife came in, an elderly woman. Behind her a young girl. The woman stood close to Linda, her face only a couple of centimetres away, and introduced herself. Said that Linda was doing well. Said she had a trainee with her, was that OK? Linda nodded and looked around for the trainee. Nodded when she saw her. The midwife said it would soon be over. And that she would have to examine her.

Linda nodded again, and looked at her like a child at her mother.

'That's great,' the midwife said. 'Good girl.'

This time she didn't scream. Lay there with big dark eyes looking into the air. I stroked her forehead, she wasn't aware of me. When the midwife took away her hand, Linda shouted, 'ARE WE THERE?'

'Bit more yet,' the midwife said. Linda patiently got up and resumed her position.

'An hour, perhaps less,' the midwife said to me.

I looked at my watch. Eleven.

Linda had been standing there for eight hours.

'We can take this off you,' the midwife said, removing all the straps and wires. Suddenly freed, she lay there, a body in a bed, and the pain she had resisted was no longer green waves and rising numbers on a screen I was watching, but something taking place inside her.

I hadn't understood that before. It was inside her, and she was completely on her own with it.

That was how it was.

She was free. Everything that happened, happened inside her.

'It's coming now,' she said, and it was from inside her it came. I pressed my hands as hard as I could against her back. There was just her and inside her. Not the hospital, not the monitors, not the books, not the medical courses, not the cassettes, not all these corridors that our thoughts had followed, nothing of that, just her and what was inside her.

Her body was slippery with sweat, her hair straggly, the white smock hanging loosely round her. The midwife said she would be back in a minute. The trainee stayed. Wiped Linda's forehead, passed her water, fetched her a Marathon bar. Linda snatched it greedily. She was on the verge, she must have sensed it, she was almost impatient in the pauses, which lasted only brief instants now.

The midwife returned. She dimmed the light.

'Lie down and rest,' she said. Linda lay down. The midwife stroked her cheek. I went to the window. Not a car on the road below. The air around the lamps thick with snow. The room completely quiet. I turned. Linda appeared to be sleeping.

The midwife smiled at me.

Linda groaned. The midwife caught hold of her arm, and Linda sat up. Her eyes were as dark as a forest at night.

'Now push,' the midwife said.

Something new happened, something was different, I didn't understand what it was, but moved behind her and began to massage her back again. The contractions lasted and lasted, Linda groped for the gas mask, inhaled greedily, but it didn't seem to help, a protracted cry seemed to be torn from her, it went on and on.

Then it subsided. Linda slumped back. The midwife wiped the sweat from her forehead and praised her, good girl.

'Would you like to feel the baby?' she asked.

Linda looked up at her and nodded slowly. Got to her knees. The midwife took her hand and guided it between her legs.

'That's the head,' she said. 'Can you feel it?'

'YES!' Linda said.

'Hold your hand there while you're pushing. Can you do that?'

'Come here,' she said and led Linda onto the floor. 'Stand here.'

The trainee took the stool that had been beside the wall.

Linda went onto her knees. I walked behind her even though I had a sense that the massage no longer made any difference.

She screamed at the top of her lungs, her whole body moved as she held the baby's head with her hand.

'The head's out,' the midwife said. 'One more time. Push.'

'Is the head out?!' Linda asked. 'Was that what you said?'

'Yes, push now.'

Another cry, as though beyond everything, issued from her.

'Would you like to hold her?' the midwife asked, looking at me.

'Yes,' I said.

'Come here, stand here,' she said.

I walked around the stool, stood in front of Linda, who watched me without seeing me.

'One more time. Push now, my love. Push.'

My eyes were swimming with tears.

The baby slipped out of her like a little seal, straight into my hands.

'Oooohhh!' I yelled. 'Oooohhh!'

The little body was hot and slippery, it almost slipped out of my hands, but the young trainee came to my aid.

'Is she out? Is she out?' Linda asked, yes, I said, lifting the little body up to her, and she put it to her chest, and I sobbed with joy, and Linda looked at me for the first time for several hours and smiled.

'What is it?' I asked.

'A girl, Karl Ove,' she said. 'It's a girl.'

She had long black hair stuck to her head. Her skin was greyish and waxen. She screamed, I had never heard such a sound before, it was my daughter's sound, and I was at the top of the world, I had never been there before, but now I was, we were there, at the top of the world. Around us everything was still, around us everything was dark, but we were there, the midwife, the trainee, Linda, me and the little baby, she was the light.

They helped Linda into bed, she found a comfortable position on her back, and the baby, her skin redder now, raised her head and looked at us.

Her eyes were like two black lamps.

'Hi . . .' said Linda. 'This is us . . .'

The child lifted one arm and lowered it again. The movement was reptilian, a crocodile's, a monitor lizard's. Then the other one. Up, out a bit, down.

The black eyes looked straight at Linda.

'Yes,' Linda said. 'I'm your mummy. And there's your daddy! Can you see?'

The two women began to tidy up around us as we watched this creature that was suddenly here. Linda had blood over her stomach and legs, the girl was covered with blood as well, and a sharp, somehow metallic, smell came from them both, which did not lose its unfamiliarity with every breath I took.

Linda put the girl to her breast, but she wasn't interested, she had enough to do looking at us. The midwife came in with a tray of food, a glass of apple juice and a Swedish flag. They took the child to measure and weigh while we ate, she screamed, but went quiet when she was put on Linda's chest. The way Linda opened up, the consummate care that was in her every move-ment; these were new experiences for me.

'Is this Vanja?' I said.

Linda looked at me.

'Yes, of course, can't you see?'

'Hiya, little Vanja,' I said. I looked at Linda. 'She looks like something we've found in the forest.'

Linda nodded.

'Our little troll.'

The midwife came to the bed.

'It's time for you both to go to your room,' she said. 'Perhaps put some clothes on her?'

Linda stared at me.

'Would you?'

I nodded. Picked up the tiny slim body and laid her on the bed, took the pyjamas from the bag and started to dress her with infinite care while she cried with her strange little voice.

'You really know how to give birth,' the midwife said to Linda. 'You should do it more often!'

'Thank you,' Linda said. 'I think that's the nicest compliment I've ever received.'

'And think what a start she's been given. She'll carry that all the way through her life.'

'Do you think so?'

'Oh yes. There's no doubt it has meaning. Well, goodnight both of you, and congratulations. I might pop by tomorrow morning, but it's not certain.'

'Thank you very, very much,' Linda said. 'You were all fantastic.'

A few minutes later Linda staggered through the corridor on her way to the room while I walked beside her with Vanja close to my chest. She was staring at the ceiling with wide-open eyes. Once inside the room we turned off the light and went to bed. For a long time we lay chatting about what had happened, while Linda kept putting Vanja to her breast, although she didn't seem to be very interested.

'Now you won't ever need to be afraid of anything,' I said.

'That's exactly how I feel,' Linda said.

Eventually they fell asleep while I lay awake, brimming with restlessness and the urge to do something. I hadn't done anything. Perhaps that was why. I took the lift down, sat outside in the cold, smoked a cigarette and called my mother.

'Hi, it's me, Karl Ove,' I said.

'How's it going?' she said quickly. 'Are you at the hospital?'

'Yes, we've got a girl,' I said, and my voice broke.

'Ooohh,' mum said. 'Just imagine, a girl! Did Linda get on OK?'

'Yes, it went really well. Really well. Everything's hunky-dory.'

'Congratulations, Karl Ove,' she said. 'That's great news.'

'Yes,' I said. 'But I just wanted to let you know. We'll talk again tomorrow. I'm . . . Yes . . . I'm not sure I can say much now.'

'I understand,' mum said. 'Give Linda my love and congratulate her from me.'

'Will do,' I said and rang off. I called Linda's mother. She cried when I told her. I lit another cigarette and told her the same. Rang off, called Yngve. Lit another cigarette, it was easier to talk to him, walked round the illuminated car park with the phone to my ear for several minutes, warm, even though it had to be minus ten and I was in a shirt, rang off, stared around me wildly, wanting what was around me to correspond in some way to what was inside me, but it didn't, and I began to walk again, to and fro, lit another cigarette, threw it away after a couple of drags and ran to the front entrance, what was I thinking of, they were *upstairs*! Now! They were there now!

Linda was asleep with the little one on top of her. I watched them for a moment, took out my notebook, switched on a lamp, sat down in the chair and tried to write something about what had happened, but it was too stupid, it didn't work, instead I went to the TV room, I suddenly remembered that you had to stick a pin in a chart with the date of every child born, pink for girls, blue for boys, did it, a pin for lovely Vanja, wandered up and down the corridor a couple of times, took the lift down for another cigarette, which soon became two, came back up, went to bed, couldn't sleep, something inside me had opened, all of a sudden I was receptive to everything, and the world I found myself in was laden with meaning. How could you sleep?

Well, in the end I could.

This was all so new and fragile that just dressing her was a major project. While Helena, who had come to collect us in her car, waited down below it took us half an hour to get her ready, only to be met by Helena's laughter as we emerged from the lift with 'You're not going to take her out into the cold wearing those clothes, are you?'

Ah, we hadn't thought about that.

Helena wrapped her up in her Puffa jacket, and then we ran across the car park with me holding the car seat in one hand and Vanja swinging to and fro. Alone in the flat, Linda began to cry, she sat with Vanja in her arms crying for all the good and all the bad in her life now. I was filled with the same immense urge to be active, I couldn't sit still, had to do something, cook, wash up, run out and go shopping, anything, as long as there was movement involved. Linda, for her part, just wanted to sit still, motionless, with the baby at her breast. The light did not leave us, nor the silence, it was as though a zone of peace had sprung up around us.

It was fantastic.

I walked around for the next ten days full of peace and tranquillity, as well as the same uncontrollable urge to be active. Then I had to start work again. Drop everything that had happened in my life and was going on right now in the flat, and write about Ezekiel. Open the door in the afternoon to the little family and think that this was my little family.

Happiness.

Everyday life, with all the new demands the little child made, began to run its course. Linda was worried about being on her own with her, she didn't like it, but I had to work, the novel had to be out for the autumn, we needed the money.

But a novel about sandals and camels, that was no good.

Once I had written in a notebook, 'The Bible enacted in Norway' and 'Abraham in the Setesdal Hills'. It was an idiotic thought, both too small and too large for a novel, but now that it was suddenly back in my mind I needed it in a completely different way and thought, to hell with it, I'll start and see what happens. I had Cain hitting a rock with a sledgehammer in a Scandinavian landscape at dusk. Asked Linda if I could read it to her, she said yes, of course, I said, but it's so unbelievably stupid, you know, she said, that's often when you're good, well, I said, but not this time. Come on, read it! she said from the chair. I read it. She kept saying, that's fantastic, that's absolutely fantastic, you have to go on, and I did, kept writing until the day of Vanja's christening in May, which was held at my mother's in Jølster. When we returned we went to Idö in the archipelago outside Västervik, where Vidar, Ingrid's partner, had a summer house. While Linda and Ingrid were together with Vanja I sat writing, it was June, the novel had to be done and dusted in six weeks, but even though the Cain and Abel story was ready it was still too little. I lied to my editor for the first time, said I only had some fine-tuning to do, while in fact I launched into a story I knew would become the *real* novel. I wrote like a madman, this was never ever going to work, I had lunch and dinner with Linda and the others, watched the European football championships with her in the evenings, otherwise I was in a small room hammering away at the keyboard. After we came home from Idö I realised that this was all or nothing, I told Linda I was moving into the office, I would have to write day and night. You can't do that, she said, that's not on, you've got a family, or have you forgotten? It's summer, or have you forgotten? Am I supposed to look after your daughter on my own? Yes, I said. That's the way it is. No, it isn't, she said, I won't let you. OK, I said, but I'll do it anyway. And I did. I was totally manic. I wrote all the time, sleeping two or three hours a day, the only thing that had any meaning was the novel I was writing. Linda went to her mother's and called me several times a day. She was so angry that she *screamed*, actually *screamed* down the phone. I just held it away from my ear and kept writing. She said she would leave me. Go, I said. I don't care, I have to write. And it was true. She would have to go if that was what she wanted. She said, I will. You'll never see us again. Fine, I said. I wrote twenty pages a day. I didn't see any letters or words, any sentences or shapes, just countryside and people, and Linda rang and screamed, said I was a sugar daddy, said I was a bastard, said I was an unfeeling monster, said I was the worst person in the world and that she cursed the day she had met me. Fine, I said, leave me then, I don't care, and I meant it, I didn't care, no one was going to stand in the way of this, she slammed down the phone, she rang two minutes later and continued to swear at me, I was on my own now, she would bring up Vanja alone, fine by me, I said, she cried, she begged, she pleaded, what I was doing to her was the worst thing anyone could do, leaving her alone. But I didn't care, I wrote night and day, and then out of the blue she rang and said she was coming home the following day, would I go to the station and meet them?

Yes, I would.

At the station she came towards me with Vanja asleep in the buggy, gave a terse greeting and asked how things were, fine, I said, she said she was sorry about everything. Two weeks later I rang to say the novel was finished, by some miracle on the exact day I had been given as a deadline by the publishing house, 1 August, and when I went home she was standing in the hallway with a glass of Prosecco for me, my favourite music playing in the living room and my favourite meal on the table. I had finished, the novel was written, but I was not finished with what I had experienced, that is, the place where I felt I had been. We went to Oslo, I went to the press conference, got so drunk at the dinner afterwards that I was flat on my belly spewing up in the hotel room all morning and only just managed to make it to the airport, where a delay was the last straw for Linda, at the airline counter she gave the staff a piece of her mind, I hid my head in my hands, were we back there again? The plane went to Bringelandsåsen, where mum was waiting for us, for the whole of the next week we went on long walks beneath the beautiful mountains, and everything was great, everything was as it should be, yet not good enough, I longed to be back where I had been, I ached for it, to the maniacal, the lonely, the happy place.

When we returned to Sweden, Linda started her second year

at the Dramatiska Institut while I stayed at home looking after Vanja. She was pumped full of milk in the morning, I dropped by the DI at lunch, where she was pumped full again, and in the afternoon Linda cycled back as fast as she could. I couldn't complain, everything was good, the book received good reviews, the rights were bought by foreign publishers, and while that went on I was pushing a buggy around the fine city of Stockholm with a daughter I loved above all else, while my true love was on her course, pining to be with us.

Autumn passed into winter, life with baby food and baby clothes, baby cries and baby vomit, utterly wasted mornings and empty afternoons began to take their toll, but I couldn't complain, couldn't say anything, I just had to keep my mouth shut and do what I had to do. In the block of flats the minor harassment continued, the events of New Year's Eve had not changed the Russian's attitude towards us. Any idea that she would no longer do her utmost to torment us proved to be naïve, the opposite occurred, the frequency increased. If, one morning, we switched on the bedroom radio, if I dropped a book on the floor, if I hammered a nail into the wall, the pipes reverberated straight afterwards. Once I left an Ikea bag of clean clothes in the cellar and someone had put it under the sink, loosened the down pipe so that all the water that ran through the plug – and it was mostly dirty water – ended up in the bag. One morning towards the end of the winter Linda received a phone call from the company that owned the block, they had received a letter of complaint about us, a whole list of serious points, would we be so kind as to explain them? First of all, we played loud music at unsociable hours. Secondly, we left bags of rubbish in the corridor outside our door. Thirdly, the buggy was always there. Fourthly, we smoked in the backyard and dropped cigarette ends everywhere. Fifthly, we left clothes in the cellar, didn't clean up after us and washed at times other than those allocated to us. What could we say? That a neighbour had it in for us? It was our word against hers. And besides she was not the only person to sign the complaint, her girlfriend on the floor above had also signed. Furthermore, some of the points were factually correct. Since everyone else in the block put rubbish bags outside the door at night, we did too. Nor could we deny it; the two busybodies had taken a photo of our door with the bag outside. And we put the buggy outside the door as well, that was correct, did they imagine we would carry the baby and everything she needed from the cellar several times a day? It was quite possible that we forgot our washing times, but didn't everyone? Well, we should be more attentive. They would let it go this once, but if there were any more complaints our contract would be reviewed. In Sweden you have a rental contract for life, they are hard to get, and for one like ours, in a city-centre location, you had to either work your way up over a long life or buy it for up to a million on the black market. We had got ours through Linda's mother. If we lost this contract it would be like losing the only asset we had of any value. All we could do, from now on, was make sure that everything we did was by the book. For Swedes this is in their blood. Swedes who don't pay their bills on the dot don't exist because unless they pay, they get a reprimand, and if they get a reprimand, however small the sum involved, they cannot get a bank loan, they cannot get a mobile phone subscription and they cannot rent a car. For me, someone who was not so punctilious and who was used to incurring a couple of debts every six months, this was of course a different matter. I only appreciated the gravity of this a few years later when I needed a loan and was refused point blank. A loan, *you*! But the Swedes, they clenched their teeth, they had order in their lives and were contemptuous of those who didn't. Oh, how I hated this shitty little country. And how smug they were! The way everything was in Sweden was normality; anything different was abnormal. And this at the same time as embracing all the multi-cultural and minority issues! The poor black people who came from Ghana or Ethiopia to the Swedish basement laundry room! Having to book a slot two weeks in advance and then getting your ears chewed off if you left a sock in the tumble drier. Or being subjected to a man appearing at the door with one of those bloody Ikea bags in his hand and sarcastically asking if by any chance it was yours! Sweden hasn't had a war on its soil since the seventeenth century and how often did it cross my mind that someone ought to invade Sweden, bomb its buildings, starve the country, shoot down its men, rape its women, and then have some faraway country, Chile or Bolivia for example, embrace its refugees with kindness, tell them they love Scandinavia and dump them in a ghetto outside one of the cities there. Just to see what they would say.

Perhaps the worst aspect of all this was that Sweden was so admired in Norway. I had been the same when I lived there. I knew nothing of course. But now that I knew and tried to tell people at home in Norway, no one understood what I meant. It is impossible to describe exactly how conformist this country is. Also because the conformity is laid bare by an absence, opinions diverging from the norm do not in fact *exist* in public. It takes time for you to notice.

Such was the situation on that evening in February 2005 when, with a book by Dostoevsky in one hand and an NK carrier bag in the other, I passed the Russian on the stairs. For her to avoid my gaze was not so unusual. When we put the buggy in the cycle room in the afternoon, the following day we often found it pushed against the wall, with the hood pressed down on one side or the other, sometimes the duvet had been slung on the floor, all obviously done in haste and a bout of fury. Once the sporty little model we had bought second-hand was placed under the sign *grovsopor*, bulky rubbish, so the dustcart had taken it in the morning. It was hard to imagine anyone else could be behind that. But it was not impossible. None of the other neighbours exactly greeted us with warmth either.

I opened the door, went in, leaned forward and unlaced my boots.

'Hello?' I said.

'Hello,' Linda said from inside the living room.

No unfriendliness in her voice.

'Sorry I'm late,' I said and stood up, took off my scarf and jacket and hung them on the clothes hanger in the wardrobe. 'But I lost track of time while I was reading.'

'No problem,' Linda said. 'I gave Vanja a leisurely bath and put her to bed. It was wonderful.'

'Good,' I said, and joined her in the living room. She was sitting on the sofa and watching TV, wearing my dark green woollen jumper.

'Are you wearing my jumper?'

She turned off the television with the remote and got up.

'Yes?' she said. 'I miss you, you know.'

'I do live here,' I said. 'I'm here all the time.'

'You know what I mean,' she said, reaching up to give me a kiss. We hugged each other for a while.

'I remember Espen's girlfriend complaining that his mother used to wear his jumpers while she was there,' I said. 'I think she thought the mother was communicating a kind of possession over him. That it was a hostile act.'

'Which it obviously was,' she said. 'But this is just you and me. And we aren't enemies, are we?'

'No, not at all,' I said. 'I'll go and make some food. Would you like a glass of red in the meantime?'

She looked at me askance.

'Oh, that's right, you're breastfeeding,' I said. 'But a glass wouldn't be a problem, would it? Come on.'

'Would be nice, but I think I'll wait. You have one!'

'I'll just have a peep at Vanja first. She's asleep, isn't she?'

Linda nodded, and we went into the bedroom, where she lay in her cot beside our double bed. She slept in a sort of kneeling position with her bottom in the air, her head boring into the pillow and her arms out to the side.

I smiled.

Linda covered her with the blanket and I went to the hallway, carried the bag to the kitchen, switched on the oven, washed the potatoes, forked them one by one, placed them on the tray which I had greased with a bit of oil, put it in the oven and filled a pan with water for the broccoli. Linda came in and sat at the table.

'I finished an edit today,' she said. 'Could you listen to it afterwards? I might not have to do any more to it.'

'Of course,' I said.

She was working on a documentary about her father which she had to hand in on Wednesday. She had interviewed him a few times over recent weeks, and so he had entered her life again after having been absent for some years, despite the fact that he lived in a flat fifty metres from us.

I put the entrecôte steaks on a broad wooden board, tore off some kitchen roll and dried them.

'That looks good,' Linda said.

'I hope so,' I said. 'I daren't tell you what the price per kilo was.'

The potatoes were so small they barely needed more than ten

minutes in the oven, so I took the frying pan, put it on the hotplate and dropped the broccoli into the saucepan, where the water had started to boil.

'I can set the table,' she said. 'We're eating in the living room, aren't we?'

'Can do.'

She got up, reached down two of the green plates, took two wine glasses from the cupboard and carried them into the living room. I followed with the bottle of wine and the mineral water. As I entered she was putting out the candlestick.

'Have you got a lighter?'

I nodded, dug it up from my pocket and passed it to her.

'That's cosier now, isn't it?' she said with a smile.

'Yes, it is,' I said. Opened the wine and poured it into one glass.

'Shame you can't have any,' I said.

'I suppose I could have a mouthful,' she said. 'To taste it. But I'll wait until the food's ready.'

'OK,' I said.

On the way to the kitchen I stopped by Vanja's bed again. Now she was lying on her back, with her arms out, as though she had been thrown there from a great height. Her head was as round as a ball and her short body more than well padded. The health visitor who examined Vanja suggested last time that we should try to slim her down. That maybe she didn't need milk *every* time she cried.

They were crazy in this country.

I supported myself on the bed and leaned over her. She was sleeping with her mouth open and exhaling little wheezes. Now and then I could see Yngve in her face, but only in flashes; otherwise she didn't have the slightest resemblance to me or anyone in my family.

'Isn't she lovely?' Linda said, stroking my shoulder as she passed.

'Mm,' I said. 'Whatever that means.'

When the doctor had examined her, a few hours after birth, Linda had tried to make her say she was not only a lovely child but an *especially* lovely child. The doctor complied, but Linda was not happy with her low-key response. I had glanced at her in some surprise. Was this how maternal love expressed itself, forcing all considerations to cede to it?

Oh, what a time this had been. We were so unused to dealing with small babies that every little operation was a mixture of anxiety and pleasure.

Now we were more used to it.

In the kitchen the butter in the pan was smoking and had turned dark brown. Steam was rising from the saucepan beside it. The lid was banging against the edge. I put the two pieces of meat in the pan with a hiss, removed the potatoes from the oven and slid them into a bowl, drained the water from the broccoli, kept it on the hotplate for a few seconds, turned the steaks, remembered I had forgotten the mushrooms, got out another frying pan, put them in with two tomato halves and turned on the heat full. Then I opened the window to get rid of the frying fumes, which were sucked out of the room at once. Placed the steaks on a white dish with the broccoli and poked my head out of the window while waiting for the mushrooms. The cold air settled on my face. The offices opposite were empty and dark, but on the pavement below people drifted past, well wrapped up and silent. Some sat around a table at the back of a restaurant, which had to be doing badly, while the chefs in the adjacent room, invisible to them but not to me, shuttled back and forth between worktops and stoves, their movements unerring and fleet. A little queue had formed in front of the entrance to the adjacent jazz club, Nalen. A man wearing a cap got off the Swedish Radio bus and went through the door. Something hung from some string around his neck, probably an ID card. I turned and shook the pan of mushrooms to turn them over. Almost no one lived in this district, it consisted of office buildings and shops in the main, so when they closed at the end of the afternoon street life died. People walking here in the evening were going to restaurants, of which there was a plethora. Bringing a child up here was unthinkable. There was nothing for them.

I switched off the hotplate and put the small white mush-rooms, which were now streaked with brown, on the dish. It was white with a blue line round and outside that there was a further line, of gold. It wasn't very attractive, but I had brought it here after Yngve and I had divided the few items dad had left behind. He must have bought them with the money he got when he divorced and mum bought his share of the house in Tveit. He bought all his household requirements in one fell swoop, and something about that, the fact that everything he possessed stemmed from the same period of time, divested it of meaning, it had no aura other than one of recent domesticity and a soli-tary existence. For me it was different: dad's goods and chattels which, beyond this crockery service, consisted of one pair of binoculars and one pair of rubber boots, helped to preserve him in my memory. Not in any strong, clear sense, it was more like a regular confirmation that he was also a part of my life. In my mother's house objects played a very different role. There was, for example, a plastic bucket that they had bought some time in the 1960s when they were students and lived in Oslo, which had been placed too near a fire in the 1970s and had melted on one side into a form, I thought as a boy, that resembled a man's face, with eyes, a crooked nose and a twisted mouth. This was still *the* bucket, the one she used when she washed something, and still it was the face I saw when I went to fill it with water and not a bucket. First hot water and then soap were poured onto the poor man's head. The ladle she stirred porridge with was the same one she had used to stir porridge for as long as I could remember. The brown plates which we ate breakfast from when we were there were the same ones I had eaten breakfast from when I was small, sitting on the kitchen stool with my legs dangling down, in Tybakken in the 1970s. The new items she had bought were added to the rest and belonged to her, unlike dad's possessions, which were expendable. The priest who buried him mentioned this in his sermon, he said that you have to ground your gaze, ground yourself in the world, by which he meant that my father had not done this, and he was absolutely right. But it was several years before I understood that there were also many good reasons for loosening your grip, not grounding yourself at all, just letting yourself fall and fall until you were ultimately smashed to pieces at the bottom.

What was it about nihilism that could draw minds to it in this way?

In the bedroom Vanja started to wail. I poked my head through the door and saw her standing with her hands around the rails and jumping up and down with frustration as Linda dashed across the floor towards her.

'Food's ready,' I said.

'Typical!' she said, lifting Vanja up, lying on the bed with her, raising her sweater on one side and loosening the bra cup. Vanja instantly went quiet.

'She'll be back to sleep in a few minutes,' Linda said.

'I'll wait,' I said, and went back into the kitchen. Closed the window, turned off the fan, took the dishes and carried them into the living room through the hall so as not to disturb Linda

and Vanja. Poured some mineral water into a glass and drank
it in the middle of the floor while looking around. Some music
wouldn't be a bad idea. I stood in front of the CD racks. Picked
out Emmylou Harris's *Anthology,* which we had played a lot in
recent weeks, and put it on. It was easy to protect yourself against
music when you were prepared or just had it on as background,
because it was simple, undemanding and sentimental, but when
I was not prepared, like now, or was really listening, it hit home
with me. My feelings soared and before I knew what was
happening my eyes were moist. It was only then that I realised
how little I normally felt, how numb I had become. When I was
eighteen I was full of such feelings all the time, the world seemed
more intense, and that was why I wanted to write, it was the
sole reason, I wanted to touch something music touched. The
human voice's lament and sorrow, joy and delight, I wanted to
evoke everything the world had bestowed upon us.

How could I forget that?

I put down the CD box and went to the window. What was it
that Rilke wrote? That music raised him out of himself, and
never returned him to where it had found him, but to a deeper
place, somewhere in the unfinished?

It was unlikely he had been thinking about country music . . .

I smiled. Linda came through the door in front of me.

'Now she's asleep,' she whispered, pulled out a chair and sat
down. 'Ah, lovely!'

'It's probably a little cold now,' I said, sitting on the opposite
side of the table.

'That doesn't matter,' she said. 'Can I start? I'm famished.'

'Go on,' I said, poured a glass of wine and put some potatoes
on my plate while she helped herself to meat and vegetables.

She chatted about the projects chosen by colleagues in her
class whose names I barely knew despite there being only six of

them. It had been different when she started the course, then I met them regularly, up at Filmhuset and in various pubs where they gathered. It was a relatively mature class, many were in their late twenties and already established. One of them, Anders, was in *Doktor Kosmos*, another, Özz, was a well known stand-up comedian. But when Linda became pregnant with Vanja she took a year off, and then she found herself in a new class which I didn't feel like getting to know.

The meat was as tender as butter. The red wine tasted of earth and wood. Linda's eyes glinted in the glow from the candles. I put my knife and fork down on the plate. It was a few minutes to eight o'clock.

'Do you want me to listen to the documentary now? I asked.

'You don't have to if you don't want to,' Linda said. 'You can do it tomorrow, you know.'

'But I'm curious,' I said. 'And it's not very long, is it?'

She shook her head and got up.

'I'll get the player then. Where do you want to sit?'

I shrugged.

'There perhaps?' I said, motioning towards the chair by the bookshelves. She took out the DAT player, I fetched a pen and paper, sat down and put on the headset, she raised her eyebrows, I nodded and she pressed play.

After she had cleared the table I sat there alone listening. I already knew her father's story, but it was something else to hear it from his own mouth. His name was Roland and he was born in 1941 in one of the towns up in Norrland. He grew up without a father, with his mother and two younger siblings. His mother died when he was fifteen and from then on he was responsible for his little brother and sister. They lived alone without any adult support except for a woman who came to clean and cook for them. He went to school for four further years, became what was known in Sweden as a *gymnas* engineer, started working, played football in his free time, as goalkeeper for his local club, and thrived up there. At a dance he met Ingrid; she was the same age as him, had been to a domestic science college, worked as a secretary in a mining company office and was exceptionally beautiful. They became a couple and got married. Ingrid, however, had acting dreams, and when she was accepted for drama school in Stockholm, Roland abandoned the whole of his former life and moved with her to the capital. The life that awaited her, as an actress at the Royal Dramatic Theatre, had nothing to offer him, there was a gulf between his life as a goalkeeper and *gymnas* engineer in a provincial Norrland town and the one he had now, as the husband of a beautiful actress on the country's most important stage. They had two children in quick succession, but that was not enough to keep them together, they soon divorced and straight afterwards he fell ill for the first time. The illness he had was boundless and caused him to fluctuate between manic heights and depressive abysses, and once it had him in its grip it never let go. From then on he was in and out of institutions. When I met him for the first time, in the spring of 2004, he hadn't worked since the mid-1970s. Linda had not met him for many years. Even though I had seen photographs of him I still wasn't ready for what was awaiting me when I opened the door and he stood outside. His face was utterly open: it was as though there was nothing between him and the world. He had no protection against it, he was wholly defenceless, and to see that hurt you deep into your soul.

'So you're Karl Ove, are you?' he said.

I nodded and shook his hand.

'Roland Boström,' he said. 'Linda's father.'

'I've heard a lot about you,' I said. 'Come in!'

Behind me stood Linda with Vanja in her arms.

'Hi, dad,' she said. 'This is Vanja.'

He stood quite still and looked at Vanja, who looked back, equally still.

'Oohh,' he said. His eyes glistened.

'Let me take your coat,' I said. 'Then we can go in and have a cup of coffee.'

His face was open, but his movements were stiff, almost mechanical.

'Did you do the painting?' he said as we entered the living room.

'Yes,' I said.

He went to the nearest wall and stared at it.

'Did you do the painting, Karl Ove?'

'Yes.'

'You made a grand job of it! You have to be very precise when you paint, and you have been. I'm painting my flat now, you see. Turquoise in the bedroom and creamy white in the sitting room. But I haven't got any further than the bedroom, the back wall.'

'That's good,' Linda said. 'I'm sure it'll be lovely.'

'Yes, it will be, that's for certain.'

Something I had never seen before had come over Linda. She adapted to him, she was subordinate to him somehow, she was his child, she gave him attention and her company while also being above him in the sense that she was constantly trying to hide – although never quite succeeding – her shame. He sat down on the sofa, I poured the coffee, went to the kitchen for the cinnamon snails we had bought that morning and returned with a dish. He ate in silence. Linda sat beside him with Vanja on her lap. She showed him her child. I had never imagined it would mean so much to her.

'Nice buns,' he said. 'And the coffee was good too. Did you make it, Karl Ove?'

'Yes.'

'Have you got a coffee machine?'

'Yes.'

'That's good,' he said.

Pause.

'I wish you all the best,' he went on to say. 'Linda's my only daughter. I'm happy and grateful that I can come and visit you.'

'Do you feel like seeing some photos, dad?' Linda asked. 'Of Vanja when she was born?'

He nodded.

'Take Vanja for a bit, will you,' she said to me. The hot little bundle was placed into my arms, her eyes rolled on the brink of sleep while Linda got up and went to the shelves for the photo album.

'Mhm,' he said to every picture he was shown.

When they had been through the whole album he stretched out a hand for his cup of coffee on the table, raised it to his mouth in one slow, careful, well-considered movement and drank two big gulps.

'I've been to Norway only once, Karl Ove,' he said. 'To Narvik. I was in goal for some football club, and we went there to play a Norwegian team.'

'Oh yes!' I said.

'Yes,' he said, nodding.

'Karl Ove has also played football,' Linda said.

'Long time ago now,' I said. 'And at a very modest level.'

'Were you in goal?'

'No.'

'Right.'

Pause.

He took another swig of coffee in the same, somehow scrupulously planned, way.

'Well, this has been nice,' he said when the cup was back on his coaster. 'But now I'd better think about getting home.'

He stood up.

'But you've only just come!' Linda said.

'It was perfect,' he said. 'I'd like to invite you to a meal. It's my turn. Is Tuesday convenient?'

I met Linda's eyes. It was her decision.

'It is,' she said.

'Then that's a deal,' he said. 'Five o'clock on Tuesday.'

On the way to the hall he peered through the open bedroom door and stopped.

'Did you do the painting here as well?'

'Yes,' I said.

'May I see?'

'Of course,' I said.

We followed him in. He stood in front of the wall and looked up behind the enormous wood burner.

'It wasn't easy to paint there, I can see,' he said. 'But it looks good!'

Vanja made a little noise. She was lying on my arm so I couldn't see her face, and I laid her down on the bed. She smiled. Roland sat on the edge of the bed and put his hand around her foot.

'Don't you want to hold her?' Linda asked. 'You can if you want.'

'No,' he said. 'I've seen her now.'

Then he got up, went into the hallway and put on his coat. As he was about to leave he hugged me. His stubble rubbed against my cheek.

'Nice to meet you, Karl Ove,' he said. He hugged Linda, grabbed Vanja's foot again and set off down the stairs in his long coat.

Linda avoided my gaze as she passed Vanja to me and went into the living room to clear the table. I followed.

'What do you think of him?' she asked airily on her way.

'He's a nice man,' I said. 'But he has absolutely no filter against the world. I don't think I've ever seen anyone who radiates such immense vulnerability.'

'He's like a child, isn't he.'

'Yes, he is. There's no doubt about that.'

She walked past me with three coffee cups on top of each other in one hand, the cake basket in the other.

'That's quite some grandfather Vanja has got,' I said.

'Yes, what is it going to be like?' she asked. There was no irony in her voice; the question came straight from the darkness of her heart.

'It'll be fine of course,' I said.

'But I don't want him in our life,' she said, putting the cups in the dishwasher.

'If it's like this I'm sure it'll be fine,' I said. 'No harm in him dropping by for coffee once in a while. And then the odd meal at his place. He is her grandfather after all.'

Linda closed the dishwasher door, took a transparent plastic bag from the bottom drawer of a cabinet and put the three remaining cakes in it, tied a knot and went past me to put it in the hall freezer.

'But he won't be happy with that, I know. Now he's made contact he'll start ringing. And he only does that when he's in a mess. There are no limits for him. You have to understand that.'

She went into the living room for the last plates.

'We can try at any rate,' I said following her. 'And see what happens?'

'OK,' she said.

At that moment there was a ring at the door.

What could that be? The crazy neighbour again?

But it was Roland. His eyes were frantic.

'I can't get out,' he said. 'I can't find the buzzer for the lock. I've searched and searched. But it isn't there. Can you help me?'

'Of course I can,' I said. 'I'll just pass Vanja over to Linda.'

After doing that I put on my shoes and followed him down to the front hall, showed him where the buzzer was, on the wall to the right of the first door.

'I'll make a note of that,' he said. 'For next time. On the right of the first door.'

Three days later we had a meal in his flat. He showed us the wall he had painted, and glowed with satisfaction when I praised his handiwork. He hadn't started cooking yet, and Vanja was asleep in the buggy in the hall, so Linda and I sat alone in the sitting room chatting while he was busy in the kitchen. On the wall were childhood pictures of Linda and her brother, and beside them newspaper articles and cuttings of interviews they had given when they made their debuts. Her brother had also had a book published, in 1996, but, like Linda, he hadn't produced anything since.

'He's so proud of you,' I said to Linda.

She looked down at the table.

'Shall we go out onto the balcony?' she suggested. 'So that you can have a smoke?'

There wasn't a balcony but a roof terrace, from which, between two other roofs, you could see over Östermalm. A roof terrace right by Stureplan; how many millions must the flat be worth? True, it was dark and smoke-infested, but that was easy enough to sort out.

'Does your father own the flat?' I asked, lighting a cigarette with my hand cupped over the lighter flame.

She nodded.

I had never lived in a place where the right address and elegant apartments meant as much as they did in Stockholm. Somehow it was a concentrate of everything. If you lived outside, well, you weren't really included. The question of where you lived, which came up again and again, was therefore charged in Stockholm in a way that was quite different to Bergen, for example.

I walked to the edge to see below. There were still small piles of snow and patches of ice left on the pavement after the winter, almost completely eroded by the mild weather and grey from the sand and exhaust fumes. The sky above us was also grey, laden with cold rain that lashed the town at regular intervals. Grey but with a different light in it from the grey winter sky, for it was March, and March light was so clear and strong that it penetrated the cloud cover, even on a muggy day like this, and opened all the gates of darkness, as it were. There was a gleam in the walls in front of me and in the tarmac on the road beneath. The parked cars glinted, each in its own colour. Red, blue, dark green, white.

'Hold me,' she said.

I stubbed out my cigarette in the ashtray on the table and put my arms around her.

When, a moment later, we went back in, the sitting room was still empty and we entered the kitchen. He was by the stove pouring the contents of a tin of mushrooms into the frying pan. The liquid hissed as it met the hot pan. Then he added a diced courgette. A pan of spaghetti was boiling next to it.

'That looks good,' I said.

'Yes, it is good,' he said.

On the worktop there was a tin of shrimps in brine and a tin of double cream.

'I usually have dinner down at Vikingen. But on Fridays, Saturdays and Sundays I eat here. Then I cook for Berit.'

Berit was his girlfriend.

'Is there anything we can help with?' Linda asked.

'No,' he said. 'Have a seat and I'll bring the food when it's ready.'

The food tasted like something I could have made when I was a student and ate alone in my bedsit in Absalon Beyers gate during my first year at Bergen University. Linda's father talked more about the time when he played in goal for the team in Norrland. Then he talked about what his job had been, planning and designing warehouses. Then he talked about the horse he had once owned, which had been injured just as it looked as if it was going to start winning. He recounted everything in very precise, elaborate terms as if every detail was of the uttermost significance. At one point in the conversation he went to fetch a pen and paper so that he could show us how he had come to the precise number of days he had left to live. I sought Linda's eyes, but she would not meet mine. We had determined in advance that the visit should be brief, so when dessert, a two-litre carton of ice cream served up on the table, was over we got to our feet and said we were afraid we had to go, Vanja had to be taken home and fed and changed. This appeared to please him. The visit had already lasted an infinity. I went into the hall and put on my outdoor clothes while Linda and he exchanged a few words in private. He said something about her being his girl and that she had grown so much. Come here and sit on my lap for a bit. I tied the last shoelace, got up, went to the crack in the door and looked into the room. Linda was sitting on his lap, he had his arms around her waist while saying something I was unable to catch. There was something grotesque about the sight, she was thirty-two years old, the girlish pose she struck was much too young for her, which she knew of course, her lips were pursed in disapproval, her whole being screamed with ambivalence. She didn't want to go along with this, but she didn't want to reject him either. He would not have understood a rejection, it would have hurt him, so she had to sit through it while he patted her until it would no longer seem like a rejection to get up and she was standing in front of him again.

I stepped back so that I would not make the situation worse for her by being a witness to it. When she came into the hall I was studying the pictures hanging on the wall. She put on her things. Her father came out to say goodbye, he gave me a hug, as before, looked at Vanja sleeping in the buggy, embraced Linda, stood in the doorway and watched us as we went into the lift, raised his hand for a last time and went inside as the lift door closed and we sank down through the building.

I never uttered a word regarding the little scene I had witnessed between them. In the way she had subordinated herself to him she had been a ten-year-old girl, I saw that; in the way she had fought against it, an adult woman. But the very fact that she'd had to fight somehow disqualified the notion of adulthood. Surely no adult would end up in a situation like this? He had no such thoughts, he was of the boundless kind, for him she was a daughter, nothing else, a creature of all ages.

And, as she had predicted, after that he began to ring us. It could be at any time of the day and in any state of mind, so Linda struck a deal with him: he would ring at a particular hour on a particular day. He seemed to like that. But it was also a commitment: if we didn't answer the phone he might be terribly offended and regard the contract as null and void, so he would be free to ring us whenever he wanted again, or never ring again. As for myself, I spoke to him only a handful of times. Once he asked me if he could sing me a song. He had written it himself, and it had been performed on stages in Stockholm and on the radio, he said. I didn't know what to believe. But there was no reason why he shouldn't be allowed to sing. He launched into song, his voice was powerful, his energy immense and even though he didn't hit all the notes to perfection the performance was still impressive. The song had four verses and was about a migrant worker building a road in Norrland. When he had finished I didn't know what else to say except that it was a wonderful song. Presumably he had expected more because he was quiet for a few seconds. Then he said, 'I know you write books, Karl Ove. I haven't read them yet, but I've heard a lot of good things about them. And I want you to know that. I'm hugely proud of you, Karl Ove. Yes, I am . . .'

'I'm happy to hear that,' I said.

'Are you and Linda OK?'

'Yes, we are.'

'Are you kind to her?'

'Yes.'

'That's good. You must never leave her. Never. Do you understand?'

'Yes.'

'You must take care of her. You must be kind to her, Karl Ove.' Then he burst into tears.

'We get on well,' I said. 'There's nothing to worry about.'

'I'm just an old man,' he said. 'But I've experienced a lot, you see. I've experienced more than most. My life isn't anything to shout about now. But I've counted how many days I have left. Did you know?'

'Yes, you showed us how you had worked it out when we were at your place.'

'Ah, yes, yes. But you haven't met Berit, have you.'

'No.'

'She's so kind to me.'

'So I gather,' I said.

He was suddenly on his guard.

'Eh? How?'

'Well, Linda has told me a bit about her. And Ingrid. You know . . .'

'I see. I won't bother you any more, Karl Ove. I'm sure you have important things to do.'

'Not at all,' I said. 'You're not bothering me at all.'

'Tell Linda I called. Take care.'

He rang off before I had a chance to wish him the same. On the display I saw that the whole conversation had not taken more than eight minutes. Linda snorted when I told her.

'You don't have to listen to that stuff,' she said. 'Don't answer the phone next time he rings.'

'It doesn't bother me,' I said.

'But it does bother me,' she said.

Linda's documentary contained nothing of this. She had edited out everything except his voice. However, therein lay everything. He talked about his life, and his voice was filled with sorrow when he spoke of his mother's death, happiness when he spoke of his first years of adulthood, resignation when he spoke about his move to Stockholm. He spoke about the problems he'd had with the telephone, what a curse the invention had been for him, how for long periods he had kept it in a cupboard. He spoke of his daily routines, but also about his dreams, of which the greatest was to run a stud farm. Here he came into his own, and there was something hypnotic about his account, you were sucked into his world from the very first sentence. But most of all of course it was about Linda. Hearing what she did or reading what she wrote, I came so close to the person she was. It was as though those special qualities that stirred within her only then became visible. In our daily lives they were lost in whatever we were doing, which was the same as everyone else did, I saw nothing of the person I had fallen in love with. If I hadn't actually forgotten, I certainly didn't give it a thought.

How was that possible?

I looked at her. She tried to hide the anticipation in her eyes. Dropped her gaze too easily to the DAT player on the table and the mass of wires beneath.

'You don't need to change anything,' I said. 'It's completely finished.'

'Is it good, do you think?'

'Oh yes. Brilliant.'

I placed the headset on the player, stretched and blinked a few times.

'I was moved,' I said.

'By what?'

'His life is a tragedy, in a way. But when he talks about it, he fills it with life, we know this is a *life*. With a value all of its own, irrespective of what happened to him. Obvious perhaps, but it's one thing to know this and another to feel it. And I did when I was listening to him just now.'

'I'm so pleased,' she said. 'So perhaps I don't need to do any more than adjust the sound levels. I can do that on Monday. But are you sure?'

'As sure as I can be,' I said, getting up. 'Now I'm going for a smoke.'

Downstairs, in the backyard, the wind was cold. The only two children in the block, a boy of nine or ten and his sister of eleven or twelve, were kicking a ball to each other by the gate at the other end. Intense loud music was coming from the Glenn Miller Café beyond the wall in the street behind them. Their mother, who lived alone with them on the top floor and looked seriously tired, had the window open. From the characteristic clinks and clunks I could hear she was washing up. The boy was plump, and probably to compensate had his hair cropped to make him seem tough. He always had blue bags under his eyes. When his sister had friends at home he performed ball tricks or ostentatious climbing feats on the monkey bars. On evenings like this, when they were alone and she had nothing better to do than play with her brother, he was happier, more energetic and keener to play well. Now and then they shouted and screamed up there, sometimes all three of them, but usually it was just him and his mother. I had seen the father come a couple of times to collect them – a small thin sickly guy with a moustache who obviously drank too much.

The sister went to the fence and sat down. She took a mobile phone from her pocket and it was so dark where she was sitting that the blue light of the display lit up the whole of her face. Her brother began to kick the ball against the wall, again and again. Bang. Bang. Bang.

His mother poked her head out of the window.

'Will you stop that!' she yelled. The boy bent forward quietly, picked up the ball and sat beside his sister, who turned away without changing the focus of her attention for a second.

I looked up at the two illuminated towers. A stab of tenderness and pain went through me.

Oh Linda, oh Linda.

At that moment the neighbour who lived next door to us came through the entrance. I watched her as she lightly closed the gate behind her. She was in her fifties and the way that women of this age are nowadays, that is with a certain artificially maintained youthfulness. She had a mass of dyed blonde hair, was wearing a fur jacket and pulling a small inquisitive dog on

a taut leash. Once she had told me she was an artist, although
I was none the wiser about what it was she did. She wasn't
exactly the Munch type. Sometimes she could be very chatty,
telling me she was going to Provence in the summer or had a
weekend trip to New York or London planned. Sometimes she
said nothing and could walk past me without saying a word.
She had a teenage daughter who had given birth at the same
time as Linda and whom she bossed around.

'Weren't you going to give up smoking?' she asked, not slowing
her pace.

'The clock hasn't chimed twelve yet,' I said.

'Ah,' she said. 'It's going to snow tonight. You mark my words.'

She let herself in. I waited, then threw my cigarette end in
the flower pot someone had put by the wall for this purpose
and followed. My knuckles were red from the cold. I bounded
up the stairs three at a time, opened the door, took off my coat
and went into Linda, who was watching TV on the sofa. I leaned
forward and kissed her.

'What are you watching?' I asked.

'Nothing much. Shall we watch a film?'

'Yes, let's.'

I went to the DVD rack.

'What would you like to see?'

'No idea. You choose.'

I ran my eye along the row. When I bought films it was always
with the idea that they should broaden my horizons. They
should have their own special imagery I could assimilate, or
forge a relationship with places whose potential I hadn't considered or be set in an unfamiliar time or culture. In short, I chose
films for all the wrong reasons, because when evening came
and we wanted to see one of them we could never be bothered
to watch two hours of some Japanese event from the 1960s in

black and white or the great open expanses of Rome's suburbs, where the only thing that happened was that some stunningly beautiful people met who were fundamentally alienated from the world, as tended to be the case with films of that era. No, when evening came and we sat down to watch a film we wanted to be entertained. And it had to be with as little effort and inconvenience as possible. It was the same with everything. I hardly read books any more; if there was a newspaper around I preferred to read that. And the threshold just kept rising. It was idiotic because this life gave you nothing, it only made time pass. If we saw a good film it stirred us and set things in motion, for that is how it is: the world is always the same, it is the way we view it that changes. Everyday life, which could bear down on us like a foot treading on a head, could also transport us with delight. Everything depended on the seeing eye. If the eye saw the water that was everywhere in Tarkovsky's films, for example, which changed the world into a kind of terrarium, where everything trickled and ran, floated and drifted, where all the characters could melt away from the picture and only coffee cups on a table were left, filling slowly with the falling rain, against a background of intense, almost menacing green vegetation, yes, then the eye would also be able to see the same wild existential depths unfold in everyday life. For we were flesh and blood, sinews and bone, around us plants and trees grew, insects buzzed, birds flew, clouds drifted, rain fell. The eye which gave meaning to the world was a constant possibility, but we almost always decided against it, at least it was like that in our lives.

'Are we up for *Stalker*?' I asked, turning to her.

'OK as far as I'm concerned,' she said. 'Put it on and let's see.'

I inserted the DVD in the player, switched off the ceiling light, poured a glass of red wine, sat down beside Linda, took the remote and chose the language of the subtitles. She cuddled up to me.

'Does it matter if I fall asleep?' she asked.

'Not at all,' I answered, putting my arm around her.

I had seen the introduction with the man who wakes up in the dark damp room at least three times. The table with all the small objects shaking as a train passes. The man shaving in front of the mirror, the woman who tries to hold him back but fails. I had never got much further than that.

Linda placed her hand on my chest and looked up at me. I kissed her, and she closed her eyes. I stroked her back, she held me tight, almost clung to me, I laid her down, kissed her neck, cheek, mouth, rested my head on her bosom, heard her heart pounding, removed her soft jogging pants, kissed her stomach, her thighs . . . She looked at me with her dark gaze, with her beautiful eyes which closed as I penetrated her. We don't have any protection, she whispered. Do you want to get it? No, I said. No. And when I came, I came inside her. That was all I wanted.

Afterwards we lay close to each other for a long time without speaking.

'Now we'll have another child,' I said at length. 'Are you ready for that?'

'Yes,' she said. 'Oh yes. I am.'

The next morning Vanja woke at five as usual. Linda brought her into our bed to sleep for a few more hours with her while I got up, took out my laptop and started to work on the translation on which I was writing a report. The work was tedious and unending, I had already written thirty pages, and that about a short story of no more than one hundred and forty. Nevertheless, I was looking forward to the work and enjoyed sitting there. I was alone and working on a text. I needed nothing else. Then there were the little moments of pleasure: putting on the coffee machine, hearing the gurgle of water trickling through, the aroma of freshly brewed coffee, standing outside in the darkness of the backyard before anyone had got up, drinking a cup and smoking the first cigarette of the day. Back upstairs and working while the gap between the houses gradually grew light and activity increased in the street. This morning the brightness of dawn was different and with it the atmosphere in the flat, for a thin layer of snow had fallen in the night. At eight o'clock I switched off my laptop, put it in my bag and walked to the little bakery a hundred metres down the street. The shop awnings along the line of buildings flapped above me. On the road the snow had already melted, but it was still on the pavement, peppered with the footprints of those who had wandered past during the night. Now the street was deserted. The bakery was tiny and run by two women of my age. Stepping inside was like stepping inside one of those noir films from the 1940s in which all the women, even those working in kiosks or washing floors in office blocks, are strikingly beautiful. One of them was red-haired, with white skin and freckles, pronounced facial features and green eyes. The other had long dark hair, a slightly square face and friendly dark blue eyes. Both were tall and slim, their bodies flecked with flour. On their foreheads, cheeks, hands or aprons. Newspaper cuttings on the wall told of how they had swapped their creative professions for this, which had always been their dream.

The red-haired woman came from behind the counter when the doorbell rang, I said what I wanted, one of the big sourdough loaves, six of the wholemeal rolls, two cinnamon snails. I pointed at the same time, because even the simplest Norwegian words were met with a 'What?' She put everything in a bag and rang up the total on the till. With the white carrier bag in my hand,

I hurried back to the flat, wiped the snow off my feet on the hall mat, heard as soon as I opened the door that they were up and sitting in the kitchen having breakfast.

Vanja sat waving her spoon in the air and smiled at me when I entered the room. She had porridge all over her face. It was a long time since she had let us feed her. I reacted instinctively, wanted to wipe up the mess – from her face as well – I didn't like her sitting there all sticky. It was in my blood. Linda had criticised my reaction from the very beginning, it was important there were no rules or restrictions as far as food was concerned, it was a sensitive area, she should be allowed to do exactly what she wanted. Of course, Linda was right, I did understand, and on a purely theoretical level I could accept the greediness, the freedom and the soundness of a child being allowed to eat noisily and make a mess, but on a practical level my first impulse was to modify her behaviour. That was my father in me. He didn't tolerate as much as a breadcrumb on the table when I was growing up. But I knew that, I had experienced it myself and hated it with every fibre in my body, so why did I instinctively want to persist at all costs?

I cut some slices of bread, put them in a basket with the rolls, filled the kettle and sat down to have breakfast with them. The butter was a little hard, and as I tried to spread it with the knife the bread tore. Vanja was staring at me. I spun my head round and fixed my eyes on her. She gave a start in her chair. Then, fortunately, she began to laugh. I did the same again, looked down at the table in front of me for a long time until she had begun to give up hope that anything would happen and thought my mind was busy elsewhere, then, as quick as a flash, I stared into her eyes, they widened with alarm and she jumped in fright. Then she burst into laughter again. Linda and I laughed too.

'How funny our Vanja is,' Linda said. 'You're so funny, you are! My little bunny rabbit!'

She leaned forward and rubbed her nose against Vanja's. I grabbed the culture section of the newspaper lying open on the table in front of Linda, took a mouthful of bread and chewed as I scanned the headlines. On the worktop behind me the kettle boiled and switched itself off. I got up, put a tea bag in a cup, poured the steaming water over it, went to the fridge to get a carton of milk, then sat down. Dunked the tea bag a few times until the brown billowing liquid slowly issuing from it had completely changed the colour of the water. Poured in a splash of milk and flicked through the paper.

'Have you seen what they say about Arne?' I said, looking at Linda.

She nodded and gave a little smile, but to Vanja, not me.

'The publishers are withdrawing the book. What a defeat.'

'Yes,' she said. 'Poor Arne. But he only has himself to blame.'

'Do you think he knew it was lies?'

'No, not at all. He didn't do it intentionally, I'm sure. He must have thought that was how it was.'

'Poor devil,' I said, raising the cup and sipping the mud-coloured tea.

Arne was one of Linda's mother's neighbours in Gnesta. He had written a book about Astrid Lindgren, which had come out this autumn, loosely based on conversations he'd had with her before she died. Arne was a spiritual person, he believed in God, although not in a conventional sense, and it must have surprised many people that Astrid Lindgren shared this unconventional belief in God. The papers were beginning to take an interest in the affair. No one else had been present during the conversations, so even if Lindgren had never expressed such attitudes to anyone else it could not be proved that they had been fictionalised for the occasion. But there were other things in the press, among them Arne's readings of Lindgren, which turned out to be anachronistic: at the time he said that he had read *Mio my Mio* the book hadn't been published. And so it continued throughout his book. The Lindgren family denied that she had such attitudes; she could not have said this. The papers did not leave Arne with much honour, the subtext was that he was a liar, as good as a pathological liar, and now the publishing house had decided to withdraw the book. The book that had kept Arne going for the last few illness-plagued years and of which he was so proud.

But Linda was right: he had only himself to blame.

I buttered another slice of bread. Vanja stretched her hands into the air. Linda lifted her out of the chair and carried her into the bathroom, from where soon there came the sounds of running water and Vanja's little squeals of protest.

The phone rang in the living room. I froze. Even though I knew at once it had to be Ingrid, Linda's mother – no one else would ring us at this time – my heart beat faster and faster.

I sat motionless until the ringing stopped, as suddenly as it had started.

'Who was that?' Linda asked when she emerged from the bathroom with Vanja hanging from her arms.

'No idea,' I said. 'I didn't answer it. But it was probably your mother.'

'I'll call her,' she said. 'I had planned to anyway. Will you take Vanja?'

She held her out as if my lap was the only other place she could be in the flat.

'Just put her on the floor,' I said.

'Then she'll scream.'

'Let her scream. It's no problem.'

'O-K,' she said, the way that meant the opposite. This is not OK, but I'm doing it because you say so. Then you'll see what happens.

Of course, she started to cry as soon as Linda put her down on the floor. I stretched my arms out for her, then fell hands first onto the floor. Linda didn't turn round. I pulled open a drawer, which I could reach now from a sitting position, and took out a whisk. Vanja wasn't interested, even if I could make it vibrate. I held up a banana in front of her. She shook her head as the tears ran down her cheeks. In the end I lifted her up and carried her to the bedroom window, where I stood her on the sill. That did the trick. I named all the things we saw, she stared with interest and pointed at every car that passed.

Linda poked her head through the doorway with the phone held to her chest.

'Mummy asks if we would like to eat there tomorrow. Would we?'

'Yes,' I said. 'That's fine.'

'Then shall I say yes?'

'Go for it.'

I lifted Vanja carefully down to the floor. She could stand but not walk yet, so she squatted and crawled towards Linda. This child could not show a second of dissatisfaction before her needs were fulfilled. For close on the whole of her first year she had woken up in the night every two hours and been fed. Linda had been almost out of her mind with tiredness, yet she wouldn't make Vanja sleep in her own bed because then she would scream. I was in favour of a brutal course of action, putting her in her own bed and letting her scream as much as she wanted the whole night through, so that the next time she would understand that no one was going to come whatever she did, and resigned and perhaps angry, she would settle down to sleep on her own. I might just as well have told Linda that I would beat Vanja over the head until she was quiet. The compromise was that I rang my mother's sister, Ingunn, who was a child psychologist and had experience of such things. She suggested a gradual weaning, emphasising that Vanja had to be patted and stroked a lot if she wanted to be fed or to get up but was not allowed, and that bit by bit we should defer the time when she was given the day's final feed. So there I was, by her bed at night with a notepad, jotting down the exact times and patting and stroking her while she screamed her head off and glowered at me furiously. It took ten nights for her to sleep through. It could have been done in one. Because surely it didn't hurt her to cry a little? The same happened in the play area. I tried to make her stay there alone so I could sit on a bench and read, but that was out of the question: a few seconds on her own and she was searching for me with her eyes and holding out imploring arms.

Linda rang off and came out with Vanja in her arms.

'Shall we go for a walk?' she suggested.

'I don't suppose there's much else we can do,' I said.

'What do you mean?' she asked warily.

'Nothing,' I said. 'Where shall we go?'

'Skeppsholmen maybe?'

'OK, let's do that.'

Since I'd had Vanja in the week, Linda took care of her now. She sat Vanja on her lap, dressed her in a small red knitted jumper we had inherited from Yngve's children, brown corduroy trousers, the red romper suit Linda's mother had bought for us, the red cap with the strap under the chin and the white brim and a pair of white woollen mittens. Until a month ago she had always sat still when we changed her, but of late she had begun to wriggle and squirm in our hands. It was particularly difficult when you had to change her nappy, the crap could end up anywhere as she kept wriggling, and more than once I had raised my voice. LIE STILL! Or LIE STILL FOR CHRIST'S SAKE! And my grip on her tightened more than was necessary. For her part, she thought it was funny to try and wriggle away, she always smiled or laughed whenever she succeeded and at first she simply did not understand the loud irritated voice. Sometimes she ignored it totally, or she stared at me in surprise, now what was that meant to be? Or she cried. First the lower lip puckered and started to quiver, then the tears flowed. What on earth was I doing? I thought. Had I gone completely mad? She was one year old, as innocent as only the innocent can be, and there I was, *yelling* at her!

Luckily she was easy to comfort, easy to make laugh, and luckily she had a short memory. From that perspective, it was worse for me.

Linda had more patience, and after five minutes Vanja was fully dressed in her arms with an expectant smile on her lips. In the lift she tried to press the buttons, Linda pointed to the right one and guided her hand. The button lit up, the lift set off. While Linda went into the bicycle room with her, where the buggy was, I lit a cigarette outside. The wind was still strong and the sky heavy and grey. The temperature was around zero or minus one.

We walked down Regeringsgatan, into Kungsträdgården, past the National Museum, and turned left onto the island of Skeppsholmen, along the quays where all the houseboats were. A couple of them were from the turn of the last century and in their heyday had plied between the many islands outside Stockholm. There was also a kind of small boatyard here, or so it seemed, with a keel and timbers arranged like a skeleton inside a wooden warehouse. Now and then a bearded face poked out as we walked past, otherwise the area was deserted. Up on a small hill was the Moderna Museet, where Vanja had spent, considering the length of her short life, a disproportionately large number of days. But admission was free, the restaurant was good and child-friendly, there were play areas and some of the art was worth seeing.

The water in the harbour was black. The clouds were dense and low in the sky. The thin layer of snow on the ground seemed to make everything harder and more naked, perhaps because it removed the little colour that was left in the townscape. All the museum buildings here had once been military and they still bore the hallmarks – low and closed, they ran alongside the short untrafficked roads or stood at the end of what must have been parade grounds.

'That was great yesterday,' Linda said, wrapping an arm around me.

'Yes,' I said. 'It was. But do you really want another child now?'

'Yes, I do. But the odds are against it.'

'I'm sure you're pregnant,' I said.

'As sure as you were that Vanja was a boy?'

'Ha ha.'

'I'd be so happy,' she said. 'Imagine I was! Imagine we were going to have another child!'

'Yes . . .' I said. 'What do you say to that, Vanja? Would you like a little brother or sister?'

She looked up at us. Then she turned her head to the side and pointed to three seagulls bobbing up and down on the waves, their wings tucked into their sides.

'Deh!' she said.

'Yes, there,' I said. 'Three seagulls!'

One child was absolutely out of the question for me, two was too few and too close together, but three, I reckoned, was perfect. Then the children outnumbered the parents, there were lots of permutations possible, then we were a gang. I had nothing but contempt for precise plans to pinpoint the most suitable time, both as far as our own lives were concerned and which ages went best together. After all this was not a business we were running. I wanted to let chance decide, let what happened happen, and then deal with the consequences as they emerged. Wasn't that what life was about? So when I walked down the street with Vanja, when I fed and changed her, with these wild longings for a different life hammering away in my chest, this was the consequence of a decision and I *had* to live with it. There was *no* way out, other than the old well-travelled route: endurance. The fact that I cast a pall over the lives of those around me in doing so, well, that was just another consequence which had to be endured. If we had another child, and we would, regardless of whether Linda was pregnant now or not, and then another, which was equally inevitable, surely this would transcend duty, transcend my longings and end up as something wild and free in its own right? If not, what would I do then?

Be there, do what I had to do. In my life this was the only thing I had to hold on to, my sole fixed point, and it was carved in stone.

Or was it?

A few weeks ago Jeppe had phoned me, he was in town, could we meet for a few beers? I had a lot of respect for him, but I had never managed to talk to him, as was the case with so many people, but we loosened up after I had knocked back several beers in quick succession. I told him what my life was like now. He looked at me and said with that natural authority which was typical of him, 'But you must *write*, Karl Ove!'

And when push came to shove, when a knife was at my throat, this was what mattered most.

But why?

Children were life, and who would turn their back on life?

And writing, what else was it but death? Letters, what else were they but bones in a cemetery?

The Djurgård ferry rounded the spit at the end of the island. On the other side was Gröna Lund, the vast amusement park, with all the machines empty and motionless, some covered with tarpaulins. A couple of hundred metres away was the building that housed the Vasa ship.

'Shall we take the ferry across?' Linda asked. 'Then we can have lunch at Blå Porten.'

'We've only just had breakfast,' I said.

'A coffee then.'

'Yes, we can. Have you got any cash on you?'

She nodded, and we waited where the ferry berthed. After only a few seconds Vanja started complaining. Linda found a banana in the bag and handed it to her. Happy, she sat back in the buggy and stared across the sea while stuffing bits of banana into her mouth. I was reminded of the very first time I had been out with her on my own, because this was where we came. She had been a week old. I had almost run around the island with the buggy in front of me, frightened she would stop breathing, frightened she would wake up and scream. At home we had the situation under control: there was breastfeeding, sleeping, changing nappies in a soporific yet somehow quietly triumphant system. Away from home, we no longer had a structure to cling to. The first time we took her out was the third day, she had to go for a check-up and it was like we were transporting a bomb. Obstacle number one was all the clothes she had to wear because the temperature outside was more than fifteen degrees below. The second was the child seat. How do you attach it in a taxi? The third was the eyes that studied us in the reception area. But all went well, we survived, albeit with an immense amount of fuss, but it was all worth it when some minutes later she was placid and gently kicking her legs on the changing table as she was being examined. She was in perfect health and in an irresistibly good mood because she suddenly smiled at the nurse bent over her. That was a smile, the nurse said. It wasn't gripe. It's rare for babies to smile so early on! We luxuriated in the compliment, it said something about us as parents, only several months later did it strike me that the line, it's rare for babies to smile so early on, was probably used to accomplish that very effect. But, oh, the low, somehow timid January light that fell through the window and over our daughter on the table, whom we still weren't remotely used to, the ice outside glinting in the freezing temperatures, Linda's utterly open relaxed face, made this one of the few memories that did not contain the slightest trace of ambivalence. It lasted until we were in the corridor and ready to go, and Vanja began to scream her head off. What should we do? Pick her up? Yes, we had to. Should Linda give her a feed? If so, how? She was wearing so many clothes she looked like a balloon. Should we undress her again? *While* she was screaming? Was that what you did? What about if she didn't calm down?

Oh, how Vanja screamed as Linda fiddled with her clothing in her nervous, irresolute way.

'Let me do it,' I said.

Her eyes flashed as they met mine.

Vanja went silent for some seconds as her lips closed around the nipple. But then she jerked her head back and continued to scream her head off.

'Not that then,' Linda said. 'What is it? Is she ill?'

'No, I doubt that,' Linda said. 'After all, she's just been checked over by a doctor.'

Vanja screamed and screamed. The whole of her little face was in convulsion.

'What shall we do?' Linda said in desperation.

'Hold her for a while and we'll see,' I said.

The second couple, the ones after us, came out with their baby in a car seat. They studiously avoided looking at us as they passed.

'We can't stand here,' I said. 'Let's go. Come on. She'll just have to scream.'

'Have you rung for a taxi?'

'No.'

'Then do it!'

She looked down at Vanja, whom she was hugging, not that it helped, there wasn't much reassurance in the contact between Vanja's romper suit and Linda's Puffa jacket. I took out my mobile and tapped in the taxi number, holding the car seat in my other hand, and walked towards the stairs at the end of the corridor.

'Hang on,' Linda said. 'I just have to put on her hat.'

She screamed all the time we waited for the taxi. Fortunately it arrived a few minutes later. I opened the rear door, put the seat in and tried to secure it with the seat belt, which I had managed an hour earlier without a problem, but now it appeared to be absolutely impossible. I tried attaching it in every conceivable way, through, over and under the bloody seat, and none worked. All with Vanja screaming and Linda looking daggers at me. In the end the driver got out to help me. At first I refused to move, I could damn well manage this on my own, thank you, but after another minute's fumbling I had to concede defeat and let him, a moustachioed Iraqi-looking man, fasten it at a stroke.

All the way through snowy glistening Stockholm she screamed. Only when we were through the door, at home and she was lying undressed on the bed with Linda did she stop.

We were both drenched in sweat.

'That was a bit of an ordeal!' Linda said as she got up from Vanja, asleep on the bed.

'Yes,' I said. 'There's some life in her anyway.'

Later that day I heard Linda telling her mother about the medical check-up. Not a word about all the screaming or the panic we had felt, no, what she told her was that Vanja smiled when she was on the table being examined. How happy and proud Linda was! Vanja had smiled, she was in perfect health, and the low sunlight outside, seemingly elevated by the snow-covered surfaces, made everything in the room soft and shiny, even Vanja, as she lay naked on the blanket kicking her legs.

What had happened afterwards was passed over in silence.

Now, waiting in the wind for the ferry, close to a year later, the whole scene appeared bizarre. How was it possible to be so ignorant? But that was how it had been, I could still remember how I felt inside then, how fragile everything had been, also the happiness that was radiated everywhere. Nothing in my life had prepared me for having a baby, I had barely seen one before, and the same was true for Linda, she had not had a single baby near her during her adult life. Everything was new, everything had to be learned on the hoof, also the mistakes that were bound to be made. Quite soon I began to regard various elements of childcare as challenges, as though I were participating in a kind of competition the point of which was to tackle as much as possible at once, and I had continued doing this when Vanja became my responsibility during the day, until there were no new elements left, the little field was conquered, and all that remained was routine.

The engine on the ferry was thrown into reverse as it slowly glided the last metres towards the quay. The ticket collector opened the gate and we, apparently the only passengers, pushed the buggy on board. Bubbles of grey-green water rose to the surface around the propellers. Linda took her wallet from the inside pocket of her blue jacket and paid. I held the railing and looked back towards the town. The white projection which was the Royal Dramatic Theatre, the ridge of hills that separated Birger Jarlsgatan from Sveavägen, where our flat was. The vast mass of building that filled almost all the space in the countryside. How a different perspective, which knew nothing of the purpose of houses and roads, but which considered them as forms and mass, the way pigeons must see the town they fly over and land on, saw the town, how this view in one fell swoop made everything alien. An enormous labyrinth of passages and cavities, some under an open sky, others enclosed, others again under the ground, in narrow tunnels through which trains raced like larvae.

Well over a million people lived their lives there.

'Mummy said she could look after Vanja on Mondays if you wanted. Then you'd have the day to yourself.'

'I'd like that of course,' I said.

'No of course about it,' she said.

Mentally, I rolled my eyes.

'But then we can sleep there,' she went on. 'And then come back together early in the morning. If you want, that is. And mummy can bring Vanja in the afternoon.'

'Sounds like a good plan,' I said.

When the ferry moored on the other side we walked up the street beside the fair, which in the summer months was always full of people, queuing in front of the ticket windows or hot dog stands, eating in one of the fast food restaurants across the way or just walking. The tarmac was littered with tickets and brochures, ice cream wrappers and hot dog paper, serviettes and drinking straws, Coke cups and juice cartons and everything else people enjoying their leisure tended to drop. Now the street ahead was quiet, empty and clean. Not a soul to be seen anywhere, not in the restaurants on one side, nor in the fair on the other. On a little hill at the other end was Circus, the concert venue. I had been to the restaurant there once with Anders, we had been on the lookout for somewhere showing the Premier League. They had the match we wanted to see on the TV at the back. There was only one other person inside. The light was dim, the walls dark, yet he was wearing sunglasses. It was Tommy Körberg. All the newspapers had his face plastered over the front pages that day, he had been caught drink-driving, you could hardly walk a metre in Stockholm without seeing his face. Now he was hiding in here. The flagrant stares must have been as unpleasant for him as the carefully averted eyes, he left a short time after we entered, even though neither of us had glanced in his direction once.

Compared with what he appeared to be going through, my worst attacks of post-alcoholic angst paled into insignificance.

My mobile rang in my pocket. I took it and looked at the display. Yngve.

'Hi?' I said.

'Hi,' he answered. 'How's it going?'

'Fine. How about you?'

'Yep, fine.'

'Good. Yngve, we're about to go into a café. Can I ring you later? This afternoon some time? Or was there something in particular?'

'No, nothing. We can talk later.'

'Bye.'

'Bye.'

I put the mobile back in my pocket.

'That was Yngve,' I said.

'Is he all right?' Linda asked.

I shrugged.

'I don't know. But I'll call him afterwards.'

Two weeks after he turned forty Yngve left Kari Anne and moved into a house on his own. It had all happened very suddenly. Only when he had been here last time had he told me about his plans. Yngve seldom talked about personal matters, he kept almost everything to himself – unless I asked him direct questions, that is. But that didn't always happen. Besides, I didn't need him to confide in me to know that he had been living a life he didn't want. So when he told me it was over, I was happy on his behalf. Nonetheless, I couldn't help thinking about dad, who had left my mother just a few weeks before he turned forty. The age coincidence, which in this case was down to a week, was neither a family nor a genetic matter and the midlife crisis was not a myth: it had begun to hit people around me, and it hit them hard. Some went almost crazy in their despair. For what? For more life. At the age of forty the life you have lived so far, always pro tem, has for the first time become *life* itself, and this reappraisal swept away all dreams, destroyed all your notions that real life, the one that was meant to be, the great deeds you would perform, was somewhere else. When you were forty you realised it was all here, banal everyday life, fully formed, and it always would be unless you did something. Unless you took one last gamble.

Yngve had done it because he wanted a better life. Dad did it because he wanted a radically different one. That was why I wasn't worried about Yngve, and actually never had been, he would always manage.

Vanja had fallen asleep in the buggy. Linda stopped, laid her on her back and glanced at the board on the pavement outside Blå Porten showing the meal of the day.

'In fact, I am hungry,' she said. 'How about you?'

'We could have some lunch,' I said. 'The lamb meatballs are good.'

It was a nice place. There was an open area in the middle, full of plants with a fountain, where you could sit in the summer. In the winter the centrepiece was a long corridor with glass walls. The only downside was the clientele, which for the most part consisted of cultured women in their fifties and sixties.

I held the door open for Linda, who pushed the buggy in, then grabbed the bar between the wheels and lifted it down the three steps. The room was just over half full. We chose the table furthest away in case Vanja woke up, and went to order. Cora was sitting at the window table at the back. She got up with a smile when she saw us.

'Hi!' she said. 'How good to see you both!'

She hugged first Linda, then me.

'Well?' she said. 'How are things?'

'Good,' Linda said. 'How about you?'

'Good. I'm here with my mother, as you can see.'

I nodded to her mother, whom I had met once, at one of Cora's parties. She nodded back.

'Are you here alone?' Cora asked.

'No, Vanja's over there,' Linda answered.

'Oh yes. Are you going to be here for a while?'

'Ye-es, I think so . . .' Linda said.

'I'll come over afterwards,' Cora said. 'Then I can have a peep at your daughter. Is that all right?'

'Of course,' Linda said, and went to the end of the counter, where we took our turn in the queue.

Cora was the first of Linda's friends I had met. She loved Norway and all things Norwegian, had lived there for some years and was prone to speaking Norwegian when she was drunk. She was the only Swede I had met who understood that there were big differences between our two countries, and she understood in the only way it could be understood, physically. The way people bump into each other in the street, in shops and on public transport. The way people in Norway always chat, in kiosks, queues and taxis. Her eyes had widened in surprise when she read Norwegian newspapers and saw the tone of debates. They really give each other a tongue-lashing! she said with enthusiasm. They give it everything they've got! They're not afraid of anything! Not only have they got every opinion under the sun and the courage to say things no Swede would ever say, they also do it while going at each other hammer and tongs. Oh, how liberating that is! Her reaction made it easier to get to know her than Linda's other friends, who were sociable in quite a different, formal and more polished way, not to mention the office collective where she had got me in. They were kind and friendly, often invited me to lunch, and just as often I declined, apart from a couple of occasions when I sat silently listening to their conversations. On one of the occasions they were discussing the imminent invasion of Iraq and the neighbouring eternal conflict between Israel and Palestine. Discussing is perhaps not the right word; it was more like small talk about the food or the weather. The following day I met Cora, and she told me her friend had resigned her post at the collective in a fury. Apparently there had been a heated exchange of opinions about the relationship between Israel and Palestine, she had lost her temper and resigned her post on the spot. And sure enough, her place had been cleared the next day. But I had been present! And I hadn't noticed anything! No aggression, no irritability, nothing. Only their friendly chatty voices and their elbows sticking out like chicken wings as they plied their knives and forks. This was Sweden, these were the Swedes.

But Cora also got annoyed that day. I told her that Geir had gone to Iraq two weeks before to write a book about the war. She said he was a conceited egotistical idiot. She wasn't a political person, so I was surprised by her violent reaction. In fact, there were tears in her eyes as she cursed him. Was her empathy that strong?

Her father had gone to the war in the Congo in the 1960s, she said then. He had worked as a war correspondent. It had destroyed him. Not that he had been injured or anything like that, nor that the experiences had shaken him in such a way that he bore mental scars; more the opposite, he wanted to go back, he wanted to have more of the life he had lived there, close to death, a need nothing in Sweden could fulfil. She told us a strange story about how he had ridden a motorbike at a circus afterwards, *the motorbike of death* she called it, and of course he had started drinking. He was destructive and had died by his own hand when Cora was young. The tears in her eyes were for him, she was grieving for him.

Fortunate then that she had such a strong, authoritative and strict mother?

Well, not necessarily . . . My impression was that she viewed Cora's life with some disapproval, and Cora took that more to heart than she should. Her mother was an accountant, and it was clear that Cora's wanderings in a vaguely cultural landscape did not quite correspond to her expectations of what constituted a suitable life for her daughter. Cora had earned her corn as a journalist on a variety of women's magazines, although that didn't leave much of a mark on her self-image, and she wrote poems, she was a poet. She had been to Biskops-Arnö, the writing school where Linda had also been, and she wrote good poetry from what I could judge; I heard her do a reading once and was surprised. Her poems were neither language poetry, which most young Swedish poets went in for, nor delicate or sensitive, like

those of the others, but something else, unrestrained and explor-
atory in a non-personal way, written in expansive language it
was difficult to associate with her. She remained, however,
unpublished. Swedish publishers were infinitely more budget-
conscious than their Norwegian counterparts and much more
careful, so if you didn't align yourself perfectly with the literary
surroundings you didn't have an earthly. If she held her nerve
and worked hard she would succeed in the end because she had
talent, but when you looked at her, endurance was not the first
quality to leap up at you. She was given to self-pity, spoke in a
low voice, often about depressing matters, although she could
also turn on a five-øre piece and be lively and interesting. When
she drank she could take centre stage and make a scene, the
only one of Linda's friends who would. Perhaps that was why I
found her so congenial?

Long hair hung down on either side of her face. The eyes
behind the small glasses had a kind of dog-like melancholy about
them. Whenever she drank, and occasionally when sober as well,
she expressed her great admiration for and feelings of identity
with Linda. Linda never really knew quite how to react.

I gently stroked Linda's back. The table we were standing beside
was covered with cakes of all shapes and sizes. Dark brown
chocolate, light yellow custard cream, greenish marzipan, pink
and white meringue kisses. A little flag with the name on every
dish.

'What would you like?' I asked.

'I don't really know . . . Chicken salad maybe. And you?'

'Lamb meatballs. I know what I'm getting then. But I can order
yours. You go and sit down.'

She did. I ordered, paid, poured water into two glasses, cut
some slices from the loaves at the end of the enormous cake
table, took some cutlery, grabbed a couple of small packets of

butter and some serviettes, put everything on a tray and stood beside the counter to wait for the food to be brought from the kitchen, the top half of which I could see over the swing door. In the atrium-style courtyard, tables and chairs stood unoccupied between all the green plants, which the grey concrete floor and the grey sky set off to perfection. The combination of these particular colours, grey and green, drew your eye. No artist would have known how to exploit them better than Braque. I remembered the prints I had seen in Barcelona when I was there with Tonje, of some boats on a beach under an immense sky, their almost shocking beauty. They had cost a few thousand kroner, too much, I had thought. When I reconsidered, it was too late: the next day, our last in Barcelona, a Saturday, I stood vainly pulling at the gallery door.

Grey and green.

But also grey and yellow, as in David Hockney's fantastic painting of lemons on a dish. Detaching colour from motif was modernism's most important achievement. Before it, pictures like Braque's or Hockney's would have been unthinkable. The question was whether it was worth the price, bearing in mind all the baggage it brought to art.

The café I was in belonged to Liljevalch's art gallery, whose rear was formed by the fourth and last wall of the garden area, and the cloistered passage at the top of the steps was a part of it. The last exhibition I had seen there was of Andy Warhol's work, which I was out of my depth to judge as far as quality was concerned, whatever perspective I took. This made me feel ultra-conservative and reactionary, which I certainly did not want to be and definitely didn't want to cultivate being. But what could I do?

The past is only one of many possible futures, as Thure Erik was wont to say. It wasn't the past you had to avoid and ignore, it was its ossification. The same applied to the present. And when the movement art cultivated became static, that was what you had to avoid and ignore. Not because it was modern, in tune with our times, but because it wasn't moving, it was dead.

'Lamb meatballs and chicken salad?'

I turned. A young man with pimples, a chef's hat and an apron stood behind the counter looking around with a plate in each hand.

'Yes, here,' I said.

I put the plates on the tray and carried it through the room to our table, where Linda was sitting with Vanja on her lap.

'Did she wake up?' I asked.

Linda nodded.

'I can take her,' I said. 'Then you can eat.'

'Thanks,' she said.

The offer didn't spring from altruism but self-interest. Linda often suffered from low blood glucose and became more and more irritable the longer it lasted. Having lived with her for close on three years I picked up the signals long before she herself was aware of them, the secret lay in details, a sudden move, a hint of black in her gaze, a touch of curtness in her responses. Then all you had to do was put food in front of her and it passed. Before coming to Sweden I had never even heard of this phenomenon, had no idea low blood glucose existed and was perplexed the first time I noticed the condition in Linda, why did she snap at the waitress? Why did she give a brief nod and look away when I asked her about it? Geir thought this phenomenon, which was widespread and well documented, was caused by the fact that all Swedes went to nursery schools and were given *mellanmål*, 'between-meals', all through the day. I was used to people getting moody because something had gone wrong or somebody had made an offensive remark or suchlike, in other words for more or less objective reasons, and I knew the moods of younger children were affected by whether they were hungry or not. I clearly had a lot to learn about the ways of the human mind. Or was it the Swedish mind? The female mind? The cultural middle-class mind?

I lifted Vanja and went to fetch one of the children's chairs inside the door by the entrance. With my daughter in one hand and the chair in the other I went back, took off her hat, romper suit and shoes and put her down. Her hair was unkempt, her face sleepy, but there was a glint in her eyes that offered hope of a quiet half an hour.

I cut off some bits of the meatballs and put them on the table in front of her. She tried to knock them away with a sweep of her arm, but the edge of the plastic table prevented her. Before she had time to pick them up and throw them one by one, I put them back on my plate. I leaned over and rummaged through the bag to see if there was something that might keep her occupied for a few minutes.

A tin lunch box, would that do the trick?

I removed the biscuits and put them on the edge of the table, then placed the box in front of her, took out my keys and dropped them in.

Objects that rattled and you could take out and put down were just what she needed. Satisfied with my solution, I sat at the table and began to eat.

The room around us was filled with the buzz of voices, the clink of cutlery and occasional muted laughter. In the short time that had elapsed since we arrived, the café had become almost full to the rafters. Djurgården was always crowded at the weekends and had been so for more than a hundred years. Not only were the parks spacious and beautiful, with more trees than park in some places, there were also lots of museums here. The Thielska

Gallery, with its death mask of Nietzsche and paintings by Munch, Strindberg and Hill; Waldemarsudde, the former residence of Prince Eugen, also an artist, the Nordic Museum, the Biological Museum, Skansen of course, with its zoo of Nordic animals and buildings from the whole of Sweden's history, all brought to light in the fantastic period at the end of the nineteenth century and the beginning of the twentieth, a strange mix of middle-class respectability, national romanticism, health fanaticism and decadence. The sole remnant was health fanaticism; Sweden had distanced itself from the rest, particularly national romanticism; now the ideal was not human uniqueness but equality, and not cultural uniqueness but multicultural society, hence all the museums here were museums of museums. This was especially true of the Biological Museum, which had stood unaltered since it was built some time at the beginning of the previous century and had the same display as then, various stuffed animals in a pseudo-natural environment against backgrounds painted by the great animal and bird artist Bruno Liljefors. In those days there were still enormous tracts of the planet untouched by humans, so its re-creation was not prompted by any necessity other than to provide knowledge; and the view it offered of our civilisation, namely that everything had to be translated into human terms, was occasioned not by need but by desire, by thirst; and the fact that this desire and thirst for knowledge, which was meant to expand the world, at one and the same time made it smaller, also physically, where what then had only just been started, and was therefore striking, had now been completed, made me want to cry every time I was there. The crowds of people walking along the canals and on the gravel paths, across the lawns and through the copses of trees at the weekend were in principle the same as at the end of the nineteenth century, and this reinforced the feeling: we were like them, just more lost.

A man of my age stood before me. There was something familiar about him, although I was unable to put my finger on what. He had a strong jutting chin and had shaved his head to hide the fact that he was beginning to go bald. His earlobes were podgy and there was a vaguely pink glow to his face.

'Is that chair free?' he asked.

'Yes, help yourself,' I said.

He carefully lifted it and carried it to the table adjacent to ours, where two women and a man in their sixties were sitting with a woman in her thirties and what had to be her two small children. A family outing with grandparents.

Vanja unleashed one of her dreadful screams, which she had started to do in recent weeks. She launched it from the bottom of her lungs. It went right through my nervous system and was unbearable. I looked at her. Both the tin box and the keys were on the floor beside the chair. I picked them up and placed them in front of her. She grabbed them and threw them down again. It could have been a game had it not been for the ensuing scream.

'Don't scream, Vanja,' I said. 'Please.'

I forked the last bit of potato, yellow against the white plate, and raised it to my mouth. While I was chewing I gathered the remaining pieces of meat on my plate, loaded them onto my fork with the knife, together with some onion rings from the salad, swallowed and lifted it to my mouth. The man who had taken the chair was on his way to the counter with the older man, whom I guessed to be his wife's father, since none of his facial features were recognisable in the older man's more ordinary face.

Where had I seen him before?

Vanja screamed again.

She was just impatient, no reason to get excited, I thought, as anger mounted in my chest.

I placed the cutlery on my plate and got up, looked at Linda, who would soon have finished as well.

'I'll take her for a little walk,' I said, 'just through the cloisters. Would you like a coffee afterwards or shall we have one elsewhere?'

'We can have one somewhere else,' she said. 'Or stay here.'

I rolled my eyes and leaned forward to pick up Vanja.

'Don't you roll your eyes at me,' Linda said.

'But I asked you a simple question,' I said. 'A yes-or-no question. Do you want to, or don't you? And you can't even answer.'

Without waiting for her response, I put Vanja down on the floor, took her hands and started to walk, with her leading the way.

'What do *you* want then?' Linda asked behind me. I pretended to be too busy with Vanja to hear. She moved one leg in front of the other, more in enthusiasm than pursuit of a particular destination, until we reached the steps, where I carefully let go of her hands. For a moment she stood upright and swayed. Then she went down on her knees and crawled up the three steps. Set off at full speed for the front door like a little puppy. When it was opened, she sat back on her haunches and peered up at the newcomers with saucer eyes. They were two elderly women. The one at the back stopped and smiled at her. Vanja cast down her eyes.

'She's a bit shy, isn't she?' the woman said.

I smiled politely, lifted Vanja and carried her into the courtyard outside. She pointed to some pigeons pecking at crumbs under a table. Then she looked up and pointed at a seagull sweeping past in the wind.

'Birds,' I said. 'And look over there, behind the windows. All the people.'

She glanced at me, then stared at the people. Her eyes were

alive, as expressive as they were open to impressions. When I looked into them I always had a sense of who she was, this very determined little person.

'Brr, it's so cold,' I said. 'Let's go in, shall we?'

From the steps I saw Cora had gone over to our table. Fortunately she hadn't sat down. She was standing behind the chair with her hands in her pockets and a smile on her lips.

'How big she is!' she said.

'Yes,' I said. 'How big is Vanja?'

Usually Vanja was proud when she could answer the question by stretching her arms above her head. But now she just leaned her head against my shoulder.

'We're on our way home. Aren't we?' I said, looking at Linda. 'It'll take half an hour to get a coffee now.'

She nodded.

'Yes, we have to go soon as well,' Cora said. 'But I've just arranged with Linda to pop round one day. So I'll see you soon.'

'That's nice,' I said. I sat Vanja on my lap and started to put on her romper suit. Smiled at Cora so as not to appear stand-offish.

'What's it like being a house husband?' she asked.

'Dreadful,' I replied. 'But I'm hanging in there.'

She smiled.

'I mean it,' I said.

'I got the message,' she said.

'Karl Ove's hanging in there,' Linda said. 'That's his method in life.'

'It's an honest answer, isn't it?' I said. 'Or would you rather I lied?'

'No,' Linda said. 'I'm just sorry you dislike it so much.'

'I don't dislike it *so much*,' I said.

'Mum's waiting over there,' Cora said. 'Nice to see you. And see you again soon.'

'Nice to see you too,' I said.

As she left I met Linda's glare.

'I didn't say anything out of place, did I?' I said, and put Vanja in the buggy, tightened the belt and kicked up the lever on the wheel.

'No,' Linda said with such vehemence that I knew she meant the opposite. Tight-lipped, she bent down and lifted the buggy when we came to the steps; tight-lipped, she walked beside me out of the courtyard and onto the road to the centre. It felt as if the wind was blowing straight into our bone marrow. Around us, everywhere was teeming with people. The bus stops on both sides were packed with shivering people clad in black, not unlike birds from a certain angle, the ones that hunch together and stand motionless on some cliff in the Antarctic, staring into the sky.

'It was so lovely and romantic yesterday,' she said at length as we passed the Biological Museum and caught fleeting glimpses of the gleaming black canal between the branches. 'And then there's nothing left of it today.'

'I'm not the romantic type, as you know,' I said.

'No, what type are you exactly?'

She wasn't looking at me as she said it.

'Cut it out,' I said. 'Don't start on that stuff again.'

I met Vanja's eyes and smiled at her. She lived in her own world, which was connected to ours through emotions and perceptions, physical touch and the sound of voices. Alternating between worlds, as I was now, being cross with Linda one moment and being happy with Vanja the next, was strange; it felt as though I was leading two quite separate lives. But she had only one, and soon she would be growing up into the second, when innocence was a distant memory and she understood what was going on between Linda and me at moments like this.

We reached the bridge over the canal. Vanja's head moved back and forth from one passer-by to the next. Whenever a dog came along or she saw a motorbike she pointed.

'The thought that we might be having another child made me so happy,' Linda said. 'It did yesterday and it does today. I've been thinking about it almost non-stop. A shot of happiness in my stomach. But you don't feel the same way. That makes me sad.'

'You're mistaken,' I said. 'I was happy too.'

'But you aren't now.'

'No,' I said. 'But is that so strange? I'm not in such a great mood.'

'Because you're at home with Vanja?'

'Among other things, yes.'

'Will it be better if you can write?'

'Yes.'

'Then we'll have to start Vanja at a nursery,' she said.

'Do you mean that?' I asked. 'She's so small.'

It was the middle of the rush hour for pedestrians, so on the bridge, which was a bottleneck on the route towards Djurgården, we were obliged to walk slowly. Linda held the buggy with one hand. Even though I hated that, I said nothing, it would have been too petty, especially now, during our discussion.

'Yes, she is much too small,' Linda said. 'But there's a waiting list of three months. By which time she'll be sixteen months old. She'll be too small then as well, but . . .'

We turned left when we came to the other side and walked along the quayside.

'What are you actually saying now?' I asked. 'On the one hand, you're saying she should go to a nursery. On the other, you're saying she's too small.'

'I think she's too small. But if it's absolutely imperative for

you to work then she'll have to go anyway. I can't exactly drop
my course.'

'There has never been any question of that happening. I've
said I would look after Vanja until the summer. And that she
can start nursery in the autumn. Nothing has happened to
change that.'

'But you're not happy.'

'Yes, but that's not perhaps such a big issue. At any rate, I
don't want to be Mr Nasty and send my child to the nursery too
early. Against Mrs Nice's will. For my own benefit.'

She stared at me.

'If you could choose, what would you do?'

'If I could choose, Vanja would start on Monday.'

'Even though you think she's too small?'

'Yes. But this is not only my decision, I believe?'

'No, but I agree. I'll phone on Monday and put her name on
the waiting list.'

We continued walking for a while in silence. To our right were
the most expensive and exclusive apartments in Stockholm. It
was impossible to have a more prestigious address. The buildings
reflected this. The façades gave nothing away, nothing penetrated
the walls, they could be best likened to castles or fortresses.
Inside were vast apartments containing twelve to fourteen rooms,
I knew that. Chandeliers, nobility, massive quantities of money.
Lives that were foreign to me.

The harbour was on the other side, pitch black to the edge of
the quay, white froth on the tips of the waves further out. The
sky was heavy and dark, the lights from the mass of buildings
on the other side dots in the vast greyness.

Vanja was whimpering and squirming in the buggy. She
slipped down and ended up on her side, which only made her
whimper more. When Linda bent forward and pulled her up,

she thought for an instant she would be lifted out of the buggy and let out a scream of frustration when that proved not to be the case.

'Stop for a moment,' Linda said. 'I'll see if we've got an apple or something in the bag.'

There was, and the very next second the frustration was gone. Vanja sat happily gnawing at the green apple while we continued towards the ferry.

Three months, that would be May. So I hadn't gained much more than two months. But it was better than nothing.

'Perhaps mummy can take Vanja for a couple of days a week as well,' Linda said.

'Well, that would be brilliant,' I said.

'We can ask her tomorrow.'

'I have a feeling she will say yes,' I said with a smile.

Linda's mother dropped everything and raced off as soon as one of her children needed help. And if there had been any limits before, they had certainly been removed now that a grandchild had come into the world. She worshipped Vanja and would do anything, absolutely anything for her.

'Are you happy now?' Linda asked, stroking my back.

'Yes,' I said.

'She'll be quite a lot bigger,' she said. 'Sixteen months. That's not *so* small.'

'Torje was ten months old when he started at nursery,' I said. 'And it doesn't seem to have left any visible scars at least.'

'And if I *am* pregnant, the birth will be in October. Then it'll be good if Vanja has some structure to her day.'

'I think you are.'

'I do too. No, I *know* I am. I've known ever since yesterday.'

When we reached the square in front of the Royal Dramatic Theatre and stopped to wait for the lights to change to green it

started snowing. The wind gusted round corners and over rooftops, leafless branches swayed, flags flapped wildly. The poor
birds on the wing were blown hopelessly off course above us.
We walked to the marketplace at the end of Biblioteksgatan,
where the hostage drama that shook all of Sweden and gave rise
to the concept of the Stockholm syndrome had taken place some
time in the innocent 1970s, and we followed one of the back-
streets up to NK, where we were going to do our food shopping
this evening.

'You can take her home if you like while I do the shopping,'
I said because I knew how much Linda disliked shops and malls.

'No, I want to be with you,' she said.

So we took the lift down to the food section in the basement,
bought Italian sausage, tomatoes, onions, leaf parsley and two
packets of rigatoni pasta, ice cream and frozen blackberries, took
the lift up to the floor where the Systembolaget was and bought
a litre carton of white wine for the tomato sauce, a carton of
red wine and a small bottle of brandy. On the way I bought the
Norwegian newspapers that had just appeared – *Aftenposten,
Dagbladet, Dagens Næringsliv* and *Verdens Gang* – as well as the
Guardian and *The Times* in case, but it was by no means guaran-
teed, I had an hour free to read over the weekend.

We arrived home at a few minutes past one. Sorting out the
flat, tidying up and cleaning took exactly two hours. On top of
that, there was an enormous pile of clothes that had to be
washed. But we had plenty of time: Fredrik and Karin wouldn't
be here before six.

Linda sat Vanja in her chair and heated a tin of baby food in
the microwave while I picked up all the rubbish bags that had
accumulated, not least the one in the bathroom, where the
nappies not only filled the bin and forced the lid into a vertical
position but also spilled out onto the floor, and carried them to

the refuse room on the ground floor. As it was the end of the week, the bulk containers were full to the brim. I opened all the lids and threw the various types of rubbish into their respective places: cardboard there, coloured glass there, clear glass there, plastic there, metal there, the rest to over there. As always I was able to confirm that a lot of drinking went on in this building; much of the cardboard was wine cartons and almost all the glass was wine and spirits. In addition, there were always big piles of illustrated magazines, the cheap newspaper supplements and the thicker, more specialist editions. In particular, fashion, interior design and country houses in this block. In the corner on the shortest wall there was a hole, provisionally nailed up, where some men had sawn through to get to the hairdressing salon next door. I had almost stumbled over them. One of the mornings when I got up at five I had been on my way outside with a cup of coffee in my hand and had heard the ear-piercing alarm in the salon as soon as I entered the hallway. Downstairs there was a security guard with a telephone to her ear. She stopped talking the second I appeared and asked if I lived here. I nodded. She said someone had just broken into the hairdressing salon and the police had been alerted. I went with her to the bicycle room, where the door had been smashed open, and I saw the half-metre-wide hole in the stud wall. I had a few jokes about vain thieves on the tip of my tongue, but I bit it. She was Swedish, either she wouldn't understand what I said or she wouldn't get the joke. One of the consequences of living here, I mused as I banged the container lids shut and unlocked the door to have a cigarette outside, was that I simply said less. I had stopped almost all the small talk, chatting to assistants in shops, waiters in cafés, conductors on trains and strangers in chance encounters. This was one of the best parts about returning to Norway: the ease of dealing with people I didn't know returned and my shoulders dropped. And also all the knowledge you possessed about your compatriots, which overwhelmed me when I stepped into the arrivals hall at Gardermoen, Oslo Airport: he comes from Bergen, she comes from Trondheim, him, he must be from Arendal, and her, wasn't she from Birkeland? The same applied to all nuances of society. What jobs people did, what their backgrounds were, everything was clear in seconds, while in Sweden it was always hidden from me. A whole world disappeared in this way. What must it be like to live in an African village? Or a Japanese village?

Outside, the wind buffeted me. The snow that had fallen was thick and wound its way across the tarmac in twists and turns, here and there it swirled up in veils, as though this was a mountain plateau I had stepped onto and not an urban backyard near the Baltic. I stood under the porch by the front entrance, where only sporadic, particularly wild, gusts of stinging snow could reach me. The pigeon stood motionless in its corner, totally unaffected by my presence and movements. The café on the other side of the street was packed, I could see, mostly with young people. Occasional passers-by walked, bent double, into the wind. All of them turned their heads towards me.

The break-in I had nearly witnessed was not an isolated example. As the block was in the city centre it was sometimes used by tramps. One morning I came across one in the basement laundry room, at the back, lying asleep by a washing machine, whose heat he had probably sought, like a cat. I had slammed the door, gone upstairs and waited for a few minutes, and when I returned he had left. Also in the basement I had bumped into a tramp one evening at around ten. I wanted something or other from our storage room and there he was, sitting against the wall, bearded with intense eyes, staring at me. I nodded, unlocked our door and left when I had got what I wanted. Of course, you should ring the police, there was an implicit fire risk, but they didn't bother me, so I let them be.

I stubbed my cigarette out on the wall and like a good tenant took it to the big ashtray, thinking seriously I would have to stop smoking soon. These days my lungs seemed to be burning. And how many years had I woken up in the morning with my throat full of thick mucus? But not today, it was never today, I said to myself half out loud, as I had got into the habit of doing lately, and let myself in.

While I was cleaning the flat I could always hear what Linda was doing with Vanja. She read to her, she found toys for her, which were mostly banged on the floor again and again – several times I was on the point of intervening, but our neighbour obviously wasn't in, so I let it go – she sang songs to her, she ate 'between-meals' with her. Sometimes they came to see me, Vanja dangling from Linda's arms, sometimes Linda tried to read a newspaper while Vanja was playing on her own, but not many minutes passed before she began to demand Linda's full attention. Which she always gave her. But I had to be wary about going in and giving my opinion, it didn't take much for it to be regarded as criticism. Having another child might loosen the tense dynamics. Having two certainly would.

When I had finished I sat down on the sofa with a pile of newspapers. The only jobs left were to iron the tablecloth, set the table and cook the food. But it was a simple meal, wouldn't take more than half an hour, so I had plenty of time. Darkness was drawing in. From the flat across the way came the sound of a guitar, it was the bearded forty-something practising his blues songs.

Linda stood in the doorway.

'Can you take Vanja?' she said. 'I need a break as well.'

'I've just sat down,' I said. 'I've cleaned the whole bloody flat, as I'm sure you've noticed.'

'And I've had Vanja,' she said. 'Do you consider that less demanding?'

Well, in fact, I did. I could have Vanja on my own *and* clean the flat. There were a few tears, but it worked fine. However, that was not a line I could take unless I wanted a head-on confrontation.

'No, I don't,' I said. 'But I have Vanja all week.'

'Me too,' she said. 'In the morning and in the afternoon.'

'Come on,' I said. 'I'm the one who's at home with her.'

'When I was at home with her, what did you do? Did you take her in the mornings and the afternoons? And did I perhaps go to the café every day when you came home, like you do now?'

'OK,' I said. 'I'll have her. Sit down.'

'Not if you take that kind of attitude. I'll have her myself.'

'Surely it doesn't matter what kind of attitude I have? I take her, you get a break. Simple. Everyone happy.'

'And you keep going out and having cigarette breaks. I don't. Have you thought about that?'

'You'll have to start smoking then,' I said.

'Perhaps I will,' she said.

I walked past her, without meeting her stare, to Vanja, who was sitting on the floor and blowing into a recorder which she held in one hand while waving the other up and down. I stood by the windowsill and crossed my arms. I was definitely not going to fulfil Vanja's every little wish. She had to be able to survive a few minutes without being fully occupied, like other children.

From the living room I could hear Linda flicking through the newspaper.

Should I tell her she could iron the tablecloth, set the table and cook the food? Or act surprised and say she was responsible for that now, when she came to take care of Vanja again? We had swapped, hadn't we?

An acrid fetid smell began to spread through the room. Vanja had stopped blowing into the recorder and was sitting still and staring into the distance. I turned and looked out of the window. Snowflakes being blown through the street below, where the gleam from the hanging lights picked them out, but which were invisible until the moment they hit the window with a tiny, barely perceptible tap. The door of US Video forever opening and closing. Cars going past at intervals regulated by traffic lights out of my eyeshot. Windows in the flats opposite, which were so far away that residents were only visible as vague intrusions in the subdued light of the panes.

I turned back.

'Have you finished now?' I asked Vanja and met her eyes. She smiled. I took her under my arms and threw her onto the bed. She started laughing.

'I'm going to change you now,' I said. 'It's important that you lie still. Have you got that?'

I lifted her and threw her again.

'Have you got that, you little troll?'

She laughed so much she could hardly breathe. I pulled off her trousers and she wriggled round and tried to crawl up the bed. I grabbed her ankles and dragged her back.

'Lie still, will you. Do you understand?' I said, and for a moment it was as though she did understand, because she was lying quite still and staring at me with her round eyes. With one hand I lifted her legs into the air while releasing the tabs with the other and removing her nappy. Then she tried to wriggle free, squirmed round and because I had a tight grip on her, she contorted like some epileptic.

'No, no, no,' I said, throwing her back onto the bed. She laughed, I pulled some wipes from the packet as fast as I could, she swung round again, I pressed her down and wiped her clean while breathing through my nose and trying not to react to the irritation I could feel was brewing inside me now. I had forgotten to put the full nappy away, she had her whole foot in it, I nudged it to the side and wiped her foot, somewhat half-heartedly, because I knew wipes were no longer up to the job. I lifted her and carried her to the bathroom, where with Vanja kicking and struggling under my arm I took the showerhead from the holder, turned on the water, adjusted it until it was warm on the back of my hand and began to spray the lower half of her body carefully while she gripped the ends of the yellow shower curtain. Once this was done I dried her with a towel and got her into a new nappy, after thwarting another bid for freedom. All that was left to do was to dispose of the used one, put it in a plastic bag, tie a knot and chuck it outside the front door.

Linda was skimming through the newspaper in the living room. Vanja banged one of the building bricks she had been given as an autumn present by Öllegård on the floor. I lay back on the bed with my arms behind my head. The next moment there was a thunderous knocking on the pipes.

'Don't take any notice of her,' Linda said. 'Let Vanja play as she likes.'

But I couldn't. I got up, went over to Vanja and took the brick from her. And handed her a cloth lamb instead. She threw it away. Even when I put on a silly voice and bounced the lamb back and forth she still wasn't interested. It was the brick she wanted; she was attracted by the sound of it banging on the floor. Well, she can have it then. She took two from the box and began to bang them on the floor. The very next second the pipes thundered again. What was this? Was she standing there and *waiting*? I took one of the bricks from the box and hammered it with all my strength against the radiator. Vanja watched me and laughed. The next second I heard the door below slam again. I went through the living room into the hallway. When the bell rang I snatched open the door. The Russian was looking at me with a furious expression on her face. I stepped out so that I was only a few centimetres from her.

'What the HELL do you want?' I shouted. 'What do you BLOODY mean by coming up here? I don't want you here. Don't you UNDERSTAND?'

She hadn't expected that. She recoiled, tried to say something, but as the first word escaped her lips I went on the attack again.

'NOW PISS OFF!' I shouted. 'IF YOU COME HERE AGAIN I'LL CALL THE POLICE.'

At that moment a woman in her fifties came up the stairs. She was one of the people who lived on the floor above. She looked down at the floor as she passed. Nevertheless, a witness. Perhaps that gave the Russian courage because she didn't go.

'DON'T YOU UNDERSTAND WHAT I SAID? OR ARE YOU A RETARD? GO AWAY, I SAID. GO, GO, GO!'

After saying this I took another step towards her. She turned and set off down the stairs. After a couple of steps she turned back to me.

'This will have consequences,' she said.

'I don't give a shit,' I said. 'Who do you think they'll believe? A lonely alcoholic Russian or an established couple with a small child?'

Then I closed the door and went back in. Linda stood looking at me from the living-room doorway. I walked past without a glance.

'That wasn't perhaps the wisest move,' I said. 'But it felt good.'

'I can imagine,' she said.

I went into the bedroom and took the bricks from Vanja, put them in the box, which I put on top of the dresser so that she couldn't reach them. To distract her from the despondency she felt I lifted her and put her on the windowsill. We watched cars for a while. But I was too angry to be able to stand still for long, so I sat her back on the floor and went into the bathroom, where I washed my hands – they were always so cold in winter – in warm water, dried them, studied my reflection, which did not betray a single one of the thoughts or feelings stirring inside me. Perhaps my clearest childhood legacy was that loud voices and aggression frightened me. I hated rows and scenes. And for a long time I had managed to avoid them in my adult life. There hadn't been any slanging matches in any of the relationships I'd had; any disagreements had proceeded according to my method, which was irony, sarcasm, unfriendliness, sulking and silence. It was only when Linda came into my life that this changed. And how it changed. As for me, I was afraid. It wasn't a rational fear, physically I was stronger than she was, of course, and as far as the balance of the relationship was concerned she needed me more than I needed her, in the sense that I had no problem being alone, being alone was not only an option for me, it was also an enticement, whereas she feared being alone more than anything; however, despite the fact that I was in a stronger position, I was afraid when she had a go at me. Afraid in the way I was afraid when I was a boy. Oh, I was not proud of this, but so what? It wasn't something I could control by thought or will, it was something quite different, which was released in me, anchored deeper, down in what was perhaps the very foundation of my personality. All of this, though, was unknown to Linda. You couldn't see that I was frightened. When I defended myself my voice would break because I was on the verge of tears, but to her that could easily have been caused by my anger, for all I knew. No, now that I came to think about it, somewhere inside her she must have known. But perhaps not the precise extent of how awful the experience was for me.

I suppose I must have learned from it. To shout at someone, the way I had done with the Russian, would have been inconceivable only a year ago. In this case, however, there would never be any reconciliation. From now on further escalation was the only possible outcome.

And so?

I took the four blue Ikea bags full of dirty laundry, which I had completely forgotten, and carried them into the hall. Put on my shoes and said aloud that I was going down to the basement to do the washing. Linda came to the door.

'Do you have to do it now?' she asked. 'They'll be coming soon. And we haven't started cooking yet . . .'

'It's only half past four,' I said. 'And we don't have another washing slot until Thursday.'

'OK,' she said. 'Are we friends?'

'Yes,' I answered. 'Of course.'

She came to me and we kissed.

'I love you, you know,' she said.

Vanja crawled in from the living room. She grabbed hold of Linda's trouser leg and pulled herself up.

'Hello, do you want to join us?' I said, lifting her up. She put her head between ours. Linda laughed.

'Good,' I said. 'Then I'll go and get a machine started.'

With two bags in each hand I staggered down the stairs. I put out of my mind the unease I felt at thoughts of the neighbour, the fact that she was totally unpredictable and now, in addition, deeply hurt. What was the worst that could happen? She wasn't exactly going to launch herself at me with a knife. Revenge behind closed doors, that was her forte.

The staircase was empty, the hallway was empty, the laundry room was empty. I switched on the light, sorted the clothes into four heaps, coloureds forty, coloureds sixty, whites forty, whites sixty, and shoved two of the piles into the two big machines, poured powder into the detachable drawer on the control panel and switched them on.

When I went back up Linda had put some music on, one of the Tom Waits CDs that had come out after I lost interest in him and with which I therefore had no associations other than that they were Tom Waits-like. Once Linda had reworked some Waits texts for a performance in Stockholm, which she said was among the most entertaining and satisfying stuff she had done, and she still had an intense, indeed intimate, relationship with his music.

She had fetched glasses, cutlery and plates from the kitchen and put them on the table. A cloth was there too, still folded, and a pile of creased serviettes.

'Think we'll have to iron them, don't you?' she said.

'Yes, if we're going to have a tablecloth. Could you iron it and I'll make a start on the cooking?'

'OK.'

She fetched the ironing board from the cupboard while I went to the kitchen and took out the ingredients. Put a cast-iron pot on the stove, switched on the hotplate, poured in some oil, peeled and chopped garlic, then Linda came in for the spray in the cupboard under the sink. She shook it a little to see if there was any water in it.

'Are you cooking without a recipe?' she asked.

'I know it off by heart now,' I answered. 'How many times have we made this meal now? Twenty?'

'But they haven't had it before,' she said.

'No,' I said, holding the chopping board over the pot and

letting the tiny cubes of garlic fall into it while she went back to the living room.

Outside, it was still snowing, quieter now though. It struck me that in two days I would be back in the office and a frisson of pleasure ran through me. Perhaps Ingrid would even be able to have Vanja three times a week and not just twice? I desired no more of life, in fact. I wanted to have some peace, and I wanted to write.

Of Linda's friends, Fredrik was the one she had known longest. They had met when they were working on costumes at the Royal Dramatic Theatre as sixteen-year-olds and had maintained contact ever since. He was a film director working mostly on commercials while waiting to make his first feature film. His clients were big names, the adverts were constantly on TV, so I assumed he was good at what he did and earned a packet. He had made three shorts, for which Linda had written the scripts, and a slightly longer film. He had close-set blue eyes and blond hair. His head was big, his body thin and there was something evasive about his character, also vague perhaps, which made it difficult for you to know where you were with him. He giggled rather than laughed and had a cheery disposition, both of which could lead you to draw hasty conclusions about him. His cheery nature didn't necessarily hide greater depths or gravity, rather it functioned in ways that were not readily apparent. There was something latent in Fredrik, what, I didn't know, but the fact that there was, which one day would metamorphose into a brilliant film perhaps, perhaps not, intrigued me. He was astute and fearless, and must have discovered many years ago that he didn't have much to lose. At least that was how I read his character. Linda said that his greatest strength as a director was that he was so good at dealing with actors, giving them exactly what

they needed to achieve optimal performances, and when I saw
him I could see that, for he was a friendly soul who flattered
everyone he met, and his innocuous appearance allowed you to
feel strong while the calculating side of his nature knew how
to exploit the benefits this accrued. The actors were welcome to
discuss their characters and attempt to find what made them
tick, but they were not allowed to see the entirety, where the
meaning lay, no one knew that apart from him.

I liked him, but couldn't talk to him and I tried to avoid any
situations where we were left in each other's company. As far
as I could gather, he did the same.

I didn't know Karin, his partner, so well. She was at the same
college as Linda, at DI, but on a screenplay-writing course. Since
I also wrote I ought to have been able to relate to her work, but
the craft side was so prominent in writing a screenplay, where
it was about all manner of ebbs and flows of tension, character
development, plots and subplots, intros and turning points, I
assumed I would have little to contribute in that respect and
never mobilised more than polite interest. She had black hair,
narrow brown eyes and her face, also narrow, was white. She
radiated a business-like manner which went well with Fredrik's
more flippant and childlike character. They had one child and
were expecting another. Unlike us, they had everything under
control, there was order in the home, they went out with their
child and organised interesting activities. After we had been to
theirs, or they had been to ours, that was often what Linda and
I discussed: how on earth what appeared to be so simple for
them could be so utterly beyond our capability.

There was a lot to suggest we could make friends with them
as a couple: we were the same age, we worked in the same areas,
belonged to the same culture and we both had children. But
there was always a piece missing, it was always as though we

were standing on opposite sides of a small chasm, the conversation was always tentative, we never really found the right tone. But the few times we did it was to everyone's relief and pleasure. Much of the reason it did not really work was me: my great expanses of silence and the slight discomfort that came over me when I did say something. This evening proceeded by and large as always. They arrived at a few minutes after six, we exchanged polite pleasantries, Fredrik and I each had a gin and tonic, we sat down and ate, asked one another about various matters, how this and that were going, and it was, as always, clear how much more adept they were at this than we were, or at least than I was. Taking the initiative – suddenly talking about something I had experienced or thought in an attempt to get the conversation going – was beyond me. Linda didn't do this very often either, her strategy was rather to home in on them, ask about something and play it by ear from there, unless she felt so secure and good in herself that she held the floor with the same ease that I did not. If she did, it was a great evening; there would be three players who didn't give the game a single thought.

They praised the food, I cleared the table, put on some coffee and set the table for dessert while Karin and Frederik settled their child down in the bedroom beside where Vanja was already asleep in her cot.

'By the way, your flat was on Norwegian TV just before Christmas,' I said when their son had fallen asleep and they had both sat down again and helped themselves to hot blackberries and ice cream.

'Your flat' was my office, actually a one-room flat with a bathroom and a small kitchenette which I rented from Fredrik.

'Oh yes?' he said.

'I was interviewed by *Dagsrevyen*, the Norwegian TV news programme. At first they wanted to do it here. I said no, of course. Then they'd heard I was looking after our child at the moment and wondered if they could film me with Vanja. I said no again, of course. But they persisted. They didn't need to film her, the buggy would be enough. What about if I pushed the buggy through town and then handed Vanja over to Linda – before the interview started as it were? What could I say?'

'What about no?' Fredrik said.

'But I had to throw them a bone. They absolutely refused to do it in a café or anything like that. It had to be *about* something. So the interview was in your office, plus I went looking for an angel to buy for Vanja in the Old Town. Oh, it was so stupid it could drive you to tears. But that's what it's like. They need to have something.'

'Turned out well though,' Linda said.

'No, it didn't,' I said. 'But I find it hard to understand how it could have been better in fact. Under the circumstances.'

'So you're big in Norway then, are you?' Fredrik said with a knowing look.

'No, no, no,' I said. 'It's just because I was nominated for a prize.'

'Aha,' he said. Then he laughed. 'I was just winding you up. But in fact I've just read an excerpt from your novel in a Swedish journal. It was immensely evocative.'

I smiled at him.

To divert attention from the fact that there had been a touch of smugness about the theme I had just introduced, I got up and said, 'Ah, I almost forgot. We bought a little bottle of cognac for the meal today. Would you like some?' And I was on my way to the kitchen before he could answer. On my return, the conversation had turned to alcohol and breastfeeding, which a doctor had told Linda was not a problem, at least in moderation, but she wasn't taking any chances as the Swedish health authorities recommended total abstinence. Alcohol and pregnancy were one thing, when the foetus was in direct contact with the mother's blood, breastfeeding was quite another. From there it was a swift jump to pregnancies in general and then to births. I chimed in with something or other, added a snippet here and there and otherwise listened in silence for the main part. Births are an intimate and sensitive topic of conversation for women, there is a lot of covert prestige, and as a man the only possible option is to keep well away. To refrain from expressing an opinion. Which both Fredrik and I did. Until the subject of Caesareans came up. Then I couldn't restrain myself any longer.

'It's absurd that Caesareans are an alternative form of giving birth,' I said. 'If there are no medical grounds for it, if the mother is hale and hearty, why should you cut open the belly and take the baby out that way? I watched an operation on TV once and, hell, it was cruel: one minute the baby's inside, the next it's out in the light. That must be a terrible shock for the child. And for the mother. Birth is a transition and it's slow. It's meant to be a way of preparing the mother and the baby. I don't doubt for a second that it happens in this way for a reason, that there's some meaning in it. However, like this, you forgo the whole process and everything that is set in motion within the child during that time and which takes place completely outside our control, because it's simpler to cut open the belly and take out the baby. It's sick, if you ask me.'

Silence. The mood was broken. Linda looked embarrassed. I gathered that I had unwittingly crossed a line. The situation had to be saved, but as I didn't know what I had done wrong, it wouldn't be by me. Instead it was Fredrik.

'A genuine reactionary Norwegian!' he said with a smile. 'And an author on top of that. Hail Hamsun!'

I eyed him in amazement. He winked at me and smiled again.

For the rest of the evening he called me Hamsun. Hey, Hamsun, is there any coffee left in the pot? he would say, for example. Or: What do you reckon, Hamsun? Should we move into the country or continue living in towns?

The latter was a topic we often discussed, for not only were we thinking about moving from Stockholm, perhaps to one of the islands along the south or west coast of Norway, but Fredrik and Karin were also toying with the idea, especially Fredrik, who cherished romantic notions of a life on a smallholding in a forest somewhere and would occasionally even show us places for sale they had found on the Net. But the Hamsun twist at the end suddenly cast our motivation in a completely new light. And all because I had said that a Caesarean might not be the best way to give birth to a child.

How was it possible?

After they had gone, effusive with their 'Thanks for a nice evening' and 'We must do this again,' and after I had tidied the room, cleared the table and switched on the dishwasher I sat up for a bit while Linda and Vanja slept in the bedroom. I wasn't used to drinking any more, so I could feel the cognac, a warm flame burning behind my thoughts and casting a glow of abandon over them. I wasn't drunk though. After sitting still on the sofa for half an hour, without thinking about anything special, I went into the kitchen, drank a few glasses of water, took an apple and sat down in front of the computer. When it started I went into Google Earth. Slowly rotated the globe, found the tip of South America and moved gently upwards, first from a great distance, until I saw a fjord cutting into the land mass and zoomed in. A river came down a valley, rugged mountains soared sharply on one bank, on the other the river branched into what appeared to be a wetlands area. Further out, by the edge of the fjord, lay a town, Rio Gallegos. The streets dividing it into blocks were as straight as a ruler. From the size of the cars I concluded the buildings were low. Most of them had flat roofs. Broad streets, low buildings, flat roofs: the province. The habitations became more and more sparse closer to the sea. The beaches seemed abandoned with the exception of some harbour areas. I zoomed out again and saw the green gleam of scattered patches of shallow water off the shoreline and the dark blue where it was deeper. The clouds hanging over the surface of the sea. Then I continued up the coast of this desolate countryside, which must have been Patagonia, and stopped by another town, Puerto Deseado. It was small and had something desert-like and golden about it. There was a mountain in the centre, with very few buildings, and there were two lakes, which looked dead. By the sea was a refinery plant with quays alongside huge tankers. The countryside around the town consisted of tall unoccupied vegetation-less mountains, the odd narrow road winding inwards, a lake or two, a valley or two with rivers, trees and houses. I moved away again and zoomed in on Buenos Aires on the Rio Plata opposite Montevideo, chose a place by the coastline and focused on the airport. The planes stood close to the terminal like a flock of white birds, a stone's throw from the water, which was bordered by a tree-lined road. I followed it and arrived at what seemed like three enormous swimming pools in the middle of a park. What could it be? I zoomed in closer. Aha! An aqua park! Beyond, I knew, on the other side of the road in the great open space it traversed was the River Plate Stadium. The width of it was striking, there was not only a running track around the pitch, outside it on two sides were also two semicircles of turf before the towering stands. The World Cup final between Holland and Argentina, which was played here in 1978, was one of the first I could remember seeing on TV. All the white confetti, the huge crowd, Argentina's blue and white striped shirts and

Holland's orange against the green of the grass. Holland, who lost a second final in a row. Then I came out again, found the river a bit further up and followed it downwards. Heavy industry on both sides, docks with cranes and big ships, crossed by road and rail bridges. Several football pitches here too. Where the river flowed into the centre of town the boats appeared to be more for pleasure. Behind it was the district with all the colourful timber buildings, I knew that. La Boca. Beneath it an eight-lane motorway crossed the river, and I followed that instead. It bordered the harbour for a while. Great barges on both sides. Perhaps ten blocks further was the city centre with its parks, monuments and magnificent buildings. I zoomed in on where the Teatro Cervantes ought to be, but the image resolution was too poor, everything blurred into contourless green and grey, so I switched off, had a final glass of water in the kitchen, went to the bedroom and lay down beside Linda.

The next morning we went to Central Station early to catch the suburban train to Gnesta, where Linda's mother lived. A roughly five-centimetre layer of snow covered the streets and roofs. The sky above us was leaden grey with glimmers of light in places. There were not many people up and about, naturally enough, it was a Sunday morning. The odd partygoer wending his way home, the odd pensioner walking a dog and as we approached the station the odd prospective passenger trundling a bag. A young man sat on the platform and slept with his chin resting on his chest. Behind him a crow was pecking in a rubbish bin. Further away, a train drew alongside the platform without stopping. The electronic display board above us showed no signs of life. Linda walked up and down the edge of the platform wearing the white calf-length coat I had bought in London for her thirtieth birthday, a white woollen hat and a white scarf with some rose-like embroidery, which I had given her for Christmas and I gathered she didn't really like, even though it suited her very well. Both the colour – she always looked good in white – and the pattern were as romantic as she was. The cold made her cheeks red, her eyes moist and shiny. She clapped her hands a couple of times and jogged on the spot. From the escalator came a fat woman in her fifties with a roller bag on either side of her. Behind her was a girl of around sixteen dressed in dark clothes with black mascara round her eyes, black finger mittens, black hat and long blonde hair. They stood next to each other by the edge of the platform. Mother and daughter they must have been, even though it was hard to discern any similarity.

'Tu whoo tu whoo!' Vanja said, pointing to two pigeons that strutted over. She had just learned to imitate an owl in one of the books we were reading to her, and now it was the sound all birds made.

Her facial features were so small, I thought. Small eyes, small nose, small mouth. Not that she was small, but she would always have small facial features, you could already see. Not least when you saw her beside Linda. They didn't resemble each other in any direct, obvious way, but the family likeness was still apparent, especially in the proportions of their features. Linda also had small eyes and a small mouth and nose. My features were, apart from eye colour and perhaps the almond-shaped upper part of the eye, nowhere to be seen. But now and then she had expressions I recognised – they were Yngve's, he'd had that look when he was growing up.

'Yes, two pigeons,' I said, crouching in front of her. She looked at me expectantly. I lifted the flap of her leather hat and whispered in her ear. She laughed. At that moment the board above us came to life. Gnesta, track two, three minutes.

'Doesn't look like she wants to sleep,' I said.

'No,' said Linda. 'It's a bit too early.'

Sitting still and being strapped in were not Vanja's favourite pastimes, unless she was in the buggy and moving, so on trips to Gnesta, which took an hour, we had to keep her constantly occupied. To and fro down the aisle, up to the windows and the glass in the doors, if we couldn't hold her attention with the aid of a book, a game or a packet of raisins, which might divert her for up to half an hour. Provided the train was not crowded this was not a problem, as long as you hadn't planned to read a newspaper, as I had today, the entire pile from yesterday was in my bag, but in the rush hour when these carriages were packed with people it could be unpleasant, a tired child screaming for an hour, nowhere to walk with her, it was a wearing experience. We often did this journey. Not only because Linda's mother could look after Vanja and we would have a few hours to ourselves, but also because we, or at least I, liked being there so much. Farms, animals grazing, vast forests, small gravel paths, lakes, clear fresh air. Dense black night, starry sky, total silence.

The train drew slowly into the platform, we got on board and sat on the seats by the door, where there was room for the buggy, I lifted Vanja and let her stand on the seat with her hands against the window to watch as the carriages slipped through the tunnel and onto the bridge over Slussen. The ice-bound snow-covered water shone white against the yellow and reddish brown of the houses and the steep black mountainside of Mariaberget, where the snow had not settled. The clouds in the sky to the east had a gentle golden hue, as though lit from the inside by the sun, which was behind them. We entered the tunnel underneath Söder and when we emerged we were high above the water on a bridge leading to the land on the other side, at first a mass of high-rise buildings and one satellite town after another, thereafter residential areas and detached houses until the ratio of buildings to nature was inverted and it was villages which appeared as small units in great expanses of forest and lake.

White, grey, black, isolated patches of dark green, those were the colours of the countryside through which we passed. Last summer I came here every day. We lived with Ingrid and Vidar for the last two weeks of June and I commuted between Gnesta and Stockholm, where I wrote. It was the perfect life. Up at six, a slice of bread for breakfast, a smoke and a cup of coffee on the front doorstep, pre-warmed by the sun, with a view of the meadow up to the edge of the forest, then cycle to the station, the sandwiches Ingrid had made for me in my rucksack, read on the train into Stockholm, walk to the office, write, travel back at around six through the vibrant sun-filled forest, cycle across the fields to the little house, where they were waiting with dinner, perhaps have an evening dip in the lake with Linda, sit outside reading and go to bed early.

One day the forest had been on fire alongside the railway line. That had also looked fantastic. A whole hillside, only a few metres from the train, ablaze. Flames licking up tree trunks, other trees fully alight. Orange tongues drifting across the ground, shrubs and bushes, everything illuminated by the same summer sun, which along with the thin blue sky seemed to make what was happening transparent.

Oh, this fulfilled me, it was sublime, it was the world opening up.

Vidar got out of his car in Gnesta station car park as the train pulled in and he was waiting for us with a little smile playing on his lips as we walked towards him a moment later. He was seventy-something years old, had a white beard and white hair, was a touch stooped but in robust health, which was borne out by his tanned complexion, a product of a life spent very much outdoors, and the sharp, intelligent, yet somewhat evasive, blue eyes. I knew next to nothing about what he had done in life, apart from the little Linda had told me and what I could deduce from appearances. Although he touched on many topics in the course of a weekend, it was rare for them to include anything about himself. He had grown up in Finland and still had family there, but spoke Swedish without an accent. He was an authoritative but in no way domineering man who liked to socialise with people. He read a lot, both newspapers, which he scoured from front to back, and literature, in which he was uncommonly well versed. His age revealed itself perhaps first and foremost in the viewpoints he stoutly defended; although there were not many, they could, as I had seen, occupy a great deal of space. These sides of his personality didn't affect me, only Ingrid and Linda, whom he treated as one, and Linda's brother. I suppose this was partly because I was new to the family and partly, I assumed, because I liked to hear him talk and was actually interested in what he had to say. The fact that our conversations were one-sided, as my contributions amounted to no more than questions and an unending series of short responses such as 'Yes,' 'Oh, yes,' 'Really?' 'Mm,' 'I see,' 'How interesting,' seemed to me only natural, for we were not equal, he was twice my age and had a long life behind him. Linda didn't really understand this. Many was the time she called for me or came to get me, convinced that I needed to be saved from a boring conversation I was too polite to extricate myself from on my own. Now and then this was indeed the case, but more often than not my interest was genuine.

'Hi, Vidar,' Linda said, pushing the buggy behind the car.

'Hi,' he said. '*Trevligt* to see you again.'

Linda lifted Vanja out, I folded up the buggy and put it in the boot, which Vidar opened for me.

'And now the car seat,' I said, passing it through the rear door, lifting Vanja in and attaching the seat belts.

Vidar drove as many older men did, hunched over the wheel, as though the few extra centimetres closer to the windscreen were decisive for good vision. In daylight he was a good driver – that spring, for example, we had been with him for four hours in one stretch when we went to Idö, where his country house was – but as darkness descended over the roads I felt a lot less secure. A few weeks ago we had almost run over one of the neighbours walking by the gravel track. I saw him from afar and assumed Vidar had done so as well and hadn't changed course because he was going to veer away a few metres before. But this wasn't the case, he hadn't seen him, and only a combination of my shout and the neighbour's presence of mind – he jumped into a bush – prevented an accident.

We turned out of the station car park and onto the main road, which was the only one in Gnesta.

'Everything all right with you?' Vidar enquired.

'Yes,' I answered. 'Can't grumble.'

'We had frightful weather last night,' he said. 'Several trees keeled over. Then the power went at home. But I suppose they'll fix it during the morning. What was it like in town?'

'Well, there was a bit of a wind as well,' I said.

We turned left, crossed the little bridge and came to the huge field where white hay bales were still piled up by the road. After a kilometre we turned off again and drove onto the gravel track through the forest, which mostly consisted of deciduous trees, between whose trunks a meadow looking like a small lake was visible on one side, bordered by bare rock and a swathe of evergreens growing over it. Hardy longhorn cattle grazed here all year round. A hundred metres further on there was a grass track leading up to Ingrid and Vidar's house, while the road continued for a couple of kilometres or so until it ended by grassland in the middle of the forest.

Ingrid was waiting for us outside the house when we arrived. She hurried over to the car as it stopped and opened the rear door where Vanja was.

'Oh, my little sweetheart!' she said with her hand on her bosom. 'How I have been looking forward to seeing you!'

'Just pick her up if you want,' Linda said, opening the door on the other side. While Ingrid lifted Vanja and held her out to have a look at her and then hugged her, I removed the buggy from the boot, unfolded it and pushed it towards the front door.

'Hope you're hungry,' Ingrid said. 'Because lunch is ready.'

The house was small and old. There was forest on all sides of the property, apart from at the front, where there was an open field. In the evenings and at dawn the deer would emerge there from the forest on the other side and frolic. I had also seen foxes running and hares leaping around. Originally the house had been a smallholding and it still bore the marks: even though the two rooms constituting the house had been augmented with a kitchen and bathroom annexe, Ingrid and Vidar still didn't have many square metres to live in. The living room was dark and crammed with all sorts, and in the bedroom behind there was scarcely space for much more than two built-in beds and some shelves of books on one wall. In addition, there was an earth cellar some way behind the house, a newly erected cabin with two beds and a television, and at the very top of the plot a combined workshop and wood store. When we came to stay Vidar and Ingrid moved into the cabin so we had the house to ourselves in the evening. There was little I liked better than being here, lying on the bed near the coarse old wooden beams with the starry sky visible through the window above, surrounded by darkness and silence. The last time we had been here I had read Calvino's *The Baron in the Trees*, the time before that Wijkmark's *The Draisine*, and what made both of these reading experiences fantastic must have been as much to do with the surroundings and the atmosphere I was imbued with as the actual content of the books. Or was it rather that the atmospheric space these books created had a special resonance in the world in which I found myself? For I had read a novel by Thomas Bernhard before Wijkmark and nothing in it came even close to charging me in the same way. No space was opened to me in Bernhard, everything was closed off in small chambers of reflection, and even though he had written one of the most frightening and shocking novels I had read, *Extinction*, I didn't want to look down that road, I didn't want to go down that road. Hell, no, I wanted to be as far from that which was closed and mandatory as it was possible to be. *Come on! Into the open, my friend*, as Hölderlin had written somewhere. But how, how?

I sat down on the chair by the window. A pot of meat broth was steaming in the middle of the table. A basket of fresh home-made bread rolls beside it, along with a bottle of mineral water and three cans of *folköl*, Swedish low-alcohol beer. Linda put Vanja in the baby seat at the end of the table, sliced a roll in half, gave it to her and then went to warm up a jar of baby food in the microwave. Linda's mother took over and Linda sat down next to me. Vidar sat on the opposite side of the table rubbing his bearded chin between thumb and forefinger and watching us with a little smile on his face.

'OK,' Ingrid shouted from the kitchen. 'Just start all of you!'

Linda stroked my arm. Vidar nodded to her. She began to ladle soup into the bowls. Pale green rings of leek, orange slices of carrot, yellowy pieces of kohlrabi and large grey pieces of meat, with reddish fibres in places, shiny, bluish surfaces in others. The flat white bones it was attached to, some smooth like polished stones, others coarse and porous. All swimming in the hot broth, in the fat that would stiffen as soon as the heat was gone, but which was floating around now like small almost transparent beads and bubbles in the cloudy liquid.

'It's as delicious as always,' I said, looking at Ingrid, who was sitting beside Vanja and blowing on the food for her.

'Good,' she said, and met my eyes fleetingly, then put the plastic spoon in the plastic dish and held it to Vanja's mouth, which, for a change, was as open as a fledgling chick's. When we came here Ingrid would automatically take over everything to do with Vanja. Food, nappies, clothes, sleep, fresh air, she wanted to do the lot. She had bought a high chair, children's plates and cutlery, feeding bottles, games and even an extra buggy, which was always here ready for use, as well as all the jars of baby food, baby porridge and purée in the cupboard. If we were short of something, if Linda for example asked for an apple or was concerned that Vanja might have a bit of a temper-ature, she jumped on her bike and cycled the three kilometres to the shop or chemist and returned with apples or a thermom-eter or temperature-reducing medicines in the little basket on the handlebars. And when we came here she had carefully planned and done the shopping for all the meals, which often consisted of two courses for lunch and three for dinner. She got up when Vanja woke at six, baked some bread rolls, perhaps went for a walk with her and slowly began to prepare lunch. When we got up at nine there was a lavish breakfast table set, with fresh rolls, boiled eggs, often an omelette if for example she had it in her head that I liked them, coffee and juice, and when I sat down she would always put the newspaper she had bought for me by my place. She was extraordinarily positive, extraordinarily understanding about everything, the word 'no' didn't exist in her mouth and there was nothing in the world she couldn't help us with. Her freezer was filled with an infinite number of tubs of ice cream and plastic buckets of herring as well as various meals she had made and labelled: Meatball Sauce, Jansson's Temptation, Beef and Potato Stew, Rissoles, Stuffed Peppers, Stuffed Pancakes, Pea Soup, Lamb Chop with Crispy Wedge Potatoes, Beef Bourgignon, Salmon Pudding, Cheese and Leek Pie . . . If there was a chill in the air and she was out walking with Vanja, well, she was quite likely to go to a shoe shop and buy her new boots.

'How's your mother?' she asked. 'Is she OK?'

'Yes, I think so,' I said. 'She'll soon have finished her dissertation, from what I understand.'

I wiped some soup off my chin with the serviette.

'But she won't let me read it,' I added with a smile.

'I take my hat off to her,' Vidar said. 'There aren't many sixty-year-olds with enough curiosity left to study at university, that's for sure.'

'I think she probably has mixed feelings about that,' I said. 'She's always wanted to, you see, and she does it when her career's almost over.'

'Nevertheless,' Ingrid said. 'It's not easy what she's done. She's tough, your mother is.'

I smiled again. The distance between Sweden and Norway was much greater than they imagined, and for a moment I saw my mother through Swedish eyes.

'Yes, perhaps she is,' I said.

'Send her our regards,' Vidar said. 'And the rest of the family as well, by the way. I liked them so much.'

'Vidar has been talking about them ever since we were there for the christening,' Ingrid said.

'There were some real characters!' Vidar said. 'Kjartan, the poet. He was an interesting and unusual man. And what were they called, the people from Ålesund, the child psychologists?'

'Ingunn and Mård?'

'Exactly. So nice! And Magne, wasn't that his name? Your cousin Jon Olav's dad? The director of development?'

'Yes, that's right,' I said.

'A man with authority,' Vidar said.

'Yes,' I said.

'And your father's brother. The teacher from Trondheim. He was a fine man too. Is he like your father?'

'No,' I replied. 'He's probably the least like him, I would say. He's always kept his distance, and I think that was a smart move.'

There was a pause. The slurping of soup, Vanja banging her cup on the table, her gurgles of laughter.

'They still talk about both of you,' I said, looking at Ingrid. 'Especially the food you made!'

'It's so different in Norway,' Linda said. 'It really is. Particularly on 17 May. People were wearing traditional costumes and medals on their chests.'

She laughed.

'At first I thought it was meant to be ironic, but no, it wasn't. It was quite genuine. The medals were worn with dignity. No Swedes would do that, that's for certain.'

'I'm sure they were proud,' I said.

'Yes, precisely. But you wouldn't catch a Swede admitting that, nowhere, not even to themselves.'

I angled the bowl to spoon up the last remnants of the soup as I looked out of the window, at the rectangular snow-covered meadow beneath the grey sky, the line of black deciduous trees on the edge of the forest behind, broken here and there with luxuriant green spruces. The dark dry twig-strewn forest floor in which they grew.

'Henrik Ibsen was obsessed with medals,' I said. 'There wasn't a decoration for which he was not willing to grovel. He wrote letters to every conceivable king or regent to get them. And then he wore them at home in his living room. Strutted round with his little chest plastered with them. Heh heh heh. He also had a mirror in his top hat. So he sat in his café surreptitiously staring at himself.'

'Did Ibsen do that?' Ingrid asked.

'He did,' I said. 'He was extremely vain. And isn't that a much more fantastic form of excess than Strindberg's? With him it was all about alchemy, madness, absinthe and women's hats, which is just the typical artist myth. But with Ibsen it was bourgeois vanity taken to an extreme. He was a great deal madder than Strindberg.'

'While we're on the subject,' Vidar said, 'have you heard the latest about Arne's book? The publishers have withdrawn it.'

'And they were probably right,' I said. 'There were so many errors.'

'Yes, I suppose there were,' Vidar said. 'But the publishers should have helped him with them. After all, he'd been ill. He couldn't draw a line between his own fantasies, wishful thinking and reality.'

'So in your opinion he really thought he was writing the truth?'

'Oh yes, no doubt about it. He's a good man. But there is something of the pathological liar in him. He eventually begins to believe his own stories.'

'How is he taking it?'

'I don't know. Right now that's not the first thing you talk about with Arne.'

'Of course,' I said with a smile. I drank the last drop of *folkøl*,
ate a roll and leaned back in my chair. I knew there was no
question of me being allowed to help with the washing-up or
anything like that, so I didn't even bother to offer my services.

'Shall we go for a walk?' Linda suggested, looking at me. 'Then
Vanja might go to sleep.'

'OK,' I said.

'She could stay here with me,' Ingrid said, 'if you want to be
on your own.'

'No, it's all right, thanks. We'll take her with us. Come here,
my little troll, we're off now,' she said, lifted Vanja and went to
wash her mouth and hands while I put on my outdoor clothes
and prepared the buggy.

We took the path leading down to the lake. A cold wind blew
across the fields. On the other side some crows or magpies were
hopping around. Up above them, among the trees, large motionless cows stood staring into the distance. Some of the trees were
oaks, and they were old, from the eighteenth century, I would
have thought, perhaps even older, what did I know? Behind them
ran a railway line, and a roar came every time a train passed
and resounded across the countryside whenever a train passed.
The path ended by a beautiful small brick house. In it lived an
old priest – the father of Lars Ohly, chairman of the left-wing
Swedish *Vänster* party – who was said to have once been a Nazi.
Whether that was true or not I had no idea, rumours of that
nature sprang up so easily around famous figures. But now and
then he hobbled around, hunchbacked and stooped.

Once in Venice I had seen an old man whose head was so bowed
it was horizontal. His neck was at ninety degrees to his shoulders.
All he could see was the ground in front of his feet. It took him
an eternity to shuffle across the piazza. It was in Arsenale, next

to a church where a choir was practising, I was sitting in a café smoking, unable to take my eyes off him from the moment I spotted him. It was an evening at the beginning of December. Apart from the two of us and the three waiters standing with their arms crossed by the entrance, there wasn't a person in the vicinity. Mist hung above the roofs. The cobblestones and all the old stone buildings, which were covered in moisture, glinted in the light from the lamps. He stopped by a door, produced a key, and he *tipped* his whole body backwards so that he could see where, roughly, the lock was. His fingers groped their way to the keyhole. The deformity meant that none of his body's movements seemed to belong to him, or rather the unmoving downward-facing head became the focus of attention, which as a result became a kind of centrepiece, a part of the body, though independent of it, where all the decisions were taken and all the movements were decided.

He opened the door and went in. From behind, it looked as if his head was missing. And then, with an unexpectedly violent movement which I would have considered impossible, he slammed the door.

It was eerie, eerie.

A red estate car came up the hill a few hundred metres in front of us. The snow swirled after it in the undertow. We moved to the side as it approached. The rear seats had been taken out and two white dogs ran around barking in the freed space.

'Did you see them?' I said. 'They looked like huskies. But they can't be, can they?'

Linda shrugged.

'I don't know,' she said. 'But I think they're the ones in the house by the bend, aren't they? The ones that are always barking.'

'Never been any dogs there when I walked past,' I said. 'But I know you've said that before. Were you afraid of them? Was that what it was?'

'I don't know. Maybe a little,' she said. 'It's pretty unpleasant. They're on retractable leashes and then they come bounding . . .'

She had lived here for lengthy periods when she was so depressed she couldn't look after herself. By and large she had spent all day watching TV from her bed in the guest cabin. She hardly spoke to Vidar and her mother, didn't want anything, couldn't do anything, everything inside her had come to a halt. I didn't know how long this had lasted. She had barely said a word about it. But I saw it in many places, such as the concern for her I noticed in neighbours' eyes or voices.

In the valley we walked past the manor – which was not grand and the buildings were somewhat dilapidated – where the elderly, shrunken patriarch lived. Light shone in the windows, but there was no one to be seen inside. In the drive between the barn and the house were three old cars, one on blocks. They were covered in snow.

It was scarcely credible that we had once sat there, at a set table, beside the swimming pool, one hot dark August evening, gorging on crabs. But indeed we had. Paper lanterns glowing in the darkness, happy voices, a bulging pile of red glistening crabs at each end of the long table. Beer cans, bottles of aquavit, laughter and song. The sound of grasshoppers, distant traffic. Linda had surprised me that night, I remembered, she tapped her glass, stood up and sang a drinking song. Twice she did it. She said this was required of her here, she had always done it. She had been the type of child who performed for adults. She had performed in *The Sound of Music* for more than a year at a theatre in Stockholm when she was at school. Also at parties at home, I supposed. An exhibitionist, as I had been, and equally happy to hide.

Ingrid also made an appearance. When she mingled with the neighbours, hugged everyone, showed the food she had brought along, chatted and laughed she became the centre of attention and everyone had a word to say to her. When there were social arrangements in the district, she always gave a hand, by baking or cooking something, and if anyone was ill or in need of help she cycled over to see them and do what she could.

The party began, everyone sat hunched over their dish of crabs, which had been caught in the lake below, and tossed their heads back now and then as they sank what Swedes call a *nubbe*, a schnapps. The atmosphere was festive. Then came the sudden sound of voices from the barn, a man shouting at a woman, the mood round the table evaporated, some looked, some tried to avoid looking, but everyone knew. It was the son of the old man who owned the manor, he was known to have a violent temper, and now he was taking it out on his teenage daughter, who had been smoking. Ingrid stood up at once and walked over with firm swift steps, her whole body quivering with suppressed fury. She stopped in front of the man, he was about thirty-five, well built, strong, with hard eyes, and railed at him with such vehemence that he shrank before her. After she had finished and he had driven off she put her hand on the daughter's shoulder – she had been standing close by and crying – and led her to the table. The second Ingrid sat down she tuned into the previous mood and started chatting, laughing and pulling the others along with her.

Now everything was white and still.

Below the manor the path led up to holiday cabins. The snow hadn't been cleared; no one was here at this time of the year.

During my work on *A Time to Every Purpose Under Heaven* it was Ingrid I had in mind when I was writing about Anna, Noah's sister. A woman who was stronger than all of them, a woman who, when the flood came, took the whole family up the mountain, and, when the water reached them, took them higher until they could go no further and all hope was lost. A woman who never gave up and who would sacrifice everything for her children and grandchildren.

She was a remarkable person. She filled the room when she appeared while still remaining humble. She might give the impression she was superficial, yet there was a depth in her eyes which contradicted that. She tried to keep her distance, she always kept to the background, always set great store by not getting in the way, yet she was the person closest to us.

'Do you think Fredrik and Karin had a good time last night?' Linda said, looking up at me.

'Ye-es, I think they did,' I said. 'It was very nice.'

Somewhere in the distance there was a roar.

'Even though he called me Hamsun a couple of times too often,' I continued.

'He was just messing around!'

'I did understand that.'

'They like you very much, both of them.'

'That, however, I don't understand. I say almost nothing when we meet.'

'Oh, you do. Anyway, you're so attentive it doesn't seem like that.'

'Mhm.'

Sometimes I had a bad conscience about being so quiet and uninvolved with Linda's friends, about my lack of interest in them; it was enough to be present when they were there, like a duty. For me it was a duty, but for Linda it was life, and I didn't take part. She had never complained, but I had a feeling she wished it were different.

The roar increased in volume. From the crossing bells began to go off. *Ding ding ding ding.* Then I glimpsed movement between the trees. The next moment a train shot out from the forest. Snow rose like a cloud around it. It ran alongside the lake for a few hundred metres, a long line of goods wagons carrying containers of various colours gleaming in all the whiteness and greyness, and then it was gone behind the trees in the forest on the other side.

'Vanja should have seen that,' I said. But she was asleep and oblivious to the world. Her face was almost completely submerged beneath the executioner's cap that went round her neck like a collar and, over it, the red polyester hat with white lining and thick earflaps. She had a scarf as well and padded red overalls with a woollen jumper and woollen trousers underneath.

'Fredrik was so good to me when I was ill,' Linda said. 'He used to come into the ward and fetch me. Then we went to the cinema. Didn't say a lot. But it was a great help, just getting out. And his taking care of me like that.'

'All your friends must have done that, didn't they?'

'Yes, each in their own way. And there was something about . . . I suppose I understood that I've always been on the other side, always been the one to help, the one to understand, the one to give . . . Not unconditionally of course, but in the main. My brother when we were growing up, my father and also my mother, sometimes. And then everything was turned on its head: when I fell ill I was on the receiving end. I had to accept help. The strange thing is . . . Well, the only moments I've had of freedom, where I've done what I wanted, were when I was manic. But the freedom was so great I couldn't handle it. It hurt. There was something good about it though. Finally being free. But of course it couldn't work. Not like that.'

'No,' I said.

'What are you thinking about?'

'Two things actually. One has nothing to do with you. But it was what you said about receiving. It struck me that if I'd been in your position I wouldn't have accepted anything. I wouldn't have wanted anyone to see me. And definitely not to help me. This is so strong in me you have no idea. Receiving is not for me. And it never will be, either. That's one thing. The second was wondering what you did when you were manic. I mean, since you connect it with freedom so much. What did you do when you were free?'

'If you won't receive how can anyone reach you?'

'What makes you think I want to be reached?'

'But that's no good.'

'Come on, you answer my question first.'

On the left the festival green came into sight. It was a small patch of grass with a few benches and a long table at the back which was generally used only on Midsummer Night, when everyone in the area gathered together to dance round the tall leaf-bedecked pole in the middle, to eat cake, drink coffee and participate in a quiz with an award ceremony concluding the formal part of the evening. I joined in for the first time that summer and waited intuitively for someone to set fire to the post. Surely there couldn't be a Midsummer celebration without a fire? Linda laughed when I told her. No, no fire, no magic, just children dancing to the 'Little Frogs' song around the enormous phallus and drinking fizzy drinks, as everyone did in the smaller communities all over Sweden that night.

The pole was still there. The leaves were withered and reddish-brown with white streaks of snow.

'It wasn't so much what I did as how I felt,' she said. 'The feeling that anything was possible. That there were no hindrances. I could have been president of the USA, I told mummy once, and the worst of it is that I meant it. When I went out, the social side was not a hindrance; quite the contrary, it was an arena, a place where I could make things happen and be completely and utterly myself. All my inclinations were valid, there wasn't a speck of self-criticism, there was a sense of anything goes, right, and the point was that anything also *became true*. Do you understand? Anything really *did* go. But I was incredibly restless, of course, there was never enough happening, I had a hunger for more, it mustn't end, it was not allowed to end, because somewhere I must have had an inkling it would, the trip I was on, that it would end with a fall. A fall into the absolutely immovable. The greatest hell of them all.'

'That sounds dreadful.'

'It certainly was. But it wasn't only dreadful. It's fantastic to feel so strong. So confident. And somewhere it is *also* real. In other words, it exists in me. But you know what I mean.'

'In fact, I don't,' I said. 'I've never reached that point. I know the feeling. I think I've experienced it once, but, heck, that was while I was writing, sitting quietly behind a desk. That's quite different.'

'I don't think so. I think you were manic. You weren't eating, you weren't sleeping, you were so happy you didn't know what to do with yourself. But you have some kind of boundary nevertheless, some security inside you, and this is a lot about not going beyond what you actually, and it is a big actually, can tolerate. If you do something for long enough without the tolerance there are major consequences. You have to pay. It doesn't come free.'

We had joined the path running alongside the lake and into the forest. The wind had laid bare great swathes of ice. In places it was as shiny as glass and reflected the dark sky like a mirror, in others it was grey, greenish and grainy, like frozen slush. Now that the train had passed and the warning bell had stopped ringing there was almost complete silence in the forest. Just some rustling and cracking as branches rubbed or the occasional thwack. The squeaking of the buggy wheels, our own brittle footsteps.

'At the hospital there was one thing they said which became important for me,' Linda continued. 'It was a simple matter. But what they said was that I had to try to remember I was actually fed up with myself when I became manic. That I was deeply depressed. And just that, the thought that I existed, helped. This is a lot of what it's about, completely losing sight of who you are. In fact, and I think this might have been the most significant reason for it going so far, I had never actually lived. Had never had an inner life, that is. It had always been an external life. And things went fine for a long time, I pushed it further and further, and then in the end it wouldn't go any further. It came to a stop.'

She looked at me.

'I think I was pretty ruthless in those days. Or there was something ruthless inside me. I had cut myself off from others, if you know what I mean.'

'I think that's true,' I said. 'When I met you for the first time you had a completely different aura from today. Yes, ruthless, that fits. Attractive and dangerous is what I thought. I don't think that about you now.'

'I was on my way down. It was during those weeks it happened, that I started to lose control. I'm so pleased we didn't get together then! It would never have worked. It couldn't have worked.'

'No, probably not. But I was a bit surprised when I found out exactly how romantic you were, I must say. And how close you want those who are around you. How important it is for you.'

We were silent for a while.

'Would you rather have been with me when I was like that?'

'No.'

I smiled. She smiled. Around us all was perfectly still, apart from the occasional whoosh as the wind gusted through the forest. It was good to walk here. For the first time in ages I had some peace in my soul. Even if snow lay thick on the ground everywhere and white is a bright colour, the brightness didn't dominate the terrain, because out of the snow, which so sensitively reflects the light from the sky and always gleams, however dark it is, rose tree trunks, and they were gnarled and black, and branches hung above them, also black, intertwining in an endless variety of ways. The mountainsides were black, the stumps and debris of blown-down trees were black, the rock faces were black, the forest floor was black beneath the canopy of enormous spruces.

The soft whiteness and the gaping blackness, both were perfectly still, all was completely motionless, and it was impossible not to be reminded of how much of what surrounded us was dead, how little of it all was actually alive and how much space the living occupied inside us. This was why I would have loved to be able to paint, would have loved to have the talent, for it was only through painting this could be expressed. Stendhal wrote that music was the highest form of art and that all the other forms really wanted to be music. This was of course a Platonic idea, all the other art forms depict something else, music is the only one which is something in itself, it is absolutely incomparable. But I wanted to be closer to reality, by which I meant physical, concrete reality, and for me the visual always came first, also when I was writing and reading, it was what was behind letters that interested me. When I was outdoors, walking, like now, what I saw gave me nothing. Snow was snow, trees were trees. It was only when I saw a picture of snow or of trees that they were endowed with meaning. Monet had an exceptional eye for light on snow, which Thaulow, perhaps the most technically gifted Norwegian painter ever, also had, it was a feast for the eyes, the closeness of the moment was so great that the value of what gave rise to it increased exponentially, an old tumbledown cabin by a river or a pier at a holiday resort suddenly became priceless, the paintings were charged with the feeling that they were here at the same time as us, in this intense here and now, and that we would soon be gone from them, but with regard to the snow, it was as if the other side of this cultivation of the moment became visible, the animation of this and its light so obviously ignored something, namely the lifelessness, the emptiness, the non-charged and the neutral, which were the first features to strike you when you entered a forest in winter, and in the picture, which was connected with perpetuity and death, the moment was unable to hold its ground. Caspar David Friedrich knew this, but this wasn't what he painted, only his idea of it. This was the problem with all representation, of course, for no eye is uncontaminated, no gaze is blank, nothing is seen the way it is. And in this encounter the question of art's meaning as a whole was forced to the surface. Yes, OK, so I saw the forest here, so I walked through it and thought about it. But all the meaning I extracted from it came from me, I charged it with something of mine. If it were to have any meaning beyond that, it couldn't come from the eyes of the beholder, but through action, through something happening, that is. Trees would have to be felled, houses built, fires lit, animals hunted, not for the sake of pleasure but because my life depended on it. Then the forest would be meaningful, indeed so meaningful that I would no longer wish to see it.

Around the bend, perhaps twenty metres ahead of us, came a man dressed in a red anorak. He had a ski stick in each hand. It was Arne.

'Hi, so it's you out walking, is it!' he said as he got closer.

'Hi, Arne. Been a long time,' Linda said.

He stopped beside us and cast a glance into the buggy. The scandal didn't appear to have crushed him.

'She's so big,' he said. 'How old is she now?'

'Turned one two weeks ago,' Linda said.

'Really! Time goes so quickly,' he said, meeting my gaze. One of his eyes was rigid and filled with water. In recent years he had been plagued by all manner of illness, there had been a brain tumour, and after it had been removed he hadn't been able to shake the taste he had acquired for morphine, so he was taken into rehab for a while. When this was over he suffered a stroke. Now it was pneumonia he'd just had, wasn't it?

But even though he looked wilder and more ravaged every time I saw him, even though he walked with greater difficulty and his movements were slower, he did not seem any weaker, there was no shortage of energy, a lust for life still burned inside him, he marched on with all his defects, and he still put to shame what could have been said about him two years ago, that he hadn't got long left. It must have been this spark, this lust for life, which had kept him going. Almost anyone else exposed to what he had experienced would have been two metres under the ground.

'Your book's going to be translated into Swedish, Vidar told me,' he said.

'Yes,' I said.

'When? I really don't want to miss it.'

'Next autumn they're telling me, but it'll probably be the autumn after.'

'I'll wait then,' he said.

How old was he? Late sixties? It was hard to say, there was nothing old-man-ish about him, the one eye that worked glinted with youthfulness, and even though it was the sole feature of his face that did and even though other parts were wrinkled and worn, bloodshot and blotchy, life shone through in other ways, most of all in his enthusiastic tone of voice, which was forced into a slowness that didn't suit it, but also in the total impression he gave, his aura, which strangely enough, despite all the resistance his body offered, appeared indefatigable. He had grown up in an orphanage but hadn't wandered off the straight and narrow like his friends. He had played football at a high level, at least if you believed what he told you, and worked as a journalist on *Expressen* for many years. Furthermore, he had published several books.

His wife always sent him indulgent glances when he made comments, in the way that all women married to boys do. She was a nurse and was approaching the limits of her tolerance, for in addition to an ailing husband she had to look after their child, who had just had twins and needed lots of support.

'Right,' he said. 'Nice to meet you, Linda, and you, Karl.'

'Same to you,' I said.

He raised his hand to his brow and then he set off, his sticks raised high with every stride he took.

His rigid watering eye, which had stared ahead during the whole conversation, might have belonged to a troll or some mythological creature, and even though I didn't have the image constantly in front of me the feeling it generated lasted all day.

'He didn't exactly seem crushed, did he?' I said after he had disappeared round the bend and we had started walking again.

'No,' Linda said. 'But it's never easy to see how people really are.'

Another roar sounded in the distance, from the other side now. I sat Vanja up as she lay blinking in the buggy, and turned her so that she could see when, soon after, the train sped past us between the trees. It didn't go by unnoticed; she pointed and shouted as it passed, so close that a thin layer of powdery snow was blown against my face, to melt in a trice.

Barely a kilometre later, by a railway embankment, the path came to an end. The field on the other side, where horses grazed in the summer, lay white and untouched like a tablecloth between the trees. To the left, in the east, there was a clump of houses, behind them a path, and if you followed it you came to a beautiful large manor owned by Olof Palme's brother. One summer evening Linda and I had been out for a bike ride and we ended up there, lost, pushing our bikes down the gravel road between the houses where a white-clad party was sitting outdoors and eating with a view of the great lake and Gnesta town centre far on the other side. However careful I had been to look in another direction, I still had the image of the party on my retina: them sitting there so Bergman-like on the white garden furniture and eating, between austere white farmhouses and modern red office buildings, in the midst of the green rolling Södermanland countryside.

I took Vanja from the buggy and held her in my arms as we turned to walk back the same way we had come.

Arriving half an hour later on the incline in front of the house, we heard loud voices coming from indoors. Through the kitchen window I saw Ingrid and Vidar standing on either side of the sitting-room table shouting at each other. I suppose we had come earlier than they had expected, and the snow had muffled our arrival. It was only when I stamped my boots a few times on the front doorstep that the voices stopped. Linda took Vanja, I pushed the buggy into the garage beside the house that Vidar had built in the spring and summer. When I returned he was standing in the hall and putting on his overalls.

'Well?' he said with a smile. 'Did you walk far?'

'No,' I said. 'Just a little way. The weather's really grim!'

'Yes, it is that,' he said, stepping into tall brown rubber boots. 'I'm just off to fix a few things.'

He slipped past me and walked slowly up the slope to his workshop. In the kitchen, which started half a metre from where I was removing my outdoor clothes, Ingrid had put Vanja in a high seat by the worktop while she peeled potatoes. I put my hat and gloves on the hat shelf, kicked my boots off against the door frame, she put a bowl of water and some plastic measuring spoons in front of Vanja. That could occupy her for hours, I knew. I hung my coat on a hanger and pushed it between all the other jackets, capes and coats hanging there and walked past them.

Ingrid looked upset. But her movements were considered and calm, her voice to Vanja was gentle and kind.

'What's for dinner? Something nice?' I asked.

'Lamb,' she said. 'Wedge potatoes. And red wine sauce.'

'Ah, that sounds good!' I said. 'Lamb's my favourite.'

'I know,' she said. Her eyes, enormous behind glasses, regarded me with a smile.

Vanja smacked the set of measuring spoons against the water.

'You're having a good time here, Vanja, aren't you,' I said. Tousled her hair. Looked at Ingrid. 'Has Linda gone for a lie-down?'

Ingrid nodded. From the sleeping alcove, which was out of eyeshot, although no more than four metres away, came Linda's voice: 'I'm in here!'

I went in. The two beds were at ninety degrees to each other and took up almost all the room. She was on the one further away with the duvet pulled up under her chin. Even though the curtains were not drawn it was dim, almost murky inside. The dark coarse-wood walls soaked up all the light.

'Brr!' she said. 'Are you going to have a nap?'

I shook my head.

'Think I'll do some reading. But you sleep.'

I sat on the edge of the bed and stroked her hair. On one wall there were photos of Vidar's children and grandchildren. The other was covered in books. An alarm clock and a photo of Vidar's youngest daughter were on the windowsill. I always felt uncomfortable in other people's bedrooms, I always saw something I didn't want to see, but that was not the case here.

'I love you,' she said.

I leaned forward and kissed her.

'Sleep tight,' I said, got up and left the room. Found the books I had packed, couldn't face Dostoevsky, too difficult to get into at this moment, instead took a biography about Rimbaud which I had long thought I should read and reclined with it in my hand on the sofa under the window. What excited my interest was his Africa connection. That, and the times in which he lived. I wasn't so bothered about his poetry, except for what it could say about his unusual, unique character.

In the kitchen Ingrid was chatting to Vanja while she worked. She was so good with her, managing to turn even the worst chore into an exciting adventure, not least because she put aside her own needs when they were together. Everything was about Vanja and her experiences. But there was no sense of it being a sacrifice, the pleasure she reaped from it seemed to be deeply heartfelt.

I doubted there was a woman more different from my mother than Ingrid. Mum put aside her own needs as well, but the distance to Vanja and what they did together was so much greater, and she obviously didn't derive the same pleasure from it. Once when I had been to a play area with them her faraway look had caused me to ask if she was bored;

she was, she said, and she always had been, also when we were young.

If she wanted, Ingrid could capture any child's attention, there was something in her nature that facilitated immediate contact. She had a powerful aura; she couldn't enter a room without making a difference. She took it captive. My mother could sit in a room without anyone knowing she was there. Ingrid had once been an actress on the country's most important stage, lived a big life, an active life. My mother observed, deliberated, read, wrote, reflected and lived a contemplative life. Ingrid loved to cook; my mother did it because it was necessary.

Vidar walked past the bedroom window, a trifle stooped in his blue overalls, taking careful steps so as not to go flying on the path. A moment later he came into view through the living-room window, on his way to the garage. In the kitchen Vanja was standing and supporting herself on the cupboard while Ingrid lifted a steaming hot pan of potatoes from the stove. I got up and went into the hall, put on my jacket, hat and boots, opened the door and sat down on the chair by the wall to have a smoke. Vidar came out of the garage with a bucket in one hand.

'Could you give me a hand afterwards, do you reckon?' he said. 'In about ten minutes?'

'Course,' I said.

He nodded, and continued round the corner of the house. I stared into the distance. The light beneath the sky was losing its lustre. The approaching darkness was unevenly distributed across the landscape, the already dark areas were sucking it in more and more greedily, such as the trees at the edge of the forest, the trunks and branches were completely black now. The weak February light faded without a fight, without resistance, not even a last flicker could it rouse, just a slow, imperceptible decline until everything was darkness and night.

A sudden feeling of happiness gripped me.

It was the light over the field, the chill in the air, the silence in the trees. The darkness that was waiting. It was a February afternoon breathing its atmosphere into me, and it evoked memories of all the other February afternoons I had experienced or rather the resonance of them, for the memories themselves had long faded. It was so immensely rich and replete because all of life was gathered there. It seemed to slice through the years; the special light spread out like ripples in my memory.

The feeling of happiness segued into an equally strong feeling of sorrow. I stubbed out my cigarette in the snow and threw it towards the barrel underneath the downpipe, told myself I had to get rid of the butts before we left and walked up to the back of the house, where Vidar was in the hut above the earth cellar screwing a lid onto a freezer cabinet.

'We have to carry this over to the cabin,' he said. 'It's a bit slippery, but if we take care it should be all right.'

I nodded. A crow cawed behind us. I turned round, stared at the line of trees on the other side, but couldn't see where the sound had come from. Today all their movements in the snow were visible. Their tracks followed the paths from the front door of the house and up to all the small outhouses. The rest was white and untouched.

Vidar started on the third screw. His fingers were supple and well coordinated. He did all the small repairs, the smaller the better, by the looks of things. Personally, I lost patience with anything I couldn't grip with the whole of my hand. Assembling Ikea furniture drove me mad.

As he worked his lips parted. The bared crooked teeth together with his narrow eyes and the triangular-shaped face that emphasised his goatee made him look like a fox.

The bucket he had fetched, which was full of sand, was next to him, pale red against the grey concrete floor.

'Were you going to sand the paths?'

'Yes,' he said. 'Would you like to do it?'

'No problem,' I said.

I lifted the bucket, grabbed a handful of sand and sprinkled it over the footprints as I walked down. Ingrid came out of the house, taking her usual short hurried steps through the snow, dressed in an open green windcheater, heading towards the earth cellar. Even at such an insignificant moment there was an aura of intensity about her. Linda must be up, I thought. Unless Vanja had gone to sleep with her.

There were still a few apples hanging from the two trees below the path. Their skins were wrinkled and covered with black spots, and the colour that was still intact, a muted dark red and green, seemed to have grown into them and was enhanced by the surrounding black leafless branches. If you viewed them with the meadow and forest as a background, where there was no colour, they glowed. If you viewed them with the red huts behind, the colours were matt and hardly visible.

Ingrid came out of the earth cellar with two 1.5-litre bottles of mineral water in her hands and three cans of beer squeezed under her arm, she put down one bottle in the snow so as to slip the hook into the eye of the door lock, the cap and the label so yellow against the white snow, picked it up again and shuffled back to the house. I had reached the shed and sprinkled the remaining sand on the way back. As I put the bucket down on the ground I suddenly remembered who the man I had seen in the café the previous day looked like. Tarjei Vesaas! He had been the spitting image. The same square chin, the same gentle eyes, the same bald patch. But his complexion had been different, conspicuously pink and baby-soft. It was as though Vesaas's cranium had been recreated, or the same code had been reused in one of nature's many caprices, but with different skin stretched over.

'There we are,' Vidar said, putting the little screwdriver on the lathe behind him. 'Let's do it then. I'll tip it this way and then you lift the other end, OK?'

'OK,' I said.

I lifted, and saw that when the weight shifted towards Vidar his body seemed to tense. I would have liked to take the bulk of the weight, because it wasn't heavy, but that was clearly not possible. We walked down the little hill taking tiny steps, then we turned and walked side by side up the gentle slope to the hut, where we at first put it down in the middle of the floor, then coaxed it into position in the corner.

'Thank you,' Vidar said. 'It's great to get this done.'

Since he had no one to help him, little jobs of this kind were often waiting for me when we came.

'My pleasure,' I said.

He put in the plug and immediately the freezer started humming. There were two other similar-looking cabinets in there, as well as two big chest freezers. All of them full of food. Elk meat and venison, veal and lamb. Pike and perch and salmon. Vegetables and berries. All manner of home-made meals. This was an attitude to food and money completely alien to us. In addition to being as self-sufficient as possible, Ingrid always bought huge quantities of items that were on offer, turned every krone over twice and made it a point of honour. It was all about exploiting resources. For example, she had an arrangement with a supermarket to take fruit off their hands if they were going to throw it out, to make juice or jam or cakes or whatever occurred to her to do with it. Now and then she would say what she had paid for the meat during the meal we were eating, the point of which was to underline the difference between the value of the meal before and after she had applied her culinary arts. The cheaper, the better. However, she was by no means a greedy person; she showered us with every possible, and impossible, present, regardless of her own financial position. What was at the bottom was something else, perhaps a housewife's pride and honour, because she had been to a home economics school, and after her acting career was over she had obviously reverted to the life she'd once had.

So the room buzzed and hummed with freezer chests and cabinets, so the earth cellar was full of vegetables, fruit, jars of jam and pickle, so we were served with incredible food every time we came, largely meals that used to be eaten in this country a generation or two ago, but also Italian, French and Asian meals, all of which had one feature in common: they were rustic in some way.

When we were preparing for Vanja's christening, Ingrid wanted to help with the cooking. The event was to take place in Jølster, at my mother's, and as Ingrid knew neither the kitchen nor the shops she suggested making the food at home and bringing it with her. To me that sounded like an absolutely absurd idea, transporting food more than a thousand kilometres for a small gathering, but she insisted, said it was easiest, so that was how it was left. As a consequence, Ingrid and Vidar, in addition to the usual luggage, had had three full freezer bags with them when they arrived at Bringelandsåsen Airport outside Førde one day at the end of May the previous year. There were to be two celebrations, first my mother's sixtieth birthday on the Friday, then Vanja's christening on the Sunday. Linda and I had arrived a few days earlier, not without some turmoil, because mum had been renovating the living room for the festivities and still hadn't finished tidying up, so it looked like a building site, which disappointed and enraged Linda. When she saw the state of the place she knew it would take me at least three days to sort it out. I understood her anger, if not the vehemence, but could not accept it. We went for a walk with Vanja in the valley, and Linda was cursing my mother – this was not the situation we had been led to expect; had she known we would never have had the christening here, we would have had it at home in Stockholm.

'Sissel is mean-spirited, unwelcoming, cold and closed,' Linda shouted in the green sun-drenched valley. 'That's the truth about her. You say I can't see my mother as she is, you say a gift is never a gift and that she makes me dependent on her, and you may be right, you may be, but you can't see your *bloody* mother, either.'

My stomach churned with despair, as always when I had to counter her fury, which I considered completely unreasonable, close on insane in fact, with arguments and objectivity.

We were almost running down the valley road as we pushed the buggy with Vanja asleep inside.

'It's *our* daughter being christened,' I said. 'Of course the house has to be done up! Mum works, as you know, unlike your mother, that's why she hasn't been able to finish. She can't spend all her time on us and what we're doing. She has her own life.'

'You're blind,' Linda said. 'You always have to work when we come here, she exploits the situation, and we can never be alone when we're here.'

'But we're always alone!' I said. 'We have nothing else but time alone. It's the only sodding thing we do have!'

'She never gives us any space,' Linda said.

'She what?!' I said. 'Space? If anyone gives us space it's her. It's *your* mother who doesn't give us space. Not one bloody centimetre. Do you remember when Vanja was born? You said you didn't want anyone there for the first few days, you wanted us to be alone with her?'

Linda didn't answer; she just glared.

'Mum wanted to come, of course. Yngve too. But then I rang and said they couldn't come for the first two weeks, any time afterwards though. And what happened? Who comes in the door, at your invitation? Your mother. And what did you say? "It's only mummy!" Bloody hell! Yes, those were your precise words. The "only" says everything. You don't see her. You're so used to her coming and helping you that you don't notice. *She* can come, my mother can't.'

'But your mother never came to see Vanja. Months went by.'

'And why do you think that was? I told her not to!'

'Love, Karl Ove, is stronger than any sense of rejection.'

'Oh, for God's sake,' I said.

And then we were silent.

'Yesterday, for example,' Linda said, 'she sat with us until we went to bed.'

'And?'

'Would mummy have done that?'

'No, she'd go to bed at eight, she would, if she thought you wanted her to. And she does everything when we're there, that's true enough. But it doesn't damn well mean it's nature's order. I've helped mum with bits and bobs ever since I left home. Painted the house, cut the grass and cleaned. Is there anything wrong with that now? Being helpful, is there anything wrong with that? Eh? And this time it's not even her I'm helping but us! It's our christening. Don't you understand?'

'You don't understand what this is about,' Linda said. 'We haven't come here for you to work and me to take Vanja around on my own. That's what we've left behind. And your mother isn't as innocent as you make out. She's given this some thought and counted on it.'

Oh, fucking hell, I thought as we walked along the road in silence after the last word had been spoken. What a total fucking mess this was. How the hell did I end up in this shit?

The sun burned in the clear blue sky above us. The cliffs rose steeply on both sides of the river, which, swollen with melt water, roared down towards Lake Jølstravannet, so glassy-smooth and silent between the mountains. At the top of one an arm of the Jostedal glacier glistened. The air was pure and sharp, the meadows above and beneath us green and full of bell-jingling sheep, the upper reaches of the mountains bluish, dotted with large flecks of white snow. It was so beautiful it hurt. We walked with Vanja asleep in the buggy arguing about whether I should spend a few days fixing up my mother's house or not.

Linda's unreasonableness knew no bounds. There was no point at which she thought, no, now I've gone too far.

What was going through her head?

Oh, I knew. She was all alone with Vanja during the day, from when I went to my office until I returned, she felt lonely, and she had been looking forward so much to these two weeks. Some quiet days with her little family gathered around her, that was what she had been looking forward to. I, for my part, never looked forward to anything except the moment the office door closed behind me and I was alone and able to write. Especially now that after six years of failure I had finally got somewhere and I felt it wouldn't stop here, there was more. This was what I longed for, this filled my thoughts, not Linda and Vanja and the christening in Jølster, which I took as it came. If it was good, fine, then it was good. If it wasn't good, well then it wasn't good. The difference did not matter much to me. I should have been able to categorise the row in this way, but

I couldn't, my feelings were too strong, they had me under their control.

Friday came, I had sat up all night writing a speech for my mother's birthday and I was tired as we drove through the vertiginous countryside of fjords, mountains, rivers and farms up to Loen in Nordfjord, where she had rented an old manor-style building belonging to the Nurses' Association as the venue for the celebrations. The others went up to the Briksdal glacier; Linda and I stayed in our room with Vanja to have a little sleep. The beauty of the scenery around us was stupendous and alarming. All this blue, all this green, all this white, all this depth and all this space. I hadn't always experienced it in this way; before, I remembered, the scenery was routine, almost inconsequential, something you had to pass through to get from one place to another.

There was the sound of a rushing river. A tractor driving in a field nearby. The drone rising and falling in volume. Now and then voices from the front of the building. Linda lay asleep beside me with Vanja on her chest. For her our row was long forgotten. It was just me who could be gruff and sullen for several weeks, just me who could nourish resentment for several years. Against no one else but her though. Linda was the only person I argued with, she was the only person I held grudges against. If my mother, my brother or my friends said something offensive, I let it go. Nothing of what they said touched me or mattered very much to me, not really. I assumed it was part of my life as an adult that I had succeeded in muting all the overtones and undertones of my character, which at first had been explosive, and I would therefore live the rest of my life in peace and tranquillity, and solve any cohabitation problems with irony, sarcasm and the sulky silence I had honed to perfection after the three lengthy relationships I'd had. But with Linda it was as though

I had been cast back to the time when my feelings swung from wild elation to wild fury to the pits of despair and desperation, the time when I lived in a series of all-decisive moments, and the intensity was so great that sometimes life felt almost unlivable, and when nothing could give me any peace of mind except books, with their different places, different times and different people, where I was no one and no one was me.

That was when I was young and had no options.

Now I was thirty-five years old and wanted as few disturbances and as little mental agitation as possible, I should be able to have that, shouldn't I, or at least be in a position to get it?

Didn't really look like it.

I sat on a rock outside and smoked a cigarette while skimming through the speech I had written. I had hoped to the very last minute I would slip through the net, but there was no escape – Yngve and I had decided she would get a speech from both of us. I dreaded it like the plague. Sometimes when I had to do a reading or an interview or participate in a discussion on stage I was so nervous I could barely walk. But 'nervous' in no way covered my state, nervousness was a transient phase of nerves, a minor aberration, a quivering of the spirit. This was painful and unyielding. It would pass though.

I got to my feet and trudged down to the road, from where you could see the whole district. The fertile moisture-green fields between the mountainsides, the wreath of deciduous trees growing beside the river, the tiny village centre on the plain with its handful of shops and residential blocks. The adjacent fjord, bluish-green and totally still, the mountains that towered up on the other side, the few farms, high on the slopes, with their white walls and reddish roofs, their green and yellow fields, all gleaming in the bright light from the sun, which was sinking and would soon disappear in the sea far beyond. The bare mountains above the farms, dark blue, black here and there, the white peaks, the clear sky above them, where the first stars would soon appear, imperceptible initially, a vague lightening of colour, then they became clearer and clearer until they hung there twinkling and shining in the darkness above the world.

This was beyond our comprehension. We might believe that our world embraced everything, we might do our thing down here on the beach, drive around in our cars, phone one other and chat, visit one another, eat and drink and sit indoors imbibing the faces and opinions and the fates of those appearing on the TV screen in this strange semi-artificial symbiosis we inhabited and lull ourselves for longer and longer, year on year, into thinking that it was all there was, but if on the odd occasion we were to raise our gaze to this, the only possible thought was one of non-comprehension and impotence, for in fact how small and trivial was the world we allowed ourselves to be lulled by? Yes, of course, the dramas we saw were magnificent, the images we internalised, sublime and sometimes also apocalyptic, but be honest, slaves, what part did we play in them?

None.

But the stars twinkle above our heads, the sun shines, the grass grows and the earth, yes, the earth, it swallows all life and eradicates all vestige of it, spews out new life in a cascade of limbs and eyes, leaves and nails, hair and tails, cheeks and fur and guts, and swallows it up again. And what we never really comprehend, or don't want to comprehend, is that this happens outside us, that we ourselves have no part in it, that we are only that which grows and dies, as blind as the waves in the sea are blind.

Four cars came from behind me down the valley. These were my mother's guests – her sisters, their husbands and children, as well as Ingrid and Vidar. I walked up to the house, saw how excited and happy they were, getting out of their cars, clearly the glacier had been a fantastic sight. For the next hour they were going to arrange their rooms, then we would collect in the living room and eat venison and drink red wine, listen to speeches, drink coffee and cognac, gather in small groups and chat and take it easy as the evening turned into the light summer night.

Yngve was the first to take the floor. He handed over our present, which was a single-lens reflex camera, and gave a speech. I was so nervous I didn't catch a scrap of it. He concluded by saying that she had always had great confidence in herself as a photographer, but her confidence had always been unjustified as she had never owned a camera. Hence the present.

Then it was my turn. I hadn't managed to swallow any of the food. And that despite the fact that I had known virtually all of those who were now staring at me all my life, and their expressions were without exception friendly. But the speech had to be given. I had never told my mother that she meant anything at all to me. I had never said I loved her or that I liked her. The mere thought of saying something like that could make my stomach turn in disgust and abhorrence. Of course I wasn't going to say that now either. But today she was sixty years old, and I, her son, had to honour her with a few words.

I rose to my feet. Everyone looked at me, most with a smile. I had to concentrate with all my might to be able to hold the piece of paper, for my hands not to tremble.

'Dear mum,' I said, and turned to her. She sent me an encouraging smile. 'I'd like to start by thanking you,' I went on. 'I'd like to thank you for being such an unbelievably good mother. That you've been an unbelievably good mother is just one of the things I know. But of course it's not always easy to put into words what we know. In this instance it is especially difficult because the qualities you possess are not always so easy to see.'

I swallowed, stared down at my glass of water, decided not to take it, raised my head and looked at the eyes staring at me.

'There's a film by Frank Capra about this precise point. *It's a Wonderful Life*, from 1946. It's about a good man in a small American town who, at the outset of the film, is in deep crisis, and he wants to give up everything he has. Then an angel intervenes and shows him what the world would have been like *without* him. It's only *then* that he can see what significance he in fact has for other people. I don't think *you* need the assistance of an angel to understand how important you are for us, but perhaps now and then *we* might. You give everyone the space to be themselves. Now that might sound like a commonplace, but it isn't; on the contrary, it is a very rare quality. And sometimes it's hard to see. It's easy to see those who push themselves forward. It's easy to see those who set limits. But you never push yourself forward and you never set limits for others; you take them as they are and adapt to *that*. Which I think everyone in this room has experienced.'

A mumble ran around the table.

'When I was sixteen or seventeen, this quality was so important for me. We were living alone in Tveit, and it was a tricky period, I think, but I always felt that you had confidence in me, that you trusted me, and, not least, that you believed in me. You allowed me to learn from my own experiences. While this was happening, of course, I didn't realise this was what you were doing. I didn't have a picture of either you or myself, I don't think. But I do now. And I'd like to thank you for that.'

In so saying, I met my mother's gaze and my voice cracked. I took the glass, gulped down water, tried to smile, but it was not so easy, I had a sense that some sort of sympathy for me had arisen around the table, and I found it difficult to cope with. All I wanted to do was give a speech, not plumb the depths of my own sentimentality.

'Well,' I said. 'Now you're sixty. The fact that you're not planning life as a pensioner and that you've just finished your main subject in your studies says a lot about who you are: first of all, you're lively and energetic and you have intellectual curiosity; secondly, you never give up. That applies to you in your life, but it also has something to do with how you are with others: things have to take time. Things have to take the time they need. When I was seven and about to start school, I didn't know how to appreciate this. You drove me to school on my first day, I remember it well, you weren't a hundred per cent sure of the way to school, but you were sure we would be fine. We ended up in a residential area. Then in another. I sat there in my light blue suit with my satchel on my back, hair combed, and we drove around Tromøya while my new friends stood in the school-yard listening to all the speeches. When we finally made it to the school it was all over. There's an endless list of similar anecdotes I could tell. For example, you've driven a fair few kilometres completely lost, literally, kilometre after kilometre through unfamiliar territory without realising you were not on the Oslo road until you ended up on a tractor path in a dark field at the end of some remote valley. There are so many of these I'll limit myself to the most recent. A week ago, on your sixtieth birthday, you invited colleagues to your house for coffee. They came, but you'd forgotten to buy coffee, so all of you had to sit there drinking tea. Sometimes I think the absent-minded side of your personality is the very precondition for you to be so present in our conversations and in those you have with others.'

Again I was stupid enough to meet her gaze. She smiled at

me, my eyes moistened and then, no, oh no, she got up and wanted to give me a hug.

The other guests clapped, I sat down again, full of disgust with myself, because even though losing control of my emotions made a good impression, gave extra emphasis to what I had said, I was ashamed that I had revealed such weakness.

A few seats down, mum's eldest sister, Kjellaug, got to her feet, she spoke about the autumn of our lives and was met with a couple of good-natured boos, but her speech was good and full of warmth, and after all sixty wasn't forty, was it.

During the speech Linda came in, sat down beside me and placed her hand on my arm. Everything all right? she whispered. I nodded. Is she asleep now? I whispered, and Linda nodded and smiled. Kjellaug sat down, and the next speaker rose, and so it went on until all the guests around the table had spoken. The exceptions were Vidar and Ingrid, of course, since they didn't know my mother at all. But they were enjoying themselves, at least Vidar was. Gone was the slightly rigid old man's slow-wittedness, occasionally noticeable when he was at home; here he was at his ease, happy and smiling, his cheeks and eyes ablaze, with something to say to everyone, genuinely interested in what people said and quick to respond with a rich variety of anecdotes, stories and arguments. It was harder to say how Ingrid felt. She seemed excited, laughed out loud and cast around superlatives to excess – everything was wonderful and fantastic – but that was as far as she got, she seemed to be stuck there, she didn't really get into, or come down into, the mood of the evening either because she was unable to tune in, they weren't people she knew, or because her state of mind was too exalted, or simply because the distance from the life she usually led was too great. I had seen that many times with old people: they couldn't manage abrupt change very well, they didn't like being moved from their environment, but first of all something stiff and regressive came over them, which did not exactly describe Ingrid's behaviour, it was more the opposite, and secondly Ingrid was not old, at least not by today's yardstick. When we travelled back next day to get ready for the christening her manner persisted, but with more space around her it was less conspicuous. She was anxious about the food, tried to prepare as much as possible the night before, and when the day of the christening arrived she was afraid the door of the house might be locked and she wouldn't be able to have everything ready for the guests, and, on her own in the kitchen, she might not find the necessary equipment.

The priest was a young woman, we stood around her by the font, Linda held Vanja as her head was moistened with water. Ingrid left when the ceremony was over, the rest of us stayed seated. It was a communion. Jon Olav and his family stood up and knelt before the altar. For some reason I got up and followed suit. Knelt before the altar, had a wafer placed on my tongue, drank the communion wine, was given the blessing, got up and went back, with mum's, Kjartan's, Yngve's and Geir's eyes on me, disbelieving to varying degrees.

Why had I done it?

Had I become a Christian?

I, a fervent anti-Christian from early teenage years and a materialist in my heart of hearts, had in one second, without any reflection, got to my feet, walked up the aisle and knelt in front of the altar. It had been pure impulse. And, meeting those glares, I had no defence, I couldn't say I was a *Christian*. I looked down, slightly ashamed.

Many things had happened.

When dad died I had spoken to a priest, it had been like a confession, everything poured out of me, and he was there to listen and to give solace. The funeral, the ritual itself, was almost physical, something to hold on to for me. It turned dad's life, so miserable and destructive towards the end, into a life.

Wasn't there some solace in that?

Then there was what I had been working on over the last year. Not what I wrote, but what I was slowly realising I wanted to explore: the sacred. In my novel I had both travestied and invoked it, but without the hymnic gravity I knew existed in these tracts, in these texts I had started to read; and the gravity, the wild intensity in them, which was never far removed from the sacred, to which I had never been or would ever go, yet which I sensed all the same, had made me think differently about Jesus Christ, for it was about flesh and blood, it was about birth and death, and we were linked to it through our bodies and our blood, those we beget and those we bury, constantly, continually, a storm blew through our world and it always had, and the only place I knew where this was formulated, the most extreme yet simplest things, was in these holy scriptures. And the poets and artists who dealt with similar themes. Trakl, Hölderlin, Rilke. Reading the Old Testament, particularly the third Book of Moses with its detailed accounts of sacrificial practices, and the New Testament, so much younger and closer to us, nullified time and history, it was just a swirl of dust, and brought us to what was always there and never changed.

I had thought a lot about this.

And then there was the trivial matter of the local priest being somewhat reluctant to christen Vanja because we weren't married, I was divorced and when she enquired about our faith and I couldn't say, yes, I am a Christian, I believe that Jesus was God's son, a wild notion I could never entertain as a belief, and instead just skirted round it, tradition, my father's funeral, life and death, the ritual, I felt hypocritical afterwards, as though we were christening our daughter under false pretences, and when the communion came I suppose I wanted to revoke this, with the result that I appeared even more hypocritical. Not only had I had my daughter christened without being a Christian, now I was taking bloody communion as well!

However, the sacred.

Flesh and blood.

Everything that changes and is the same.

And last but not least, the sight of Jon Olav walking past and kneeling up there. He was a whole person, a good person, and in some way it also drew me up the aisle as well and down on my knees: I so much wanted to be whole. I so much wanted to be good.

On the church steps we, the parents, the child, the godparents, stood for photographs. Vanja's great-grandmother had been christened in the dress she was wearing here in Jølster. Some of my maternal grandmother's sisters were there, among them Linda's favourites, Alvdis and her husband Anfinn, all of mum's sisters, some of their children and grandchildren, in addition to Linda's friends from Stockholm, Geir and Christina, and of course Vidar and Ingrid.

And while we were standing there Ingrid came running up the hill. The fear she'd had that the house would be locked was not ungrounded, for mum, who was so scatter-brained, had indeed locked the door. Ingrid was handed the key and dashed back. When we arrived half an hour later she was in despair over some dish she could not find. But all was well, of course, the weather was brilliant, we held the celebration in the garden with a view of the lake, in which the mountains were reflected, and the food was praised by everyone. But once the food had been served and Vanja wandered from lap to lap without needing any one-to-one supervision, Ingrid had nothing to do, and perhaps that was what was difficult for her. At any rate she went up to her room and there she stayed until we began to miss her, at five, half past five, when the first guests had already left. Linda went to find her. She was sleeping and almost impossible to wake. She had always been like this, I knew. Linda had told me before how scary it was when she was fast asleep and how impossible it was to have any contact with her for the first five to ten minutes after she woke up. Linda had a theory that sleeping tablets were involved. When she did come outside she almost staggered across the lawn, and her laughter was inappropriate, in the sense that it was too loud for what was going on around the table where she sat and slightly out of synch with the places where the others laughed. I was concerned to see her like that, there was something wrong, it was obvious. She wasn't really present, she was loud and overwrought, with glittering eyes and a flushed complexion. Linda and I talked about this after all the others had settled down for the night. It was the sleeping medicine, as well as all the stress in connection with the party. After all, she had made food for and served twenty-five guests. And everything was new and strange for her.

The next time I met them was here, and all her fluster and unease was completely gone. And Vidar was back into his routines.

Now he was standing with his hands on his hips for a moment contemplating his handiwork. The sound of a train approaching carried from the other side of the ridge, faded, returned a few seconds later on the other side, louder and fuller, as Linda came walking up the slope towards us.

'Food's ready!' she shouted, on catching sight of us.

*

Early next morning Vidar drove us to the railway station. We arrived just before the train was about to depart, so I had no chance to buy a ticket. Ingrid, who had joined us to look after Vanja for the next three days, had a monthly ticket while Linda had enough left on her strip for the return to Stockholm. I sat down by the window and took out my pile of newspapers, which I still hadn't managed to read. Ingrid took care of Vanja, Linda sat looking out of the window. The conductor didn't come until several stations after we had changed trains at Södertälje. Ingrid showed her card, Linda passed him her strip and I dug in my pocket for loose change. When he turned to me, Ingrid said, 'He got on at Haninge.'

What?

Was she fiddling the fare on my behalf?

What the hell was she doing?

I met the conductor's eyes.

'To Stockholm,' I said. 'From Haninge. How much is that?'

I couldn't say that actually I had got on at Gnesta. How would that make Ingrid feel? Nevertheless, I always made it a rule to pay for myself; if I was in a shop for example and was given too much change, I always pointed this out to the assistant. Fare dodging was the last thing I would do.

The conductor passed me the ticket and my change, I thanked him and he merged into the throng of early-morning commuters.

I was furious, but I continued reading and said nothing. After we had arrived at Stockholm Central and I had lifted the buggy onto the platform I offered to take her suitcase to the office so that she wouldn't have to drag it up to ours first of all, then back down to the office, which is where she usually stayed when she visited us in the afternoon. She was pleased. I said goodbye to them in the concourse, made my exit by the airport trains, walked to the marketplace with the fortress-like trade union building, hurried up Dalagatan, one hand pulling the roller suitcase, the other holding the bag containing my computer, and unlocked the office door five minutes later.

The place had already become full of memories. The period when I wrote *A Time to Every Purpose Under Heaven* flooded towards me from all sides. Oh, how happy I had been then.

I made room for Ingrid's suitcase in the cupboard under the sink, I didn't want to have to look at it while I was working, then I went to the toilet for a pee.

And what did I see there? Ingrid's shampoo and hair conditioner. And what was that at the bottom of the rubbish bag? Ingrid's Q-tips and dental floss.

What the HELL! I shouted, grabbing the two bottles and throwing them in the kitchen bin. That bloody DOES it, I yelled, snatched at the bag in the wastepaper basket, bent over and took the little clump of hair from the plug hole, it was hers, for Christ's sake, this was my office, the only place I had that was all mine, where I was completely alone, and even there she came with all her bits and bobs and all her odds and ends, even there I was invaded, I thought, slung her hair as hard as I could into the bag, crumpled it up and stuffed it deep, deep, down in the rubbish bin under the worktop in the kitchen.

Well, screw that.

Then I switched on the computer and sat down at the desk. Waited impatiently for it to boot up. On the wood floor there was the thorn-crowned Jesus Christ. On the wall behind the sofa hung the poster of Balke's night scene. Over the desk Thomas's two photos. On the wall behind me the dissected whale and the almost photographically precise drawings of beetles from the same eighteenth-century expedition.

I couldn't write here. That is, I couldn't write anything new.

But that wasn't what I was going to do this week. On Saturday morning I would be giving a lecture about my 'authorship' in Bærum of all places, and that was what I would be working on for the next three days. It was a meaningless job, but I had accepted it ages ago. The enquiry had come the same day it became clear that my book had been nominated for the Nordic Council's Literature Prize. They wrote that it was a tradition for the Norwegian nominee to go and talk about their book or their authorship, and as my defences had been low at that point, I said yes.

And now here I was.

Ladies and gentlemen. I don't give a shit about you, I don't give a shit about the book I've written, I don't give a shit if it wins a prize or not, all I want is to write more. So what am I doing here? I allowed myself to feel flattered, I had a moment of weakness, I have lots of them, but now this is the end of feeling flattered and having moments of weakness. To mark the occasion in a suitably unambiguous way I've brought along a few newspapers with me. I'm going to place them on the floor in front of the rostrum and have a shit. I've saved it up for a few days so that I can make the point with force. So here we go. Right. Oooh. There we are. Now I'll just wipe my arse and that's that. May I now pass over to the second nominee, Stein Mehren? Thank you.

I erased that, went to the kitchenette, filled the kettle, poked a spoon into the jar of freeze-dried coffee, loosened some clumps and sprinkled them into the cup, which I filled with boiling water straight afterwards. Then it was on with my outdoor clothes and out to the bench opposite the hospital across the street, where I smoked three cigarettes in quick succession while observing people and cars passing by. The sky was a dreary grey, the air cold and raw and the snow by the kerb dark with exhaust fumes.

I took out my mobile and tapped to and fro until I had written a verse I could send to Geir.

> *Geir, Geir, I have to say*
> *That stiffy of yours has had its day*
> *But fret you not*
> *A child you begot*
> *A girl who never says no to a lay*

Then I went indoors and sat down in front of the computer again. The aversion I felt, along with the fact that there were three whole days until I had to be finished, made it difficult, if not impossible to motivate myself. What should I say? Blah, blah, blah, *Out of the World*, blah, blah, blah, *A Time for Everything*, blah, blah, blah, happy and proud.

The mobile in my jacket pocket went off. I grabbed it and clicked on Geir's message.

Quite right, died in a car accident this morning. Didn't know it was already news. You can have my porn mags. I won't need them any longer. I'm stiffer now than I've ever been. Fine epitaph, by the way. But surely you can do better than that?

Certainly can, I wrote back. *What about this?*

> *Here lies Geir in his final abode*
> *He was driving his Saab when it left the road*
> *His eyes were extinguished, his heart beat on*
> *Yet nobody knew he'd actually gone*
> *Though his bones were smashed, his ribcage crushed*

Talk of his death was always hushed
Till the coffin was lowered and all went black
As his soul took flight, that wonderful hack!

It wasn't outrageously funny, but at least it helped to pass the time. And gave Geir a cheap laugh in his university office. After I had sent it I went to the supermarket and did some food shopping. Ate, slept for an hour on the sofa. Finished reading the first volume of *The Brothers Karamazov*, started the second, and when I had finished that it was completely dark outside and the house was filled with its early-evening sounds. I felt as I had in my childhood, when I also used to lie on my bed reading for several hours at a stretch, my head somehow cold, as though rising from a sleep, a cold sleep, in the afterglow of which my surroundings appeared hard and inhospitable. I rinsed my hands in hot water, dried them thoroughly, switched off the computer and put it in my bag, knotted a scarf around my neck, pulled a hat over my head, put on a coat and shoes, locked the door behind me, put on gloves and went into the street. I had just over half an hour before I was due to meet Geir at Pelikanen, so there was plenty of time.

The snow on the pavement was yellowish-brown with a fine-grained consistency like semolina, which meant it slipped when you stepped on it. I walked up Rådmannsgatan towards the Metro station, where it crossed Sveavägen. It was half past six. The streets around me were as good as deserted, permeated with that elusive darkness that is only found in the gleam of electric light and which here was reflected from every window, every street lamp, across snow and tarmac, stairs and railings, parked cars and bicycles, façades, window ledges, street signs and lamp posts. I could equally well have been someone else, I thought as I walked, there was nothing in me now that felt

precious enough for it not to be taken for something else. I
passed Drottninggatan, which at its lower end was teeming
with dark beetle-like people, descended the steps beside
Observatorielunden Park, along the part of the street where
there was the repugnant sign outside the Chinese restaurant
exhorting us to 'guzzle', and down the stair shaft to the underground. There were perhaps thirty to forty people on the two
platforms, most on their way home from work judging by the
bags they were carrying. I stood where there was most space,
placed my bag on the floor between my legs, leaned against
the wall with one shoulder, took out my mobile and rang
Yngve.

'Hello?' he said.

'Hi, Karl Ove here,' I said.

'I could see that,' he said.

'You rang?' I said.

'On Saturday, yes,' he said.

'I was going to call back, but things got a bit hectic. We had
people round and then I forgot.'

'No problem,' Yngve said. 'It wasn't anything special.'

'Has the kitchen arrived yet?'

'Yes, it came today in fact. It's right beside me. And I've bought
a new car.'

'Have you!'

'I had to. It's a Citroën XM, not very old. It was a hearse.'

'You're joking!'

'No, I'm not.'

'Are you going to drive around in a hearse?'

'It's been modified, of course. There isn't any room for coffins
in it now. It looks quite normal.'

'Nevertheless. Just the fact that there have been *bodies* in it
. . . That's the creepiest thing I've heard in a long while.'

Yngve snorted.

'You're so sensitive,' he said. 'It's a very normal car. And I could afford it.'

'Yeah, yeah,' I said.

There was a silence.

'Any other news?' I asked.

'Nothing special. How about you?'

'No, nothing. I was at Linda's mother's yesterday.'

'Oh, yes.'

'Yuh.'

'And Vanja? Has she started walking yet?'

'A couple of steps. But it's more falling than walking, to tell the truth,' I said.

He chuckled at the other end.

'How are Tore and Ylva?'

'They're fine,' he said. 'Tore's written you a letter, by the way. From school. Have you received it?'

'No.'

'He didn't want to tell me what he'd written. But you'll find out.'

'Right.'

From the tunnel the headlights of a train came into view. A light wind swept across the platform. People began to move towards the edge.

'The train's coming,' I said. 'Talk to you soon.'

The train braked slowly in front of me. I lifted my bag and took a few steps forward.

'OK,' he said. 'Take care.'

'And you.'

The doors opened and passengers began to spill out. As I lowered my hand with the mobile someone nudged my elbow from behind and sent the phone flying into the crowd by the door – I didn't see where, I had automatically turned to the person who had knocked me.

Where was it?

There was no clink as it hit the ground. Perhaps it had hit a foot? I crouched down and searched the platform in front of me. No telephone anywhere. Had someone kicked it further away? No, I would have noticed, I thought, standing up, and I craned my head towards those heading for the exit. Could it have fallen into someone's bag? There was a woman walking with an open handbag hanging from her arm. Could it have landed in there? No, that sort of thing doesn't happen.

Does it?

I began to walk after her. Could I gently tap her on the shoulder and ask to see in her bag, I've lost a phone, you see, and think it might have ended up there.

No, I couldn't.

The warning signal that the doors were closing sounded. The next train wouldn't be here for another ten minutes, I was already late, and my mobile was an old model, I had time to think before jumping through the doors, which were already half-closed. Dazed, I sat down on a seat beside a goth-clad twenty-year-old as the station lights flashed through the carriage and were suddenly replaced by pitch darkness.

Fifteen minutes later I got off at Skanstull, withdrew some cash from the ATM outside, crossed the road and went into Pelikanen. It was a classic beer hall, with benches and tables along the walls, chairs and tables close together on the black and white chequered floor, brown wooden wall panels, paintings on the plaster above them and on the ceiling, a few broad supporting pillars, also clad with brown panelling at the bottom and surrounded by benches, and a long wide bar at the end. The waiters were almost all old and wore black clothes and white aprons. There was no music, but the noise level was loud nevertheless, the buzz of voices and laughter and the clinking of cutlery and glasses lay like cloud cover above the tables, unnoticed when you had been there a while, but conspicuous and also often intrusive when you opened the door and came in from the street, when it sounded like thunder. Among the clientele there was still the odd drunk who might conceivably have been drinking here since the 1960s, the odd elderly man who had his dinner here, but they were dying out, the predominant types were, as everywhere else in Södermalm, men and women from the culture-creating middle classes. They were not too young, not too old, not too attractive, not too ugly, and they were never too drunk. Cultural correspondents, postgraduates, humanities students, employees from publishing houses, backroom staff for radio and television, the occasional actor or writer, but rarely any high-profile figures.

I stopped a few metres inside the door and scanned the clientele as I loosened my scarf and unbuttoned my jacket. Glasses sparkled, bald heads gleamed, white teeth flashed. Beer in front of all of them, an ochre colour against the brown tabletops. But I couldn't see Geir.

I walked over to one of the cloth-covered tables and sat down with my back to the wall. Five seconds later a waitress arrived and passed me a thick imitation-leather menu.

'There are two of us,' I said. 'So I'll wait before ordering food. But could I have a Staropramen in the meantime?'

'Of course,' the waitress said, a woman of about sixty with a large fleshy face and big auburn hair. 'Pale or dark?'

'Pale, thanks.'

Oh, how nice it was here. The typical pure beer hall style led my mind elsewhere, to more classical periods, not that the place came across as museum-like for that reason, there was nothing forced about the atmosphere, people came here to drink beer and chat the way they had done ever since the 1930s. This was one of Stockholm's great virtues – there were so many places from different epochs which were still in operation without their making a great song and dance about it. Van der Nootska Palace from the seventeenth century, for example, where Bellman was supposed to have got drunk for the first time, when the place was already a hundred years old – sometimes I had lunch there, I first went the day after Foreign Minister Anna Lindh had been murdered, and the mood in the town was strangely muted and wary – and then there was the eighteenth-century restaurant Den Gyldene Freden in the Old Town, the nineteenth-century Tennstopet and Berns Salonger, where the Red Room described by Strindberg was to be found, not to mention the beautiful art nouveau Gondolen bar, which stood, unaltered from the 1920s, on top of the Katharina Lift with a panorama of the whole town, where you felt as though you were on board an airship, or perhaps in the lounge of an Atlantic liner.

The waitress came with a tray of full glasses in her hand, put one down on a hastily lobbed beer mat, smiled and continued towards the many noisy tables, where she, perhaps once every second, was greeted with some witty comment.

I raised the glass to my mouth and felt the froth touch my lips, the cold slightly bitter liquid fill my mouth – which was so unprepared for all this taste that a shiver ran through me – and slip down my throat.

Ahh.

When you visualised the future and conjured up a world in which urban life had spread everywhere and man had achieved his long-desired symbiosis with the machine, you never took account of the simplest elements, beer for example, so golden and flavoursome and robust, made from grain in the field and hops in the meadow, or bread, or beetroot with its sweet but dark earthy taste, all this which we had always eaten and drunk at tables made of wood, inside windows through which beams of sunlight fell. What did people do in those seventeenth-century palaces, with their liveried servants, high-heeled shoes and powdered wigs pulled down over skulls full of seventeenth-century thoughts, what else if not drink beer and wine, eat bread and meat and piss and shit? The same applied to the eighteenth, nineteenth and twentieth centuries. Conceptions of humanity changed constantly, conceptions of the world and nature too, all manner of strange ideas and beliefs emerged and vanished, useful and useless objects were discovered, science penetrated ever deeper into the world's mysteries, machines grew in number, speeds increased and ever greater areas of old lifestyles were abandoned, but no one dreamed of discarding beer or changing it. Malt, hops, water. Field, meadow, stream. And basically that was how it was with everything. We were rooted in the archaic past, nothing radical about us, our bodies or needs had not changed since the first human saw the light of day somewhere in Africa 40,000 years ago or however long *Homo sapiens* had existed. But we imagined it was different, and so strong was our imaginative power we not only believed that but we also organised ourselves accordingly, as we sat getting drunk in our cafés and darkened clubs, and dancing our dances that presumably were even more clumsy than those performed, shall we say, 25,000 years ago in the glow of a fire somewhere along the Mediterranean coast.

How could the notion that we were modern even arise when people were dropping all around us, infected with illnesses for which there were no remedies? Who can be modern with a brain tumour? How could we believe we were modern if we knew that everyone would soon be lying somewhere in the ground and rotting?

I raised my glass to my mouth again and took long deep draughts.

How I loved drinking. I barely had half a glass before my brain would start toying with the thought of really going for it this time. Just sit there knocking them back. But should I?

No, I shouldn't.

The few minutes I was there a regular stream of people came through the door. Most of them did as I had done, they stopped a few metres inside and studied the clientele while fumbling with their coats.

At the back of the last crowd I recognised a face. Yes, it was Thomas!

I waved to him, and he came over.

'Hi, Thomas,' I said.

'Hi, Karl Ove,' he said, shaking hands. 'It's been a long time.'

'Yes, it has. Everything OK with you?'

'Yes, pretty good. How about you?'

'Yup, everything's fine.'

'I'm meeting some people here. They're over there in the corner. Join us if you want.'

'Thanks, but I'm waiting for Geir.'

'Right! Yes, I think he said he was meeting you. I talked to him yesterday. I'll come over and say hello afterwards if that's OK.'

'Of course,' I said. 'See you.'

Thomas was one of Geir's friends, and the one I indisputably liked best. He was in his early fifties, bore a striking resemblance to Lenin, everything from the beard and the bald patch to the Mongolian eyes matched to a T, and he was a photographer. He'd had three books published, the first pictures of coastal rangers, the second pictures of boxers – it was in this setting he had met Geir – and the last a series of pictures of animals, objects, landscapes and people over whom there hung a dark shadow and where the emptiness in and around them was the most striking feature. Thomas was friendly and undemanding in social contexts – there was, as it were, nothing to lose when you spoke to him, perhaps because he didn't take himself very seriously, although he was self-confident, or possibly that was the reason why. He cared about others, that was the impression he gave. However, in his work he was extremely stringent and demanding, always aiming for perfection, with photos orientated towards stylisation rather than improvisation. The ones I liked best were those occupying the middle ground: improvised stylisation, chance frozen in time. They were brilliant. Some of the boxing photos reminded me of ancient Greek sculptures in the balance of the bodies and the fact that they were caught in activities outside the ring; others possessed a great sombreness, and violence, of course. I had bought two of his photos in the winter, they were going to be presents for Yngve's fortieth birthday. I had sat in Thomas's lab flicking through the series that made up his last book, humming and hawing for a long time, but in the end I chose two. When I gave them to Yngve I could see from his face he didn't really like them, so I said he could choose two others, and I would keep the first two, which are now hanging in my office. They were brilliant but also sinister, for what they exuded was death, so I could well understand that Yngve didn't want them in his living room, even though of course I was a little offended. More than a little, actually. When I went to pick up the photos Yngve had finally chosen and I knocked on the door of the cellar, with massive sixteenth-century stone walls, in the Old Town, where Thomas had his lab, his colleague, an unkempt somewhat shabbily dressed man in his sixties, opened the door. Thomas wasn't there, but I could go down and wait if I wanted. It was Anders Petersen, the photographer Thomas shared his lab with, who for me was best known as the creator of the photo on Tom Waits' record *Rain Dogs*, but who'd had a name since the 70s, when he broke through with *Café Lehmitz*. His work was raw, intimate, chaotic and as close to real life as you could get. He sat down on the sofa in the room above the labs, asked if I wanted some coffee, I didn't, and he resumed his activity, leafing through a pile of contact prints and humming. I didn't want to get in the way or appear intrusive, so I stood in front of a board covered with photos and looked at them for a while, not untouched by his aura, which might have dissolved if there had been more people in the room, but there were just the two of us, and I was aware of every movement. He radiated naïvety, but not as though from inexperience; quite the contrary, he gave every impression of having experienced a great deal, it was more as if all the experiences were there but he hadn't drawn the consequences, as though they had left him unaffected, so to speak. That probably was not the case, but it was the feeling I had when meeting his gaze and watching him sit there working. Thomas returned a few minutes later and seemed glad to see me, the way he undoubtedly was with everyone. He grabbed some coffee, we sat down on a sofa by the stairs, he produced the photos, scrutinised them carefully one last time, put them in their plastic covers, which he placed in an envelope, while I passed the envelope of money to him across the table so discreetly that I wasn't even sure he had noticed. There was something about private cash transactions that embarrassed me, the natural balance was upset in some way, or even rendered null and void, without my quite knowing what it was all about. I put the photos in my bag, we chatted about this and that; apart from Geir, we had another connection, Marie, the woman he lived with, who was a poet, she had taught Linda at Biskops-Arnö many years ago and now she was a kind of mentor to Linda's friend Cora. She was a good poet, classical in a way; truth and beauty were not irreconcilable entities in her poems, and meaning was not just something to do with language. She had translated some Jon Fosse plays into Swedish and was working now on poems by Steinar Opstad, among other things. I had only met her a couple of times, but to me she seemed to have many sides, there was a wealth of nuance in her personality, and you intuited a psychological depth with no apparent signs of neuroticism, the constant companion of sensitivity of course, at least not obtrusively. But when she stood opposite me that was not what engaged my mind, for in her right eye the pupil seemed to have detached itself and slipped down, it lay somewhere between the iris and the white of the eye, and this was so fundamentally alarming that it completely dominated my first impression of her.

Thomas said they would invite Linda and me to dinner one evening, I said that would be very nice, got up and took my bag, he got up as well and we shook hands, and since it did not appear that he had seen the envelope containing the money I told him, there's the money for the photos, he nodded and thanked me as though I had forced him to express this gratitude, and slightly ashamed I went up the stairs and out into the Old Town's wintry streets.

That was almost two months ago now. I wasn't much bothered by the fact that no invitation had appeared yet; one of the first things I had heard about Thomas was that he was very forgetful. I am too, so I didn't hold that against him.

When he sat down at a table at the very back of the room it was as a thin well-dressed man wearing a Lenin mask. I took the yellow Tiedemanns pouch of tobacco from my bag, rolled a cigarette with fingertips that were for some reason so sweaty that shreds kept getting stuck to them, swallowed long gulps of beer, lit the roll-up and through the window saw Geir's figure passing by in the street.

He spotted me as soon as he came in the door, but still surveyed the room as he walked towards the table, as though searching for other options. Not unlike a fox, one might imagine, incapable of selecting a place where there weren't several exits.

'Why don't you answer your bloody phone?' he said, stretching out his hand and meeting my eyes for a fleeting instant. I got up, shook hands and then sat down again.

'Thought we said seven o'clock,' I said. 'It's gone half past now.'

'Why do you think I wanted to call you? To tell you to mind the gap between the train and the platform?'

'I lost my mobile at the Metro station,' I said.

'Lost it?' he queried.

'Yes, someone knocked my elbow and sent it flying. I reckon it must have landed in a bag because I never heard it hit the ground. And a woman was passing with an open bag at precisely that moment.'

'You're unbelievable,' he said. 'I assume you didn't ask her if you could have it back?'

'No-o. Because, firstly, the train arrived at that precise moment and, secondly, I wasn't sure that was what had happened. And you can't just ask women if you can have a rummage through their handbags.'

'Have you ordered?' he asked.

I shook my head. He took hold of the menu and looked around for a waiter.

'She's over there by the pillar,' I said. 'What are you going to have?'

'What do you reckon?'

'Pork and onion sauce maybe?'

'Yes, maybe.'

Whenever I met Geir there was always a distance, it was as though he couldn't absorb the fact that I was there, so he tried to keep me at arm's length. He didn't meet my eyes, he didn't pursue my topics of conversation, he seemed to throttle them by turning his attention to something else, he could be sarcastic and his whole being radiated arrogance. Sometimes that put me out, and when I was put out, I said nothing, which he could easily find it in himself to criticise. 'My God, you're hard graft today, you are,' 'Are you going to sit there gaping into eternity all evening?' or 'Well, you were fun this evening, Karl Ove.' It was a kind of preliminary psychological skirmish he orchestrated inside himself, for after a while, perhaps half an hour, perhaps an hour, perhaps only five minutes, he changed, cast his defences aside and seemed to attune to the situation, become attentive, considerate and present, and the laughter, hitherto cold and hard, was warm and sincere, in a transformation that also encompassed his voice and eyes. When we spoke on the telephone there were no defences, then we chatted on an equal footing from the moment the receiver was lifted. He knew more about me than anyone else, in the same way that probably, but it was by no means certain, I knew more about him than anyone else.

The difference between us, which had diminished over the years but was never completely erased because it had nothing to do with opinions or attitudes, it was basic character, buried deep in the forever un-influence-able, manifested itself in all its clarity in a present Geir gave me after I had finished writing *A Time to Every Purpose Under Heaven*. It was a knife, the model that US Marines use, which couldn't be used for much else apart from killing someone. He didn't do this as a joke, it was simply the finest object he could imagine. I was pleased, but the knife, so intimidating with its polished steel, sharp blade and deep indentations to enable blood to flow, remained in its box behind some books on an office shelf. He may have realised how alien this object was to me because when *A Time to Every Purpose Under Heaven* came out a few months later, he gave me another present, a replica edition of an eighteenth-century *Encyclopaedia Britannica* – profoundly fascinating for all the objects and phenomena it did not describe since they did not yet exist – which of course was more up my street.

He took out a polysleeve containing a few sheets of paper and passed it to me.

'It's just three pages,' he said. 'Could you read it and tell me if it's better?'

I nodded, pulled the sheets from the sleeve, stubbed out my cigarette and began to read. It was the opening of the essay I had been looking for when I went through his manuscript. It was based on Karl Jaspers' concept of *Grenzsituationen*, border situations. The point where life is lived at maximum intensity, the antithesis of everyday life in other words, close to death.

'This is good,' I said when I had finished.

'Sure?'

'Definitely.'

'Good,' he said, replacing the papers in the sleeve and dropping it in the bag on the chair beside him. 'You'll get more to read later.'

'I'm sure I will.'

He pulled his chair closer, rested his elbows on the table and folded his hands. I lit another cigarette.

'Your journalist rang me today, by the way,' he said.

'Who's that?' I asked. 'Oh, that *Aftenposten* guy.'

Since the journalist was writing a portrait he had asked if he could talk to a couple of my friends. I had given him Tore's

number, who was a bit of a loose cannon in that respect, likely
to say anything at all about me, and Geir's, as he knew more
about my present situation.

'What did you say then?' I asked.

'Nothing.'

'Nothing? Why not?'

'Well, what should I have said? If I'd told him the truth about
you, he would have either not understood it or totally distorted
it. So I said as little as possible.'

'What was the point of that?'

'How should I know? It was you who gave him my number . . .'

'Yes, so that you could say something. Anything, I told you, it
doesn't matter what they print.'

Geir eyed me.

'You don't mean that,' he said. 'Well, actually, I did say one
thing about you. Perhaps the most important, in fact.'

'And that was?'

'That you have high morals. Do you know what the idiot
answered? "Everyone has." Can you imagine that? That's exactly
what they *don't* have. Next to *no one* has high morals or even
knows what they are.'

'That just means he has a different interpretation of morals
from you.'

'Yes, but he was only after a bit of scandal. A few anecdotes
about how drunk you once were and stuff like that.'

'Oh well,' I said. 'We'll see tomorrow. It can't be *that* awful.
This is *Aftenposten* after all.'

Geir, sitting on the other side of the table, shook his head.
Then his eyes went in search of the waitress, who came over at
once.

'Pork and onion sauce, please,' he said in Swedish. 'And a pale
Staropramen.'

'I'll have the meatballs, please,' I said and raised my glass. 'And another of these.'

'Thank you, gentlemen,' the waitress said, putting her tiny notebook in her breast pocket and heading for the kitchen, which you could glimpse through the ever-swinging doors.

'What do *you* mean by high morals?' I asked.

'Well, you're a deeply ethical person. There is an ethical foundation at the base of your personality and it is irreducible. You react in a purely physical way to inappropriate behaviour, the shame that overwhelms you is not abstract or conceptual but a hundred-per-cent physical, and you cannot escape it. You're not a dissembler. Nor a moralist though. You know I have a predilection for Victorianism, their system with the front stage where everything is visible and a back stage where everything is hidden. I don't think that kind of life makes anyone happier, but there is more life. You're a Protestant through and through. Protestantism, that's inner life, that's being at one with yourself. You couldn't live a double life even if you wanted to, it's not something you can make happen. There's a one-to-one relationship between life and morality in you. So you are ethically unassailable. Most people are Peer Gynt. They fudge their way along life's road, don't they? You don't. Everything you do you do with the uttermost seriousness and conscientiousness. Have you ever skipped a line of the manuscripts you read, for example? Has it ever happened that you haven't read them from the first page to the last?'

'No.'

'No, and there's something in that. You can't fudge anything. You *can't*. You're an arch-Protestant. And as I've said before, you're an auditor of happiness. If you have some success, generally something others would die for, you just cross it off in the ledger. You're not happy about anything. When you're at one with yourself, which you are almost all the time, you're much, much more disciplined than me. And you know what I'm like with all my systems. There are unmapped areas in your mind where you can lose control, but when you don't go there, and nowadays invariably you don't, you are absolutely ruthless in your morality. You are exposed to temptations far more than me or anyone else. If you had been me you would have lived a double life. But you can't do that. You are doomed to a simple life. Ha ha ha! You're no Peer Gynt and I think that is the heart of your nature. Your ideal is the innocent, innocence. And what is innocence? I'm right at the other end. Baudelaire writes about it, about Virginia, do you remember, the picture of pure innocence, which is confronted with the caricature, and she hears coarse laughter and realises that something dishonourable has happened, but she doesn't know what. She doesn't know! She folds her wings around herself. And then we're back to the painting by Caravaggio, you know, *The Cardsharps*, where he's tricked by all the others. That's you. That's innocence as well. And in that innocence, which in your case also lies in the past, the thirteen-year-old you wrote about in *Out of the World*, and the crazy nostalgia trip you have for the 1970s . . . Linda has some of this too. How was it she was described? Like a mixture of Madame Bovary and Kaspar Hauser?'

'Yes.'

'Kaspar Hauser, he's the enigma of course. Now I never met your previous wife, Tonje, but I've seen photos of her, and although she's not like Linda there was something innocent about her, her appearance. Not that I think she is innocent, necessarily, but she gives that impression. Innocence of this kind is typical of you. Purity and innocence don't interest me. However, it's very clear in you. You're a deeply moral and a deeply innocent person. What is innocence? It is that which has not been touched by the world, that which has not been destroyed, it is like water into which a stone has never been thrown. It's not that you don't have lusts, that you don't have desire, for you do, it's just that you conserve innocence. Your insanely huge longing for beauty comes in here as well. It wasn't by chance that you chose to write about angels. That's the purest of the pure. You can't get purer than that.'

'But not in my novel. There it's about the bodily, the physical side of them.'

'Well, nevertheless, they are the very symbol of purity. And of the fall. But you have made them human, allowed them to fall, not into sin, but into human-ness.'

'If you take an abstract view of this, in a way you're right. The thirteen-year-old, that was innocence, and what happened to it? It had to be made physical.'

'What a way to put it!'

'Yeah, well, OK. She had to be screwed then. And the angels had to become human. So there's a connection. But all this takes place in the subconscious. Deep down. So, in that sense, it's not real. I might be heading in that direction, but I'm not aware of it. Of course, I didn't know I had written a book about shame before reading the blurb on the cover. And I didn't think about innocence and the thirteen-year-old until long after.'

'It's there though. Perfectly obvious and not a shred of doubt.'

'OK. But hidden from me. And it strikes me there's something you're forgetting. Innocence is related to stupidity. What you're talking about is stupidity, isn't it? About ignorance?'

'No, no, far from it,' Geir said. 'Innocence and purity have become a *symbol* of stupidity, but that's nowadays. We live in a culture where the person with the most experience wins. It's sick. Everyone knows which way modernism is going, you create a form by breaking up a form, in an endless regression; just let it continue, and for as long as it does, experience will have the upper hand. The unique feature of our times, the pure or independent act, is, as you know, to renounce, not to accept. Accepting is too easy. There's nothing to be achieved by it. That's more or less where I place you. Almost saint-like, in other words.'

I smiled. The waitress came with our beer.

'*Skål*,' I said.

'*Skål*,' he said.

I took a long swig, wiped the froth from my mouth with the back of my hand and put the glass on the beer mat in front of me. There was something uplifting about the light, golden colour, it seemed to me. I looked at Geir.

'Saint-like?' I repeated.

'Yes. Saints in the Catholic faith could have been close to your way of believing and thinking and acting.'

'You don't think you're going a little too far now?'

'No, not at all. For me, what you do is utter mutilation.'

'Of what?'

'Of life, of opportunities, of living, of creating. Creating life, not literature. For me, you live in an almost frightening asceticism. Or rather, you wallow in asceticism. As I see it, it's extremely unusual. Extremely deviant. I don't think I've ever met anyone, or heard of anyone . . . well, as I said, then I have to go back to the saints or the Church fathers.'

'Stop right there.'

'You did ask. There's no other conceptual framework for you. There are no external characteristics, there's no morality at stake, there's no social morality, that's not where it is. It's in religion. Without a god though, that's clear. You're the only person I know who can take communion despite not believing in God and not commit blasphemy. The only person I know.'

'No one else you know has done it, I suppose?'

'They have, but not with purity! I did it when I got confirmed. I did it for money. Then I renounced the Church. What did I spend the money on? Well, I bought a knife. But that's not what we were talking about. What were we talking about again?'

'Me.'

'Yes, that's right. You have something in common with Beckett, in fact. Not in the way you write, but in the saintliness. It's what Cioran says somewhere: "Compared with Beckett I'm a whore." Ha ha ha! I think that's absolutely spot on. Ha ha ha! And by the way Cioran was reckoned to be one of the most incorruptible people around. I look at your life and regard it as totally wasted. For that matter, I think that of everyone, but your life is even more wasted because there is more to waste. Your morality is not about tax declarations, as that idiot thought, but about your nature. Your nature, nothing less. And it is this enormous discrepancy between you and me which allows us to talk every day. *Sympatio* is the right term for it. I can sympathise with your fate. Because it is a fate, there is nothing you can do about it. All I can do is watch. Nothing can be done for you. There is nothing anyone can do. I feel sorry for you. But I can only view it as a tragedy unfolding at close quarters. As you know, a tragedy is when a great person goes through bad times. In contrast to a comedy, which is when a bad person goes through good times.'

'Why tragedy?'

'Because it is so joyless. Because your life is so joyless. You have such unbelievable reserves and so much talent, which stops there. It becomes art, but never more than that. You're like Midas. Everything he touches turns to gold, but he gains no pleasure from it. Wherever he goes everything around him sparkles and glitters. Others search and search, and when they find a nugget, they sell it to acquire life, splendour, music, dance, enjoyment, luxury, or at least a bit of pussy, right, throw themselves at a woman just to forget they exist for an hour or two. What you lust for is innocence and this is an impossible equation. Lust and innocence can never be compatible. The ultimate is no longer the ultimate when you've stuck your dick in it. You have been allotted the Midas role, you can have everything and how many people do you think can have that? Almost no one. How many would turn it down? Even fewer. One, to my knowledge. If this isn't a tragedy, then I don't know what is. Could your journalist have made anything of this, do you reckon?'

'No.'

'No. He has his journo scales with which he weighs everything. Everyone is lumped into the same pot by journalists. That's the basis of the whole system. But like that he won't get close, not even close, to you or who you are. So we can forget it.'

'It's the same for everyone, Geir.'

'We-ell, maybe, maybe not. Your distorted self-image and your yearning to be like everyone else also come into this.'

'That's what you say. I say that the picture you paint of me is one only you could have painted. Yngve or mum or any one of my relatives or friends wouldn't have had a clue what you were talking about.'

'That doesn't make it any less true, does it?'

'No, not necessarily, but I'm reminded of what she said about you once, that you big up everyone around you because you want your own life to be great.'

'But it is. Everyone's life is as great as they make it. I'm the hero in my own life, aren't I. Well-known people, famous people, people everyone knows, they aren't well known or famous in themselves, in their own right; someone has made them well known, someone has written about them, filmed them, talked about them, analysed them, admired them. That's how they become great for others. But it's just scene-setting. Should my scene-setting be any the less true? No, quite the opposite, because the people I know are in the same room as me, I can touch them, look them in the eye when we talk, we meet in the here and now, and of course we don't do that with any of all those names swirling around us all the time. I'm the Underground Man and you're Icarus.'

The waitress came towards us with the food. A piece of pork protruded from a sea of white onion sauce like an island on the plate she put down in front of Geir. On mine there was a dark heap of meatballs beside bright green mushy peas and red lingon-berry sauce, all in a thick cream sauce. The potatoes were served in a separate dish.

'Thank you,' I said, looking up at the waitress. 'May I have another please?'

'A Staro, yes,' she said, and looked at Geir. He unfolded the serviette over his lap and shook his head.

'I'll wait, thanks.'

I drained the last drop from the glass and put three potatoes on my plate.

'That wasn't a compliment in case you thought it was,' Geir said.

'What wasn't?' I said.

'The saint image. No modern person wants to be a saint. What is a saintly life? Suffering, sacrifice and death. Who the hell would want a great inner life if they don't have any outer life? People only think of what introversion can give them in terms of external life and success. What is the modern view of a prayer? There is only one kind of prayer for modern people and that is as an expression of desire. You don't pray unless there is some-thing you want.'

'I want loads of things.'

'Yes, of course. But they don't give you any pleasure. Not to strive for a happy life is the most provocative thing you can do. And again this is not a compliment. Not at all. I want life. It's all that counts.'

'Talking to you is like going to the devil for therapy,' I said, putting the dish of potatoes in front of him.

'But the devil always loses in the end,' he said.

'We don't know,' I said. 'It's not the end yet.'

'You're right. But there's nothing to indicate that he's going to win. At any rate, not that I can see.'

'Even when God is no longer among us?'

'Among us is the right expression. Before, he wasn't here, he was above us. Now we've internalised him. Incorporated him.'

We ate in silence for a few minutes.

'Well?' Geir said. 'How has your day been?'

'It hasn't really been a day,' I said. 'I tried to write a speech, you know the one, but it was just rubbish, so I've been reading instead.'

'I suppose you could have done worse.'

'Yes, probably. But I've noticed how angry I am at all that. You'll never understand, by the way.'

'What's "all that"?' Geir asked, putting down his glass.

'In this particular case it's the feeling I have when I'm forced to write about my two books. I'm *forced* to pretend it's meaningful, otherwise it's impossible to talk about them, and it's a bit like patting yourself on the back, isn't it. It's repugnant because then I have to stand there talking in complimentary terms about my own books, and those listening are actually *interested*. Why? Afterwards they come to me wanting to tell me how fantastic the books are and what an unbelievably wonderful talk it was, and I don't want to meet their eyes, I don't want to see them, I want to escape from the hell, because I'm a prisoner there, do you understand? There is no worse fate than being subjected to bloody praise. Georg Johannesen spoke about "praise competence". The distinction is redundant, it implies that valuable praise *exists*, but it doesn't. And the higher the authority, the worse it is. At first I'm embarrassed, I have nothing to hide behind, and then I lose my temper. When people start treating me in that special way. You know what I mean. Oh no, shit, you don't know what I mean at all! You're right at the bottom of the ladder, aren't you! You *want* to climb. Ha ha ha.'

'Ha ha ha.'

'That stuff about praise is not quite true, by the way,' I continued. 'If you say something is good, that has meaning. If Geir praises me, it has meaning. And Linda, of course, and Tore and Espen and Thure Erik. All those who are close to me. It's all the outsiders I'm talking about. Where I no longer have any control. I don't know what it is . . . All I know is that success is not to be trusted. I notice that I get angry just talking about it.'

'There are two things you've said that I've taken note of and have made me think a lot,' Geir said, looking at me with his knife and fork hovering over his plate. 'The first was when you were talking about Harry Martinson's suicide. He cut open his stomach after receiving the Nobel Prize. You said you could understand exactly why.'

'Yes, but that's obvious,' I said. 'Getting the Nobel Prize for literature is the greatest dishonour of all for a writer. And his prize was systematically called into question. He was Swedish, he was a member of the Swedish Academy, it was clear there was some kind of cronyism going on, that he didn't really deserve it. And if he didn't deserve it, the whole affair was a mockery. You have to be bloody strong if you're going to get over that sort of mockery. And for Martinson, with all his inferiority complexes,

it must have been unbearable. If that was why he did it. What
was the second?'

'Hm?'

'You said there were two things I'd said which had stuck in
your mind. What was the second?'

'Oh, that was Jastrau in Tom Kristensen's *Havoc*. Do you
remember?'

I shook my head.

'There's no safer place for secrets than in you,' he said. 'You
forget everything. Your brain's like Swiss cheese without the
cheese. You told me *Havoc* was the scariest book you'd ever read.
You said the fall in it wasn't a fall. He just let go, let himself go,
gave up everything he had, to drink, and in the book that seemed
like a real alternative. A good alternative, that is. Just letting go
of everything you have, letting yourself go. Like from the quayside.'

'Now I remember. He writes so well about what it's like to be
drunk. How fantastic it can be. And then you have the feeling
it's not such a big deal. I hadn't thought about the lazy, unre-
sisting side of the fall before. At the time I saw it as something
dramatic, something far-reaching. And it was shocking to think
of it as everyday routine, arbitrary and maybe even wonderful.
Because it is indeed wonderful. The second day of inebriation,
for example. The thoughts that come into your mind . . .'

'Ha ha ha!'

'You could never let go,' I said. 'Could you?'

'No. Could *you*?'

'No.'

'Ha ha ha! But almost everyone I know has done. Stefan boozes
all the time on his farm, doesn't he. Boozes, grills whole pigs
and drives a tractor. When I was at home this summer Odd
Gunnar was drinking whisky from a milk tumbler. The pretext

for filling it to the brim was that I was visiting him. But I didn't drink. And then there's Tony. But he's a drug addict, that's a bit different.'

From one of the tables on the other side a woman who'd had her back to us until now stood up, and as she headed for the door where the toilets were I saw it was Gilda. In the few seconds I was within her sight I bowed my head and studied the table. Not that I had anything against her, I just didn't want to talk to her right now. She had been one of Linda's best friends for years, they had even lived together for a while, and at the beginning of our relationship we spent quite a bit of time in one another's company. She'd had a lot to do with the Vertigo publishing house for a period, I never quite worked out what she did there, but at any rate there were photographs of her on one of their covers, a book by the Marquis de Sade; otherwise she worked at Hedengrens bookshop a few days a week, and recently she had started a company with a girlfriend who also had some connection with literature. She was unpredictable and volatile, but not in any pathological way, it was more a surfeit of life, which meant you never knew what she was going to say or do. One side of Linda was a perfect match. The way they met was typical. Linda had spoken to her in the street, they had never seen each other before, but Linda thought Gilda looked interesting, went over to her and they became friends. Gilda had wide hips, a large bosom, dark hair and Latin features, in appearance she was reminiscent of a 1950s female type, and had been courted by more than one well-known Stockholm writer, but a conspicuous girlishness often shone through this façade, an ill-mannered sullen wild quality. Cora, a more fragile nature, had once said she was frightened of her. Gilda was with a literature student, Kettil, who had just begun a doctorate. Having had a proposal about Herman Bang turned down, he had gone for what they wanted, what they would not reject, namely Holocaust literature, which went through without a problem of course. The last time we had seen each other had been at a party at their place, he had just been to a seminar in Denmark where he had met a Norwegian who studied in Bergen, what was his name? I had asked, Jordal he had said, not Preben by any chance? I had said, yes, that was his name, Preben Jordal. I said he was a friend of mine, we had edited *Vagant* together and I had a high opinion of him, he had both wit and flair, to which Kettil answered nothing, and from the way he said nothing, the slight embarrassment that came over him, a sudden urge to fill my glass and thus create a distance to make the breakdown in communication less obvious, I gathered that Preben might not have mentioned me in equally glowing terms. Then the thought flashed through my mind that he had panned my last book with such vehemence, and twice at that, first in *Vagant*, afterwards in *Morgenbladet*, and that this must have been the topic of conversation in Denmark. Kettil was ill at ease because my name had been dragged through the mud. True, this was little more than a theory, yet I was fairly sure there was something in it. It was strange that I hadn't remembered the panning straight away, but no stranger than my recognition of what lay behind it: Preben belonged to the Bergen section of my memory, that was where he was, while the panning belonged to the Stockholm period, the present, and was tied to the book, not the life around it. Oh, it had hurt, it had been like being stabbed in the heart, or perhaps back would be more apt since I knew Preben. However, I didn't blame Preben so much, more the fact that my book was not infallible, it was not immune to that kind of criticism, in other words, it was not good enough, and at the same time I was also afraid this verdict would be the one that would be passed on the book, these words the ones that would be remembered.

But surely that wasn't why I didn't want to talk to Gilda? Or was it? For me incidents like this lay like a shadow over all those involved. No, it was her company I didn't want to hear about. It was some kind of link between publishing houses and bookshops, as far as I was informed. Some event management stuff? Festivals and stunts . . . ? Whatever it was I didn't want to hear about it.

'Nice evening at your place, by the way,' Geir said.

'Was that the last time we saw each other?'

'Why?'

'That was five weeks ago. Strange you should bring it up now.'

'Ah, I see. I was talking about it with Christina yesterday, perhaps that's why. We were thinking of inviting you all over soon.'

'Good idea,' I said. 'By the way, Thomas is here. Have you seen him? He's at the back there.'

'Oh? Have you talked to him?'

'Briefly. He said he'd come over later.'

'He's reading your book now. Did he say?'

I shook my head.

'He really liked the essay about angels. Thought it should have been much longer. But that's typical of him not to say anything to you. He must have forgotten you wrote it. Ha ha ha! He's so terribly forgetful.'

'I suppose he's just immersed inside himself,' I said. 'The same happens to me. And, for Christ's sake, I'm only thirty-five. Do you remember when I came here with Thure Erik? We stayed here drinking all day and night. As the hours passed he began to talk about his own life. He told me about his childhood, his mother, father and sisters, about generations of his family. Firstly he's pretty damned good at storytelling, and secondly there were a couple of quite sensational things he said. However, even though I listened very carefully and even though I thought to

myself, this is bloody fantastic, by the following day I had
forgotten everything. All that was left was the narrative structure. I remembered that he had talked about his childhood, his
father and his family. And that it had been sensational. But I
couldn't remember *what* it was that constituted the "sensational".
Not a thing! A black hole!'

'You were drunk.'

'That's got nothing to do with it. I remember Tonje was always
talking about something terrible that had happened in her life,
many years ago, she was forever harking back to it, but she
wouldn't say what it was, we didn't know each other well enough,
it was *the* great secret of her life. Do you understand? Two years
went by before she finally told me what it was. There wasn't any
alcohol involved. And I was completely and utterly present, I
listened attentively to every word she had to say, and afterwards
we discussed it at length. But then it was gone. A few months
later nothing was left. I don't remember a thing. And that put
me in an extremely tricky position because this was so unbelievably painful for her, it was such a raw topic she would have left
me if I'd said I was sorry, I couldn't remember anything. So then
I had to pretend I knew the whole story whenever it came up.
And this forgetfulness can arise anywhere. Once, for example, I
suggested to Fredrik at Damm that they should publish a book
of Norwegian short prose, and in his next email he continued
the conversation without referring directly to the idea and I
didn't have a clue what he was talking about. It had totally gone
from my mind. There are writers who have told me what they
are writing about with great passion and intensity, and I have
responded, chatted with equal passion for perhaps half an hour
or an hour at a stretch. A few days later, totally gone. I *still* don't
know what my mother actually wrote her dissertation on. At a
certain point you can no longer ask without causing great

offence, right, so I pretend. I sit there nodding and smiling, wondering what the hell it was again. It's like that for me in all areas of life. You may think it's because I don't care enough, or I'm not present enough, but that's not true, I do care and I am present. Nevertheless, puff, gone. Yngve, on the other hand, can remember everything. Everything! Linda remembers everything. And you remember everything. However, to complicate matters, there are also things that have never been said or have never happened which I'm sure actually took place. Thure Erik again: do you remember when I met Henrik Hovland at Biskops-Arnö?'

'Naturally.'

'It turned out that he came from a farm very close to Thure Erik's. He knew them well and talked a bit about Thure Erik's father. Then I said that Thure Erik's father was dead now. Oh? said Henrik Hovland, it was the first he had heard. But he didn't have much contact with people in the area any more, he said. Nevertheless, he was obviously surprised. He had no doubt it was true. Why would I say Thure Erik's father was dead if he wasn't? Because he wasn't. The next time I met Thure Erik, he spoke about his father in the present tense, with no hesitation or anguish. He was very much alive. So what had made me think he was dead? Enough for me to proclaim it as a fact? I do not know. I haven't a clue. But it meant I was nervous whenever I met Thure Erik after that, for what if he had bumped into Hovland and Henrik had offered his condolences, and Thure Erik had sent him a bemused look, what was he talking about, well, your father, he died so suddenly, didn't he, my father, where the hell did you get that from? Er, Knausgaard told me. Is he alive? Is that what you're saying? But Knausgaard said . . . ? No one on earth would accept I said that by mistake, that I really believed it, because why would I believe it, no one could have told me, no other fathers of people I knew had died, so there was no chance of my being confused. It was pure fantasy, but I thought it was the truth. It's happened a few times, but not because I'm a mythomaniac, I really do believe what I say. God knows how often I go round believing facts that are just nonsense!'

'Good job I'm such a monomaniac and talk about the same stuff all the time. In that way I hammer it home and you can't make a mistake.'

'Are you sure? When was the last time you spoke to your father?'

'Ha ha.'

'It's a disability. It's like poor vision. Over there, is that a person? Or a small tree? Ouch, I've just bumped into something. A table. Aha, it's a restaurant! Keep close to the wall on the way to the bar. Whoops! Something soft? A person? Sorry! Do you *know* me? Oh, Knut Arild! Oh shit! I didn't recognise you straight away . . . And the terrible thought that arises from this is that everyone has such disabilities. Their inner, private, secret black holes which they expend so much energy on trying to hide. And that the world is full of inner cripples bumping into one another. Yes, behind all the attractive and less attractive, though at least normal and non-frightening faces we confront. Not psychologically or spiritually or psychically, but in a conscious manner, physiognomically. Defects in thoughts, consciousness, memory, perception and comprehension.'

'But that *is* how it is. Ha ha ha! That's how it *is*! Look around you, man! Wake up! How many comprehension deficiencies do you think there are just in here? Why do you think we have established forms for everything we do? Forms of conversation, address, lectures, serving, eating, drinking, walking, sitting and even sex. You name it, it's there. Why do you think normality is so sought after if not for this very reason? It's the only place where we can be sure of meeting. But even there we don't meet. Arne Næss once described how, when he knew he was going to meet an ordinary, normal person, he would make a supreme effort to be ordinary and normal while this normal person, from his side, presumably exerted himself to the utmost to reach Næss. Yet they would never meet, according to Næss, the chasm that existed between them could not be bridged. Formally, yes, but not in reality.'

'But wasn't it Arne Næss who also said that he could parachute from a plane anywhere on the planet and know that he would always be greeted with hospitality? Always have a meal and a bed somewhere?'

'Yes, it was. I wrote about it in my thesis.'

'That must be where I've got it from. The world is small.'

'At least ours is,' Geir said with a smile. 'But he's quite right. This is my experience too. There is a kind of minimum common humanity which you meet everywhere. In Baghdad it was very much like that.'

Gilda came behind him across the floor in low heels and a flowery summer dress.

'Hi, Karl Ove,' she said. 'How are you?'

'Hi, Gilda,' I said. 'Very well. How about you?'

'Fine too. Working a lot now, you know. How are things at home? With Linda and your little daughter? It's terrible how time has flown since we last talked. Is she OK? Is she doing well?'

'Yes, she is. She's busy with her course at the moment. So I'm busy taking Vanja out in the buggy during the day.'

'And what's that like?'

I shrugged.

'OK.'

'I'm wondering about it myself, you see. What it's like to have a child. I think they're a bit repellent. And the enormous belly and the milk in your breasts – that bothers me, to tell the truth. But Linda's happy?'

'Oh yes.'

'Well, there you go. Say hello to her. I'll ring her one day. Tell her!'

'I will. Regards to Kettil!'

She raised a hand in a wave and went back to her seat.

'She's just taken her test,' I said. 'Did I tell you that? The first time she drove on her own she was behind a lorry and two lanes merged into one, but she thought she had time to overtake, accelerated and moved out, only to see that she couldn't. Her car was forced against the crash barrier, ended up on its side and skidded along for several hundred metres. But she was unhurt.'

'That one's going to live to be an old lady,' Geir said.

The waitress came and cleared the table. We ordered two more beers. Sat for a while without saying anything. I smoked a cigarette and manoeuvred the soft ash into a little pile in the shiny ashtray with the tip.

'I'm paying today, just so that you know,' I said.

'OK,' Geir said.

If I didn't say straight out I was seeing to the bill he would, and when he had made up his mind it was impossible to change it. Once we had been out, all four of us, Geir and Christina and Linda and me, to a Thai restaurant at the end of Birger Jarlsgatan, and he had said he was going to pay, and I had said no, we should at least share, no, he said, I'm paying and that's that. After the waiter had taken his card I had pulled out half the sum in cash and put it on the table in front of him. He made no move to take it, in fact, it didn't seem as if he had even seen it. The coffee came, we drank it and as we got up to go, ten minutes later, he still hadn't touched the money. Hey, take the money, I said, we're sharing this one. Come on now. No, I'm paying, he repeated. It's your money. You take it. So I had no choice but to pick up the money and stuff it back into my pocket. If I hadn't it would have been left there, I knew. Then he smiled his most obnoxious I-knew-you-would smile. And I regretted not having paid. No sacrifice was too great for Geir when it was about not losing face. But from Christina's face, which was so incredibly sensitive and betrayed all her thoughts, she appeared to be ashamed of him. Or at least found the situation embarrassing. I had never entered into open conflict with him. Wisely, perhaps, for there was something in him I would never defeat. If we had a competition to outstare each other, the way you do when you're young, he would have held my stare for a week if need be. I would have held his as well, but sooner or later I would have thought this was unnecessary and looked down. He would never entertain such an idea.

'Well,' I said. 'How has *your* day been?'

'I've been writing about the *Grenzsituation*, the border situation. To be precise, about Stockholm in the eighteenth century. How high the mortality rate was, how short their lives were and what they did with the lives they had, compared with ours. Then Cecilia came into the office wanting to chat. We went for lunch together. She had been out last night with her partner and his friend. She had flirted with the friend all evening, she said, and her partner had been livid when they got home, of course.'

'How long have they been together?'

'Six years.'

'Was she thinking of leaving him?'

'No, not at all. On the contrary, she wants children with him.'

'So why the flirting?' I asked.

Geir looked at me.

'She wants to have her cake and eat it, obviously.'

'What did you say to her? I assume she went to you for advice?'

'I said she should deny it. Deny everything. She hadn't been flirting, she'd just been friendly. Say no, no, no. And then don't be so bloody stupid next time, wait for an opportunity to offer itself and go about it calmly and collectedly. I don't blame her for doing what she did. I blame her for being inconsiderate. She hurt him. That was uncalled for.'

'She must have known you would say that. Otherwise she wouldn't have gone to you.'

'I agree. Had she gone to you, on the other hand, it would have been to get advice about admitting everything, going down on her knees and begging for forgiveness and then sticking to her lawful husband from then on.'

'Yes, either that or leaving him.'

'The worst is that you mean it.'

'Of course I mean it,' I said. 'The year after I was unfaithful to Tonje and didn't say anything was the worst year I've ever experienced. It was blackest night. One long, endless bloody night. I thought about it all the time. Jumped out of the chair in alarm whenever the phone rang. And if the word infidelity was mentioned on TV I blushed from head to toe. I was on fire inside. When we hired films I studiously avoided anything connected with it because I knew that sooner or later she would notice me squirming like a grub whenever the topic came up. And the fact that I had been guilty destroyed everything else in my life, I couldn't say anything with heartfelt sincerity, it was all lies and pretence. It was a nightmare.'

'Would you own up now?'

'Yes.'

'What about the events on Gotland?'

'That wasn't infidelity.'

'But it still torments you?'

'Yes, it does.'

'Cecilia wasn't unfaithful. Why should she tell her partner what she was thinking of doing?'

'That's not what this is about. It's about intent. As long as it's there you have to take the consequences.'

'What about your intentions on Gotland?'

'I was drunk. I wouldn't have done it if I'd been sober.'

'But you would have thought it?'

'Maybe. It's a huge leap, though.'

'Tony's a Catholic, as you know. His priest said once, and I took note, sinning is putting yourself in a position where a sin becomes possible. Getting drunk, when you know what's on your mind and what pressure there is inside you, is putting yourself in such a position.'

'Yes, but I thought I was absolutely safe before I started drinking.'

'Ha ha ha!'

'It's true.'

'Karl Ove. What you did was nothing. A bagatelle. And everyone understands that. Everyone. What did you do actually? Knock on a door?'

'For half an hour, yes. In the middle of the night.'

'But she didn't let you in?'

'No, no. She opened the door and gave me a bottle of water, and closed it again.'

'Ha ha ha! And for that you sat shaking, white-faced, when I met you. You looked as though you'd killed someone.'

'It felt like it.'

'But actually it was nothing, was it?'

'Possibly. But I can't forgive myself. And that's the way it will be until my dying day. I have a long list of things I've done when I didn't behave well. And that's what it's about. For Christ's sake, you shouldn't cheat. And one would have thought it was an easy ideal to uphold. For some it is. I know some people, not many, but some who always do the right thing. Who are always good, decent people. I'm not talking about those who don't do anything wrong because they don't do anything, because the lives they lead are so trivial that nothing can be destroyed, for they exist as well. I'm talking about those people who are fair to the last fibre of their being, and those who always know the best way to act in every situation. Those who don't put themselves first, who don't betray their principles. You've met them as well. People good through to the core, right? And they wouldn't know what I was talking about. Precisely because it's not something they have given any thought to, they don't think like that, that they should be good; they just *are*, and are unaware of it. They take care of their friends, they're considerate to their partners, they're good parents, but not in a feminine way, always do a good job, they want whatever is good and do whatever is good. Whole people. Jon Olav, for example, you know, my cousin.'

'Yes, I've met him.'

'He's always been an idealist, but not in order to achieve anything for himself. He's always stood up for everyone who's needed him. And he's not in the slightest bit corrupt. The same applies to Hans. His integrity – yes, that's the word I was after. Integrity. If you have integrity you do the right thing. I have so little integrity, there's always something . . . well, not sick exactly, but something base, fawning, creeping, it oozes out of me. If I get into a situation that requires prudence, where everyone knows prudence is required, I can just steam in, right, and why? Because I only think about myself, only see myself, ooze out of myself. I can be good to others, but then I need to have it formulated in advance. It's not in my blood. It's not in my nature.'

'And where do you place me in this system of yours?'

'You?'

'Yes.'

'Oh, you're a cynic. You're proud and ambitious, perhaps the proudest person I know. You would never do anything openly debasing, you'd rather starve and live on the street. You're loyal to your friends. I trust you blindly. At the same time you look after yourself and can be ruthless to others if for some reason you have something against them, or if they've done something to you, or if there is something greater to gain by it. Isn't that true?'

'Yes, but I'm always considerate to those I like. Really. Scrupulous might be a more accurate expression. There is in fact an important distinction.'

'Scrupulous then. But let me mention one example. You lived with the human shield in Iraq, travelled with them all the way from Turkey, shared everything with them in Baghdad. Some of them became your friends. They were there because of their convictions, which you didn't in fact share, but they didn't know that.'

'They had a suspicion,' Geir said with a smile.

'So when the US Marines come, you simply say goodbye to your friends and go over to their enemies without a backward glance. You betrayed them. There is no other way to see it. But you didn't betray yourself. I place you somewhere around there. It's a free, independent place, but the price of getting there is high. People lie strewn around you like skittles. That wouldn't be possible for me. Social pressure from all sides starts when I get up from my office chair and by the time I'm in the street I'm bound hand and foot by it. I can hardly move. Ha ha ha! But it's true. At bottom, and I don't think you have understood this, it's not saintliness or high morals but cowardice. Cowardice and nothing else. Don't you think I'd like to cut all my ties to everyone and do what I want, not what they want?'

'Yes, I do.'

'Do you think I'm going to do that?'

'No.'

'You're free. I'm not. It's as simple as that.'

'No, it isn't, not by a long chalk,' Geir said. 'You may be trapped by social pressure, which sounds strange, after all you never meet anyone. Ha ha ha! But I understand what you mean, and you're right, you try to take account of everyone all at once. I've seen it with my own eyes, how you run around when we come to yours for a meal. However, there are many ways to be trapped; there are many ways of not being free. You have to remember that you've had everything you wanted. You've had your revenge on those you targeted. You have status. People sit waiting for what you do and wave palm leaves as soon as you show your face. You can write an article about something that interests you and it will be in print in the newspaper of your choice a few days later. People ring and want you to go here, there and everywhere. Newspapers ask you for a comment on all sorts of matters. Your books will be published in Germany and England. Do you understand the freedom there is in that? Do you understand what has opened in your life? You talk about a longing to let go and fall. If I let go I would be standing in the same place. I'm standing right at the bottom. No one's interested in what I write. No one's interested in what I think. No one invites me anywhere. I have to force my way in, right? Whenever I enter a room full of people I have to make myself interesting. I don't pre-exist, like you, I don't have a name, I have to create everything from scratch every time. I'm sitting at the bottom of a hole in the ground and shouting through a megaphone. It doesn't matter what I say, no one is listening. And you know that whatever I say from the outside contains a criticism of what is inside. And then by definition you're self-opinionated. The embittered querulous type. Meanwhile the years pass. I'll soon be forty and I don't have *any* of what I wanted to have. You say it's brilliant and unique, and perhaps it is, but what good is that? You have everything you want, and you can dispense with it, leave it, make no use of it. But I can't. I *have* to get in. I've spent twenty years trying. The book I'm busy with now is going to take three years at least. I can already feel how the world around me is losing belief and hence any interest. I'm becoming more and more like a madman refusing to drop his mad project. Everything I say is measured against that. When I said something after my doctorate it was measured against that, that was when I was academically and intellectually alive, now I'm dead. And the more time that passes the better the next book has to be. It's not enough for the next book to be all right, pretty OK, very good, because I've spent a lot of time on it and because my age is, relatively speaking, so advanced that it has to be outstanding. From that perspective, I'm not free. And to link up with what we were talking about before, the Victorian ideal, which wasn't an ideal but a reality, namely a double life. Therein lies a sorrow too because such a life can never be whole. And of course that's what everyone dreams of, one love affair, or falling in love with someone, when cynicism and calculation are absent, when everything is whole. Yes, you know. Romance. A double life is a passable resolution of a problem, but it is not unproblematic, if that's what you reckoned I went around thinking. It's practical, provisional, pragmatic, in other words, part of life. But it's not whole, and it's not ideal. The most important difference between us is not that I'm free and you aren't. For I don't believe this to be the case. The most important difference is that I'm happy, a glad soul. And you aren't.'

'I don't think I'm that unglad—'

'Exactly! Unglad. Only you can use a word like that! It says everything about you.'

'Unglad is a good word. I've seen it in the old Norwegian saga *Heimskringla*, in point of fact. And the Storm translation is a hundred years old. But perhaps it's time we changed the subject?'

'If you'd said that two years ago I would have understood.'

'OK. I can go on. After everything finished with Tonje I went to an island and lived there for two months. I had been there before, I just had to get on the phone and everything was arranged. A house, a small island, right out in the sea, three other people there. It was the end of the winter, so the whole island was frozen and stiff. I walked all over it thinking. And what I thought was that I would have to do everything I could to become a good person. Everything I did should be to that end. But not in the abject, evasive manner that had characterised my behaviour so far, you know, being overcome by shame at the smallest trifle. The indignity of it. No, in the new image I was drawing of myself there was also courage and backbone. Look people straight in the eye, say what I stood for. I had become more and more hunched, you see, I wanted to occupy less and less space, and on the island I began to straighten my back, quite literally. No joking. At the same time I read Hauge's diaries. All 3,000 pages. It was an enormous consolation.'

'He went through worse times, didn't he?'

'He certainly did. But that wasn't the point. He fought *without cease* for the same, for the ideal of how he should be, as compared with the person he was. The determination to fight was extraordinarily strong in him. And that in a man who didn't really do anything, didn't really experience anything, just read, wrote and fought his inner struggle on a stupid little farm by a stupid little fjord in a stupid little country on the margin of the world.'

'No wonder he was prone to going absolutely bananas.'

'You get the impression it was also a relief. He gave in, and part of the velocity with which he was hurled off course was born of happiness. He escaped the iron grip on himself and relaxed, so it seemed.'

'The question is whether it was God,' Geir said. 'The feeling of being seen, of being forced to your knees by something that can see you. We just have a different name for it. The superego or shame or whatever. That was why God was a stronger reality for some than others.'

'So the urge to give yourself to baser feelings and wallow in pleasure and vice would be the devil?'

'Exactly.'

'That's never attracted me. Apart from when I drink, that is. Then everything goes overboard. What I want to do is travel, see, read and write. To be free. Completely free. And I had a chance to be free on the island because the reality was that I had finished with Tonje. I could have travelled anywhere I wanted – Tokyo, Buenos Aires, Munich. But instead I headed out there, where there wasn't a soul. I didn't understand myself, I had no idea who I was, so what I resorted to, all these ideas about being a good person, was simply all I had. I didn't watch TV, I didn't read newspapers, and all I ate was crispbread and soup. When I indulged myself out there it was with fishcakes and cauliflower. And oranges. I started doing press-ups and sit-ups. Can you imagine? How desperate do you have to be to start doing press-ups to solve your problems?'

'This is all about purity, nothing less. Through and through. Asceticism. Don't be corrupted by TV or the newspapers, eat as little as possible. Did you drink coffee?'

'Yes, I drank coffee. But it's true what you said about purity. There is something almost fascist about it all.'

'Hauge wrote that Hitler was a great man.'

'He wasn't so old then. But the worst of it is that I can understand: that need to rid yourself of all the banality and small-mindedness rotting inside you, all the trivia that can make you angry or unhappy, that can create a desire for something pure and great into which you can dissolve and disappear. It's getting rid of all the shit, isn't it? One people, one blood, one earth. Now precisely this has been discredited once and for all. But what lies behind it, I don't have any problem understanding that. And as sensitive to social pressure, as governed by what others think of me as I am, God knows what I would have done if I'd lived through the 1940s.'

'Ha ha ha! Relax. You don't do what everyone else does now, so you probably wouldn't have then.'

'But when I moved to Stockholm and fell in love with Linda, everything changed. It was as though I had been raised above trivia, none of it mattered, everything was good and there were no problems anywhere. I don't know how to explain . . . It was as though my inner strength was so great everything outside it was crushed. I was invulnerable, do you understand? Filled with light. Everything was light! I could even read Hölderlin! It was an utterly fantastic time. I've never been happier. I was bursting with happiness.'

'I can remember. You were up in Bastugatan and positively glowing. You were almost luminous. You played Manu Chao again and again. It was barely possible to talk to you. You were running over with happiness. Sitting in bed like some bloody lotus flower, beaming all over your face.'

'The point is that all this is about perspectives. Seen in one way, everything offers pleasure. Seen in another, just sorrow and misery. Do you think I cared about all the rubbish TV and the press stuff us with while I sat up there being happy? Do you

think I was ashamed of anything at all? I was tolerant of everything. I couldn't bloody lose. That was what I told you when you
were so terribly depressed and beyond yourself the following
autumn. It was all about perspective. Nothing in your world had
changed or become an urgent problem except for the way you
saw it. But of course you didn't listen to me; you went to Iraq
instead.'

'The last thing you want to hear when you're in the darkness
of depression is the babbling of some happy tosser. But I was
happy when I returned. It got me out of it.'

'Yes, and now the roles are reversed again. Now I'm sitting
here and complaining about the wretchedness of life.'

'I think it's the natural order,' he said. 'Have you started doing
press-ups again?'

'Yes.'

He smiled. I smiled too.

'What the hell am I going to do?' I said.

We left Pelikanen an hour later, took the same Metro train to
Slussen, where Geir changed to the red line. He placed his hand
on my shoulder, told me to take care and say hello to Linda and
Vanja. I slumped back into the seat after he had gone, wishing
I could sit there for hour after hour and travel through the
night, not like now, having to stand up and get off at Hötorget,
only three stations along.

The carriage was nearly empty. A young man with a guitar
case on his back stood holding the pole by the door, thin as a
toothpick with curly black hair falling from under his hat. Two
girls of around sixteen on the seat at the back were showing
each other text messages. An elderly man in a black coat, rust-
red scarf and the kind of grey woollen almost square hat worn
in the 1970s sat on the opposite side. Facing him was a small

dumpy woman with South American features in a large Puffa jacket, cheap dark blue jeans, suede boots with an edge of synthetic wool at the top.

I had forgotten the telephone business until Geir reminded me just before we left. He handed me his mobile and said I should ring my phone, which I did, but no one answered. We agreed he would write a text asking her to ring my home number and send it in half an hour, by which time I should be at home.

Perhaps she might think this was some kind of pick-up? I had intentionally put the phone in her bag so that I could ring her later?

At T-Centralen Metro station the place was heaving. Mostly young people, a few boisterous gangs, a number of loners with small headsets over their ears, some with sports bags between their feet.

They probably all slept at home.

The idea came from nowhere and tingled.

This was my life. This was what my life was.

I had to pull myself together. Chin up.

A train passed on the parallel track, for a few seconds I saw straight into an aquarium-like carriage with passengers sitting immersed in their own thoughts, then they were propelled upwards on their path while we were hurled down a tunnel where there was nothing to see but the reflection of the carriage and my vacant face. I stood up and went to the door as the train slowed. Crossed the platform and took the escalator up to Tunnelgatan. The fat blonde woman in her thirties who had long been anonymous to me until Linda had greeted her once and said she had been at Biskops-Arnö with her sat in the ticket office window. As our eyes met she looked down. Fine by me, I thought, pushing the barrier aside with my thigh and leaping up the last steps.

Whenever I climbed the long staircase up to Malmskillnadsgatan it went through my mind that my homeward route was probably the same one that Olaf Palme's murderer had followed. I remembered every detail of the day when the murder had been made public. What I had been doing, what I had been thinking. It had been a Saturday. Mum had been ill and I had caught the bus to town with Jan Vidar. We had been seventeen years old. If the Palme murder had not taken place the day would have vanished, as all the others had. All the hours, all the minutes, all the conversations, all the thoughts, all the events. Into a pool of oblivion with everything else. And then the little that was left would have to represent the whole. How ironic was it that the only reason it remained was that it stood out from the rest?

In the KGB restaurant a few long-haired men sat by the window drinking. Otherwise it appeared to be empty. But perhaps all the action was in the cellar this evening.

Two black shiny taxis raced past towards the centre. Snowflakes swirled up, settling seconds later on my face, which was level with the road. I crossed, jogged the last metres to the front door and let myself in. Luckily, no one was in the front hallway or the stairwell. The flat was silent.

I took off my coat and shoes, walked quietly through the living room and opened the bedroom door. Linda opened her eyes and looked at me in the semi-darkness. She stretched out her arms towards me.

'Did you have a nice evening?'

'Yes,' I said, bending forward to kiss her. 'Everything OK here?'

'Mhm. We missed you. Are you coming to bed now?'

'I'll grab a bite to eat first. Then I'll come. OK?'

'OK.'

Vanja lay in her cot with her backside in the air and her face pressed against the pillow as usual. I smiled as I walked past. I drank a glass of water in the kitchen, stared into the fridge for a while before taking out some margarine and a packet of ham. Took the bread from the cupboard next to it. As I was about to close the door I glanced at the bottles on the top shelf. There was nothing casual about my glance. The bottles were not standing in their usual positions. The half-full bottle of aquavit from Christmas had changed places with the Calvados. The grappa that had been at the back was now to one side near the Dutch gin. Had that been all, I would not have given it a second thought, I would have concluded I must have cleaned the shelf on Saturday, but now that I was looking, the bottles also seemed to be less full. The very same thought had struck me only a week ago, but I had dismissed it. We must have drunk more than I remembered when we'd had people round. Now, on top of every-thing else, they were in different positions.

I stood for a while rotating the various bottles in my hands wondering what could have happened. The grappa had been almost full, hadn't it? I had poured three small shots after a dinner we'd had a few weeks ago. Now it was right down by the label. And the aquavit, surely there had been more than a bit at the bottom? And the cognac, surely there had been a bit more as well?

These were bottles I brought back with me when I had been travelling or ones we had been given. We never drank from them, except when we had guests.

Could it be Linda?

Was she having a drink when she was alone here?

On the quiet?

No, no, no, absolutely no chance. She hadn't had a drop of alcohol since she became pregnant. And as long as she was breastfeeding she wouldn't touch it.

Was she lying?

Linda?

No, hardly likely. I couldn't be that blind.

I put the bottles back, exactly as they had been, in positions I would remember. I also tried to memorise more or less how much was left in each of them. Then I closed the cupboard door and sat down to eat.

Probably my memory had been playing tricks on me. Probably we had drunk more than I had realised in recent weeks. I didn't know exactly how much there was left. Then the bottles had been moved around when I cleaned the cupboard on Saturday. It was quite normal not to remember. Wasn't it Tolstoy who wrote about this in his diaries, according to Shklovsky? About not being able to remember whether he had dusted the living room or not? If he had, what status did the experience have, and what time did it occupy?

Oh, Russian formalism, where have you been all my life?

I got up and was just about to clear the table when the telephone rang in the living room. Fear gripped my chest. But then I remembered the text message Geir had sent to my mobile. Nothing to be concerned about.

I hurried to the phone and picked it up.

'Hello, Karl Ove here,' I said.

The other end of the line was quiet for some seconds. Then a voice said, 'Are you the person who has lost a mobile phone?'

The voice belonged to a man. He spoke broken Swedish, and if the tone was not aggressive, it was not particularly friendly either.

'Yes, that's me. Have you found it?'

'It was in my fiancée's bag when she came home. Now would you mind telling me how it ended up there?'

The door opened in front of me. Linda came through and sent me a worried stare. I raised my hand in defence and smiled.

'I had the phone in my hand on the platform at Rådmannsgatan when someone knocked me from behind and I lost it. I turned to the man who had nudged me and didn't see where it landed. But I never heard it hit the ground. Then I saw a woman with an open bag over her arm and guessed that it had to be there.'

'Why didn't you say anything to her? Why did you want her to contact you?'

'The train arrived at that moment. And I didn't have the time. Besides, I wasn't sure that was where it had landed. I couldn't go over to a stranger and ask her if I could look in her bag, could I.'

'Are you Norwegian?'

'Yes.'

'OK. I believe you. You can have your phone back. Where do you live?'

'In the city centre. Regeringsgatan.'

'Do you know where Banérgatan is?'

'No.'

'Östermalm, one street up from Strandgatan, right by Karlaplan. There's an ICA shop there. Be there at twelve. I'll be outside. If I'm not, your mobile will be at the cash desk. Just ask the assistant. OK?'

'Fine. Thanks.'

'Don't be so cack-handed next time.'

Then he rang off. Linda, who had sat down on the sofa with a blanket over her lap, raised her eyebrows.

'What was that about?' she asked. 'Who was it, ringing at such a late hour?'

She laughed when I told her what had happened. Not so much at the sequence of events as at the suspicion it had been greeted with. If you wanted to meet a woman whose telephone number you didn't know, what better way than to drop a phone in her bag and then ring her up?

I sat down beside her on the sofa. She snuggled up to me.

'Now Vanja's on the waiting list for the nursery,' she said. 'I rang them today.'

'Did you? That's great!'

'I have mixed feelings, I must confess,' she said. 'She's so small. But maybe we can send her for half a day to start with?'

'Of course.'

'Little Vanja.'

I looked at her. It was as though her face was tired from the sleep she had just woken up from. Narrow eyes, doughy skin. Surely she couldn't be drinking on the sly? With the immense affection she had for Vanja and the seriousness she brought to the maternal role?

No, definitely not. How could I even think it?

'There's something mysterious going on in the kitchen cupboard,' I said. 'Whenever I see the bottles there seems to be less in them. Have you noticed?'

She smiled.

'No, but we're probably drinking more than you realise.'

'Seems so,' I said.

I laid my forehead against hers. Her eyes, which looked straight into mine, filled me to the brim. In this short second they were all I saw, they shone with her life, the way she lived it inside her.

'I miss you,' she said.

'I'm here,' I said. 'What is it? Do you want all of me?'

'Yes, that's what I want,' she said, taking my hands and drawing me down onto the sofa.

Next morning I got up at half past four as usual, worked on editing the translated collection of short stories until seven and had breakfast with Linda and Vanja without saying a word. At eight Ingrid came to collect Vanja. Linda went to her course and I sat reading the online newspapers for half an hour before starting to answer the emails that had accumulated. Then I showered, dressed and went out. The sky was blue, the low sun shone across the town and although it was still cold, the light presaged a sense of spring, even deep down in the shadowy street I followed on the way towards Stureplan. Obviously I was not the only person to feel this; whereas the previous day people had walked with lowered heads and stooped shoulders, now they lifted their faces and in the eyes they viewed the world with there was both curiosity and happiness. Was this open cheery town the same as the enclosed depressed one we were walking around yesterday? While the muted winter light that had forced its way through the clouds seemed to draw all the colours and flat surfaces towards one another and minimise the differences between them with its greyness and frailty, this clear, direct sunlight emphasised them. Around me the town exploded with colour. Not the warm biological colours of the summer but the mineral colours of the winter, cold and synthetic. Red brick, yellow brick, dark green car bonnets, blue signs, an orange jacket, a purple scarf, grey-black tarmac, verdigris metal and shiny chrome. Sparkling windows, glowing walls and glinting gutters on one side of a building; black windows, dark walls, toned down almost invisible gutters on the other. In Birger Jarlsgatan the snow lay heaped along the side of the street, sometimes gleaming, sometimes grey and mute, all depending on how the sunlight fell. Towards Stureplan and into Hedengrens bookshop, where a young man was unlocking the door as I arrived. I went down to the basement, drifted between shelves and collected a pile of books which I sat down to flick through. I bought a biography of Ezra Pound because I was interested in his theory about money and hoped it would be included, a book about science in China from 1550 to 1900, a book about the economic history of the world written by a certain Rondo Cameron, and a book about native Americans which described all the tribes existing before the Europeans arrived, a magnificent work of 600 pages. In addition, I found a book about Rousseau by Starobinski, and a book about Gerhard Richter, *Doubt and Belief in Painting,* which I bought. I knew nothing about Pound, economics, science, China or Rousseau, nor whether I was interested, but I was about to write a novel soon, and I had to start somewhere. I had been thinking about the Indians for a long time. Some months ago I had seen a picture of some Indians in a canoe. They were paddling across a lake, in the bow was a man dressed like a bird with its wings outstretched. The picture penetrated all the layers of conceptions I had about Indians, everything I had read in books and comics and seen in films, straight through to reality: they had existed. They had indeed lived their lives with their totem poles, spears and bows and arrows, alone on an enormous continent, blissfully unaware that lives other than theirs were not only possible but also existed. It was a fantastic thought. The romance this picture evoked, with its wildness, this birdman and this untouched nature therefore evolved from reality and not vice versa, which was otherwise always the case. It was shocking. I can't explain it in any other way. I was shocked. And I knew I would have to write about it. Not about the picture itself but what it contained. Then all the counter-arguments seeped through. They might have existed once, but they didn't any more, they and their culture had long since been wiped out. Why write about it then? Their time was gone and it would never return. If I created a new world in which elements of their culture were to be found, it would just be literature, just fiction, and worthless. However, I could counter that Dante, for example, had written just fiction, that Cervantes had written just fiction and that Melville had written just fiction. It was irrefutable that being human would not be the same if these three works had not existed. So why not write just fiction? The truth did not, of course, have a one-to-one relationship with reality. Good arguments, but they didn't help, just the thought of fiction, just the thought of a fabricated character in a fabricated plot made me feel nauseous, I reacted in a physical way. Had no idea why. But I did. The Indians would have to wait. I was aware I might not always feel like this.

After I had paid for the books I went down to the lower section of Sergels torg, to the music and film shop, where I bought three DVDs and five CDs, next up to Akademi bookshop, where I found a dissertation on Swedenborg published by Atlantis, which I bought along with a couple of journals. I wouldn't get round to reading much of this, which did not prevent me from feeling good, however. I went home, unloaded my purchases, had a couple of sandwiches standing by the kitchen worktop and went out again, this time across Östermalm to the shop in Banérgatan, where I arrived at twelve on the dot.

No one was there. I lit a cigarette and waited. Searched the faces of passers-by, but no one stopped or came over. After fifteen minutes I went into the shop and asked the female assistant if anyone had handed in a mobile phone today. Yes, indeed, it was here. Could I describe it?

I did, and she took it from a drawer beside the till and passed it to me.

'Thank you,' I said. 'Who handed it in? Do you know?'

'Yes, well, I mean I don't know his name. But he's a young guy. He works at the Israeli Embassy just over there.'

'At the *Israeli* Embassy?'

'Yes.'

'Oh, right. Thank you again. Bye.'

'Bye.'

I sauntered down the street grinning to myself. The Israeli Embassy! No damn wonder he had been suspicious! The phone must have been examined outside and in. All the text messages, all the phone numbers . . . heh heh heh!

I switched it on and rang Geir.

'Hello?' he said.

'Someone rang about my mobile yesterday,' I said. 'He was very suspicious, but in the end agreed to give it back to me. So now I've just picked it up. He left it at a shop till. I asked the girl working there if she knew who he was. Do you know what she said?'

'Of course not.'

'He worked in the Israeli Embassy.'

'You're joking!'

'I'm not. When I dropped my phone it didn't land on the platform, it landed in a bag. And when I dropped it into a bag it wasn't just anyone's bag but one belonging to the girlfriend of someone working at the Israeli Embassy. Bizarre, eh?'

'I think you can forget the girlfriend idea. It's more likely she works at the Israeli Embassy and contacted them when she found your mobile. So they sat there looking at this phone wondering who the hell could have planted it. And what was it? A bomb? A microphone?'

'And what on earth did the Norwegian connection signify? Something to do with heavy water? Revenge for the Lillehammer Affair?'

'It's unbelievable how you manage to get caught up in things. Russian prostitutes and Israeli agents. That writer you invited to dinner, who weighed all the food before she ate it, what was her name?'

'Maria. She has a Russian connection too, by the way.'

'And who had to ring someone and tell them exactly what she had eaten after the meal. Ha ha ha!'

'What's that got to do with anything?'

'I don't know. That weird things happen when you're around perhaps? Linda's other friend who's in love with a drug addict whose sister lives in your building? The flat you got in the block where Linda lived? Your computer being exposed to all sorts, getting drenched in the rain, being dropped from a train onto the rails and it isn't damaged. You losing your phone and it turning up in an Israeli Embassy worker's bag slots neatly into the frame.'

'That all sounds very intense and jolly,' I said. 'But the truth about my life is quite different, as you know.'

'Oh, come on, can't we pretend for once?'

'No. What are you doing?' I asked.

'What do you think?'

'Sounds very much like you're messing around backstage. So I suppose you're writing.'

'I suppose I am. And you?'

'I'm on my way to Filmhus. Going to have lunch with Linda. Catch you later.'

'OK.'

I rang off, put the phone in my pocket and picked up the pace. Walked past the drained fountain in Karlaplan, through Feltöversten, into Valhallavägen to Filmhus, which was on the edge of the semi-snow-covered Gärdet district and glittered in the sun.

After lunch I caught the Metro to Odenplan and walked from there to my office, mostly to have somewhere to sit in peace. Ingrid had a key for the flat and would probably be there with

Vanja. I wasn't in the right frame of mind for cafés either, with all the unfamiliar faces and restless eyes. So I sat behind the desk and tried for a while to write my talk, but I just became depressed. Instead I lay down on the sofa and fell asleep. When I awoke the street outside was dark and it was ten minutes past four. The *Aftenposten* journalist was coming at six, so I had no choice but to put my coat on and go home if I wanted to see anything of Vanja and Linda that day.

'Anyone at home?' I called as I opened the door. Vanja crawled through the hall towards me at full speed, laughing, and I threw her up in the air a few times before carrying her into the kitchen, where Linda was stirring a saucepan.

'Chickpea stew,' she said. 'Best I could manage.'

'Oh, that's good,' I said. 'How's it been with Vanja today?'

'Fine, I think. They spent the whole morning in the children's museum. Mummy's just left. Did you bump into her?'

'No,' I said, and took Vanja to our bed, tossed her around until I was tired, sat her down, flushed and sweaty from laughing, on the chair by the kitchen worktop and went into the living room to check my emails. After reading them I switched off the computer and gazed down at the flat across the street on the floor beneath ours, where another computer was lit. Once I had seen a man masturbating in front of the screen there. He thought he couldn't be seen, hadn't realised he was visible from here. He was alone in the room, but not in the flat; on the other side of the wall was a kitchen, where a man and a woman were sitting. It was strange to see how close private and open areas were to one another.

Now the room was empty. Just pixels jumping about on the screen, the light of a lamp in the corner falling across a chair, and a little table with a book face up.

'Food's ready!' Linda shouted from the kitchen. I got to my feet and joined them. It was already a quarter past five.

'When are they supposed to be coming?' Linda asked. She must have noticed me glance at the clock.

'At six. But we'll go out straight away. You won't need to show your face. Well, you can say hello to them if you like, but you don't have to.'

'I think I'll stay here. Out of sight. Are you nervous?'

'No, but I'm not in the mood. You know what it's like.'

'Don't give it a thought. Just chat with them, say what you want and don't be hard on yourself. Relax.'

'I spoke to that Majgull Axelsson, you know, the writer? She was at the lectures in Tvedestrand and Gothenburg. During the tour she took me under her maternal wing a bit. She said she made it a rule never to read what was written about her, never to watch herself on TV and never to listen to herself on the radio. Treat them as one-offs. Just concentrate on the moment it's happening, she said. They were meetings with people then, that was all, easy, no complications. That made sense to me. But there was all the vanity business, wasn't there? Am I being presented as a complete idiot now, or just an idiot? And is it the presentation or is it me?'

'I wish you would drop all this,' Linda said. 'It's so unnecessary! It takes so much out of you. It occupies you all the time.'

'Yes, I know. But I will stop doing it. I'll refuse everything.'

'You're such a wonderful person. If only you could see that.'

'My basic feeling is the opposite. In fact, it pervades everything. And don't say I should have therapy.'

'I didn't say a word!'

'You feel the same,' I said. 'The only difference is that you also have periods when your self-esteem is intact, not to put too fine a point on it.'

'Just hope Vanja will be spared this,' Linda said, looking at her. She smiled at us. The whole table was covered with rice, and the floor under the chair. Her lips were red with sauce, and white grains were stuck around her mouth.

'But she won't be,' I said. 'It's impossible. Either she has it from the start or she picks it up on the way. It's impossible to hide. But it might not mark her. It doesn't have to, does it?'

'I hope not,' Linda said.

Her eyes were moist.

'That was delicious anyway,' I said, getting up. 'I'll do the washing-up. Should manage it before they come.'

I turned to Vanja.

'How big is Vanja?' I asked.

She stretched her arms above her head proudly.

'So big!' I said. 'Come on, and I'll give you a little wash.'

I lifted her off the chair and carried her into the bathroom, where I rinsed her face and hands. Held her up in front of the mirror and rested my cheek against hers. She laughed.

Then I changed her nappy in the bedroom, set her down on the floor and went in to clear the table. After it was done and the dishwasher was humming beneath the worktop I opened the cupboard to check in the unlikely event that something had happened to the bottles.

It had. Someone had drunk from the grappa bottle since yesterday, and I was absolutely certain because the contents had been level with the edge of the label. The cognac was standing in a different position and although I wasn't quite so sure of this, it appeared some had been drunk.

What the hell was going on?

I refused to believe that Linda was behind this. Especially after we had been chatting about it the night before.

But there was no one else here.

It wasn't as if we had a home help or anything.

Oh shit, no.

Ingrid.

She had been here today. And yesterday. It had to be her, it was obvious.

But was she drinking while she was looking after Vanja? Was she sitting here with her grandchild around her legs and knocking back the juice?

If so, she would have to be an alcoholic. Vanja was everything to her. She wouldn't risk anything, for Vanja's sake. But if she was still drinking, the urge had to be stronger in her, it had to be, she was willing to risk everything for it.

Oh, Lord above, please be merciful.

From the bedroom floor I could hear Linda's footsteps approaching, so I closed the cupboard door, went to the worktop, took a cloth and began to wipe down the surface. It was ten minutes to six.

'I'll go down for a smoke before they come. Is that OK?' I said. 'There's a bit left to do, but . . .'

'Of course. Off you go,' Linda said. 'Take the rubbish down on the way, will you?'

At that precise moment the doorbell rang. I went to open up. A young man with a beard and a shoulder bag stood there smiling. Behind him was another man, older, dark-skinned, with a large camera bag over his shoulder and a camera in one hand.

'Hi,' the young man said, proffering his hand. 'Kjetil Østli.'

'Karl Ove Knausgaard,' I said.

'Pleased to meet you,' he said.

I shook the photographer's hand and asked them in.

'Would you like a coffee?'

'That would be nice. Thank you.'

I went into the kitchen, fetched the Thermos of coffee and three cups. When I returned they were looking around the living room.

'Getting snowed in wouldn't be a problem here,' the journalist said. 'You've got the odd book or two!'

'Most of which I haven't read,' I said. 'And the ones I have I don't remember a thing about.'

He was younger than I had thought, probably no more than twenty-six or twenty-seven, despite the beard. His teeth were large, his eyes jovial and his personality was easy-going and cheery. This type was not unfamiliar to me, I had met several people who reminded me of him, but only in recent years, never when I was growing up. It might have had something to do with class, geography or generation, probably all of them at once. South-east Norway, middle class, I guessed, possibly academic parents. Well brought up, self-confident manner, sharp-witted, good social skills. Someone who had not been buffeted by adversity yet, that was the impression he gave in the first few minutes. The photographer was Swedish, thereby evading any chance I had of detecting nuances in the way he presented himself.

'In fact, I had decided to turn down all interviews from now on,' I said. 'But they said at the publisher's you were so good that I absolutely mustn't let the opportunity slip through my fingers. Hope they're right.'

Bit of flattery never hurts.

'I hope so too,' the journalist said.

I poured them a cup of coffee.

'Could I take a few shots here?' the photographer asked.

As I hesitated he assured me they would only be of me and nothing else.

At first the journalist had wanted to do the interview at home, and I had said no, but when he rang to arrange where to meet I said they should come up after all. Then we could take it from there. I could hear he was pleased.

'OK,' I said. 'Here?'

I stood in front of the bookshelves with a cup of coffee in my hand, he walked round taking photos.

What a load of shite this was.

'Could you raise your hand a bit?'

'Doesn't that look a bit artificial?'

'OK then. We'll let that one go.'

From the hallway I heard Vanja crawling in. She sat up in the doorway and looked at us.

'Hi, Vanja!' I said. 'Are there lots of scary men here? But you know me, don't you . . .'

I lifted her up. At that moment Linda came in. She gave a perfunctory greeting, took Vanja and went back into the kitchen.

Everything I didn't want to be seen was seen. Everything that was me and mine became stiff and stilted. I didn't want it to be like this. No bloody way. But there I went again, grinning like an imbecile.

'Can I have a couple more?' the photographer asked.

I posed again.

'A photographer once told me that taking pictures of me was like taking pictures of a lump of wood,' I said.

'Must have been a rotten photographer,' said the photographer.

'But you know what he meant?'

He stopped, took the camera away from his face, smiled, put it back and continued.

'I think we should go to Pelikanen,' I said to the journalist. 'That's my local. And there's no music. Should do the trick.'

'Fine by me.'

'Let's do a few shots outside first. Then I'll let you two get on with it,' the photographer said.

At that moment the journalist's mobile rang. He scrutinised the number.

'I'll have to take this,' he said. The conversation, which lasted no more than one, maximum two, minutes, was about snowfall, a car, train times, a skiing hut. He rang off and met my glance.

'I'm going skiing with some friends for the weekend. That was our lift from the train to the hut. An old boy who's always helped us out.'

'Sounds nice,' I said.

A hut, skiing with friends, that was something I had never done. While I was at *gymnas* and for a couple of years into the course at university, this had been a sore point. I barely had any friends. And the few I had didn't know each other. Now I was too old to bother about that sort of thing, but nevertheless I did feel a stab of pain, on behalf of the old me, as it were.

He put the mobile into his pocket and set the cup down on the table. The photographer was packing away his gear.

'Shall we go then?' I said.

It was a bit awkward standing together and getting dressed to go out, the hall was too narrow, they were too close, no one said anything. I called goodbye to Linda and we went down the stairs and out. On the front doorstep I lit a cigarette. The temperature was biting cold. The photographer drew me over to the step across the street, where I posed for a few minutes with the cigarette cupped behind my hand until the photographer said he would like it in the picture, if I didn't mind. I understood what he meant, it gave a bit of life, so I stood on the step smoking while he clicked away and I moved according to his instructions, all of which was registered by the many passers-by, then we walked to the tunnel entrance, where he continued for a further five minutes until he was happy. He left, and I walked in silence with the journalist over the hill and down to the Metro station on the other side. A train pulled into the platform at once, we stepped on and sat by the window facing each other.

'Taking the Metro still reminds me of the Norway Cup,' I said.

'When I catch a whiff of that special smell in the concourses that's what I think of. I come from a small town, you see, and then the Metro was the most exotic invention in existence. And Pepsi-Cola. We didn't have that either.'

'Did you play football for a long time?'

'Until I was eighteen. But I was never any good. It was a very low level, all of it.'

'Is everything you do at a low level? You said you hadn't read any of your books. And in interviews with you that I've seen you often talk about how poor what you do is. Aren't you being a bit too self-critical?'

'No, I don't think so. It depends how high you set the bar, of course.'

He peered out of the window as the train emerged from the tunnel at T-Central.

'Do you think you're going to win the prize?' he asked.

'The Nordic Council one?'

'Yes.'

'No.'

'Who will then?'

'Monica Fagerholm.'

'You seem sure?'

'It's a very good novel, the author's a woman and it's ages since Finland has won it. Of course she's going to get it.'

The conversation went quiet again. The time before and after an interview was always uneasy; he, and I didn't know him, was there to elicit my innermost thoughts, but not yet, the situation hadn't arisen, the roles hadn't been allocated, we were on an equal footing, but there were no points of contact, nonetheless we had to talk.

I thought about Ingrid. I couldn't say anything to anyone, not even Linda, until I was absolutely sure that I was right. I would

simply have to mark the bottles. Would have to do it this evening.
Then have a look tomorrow. If the levels were down I would have
to take it from there.

We arrived in Skanstull, and with the town glittering in the
darkness around us we walked in silence to Pelikanen, where
we found ourselves a table at the back of the pub. We sat chatting for an hour and a half about me and my work, then I got
up and left while he, not having to fly back to Norway until the
next day, remained where he was. As always after long interviews
I felt empty, drained like a ditch. As always, it felt as though I
had betrayed myself. Merely by sitting there I had gone along
with the premise, which was that the two books I had written
were good and important, and that I, the writer, was an unusual
and interesting person. That was the starting point for the conversation: everything I said was important. If I didn't say anything
important, well, then I was just hiding it. Because it obviously
had to be somewhere! So when I told stories about my childhood,
for example, some perfectly normal, ordinary story everyone had
experienced, it was important because it was me who said it. It
said something about me, the writer of two good and important
books. And I not only went along with this view, which formed
the basis for the conversation, but did it with great enthusiasm.
I sat there jabbering away like a parrot in the zoo. All while
knowing the reality of the situation. How often did a good
meaningful novel come out in Norway? Somewhere between
every ten to twenty years. The last good Norwegian novel was
All Ablaze by Kjartan Fløgstad, and that was published in 1980,
twenty-five years ago. The last good one before that was *The Birds*
by Vesaas, which appeared in 1957, so a further twenty-three
years previously. How many Norwegian novels had there been
in the meantime? Thousands! Yes, thousands! Some of them
good, a few more passable, most weak. That's how it is, nothing

to shout about, everyone knows this. The problem is what
surrounds all these authorships, the flattery that mediocre
writers thrive on and, as a consequence of their false self-image,
everything they are emboldened to say to the press and TV.

I know what I'm talking about. I'm one of them myself.

Oh, I could cut off my head with bitterness and shame that
I have allowed myself to be lured, not just once but time after
time. If I have learned one thing over these years which seems
to me immensely important, particularly in an era such as ours,
overflowing with such mediocrity, it is the following:

Don't believe you are anybody.

Do not bloody believe you are somebody.

Because you are not. You're just a smug mediocre little shit.

Do not believe that you're anything special. Do not believe
that you're worth anything, because you aren't. You're just a
little shit.

So keep your head down and work, you little shit. Then at
least you'll get something out of it. Shut your mouth, keep your
head down, work and know that you're not worth a shit.

This, more or less, was what I had learned.

This was the sum of all my experience.

This was the only true bloody thought I'd ever had.

This was one side of the coin. The other was that I was preoccupied, to an unusually high degree, by being liked, and always
had been, ever since I was small. I had attached huge importance
to what other people thought about me ever since I was seven.
When newspapers showed some interest in what I was doing
and who I was, it was, on the one hand, confirmation that I was
liked and therefore something part of me accepted with great
pleasure while, on the other, it became an almost unmanageable
problem because it was no longer possible to control other
people's opinions of me, for the simple reason that I no longer

knew them, no longer saw them. So whenever I had done an interview and there was something in the interview I hadn't said or what I had said was cast in a different light, I moved heaven and earth to change it. If it wasn't possible, my self-image burned with shame. The fact that despite all this I went on giving interviews, and once again sat facing a journalist some-where, was the result of my desire for flattery being stronger than both my fear of looking an idiot and any ideals of quality I had, as well as acknowledging that it was important for the books to reach a readership. When I had written *A Time to Every Purpose Under Heaven* I said to Geir Gulliksen that I didn't want to do any interviews, but after talking to him I decided to do them after all, such was the effect he had on me, and I justified the about-turn with the excuse that I owed the publishing house nothing less. But it was no good: I was a writer, not a salesman or a whore.

All this turned into one unholy mess. I often complained I was presented as an idiot in the newspapers, but it was no one's fault but my own because I saw how other writers were presented – for example Kjartan Fløgstad – they definitely never came across as idiots. Fløgstad was a man of integrity, he stood as tall as a tree whatever was going on around him, and had to belong, I guessed, to that rare breed of whole person.

And then he didn't talk about himself.

What had I just done, if not that and only that?

I gave my ticket to the black man in the ticket office window, he stamped it hard and pushed it back with expressionless eyes, and I went back down the escalator to the underground, through the tunnel and onto the narrow platform, where, after confirming that the next train was due in seven minutes, I sat down on a bench.

In late autumn, when *Out of the World* was published, *TV2 News* wanted to do an interview. They came to my home to collect me, we drove down to the Hurtigruten terminal, where the interview was going to take place, and on the way there, by the Technology Centre at the end of Nygårdsparken, the journalist turned and asked who I was.

'Who are you actually?' he asked.

'What do you mean?' I answered.

'Well, Erik Fosnes Hansen is the sage, the cultural conservative, the child prodigy. Roy Jacobsen is the Socialist Party writer. Vigdis Hjort is the wanton and drunken female writer. Who are you? I know nothing about you.'

I shrugged. The sun was glittering on the snow.

'I don't know,' I said. 'I'm just an ordinary fellow.'

'Come on! You've got to give me something. Something you've done?'

'Had a few odd jobs. Studied a bit. You know . . .'

He turned round in his seat. Later that day he solved the problem by showing rather than telling: towards the end of the interview he pieced together a series of pauses and hesitations to represent my personality, and brought it to a conclusion with my statement: 'Ibsen said that he who stood alone was strongest. I think that's wrong.'

Sitting on the bench, I threw up my hands and took a deep breath as the memory of what I had said overcame me.

How could I have said anything like that?

Had I believed it?

Yes, I had. But it was my mother's ideas I was expressing, she was the one who was preoccupied by human relationships, who thought that was where value lay, not me. That is, at the time I was, at the time I believed it. But not from any personal experience, it was just one of the things that were as they were.

Ibsen had been right. Everything I saw around me confirmed

it. Relationships were there to eradicate individuality, to fetter freedom and suppress that which was pushing through. My mother was never so angry as when we discussed the concept of freedom. When I expressed my opinion, she snorted and said that was just an American notion without any content, vacuous and fallacious. We were here for others. But this was the idea that had led to the systematised existence we had now, where unpredictability had vanished and you could go from nursery to school to university and into working life as if it were a tunnel, convinced that your choices had been made of your own free will, while in reality you had been sieved through like grains of sand right from your very first school day: some were sent into practical jobs, some into theoretical, some to the top, some to the bottom, all while being taught that everyone was equal. This was the idea that had made us, at least my generation, have *expectations* of life, to live in the belief that we could make demands, make real demands and blame every possible circumstance other than ourselves if it didn't turn out the way we had imagined, that made us rage against the state if a tsunami came and you didn't receive immediate help. How pathetic was that? Become embittered if you didn't get the job you had merited. And this was the thinking that meant the fall was no longer a possibility, except for the very weakest, because you could always get money, and pure existence, one where you stand face to face with a life-threatening emergency or peril, had been completely eliminated. This was the thinking that had spawned a culture in which the greatest mediocrities, warm and with a well-fed stomach, trumpeted their cheap platitudes, thus allowing writers such as Lars Saabye Christensen or whoever to be worshipped as if Virgil himself were sitting on the sofa and telling us whether he had used a pen or a typewriter or a computer and what times of the day he wrote. I hated it, I didn't want to know about it. But who was talking to journalists about how he wrote his mediocre books as though he were some literary giant, a champion of the written word, if not myself?

How can you sit there receiving applause when you know that what you have done is not good enough?

I had *one* opportunity. I had to cut all my ties with the flattering, thoroughly corrupt world of culture in which everyone, every single little upstart, was for sale, cut all my ties with the vacuous TV and newspaper world, sit down in a room and read in earnest, not contemporary literature but literature of the highest quality, and then write as if my life depended on it. For twenty years if need be.

But I couldn't grasp the opportunity. I had a family and I owed it to them to be there. I had friends. And I had a weakness in my character which meant that I would say yes, yes, when I wanted to say no, no, which was so afraid of hurting others, which was so afraid of conflict and which was so afraid of not being liked that it could forgo all principles, all dreams, all opportunities, everything that smacked of truth, to prevent this happening.

I was a whore. This was the only suitable term.

Half an hour later, after I closed the door behind me at home, there was a sound of voices in the living room. I poked my head in and saw that Mikaela was there. They were curled up on the sofa with a cup of tea in their hands. On the table in front of them was a candlestick with three lighted candles, a dish with three pieces of cheese in it and a basket full of various biscuits.

'Hi, Karl Ove, how was it?' Linda asked.

They smiled at me.

'OK,' I said with a shrug of the shoulders. 'Nothing worth talking about anyway.'

'Would you like a cup of tea and some cheese?'

'No, thanks.'

I unwound my scarf as I stood there, hung it in the wardrobe with my jacket, untied my laces and put my shoes on the shelf by the wall. The floor underneath was grey with sand and gravel. I would have to join them for a while so as not to appear totally unsociable, I thought, and went into the living room.

Mikaela was talking about a meeting she'd had with the minister of culture, Leif Pagrotsky. He was a tiny man and had been sitting on a large sofa, she said, with a huge cushion on his lap, which he hugged as he sat there, and even, according to her, sank his teeth into. But she had the greatest respect for him. He had a razor-sharp mind and an enormous capacity for work. I wasn't sure what qualifications Mikaela had, since I had only met her in contexts like this, but whatever they were they obviously worked well for her: barely thirty years old, she went from one top post to the next. Like so many women I had met she was close to her father, who had something or other to do with literature. With her mother, a demanding lady who lived alone in an apartment in Gothenburg, from what I had gathered, she had a more complicated relationship. Mikaela often changed her partners, and no matter how different they were they had one thing in common: they were always inferior to her. Of all the stories she had told over the three years since I first met her there was one in particular that stood out in my mind. We were sitting in the bar at Folkoperan and she told us about a dream she'd had. She had been to a party and had gone without any trousers on, so she was naked from the waist down, like Donald Duck. It had made her feel uneasy, she said, but that wasn't all, there had also been something alluring about it, and then she simply lay down on a table with her naked backside in the air. What did we think the dream could mean?

Ye-es, what could it mean?

When she told us this I didn't think it was true, or that the others around the table knew something I didn't, because surely what the dream said about her was something she would not want everyone to know? From then on, this trace of naïvety, which had appeared so unexpectedly in her otherwise sophisticated demeanour, led me to view her with affection and wonderment. Was that perhaps the intention? Whatever the reason, she had a high opinion of Linda, turned to her sometimes for advice because, like me, she knew about Linda's unfailing intuition and taste. That on occasions like this she could become a little too self-centred didn't strike me as much of a surprise, and it was perfectly forgivable. Besides, what she told us about life in the corridors of power was always interesting, at least for me, so far removed on the periphery. If you switched perspective and took her point of view, she was visiting a close but fragile friend and her taciturn husband, and what option had she but to take the initiative and embrace this small family with some of her happiness and energy? She was Vanja's godmother and had been at the christening, where she had made such a good impression on my mother that she still asked after her. She had been interested in what mum had to say and went into the kitchen to help with the washing-up when the party was coming to an end, thereby revealing an understanding of the situation, which Linda had never shown in the same way, with all the latent friction that this caused between her and my mother. This is what we have forms for, they help us to co-exist, they are in themselves signs of friendship or goodwill, and with them in place greater personal divergence is tolerated, more idiosyncrasy, which unhappily idiosyncratic individuals never understand since it is in the very nature of idiosyncrasy not to understand. Linda did not want to serve anyone, she wanted to be served, and the consequence of that was she wasn't served. Whereas Mikaela served, and so she was served. Simple as that. It grieved me that mum was so taken with her, also because there was quite a different richness and unpredictability in Linda's personality. Sudden precipices, unexpected blasts of wind, enormous walls of resistance. Getting things to run smoothly, working to achieve a lack of resistance, this is the antithesis of art's essence, it is the antithesis of wisdom, which is based on restricting or being restricted. So the question is: what do you choose? Movement, which is close to life, or the area beyond movement, which is where art is located, but also, in a certain sense, death?

'I'll have a cup of tea after all,' I said.

'It's herbal tea,' Linda said. 'You don't want that, do you? But the water's probably still hot.'

'No, preferably not,' I said, and went into the kitchen. While I was waiting for the water to boil I took a pencil, positioned myself on a chair in front of the cupboard and marked all the bottles. A little dot on the labels, nothing more, so small that to see it you had to know it was there.

I was behaving like the father of a teenager and felt somewhat stupid standing there, yet I couldn't see what else I could do. I didn't want the woman who was looking after my child and the person who had most to do with her apart from Linda and me to drink alcohol when she was with her.

Then I popped a tea bag in the cup and poured water on it. I looked down at Nalen, where the cooks were hosing the floor and the dishwashers were steaming. From the departure sounds in the living room I gathered Mikaela was on her way home. I went into the hall and said goodbye to her. Then I sat down in front of the computer, accessed the Net, checked my emails, nothing, went onto a few websites and googled myself. There were over 29,000 hits. The figure rose and sank like a kind of index. I surfed and clicked at random. Steered clear of interviews

and reviews, clicked on some of the blogs. Someone wrote that
my books weren't even worth wiping your arse with. Elsewhere
I found the homepage of a small publishing house or journal.
My name appeared in a caption under a picture of Ole Robert
Sunde which said he was telling anyone who would listen how
bad Knausgaard's last book was. Then I stumbled on the docu-
ments of a boundary dispute between neighbours in which a
relative had clearly been involved. The cause was a garage wall
a few metres too short or too long.

'What are you doing?' Linda asked behind me.

'Googling myself. It's a bloody Pandora's box. You wouldn't
believe what people come out with.'

'You shouldn't do it,' she said. 'Come here and sit down.'

'Coming,' I said. 'Just got a couple of things to check.'

The next morning I left for the office when Ingrid came to pick
up Vanja at eight. Sat there until three writing the speech, was
back home by half past three. Linda was in the bath, she was
going out for a meal with Christina. I went into the kitchen and
monitored the bottles. Two of them had been drunk from.

I went in to Linda and sat on the toilet seat lid.

'Hi,' she said with a smile. 'I bought myself a bath bomb today.'

The bathtub was full of lather. When she raised an arm to sit
up there was a ribbon of foam hanging from it.

'I can see,' I said. 'There's something we have to talk about.'

'Oh?'

'It's your mother. Remember what I told you about how the
levels in the bottles of booze were falling very noticeably of late?'

She nodded.

'I marked the bottles yesterday. So that I could be sure. And
they've gone down again. If it's not you it has to be your mother.'

'Mummy?'

'Yes, she drinks when she's here with Vanja. She's been doing it all week, and I don't think there are any grounds for believing it's just started.'

'Are you sure?'

'Ye-es, as sure as I can be.'

'What shall we do?'

'Tell her we know what's going on. And for us it's unacceptable.'

'Right.'

She fell silent.

'When are they coming back?' I asked after a while.

She looked at me.

'Around five,' she said.

'What do you suggest?' I asked.

'We'll have to tell her. Simply give her an ultimatum. If she does it again she can't be left alone with Vanja.'

'Mm,' I said.

'This must have been going on for several years,' she said, apparently engrossed in her own thoughts. 'It would explain a great deal. She's been so incredibly scratchy. It's next to impossible to have any real communication.'

I got up.

'It might not,' I said. 'Maybe it has something to do with Vidar and her. Perhaps she's stuck in a cul-de-sac out there. And she's unhappy.'

'But you don't start drinking because you're unhappy when you're over sixty,' she said. 'Must be a way of coping. Must have been going on for a long time.'

'They'll be here in about half an hour,' I said. 'Shall we let it go and tackle it later, or shall we go for it right away? Get it over and done with?'

'I don't suppose there's anything to wait for,' she said. 'But how shall we put it to her? I can't do it on my own. She'll only deny it and somehow make it all about me. Shall we do it together?'

'Bit like a family meeting, you mean?'

Linda shrugged and turned her palms face up in the foam-filled bath.

'Well, *I* don't know,' she said.

'It's too complicated. And it's two against one. Like some tribunal. I can do it. I'll go out with her and talk to her.'

'Do you want to do that?'

'Want? It's the last thing I'd want to do on this earth! She's my mother-in-law for Christ's sake. All I want is some decency, dignity and peace and quiet.'

'I'm pleased you'll do it,' she said.

'I must say you're taking this well though,' I said.

'This is almost the only time when I'm calm, when something unforeseen happens, some crisis or other. It's a hangover from childhood. Then it was the normal situation. I'm used to it. But I'm angry too, just so that you know. It's now that we need her. She has to be someone for our children. They have almost no family, as you know. She can't let us down now. She can't, even if I have to make sure she doesn't myself.'

'Children?' I said. 'Do you know something I don't?'

She smiled and shook her head.

'No, but perhaps I can feel something.'

I went out, closed the door behind me and stood in front of the living-room window. Heard the water draining down the bath plughole, looked at the torch flickering outside the café across the narrow street, the dark figures with white mask-like faces walking past. On the floor above a neighbour was playing a guitar. Linda came into the hall with a red towel wrapped round her head like a turban and disappeared behind the open cupboard door. I went to check my emails. One from Tore, one from Gina Winje. I started a reply to her, then deleted it. Went into the kitchen, put on the coffee machine and drank a glass of water. Linda was standing in front of the hall mirror putting on her make-up.

'When's Christina coming?' I asked.

'At six. But I might as well get ready now while we're alone. How was it today by the way? Did you get anything done?'

'Bit. Have to do the rest tomorrow evening and on Friday.'

'Are you going on Saturday?' she asked, leaning her head back and running the little brush across one eyelash.

'Yes.'

Outside the lift started. There weren't many residents in the building so the chances were it would be them. Yes, it was. The lift stopped, the door opened into the corridor, followed immediately by the sound of a buggy being reversed.

Ingrid opened the door and came into the hall, which was soon filled with her energetic-frenetic presence.

'Vanja fell asleep on the way,' she said. 'The little darling was worn out, poor thing. But she's done a lot today! We were at the children's museum. I bought a season ticket which you can have . . . so you've got free entrance for the whole of the rest of the year . . .'

She put down all the bags she was carrying, pulled a wallet from her jacket and took out a yellow card, which she passed to Linda.

'And then we also bought a new jumpsuit, identical to the old one, which was a bit too small for her – hope that's not a problem?'

She looked at me. I shook my head.

'And a new pair of gloves while we were at it.'

She searched through the bags and took out a pair of red gloves.

'They've got hooks you can attach to the sleeve. They're nice and warm, and big.'

She looked at Linda.

'Are you going out? Oh yes, you're off with Christina tonight.' She looked at me. 'So you and Geir will have to think of something. But I won't hold you up. I'm leaving now.'

She turned to Vanja, who was lying in the buggy behind her with her hat down over her eyes.

'She'll probably sleep for another hour. She didn't sleep much this morning, you see. Shall I put her in the living room?'

'I can do that,' I said. 'Are you going back to Gnesta, or what?'

She looked at me with raised eyebrows.

'No. I'm going to the theatre with Barbro. I had planned to borrow your office for another night. I thought . . . I told Linda. Do you need it?'

'No, no,' I said. 'I was just wondering. I wanted to have a chat with you actually. There's something I have to say.'

The large eyes behind the thick glasses examined me with unease.

'Fancy coming for a walk with me?' I said.

'All right,' she said.

'Let's go right away then. This won't take long.'

I loosened the nuts on the screws holding the double doors together, pulled the bolt fixing them to the floor, opened them and pushed in the buggy. While I was doing this Ingrid went into the kitchen for a glass of water. Then I got ready, stood a few metres away and waited, lost in my own thoughts. Linda had gone into the living room.

'You're not splitting up, are you?' she said as I closed the door behind us. 'Please don't say you're splitting up . . .'

Her face was white as she said it.

'No, we're not. My God, no. No, we're not. I want to talk to you about something completely different.'

'Ooof, I'm so relieved.'

We went into the backyard, through the gateway and into David Bagares gate, which we followed up to Malmskillnadsgatan. I said nothing, I didn't know how to articulate this, how to start. She didn't say anything either, glanced at me a couple of times, in anticipation or surprise.

'I don't quite know how to say this,' I said as we approached the crossroads and started to walk towards Johanneskyrk.

Pause.

'But it's . . . Well, I may as well blurt this straight out. I know you were drinking when you looked after Vanja today. And you were yesterday. And I . . . well, I simply can't tolerate that. It's no good. You can't do that.'

Her eyes were on me the whole time we were walking.

'I don't want to be checking on you in any way,' I continued. 'You can do what you like, of course, as far as I'm concerned. But not if you're looking after Vanja. I have to set a limit. That's no good. Do you understand?'

'No,' she said, astonished. 'I don't know what you're talking about. I've never had a drink while looking after Vanja. Never. Nor would it ever occur to me. Where have you got this idea from?'

My insides plummeted. As always when I was in situations where there was a lot at stake, agonising situations, when I went further, or was forced to go further than I wanted, I saw everything around me, also myself, with a special almost hyper-real clarity. The green tin roof of the church tower before us, the black leafless trees in the cemetery we were walking beside, the car, a gleaming blue, gliding up the road on the other side. My own slightly stooped gait, Ingrid's more energetic walk beside me. Her looking up at me. Bemused, a slight almost imperceptible shadow of reproach.

'I noticed the levels in the spirits bottles were down. To make sure, I marked the labels yesterday. When I came home I saw that more had gone. I hadn't drunk any. The only other people who have been there today are you and Linda. I know it wasn't Linda. That means it has to be you. There's no other explanation.'

'There must be,' she said. 'Because it wasn't me. I'm sorry, Karl Ove, but I haven't been drinking your spirits.'

'Listen,' I said. 'You're my mother-in-law. I wish you nothing but well. I don't want this. Not at all. The last thing I want to do is to accuse you of anything. But what can I do when I *know* what happened?'

'But you can't know,' she said. 'I didn't do this.'

My stomach ached. I had wandered into a kind of hell.

'You have to understand, Ingrid,' I said. 'Whatever you say, this will have consequences. You're a fantastic mother-in-law. You do more for Vanja, and you mean more to Vanja than anyone else. And I'm incredibly happy about that. And I want this to continue. We don't have much family around us, as you know. But if you won't come clean we can't trust you. Do you understand? Not that you won't be able to see Vanja, because you will, whatever happens. But if you won't come clean, if you don't agree to put this behind you, you won't be able to see her on your own. You'll never be alone with her. Do you understand what I'm saying?'

'Yes, I do. It's a great shame. But that's the way it'll have to be. I can't confess to doing something I haven't done. Even though I feel like it. I can't do it.'

'OK,' I said. 'We're not going to get any further with this. I suggest we drop it for a while, and then we can discuss it again and work out what to do.'

'All right,' she said. 'But it won't change anything, you know.'

'OK.'

We walked down the steps in front of the French school and followed Döbelnsgatan up to Johannesplan, along Malmskillnadsgatan and down David Bagares gate, all the way without saying a word. Me stooped with long strides, her almost jogging beside me. It shouldn't be like this, she was my mother-in-law; there was no reason in the world for me to correct her, or punish her, except this. It felt unworthy. And even more unworthy when she denied everything.

I put the key into the lock and swung the gate open for her. She smiled and went in.

How could she be so calm, and answer with such confidence?

Could it have been Linda after all?

No, of course it couldn't.

But was I wrong? Had I made a mistake?

No.

Or?

In the yard the white-clad hairdresser was smoking. I greeted her and she smiled. Ingrid stopped outside the front door, which I unlocked.

'I'm going now,' she said as we went up the stairs. 'We can discuss this later, as you suggested. Perhaps you'll have found out what happened by then.'

She took her handbag and two of the plastic bags, smiled as usual as she said goodbye, failed to give me a hug though.

Linda came into the hall after she had gone.

'How did it go? What did she say?'

'She said she hadn't been drinking when she'd been with Vanja. Not today, either. And she couldn't understand how the levels in the bottles had gone down.'

'If she's an alcoholic, denial is part of the whole picture.'

'Possible,' I said. 'But what the hell can we do? She just says no, I didn't do it. I say yes, you did, and she says no, I didn't. I can't *prove* anything. It's not as if we have CCTV in the kitchen.'

'As long as *we* know, it doesn't matter much. If she wants to play games she'll have to take the consequences.'

'Which are?'

'We-ell. We can't leave her alone with Vanja.'

'Oh, fucking hell,' I said. 'What a pile of shit. Fancy having to walk around with my mother-in-law and insist that she's been drinking. What is this?!'

'I'm glad you did. She'll probably admit to it in the end.'

'I don't think she will.'

How quickly a life sets new roots. How quickly you move from being a stranger in a town to being absorbed into it. Three years ago I had been living in Bergen, at that time I knew nothing about Stockholm and knew no one there. Then I went to Stockholm, the unknown, populated by foreigners, and gradually, day by day, though imperceptibly, I began to thread my life into theirs until now they were inseparable. If I had gone to London, which I might well have done, the same would have happened there, just with different people. It was that arbitrary, and so momentous.

Ingrid rang Linda the next day and admitted everything. She added she didn't think it was that serious herself, but since we did, she would implement the necessary measures to ensure it would never be a problem for anyone again. She already had an appointment to see an alcohol therapist and had decided to spend more time concentrating on herself and her own needs, as she thought that was where part of the problem lay, with the enormous pressure she put on herself.

Linda was desperate after the conversation because, as she

said, her mother was so optimistic and keen it wasn't possible to have proper communication with her, it was as though she had lost her grip on reality and had started to live in a kind of light, carefree future world.

'*I can't talk to her!* I have no real *contact* with her. It's just platitudes and words and how fantastic this and that is. You, for example, had praise heaped on you for the way you handled the situation. I'm fantastic and everything is wonderfully brilliant. But it comes one day after we told her we don't want her to drink while she's looking after Vanja. I'm seriously worried about her, Karl Ove. It's as if she's suffering, but she doesn't know she is, if you get me. She represses *everything*. She deserves to enjoy her twilight years. She shouldn't have to be tormented and suffer and drink to drown her sorrows. But what can I do? She obviously doesn't want any help. She won't even admit there are problems in her life.'

'But you're her daughter,' I said. 'It's no wonder she doesn't want you to help her. Or admit something is not as it should be. Her entire life has been orientated towards helping others. You, your brother, your father, her neighbours. If all of you were to help her, everything would unravel.'

'I'm sure you're right. But I just want contact with her, do you understand?'

'Yes, I do.'

Five days later I received an email with the *Aftenposten* interview attached. Reading it just made me sad. It was hopeless. I had no one to blame but myself, yet I wrote a long reply to the journalist in which I tried to expand on my side of the matter, that is give it the semblance of seriousness it had in my mind, which of course led to my faring even worse. The journalist rang me straight afterwards, suggested adding my email to the interview on the website, which suggestion I rejected, this wasn't the point. All I could do was give the newspaper a miss that day and stop thinking about how I came across as stupid. So I was stupid, OK, I would have to live with it. Close-up interviews also included photos of the featured person's private life, and as I didn't have any I asked my mother to send me some. Since they hadn't arrived by the deadline and the journalist was asking for them I rang Yngve, who scanned some and emailed them through while mum's photos came a week later, carefully glued onto thick card with detailed information underneath in her hand-writing. I could see how proud she was and despair rose inside me like a wall. Most of all I felt like disappearing into the depths of a forest somewhere, building myself a log cabin and staying there, far from civilisation and gazing into a fire. People, who needs people?

'A young Sørlander with nicotine-stained fingers and faintly discoloured teeth,' he had written. The sentence was indelibly etched in my brain.

But I got what I deserved. Had I not myself written up an interview with Jan Kjærstad many years ago entitled 'The Man Without a Chin'? And *that* without appreciating what an insult it was . . .

Ha ha ha!

No, bugger it, this wasn't worth the worry. I had to refuse everything from now on, endure the last months as a house husband with Vanja and then resume work in April. Hard, methodical, keeping an eye open for anything that imparted joy, energy and light. Cherish what I had, ignore everything else.

At that moment Vanja woke in the bedroom. I picked her up, held her against my chest and walked around for a few minutes until she had stopped crying and was ready for some food. I heated a potato and some peas in the microwave, mashed them with a little butter, hunted for something meaty in the fridge, found a bowl containing two fish fingers, heated them as well, and put this in front of her. She was hungry, and since I could see her from the living room, I went in, checked my emails again and answered a couple while keeping an ear open for any sounds of disgruntlement.

'Have you eaten everything?!' I said when I went back. She smiled with pleasure and threw her cup of water on the floor. I lifted her up and she made a grab for the wisps of beard on my chin and stuck a finger in my mouth. I laughed, tossed her up in the air a few times, fetched a nappy from the bathroom and changed her, put her on the floor and went to throw the old one in the bin under the sink. On my return she was standing in the middle of the floor and swaying. She started to walk towards me.

'One! Two! Three! Four! Five! Six!' I counted. 'A new record!'

She noticed that something extraordinary had happened because she was beaming over all her face. Perhaps she was full of the sensational feeling of walking.

I put on her outdoor clothes and carried her to the buggy in the bike room. The day was bright and spring-like, even though the sun wasn't shining. The tarmac was dry. I texted Linda about our child's first long walk. 'Fantastic!' she texted back. 'Home at half past twelve. Love you both!'

I went into the supermarket down in the Metro station by Stureplan, bought a grilled chicken, a lettuce, some tomatoes, a cucumber, black olives, two red onions and a fresh baguette, popped into Hedengrens on the way back and found a book about Nazi Germany, the first two volumes of *Das Kapital*, Orwell's *1984*, which I had never managed to read, a collection of essays by the same author, a book about Céline by Ekerwald and the latest Don DeLillo until Vanja brought my browsing to an end and I had to go and pay. The DeLillo I regretted buying the instant I was outside because even though I had been a fan of his, especially the novels *The Names* and *White Noise*, I hadn't been able to read more than half of *Underworld*, and since the next book had been terrible it was evident that he was in decline. I was on the point of going back and exchanging it, there were a couple of other books I had seen and fancied, for example, the latest Esterházy novel, *Celestial Harmonies*, which was about his father. But I preferred not to read novels in Swedish, it was too close to my own language, it constantly threatened to leach in and destroy it, so if the title was available in Norwegian I read it in Norwegian, also because I read too little in my mother tongue. Besides I was strapped for time if I was going to make lunch before Linda got home. And Vanja obviously felt that I had already looked at enough books in the shop.

Upstairs in the kitchen I made a chicken salad, sliced some bread and set the table, all while Vanja sat on the floor banging small wooden balls through holes in a board with a tiny mallet, down a slide and onto the floor.

Five minutes later she had to stop because the Russian woman started hammering on the radiators. I hated the sound, hated waiting for it, although her reaction wasn't always unjustified now, the banging could drive anyone insane, so I took the toy off Vanja, put her in the chair instead, tied a bib around her neck and was giving her some bread and butter when Linda came in the door.

'Hi!' she said, coming over to hug me.

'Hi?' I said.

'I went to the chemist this morning,' she said, looking at me with a sparkle in her eyes.

'Yes?' I said.

'I bought a pregnancy test.'

'Yes? What are you actually telling me?'

'We're going to have another child, Karl Ove!'

'Are we really?'

There were tears in my eyes.

She nodded. Her eyes were moist too.

'I'm so happy,' I said.

'Yes, I couldn't talk about anything else in therapy. Haven't thought about anything else all day. It's fantastic.'

'Did you tell your therapist before you told me?'

'Yes, and?'

'What have you got between your ears? Do you imagine it's only your child? You can't tell other people before you tell me! Is there something wrong with you or what?'

'Oh, Karl Ove, I'm so sorry. I didn't think. I was just overwhelmed. I didn't mean to. Please, don't let this come between us.'

I looked at her.

'OK,' I said. 'I don't suppose it makes much difference. In the bigger picture, I mean.'

In the night I was woken by her crying. Sobbing her heart out as only she could. I placed my hand over her neck.

'What's up, Linda?' I whispered. 'Why are you crying?'

Her shoulders shook.

She turned her face to me.

'I was only being dutiful!' she said. 'That was all it was.'

'All what was?' I asked. 'What are you talking about?'

'This morning. I went into the chemist and bought the test because I wanted to know. I couldn't wait! And so after I had the answer I had to go to therapy! It didn't occur to me that I could come home! I thought I had to go!'

She started sobbing again.

'I could have come home and told you the fantastic news! Straight away! I didn't need to go to therapy, did I!'

I stroked her back, ran my hand through her hair.

'But, Linda love, it's nothing!' I said. 'It doesn't matter! I was a bit put out, that was all. Hell, the only thing that counts is we're going to have a baby!'

She looked at me and smiled through the tears.

'Do you mean that?' she said.

I kissed her.

Her lips tasted of salt.

That November evening I sat on the balcony of our flat in Malmö in the darkness after having taken Vanja to the birthday party, and almost two years had passed. The child, barely conceived back then, had not only been born but was now a year old. We had christened her Heidi, she was a happy blonde girl, more robust than her sister in some ways, just as sensitive in others. During the christening Vanja had shouted No! No! No! so loudly it resounded around the church as the priest was about to splash water over her sister's head, and it was impossible not to laugh, it was as if she was reacting physically to the holy water, like some tiny vampire or devil. When Heidi was nine months old we moved to Malmö on a kind of impulse, neither of us had been there before, and we didn't know anyone, but we went there to have a look at a flat and made the decision after being in the town for a total of five hours. This was where we were going to live. The flat was on the top floor of a block in the centre, it was large, 130 square metres, and since it was so high up light flooded in from dawn to dusk. Nothing could have suited us better; our life in Stockholm had become darker and darker until in the end we had no choice but to get out. Away from the crazy Russian, with whom we had been engaged in an

unresolvable conflict and who continued to send complaints to
the owners of the block, who then summoned us to a meeting,
not that that led anywhere, because even though they believed
us, which in the end they did, there was nothing they could do.
We took matters into our own hands. After a further incident
when she had come up to our flat and I, holding Vanja and Heidi
in my arms, had told her to leave us in peace, to which she had
said she had a man in her flat and was going to tell him to beat
me up, we rang the police and reported her for harassment and
threatening behaviour. I never thought I would go that far, but
I did. The police couldn't do anything, but that wasn't important
because they set the social services on her, two people who came
to inspect her living conditions, and for her there could be no
greater humiliation. Oh, how I relished the thought of that! But
it didn't make relations with the neighbours any better. And
with two children in the middle of a large city, where the only
car-free green zones were parks, where we walked them like
dogs, the question was not whether but when we would move.
Linda wanted to go to Norway and I didn't, so the choice was
between two towns in Sweden, Gothenburg or Malmö, and since
Linda had negative associations with the former, having broken
off her studies at Litterær Gestaltning, the writers' school, after
a few weeks because of illness, the matter was decided: we moved
to Malmö as we liked the feeling we had in the few hours we
were there. Malmö was open, the sky above the town high, the
sea close by, there was a long beach only a few minutes from
the centre, Copenhagen was three quarters of an hour away, and
the atmosphere in the town was laid-back, in holiday mode,
quite different from Stockholm's tough, stern, careerist ambience. The first months in Malmö were wonderful, we went swimming every day, sat on the balcony eating when the children
were in bed, buoyed with optimism, closer to each other than

we had been for two years. But the darkness crept in there as well, slowly and imperceptibly it filled all the other parts of my life, the novelty wore off, the world slipped away, leaving quivering frustration.

As it did this evening. Linda and Vanja were eating in the kitchen, Heidi slept her fevered sleep in the cot in our bedroom and I was almost suffocated by the thought of the washing-up, the rooms that looked as if they had been systematically ransacked, as though someone had tipped everything from the drawers and cupboards across the floor, by the dirt and sand everywhere and the pile of dirty laundry in the bathroom. By 'the novel' I was writing, which was taking me nowhere. I had spent two years on nothing. By the oppressiveness of life in the flat. By our arguments, which were escalating and becoming more and more unmanageable. By the joy that had departed.

My angry outbursts were petty, they flared up over trifles; who cares who washed what when, as you looked back on a life, summed up a life? Linda shifted between her moods, and when she was at her lowest ebb she simply lay on the sofa or in bed, and what at the start of our relationship had aroused tenderness in me now led directly to irritation: was I supposed to do *every-thing* while she lay there moping? Well, I could, but not without conditions. I did it and had every right to be bad-tempered and grumpy, ironic, sarcastic, occasionally furious. This joylessness spread far beyond me and right into the centre of our life together. Linda said she wanted only one thing, for us all to be a happy family. That was what she wanted, that was what she dreamed about, for us to be one happy, contented family. All I ever dreamed about was for her to do her half of the housework. She said she did, so there we were, with our accusations, our anger and our longings, in the middle of life, of our lives, no one else's.

How was it possible to waste your life getting het up about housework? How was it *possible*?

I wanted the maximum amount of time for myself, with the fewest disturbances possible. I wanted Linda, who was already at home looking after Heidi, to take care of everything that concerned Vanja so that I could work. She didn't want to. Or perhaps she did, but she couldn't cope. All our conflicts and rows were in some form or other about this, the dynamics. If I couldn't write because of her and her demands, I would leave her, it was as simple as that. And somewhere she knew. She stretched my limits, according to what she needed in her life, but never so far that I reached my snapping point. I was close though. The way I took my revenge was to give her everything she wanted – I took care of the children, I cleaned the floors, I washed the clothes, I did the food shopping, I cooked and I earned all the money so that she had nothing tangible to complain about as far as me and my role in the family were concerned. The only thing I didn't give her, and it was the only thing she wanted, was my love. That was how I took my revenge. Cold and unmoved, I watched her become more and more desperate until it became untenable and she screamed at me in rage, frustration and yearning. What's the problem? I asked. Don't you think I'm doing enough? You're exhausted, you say. But I can take the children tomorrow. I can take Vanja to the nursery, and then I can go out with Heidi while you sleep and have a rest. Then I can collect Vanja from the nursery in the afternoon and look after them in the evening. That's OK, isn't it? Then you'll be able to rest as you're so drained. In the end, when she ran out of arguments she would throw objects and smash them. A glass, a plate, whatever came to hand. She was the one who should have been doing these chores for me, so that I could work, but she didn't. And since her problem was not that she was doing too much, but the fact that there was no love, only spite, moodiness, frustration and bad temper in the man she loved, which she was unable to find a way to articulate, the best revenge for me was to take her at her word. Oh, how I gloated when I caught her in the trap and could stand there agreeing to all her demands! After the eruption, which was inevitable, after we had gone to bed, she would often cry and want to be comforted. That gave me an opportunity to extract further revenge, because I wouldn't comply.

However, living like this was impossible, nor was it what I wanted, so when my anger, which was hard and implacable, abated, and all that was left was this soul in torment, as though everything I had was going to pieces, we made up, came closer to each other and lived as we once had. Then the whole process started again, it was cyclical, as in nature.

I stubbed out my cigarette, drank the last mouthful of flat Coke and got up, held the railing and stared into the sky, where a light hung motionless somewhere outside town, too low to be a star, too quiet to be a plane.

What on earth . . . ?

I stared for several minutes. Then it suddenly fell to the left, and I realised it was a plane. It was motionless because it was coming down over Øresund and maintaining a course straight for me.

Someone knocked on the window and I turned. It was Vanja, she smiled and waved. I opened the door.

'Are you going to bed now?'

She nodded.

'I wanted to say goodnight to you, daddy.'

I bent down and kissed her on the cheek.

'Goodnight. Sleep tight!'

'Sleep tight!'

She ran through the hall and into her room, a bundle of energy even after such a long day.

Better do the bloody washing-up then.

Scrape the leftovers into the bin, empty the dregs of milk and water from the glasses, take the apple and carrot peel, the plastic packaging and tea bags from the sinks, clean them and put everything on the drainer, run hot water, squirt some washing-up liquid, rest my forehead against the cupboard and start washing, glass by glass, cup by cup, plate by plate. Rinse. Then, when the stand was full, start drying to make room for more. Afterwards the floor, which had to be scrubbed where Heidi had been sitting. Tie the bin bag and take the lift down to the cellar, walk through the warm labyrinthine corridors to the waste disposal room, which was strewn with filth and slippery, which had pipes hanging from the ceiling like torpedoes, adorned with torn plastic ties and bits of insulation tape, a sign on the door proclaiming *Miljørom*, Milieu Room, a typical Swedish euphemism, throw the bags up into one of the large green rubbish containers, suddenly reminded of Ingrid, who the last time she had been here had found hundreds of small canvasses in one of them and had carried them up to the flat, imagining this would fill us with as much happiness as it did her, the idea that the children would now have enough painting material for several years into the future, close the lid and walk back to the flat, where at that moment Linda was tiptoeing out of the children's room.

'Is she asleep?' I asked.

Linda nodded.

'What a nice job you've done,' she said. Stopped at the kitchen door. 'Would you like a glass of wine? The bottle Sissel brought last time she came is still here.'

My first impulse was to say no, I definitely did not want any wine. But, strangely, the short time away from the flat had softened my attitude towards her, so I nodded.

'Could do,' I said.

Two weeks later, one afternoon while Heidi and Vanja were running wild around us, jumping on the sofa and screaming, we huddled together examining for the third time in our lives a small blue line on a small white test stick, overcome with emotion. It was John signalling his arrival. He was born late the following summer, gentle and patient from the first moment, always close to laughter, even when the storm around him was at its worst. Often he looked as if he had been dragged through a thicket, covered with scratches from the clawings Heidi gave him whenever she had the chance, usually under the pretext of a hug or an amicable pat on the cheek. What once had irked me, walking through the town with a buggy, was now history, forgotten and outlandish, as I pushed a shabby buggy with three children on board around the streets, often with two or three shopping bags dangling from one hand, deep furrows carved in my brow and down my cheeks, and eyes that burned with a vacant ferocity I had long lost any contact with. I no longer bothered about the potentially feminised nature of what I did; now it was a question of getting the children to wherever we had to go, with no sit-down strikes or refusals to go any further or any other ideas they could dream up to thwart my wishes for an easy morning or afternoon. Once a crowd of Japanese tourists stopped on the other side of the street and pointed at me, as though I were the ringmaster of some circus parade or something. They *pointed*. There you can see a Scandinavian man! Look, and tell your grandchildren what you saw!

I was so proud of the children. Vanja was wild and plucky, you would never think her thin body could have such a huge appetite for activity, that it could devour the physical world so greedily, with its trees, climbing frames, swimming pools and open fields, and her introversion, which had held her back in the first months at the new nursery, had completely gone, so much so that the next 'progress conversation' was to focus on the opposite. Now it was not that Vanja hid away or she didn't want contact with adults or she never took the initiative in games that was the problem; on the contrary, it was perhaps that she took too central a role sometimes, as they deftly put it, and was too keen to be number one. 'To be frank,' the nursery head said, 'she sometimes bullies some of the other children. The positive side of that,' he continued, 'is that in order to do so she has to be able to understand the situation and be intelligent enough to exploit it. But we're working at making her understand that she can't do that. Have you any idea where she might have picked up this rhyme: naaa-na-na-na-naaa-na? Has she seen it in a film or what? If so, we can show the film here and explain to them what it is.' After the last meeting, when they had talked about a speech therapist and treated her shyness as a flaw or a defect, I couldn't care less what they thought about her. She had only just turned four, she would be rid of it in a few months . . . Heidi wasn't quite as wild, her physical control was of another order, she seemed to be present in her body in quite a different way from Vanja, for whom fiction was simply a variant of reality and who allowed her imagination to run away with her. Vanja would lose her cool and go frantic with despair if she couldn't master something from the outset and gratefully accept help, whereas Heidi wanted to do everything herself, she would be offended if we offered our help and she would keep going and going until she succeeded. Oh, the triumph on her face then! She climbed to the top of the big tree in the playground before Vanja. The first time she wrapped her arms round the top branch. The second time, driven by tiny-tot hubris, she stood on top. I was sitting on a bench reading a newspaper and heard her scream: she was perched at the end of the branch, with nothing to hold on to, six metres above the ground. One rash move and she would fall. I shinned up and grabbed her, unable to stop laughing, what on earth were you doing *there*? She often did an extra skip when she walked, and that, I thought, was a skip of happiness. She was the only person in the family who was truly happy, it seemed, or who had a sunny disposition. She tolerated everything, apart from being told off. Then her lips quivered, the tears began to well up and it could take an hour to console her. She loved playing with Vanja, she went along with everything, and she adored riding. When she was astride the donkey at the amusement park we went to in the summer her face glowed with pride. But even the sight of Heidi was not enough to change Vanja's opinion, she didn't want to ride, she would never ride again, pushed her glasses up her nose, suddenly threw herself in front of John and let out a scream that made everyone around look at us. John liked it though, he shouted back, and then they laughed.

The sun was already low over the pine trees in the west. The sky was the same deep blue colour I remembered from my childhood and loved. Something eased inside me, soared upwards. But I couldn't make any use of it. The past was nothing.

Linda lifted Heidi off the stupid donkey. She waved goodbye to the animal and to the woman selling the tickets.

'There we are,' I said. 'Now it's straight home.'

The car was on its own in the large gravelled car park now. I sat down on the kerbstone nearby with Heidi on my lap, changing her nappy. Then I strapped in John on the front seat while Linda did the same for the girls in the back.

We had rented a big red VW. It was only the fourth time I had driven since I got my licence, so everything connected with it gave me pleasure. Starting up, changing gear, accelerating, reversing, steering. It was all fun. I had never thought I would ever drive a car, it wasn't part of my self-image, so my pleasure was all the greater when I found myself driving homewards on the motorway at 150 kph, in the regular almost drowsy rhythm that set in, indicating to pull out, overtaking, indicating to pull in, surrounded by countryside initially dominated by forest, then after a long gradual incline up an enormous hill, by cornfields as far as the eye could see, low farm buildings, magnificent coppices and small forests of deciduous trees, with the sea as a constant blue border in the west.

'Look!' I said as we reached the summit, and the Skåne countryside lay beneath us. 'So *unbelievably* beautiful!'

Golden cornfields, green beech forests, blue sea. All seemingly intensified and shimmering in the light from the setting sun.

No one answered.

I knew John was asleep. But those at the back, had they also nodded off?

I turned to look over my shoulder.

Yes, indeed. Three girls lay there with mouths agape and eyes closed.

Happiness exploded inside me.

It lasted for one second, two seconds, maybe three. Then came the shadow that always followed, this happiness's dark train.

I tapped my hand against the steering wheel and sang along to the music. It was Coldplay's latest CD, one I couldn't stand but which I had found was perfect for driving. Once I'd had the exact same feeling as now. When I was sixteen, in love, on my way through Denmark early one summer morning, heading for Nykøbing to a football training camp, all the others in the car apart from the driver and me at the front were asleep. He was playing the *Brothers in Arms* CD by Dire Straits, which had come out that spring, and with Sting's *The Dream of a Blue Turtle* and Talk Talk's *It's My Life* formed the soundtrack to all the fantastic experiences I'd had over the past months. The flat landscape, the sun rising, the stillness outside, the sleeping passengers, reinforced by a happiness that was so strong I remembered it twenty-five years later. But this happiness hadn't had a shadow, it had been pure, undiluted, unadulterated. Then life lay at my feet. Anything could happen. Anything was possible. It wasn't like that any longer. A lot had happened, and what had happened laid the ground for what could happen.

Not only were the opportunities fewer; the emotions I experienced were weaker. Life was less intense. And I knew I was halfway, perhaps more than halfway. When John was as old as I was now I would be eighty. And with one foot in the grave, if not both feet. In ten years I would be fifty. In twenty, sixty.

Was it strange that a shadow hung over happiness?

I indicated to pull out and overtook a juggernaut. I was so inexperienced that I felt uneasy when the car was buffeted by the turbulence. But I wasn't afraid, I had only been afraid once for as long as I had been driving, and that was on the day of my driving test. It took place early one midwinter morning, it was pitch black outside, I had never driven in the darkness. The rain was pelting down, and I had never driven in the pouring rain. And the examiner was an unfriendly-looking man with an unfriendly presence. Naturally, I had the compulsory safety check off by heart. The first thing he said was that we would skip the check. Just clean the condensation off the windows and we'll say that's fine. I didn't know how to do that out of the sequence I had drilled into myself, and by the time I had worked it out after two minutes' fumbling around on the dashboard, I had forgotten to switch on the ignition for the demist to work, which caused the examiner to scrutinise me, ask, 'You do know how to drive, do you?' and with a shake of the head to turn the key for me. After such an incredibly bad start I wasn't helped by the fact that my legs were wildly out of control, they were shaking and trembling, and my coordination was conspicuous by its absence, so we kangaroo-jumped rather than glided into the traffic. Pitch black. Morning rush hour. Pouring rain. After a hundred metres the examiner asked me what my day job was. I said I was a writer. Then he became really interested. He was an artist himself, he told me. He'd had an exhibition and so on. He asked me what I wrote. I had just started to tell him about *A Time to Every Purpose Under Heaven* when he gave me the name of the town I should head for. In front of us was an enormous motorway junction. I couldn't see a sign with the name. He asked if the book had come out in Swedish. I nodded. There! There was the sign. But over on the far lane! So I steered towards it and accelerated, and he jumped on the brakes, bringing us to a sudden halt.

'The lights are red!' he said. 'Didn't you see? Fire-engine red!'

I hadn't even seen any lights.

'Well, that's it then, isn't it?'

'I'm afraid so,' he said. 'If we have to intervene, you've failed. Those are the rules. Do you want to drive a bit more?'

'No. Let's go back.'

The whole test had lasted three minutes. I was home by half past nine. Linda regarded me with tense eyes.

'Failed,' I said.

'Oh no!' she said. 'Poor you! What happened?'

'Went through on red.'

'Really?'

'Yes, really! Who would have imagined when I got up early

this morning that I would jump the lights during the test! It'll be fine next time. I won't do it again in the next test.'

It wasn't a big issue. We didn't have a car, and it didn't matter whether I got my licence in January or March. And I had already squandered such an incredible amount of money on driving lessons that a handful more wouldn't make much difference. The only problem was that we had planned a trip at the end of the month. I had agreed to do a job in Søgne, in southern Norway, with the idea of going there as a family and afterwards travelling back via Sandøya, outside Tvedestrand, and staying at a guest house for a couple of days to see what it was like. In fact, I had checked out Sandøya a few years ago and thought it would be a perfect place for us to live. An island with around two hundred inhabitants, a nursery, a school with classes for children up to ten and no cars. The countryside was exactly like the area I had grown up with, and for which I felt such a deep yearning, except that it wasn't, it wasn't Tromøya or Arendal or Kristiansand, which I would not have returned to for the whole wide world, but something different, something new. Sometimes I thought the longing for the terrain we had grown up with was biological, somehow rooted in us, that the instinct which could make a cat travel several hundred kilometres to find the place it came from also functioned in us, the human animal, on a par with other deeply archaic currents within us.

Sometimes I looked at pictures of Sandøya on the Net, and the sight of the landscape gave me a rush that was so strong it completely overshadowed the potentially lonely and abandoned existence there. Not for Linda, of course, she was more sceptical, but not entirely closed to the idea. Living in a forest by the sea would suit us a great deal better than living on the sixth floor in the centre of the town. So we spent hours speculating, long enough for us to want to go there and check it out. But then I didn't get my licence, so I had to go to Søgne alone, which meant the whole point of the job was lost. What was I going to talk about?

That evening, Geir rang me as I was booking the flight online. We had already spoken during the day, but he hadn't been himself over recent weeks, in his own controlled way, so there was nothing strange about him phoning again. I sat back in my armchair and put my feet on the desk. He told me a bit about the biography he was writing, about Montgomery Clift and how he always strove to get the maximum out of life in all ways. My only reference point to Montgomery Clift was via The Clash, their line 'Montgomery Clift, honey!' from 'London Calling', and it transpired that was also where Geir had heard his name, although in a different context: in Iraq he had been living in a waterworks with Robin Banks, an English junkie who had been one of the band's best friends, he travelled with them on tour, he even had a song dedicated to him, and he had told him how Montgomery Clift had occupied an important place in their lives, which prompted Geir to find out more about him. Another reason was that *The Misfits* was one of his favourite films. I spoke about Thomas Mann's *Buddenbrooks*, which I had just started rereading, about how perfect the sentences were, how high the quality of the writing was, for which reason I enjoyed, truly enjoyed, every page, which was a rare occurrence, and about how this perfection, like the setting and the form incidentally, belonged to a different era from Thomas Mann's, which made it more like an imitation, a reconstruction, or in other words, a pastiche. What happened when the pastiche surpassed the original? *Could* it indeed? This was a classic problem; writers as far back as Virgil must have grappled with it. How closely is a style or a form tied to the particular era and the particular

culture it first appeared in? Is a style or a form destroyed as soon
as it appears? In Thomas Mann's hands it wasn't destroyed, that
was not the right word, more 'ambivalent' perhaps, endlessly
ambivalent, whence the irony, the irony that would destabilise
all foundations, flowed. From there we moved on to Stefan
Zweig's *The World of Yesterday*, the fantastic portrait of the turn
of the last century, when age and gravity and not youth and
beauty were desirable, and all young people tried to look middle-
aged with their stomachs, watch chains, cigars and bald patches.
All blown to pieces by the First World War, which, followed by
the Second World War, formed a chasm between us and them.
Geir then talked about Montgomery Clift again, his tumultuous
life, his unbridled vitalism. He realised that all the biographies
he had read over the last year had this in common: they were
all about vitalists. Not in theory, but in practice, they were always
out to get the most from life. Jack London, André Malraux,
Nordahl Grieg, Ernest Hemingway. Hunter S. Thompson.
Mayakovsky.

'I can easily understand why Sartre took amphetamines,' he
said. 'Life in the fast lane, achieve more, burn. That's how it is.
But the most consistent one of them all was Mishima. I always
go back to him. He was forty-five when he took his own life. He
was consistent. The hero had to be good-looking. Couldn't be
old. And Jünger, who went the other way. On his hundredth
birthday he sat drinking cognac and smoking cigars, as sharp
as a razor. Everything's about strength. That's all I'm interested
in. Strength, courage, determination. Intelligence? No. I think
you get that if you want. It's not important, it's not interesting.
Growing up in the 70s and the 80s is a joke. We don't do anything.
And what we do do is just rubbish. I write to recapture my lost
gravity. That's what I do. But of course it serves no purpose. You
know where I sit. You know what I do. My life is so trivial. And

my enemies, they're so trivial. It's not worth wasting your strength on. But there's nothing else. So here I sit, thrashing around in my bedroom.'

'Vitalism,' I said. 'There is another vitalism, you know, the one connected with land and kinfolk. Norway in the 1920s.'

'Oh, I'm not interested in that. There's not a trace of Nazism in the vitalism I'm talking about. Not that it would matter if there was, but there isn't. What I'm talking about is anti-liberal culture.'

'There wasn't a trace of Nazism in Norwegian vitalism either. It was the middle classes who imported Nazism, converted it into something abstract, an idea, in other words something that didn't exist. It was about a longing for a plot of land, a longing for family. What makes Hamsun so complicated was that as a person he was so rootless, so anchorless, and as such modern, in an American sense. But he despised America, mass humanity, rootlessness. It was himself he despised. The irony that results from this is a great deal more relevant than Thomas Mann's because it has nothing to do with style, it deals with basic existence.'

'I'm not a writer, I'm a farmer,' Geir said. 'Ha ha ha! But, no, you can keep your land. I'm only interested in the social world. Nothing else. You can read Lucretius and shout hallelujah. You can talk about forests in the seventeenth century. I couldn't be less interested. It's only people that count.'

'Have you seen that picture by Anselm Kiefer? It's of a forest. All you can see is trees and snow, with red stains in places, and then there are some names of German poets written in white. Hölderlin, Rilke, Fichte, Kleist. It's the greatest work of art since the war, perhaps in the whole of the previous century. What does it depict? A forest. What's it about? Well, Auschwitz of course. Where's the connection? It's not about ideas, it reaches right down into the depths of culture, and it can't be expressed in ideas.'

'Have you had a chance to see *Shoah*?'

'No.'

'Forest, forest and more forest. And faces. Forest and gas and faces.'

'The picture's called *Varus*. As far as I remember, he was a Roman army commander who lost a decisive battle in Germany. The line goes right back from the 70s to Tacitus. Schama traces it in *Landscape and Memory*. We could have added Odin, who hangs himself from a tree. Perhaps he does, I don't remember. But it's forest.'

'I can see where you're going.'

'When I read Lucretius it's all about the magnificence of the world. And that, the magnificence of the world, is of course a Baroque concept. It died with the Baroque age. It's about things. The physicality of things. Animals. Trees. Fish. If you're sorry that action has disappeared, I'm sorry the world has disappeared. The physicality of it. We only have pictures of it. That's what we relate to. But the apocalypse, what is it now? Trees disappearing in South America? Ice melting, the waters rising. If you write to recapture your gravity, I write to recapture the world. Yes, not the world I'm in. Definitely not the social world. The wonder-rooms of the Baroque age. The curiosity cabinets. And the world in Kiefer's trees. That's art. Nothing else.'

'A picture?'

'You've got me there. Yes, a picture.'

There was a knock at the door.

'I'll call you back,' I said, and rang off. 'Come in!'

Linda opened the door.

'Are you on the phone?' she said. 'I just wanted to say I was going to have a bath. Keep an ear open for the children. In case they wake up. Don't put your headphones on.'

'OK. Are you going for a sleep afterwards?'

She nodded.

'I'll join you.'

'Right,' she said, smiled and closed the door. I called Geir back.

'Well, what the hell do I know,' I said with a sigh.

'Or me,' he said.

'What have you been doing this evening?'

'Listening to some blues. Got ten new CDs in the post today. And I've ordered . . . thirteen, fourteen, *fifteen* more.'

'You're mad.'

'No, I'm not . . . Mum died today.'

'What?'

'She passed away in her sleep. So now her angst is over. What good did it do? one might ask. But dad's devastated. And Odd Steinar, of course. We're going down there in a few days. The funeral's in a week. Weren't you going to Sørland at about that time?'

'Ten days later,' I said. 'I've just booked the tickets.'

'Then we'll see each other perhaps. We're bound to stay on for a few days.'

There was a pause.

'Why didn't you tell me straight away?' I said. 'We chatted for half an hour before you told me. Were you trying to make a point out of everything being as normal?'

'No. Oh no. You've got the wrong end of the stick. No, no. I just don't want to go there. And when I talk to you I'm away from it. It was as simple as that. It's not worth talking about. I'm sure you understand that. It doesn't help at all. It's the same with blues. It's a place to escape to. Well, not that I feel a lot. But I reckon that's a feeling too.'

'It is.'

*

After we had rung off I went into the hall between the kitchen and the living room, took an apple and stood munching as I gazed at the kitchen, which had been stripped of everything. Plaster where the worktop had been, long planks leaning against the bare walls, the floor covered in dust, various tools and cables, some furniture which would soon be assembled wrapped in plastic packaging. The renovation was supposed to take another two weeks. All we had really wanted was a dishwasher, but the worktop wasn't the right size for it, and it would be simpler, the fitter said, to have the whole kitchen changed. So that's what we did. The owners of the block would pay.

A voice made me turn my head.

Had it come from the children's room?

I went over and peeped in. They were asleep, both of them. Heidi in the top bunk, with her feet on the pillow and her head on the rolled-up duvet, Vanja beneath, on the duvet as well, with her arms and legs stretched out, her body in a little X-formation. She tossed her head from one side to the other and back again.

'Mummy,' she said.

She had opened her eyes.

'Are you awake, Vanja?' I asked.

No answer.

She must have been asleep.

Now and then she woke late in the evening and cried so piercingly, but it wasn't possible to make contact with her, she just screamed and screamed, trapped inside herself, it seemed, as though we didn't exist and she was completely alone where she was. If we lifted her and held her tight, she put up a furious resistance, kicked and punched and wanted to be put down again, where she was just as wild and unapproachable. She wasn't asleep, but she wasn't awake either. It was a kind of in-between state. It was heart-wrenching to see. But when she woke next day she was in a cheery mood. I wondered whether she remembered the desperation or if it drifted away like a dream.

At any rate, she would like to hear that she had said mummy in her sleep. I would have to remember to tell her.

I closed the door and went into the bathroom, where the only light came from a small candle on the edge of the bath, flickering in the draught from the window. The steam was dense inside. Linda lay with her eyes closed and her head half under the water. She sat up slowly when she noticed me.

'Here you are in your grotto,' I said.

'It's lovely,' she said. 'Don't you want to jump in?'

I shook my head.

'Thought so,' she said. 'Who were you talking to, by the way?'

'Geir,' I said. 'His mother died today.'

'Oh, how sad . . .' she said. 'How is he taking it?'

'Well,' I said.

She leaned back in the bath.

'I suppose we're at that age now,' I said. 'Mikaela's father died only a few months ago. Your mother had a heart attack. Geir's mother has died.'

'Don't say that,' Linda said. 'Mummy will live for many years yet. Your mother too.'

'Maybe. If they get through their sixties they can live to be quite old. That's how it usually is. Anyway, it won't be long before we are the oldest.'

'Karl Ove!' she said. 'You aren't even forty yet! And I'm thirty-five!'

'I talked to Jeppe about this once,' I said. 'He's lost both his parents. I said that the worst for me would be that I no longer had anyone to witness my life. He didn't have a clue what I was talking about. And I don't really know if I meant it. Or if it's not my life I want witnessed, but our children's. I want mum to see how they get on, not just now while they're small but when they grow up. I want her to know them inside out. Do you understand what I mean?'

'Of course. But I don't know if I want to talk about it.'

'Do you remember when you came into the room and asked if I knew where Heidi was? I went out with you to look. Berit was here. She had opened the balcony door. And when I saw it, the open door, I was seized by a terrible fear. All the blood drained from my face. I almost fainted. The fear or the panic or the terror, or whatever it was, was so instantaneous. I thought that Heidi had wandered onto the balcony on her own. In those seconds I was sure we had lost her. They must be the worst seconds of my life. I've never known such a strong emotion. The wonder is that I'd never experienced it before, that something can happen and we could really lose them. In some way or other, I imagined they were immortal. Oh, yes, that was what we weren't supposed to talk about.'

'Thank you.'

She smiled. When she had her hair slicked back and didn't wear any make-up she looked so young.

'You definitely don't look thirty-five,' I said. 'You look like twenty-five.'

'Do I?'

I nodded.

'They actually asked me for ID last time I went to the Systembolaget. I suppose I should be flattered by that, but at the same time I am stopped by all manner of Christian organisations when I'm walking in the street. I'm always the one they latch on to. When I'm with other people they don't bother *them*. Then they see me and make a beeline for me. Must be something to do with the vibes I give off. There's one we can redeem. She's dying for redemption. Don't you reckon?'

I shrugged.

'Could be because you look so innocent?'

'Ha! Even worse!'

She held her nose with two fingers and ducked her whole body under the water. When she re-emerged she shook her head first. Then she looked at me with a smile.

'What's up? Why are you looking at me like that?' she asked.

'That, for example,' I said. 'What you used to do as a child.'

'What?'

'Duck your head under the water.'

In the bedroom, which was adjacent to the bathroom, John began to cry.

'Pat him on the back a bit and I'll be with you in a minute.'

I nodded and went into the bedroom. He was lying on his back and flailing with his arms as he cried. I turned him over like a turtle and stroked his back with the palm of my hand. This is what he liked best, he always went quiet then, if he hadn't had sufficient time to get himself into a real state.

I sang the five lullabies I knew. Linda came in and pulled him to her in bed. I went into the living room, put on my outdoor jacket, a scarf, a hat and shoes, which were by the balcony door, and went out. Sat down on the chair in the corner, poured myself some coffee and lit a cigarette. The wind was blowing from the east. The sky was deep and starry. Plane lights twinkled.

The summer I turned twenty mum rang one day and told me she had a large tumour in her stomach and was being admitted to hospital the following day to have it operated on. She said she didn't know whether it was malignant or not, and it wasn't possible to say how this would go. She said the tumour was so big she hadn't been able to lie on her stomach for a long time. Her voice was tired and weak. I was staying with Hilde, a girl-friend from the *gymnas*, in Søm, outside Kristiansand, where a

few minutes before I had been standing on the drive beside the
car waiting for her. We were going swimming. Then she had
called me from the balcony, your mother's on the phone, Karl
Ove. I immediately grasped the gravity of the situation, but
nothing about it aroused any emotions, I was completely cold
towards her. Rang off, went over to Hilde, who had got into the
car, opened the passenger door and got in, said mum was having
an operation and that I would have to go to Førde the next day.
It felt like an event, one I should have a part in, a role I could
play, the son who flies home to take care of his mother. I visualised the funeral, everyone passing on their condolences, how
sorry they would be for me, and I thought about the inheritance
she would bequeath. And then I thought at last I had something
of significance to write about. While all this was going on another
voice seemed to be running in parallel and saying no, this was
serious, come on, this is your mother who's dying, she means
a lot to you, you want her to live, you do, Karl Ove! Telling Hilde
would give me kudos, I felt, my importance would grow in her
eyes. She drove me to the airport the following day, I landed in
Bringelandsåsen, caught the airport bus to Førde centre and a
local bus to the hospital, where I was given mum's house keys.
She had just moved, everything was packed away in boxes, I
didn't need to bother about that, she said, just leave them where
they were, I'll sort them out when I'm back. *If* you come back,
I thought. Caught the bus up the valley through the strident
green countryside, I was alone in the house all evening and
night, went down to the hospital the next day, she was drowsy
and weak after the operation, which had gone well. After I arrived
back at the house, situated at the end of a short plain with
gently sloping fields up to a mountain on one side and a river,
a forest and another mountain on the other, I began to sort the
boxes, put the ones with cooking utensils in the kitchen and so

on. Darkness fell, the traffic on the road dwindled, the hum of the river grew, the shadow of my body flickered on walls and boxes. Who was I? A lonely person. I had just begun to learn to come to terms with it, that is minimise the significance of it, but I still had a good way to go, so every time I stopped working I would feel this chill in my head, this ice-cold evil, and perhaps put on my outdoor clothes, perhaps walk over the grass, through the garden gate, over the road to the river, which flowed past in the summer darkness, grey and black, stand between the shining-white birch trees and gaze at the water, which in some way soothed my feelings, matched them, what did I know? There must have been something to it, because that was what I did then, went out at night and searched for water. Sea, rivers, lakes, it made no difference. Oh, I was so preoccupied with myself, and I was so great, yet a nobody at the same time, quite shamefully alone and friendless, full of thoughts about *the* one, *the* woman, although I wouldn't know what to do if I got her because I still hadn't been to bed with one. Cunt, that only existed in theory for me. I would never dream of using such a word. Lap, bosom, backside, they were the words I used to describe my desire. I toyed with the idea of suicide, I had done that ever since I was small and despised myself for that reason, it would never happen, I had too much to avenge, too many people to hate and too much due to me. I lit a cigarette, and when it was finished I went back to the empty house with all the cardboard boxes. By three in the morning all the boxes were in place. I started moving the pictures in the hall to the living room. When I put one of them down a bird suddenly flew up into my face. Oh Jesus! I must have jumped a metre. It wasn't a bird, it was a bat. It darted to and fro through the room with wild, agitated movements. I was terrified. I ran out, closed the door behind me and went up to the bedroom on the first floor, where I spent the whole night. I fell asleep at about six and slept through till three the next afternoon, threw my clothes on and caught the bus to the hospital. Mum was better, but still groggy from painkillers. We sat on a terrace, she was in a wheelchair. I told her some of the terrible experiences I'd had that spring. The notion that I shouldn't worry her so soon after the operation didn't occur to me until several years later. When I returned to the house the bat was hanging from the wall. I took a washtub and put it over the bat. Heard it banging around inside and almost threw up with revulsion. Dragged the bucket down the wall and got it onto the floor without the bat escaping. So that it was trapped at least, if not dead. I did as the night before, closed the living-room door and went up to the bedroom. Lay reading Stendhal's *Le Rouge et Le Noir* until I fell asleep. The next morning I found a brick in the shed. Carefully lifted the bucket, found the bat lying still, hesitated for a second, was there a way to get it outside? Nudge it into a bucket perhaps and then cover it with a newspaper? I didn't want to crush it if I didn't have to. Before I had really made up my mind I smacked the brick down as hard as I could on the bat and squashed it against the floor. Pressed the brick down and wriggled it to and fro until I was sure there was no life left. The feeling of soft flesh against hard stone stayed with me for several days, indeed weeks. I shoved a dustpan under the bat and threw it into the ditch beside the road. Then I washed where it had been, thoroughly, and caught the bus to the hospital again. The next day mum came home, and I was a good son for two weeks. Amid the lush green of the valley, beneath the grey sky, I carried furniture and unpacked boxes until the time came for me to start university and I caught the bus to Bergen.

How much of the twenty-year-old was left in me now?

Not much, I thought, sitting and looking up at the glimmering stars above the town. The feeling of being me was the same. The person I woke up to every morning and fell asleep to every night. But the quivering panic was gone. As was the immense focus on others. And its opposite, the megalomaniac importance I ascribed to myself had become smaller. Perhaps not much smaller, but smaller nevertheless.

When I was twenty it was only ten years since I had been ten. Everything in my childhood was still close. It was still my reference point, from it I made sense of things. Not now, not any more.

I got up and went in. Linda and John were asleep, lying close together in the darkness of the bedroom. John like a little ball. I lay down beside them, watched for a while, until I too fell asleep.

Ten days later, early in the morning, I landed at Kjevik Airport, outside Kristiansand. Even though between the ages of thirteen and eighteen I had lived ten kilometres away and the countryside was full of memories, it aroused little or nothing in me this time, perhaps because it was no more than two years since I had last been there, perhaps because I was further away than ever. I descended the steps from the plane with Topdalsfjord to the left sparkling in the light from the February sun, and Ryensletta to the right, where one New Year's Eve Jan Vidar and I had dragged ourselves downhill through a snowstorm.

I walked into the terminal building, past the baggage carousel, to a kiosk, where I bought a cup of coffee and took it with me outside. Lit a cigarette, watched people coming out in dribs and drabs, heading for the airport bus or the line of taxis, everywhere I heard the southern Norwegian dialect, which filled me with such ambivalence. It belonged here, it was the very marker of belonging, both cultural and geographical, and I could still hear the smugness I had always heard in it so clearly, probably my own interpretation, because I didn't belong here myself and never had done.

A life is simple to understand, the elements that determine it are few. In mine there were two. My father and the fact that I had never belonged anywhere.

It was no more difficult than that.

I switched on my mobile phone and looked at the clock. A few minutes past ten. I was supposed to give the day's first talk at one at the new university in Agder, so I had plenty of time. The second was in Søgne, approximately twenty kilometres outside the town, at half past seven. I had decided to speak without a script. I had never done this before, and fear and nerves were washing through me about every ten minutes. I was weak at the knees too, and it felt as if the hand holding the cup was shaking. But it wasn't, I confirmed. I stubbed the cigarette out on the ash-coloured grid above the rubbish bin and went through the automatic doors, back to the kiosk, where I bought three newspapers and sat down on one of the high barstools to read them. Ten years ago I had written about this room, it was where the main protagonist in *Out of the World*, Henrik Vankel, went to meet Miriam in the final scene of the novel. I had been up in Volda, on the west coast, writing, where the view of the fjord, ferries shuttling hither and thither, the lights in the harbour and beneath the mountains on the other side was a mere shadow in the rooms and the countryside I was describing, this Kristiansand I had once wandered around and was now revisiting in my mind. I might not have remembered what people said to me, I might not have remembered what had happened where; however I did remember exactly what it looked like and the atmosphere which surrounded it. I remembered all the rooms I had been in and all the landscapes. If I closed my eyes I could invoke all the details of the house in which I had grown up, and the neighbour's house, and the countryside around, at least within a radius of a couple of kilometres. The schools, the swimming baths, the sports halls, the youth clubs, the petrol stations, the shops, my relatives' houses. The same applied to the books I had read. What they were about was gone in weeks, but the places where the plot had taken place had stayed with me for years, perhaps they would for ever, what did I know?

I flicked through *Dagbladet*, followed by *Aftenposten* and *Fædrelandsvennen*, then sat watching people pass by. I ought to have spent the time preparing. All I had done thus far was read through some old papers the night before and print the texts I was going to read. On the plane I had written down ten points I would cover. I couldn't bring myself to do any more because the thought that I was only going to talk, that there was nothing simpler, was so strong and so appealing. I was supposed to talk about the two books I had written. I couldn't do that, so it would have to be about how the books came into being, those years of nothing until something definite began to take shape, how it slowly but surely took over, in such a way that in the end every-thing came by itself. Writing a novel is setting yourself a goal and then walking there in your sleep, Lawrence Durrell had once said that was what it was like, and it was true. We have access not only to our own lives but to almost all the other lives in our cultural circle, access not only to our own memories but to the memories of the whole of our damn culture, for I am you and you are everyone, we come from the same and are going to the same, and on the way we hear the same on the radio, see the same on TV, read the same in the press, and within us there is the same fauna of famous people's faces and smiles. Even if you sit in a tiny room in a tiny town hundreds of kilometres from the centre of the world and don't meet a single soul, their hell is your hell, their heaven is your heaven, you have to burst the balloon that is the world and let everything in it spill over the sides.

That, more or less, was what I was going to say.

Language is shared, we grow into it, and the forms we use it in are also shared, so irrespective of how idiosyncratic you and your notions are, in literature you can never free yourself from others. It is the other way round, it is literature which draws us closer together. Through its language, which none of us owns and which indeed we can hardly have any influence on, and through its form, which no one can break free of alone, and if anyone should do so, it is only meaningful if it is immediately followed by others. Form draws you out of yourself, distances you from yourself, and it is this distance which is the prerequisite for closeness to others.

For the talk I was going to start with an anecdote about Hauge, the crabby old man who mumbled and was so locked inside himself, utterly isolated for all those years, yet so much closer to the centre of culture and civilisation than perhaps anyone else of his era. What conversations did he have? What places did he inhabit?

I slipped down off the stool and went to the counter for a refill. Changed a fifty-krone note into coins. I had to ring Linda before going any further, and I couldn't use my mobile phone to call from abroad.

It'll be fine, I thought as I scanned the two sheets of cues. It didn't matter too much that these were old ideas and I no longer believed in them. The important thing was that I said something.

Over recent years I had increasingly lost faith in literature. I read and thought this is something someone has made up. Perhaps it was because we were totally inundated with fiction and stories. It had got out of hand. Wherever you turned you saw fiction. All these millions of paperbacks, hardbacks, DVDs and TV series, they were all about made-up people in a made-up, though realistic, world. And news in the press, TV news and radio news had exactly the same format, documentaries had the same format, they were also stories, and it made no difference whether what they told had actually happened or not. It was a crisis, I felt it in every fibre of my body, something saturating was spreading through my consciousness like lard, not least because the nucleus of all this fiction, whether true or not, was verisimilitude and the distance it held to reality was constant. In other words, it saw the same. This sameness, which was our world, was being mass-produced. The uniqueness, which they all talked about, was thereby invalidated, it didn't exist, it was a lie. Living like this, with the certainty that everything could equally well have been different, drove you to despair. I couldn't write like this, it wouldn't work, every single sentence was met with the thought: but you're just making this up. It has no value. Fictional writing has no value, documentary narrative has no value. The only genres I saw value in, which still conferred meaning, were diaries and essays, the types of literature that did not deal with narrative, that were not about anything, but just consisted of a voice, the voice of your own personality, a life, a face, a gaze you could meet. What is a work of art if not the gaze of another person? Not directed above us, nor beneath us, but at the same height as our own gaze. Art cannot be experienced collectively, nothing can, art is something you are alone with. You meet its gaze alone.

That was as far as the thought got, it hit a wall. If fiction was worthless, the world was too, for nowadays it was through fiction we saw it.

Now of course I could relativise this as well. I could think it was more about my mental state, my personal psychology than the actual state of the world. If I spoke to Espen or Tore about it, who were now my oldest friends, whom I had known long before they made their debuts as writers, they would utterly reject my view. Each in their own way. Espen was the critical type, yet at the same time he had this burning curiosity, he had a voracious appetite for the world, and when he wrote all his energy was focused outwards: politics, sport, music, philosophy, the history of the Church, medical science, biology, painting, great events of the present, great events of the past, wars and battlefields, but also his daughters, his holiday trips, minor events he had witnessed: he wrote about everything, and with his characteristic lightness, which he had because he wasn't interested in the in-turned gaze, introspection, where his criticism, which was so fruitful on the outside, could easily contrive to destroy everything he tried to understand. It was this participation in the world that Espen liked and craved. When I first got to know him he was introverted and shy, self-contained and not very happy. I had seen the long way he had come, to the life he lived now, which he had managed so that everything that depressed him was gone. He had landed on his feet, he was happy, and if he was critical of much in the world he didn't despise it. Tore's lightness was of a different kind: he loved the present and took a great interest in it, which perhaps stemmed from his deep fascination with pop music – the anatomy of the charts, one week's top songs being replaced by others the next, the whole aesthetic of pop, big sales, high media visibility, touring with his own show. He had transferred this to literature, for which of course he was castigated, but nevertheless he carried on with typical resolve. If there was one thing he hated it was modernism because it was non-communicative, inaccessible, abstruse and endlessly self-important, though he never bothered to elaborate. But what do you say to have any impact on a man who at one time admired the Spice Girls? To influence a man who once wrote an enthusiastic essay about the sitcom *Friends*? I liked the direction he was taking, towards the pre-modern novel, Balzac, Flaubert, Zola, Dickens, but I didn't share his belief that the form could be transferred to today. Hence the only thing I was doing that he really criticised was the form, which he thought was weak. I also liked the direction Espen was taking, towards the scholarly but digressive and overflowing, all-encompassing essay which had something Baroque about it, but I disliked the standpoint he took, in which for example rationalism was lauded and Romanticism ridiculed. Nonetheless, Espen and Tore didn't do anything by halves, and I saw nothing wrong in that; on the contrary, that was what I also had to do, affirm life, in a Nietzschean sense, for there was nothing else. This was all we had, this was all that existed, and so should we say no to it?

I took out my mobile and flipped it open. The photo of Heidi and Vanja shone up at me. Heidi with her face pressed against the display, one big smile, Vanja a little more tentative behind.

It was a quarter to eleven.

I got up and went to the payphone, inserted forty kroner and dialled Linda's mobile number.

'How was it this morning?' I asked.

'Terrible,' she said. 'Absolute chaos. Uttterly out of control. Heidi clawed John again. Vanja and Heidi had a fight. And Vanja had a temper tantrum on the street as we were about to go.'

'Oh no. Oh no,' I said. 'I'm sorry to hear that.'

'And then when we got to the nursery Vanja said, "You and dad are always so angry. You're always so angry." I was so upset! So unbelievably upset.'

'I can understand that. It's terrible. We'll have to sort this out, Linda. We have to. We have to find a solution. It's no good what we're doing. I'll have to pull myself together. A lot of this is my fault.'

'Yes, we must,' Linda said. 'We'll have to talk about it when you come home. What drives me to despair is that I only want us to be happy. That's all I want. And I can't do it! I'm such a terrible mother. I can't even be alone with my own children.'

'No, that's not true. You're a fantastic mother. That's not what this is about. But we'll get there. We will.'

'Yes . . . How was the trip?'

'Fine. I'm in Kristiansand now. Off to the university soon. I'm dreading it. I really hate this. I can't think of anything worse. And then I go and do it again and again.'

'It always goes well though.'

'That's a qualified truth. Sometimes it does. But I don't want to keep grumbling. It'll be fine, and I am fine. I'll ring again tonight, OK? If there is anything, ring my mobile. It's OK for incoming calls.'

'All right.'

'What are you doing now?'

'Walking in Pildamms Park with John. He's asleep. It's nice here and I should be happy. But . . . this morning has shattered me.'

'It'll pass. You'll have a nice afternoon together. Linda, I've got to go. Bye!'

'Bye. And good luck!'

I hung up the receiver, collected my bag and went out for a last cigarette.

SHIT. SHIT, SHIT, SHIT.

I leaned against the wall and looked at the forest, the grey rock face between all the yellow and green.

I was so sad for the children. I was so angry and irritable at home. It took nothing for me to tell Heidi off, nothing to *shout* at her. And Vanja, Vanja . . . When she had her bouts of defiance and not only said no to everything but also shouted and screamed and punched, I shouted back, grabbed her and threw her onto the bed. I was completely out of control. Then came the remorse afterwards, the attempts to be patient, kind, nice, friendly, good. Good. And that was what I wanted to be, all I wanted to be, to be a good father to the three of them.

Wasn't I a good father?

SHIT. SHIT. SHIT.

I tossed the cigarette away, grabbed my bag and left. As I had no idea where the university was, nothing like it had existed when I lived here, I took a taxi all the way. It went from the car park with me on the back seat, alongside the runway at first, then over the river, past my old school, which I couldn't care less about, up and down the hills and past Hamresanden, the campsite, the beach, the hills with the estate behind, where most of my classmates had lived. Through the forest to the Timenes crossroads, where we followed the E18 to Kristiansand.

The university was on the other side of a tunnel, not so far from the *gymnas* I had attended but completely isolated from it. It lay like a little island in the forest. Large attractive new buildings. There was no doubt that money had flowed into Norway since I lived here. People were better dressed, their cars were more expensive and building projects were under way everywhere.

A bearded bespectacled lecturer-type met me at the front entrance. We shook hands, he showed me the room where the talk was to be held and went about his business. I made a beeline for the canteen, stuffed down a baguette, sat outside in the sun, drank coffee and smoked. There were students everywhere, younger than I thought they should be, they looked more like they were attending a *gymnas*. Suddenly I had a vision of myself, an ageing man with sunken eyes and a bag, sitting on his own. Forty, I would soon be forty. Hadn't I almost fallen off my chair

when Hans's pal Olli had once told us he was forty? I hadn't
believed it at first, but then his life appeared in a very new light,
what was that old boy doing with us?

Now I was the same age myself.

'Karl Ove?'

I looked up. Nora Simonhjell stood in front of me with a smile
on her face.

'Hi, Nora! What are you doing here? Do you work here?'

'Yes. I saw you were coming. Thought I would find you here.
Nice to see you!'

I got up and gave her a hug.

'Grab a seat!' I said.

'You're looking so good!' she said. 'Tell me what's new in your
life.'

I gave her the edited highlights. Three children, four years in
Stockholm, two in Malmö. Everything OK. She – I had first met
her at a department party at Bergen University the night they
were celebrating having finished their main subject, and then
bumped into her in Volda where she taught and I wrote my first
novel, which she read and was the first to comment on – had
lived for a while in Oslo, worked in a bookshop and at
Morgenbladet, published her second collection of poems and got
a job here. I told her Kristiansand had been a nightmare for me.
But a lot must have changed in the intervening twenty years.
And it was one thing to go to a *gymnas* and another to be employed
at a university.

She loved it, she said. Seemed happy. She had hung up her
quill, but not for good, you never knew what might happen. A
friend came over, she was American, we talked a little about the
differences between the old country and her new one, then went
up to the auditorium. The talk was due to start in ten minutes.
My stomach hurt, my whole body did in fact, everything ached.

And my hands, which had been trembling subconsciously all day, now really were trembling. I sat down at the desk, flicked through the books, looked up at the entrance. Two people in the hall. Me and the lecturer. Was it going to be that kind of day?

The first time I read in public, a few weeks after my debut novel had come out, was in Kristiansand. There were four people in the audience. One of them, I saw to my great satisfaction, was my old history teacher, now the headmaster, Rosenvold. I went over to chat with him afterwards. It turned out that he had almost no memory of me, but he had come to listen to and meet the second of the evening's debutants, Bjarte Breiteig.

So much for the homecoming. So much for revenge over the past.

'We-ell, I think we can begin then, can't we?' the lecturer said.

I looked along the rows of chairs. Seven people sitting there.

Nora said she was impressed when it was over, an hour later. I smiled and thanked her for her kind words, but I hated myself and my whole being, I couldn't get away fast enough. Fortunately, Geir had turned up twenty minutes before we had arranged. He was standing in the middle of the large foyer when I came downstairs. I hadn't seen him for more than a year.

'I didn't think you could lose any more hair,' I said. 'But I was wrong.'

We shook hands.

'Your teeth have gone so yellow the dogs are going to flock round you in town,' he said. 'They'll think you're their king. How was it?'

'Seven people came.'

'Ha ha ha!'

'Never mind. Otherwise, it went well. Shall we go? Have you got your car outside?'

'Yes,' he said.

Considering he had buried his mother the day before, he was in an astonishingly good mood.

'Last time I came here it was on an exercise with the Home Guard cadets,' he said as we crossed the square. 'We were given our kit near here. But there was none of this here then, of course.'

He pressed the remote key, and twenty metres away a red Saab flashed. There was a child's car seat in the back, for his son, Njaal, who was born the day after Heidi and whom I was god-father to.

'Do you want to drive?' he asked with a smile.

I couldn't think of a quick retort and just smiled. Opened the door and got in, pushed the seat back, put on the seat belt and looked at him.

'Aren't we going?'

'Where to?'

'Town, I suppose. What else is there to do?'

He turned the key, reversed and pulled onto the road.

'You seem a bit dejected,' he said. 'Didn't it go particularly well?'

'It went fine. And I'm not going to burden you with what isn't.'

'Why not?'

'Well, you know . . .' I said. 'There are small problems and then there are big problems.'

'Mum's burial yesterday does not belong to the category "problem",' he said. 'What has happened has happened. Come on now. What's eating you?'

We drove into the short tunnel and emerged on the plain by Kongsgård, which, flooded with the sharp winter light, seemed almost beautiful.

'I spoke to Linda earlier,' I said. 'She had a hard morning, well, you know what I mean. Tempers and chaos. Then Vanja said we were always angry. And she's bloody right. I can see it as soon as I'm away. In fact, I feel like going back right this minute and sorting it out. That's what's eating me.'

'Nothing new then,' Geir said.

'No.'

We drove onto the E18, pulled up in front of the toll booths, where Geir opened his window and threw coins into the grey metal cone, and went past Oddernes Church, behind it the chapel where dad had been buried, and Kristiansand Cathedral School, where I had spent three years.

'This place is packed with meaning for me,' I said. 'My grandparents are buried here. And dad . . .'

'He's in some warehouse here, isn't he?'

'Correct. How could we not have got the job done properly, eh?! Heh heh heh.'

'Sometimes blood is thinner than water. Heh heh heh.'

'Ha ha ha! Seriously, though, I'll get this sorted out soon, get him under the ground. I have to.'

'Ten years in a warehouse has never hurt anyone,' Geir said.

'Yes, it has. But no one who's been cremated.'

'Ha ha ha!'

Silence. We drove past the fire station into the tunnel.

'How was the funeral yesterday?' I asked.

'It was wonderful,' he said. 'Lots of people came. The church was packed. Loads of relatives and family friends I haven't seen for years, in fact, ever since I was a boy. It was great. Dad and Odd Steinar cried. They were devastated.'

'And you?' I said.

He glanced at me.

'I didn't cry,' he said. 'Dad and Odd Steinar hugged. I sat beside them on my own.'

'Doesn't that bother you?'

'No, why should it? I feel what I feel. They feel what they feel.'

'Turn left here,' I said.

'Left? Over there?'

'Yes.'

We came into the centre of town and drove down Festningsgaten.

'There's a multi-storey car park to the right soon,' I said. 'Shall we go there?'

'OK.'

'What do you reckon your father thinks about that?' I asked.

'About me not grieving?'

'Yes.'

'He won't give it a thought. "That's the way Geir is," he'll think. That's what he's always done. He's always accepted me exactly as I am. Did I tell you about the time he picked me up from a party once? I was sixteen and had to throw up; he stopped the car, I spewed, he drove on, didn't say a word. Total confidence. So, if I don't cry at mum's funeral or I don't put my arm round him, it doesn't mean anything to him. He feels what he feels, others feel what they feel.'

'He sounds like a nice man.'

Geir looked at me.

'Yes, he is a nice man. And he's a good father. But we live on different planets. Was that where you meant? Over there?'

'Yes.'

We drove down into the underground garage and parked. Wandered round town, Geir wanted to go to some record shops and look for blues CDs, his new obsession, and then we went to the two big bookshops before looking for somewhere to eat. The choice fell on Peppes Pizza, beside the library. Geir seemed unmoved by what had happened in his life during the last week, and while we sat eating and chatting I wondered whether it was because he was in fact unmoved, and if so, why, or whether it was because he needed to hide his feelings. During my early days in Stockholm he had written some short stories, I read them, they were characterised above all else by a great distance to the events they described, and I remembered I told him it was as though a huge sunken ship had to be raised. Lying deep in his consciousness. He didn't care about this any more, it wasn't important for him, which of course did not mean it was without significance. He didn't acknowledge it, and lived accordingly. But what status did it have? Was it repressed? Rationalised out of existence? Or was it, as he said, yesterday's news? The distance he kept from his family was related: he held everything in the past at arm's length. Their lives, which from what he said consisted of a regular series of everyday events, whose high points were trips to out-of-town shopping centres and Sunday lunch at some roadside inn, and topics of which conversation rarely rose beyond food and the weather, drove him crazy with restlessness, also because, I assumed, what he did had no place in them. They weren't in the slightest bit interested in what he did. If the relationship was going to work he had to meet them on their terms, but he didn't want to. At the same time he would often praise their warmth, their concern for their immediate world, hugs, embraces, but he invariably did that after having talked about what he couldn't stand about them, like a kind of penance, and not without jibes at my expense, for while I had everything he didn't have in the family, intellectual curiosity and constant conversation, which he called middle-class values, we didn't have the warmth and closeness that he saw as typical of the working class from which he came, nor the desire to create cosy atmospheres so disdained in academic circles, inasmuch as the taste with which it was expressed was regarded as basic, simple even. Geir loathed the middle classes and middle-class values, but was quite aware they were the ones he himself had embraced in his university career with all that that entailed, and somewhere there he was caught like a fly in a spider's web.

He was glad to see me, I noticed, and perhaps he also felt some relief that his mother was dead, not so much for his own sake as hers. One of the first things he mentioned was what importance her fear had now. None . . . but that was the point, we were as trapped in each other as in ourselves, we couldn't escape, it was impossible to free yourself, you had the life you had.

We talked about Kristiansand. For him it was only a town, for me it was a place where I was unable to stay without the old feelings welling up. Mostly they were of hatred, but there was also my own inadequacy, not being able to live up to any of the demands made of me. Geir thought this was all about the place where you were brought up, it was coloured by the time, but I disagreed, there was a big difference between Arendal and Kristiansand, even the mentality was different. Towns also have a character, psychology, mind, soul, whatever you like to call it, which you notice the moment you enter them, and it marks the people who live there. Kristiansand was a commercial town, it had a mercenary soul. Bergen also had a mercenary soul, but it had wit and irony in addition, that is to say it had incorporated the world outside, it knew very well it was not the only town.

'By the way, I read *Shallow Soil* this summer,' I said. 'Have you read it?'

'A long time ago.'

'Hamsun pays tribute to the businessman in it. He's young, dynamic, the future of the world and the great hero. He has nothing but contempt for artists. Writers, painters, they're off the scale. But the man of trade! It's amusing. Can you understand how contrary the man was!'

'Mm,' he said. 'There's a section in the biography about when he hits on serving girls. The colophon takes a prudish stand with regard to this issue, or is unable to understand. But in fact Hamsun came from the lowest echelon. That's what you forget. He was a working-class writer. He came from the poorest of the poor regions. For him serving girls were a rung up the social ladder! It's impossible to get anything out of Hamsun if you don't understand that.'

'He didn't look back,' I said. 'It's as if his parents weren't a part of his psychology, if you get what I mean. I'm left with the impression of some old grey people hugging the wall in a room somewhere in northern Norway, so old and grey that you can barely distinguish them from the furniture. And so alien to Hamsun's later life that they have no relevance at all. But it can't have been like that.'

'Can't it?'

'Well, I suppose it could, but you know what I mean, don't you? There isn't a single portrait of childhood in Hamsun apart from in *The Ring is Closed*. Nor of parents. Characters emerge from nothing in his books. Without a vestige of a past. Was it because they actually had no meaning or because their meaning had been repressed? And so these characters somehow become the first mass-produced humans, that is without their own predetermining origins. They are determined by the present.'

I took a slice of pizza, cut the long threads of cheese holding it back and bit off a mouthful.

'Try the dip,' he said. 'It's good!'

'You can keep the dip,' I said.

'When do you have to be there, by the way?'

'Seven. It starts at half past.'

'We've got an hour or two on our hands then. Shall we drive around for a bit? So that you can see some of your old haunts?

I've got a couple of Kristiansand haunts as well. Mum's uncle and his family lived in Lund. I'd like to pop by.'

'Let's have coffee somewhere else first. And then we'll go. OK?'

'There's a café close by where we used to walk when I was a boy. We can see if it still exists?'

We paid and left. Strolled down to Hotel Caledonien. I told him about the fire there, how I had stood behind the barriers, gaping up at the black façade, where it was all burned out. We ambled past the containers in the harbour to the bus station, up by the stock exchange, across Markensgate and into some arty-type café. Despite the cold, we sat outside so that I could smoke. Then we walked to the car, drove first to the house in Elvegaten, where I had lived during the winter mum and dad got divorced. The house had been sold and renovated. Then we went to grandma and grandad's house, where dad had died. Turned in the square in front of the marina, parked in the tiny street and looked up at the house. It had been painted white. The tables had been replaced. The garden was neat and tidy.

'Is that it?' Geir asked. 'What a wonderful house! Attractive, middle class, expensive. I would never have believed it. I had imagined something quite different.'

'Yes,' I said. 'That's it all right. But I have no feelings for it. It's just a house. It doesn't mean anything any more. I can see that now.'

Two hours later we parked in front of the folk high school where I was going to do the reading. It was situated in the middle of a forest outside Søgne. The sky was all black, everywhere stars twinkled and shone, somewhere nearby a river rushed and trees rustled. The sound of a car door slamming resounded between walls. Then the silence closed around us.

'Are you sure it's here?' Geir asked. 'In the middle of a forest?

Who on earth would come here to listen to you read on a Friday evening?'

'Who knows,' I said. 'But it is here. Nice, isn't it?'

'Oh yes. Full of atmosphere.'

Our footsteps crunched on the frozen gravel as we walked in. One building, a large white timber house that looked to be from the turn of the last century, was unlit. In the other, which was twenty metres away and at right angles to it, three windows were lit. Two figures were visible in one of them. They were playing the piano and violin. Then there was a large barn to the right, also unlit, where the reading was due to take place.

We wandered round for a few minutes, peered in through the darkened windows and saw a library and what seemed to be a living room. We followed the path, ended up by a stone bridge over a little river or stream. Black water and the forest like a black wall on the other side.

'We've got to have a coffee or something,' Geir said. 'Shall we ask those two in there if they have a key?'

'No, we're not asking anyone anything,' I said. 'The event organisers will come when they come.'

'We need to warm ourselves up a bit at the very least,' Geir said. 'You don't mind us doing that, do you?'

'Not at all.'

We entered the narrow house ringing with notes from the two young musicians. They must have been sixteen or seventeen. She had a soft beautiful face. He, the same age as her but pimply, ungainly and also flushed, did not seem happy to see us.

'Have you got a key or something for these buildings? He's doing a reading, and we're a trifle on the early side.'

She shook her head. But we could sit down in the adjacent room, where there was also a coffee machine. So we did.

'This place reminds me of school trips,' Geir said. 'The light in here. The cold and the darkness outside. And the forest. And the fact that no one knows where I am. No one knows what I'm doing. Yes, a kind of feeling of liberation. But there's a lot of darkness. The atmosphere inside it.'

'I know what you mean,' I said. 'For myself, I'm simply nervous. My whole body aches.'

'Because of this? Because of your talk here? Relax, man! It'll be fine.'

I held up a hand.

'See?' I said.

I was trembling like an old man.

Half an hour later I was shown into the hall where I was to give the talk. Another bearded lecturer-type, late fifties with glasses, received me.

'Isn't this wonderful?' he said as we entered.

I nodded. It really was. Inside the barn there was a large gallery like a capsule, built to give optimal acoustics, with seating for 200 people. Art on the walls of all the rooms. There was a lot of money in this country now, I reflected again. I placed my bag against the lectern, took out my papers and books, shook hands with a few others I had to greet, among them the bookseller who had come to set up shop after the talk, a charming energetic elderly woman, before going downstairs for a walk in the darkness, to the river, where I smoked two cigarettes. Then I sat on the toilet for a quarter of an hour with my head in my hands. When I went back up there was quite a turnout. Forty, maybe fifty? That was good. And there was a brass band, too, who were going to play some Baroque music. They kept it up for half an hour, in the middle of the forest on a Friday night, and then it was my turn. I stood in the centre with everyone's eyes on me, drank water, flicked through my papers, began to talk, hesitantly, swallowed words, my voice quivered, until I got into my stride and could talk freely. The audience was attentive, their interest streamed up towards me, I relaxed more and more, they laughed where they were supposed to, and I was filled with a feeling of happiness, for few things are more uplifting than talking to an audience who are on your wavelength, who don't just wish you well but are also into what you are talking about. I could see it, they were vitalised, and when I sat down to sign books afterwards they all wanted to discuss what I had said, it touched something in their lives which they were enthusiastic to tell me about. It was only when I was walking over to the car with Geir that I came down to the ground again, to where I usually was, to the place where contempt flourished. I said nothing, just got in and stared at the road winding its way through the dark landscape.

'That was good,' Geir said. 'You've got that down to a fine art. I don't know what you were moaning about. You could travel round earning money from it!'

'It went well,' I said. 'But I give them what they want. I say what they want to hear. I pander to them the way I pander to everyone and everything.'

'There was a woman in front of me,' Geir said. 'She looked like a teacher. When you started to talk about child abuse she stiffened. Then you said the word they wanted to hear. Infantilisation. She nodded. This was a concept she could handle. It smoothed over everything. But if you hadn't said it, if you hadn't gone into detail, I'm not sure everyone would have spoken to you afterwards – I'm not. And what is paedophilia, if not infantile?'

He laughed. I closed my eyes.

'And the brass band in the middle of the forest. Baroque music. Who would have expected that? Ha ha ha! It was a great evening,

Karl Ove, it was. Almost magical. The darkness and the stars and the sough of the forest.'

'Yes,' I said.

We drove around Kristiansand, over Varodd Bridge, past the animal park, past Nørholm, Lillesand and Grimstad. Chatted about this and that, arrived in Arendal, where we strolled around on the Tyholmen peninsula, I had a beer in a pub and for no particular reason felt completely out of kilter. Being here, surrounded by familiar buildings around the harbour, with the silhouette of Tromøya island on the other side of the water, in a world so crammed with memories, felt good but strange, not least because Geir, whom I connected with the Stockholm part of my life, was with me. At around twelve we drove to the island of Hisøya, he showed me some places which I looked at without being able to muster much interest, among them a quay where they had hung out in his youth, then we drove to the estate where he had grown up. He parked outside a garage, from the boot I took my bag and the bouquet I had been given and followed him to the house, which was a similar type to ours, or at least from the same period.

The hallway was full of flowers and wreaths.

'There's been a funeral, as you can see,' he said. 'If you like, you can put yours in one of these vases.'

I did as suggested. He showed me the room where I would sleep, which actually belonged to his brother, Odd Steinar, but had been tidied up for me. We had a couple of sandwiches in the kitchen, I wandered round the two living rooms looking. He had always said his parents actually belonged to the generation before our parents' generation, and when I saw how they had arranged the house I understood what he meant. Tablecloths, runners, rugs, there was something 1950s, deepest Norway, about it, and the same applied to the furniture and the pictures on the walls. A 1970s house furnished like a 1950s home, that was how it looked. Lots of family photos on the walls, a large collection of ornaments on the windowsills.

I had been in a house once before when someone had just died. It was total chaos. Here everything was as good as unaffected.

I had a smoke on the lawn. Then we said goodnight, I went to bed, I didn't want to close my eyes, I didn't want to meet what I met there, but I had to, I summoned all the strength I had to think about a neutral topic and fell asleep after a few minutes.

The following morning I was woken at seven by activity in the rooms above me. Njaal, Geir's son, and Christina had got up. I showered, dressed and went upstairs. A man of around seventy with a kind face and friendly eyes came out of the kitchen and greeted me. It was Geir's father. We talked a bit about how I had grown up here and how beautiful it was. He radiated goodness, but not in that open, almost self-exposing, way that Linda's father did. No, there was also solidity in this face. Not hardness exactly, but . . . character. That was what it was. Then Geir's brother came in, Odd Steinar. We shook hands, he sat down on the sofa and began to talk about this and that; he too was friendly and kind, but with a shyness his father didn't have and Geir definitely didn't. The father set the table for breakfast in the living room, we sat down and I kept thinking that his wife and their mother had been buried yesterday, and that it was inappropriate for me to be here, yet I was being treated with kindness and interest, any friends of Geir's were their friends, their house was an open house.

Nonetheless, I took a deep breath as I left afterwards.

The flight home was in the afternoon, we had planned to drive around, go to Tromøya where I hadn't been for a long time, not to Tybakken, where I had grown up, and then straight to the airport, but Geir's father had insisted we should go back home first. It was Saturday, he would buy some shrimps at the harbour, I would have to experience them before I went to Malmö, we didn't have shrimps like that there, did we.

So we got into the car and motored over to Tromøya. Geir talked about the places we passed, told anecdotes associated with them. A whole life emerged from this area. Then he told me about his family. About who his mother had been, who his father and his brother were.

'It was interesting to meet them,' I said. 'Now I understand more about what you've been saying. Your father and brother, they have almost *nothing* in common with you. With your temperament. Your mind and your curiosity. Your restlessness. With your father and brother there was just kindness and friendliness. So where's the connection? Someone was missing, and it was so obvious. Your mother must have been like you. Am I right?'

'Yes, you are. I understood her. But that was also why I had to get away. Shame you never met her, by the way.'

'I've arrived when it's all over.'

'The most solid connection between the three generations is probably that Njaal, dad and I all have the same head from the back.'

I nodded. We drove up the hills before Tromøya Bridge. Mountains had been dynamited, roads built, industrial plants established like everywhere in the district.

Beneath us I saw the little island of Gjerstadholmen, further behind it Ubekilen Bay. To the right, Håvard's house. The bus stop, the forest below, where in the winter we had made ski slopes and in the summer walked down to the rocks to go swimming.

'In there,' I said.

'Where? To the left? Jesus, you didn't live *there*, did you?'

Old Søren's house, the wild cherry tree, and there, the estate. Nordåsen ringvei.

My God, it was so small.

'There it is. Straight ahead.'

'Where? The red house?'

'Yes. It was brown when we lived there.'

He parked the car.

How small everything was. And so ugly.

'Not a lot to see,' I said. 'Come on, let's go on. Up the hill here.'

A woman in a white Puffa jacket was walking down pushing a buggy. Otherwise there wasn't a sign of life anywhere.

Olsen's house.

The mountain.

We had called it the mountain, but it was only a little hill. Siv's house behind it. Sverre and the others' house.

Not a soul. Yes, there was. A huddle of children.

'You've gone quiet,' Geir said. 'Are you overwhelmed?'

'Overwhelmed? No, more like underwhelmed. This is so small. There isn't anything here. I've never experienced that before. There's nothing at all. And at one time it was my everything.'

'Ye-es, Karl Ove,' he said with a smile. 'Straight on?'

'Let's drive round the island, shall we? Tromøya Church? That's wonderful. Thirteenth century. There are some fantastic headstones from the seventeenth century, with skulls and hourglasses and snakes. I used an inscription from one of them in the first decent short story I wrote. As an epigraph.'

All the places I carried inside me, which I had visualised so many, many times in my life, passed outside the windows, completely aura-less, totally neutral – the way they were, in fact. A few crags, a small bay, a decrepit floating pier, a narrow shoreline, some old houses behind, flatland that fell away to the water. That was all.

We got out of the car and went to the cemetery. Wandered around, looked across towards the sea, but even that, even the sight of the pine trees growing down to the pebble beach, smaller and smaller the closer they got to the raw wind, aroused nothing in me.

'Come on, let's go,' I said. Saw the fields where I had worked in the summer, the road leading to the water, where we could go swimming as early as 17 May. Sandum Bay. My teacher's house, what was her name? Helga Torgersen? Must be getting on for sixty now? Færvik, the petrol station, the house on the other side, where the girls in the class had got so excited at the party the night before I left, the supermarket, which I could remember them building.

There was nothing. But lives were still being lived in these houses, and they were still everything for the people inside. People were born, people died, they made love and argued, ate and shat, drank and partied, read and slept. Watched TV, dreamed, ate an apple gazing across rooftops, autumn winds shaking the tall slim pine trees.

Small and ugly, but all there was.

An hour later I was sitting at the living-room table, alone, eating shrimps at top speed, served by Geir's father, who wasn't having any himself but wanted me to have a Sørland experience before I left. Then I shook hands, thanked them for having me, got into the car beside Geir again and was driven to the airport. We took the route via Birkeland because I wanted to see what my other childhood home, the one in Tveit, was like now.

Geir pulled up outside the house. He laughed.

'Did you live *there*?' In the middle of the forest? It's completely isolated! There isn't a soul here! So deserted . . . Pure *Twin Peaks*, if you ask me. Or *Pernille and Mr Nelson*, if you can remember the TV programme? It frightened the life out of me when I was a child.'

He continued to laugh as I pointed out places. And I had to laugh too because I saw them with his eyes. All these derelict old houses, these wrecks of cars on the drives, lorries parked outside, the distances between houses and the evident poverty. I tried to explain to him how nice our house had been, how good living here had been, that everything was here, but . . .

'Come on!' he said. 'Living here must have been penal servitude.'

I didn't answer, I was piqued, I felt the need to put up a defence. But I couldn't be bothered. It was the same here, the inner experience, which made everything glow with meaning, it had no counterpart on the outside.

We shook hands in the car park, he got back into his car and I walked towards the departures hall. The flight was to Oslo, where I would change and fly to Billund in Denmark, where I would change again for Kastrup, Copenhagen. I didn't get home until ten in the evening. Linda hugged me when I arrived, a long, passionate hug, we sat down in the living room, she had made something to eat, I told her about the trip, she said the last day had been better, but she had realised we would have to do something to break the vicious circle we were in, I agreed, it couldn't go on, it couldn't, we had to find a way out and make a new path. At half past eleven I went into the bedroom and switched on my computer, opened a new document and began to write.

In the window before me I can vaguely see the image of my face.
Apart from the eyes, which are shining, and the part directly
beneath, which dimly reflects light, the whole of the left side lies in
shade. Two deep furrows run down the forehead, one deep furrow
runs down each cheek, all filled as it were with darkness, and when
the eyes are staring and serious, and the mouth turned down at
the corners it is impossible not to think of this face as sombre.

What is it that has etched itself into you?

The next day I continued. The idea was to get as close as
possible to my life, so I wrote about Linda and John sleeping in
the adjacent room, Vanja and Heidi, who were at the nursery,
the view from the window and the music I was listening to. The
next day I went to the allotment cabin, I wrote more there, some
ultra-modernistic-style passages about faces and the patterns
that exist in all big systems, sand heaps, clouds, economies,
traffic, occasionally went into the garden to smoke and watch
the birds flying hither and thither in the sky, it was February
and there was no one around in the enormous allotment
compound, just row upon row of small well-kept doll's houses
in small gardens, so perfect they looked like living rooms. In
the evening a huge flock of crows flew over, there must have
been several hundred, a dark cloud of flapping wings drifting
past and flying on. Night fell, and apart from what was lit up
by the light streaming out of the open door at the other end of
the garden, everything around me was dark. So still was I, where
I sat, that a hedgehog shuffled by half a metre from my feet.

'Well, hello there,' I said and waited until it had reached the
hedge before getting up and going in. The next day I began to
write about the spring dad moved out from mum and me, and
even though I hated every sentence I decided to persist, I had
to come to terms with it, to tell the story I had tried for so long

to tell. Back at home I continued with some notes I made when I was eighteen and for some reason had not disposed of, 'bags of beer in the ditch' caught my eye, a reference to one New Year's Eve when I was a teenager, I could use that as long as I wasn't too bothered and shelved any idea of aiming for the sublime. The weeks passed, I wrote, walked the children to the nursery or collected them, spent the afternoons with them in one of the many parks, cooked dinner, read to them and put them to bed, worked on reader reports and other odd jobs in the evenings. Every Sunday I cycled to Limhamnsfältet and played football for two hours, that was my only leisure activity, everything else was either work or children. Limhamnsfältet was an enormous grassy area outside the town, by the sea. Since the end of the 1960s a motley collection of men have gathered there every Sunday at a quarter past ten. The youngest are sixteen or seventeen while the oldest, Kai, is closer to eighty – he is on the wing and the ball has to be played to his feet, but if he gets it, there is still enough football left in him to whip in a centre, and now and then he even scores a goal. But the majority of the players are between thirty and forty, come from all walks of life and all they really have in common is the joy of playing football. The last Sunday in February Linda and the children came along, Vanja and Heidi cheered me on for a bit, then they went to the play area by the beach while I carried on playing. There had been a ground frost, the usually soft layer of grass was rock hard, and when after half an hour I was sent flying by a tackle and landed smack on my shoulder I realised at once that something was wrong. I stayed down, the others gathered round, I was nauseous with the pain, hobbled slowly, shoulder hunched, to behind the goal, the others knew that this wasn't just a little knock and the game was called off, it was half past eleven anyway.

Fredrik, a fifty-something writer and classic poacher who still

bangs in goals in Swedish non-league football, drove me to
hospital while Martin, a two-metre-plus giant of a Dane I knew
through the nursery undertook to inform Linda and the children
about what had happened. A & E was full, I took a number from
the machine and sat down to wait, my shoulder burned and
there was a stab of pain every time I moved it, but it was bear-
able for the half-hour it would take before it was my turn. I
explained the situation to the nurse in reception, who came out
to give me a quick examination, grabbed my arm and moved it
slowly to the side. I screamed from the top of my lungs.
AAAAAAgggghhh! Everyone stared at me. A man approaching
forty wearing an Argentina national shirt and football boots, his
long hair tied with an elastic band in a knot like a pineapple
on top of his head, howling with pain.

'You'd better come with me,' the nurse said. 'So we can have
you examined properly.'

I went into a room nearby, she asked me to wait, a few minutes
later another nurse came, she made the same movement with
my arm, I screamed again.

'Sorry,' I said. 'But I can't help it.'

'No problem,' she said, gently removing my tracksuit top.
'We'll have to take your shirt off as well,' she said. 'Do you think
that'll be OK?'

She pulled at the sleeve, I screamed, she paused, tried again.
Took a step back. Looked at me. I felt like an overgrown child.

'We'll have to cut it off.'

Now it was my turn to look at her. Cut up my Argentina shirt?

She came back with some scissors and cut up the sleeves, then
asked me to sit on a bed once the shirt was off and stuck a
needle in my lower arm just above the wrist. She was going to
give me a bit of morphine, she said. After it was done, although
I noticed nothing, she pushed me in a wheelchair into another

room, perhaps fifty metres deeper into the labyrinthine building, where I was left alone to wait for an X-ray, not without some dread because I thought my shoulder must have been dislocated and, if so, I knew putting it back would be painful. But it was a fracture, the doctor confirmed. It would take between eight and twelve weeks to heal. They gave me some painkillers, a prescription for more, tied a bandage in a taut figure of eight over and under the shoulders, hung my tracksuit top on me and sent me home.

When I opened the door to the flat Vanja and Heidi came towards me at a run. They were excited, daddy had been to hospital, it was an adventure. I told them and Linda, who followed with John on her arm, that I had broken my collarbone and had a sling, it was nothing major, but I couldn't lift or carry or use my arm for the next two months.

'Are you serious?' Linda asked. 'Two months?'

'Three at worst,' I said.

'You must never play football again, that's for definite,' Linda said.

'Oh?' I said. 'So that's your decision, is it?'

'It's me who has to put up with the consequences,' she said. 'How am I going to take care of the children on my own for two months, if I might ask?'

'It'll be fine,' I said. 'Relax. I've broken my collarbone after all. It hurts, and it's not as if I did it on purpose.'

I went into the living room to sit down on the sofa. I had to make every movement slowly and plan it in advance. Every little deviation sent a pain through me. Agh, Ohh, Oooh, I said, slowly lowering myself. Vanja and Heidi watched with saucer eyes.

I smiled at them while trying to put the big cushion behind my back. They came up close. Heidi ran her hand across my chest as if to examine it.

'Can we have a look at the bandage?' Vanja asked.

'Afterwards,' I said. 'It hurts a little to take clothes off and put them back on, you see.'

'Food's up!' Linda shouted from the kitchen.

John was sitting in his baby chair banging his knife and fork on the table. Vanja and Heidi stared at me and my slow, laborious movements as I sat down.

'What a day!' Linda said. 'Martin didn't know a thing, only that you'd been taken to A & E. He brought us home, luckily, but when I was opening the door the key broke. Oh my God. I visualised us having to stay with them tonight. But then I double-checked my bag, and there it was, Berit's key. What a stroke of luck! I hadn't hung it up. And then you come home with a broken collarbone . . .'

She looked at me.

'I'm so tired,' she said.

'I'm sorry,' I said. 'It'll probably only be the first few days that I can't do anything. And then one arm will be perfectly OK.'

After eating I lay down on the sofa with a cushion behind my back watching an Italian football match on TV. In the four years we'd had children I had only done something like this once. At the time I was so ill I couldn't move, I lay on the sofa for a whole day, saw ten minutes of the first Jason Bourne film, slept for a bit, saw ten minutes, slept for a bit, threw up intermittently, and even though my whole body ached and basically it was absolutely unbearable, I still enjoyed every second. Lying on the sofa and watching a film in the middle of the day! Not one single obligation! No clothes to be washed, no floor to be scrubbed, no washing-up to be done, no children to look after.

Now I had that same feeling. I was *not* in a position to do anything. However much my shoulder burned and stung and ached, the pleasure at being able to lie in total peace was greater.

Vanja and Heidi circled round me, coming close every so often and gently stroking my shoulder, then they went out of the room to play, and came back. For them this was probably unprecedented, I mused, me being completely passive and still. It was as though they had discovered a new side to me.

When the match was over I went for a bath. We didn't have a holder for the showerhead, we had to hold it in one hand, and that option was out of the question now, so all I could do was run the bath and climb into the tub with difficulty. Vanja and Heidi watched me.

'Do you need any help with washing, daddy?' Vanja asked. 'Can we wash you?'

'Yes, that would be nice,' I said. 'Can you see the cloths there? Take one each, and then dip it in the water and rub some soap into it.'

Vanja followed the instructions precisely, Heidi copied her. And they stood there, leaning over the edge of the bath and washing me with their cloths. Heidi laughed, Vanja was serious and business-like. They washed my arms, neck and chest. Heidi was bored after a few seconds and ran into the living room while Vanja stayed for a while longer.

'Is that good?' she asked at length.

I smiled. That was what I usually asked.

'Yes, it's great,' I said. 'I don't know what I'd do without you!'

She brightened up, and then she ran into the living room as well.

I wallowed in the water until it turned cold. First football on TV, then a long bath. What a Sunday!

Vanja came in a couple of times to see. I supposed she was waiting for the bandage to be put on. She spoke Swedish of course, still with Stockholm intonation patterns, but when I had been with her for a morning or an afternoon, or she felt close to me for some other reason, words from my dialect appeared more frequently in her conversation. Very often she would say *mæ* instead of the Swedish *mig*, me. '*Lyft upp mæ!*' Lift me up, she would say, for example. I laughed every time.

'Can you go and get mummy?' I said.

She nodded and ran off. I got out of the bath gingerly, and had dried myself by the time she came back.

'Could you put the bandage on?' I asked.

'No problem,' she said.

I explained how it was supposed to be, and said she had to pull it hard, otherwise it wasn't doing its job.

'Harder!'

'Doesn't it hurt?'

'A bit, but the tauter it is the less it hurts when I move.'

'OK,' she said. 'If you say so.'

And then she pulled from behind.

'Aaaaagh!' I said.

'Was that too hard?'

'No, that was good,' I said. I turned towards her.

'I'm sorry I was so grumpy,' she said. 'But I had such a terrible vision of the future, me doing everything on my own for months on end.'

'It won't be like that though,' I said. 'I'll be able to take them to school and pick them up as usual within a few days, I'm sure.'

'I know it hurts, and it's not your fault. But I'm just so tired.'

'I know. It'll be fine. Things'll sort themselves out.'

On Friday Linda was so tired that I went with John to pick the girls up from the nursery. Going there was easy, I pushed John in the buggy with my right hand while walking behind as carefully as I could. The way back was more problematic. I pulled John after me with my right hand, clutching the injured left hand to my side and somehow shunting Vanja and Heidi in the double buggy with my whole body. Occasional pains shot through me and I had no defence except to emit little screams. It must have been a bizarre sight, and people did stare at us as we trundled along. It was also a strange experience for me during those weeks. Not being able to lift or carry and finding it difficult to sit down and get up gave me a sense of helplessness that went beyond physical restrictions. Suddenly I had no authority, no strength, and the feeling of control I had taken for granted until now became manifest. I sat still, I was passive, and it was as though I had lost control of my surroundings. So, had I always felt I controlled them and had power over them? Yes, I must have done. I didn't need to make any use of the power and the control, it was enough to know that it existed, it permeated everything I did and everything I thought. Now it was gone, and I saw it for the first time. Even stranger was the fact that the same applied to writing. Also with it I had a sense of power and control, which disappeared with the broken collarbone. Suddenly I was *under* the text, suddenly *it* had power over *me,* and it was only with the greatest effort of will that I managed to write the five pages a day I had set myself as a goal. But I managed, I managed that too. I hated every syllable, every word, every sentence, but not liking what I was doing didn't mean I shouldn't do it. One year and it would be over, and then I would be able to write about something else. The pages mounted, the story advanced and then one day I came to another of the places where I had made a note in the book I had kept for the last twenty years, about a party dad had held for friends and colleagues the summer I turned sixteen, a gathering which in the late-autumn darkness merged into one with my own enormous pleasure and dad crying, it was so emotional, such an impossible evening, everything converged there, and now at last I was going to write about it. Once it was done, the rest would be about dad's death. This was a heavy door to open, it was hard being inside, but I approached it in the new way: five pages every day, regardless. Then I got up, switched off the computer, took the rubbish with me, disposed of it in the basement and went to collect the children. The horror lodged in my chest dissipated when they came running towards me across the playground. They competed with each other, seeing who could shout loudest and give me the biggest hug. If John was with us he sat smiling and shouting, for him his two sisters were the tops. They scattered their lives around him, he sat lapping it all up, and copied whatever he could, and even Heidi, who could still become so jealous of him that she would scratch or knock or thump him if we didn't keep an eagle eye open, didn't hold any fears for him, he never viewed her with fear. Did he forget? Or was there so much goodness there the rest was lost in it?

One day in March the telephone rang while I was working, the number was unfamiliar, but as it didn't come from Norway, but was Swedish, I took it anyway. It was a colleague of my mother's, they were at a seminar in Gothenburg, mum had fainted in a shop and been taken to hospital, where she was now in intensive care. I rang, she'd had a heart attack, was being operated on now and was out of danger. Late that night she rang me herself. I could hear she was weak and perhaps a touch confused. She said the pain had been so great she would rather have died than gone on living. She hadn't fainted, she had just fallen over. And not in a shop but the street. While she was lying there, she said now, convinced that this was the end, the thought had gone through her head that she'd had a fantastic life. When she said that I froze.

There was something so good about it.

In addition, she said it had been particularly her childhood that had flashed through her mind as she lay there about to die, as a kind of sudden insight: she'd had an absolutely brilliant childhood, she had been free and happy, it had been fantastic. In the ensuing days what she had said kept returning to me. In a way I was shocked. I could never have thought that. If I keeled over now, and had a few seconds, perhaps minutes, to think before it was all over I would think the opposite. That I hadn't accomplished anything, I hadn't seen anything, I hadn't experienced anything. I want to live. But why don't I live then? Why, when I'm on board a plane or in a car imagining it's going to crash or have a collision, why do I think that's not so bad? That it doesn't matter? That I might just as well die as live? For this is what I think more often than not. Indifference is one of the seven deadly sins, actually the greatest of them all, because it is the only one that sins against life.

Later that spring, when I was nearing the end of the story about dad's death, the terrible days spent at the house in Kristiansand, mum came to visit me. She had been at another seminar in Gothenburg and came over to see us afterwards. Two months had passed since she fell over in the same town. If she had fallen over at home it is unlikely she would have survived, she lived alone, and if, contrary to expectation, she had got help it was a forty-minute drive to the nearest hospital. In Gothenburg she had been attended to at once, and in no time at all she was on the operating table. Now it transpired the heart attack hadn't come out of the blue. She'd had pains, terrible intermittent pains, but she thought it was stress, pushed it to the back of her mind, thinking she would go and see the doctor when she got home, and then she fell over.

One morning she was knitting while I sat writing and Linda was out with John after having taken the girls to the nursery.

After a while I went in to see how she was and she started talking unbidden about dad. She said she had always wondered why she stayed with him, why she didn't take us and leave him, was it because she hadn't dared? Some weeks earlier she had talked to a friend about it, she told me, and suddenly she had heard herself say she loved him. Then she glanced at me.

'I *did* love him, Karl Ove. I loved him a lot.'

She had never said that before. She hadn't even been close to it. Indeed, I couldn't recall her ever using a word like love before.

It was a shock.

What is going on? I thought. What is going on? For something around me was changing. Or was it changing inside me, so that now I could see something I hadn't seen before? Or had I set something in motion? Because I talked to her and Yngve a lot about the time with dad. Suddenly it was close to me again.

That morning she went on to tell me about the first time they had met. She had been working at a hotel in Kristiansand during the summer when she was sixteen, and one day at a terrace restaurant in a large park, in the shade of a tree, her friend had introduced her to her boyfriend and his pal.

'I didn't quite catch his name, and for a long time I thought it was Knudsen,' she said. 'And at first I liked the other one better, you know. But then I fell for your father . . . It's such a good memory. The sun, the grass in the park, the trees, the shade, all the people there . . . We were so young, you know . . . Yes, it was an adventure. The beginning of an adventure. That was how it felt.'

penguin.co.uk/vintage